WESTERN

By Frank Yerby

The Foxes of Harrow
The Vixens
The Golden Hawk
Pride's Castle
Floodtide
A Woman Called Fancy
The Saracen Blade
The Devil's Laughter
Benton's Row
The Treasure of Pleasant Valley
Captain Rebel
Fairoaks
The Serpent and the Staff
Jarrett's Jade
Gillian
The Garfield Honor
Griffin's Way
The Old Gods Laugh
An Odor of Sanctity
Goat Song
Judas, My Brother
Speak Now
The Dahomean
The Girl from Storyville
The Voyage Unplanned
Tobias and the Angel
A Rose for Ana María
Hail the Conquering Hero
A Darkness at Ingraham's Crest

WESTERN

A Saga

of the Great Plains

FRANK YERBY

The Dial Press

NEW YORK

Published by
The Dial Press
1 Dag Hammarskjold Plaza
New York, New York 10017

Library of Congress Cataloging in Publication Data

Yerby, Frank, 1916–
Western : a saga of the Great Plains.

I. Title.
PS3547.E65W4   813'.54   81-19470
ISBN: 0-385-27230-8   AACR2

1

It wasn't until after Ethan Lovejoy had changed both boats and rivers in St. Louis that he noticed the girl. He conceded that she might well have been on the medium-sized sternwheeler that had brought him down the Mississippi from Rock Island, Illinois; but, if so, nothing about her had attracted his attention during that penultimate segment of his long, slow voyage. He was absolutely sure that she hadn't been a fellow passenger aboard any of the railroads and steamboat lines he had used so far to cover the immense distances between his hometown of Pittsfield, Massachusetts, and his proposed destination, Atchison, Kansas, because the mere fact that she was quite young—in her early twenties—and shockingly unaccompanied, would have aroused his curiosity if nothing else about her did. Even in this most modern and enlightened of all years, 1866, for a young woman, especially if she were decent—as this one obviously was—to make so much as an overnight trip alone was still an unheard-of thing.

He stared at her where she stood, a few yards away from him down the main passenger deck of the *Prairie Belle.* Not that he could see very much of her, because she was completely surrounded by a wolf pack of at least twenty lean, rangy young Westerners. In fact, as Ethan's Kansas friend, Phil Harris—who was going to meet him in Atchison—would have put it, "Th' pore li'l thing is fair hipboot-deep in caterwaulin' lonesome polecats!"

And it was precisely this fact that Ethan Lovejoy found astonishing. He was, as a result of the fortunes of war, compounded and complicated by the direct—if forced and accidental—intervention of his own hand in what ordinarily would have been sheer destiny, an act of God, the sole surviving son of an old manufacturing family become actually wealthy through the profits they'd obtained from the boots, shoes, and other leather accouterments supplied the Union Army during the great and terrible struggle but lately closed, and, in the circles he normally frequented, a girl who looked like this one did would have been hard put to find herself even *one* suitor, not to mention twenty.

He stared out over the Missouri's coffee-colored waters.

By then he had completely forgotten the girl; he had other, much greater problems to occupy his poor, malfunctioning head with; and, anyhow, she just wasn't his kind of girl.

But, a few moments later, he found himself compelled to turn and look at her again. He had had that prickly, almost tactile feeling that he was being stared at. Glancing in her direction, he saw that feeling hadn't been imaginary: she *was* staring at him. Openly. With something like desperation in her soft, blue eyes. And the instant she perceived she had captured his attention, she deliberately winked at him.

He was aware from the outset that she wasn't very good at that most classic of all female amatory assault tactics.

'Why,' he realized, 'she wants me to come to her rescue! And— why not? What harm can it do? Honey, you're on! But I'm warning you, you'll be engaging the fastest fall-back artist the Union Army ever produced . . .'

Very slowly, he smiled at her; almost imperceptibly, he nodded. At once, she broke free of the encircling plainsmen and headed updeck toward him, full steam ahead. He raised his black silk stovepipe hat and put out his hand to her. She clasped it fervently with a hot little palm that was both jumping and crawling with sheer nerves.

"Your name!" she hissed; "Quick, before they get here: tell me your name!"

"It's Lovejoy," he said. Then he added, with bitter quiet: "Cain Lovejoy at your service, my dear. Now, tell me: As far as those howling prairie coyotes are concerned, what am I supposed to be to you: your cousin, your brother—or your beau?"

"My—beau," she said, and flashed him a smile of pure, delighted mischief that did wonders for her anything but pretty face, made it interesting, somehow, made it come alive; "For nothing else would deter them to the necessary extent. Don't worry! It's only 'til we get to Kansas. D'you mind?"

"Not at all," he said solemnly; "Only too happy to be of help. But, in that case, don't you see a mere handshake won't do? You'd better let me kiss you to make the game seem real . . ."

She stared at him, and doubt, suspicion, anger, flared in her eyes.

"It's up to you," he drawled; "I'm not trying to take advantage, believe me. For, among several other reasons, why should I? What have I to gain by kissing a strange girl in broad open daylight on a river steamer's passenger deck?"

She said, bitterly:

"A strange, *ugly* girl, you mean. . . . Oh, go ahead, and be quick about it, for here they come!"

He bent his tall form and, without embracing her, touched her lips as lightly and as briefly as he could manage. But as he straightened up, he saw a gleam of what was unmistakably exasperation in her eyes.

"You call *that* a kiss?" she sniffed. "Oh, well, it doesn't matter, anyhow, and—"

"I'll try to do better next time," Ethan murmured; but he had no opportunity to say anything else, because by then all twenty of her self-appointed suitors were there.

"Oh, Lordy, Miss Annie," one of them groaned; "Why didn't you tell we'uns you had a Gentlem'n Acquaintance aboard? That there plain wuzn't fair, buildin' up our hopes thataway!"

"*Not* a Gentleman Acquaintance," she said, obviously pleased as punch with herself, and showing it; "My fiancé—or as you put it out here in the West, my promised. Boys, meet Mr. Kane Lovejoy—(somehow, from the very way she pronounced the name, Ethan knew that was how she was spelling it in her mind)—who, like me, is a New Englander. From my native state, Massachusetts, in fact . . ."

Ethan stared at her with astonishment. Then it came to him that neither Harvard College nor his travels had amended his Down East accent very much. Smoothed down his bluegilled, codfish twang a bit, that was all. But *her* accent wasn't Massachusetts to his ear. It sounded somehow British; but, if so, it had had the regional aspects completely educated out of it. It was London grand salon English, and very upper class.

"Wal now, Mr. Lovejoy," two or three of the Westerners chorused, "you sure Lord are one lucky man!"

"I'm not all that sure I am," Ethan said solemnly; "There have been times in the past when I'd have gladly traded her for a good riding horse . . ."

She picked him up right on cue, saying: "Kane, I'm going to hit you in a minute!" And it came to him what that accent really was: theater. The stage. It was exactly the kind of beautifully enunciated English, bell clear, musical, ringing, projecting itself effortlessly over considerable distances that all actors and actresses seem to acquire if they stay in their chosen profession very long. As such it was totally neutral. There was no way at all to tell whether she was really from Massachusetts, originally, or from South Carolina. But now she was beginning to intrigue him, in spite of himself. This poor little homely creature an *actress?* 'How the devil could she ever have got into a profession where physical beauty is the first requisite?' he thought.

"Wal, suh," another of the Lonesome Polecats groaned; "don't reckon you'n yore One'n Only could arrange to have a li'l falling-out, could y'all? One of us, enyhow, would shore Lord be mighty obliged effen y'all could!"

"Sorry," Ethan chuckled; "doesn't work that way with us, friend. Every time we have a falling out, I place her facedown across my knees and apply my razor strop to the seat of her intelligence. Cools her down in no time at all . . ."

"Well, I never!" Anne gasped.

"See that you don't even ever get tempted to," Ethan said with sardonic humor; "You heard me, Annie, me darlin', come along!"

"You," she said, "seemed to enjoy playing the villain of the piece rather a bit too much, Mister Kane Lovejoy. Or are you really that type? A wife-beater and a brute, I mean?"

Ethan studied her with eyes that were utterly bleak. Getting rid of her was fast becoming a priority on his agenda. She was, he was beginning to realize, a good bit more dangerous than she looked. 'Oh, damn all manners and conditions of women anyhow!' he thought. He said:

"And if I were?"

She bathed the craggy, rough-hewn features of his face in reflected cerulean light.

"I'd be—disappointed. Very," she said.

He went on studying her. 'This one,' he mused with a feeling that had a disquieting resemblance to actual fear, 'could convince a man of damned nigh anything if she really put her mind to it. Even that the rest of her is as beautiful as her speaking voice.' He said:

"Why? I mean, why would you be?"

"It would indicate that one of the very few abilities I've always had legitimate right to feel proud of is beginning to fail me," she said quietly. "And that's an aptitude for judging people. It's been quite necessary in my case. The very conditions of my life made knowing who could be trusted, and who couldn't be, an imperative, as it were. There have been times when my very physical safety depended upon the accuracy of my estimation of—of a man's character, say . . ."

"I can see how that would be," he said gravely; "Knocking about from pillar to post with a traveling theatrical company, right?"

Her blue eyes opened very wide.

"You do have your depths, don't you?" she said with a little laugh that was music's very self. "How did you know I'd been an actress?"

"Had been?" he countered; "Aren't you one now?"

"No," she sighed. "Now I'm a school teacher, if anything. I've been out of the theater for years. As a child I was something of a luminary of the stage. You see, when I was a little girl, I happened to have been, believe it or not, very beautiful. Therefore I was usually called on to play the part of the little angel who reformed her drunkard of a father, or reconciled her estranged parents by dying, or threatening to . . ."

"I can get the picture," Ethan said; "You had enormous masses of almost white blond curls, and huge blue eyes . . ."

"Lord!" she breathed. "Right again, Mr. Lovejoy! How on earth did you know?"

"The color your hair is now," he pointed out, "is the shade the hair of children who're a little too blond almost always darkens into. Strange, isn't it? Yellow or golden blond hair usually stays its original color, or close to it; but true towheads always darken . . ."

"Whereupon," she said bitterly, "if they're on the stage, they bleach it out again . . ."

"You didn't," he said.

"In my case, it was useless. At pubescence, my hair turned mousey brown, my hearing, eyesight, and wits all dimmed; and I became distinctly ugly. My mother was heartbroken. She was your ravishing beauty, y'know. The company's ingenue. And she'd entertained such high hopes for me. Only I had to go and spoil things by reversing that story of the ugly duckling who becomes a swan. But enough about me! Let's talk about you. Come on; tell me: Are you really a wife-beating, burly brute?"

"Let's postpone the subject, the dull and uninteresting subject of me, for a while yet," Ethan said. "For instance, why are you going to Kansas? I take it that it's not the usual reason—your joining a fiancé or a husband —because then you wouldn't have dared adopt the stratagem of having me pose as your promised to stave off those Lonesome Polecats . . ."

She laughed merrily at that. Her laughter was silvery, rich, and dead on pitch. You could have used its middle tones as standards to tune a musical instrument.

"What an apt description of them!" she said. "Oh, all right! I'm going to Kansas to join a father I thought was already dead, and four half brothers I didn't even know I had. My Aunt Sue informed me of the facts a few weeks ago, when I became of legal age. It was my poor mother's dying wish that I be so informed. By then she'd resigned herself to the fact that I'd never be an actress . . ."

"Why not?" Ethan asked her; "I think you'd have made an excellent one . . ."

"Oh, I had talent enough and to spare," she sighed; "And there are a good many parts—even important, leading parts—where looks don't particularly matter. I could have made a first-rate character actress, and that's a lifelong career, instead of being ephemeral the way a female romantic lead's always is. The truth is, Mr. Lovejoy, that the form that adolescent rebellion took in me was a longing for peace, quiet, security. . . . You realize what a sad reputation for—well—moral legerity actresses generally have, don't you?"

"Yes," he said gravely; "but I'm also intelligent enough—I hope!— to know that reputation isn't always justified . . ."

"The trouble is," she said sadly, "that all too often the public's estimation of our distressingly frail characters is quite accurate. In my mother's case, it was. Oh, no! I'm not reproaching her. She lived her life to the hilt, and enjoyed it, I suppose. Only I didn't, and don't, want that kind of a life. . . . When, to borrow your own exact phrase, you've knocked about from pillar to post, plain, dull domesticity comes to seem absolutely enchanting. Or it did. Now I've come to the conclusion that matrimony is a state I'd jolly well better forego. In short, I'll accept the sure serenity —and the peace!—of resignation, to the rather remote possibility of bliss . . ."

"A decision inflicted upon you," Ethan said quietly, "by the blindness and stupidity of some member of my sex. Am I right?"

"Quite!" she said crisply. "Except that your adjectives are wrong. He was neither blind nor stupid. His eyesight was acute enough for him to discern that, as far as beauty is concerned, I am a near or actual female disaster. And his wits were sharp enough to allow him to realize that I probably would be practically aswoon with gratitude at being the recipient of the marked, public, and apparently sincere attentions of so handsome a man as he was. Up to a point, he was right. I did so enjoy hearing some really stunning creatures give vent to maliciously audible stage whispers as we passed by: 'What on earth does he ever see in *her*?' "

"But he went too far?" Ethan said.

"Yes. And in the worst possible way. That is, he misjudged me. Underestimated my intelligence—"

"Which is of a very high order, indeed," Ethan said.

"Thank you for that," she said quietly. "At least you've the sense— and the taste—not to insult whatever order of brains I may have by praising the looks I haven't got. But let that pass—let it go! Being rather crass, he confused—well—call it physical innocence with actual igno- rance. And I wasn't ignorant; I'd seen twenty fickle, disappearing gallants pass through my mother's distressingly untidy life before he maneuvered his way into mine. All right, what I have inside me—spirit, fire, passion enough to burn as poor a creature as he was quite to cinders!—doesn't show on the outside, and you men will judge a book by its cover, won't you? And, besides, in me they're dominated by the kind of mind that can, and does, learn from vicarious experience—in my case, my mother's—and a will of solid iron. He demanded the—surrender of my body—without benefit of clergy, or support of the law, as a proof of my love for him. He was not, he declared, 'going to buy a pig in a poke'!"

"Thereby losing both you and that love forever," Ethan said.

"Exactly. But you mustn't imagine my decision was an easy one to make. He was a most attractive man, so there were some exceedingly lachrymose days and nights when the sacrifice of the pure abstraction that our virtue is to most of us women—until we lose it, and society, domi- nated, of course, by you lordly males, makes it concrete by the terrible penalties imposed upon us for having made that one small fatal slip— seemed cheap enough a price for keeping him . . ."

"Yet you didn't pay it," Ethan pointed out drily.

"I didn't pay it. *Au fond,* I suppose I was just too big a coward to. Would it have been worth it? Can the world, including that bauble reputa- tion, so unweighable, unassayable quality as one's good name, be well lost for love? I don't know. And now I'll never know. I don't mean to tread those dangerous and giddy primrose paths again . . ."

"Now you're being unfair," he said; "You're rejecting the whole male sex because of the sins of one lone man . . ."

"No, I'm not. I'm simply refusing to lower my standards. I know how much I'm worth, so I will not accept a man inferior to me in every way that counts simply because I haven't got a pretty face or an exciting figure. And since men, without notable exceptions, even those who have both brains enough and sufficient character to know better, all seem to adore painted dolls, I prefer the peace of loneliness to sure heartbreak. Does that seem odd to you?"

"No. It seems—wise. But too wise, somehow. There's something chilling, even repellant about that inhuman degree of wisdom. And yet, you're right. God grant me—in the future—a little of that kind of sense . . ."

She stood there studying him, a quizzical little half smile on her face. That smile was, at one and the same time, curiously serene and almost infinitely mocking.

"Have I, Mister Kane Lovejoy, fully convinced you that I have really retired from the lists of love," she asked, "and that nothing I may say to you is to be construed as an invitation to take what are coyly and quaintly known as 'liberties' with me? In other words, that I am *not* mounting a terribly cunning assault upon your manly honor? It's important that I know, because that's exactly what you thought when I came flying to you for help when I'd been outflanked, surrounded, and was on the verge of being overrun by sheer weight of numbers!"

"Lord!" he laughed. "So your multiple talents include clairvoyance, the reading of minds? If so, that particular gift seems to have deserted you, my dear. I *didn't* think that. Your lack of experience at that kind of infighting showed. I thought you honestly wanted and needed help, so I was perfectly willing to supply it, my clever Annie. Annie—what? Come to think of it, I still don't know *your* name . . ."

"It's Jeffreys. And it's *Anne* Jeffreys, not Annie. That Annnnn-neee business is an invention of the Lonesome Polecats. Come on, Kane, may I tell you something that you badly need to know, without that sublime male ego all you men seem cursed with, driving you to the instant assumption that I'm hurling myself at your poor, defenseless head?"

"Of course," he said with a mockery so understated, so controlled, that she wasn't entirely sure it was mockery; "You've already defined your terms, my dear. You refuse to accept your inferiors—to which category, I humbly submit, I belong. What is it that I badly need to know, and that you're fairly burning with eagerness to tell me?"

"That you're making a mistake," she said quietly. "Oh, I know that you probably couldn't help letting that beautiful creature hurt you. Your error—and believe me it's a grave one!—is letting your pain and sorrow show so clearly . . ."

He looked at her. Breathed out the one word: "Lord!"

"At first, when you came on board this morning at St. Louis, it seemed to me you were one of those dour, forbidding men of mystery with a terrible past, right out of a Brontë novel. And then I realized how Mrs. Bellamy—she's been aboard this boat ever since we left Pittsburgh—"

"Which means you came down the Ohio," Ethan said.

"Yes. And you either up or down the Mississippi, or else you wouldn't have had to change boats. But all roads lead to Rome—or rather to Kansas and Nebraska these days, don't they?"

"Roads, railroads, and rivers. In my case, I've had to use all three. No, four, because I made better than eighty percent of the trip West on the Great Lakes: Buffalo, New York, to Chicago. I hate trains, don't you? But you were telling me about a Mrs. Somebody or Other . . ."

"Mrs. Bellamy. She and her husband are going out to Kansas to homestead, they say. I don't believe them, but that's another matter. Anyhow, I saw how she was devouring you with her eyes, and that aroused my curiosity enough to make me take a second look at you. And I saw—in the sense of perceived—what she was so powerfully attracted by. So, therefore, I'd like to explain to you something about one of the subtler aspects of male-female relations that might well stand you in good stead, if my estimation of your intentions is correct. I take it that you want to avoid, well—sentimental entanglements—for the present anyhow, don't you?"

"Absolutely," he said grimly. "And as far into the future as I can see. So I would appreciate any advice you can give me to that end, my dear!"

Her eyes went petal soft, turned the hazy blue of distant mountains.

"Then never let any woman with blood in her veins catch you standing alone on a steamer's deck, staring out over the water, with that look of terrible, brooding sorrow in your eyes," she murmured. "A tall, ruggedly handsome man, possessed by a secret grief, a most romantic hurt, will derail any woman's good intentions, even erode a great deal of whatever earthworks she's managed to erect around her morals, the minute she becomes aware of him and the terribly intriguing circumstances currently surrounding his life."

He looked at her with a gaze that was pure, sardonic speculation.

"Even *you?*" he said.

"Even—I. But, as I've already told you, I've long since learned to dominate my irrational impulses, and to maintain—at any cost!—my head's stern mastery over my occasionally rebellious heart. Besides, it's obvious to me that the cause of your sorrow had to be very, very beautiful. . . . She was, wasn't she?"

He thought about Edith, then. Visualized her as she had been the last time he'd seen her—the night before he had left Pittsfield forever—lying there in the wet, wild-tangled mass of that hair of hers that was like a darkling flame, lithe-limbed, sweet curving, glistening with the sweat of their mutual labors, perfuming the night with the high-spiced musk of achieved passion, warm and soft and mother-naked, weeping her poor, disconsolate heart out in his arms that had no comfort to offer her, being themselves—like all the rest of him!—totally bereft of comfort, and wearied almost unto death. . . .

"Yes," he said quietly, "she was. Almost unimaginably so . . ."

"Tell me about her," Anne said.

"No," he said. Like that. Flatly.

She stared at him, and her eyes went bluer, softer still.

"That bad, Kane?" she said.

"You may place that interpretation on it, if you like," he said. "My slant is that I owe her the respect—and the recompense—of silence. What's done is done. That particular chapter of my life is closed—forever. I have neither the intention nor the desire to reopen it. Besides, I couldn't, anyhow. Come on, let's walk a bit, shall we? Work up a little appetite for lunch—"

"I have been shut up very nicely!" she laughed. "You're right. It's absolutely none of my business, is it? So a walk it is! I mean to profit from the occasion, by making all the she-cats aboard swoon from envy as I promenade the decks on the arm of my handsome beau! Notably Mrs. Bellamy."

"You seem concerned about her," he said. "Why don't you just forget her for a change—and enjoy the boyish exuberance of my company?"

She laughed at that.

"I am!" she said gaily; "or rather its funereal solemnity. D'you know, you're just about *the* most solitary person I've ever met? You were an only child, weren't you?"

"No," he said; "I had a brother. *One.* Come on, let's walk."

"Your brother," she said; "was he older, or younger than you?"

"Neither. Jonathan and I were twins. But we looked a great deal less alike than many first cousins do, not to mention brothers. In all our lives, people only confused our identities once, and that one time cost me my girl . . ."

"That's odd," she said, "how could it?"

"He was killed at Gettysburg in July, 1863," Ethan said grimly. "But when my parents got the War Department's notification of his death, it had *my* name on it. My fiancée mourned me a scant six months, then married someone else. Incidentally, that someone else was a very good friend of mine. Assistant Manager of my father's shoe factory in fact. . . ."

"And yet, he stole your girl," she said.

"No. He married her believing quite sincerely that I was dead. As far as I can see, he was far more grieved than *she* was. Horace was a real demon for work; and yet, when my family got the news, my old man had to give him two days off: He couldn't work at all; just sat there in his office blubbering like a kid. I hold him no rancor; I haven't any right to . . ."

"But you do hold her some, don't you?" she said. "Go on, Mister Kane Lovejoy! Demonstrate to me that your supposed fairness toward our sex is real!"

"It does seem to me that she might have mourned me a trifle longer," Ethan said.

"And it seems to me that you might have written her immediately after your brother's death," Anne said tartly. "Wouldn't that have been the logical thing for you to have done?"

"Yep. Only war and logic aren't even on speaking terms, Anne, my dear. Never have been. The day after my brother's death, I was in a stinking butcher shop of a field hospital with an assistant amateur butcher poking around in what was left of my guts with a pair of fire tongs, trying to dig out all the scrap iron, horseshoe nails, nuts and bolts, plus a rusty steel hoop or two from one of Mrs. Jeff Davis's oldest crinolines, I do believe, some Reb sharpshooter had pumped into my middle. Without opium, or ether, both of which were in mighty short supply, as usual. For the next six months, when I could lift a hand at all, it was only in a feeble effort to brush away the flies who dined upon my rotting and stinking carcass all day long. And all night, too, come to think of it. So letter writing was out of the question. The only thing that kept me alive was the belief—the naïve and stupid belief—that she was going to be waiting for me when I finally got back from hell's farthest borders. I was wrong. So chalk the whole thing up to experience. Or to life's unpleasant habit of educating us through our hides. Effective method, I have to admit . . ."

She stared at him, then abruptly, awkwardly, she whirled away from him and looked out over the mighty river. He found the gesture odd, inexplicable, even; then he saw the little shake that had got into her thin shoulders. He put his big, bony hand down on one of them and turned her very gently to face him. As he had suspected, she *was* crying. All of that warm and wonderfully homely face of hers was awash and glistening with tears.

"Now, Anne—" he said reproachfully.

"She had no right!" she said fiercely; "Absolutely no right at all to do a thing like that to any man—and especially not to *you!*"

He was no fool; he recognized at once that this chance encounter was gathering a headlong momentum of its own. And he wasn't prepared to become emotionally involved with another woman, not even one as genuinely appealing as he now admitted this odd little creature was. Not yet. Not with the unmitigated disaster of the way his affair with Edith had ended so cruelly fresh in his heart, his mind. And, being himself, being possessed of a very high order of intelligence indeed, the evasive action that he took had a marked degree of sophistication about it: he blandly pretended to be as dense and as unperceptive as women generally believe that all men are.

"On the contrary," he said quietly, "she had every right. Most people do what they must, my dear, not what they want to. You're plenty wise enough to realize that. And we—my brother Jonathan and I—had let her down very badly by dying. That I hadn't actually crossed the dark river to join the shades of my ancestors in Tartarus was a total irrelevancy, since she didn't know that and had no way of ascertaining the true state of affairs . . ."

"Go on," Anne said; "but I must admit that you're making me dislike her all the more with every passing minute . . ."

He shrugged.

"The way you feel about her is another irrelevancy, isn't it?" he said drily. "Since it's entirely unlikely to do her either good or harm. Put it this way: From the time that Jon and I were small boys, and she a baby in her crib, it was understood between our two families that Edith was to marry one of the two of us . . ."

"Edith what?" Anne said.

"Does it matter? Oh, hell, why not? Edith Craddock. Now Mrs. Horace Willoughby. . . . You see, by the time she decided to marry Horace, the War Department's original mistake had been both corrected and compounded. My family now knew that it was Jonathan, not I, who had been killed; but they'd been notified that I was 'missing in action, under such circumstances that my death must be presumed. . . .' It wasn't until fully ten months later that they found what was left of me in an even more glorified—and more abominably stinking!—butcher shop of an army hospital in Washington . . ."

Anne dabbed at the corners of her eyes with a tiny handkerchief.

"And with both the Lovejoy twins dead," she said acridly, "your darling Edith decided she just had to marry *somebody*. So, your loyal, grieving friend being available, she—"

"You put that very justly," Ethan said, "but without even a hint of mercy. There *were* mitigating circumstances, dear Anne. She did have to marry someone. She had only a finishing school education, which meant she'd been trained—exquisitely trained—only to be a rich man's wife. Her parents both died just before the War. On the advice of her lawyers, and ours, she sold the Craddock knitting mill, thereby losing the fortune that the mill—as every other textile factory in Pittsfield proved—would surely have made by manufacturing uniforms for both the Army and the Navy during the War. At the time, the fact that she was left in somewhat straitened circumstances—the mill was sold too quickly, and for far less than it was worth—didn't seem important since it was understood that she was to marry me . . ."

Anne stared at him again. Studied him, really.

"You know, Kane," she said evenly; "there's something in this tale of yours—an undercurrent of bitterness, I'd say—that's curiously like Hamlet's father's ghost parading the parapets of Elsinore. I sense something *wrong*. Terribly wrong. My evil female mind tells me that all the time it was understood that dear Edith was to marry you, she was in love with your brother Jonathan . . ."

"If you had lived in Salem sometime back," he drawled, "they'd have hanged you out of hand, Anne Jeffreys!"

"Meaning I'm a witch? Oh, yes; quite. Worse than the ones in Macbeth. So now, tell me: Since she was in love with him, why did she agree to marry you?"

"*I* was available. He wasn't. He wasn't in love with her. Not that much in love with her, anyhow . . ."

Again that dead level, still, blue gaze.

"Not enough to—marry her, eh, Kane?" she whispered. "But quite enough to—how *is* a woman supposed to say a thing like that? Oh, well, I'll brazen it out!—but quite enough to bed with her. . . . Right, my poor, abused friend?"

"I didn't say that!" Ethan said sharply.

"And now, you don't even need to," she said pityingly. "I know both my sex and yours far too well. And both can be pretty rotten sometimes, can't they?"

"I'd amend that to 'driven,' " he said sadly, "and bow my none too sturdy shoulders beneath my fair share of the guilt. Oh, hell, let's change this subject, shall we? We've got to, anyhow. From what I've been able to read between the lines of your tart remarks about her, that must be Mrs.

Bellamy bearing down upon us like a Confederate Ironclad, full steam ahead, preparing to ram . . ."

"Her usual tactics," Anne sighed; "God knows she was hiding behind the pantry door when both taste and subtlety were passed out. . . ."

Mrs. Bellamy, Ethan saw at once, was a handsome woman. Very much so. Her hair and eyes were brown; and yet the shade, rather than the color, of the first two features anyone tends to notice about a stranger, simply didn't match. Her eyes were—or seemed to be—far lighter than her hair. But, as she came closer, he realized this wasn't so. What they were was alight from within with a terrible intensity rather like what mid-century novelists were pleased to call "a devouring flame." They glittered so hotly—no other word would do!—that the lines from William Blake came crashing back into Ethan's mind: "Tiger, Tiger, burning bright in the forests of the night; What immortal hand or eye could frame thy fearful symmetry?"

She was every inch as tall as Ethan was himself; and her form, while ample, was quite shapely. She had, he saw, achieved the fashionable "hourglass figure" with only a moderate degree of help from her corsets. And, Ethan realized, not only wasn't she fat, as Anne had honestly and fairly declared, but she would never be. Whatever it was that glowed and glittered behind her eyes would always consume any really unsightly excess of flesh; growing old, she would weather into gauntness and, with her powerful, big-boned frame, become an even more impressive presence, though, surely, an ever more frightening one.

Then, raising his eyes, and thereby extending the trajectory of his gaze, Ethan saw Mr. Bellamy trotting along a little behind his wife. And understood, on the spur of that same instant, the tragedy of the big woman's existence. Bellamy was a little shorter than his wife, but what he lacked in height, he more than made up for in breadth. He was a square-built, powerful, muscular man. And yet, and yet. . . .

'He has the look of a gelding—or a mule,' Ethan decided. But by then, he had no more time, not even for thought, for the Bellamys were almost literally upon them.

One yard from him, Mrs. Bellamy stopped. Looked him up and down from head to toe. Crossed his lean body sidewise at shoulder height, then at hip level, with the curiously disquieting measure of her gaze. Then—quite unconsciously, Ethan was sure—she put out a wet and glistening tongue tip and licked her lips very, very slowly. Incongruously enough, in marked contrast to the almost menacing sensuality the rest of her projected, her lips were thin. Perhaps even cruel. But surely grimly determined.

'God grant,' Ethan thought despairingly, 'that they settle at least two hundred miles away from Marthasville. On the other side of the state. Or even in Nebraska. Because I'm going to have trouble with this woman. That's for sure!'

"*Now* do you see, Kane, dear," Anne said in a stage whisper deliberately meant to carry, "why we women feel insulted when a man undresses us with his eyes? How does it feel to be on the receiving end for a change?"

If Mrs. Bellamy heard that whisper, she chose to ignore it.

"Wonders never cease!" she laughed in a dark-toned contralto that was wondrously appropriate to her Valkyrie size and figure; "Anne, you dear little mouse, I have to admit I've underestimated you! *The* most attractive man aboard, and you grab him before we're even a full hour out of St. Louis! Tell me, dear, just how did you manage such a feat?"

"Perhaps by not trying too hard," Anne said solemnly. "Oh, all right; I'll do the honors! Kane, these good people you see before you are Tom and Cora Bellamy, to put matters upon a first-name basis from the outset. A most loving and devoted couple, I assure you! Tom and Cora, may I present Mr. Kane Lovejoy? He and I have at least our background in common, since we're both New Englanders. He's from my native state, in fact . . ."

Ethan shook hands with Tom Bellamy, raised his tall silk hat to Mrs. Bellamy, made her the sort of graceful and mocking little bow his late brother had excelled at; but he didn't offer to shake hands with her. He had both the suspicion and the fear that he'd have one devil of a time getting his own hand back if he tried that.

"And just where do you be heading, young fella?" Tom Bellamy asked.

"Kansas," Ethan said quietly. "Felt the need to change my life's direction, make a new start. But that's true of most of the people heading West these days, isn't it?"

"Or to git back to the kind of life they oughta stuck to in the first place," Tom Bellamy said. "Cora 'n me are both farm-bred, though we did meet in the city. . . . Try as I would, just couldn't seem to make a go of things in the Big Burg. On the land, it'll be different. Farming plumb comes natural to me. Inside of five years, I mean to have myself the prettiest spread in the whole blamed state. . . ."

"I'll wait," Cora Bellamy said mockingly. "Now, tell me, Mr. Lovejoy, what do you mean to do in Kansas—besides making all the women in the state mighty, mighty happy?"

"That's a tall order," Ethan chuckled; "Up until now, I haven't been able to find one who'd put up with me long enough for me to make her good and miserable. But as far as my plans are concerned, they're about the same as yours: I mean to homestead. Preëmp, too, if I can find myself two likely spreads lying side by side . . ."

Anne stared at him in unfeigned wonder.

"Now you've taken my breath away, quite," she said, "for the last thing on earth I would or could ever imagine *you* doing—or even wanting to, Kane, dear—is farming!"

"Hard as it is for me to ever agree with another female critter," Cora Bellamy said, "I have to admit that your judgment seems mighty sound to me, Anne, honey. I'd put Mr. Lovejoy down as a lawyer, or maybe even a newspaperman, but a clodhopping sodbuster? Never!"

"Looks mighty like a real city slicker, if you ask me," Tom Bellamy said with the heavy-handed joviality that the obviously defeated often assume. "Course he could be a preacher, y'know. Running tent revivals and protracted meetings all over th state. Nothing like religion to get a man next to fillies fast, young fella!"

"That's the last thing I want," Ethan said drily. " 'A burnt child dreads the fire,' you know. And in that department, I've had all the skin blistered and peeled right off me. So, no thanks! But, believe it or not, I'm far from the tyro you folks seem to take me for. As a matter of simple fact, I lived with my grandfather, Daniel Lovejoy, on his farm in the Berkshires, and helped him work it, too, for the last three years before the War . . ."

Again Anne Jeffreys held him with the cool blue penetration of her gaze.

"Why?" she said evenly; "That is: Why should you ever have done a thing like that?"

Ethan stared at her. Sighed.

"Some of it you already know," he said sadly; "And the rest I'll tell you tonight—after supper . . ."

"So now we've been put smack dab back in our places, Tom, love," Cora purred. "This tale's not for an old married couple's ears, eh, Kane?"

"It's not that, Mrs. Bellamy," Ethan said; "The only thing wrong with the story of why I left Pittsfield to immigrate to the West is that it would probably bore you stiff. There isn't even anything interestingly dishonorable about it. I quarreled with my father, who is in the business of manufacturing boots and shoes, because I didn't want to follow in his footsteps and become a sort of glorified cobbler, driven by millraces and by steam. And my grandfather cut the ground out from under what I really wanted to do—advanced, scientific farming—by converting the farm he planned to leave me into pastureland to feed his huge herd of sheep . . ."

Again Anne studied his face, his eyes.

"Why'd he do that?" she said.

"Because, old as he is, Gramps is as smart as a whip. All the things I meant to do to put the farm on a paying basis would take years to set up and get working properly. While with a war going on, and the textile mills fairly screaming for wool to make uniforms with, Gramps saw the chance of getting rich. He was right; he did get rich. But he ruined the farm I loved to do it. The Lovejoys, with the lone exception of this disgrace to the family principles you see before you, have always been great hands at piling up the cash . . ."

"And you," Anne said tartly, "violently objected to becoming—or in your case, I suspect, even remaining—rich?"

"Not violently," Ethan said. "What I object to are the methods most people—especially my old monster of a father—are willing to use to accomplish it. Besides, given my 'druthers,' I'd druther be a happy beggar than a miserable Croesus. I was the son of a greedy old miser, Anne, darling, so I know from my own experience that wealth and happiness are usually mutually contradictory states . . ."

"Ha!" Tom Bellamy laughed; "If sittin' on a heap o'money makes a fella miserable, I'm perfectly willin' to be miserable, Kane, son!"

"You know, Kane," Cora said, "somehow or other I'm getting the feeling you ain't—aren't—telling the whole truth. Sure there wasn't a pretty girl in the picture?"

"Yes," Ethan said, "there was. And she wasn't merely pretty—she was beautiful. Only while I was down South in Virginia letting the Johnny Rebs use me for target practice, she married my best friend . . ."

Anne gazed at him with a frown of womanly—and possessive!—annoyance and said, tartly:

"The real reason his sweetheart married his best friend was that Kane, here, was reported killed in action, instead of being merely as terribly wounded as he was. He was shot through the abdomen, and left for dead in the very thickest of the battle . . ."

"Wasn't a battle," Ethan said; "A little cavalry bickering way off on the flanks. And I got hit because I turned in my saddle to look at a Reb trooper I'd downed. And you didn't do a fool trick like that when you were up against J.E.B. Stuart's horsemen. Only this one had emptied his side-arm at me instead of using his sabre, forgetting that you can't hit the side of a red-painted barn with a revolver from horseback. So I gave him cold steel through his guts, jerked my blade free, swept past him, then turned to watch him fall. And all the rest of my life I'm going to wonder why I did a stupid thing like that . . ."

"Wasn't it because," Anne whispered, "your twin brother had been killed just the day before?"

"In part," Ethan said, "but only in part, dear Anne. It was—far more complicated than that, shall we say? By the way, it must already be lunch time, and—"

"It is, or almost," Anne said; "but before we descend to this 'Floating Palace's Grand Salon' explain me just one thing, and I promise to leave you in peace until tonight . . ."

"At which time you're gonna turn him every whichaway except loose, ain't you, honey?" Tom Bellamy chuckled.

"Possibly. Quite possibly," Anne said coolly. "Tell me, Mister Kane Lovejoy, how a man who was only an assistant manager in your father's factory—I'm from New England, and *know* what Yankee wages are!—could become so rich within a mere ten months that your distinctly avaricious ex-sweetheart would consent to marry him even though he was anything but an Adonis, from what I gather?"

"War profits," Ethan said grimly. "When my father saw what a genius at management Horace was, he offered him a huge raise in salary, in part because even a miserable skinflint like the Old Monster could realize how valuable Horace was. But in greater part because Horace himself engineered the whole deal; outsmarted the Old Man as nicely as you please. With exquisitely studied carelessness, he left a letter open on his desk, where my nosy old busybody of a father would be sure to see it. Mind you, that letter was entirely genuine. It was from another firm, one of my father's chief rivals in the leather goods manufacturing business, offering Horace double whatever Father was paying him at the moment to leave Lovejoy and Sons, and come to work for them. You see, Horace's reputation for hard work, and even harder dealing, had already made the rounds of the industry in Pittsfield. So, in self-defense, Father offered Horace that raise . . ."

"And?" Anne said.

"Horace wouldn't take it. He told the Old Monster that he was satisfied with what he was already getting but added that if Father wanted to show some appreciation for his efforts—he'd doubled our profits by then—a minor partnership in the business would suit him to a T. Father snapped that up like a speckled brook trout leaping for a fly. Turned out to be a good deal for both of them. Horace ploughed some of his share of the profits back into the business, notably to finance the installation of a labor-saving device *I* dreamed up and was fool enough to mention to Hor in a careless moment—"

"What was that device?" Anne asked.

"You wouldn't understand it," Ethan said.

"I would understand it. The wearing of skirts is not automatically a sign of idiocy, Kane Lovejoy!"

"Sorry," Ethan sighed. "You're right, you probably would. But don't you see that that's not what we were talking about? I'll tell you about that later, if you like, but right now, let me finish this, will you? While I still have a little appetite left for lunch, anyhow . . ."

"All right," Anne said sardonically; "Let us observe the Aristotelian unities of time, place, and action! Makes for far better dramatic structure, doesn't it? Do go on, dear Kane!"

"This here," Tom Bellamy groaned, "is sure Lord one smart little girl, ain't she, son? Trouble is, be there anybody around what can understand that highfalutin' lingo o'hern?"

"Kane can," Anne said imperturbably; "I'm sorry, I won't interrupt you again. Tell us how your friend Horace—Willoughby, wasn't it?—got rich enough to steal, or rather *buy* your girl . . ."

"You can be mean when you want to, can't you?" Ethan said. "Put it this way: Once Horace had my invention set up and working, the factory's profits were greater than ever. So he invested his own legitimate earnings—far, far greater than the raise he'd refused in the first place—in speculative stocks and bonds, and chose them so shrewdly that ten months later, when Edith had become somewhat reconciled to Jonathan's death, and completely so to mine—which wasn't all that big a mistake, because even by then the sawbones were still anything but sure that I was going to pull through—he was only a couple of hundred thousand dollars short of being an actual millionaire. Now, he *is* a millionaire. Several times over, in fact. When I left, he was offering to buy my father out, and allow the Old Man to retire . . .

He looked away from them, gazed out over the river, looked back again. His eyes were very bleak.

"Speaking of retiring, that's just what I'd like to do," he said, quietly. "For the moment, anyhow. The truth is, I'm somewhat tired. Would all of you excuse me? I'd just as soon skip lunch, if you don't mind . . ."

"But I definitely *do* mind!" Anne said with a severity that was almost comically wifely, and that would have embarrassed her past all bearing, Ethan was sure, if she had realized just how she looked and sounded then. "You're thinner than a rail fence, Kane, which means that no one has taken proper care of you in a long time. So now I'm going to, for the duration of this voyage, anyhow . . ."

"Which ain't more'n two days, Anne, honey," Tom Bellamy grinned. "We git to Kansas day after tomorrow, with any luck. You means to tell me you're jes' gonna up'n turn him loose after that?"

"That doesn't depend upon me, Tom," Anne said sadly. "As I told you, I'm looking for a job teaching school, and I'll have to take the best offer I can get. Which means I may be two hundred miles from wherever Kane is . . ."

Ethan considered that. Almost instantly he became aware that, surprisingly enough, he didn't like the idea. In fact, he disliked it intensely. He found it shocking to contemplate. More than that even, actually painful. Anne hadn't changed at all; she was still a pale, thin, distinctly plain young woman with a square-jawed, determined little face, mousey brown hair—and the biggest, softest blue eyes in the whole blamed universe, a speaking voice that was limpid music, angel-tongued, silvery, clear, and. . . .

'Good God!' he thought; 'I'm mesmerizing myself! And so is she, likely. It's the same thing, really, isn't it? We're both bouncing back after having been hurt. Edith, in my case. And in hers, whoever that bounder was. . . . Oh, Lord, I—'

"I hope not," he said quietly; "I'd like to get to know you better, Anne Jeffreys. Much better . . ."

She smiled. And became, out of the dark magic that his loneliness and his need can work upon a man, almost beautiful in that moment.

"Then start by coming down to lunch with me—with us—now," she said.

The luncheon wasn't an outstanding social success. In the first place, the Bellamys quarreled bitterly all through it, and over some question so insignificant that afterward Ethan couldn't even remember what it was. They would never need, Ethan realized sadly, any really valid motive for quarreling; by then they had come to hate each other so completely that any reason—or none at all!—would serve. Looking at Tom and Cora Bellamy, Ethan wondered if the attempt to save a marriage obviously on the skids should even be made. Wouldn't it be wiser, in the long run, for the states as individual entities, or collectively on a national scale, to bend their efforts toward the codifying and the eventual passage of reasonable and civilized divorce laws? In that year, 1866, to obtain a divorce, the lawyers for the warring couple still had to petition some senator to present a bill before the legislature of the state in which they resided, so each divorce—granted or denied—became a separate law. Curiously enough, the proposed destination of the little group lunching together that day in the *Prairie Belle*'s Grand Salon, headed the list as far as liberality—closely approaching license!—in such matters was concerned. In fact, the facility with which a Bill of Divorcement could be eased, or "greased," as Phil Harris put it, through the Kansas state legislature was a national joke.

Ethan was wondering if the real reason that the Bellamys were heading for Kansas were not to get rid of each other, when he felt Anne's gaze upon him like an azure brand.

"Kane," she said furiously, "you're not eating at all!"

"Sorry, my dear," he murmured.

"Why aren't you?" she demanded; "Has my friends' display of their abominably bad manners ruined your appetite? Or is it my unwelcome presence that disturbs you? If it is, say so, and I'll leave!"

He grinned at her with sad mockery.

"Neither," he said; "In fact, I kind of think it's one of Mrs. Jeff Davis's rusty crinoline hoops I told you about . . ."

She stared at him blankly, then she remembered.

"You mean that after all this time your wound still—bothers you?" she whispered, her voice vibrant with real concern.

"And it's likely to for the rest of my life," Ethan told her. "Mind you, it's completely healed, and I'm actually as healthy as a horse or else I wouldn't even dream of going on with my idea of becoming a farmer. But all that scrap iron that Reb pumped into me messed up my stomach more than somewhat, with the result that eating has become something of a chore. Oh, Lord, I'm not explaining this very well, am I? What I mean is that I *can* eat, but that I generally have no desire to. Doctor von Rauschnau says a lot of the nerves in my middle got cut loose so that my stomach doesn't respond to the usual stimuli of sight, taste, or smell. In a word, I have practically no appetite at all . . ."

"Cora," Anne said, "change places with me, will you?"

"Whatcha gonna do, Anne, baby—spank him?" Tom chuckled.

The two women changed places. Sitting beside Ethan, Anne proceeded to cut his steak into tiny pieces as a mother often does for a small and exceedingly naughty boy. Then, stabbing a piece of it on the end of his fork, she thrust it toward his mouth.

"Open up, Kane!" she said.

Ethan opened his mouth. Anne poked the food into it. As a matter of fact, as was usually the case, the food aboard the *Prairie Belle* was very good indeed. Steamboat cuisine very often was of better quality than that to be found in most places except a tiny minority of luxury hotels and restaurants. Ethan discovered it was possible to eat it with only a minimum of effort. But being, after all, both male and human, he decided to take advantage.

"No, Mama!" he piped in a falsetto meant to imitate a childish treble; "I won't! Not unless you give me a big kiss first, anyhow . . ."

Anne stared at him. Then a certain combative glow showed in her eyes. At least she thought at the moment that it was combative, a high-mettled response to a challenge. Afterward, she was far from sure.

She leaned swiftly forward and kissed him. Then, from her point of view, every conceivable thing went wrong. She had meant to tease him with the same sort of light and playful kiss he had given her as a means of rescuing her from the Lonesome Polecats that morning. But the glandular chemistry—or the essentially mysterious alchemy—of male-female attraction between the two of them had already grown too strong. To peck and pull away abruptly became an actual, physical impossibility, despite the appalled reproaches of her entirely conscious mind. Her lips on his went suddenly adhesive; try as she would to draw back they clung to his, moving, moving in that tactile, sensual language that every lover instinctively knows, informing him wordlessly, helplessly, hopelessly of all her terrible longing, all her aching need. What broke that kiss finally was a number of things: Tom Bellamy's delighted "Whoopie!"; a linked chorus of "Why, didya ever!" from all the women passengers; a burst of sardonic handclapping from the younger, sportier males, the Lonesome Polecats among them; and Cora Bellamy's utterly bitter:

"You didn't hear him right, Anne, baby; he said kiss, not swallow whole!"

Anne drew back. Her great blue eyes grew and grew in her small, square face until Ethan couldn't see anything else. Then they disappeared, walled out behind the sudden downrushing desolation of her tears.

She surged to her feet. Whirled, already running. Then, head down and visibly sobbing, she got out of there.

"Well, Kane," Cora purred, the sound deep, almost leonine, curiously appropriate to her great size, "if you don't have yourself the time of your life tonight, you're a bigger fool than I ever thought you were!"

But, precisely because he was anything but a fool, Ethan knew better than that. He looked up, met Cora Bellamy's probing gaze.

"Well, I never was right bright, Cora," he said.

2

Ethan Lovejoy stood by the larboard rail of the *Prairie Belle,* watching as—valises and carpetbags in hand, and even occasionally followed by roustabouts who trundled their steamer trunks along on pushcarts—those passengers whose voyage ended at Wyandotte, Kansas, bustled down the stageplank to the docks, giving themselves airs of great importance as they did so.

'To hide their disappointment, likely,' Ethan thought with wry amusement, 'for if this is Wyandotte, God, in His infinite mercy, help the rest of Kansas!'

In that year, 1866, Wyandotte was the first town within the borders of Kansas any steam packet bound upstream on the Missouri got to, for Kansas City—that little upstart of a "Kite Town," as Kansans derisively called any of the dozens of hamlets and villages that tacked the word "City" onto their names like the tail of a kite in the vain pretense of being what they not only weren't but that most of them would never even get to be—wouldn't be laid out for another two years.

Not all the passengers going ashore at Wyandotte would stay there, Ethan knew. That very year, the section of the Kansas Pacific Railroad connecting Wyandotte with Topeka had been completed; and besides, since the Kansas River, one of the bigger tributaries of the Missouri, flowed into the Big Muddy along one leg of the roughly triangular space on which Wyandotte stood—that fortunate accident of geography being the reason the founding fathers had selected it to build their town on in the first place—not a few of the travelers would transfer to shallow draft, much smaller steamboats for the voyage almost due westward on the Kansas River to the various towns and villages then existing along its banks.

Ethan studied, with some care, the passengers who were disembarking. He also examined with the same degree of attention—or even more so—the miserable-looking little town whose houses were mostly built of cottonwood, the poorest wood there is to try to build anything out of, with here and there a—to his mind anyhow!—visibly-unfit-for-human-habitation sod house, the whole dismal panorama being relieved at intervals by a neat brick structure.

'Have patience!' he admonished himself sternly; 'It's all just getting started, so what the hell did you expect: Paris or Rome? My grandsons will see a great city standing here, that's for sure. It's a magnificent location: the confluence of two rivers, with steamboats to bear our produce south and east, the railroads west—all the way to California, very soon now. . . . Maybe, after I see what Phil's little burg of Marthasville has to offer, I'll come back down here. Because what so many new settlers forget is that you not only have to grow the stuff, you have to ship it out, and in that regard, this section looks mighty good to me . . .'

Seeing that the last of the passengers who were going ashore at Wyandotte were already on the docks, he gave a long sigh of relief and turned away. Then he saw that his relief had been in part premature in the sense that there were quite a few other problems besides the one he had in mind, for only a couple of yards away from him the Bellamys stood, blocking his path completely and grinning at him.

"You don't mean to tell me, d'you, Kane, boy," Tom Bellamy said, laughing through his horselike—and hideous!—yellow teeth all the time, "that you really thought your little filly was gonna sneak ashore without so much as kissin' you good-bye?"

Ethan eyed Tom Bellamy with the expression that most people reserve for something utterly repulsive—a snake, for instance. Then he amended that thought to "a warty toad frog," because Tom, with his thickset build, just didn't fit his mental picture of a snake.

"Yes," he said slowly; "I did think that, Tom. In fact, I still do. You see, she's kept a quality all too many people have lost or forgot: the ability to feel ashamed of herself. Far more so, surely, than the occasion warranted; but the fact remains that I haven't seen her since that—incident. So I'm going to stand guard beside the stageplank at both Leavenworth and Atchison to make sure she doesn't go ashore without telling me how —and where—to find her later on . . ."

"You mean you actually don't know?" Cora Bellamy said.

"I don't know. All she told me was that she planned to join her father and her brothers who live in this state. And, at the time, it never even occurred to me to ask her what town they live in or near."

"Sure got you worked up, ain't she, boy?" Tom chuckled. "And cause o' one li'l old measly kiss at that! If I was you, I'd take it easy, 'n not go pawing the ground like a seed bull, rushing in without finding out a mighty heap more about her. 'Cause that there li'l filly has done dropped them frilly li'l drawers o' hern for many's the man afore she ever laid eyes on you, son, or I miss my guess!"

That was as far as he got. Ethan's bony, big-knuckled hand shot out and caught him by the front of his greasy waistcoat, and slammed him back against the bulkhead of the nearest cabin so hard that the planking shook.

"Tom," Ethan said quietly, "you'd better take back what you just said. And fast, at that."

"Oh, I take it back! I take it back!" Tom got out; "You ain't got no cause to be so hotheaded, Kane Lovejoy!"

Ethan turned Tom loose. Taking out his pocket handkerchief, he wiped his hands with it, slowly, and with great care. Then he threw the handkerchief over the rail and into the river. The studied contempt with which he made that gesture was abysmal. He said then, almost gently: "If the two of you will excuse me?"

And, lifting his tall silk hat, made that distinctly unsavory pair the most courteous—and the most mocking!—of all possible bows. Then he edged his way past them, and strode on down the deck.

The minute he entered the Salon, he saw Anne.

He could hardly have missed seeing her, for she was all alone in that usually masculine preserve, except for one bartender fast asleep and snoring lustily behind the bar. Even her being there wasn't really surprising since it was only a little after eight o'clock in the morning, and the breakfast tables had already been set up, mostly for the benefit of the passengers who has just gone ashore at Wyandotte, for those travelers who would disembark at Fort Leavenworth or Atchison still had time and to spare to enjoy a leisurely—and enormous!—repast at around ten or eleven, and wouldn't emerge from their staterooms, whose inner doors opened directly into the Salon, before then. Therefore, Ethan's luck was twofold. First of all, its being a meal hour, Anne could enter and sit in the main Salon without let or hindrance. At all other times in that serenely male-dominated age, ladies were strictly forbidden entrance not only to the bar but to the "Gentlemen's Cabin" as the main Salon was generally called, the only exception being a lady who admittedly was not a lady, whereupon she was welcomed! In revenge, female travelers had a "Ladies' Cabin," just aft of the main Salon, from which men were excluded, though the privilege of entry was occasionally granted to a husband, a man of the cloth, or a brother, say, and then only for five minutes' chat. And Ethan's second stroke of luck consisted in the lovely fact that the hour was sufficiently ungodly for most of the remaining passengers to only burrow deeper into their pillows for another forty winks, so he and Anne, for the moment, anyhow, were blessed with an almost perfect privacy. Which, as it turned out, was just as well!

Anne was sitting at a corner table and staring at each of the cabin doors that opened into the Salon in turn, as though she were watching for someone to come out of one of them.

When she saw him, her face became whiter than it already was, and the trace of tears on her cheeks exploded into a flood. Ethan raced toward her, reached her table in four long strides, stood there, said: "Anne!"

"Ohhhhh, Kane!" she wailed; "I thought you'd *never* come in here!"

Hearing that, the wave of joy that washed over him made him quite literally, physically, weak. He snarled at himself: 'You fool! It's the classic female flanking maneuver: stay out of sight until the poor devil is chasing his own tail round and round in a circle like a snake-bit coon dog, or baying the moon, and then—'

But his powers of analysis and his quite respectable intellect were no defenses at all against the spectacle Anne Jeffreys presented him at that moment. She was, if anything, homelier than ever. Her eyes were swollen almost shut from crying, her nose was cherry red, and her pale pink lips trembled so they made a moving blur. Pity invaded him, and, with it, tenderness. He was beaten then and he knew it, so he surrendered the rest of his life and the continued existence of the Lovejoy clan into her keeping with a certain degree of reluctance, a good many doubts and hesitations, but despite them, overcoming them, really, with what was also a high and handsome grace.

'I love her,' he thought, 'which makes not one goddamned bit of sense; but then does love, ever? So she's not pretty—hardly the rarest of all conditions or a matter of world-shaking importance.'

He said: "My dear—what's happened? What has upset you so?"

"Oh, Kane—I've made the most awful mistake!" she wept; "I should have known that when my father didn't answer my letters there had to be something terribly wrong!"

He sank into the chair beside her.

"Your father? You mean he's had an accident, or—"

"That's just the trouble; I don't know," she whispered, visibly fighting for and slowly gaining self-control. "This morning when the steward who has been bringing me up my meals—and taking them back down again mostly untasted—ever since I demonstrated to all the world —including myself!—that I am my mother's daughter and, like her, a perfect wanton at heart—"

"You didn't to me," he teased her solemnly; "but don't worry, I'll give you another chance—tonight."

She stared at him, and her heart was in her eyes, and clearly breaking there.

"Kane," she said with a conviction, a finality, that made his old wound ache, "if you should ever take advantage of my—my inherited weakness—of the awful way *you* make me feel, I'll go over the rail of this boat in midstream, and, believe me, I can't swim!"

Hearing that, his eyes lit up with suppressed laughter, but he kept his face almost lugubriously solemn as he said:

"That second splash you'll hear will be me, belly flopping in right behind you. And I can't swim either. Ever thought what a lovely pair of corpses we'll make when they lay us out side by side, smelling of Missouri River mud, with our noses nibbled off by the catfish, and—"

She said furiously: "Kane Lovejoy!"

"Anne, baby, you disappoint me," he chuckled. "If you'd ever taken a good look at me, you'd have seen by now that I haven't a pair of long black mustachios to twirl at you, and I never did learn how to leer. 'Unhand me, you dastard!' the Maiden cried, 'or I'll ddddrrrrown myself!' Oh, Lord, Anne, forget the traveling tent show melodrama and tell a fellow what's wrong, will you, please?"

She peered at him through slowing tears and a little, uncertain, almost smile tugged at the corners of her pale lips.

"Yankee humor—as dry as hard cider, eh, Kane? Oh, all right! What I started to say was that when I asked the steward who's been bringing me up my meals ever since I disgraced myself forever day before yesterday, when we were going to get to Tiltson, he said he'd never heard of it!"

"Me neither," Ethan said, poker-faced. "What the devil is Tiltson, anyhow?"

"A town," she said with noticeable exasperation, "on the Missouri River, having a population of close to two thousand people, and duly, as any town of that size would be, equipped with steamboat docks. The town where, according to my Aunt Sue—my mother's only sister—my father and my four little half brothers, all of 'em much younger than I am since he had them by his second wife, live. You see, he had no trouble in getting the Missouri legislature—he and my mother were living in St. Louis at the time—to hand him down a Bill of Divorcement, because he could produce two dozen witnesses to the fact that my mother deliberately left his bed and board on the arm of exactly the sort of creature you've just described, complete to the handlebar mustache he was always twirling!"

"Maybe," Ethan drawled, "he bussed her a good one, and she found he could kiss better than your pop . . ."

"Kane," she said bitterly, "that's unfair—and unkind. Believe me, I didn't *know* that I took—take—after her that much. That was the first time in my life that I have *ever* behaved that way. I've never even been seriously tempted to. Incidentally, I apologize—humbly. And I definitely promise to . . . to keep the base impulses I never before realized I had, under better control!"

"Your apology is not accepted," Ethan said. "At least not until you repeat the offense a couple of hundred times, and even then, I'll only take the matter under advisement . . ."

"Kane," she said quietly; "let's get one thing straight right now: I'm *not* going to kiss you anymore. Not *ever*. Not as long as the two of us shall live!"

"Want to bet?" Ethan said, and bent toward her. But she whirled away from him, leaped to her feet like a startled doe, and would have run out of the Salon, if he hadn't caught her by the arm.

"Please," he said gently; "I'll behave myself. Word of honor, Anne. . . . Right now, you'd better explain to me how you managed to misplace a whole blamed town with a couple of thousand people in it . . ."

She smiled then, really smiled, and, as always, performed the minor miracle of transforming her essential plainness into something considerably more interesting than mere physical beauty ever is. He didn't know what that something was, he would never be able to define it, but, whatever it was, it made her—to him!—infinitely desirable, incredibly precious and dear.

"*I* didn't misplace it," she said; "but it seems that somebody did because it definitely isn't there anymore. After I'd talked with the steward, I sent a note to the captain by him, asking the captain to let me have a little chat with him . . ."

"And did he?" Ethan said.

"Yes. And what's more, Captain Easkins *remembers* the town of Tiltson. Only he says that it has become a ghost town, that nobody lives there anymore. Did you know there were fourteen towns on the Missouri River in Kansas in 1849, the year my mother ran off with her actor friend —dragging me along with her because I was four years old at the time, so she had to!—and now there're only three?"

"Yes," Ethan said; "I did know that. And I also know that all of them failed for the same reasons. They were founded by bunco artists, get-rich-quick dreamers, fancy Dans with a bone-deep aversion for hard work. Those people didn't have idea one, dear heart, of just how rough life on the frontier is. Then the circumstances under which the Territory was settled—pro- and anti-slavery people rushing in, each trying to claim it exclusively for their side, and both of them fighting over it like savage dogs —didn't help a damned bit. Kansas became the dark and bloody ground. . . . But the problem now is, as I see it, that you haven't any information whatsoever about your father's present whereabouts . . ."

"None," she whispered. "He may be—dead. He was much older than my mother, anyhow. If he is, I shan't pretend to grieve for a man I don't even remember, and whose dour ways, my Aunt Sue says—and she's not one to defend immoral behavior, not even her own sister's—were a chief cause of my mother's running off. The truth is I only decided to join him and my half brothers for a while, until I could find myself a job teaching school. My real problem, I confess, is crassly economic: I simply haven't enough money to keep myself in a hotel or a boarding house for any length of time while I look for work."

He gave her a look whose gravity well hid the joy that was all but consuming him.

"The solution to that is simple: Let *me* keep you, Anne," he said.

She stared at him, and even her lips went white. In fact, the only reason he could distinguish them from the rest of her face were that they were even whiter. She tried to say something, words of protest, of bitter reproach, but he would never know what those words were because she was, at that moment, physically incapable of getting them out.

He was anything but a cruel man, yet he deliberately let her suffer for an appreciable length of time, out of a certain sense of the dramatic or perhaps a desire to heighten the suspense, before he went on gravely:

"Now you're wronging me again, Anne. Even insulting me to some extent by what you're now thinking. So suppose you tell me exactly what there is wrong about a man's keeping his own wife? Part of his normal obligations, it seems to me. Along with loving, honoring, and cherishing, that is. . . . From what I've seen of you so far, my dear, none of the items on that list seem too great a chore for me to undertake—"

"His own—wwwwife!" she whispered; "Ohhhhhh, Kane!"

"Exactly that," he said calmly; "I'm proposing matrimony, my darling Anne—generally considered to be a highly respectable state. So, now, what's wrong? Oh, I know! I'm not going about this properly, am I? Oh, well, I had to throw my handkerchief overboard, and this Salon's floor is as abominably filthy as floors generally are in this enlightened and civilized land of ours, but if you insist—"

He flopped down on both his knees before her, took her small hands —which were fluttering wildly like a pair of captured birds—in his own big, knobby-knuckled paws.

"My dearest Anne," he intoned solemnly; "will you do me the high honor, and grant me the exceedingly great joy, of becoming my lawful, wedded wife? And the mother of my sons, of course. And the grandmother of my grandsons, and the—"

"Kane Lovejoy!" she said furiously; "You get up from there!"

"No," he said, and grinned at her; "Not until you say 'Yes,' Annie, me darling!"

"Then you'll stay down there forev—an awfully long time, because I'm not going to!" she said, the anger in her voice ringing anything but true by then.

Hearing that, catching the correction she had made in midsentence from "forever" to "an awfully long time," his grin widened. "Scruples, Anne?" he said. "All right, let's test the matter. Do your scruples include the one against lying, my dear?"

She said: "Of course! I have never knowingly—or at least not willingly—told anyone a lie in my whole life."

"All right. Then tell me this: Why aren't you going to say 'Yes,' if not ever, at least not for an awfully long time? Don't you love me?"

"Kane, that's not fair!" she wailed.

"I love you," he said quietly; "I have, almost from the moment that I rescued you from the Lonesome Polecats. Only I fought against that feeling—largely because a member of your sex made me see a peculiarly unpleasant version of hell a little while back."

"Please get up from there, Kane," she said. "Thank you. Now sit here beside me. . . . That's it. Oh, Lord, Kane, I really don't know what to say . . ."

"Just say 'Yes,' " he told her solemnly. "Three short letters—Y-E-S, yes. Of course if you want to pretty it up somewhat, like say, 'Yes, Kane, dearest, I love you with all my heart and will gladly marry you as soon as we can find a minister or a justice of the peace in Atchison,' I'd greatly appreciate the additional courtesy. But a simple 'Yes' will do. C'mon, Anne, say it, and give me the semilegal right to kiss you . . ."

She half turned away from him and shook her head, more than a little desperately, from side to side.

"No, Kane," she whispered.

He stared at her. Said: "Forgive me—the presumption, my dear."

"Ohhhhhh, Lord!" she wailed. "All right! All right! I—I love you. But I'm not going to marry you, because you *don't* love me. You only think you do. Or rather you've tried to convince yourself that you do because I've compromised you so horribly by kissing you like a wanton in public, and—"

He threw back his head and roared with laughter.

"Anne the Mind-Reader!" he chuckled. "So, all right, I'm been compromised. My sacred honor and my manly virtue have both been besmirched. But not my boyish laughter, because another roving female creature robbed me of that quite some time ago. So now, don't you see, you've *got* to right matters by marrying me? Thus making this the first shotgun wedding in reverse in the whole of human history!"

Despite herself, she had to smile at that.

"You and your *awful* sense of humor!" she sniffed. "Besides, there's another problem—now . . ."

"And that problem is?" he said fondly.

"You said that women who sell themselves are—whores. Oh, well, you didn't actually say it, but that was what you meant. And that after I'd confessed to you that I'm very short of money—a problem you propose to remedy by marrying me. So, if I were to accept you, what does that make *me?*"

"My wife. Who's damned well going to cook, scrub floors, wash clothes, and present me with another little hired hand every year for the next dozen or so years. So what does all that make *me?*"

"A reactionary male—and a Simon Legree," Anne said. "Kane—no.

At least, not yet. Give me—a year. To get used to the idea. To make sure —very sure—that you really do love me . . ."

"And vice versa. *Mostly* vice versa," he said.

"No," she whispered; "I love you, all right. I'm positive of that . . ."

He put one arm around her shoulders, drew her to him. She didn't resist.

"Then why the year, Anne, dearest?" he said.

"Caution—and self-defense," she said quietly. "You—you're a very handsome man, Kane. You're both cultured and refined. From an old, old family, with generations of birth and breeding behind you, probably—and it shows . . ."

"So?" he said.

"As a woman, I'm nothing much. So all the advantages are on your side. Therefore, when you meet some lovely prairie flower of a Western girl, with cornflower blue eyes and long blond hair down to here"—she made an oddly graceful sidewise gesture with her right hand several inches below her knees—"I want you to feel—and be!—perfectly free to do what you want to, what you must, without your exaggerated notion of *noblesse oblige* getting in the way. While I can—still bear it," she added in a whisper. "That is, if I even can—now. Before we're married—if something like that happened—I *might* be able to—to stand it. Afterward, I—I simply couldn't. It would be—too awful, Kane; I'd—die . . ."

"Then you're going to live forever," he said.

And bent and kissed her. A long time. A very long time. And with a great deal more—hunger—more aching passion than he had meant to give free rein to.

She pushed him gently, but firmly, away.

"Don't kiss me like that, Kane," she said.

"Then how shall I kiss you?" he growled.

"Like this," she murmured and, reaching up, caught his face between her two slim, surprisingly strong hands. Rising, she clung her mouth to his so softly, sweetly, her lips trembling against his with such anguished tenderness, that their warmth and candor, plus the way he had already honestly come to feel about her by then, breached the last of his defenses. A rush of tears blindscalded his eyes, flooded the bony contours of his cheeks.

She drew back and stared at him, or at as much of him as she could see through her own tears, which wasn't much.

"Kane," she whispered, "*my* Kane. For now you love me. Now you really do . . ."

He laughed, a little shakily.

"Skip one year!" he said; "Tear it right out of the calendar! Of course it's going to be awfully rough—and on both of us—but we'll manage, somehow, and—"

"No," she said crisply; "Now I'm going to be the practical one. When we get married—that is, if we ever do—"

"Goddamnit!" he swore. "There's absolutely no 'if' about it, young woman!"

"So now he's swearing at me!" she said in mock despair; "How long d'you think it'll be before he starts beating on me, too?"

"Five minutes, or even less, if you keep that 'if' business up, Annie, me darlin'! Look, dear heart—let me explain matters to you so you can see what we're up against. First of all, I have to find two one-hundred-sixty-acre spreads, and they *must* lie side by side . . ."

"I can see the reason for the second requirement," she said; "Or else you'd always have to be crossing somebody else's lands to work the two halves of your own. Am I right?"

"Perfectly—and as smart as a spanking new buggy whip, as usual. The reason for *two* spreads, my darling wife-to-be, is that years ago, when I first got seriously interested in farming—"

"That's another thing you've got to explain: *why* you ever did, I mean . . ."

"Later. When we've more time. That's long—and sad—and more than a little complicated, I'm afraid. It started out as a negative response to the life I was forced to lead, then became a positive embracing of a kind of life I'd come to love. But let that go for now. As I was saying, years ago, when I first became seriously interested in farming, my grand-father, Daniel Lovejoy, taught me how to calculate the yield per acre of nearly any sort of farmlands pretty closely. Now Kansas is dry farming —or very nearly. From what Phil has told me, a hundred and sixty acres simply won't support a family of any size, in anything even approaching comfort . . ."

"Of any size!" she said with a well-feigned expression of horror; "I take it you mean to make a broodmare of me, Kane Lovejoy?"

"Something like that," he said cheerfully; "A boy every year for the first seven or eight years so we'll be able to do without hired hands. And, after that, then we'll start in on the girls. Any objections, wifie dear?"

"None," she whispered; "I was an only child, Kane, dearest—and the —loneliness was awful. I'll settle for a dozen, too . . ."

"Good! We're in perfect agreement on that score, aren't we? So *two* tracts, Anne. I'll homestead the one and preëmp the other—"

She gave him a look of almost adoring admiration that would have melted a cobblestone, not to mention anything so susceptible as a Victorian sentimentalist's heart, sighed, said:

"Now you've lost me. Remember, I was a traveling tent show brat, so I know absolutely nothing about farming . . ."

"Homesteading hasn't anything to do with farming as a science or an art," Ethan said gravely; "It's merely the method—or rather one of the two methods—that you acquire the land to do your farming on. If you homestead, you get one hundred and sixty acres free, with the minor exception, of course, of an eighteen-dollar fee you have to pay—fourteen down on filing your claim at the nearest land office, which can be ninety or a hundred miles away, Phil told me, and the other four on proving up . . ."

"Sounds simple," Anne said; "I suppose that's the reason everybody and his brother seems to be heading out this way . . ."

"Exactly that," Ethan said; "and it's why I've got to rush. The requirements are broad enough to include blamed near everybody: head of a family or, failing that, twenty-one years of age or over; a citizen of these United States or, if a 'furriner,' one who has filed his declaration of intention to become a citizen. The only restriction I've been able to discover is that you mustn't ever have borne arms against the United States Government or given aid and comfort to its enemies—which leaves poor old cornfed Johnny Reb out. But even he is allowed to preëmp . . ."

"Pre—what?" Anne said.

"Preëmp. That is, take a hundred and sixty acres under the Preëmption Act of 1841. Requirements are just about the same, with a few clauses thrown in to prevent the creation of huge estates or land speculation, but the main difference is that you've got to *buy* your land from the government. But since the asking price is about a dollar twenty-five cents the acre, that's not much of a drawback. I mean to do both—now . . ."

"Homestead and preëmp? Can you? I mean is it allowed?"

"Sure is. When they passed the Homestead Bill on May twentieth, 1862, it never occurred to Congress to repeal the Preëmption Act. So if you can find two one-hundred-sixty-acre spreads lying side by side, you can file for one as your homestead, and preëmp the other one, providing you've got the cash. I wasn't planning to take on a chore *that* big until quite a spell later on, because a hundred-sixty-acre tract is plenty enough trouble for one lone sinner to farm; but now, what with that dozen extra hungry little mouths to feed that you've promised to bless me with—"

"Thirteen!" she laughed; "I also eat, you know. Like a horse, my Aunt Sue swears. In fact, the theory among my cattier female friends is, that carting around all I pack away is what keeps me so thin. . . . Kane, tell me something: What can *we*—you and I—do about my problem? Because it's obvious to me that you're going to have to camp out, in a tent or something, 'til you get your first crop planted, weeded, and harvested. And I'd just be in the way—"

"Except at night," he told her solemnly.

"*Even* at night," she shot back at him; "because after you got through plowing all day, weeding the rows, chopping firewood, watering and feeding the stock, you'd be much too tired. I'd probably have to pinch and tickle you enough to wake you up, and then say demurely: 'Now looka-here, Friend Farmer—the first thing a husbandman is supposed to husband is his wife!' "

He laughed at that, freely, gaily, then he sobered.

"As much as I hate to admit it, that's the bitter truth you've just delivered yourself of, young woman," he said. "But I'm pretty sure Phil will be able to help us out as far as finding a teaching job for you is concerned. You see, he was one of the original founders and is the present mayor of Marthasville; named it after his wife, in fact, and—"

"Kane," she interrupted him, "that's the third or fourth time you've mentioned this 'Phil' to me. You seem to assume that I should know who he is. And I don't—for the very simple reason that, beyond mentioning his name in passing, you've told me absolutely nothing about him . . ."

"Good Lord! That's true, isn't it? Guess I have such a vivid mental picture of Phil in my mind that I feel everybody else should know him automatically. Look, honey, Phil—for Philip, of course—Harris was a fellow patient in the same ward with me in that butcher shop in Washington. He was there even before me, with his right arm so badly mangled by grapeshot that all those amateur butchers wanted to take it off. Only Phil was conscious the whole time—unlike me—and he fought so hard to save his arm—on the score that as a farmer he damned well couldn't do without it—that he actually touched the head butcher's ironclad heart. So they let him keep it with the charming assurance that since it was going to be paralyzed anyhow, he'd be better off without it. . . . Only he fooled 'em."

"How?" Anne said.

"Sheer willpower—plus a miracle of God. He forced that crooked, badly withered arm to work, Anne. Don't ask me how, but he did. He did a powerful lot of cussing, and a sight less of praying, and one of the two did the trick . . ."

"The prayer, surely," Anne said. "I take it he's from Kansas?"

"Phil," Ethan said, "is just about as close to a native son of Kansas as any white man can get to be so far. His family came out here with the New England Emigrant Aid company in 1854. Phil was all of fourteen years old at the time. Four years later, he was already an orphan. Charlie Hamelton's band of pro-slavery ruffians rounded up eleven Free State men —among them Tim Harris, Phil's father—and dragged them off to a ravine near the Marais des Cygnes River and shot them down. Phil's mother was dead within two more months. Phil thinks her grief affected her mind. He strongly suspects, without being able to prove it, that it was she herself who set their little cottonwood shack afire. Anyhow, she died in the flames. Neighbors saved Phil by physically restraining him from rushing into the fire in what would have surely been a fatally unsuccessful attempt to save his mother . . ."

"The poor man," Anne said; "He must be a terribly sad person, with a tragic family history like that one . . ."

"The funny part about it is, he's not. By the time I got to know him well, he'd even got over his monumental—and well justified!—hatred for everything Southern. Was always saying: 'Looks like we're going to win, and when we do I vote we let bygones be bygones and start binding up the wounds . . .' "

"You know," Anne whispered, "I'm going to *like* Phil Harris."

"Thank the Lord he's married, and to quite a beauty at that," Ethan said with a grin. "Incidentally, he's meeting us in Atchison—"

"Us!" she sniffed; "who told you I was going as far as Atchison, Kane Lovejoy?"

"Well, you are. Only sensible thing to do. First of all, even if there aren't enough kids yet in Marthasville—and I'm advancing that as a supposition, merely, dearest, as there probably are—to make hiring a schoolmistress feasible, there certainly are in Atchison itself. In fact, Phil suggested that *I* hire myself out as schoolmaster this winter, because even if I do find my two likely spreads, it will be far too late for me to get in a crop this year. But," Ethan added with a wry chuckle, "he's probably overestimating my prowess by far, for the chief requirement for a school-master seems to be the ability to knock down the biggest boy in the class in a bare-knuckles fistfight. And since the biggest boy in a Kansas one-room schoolhouse can be an oaf weighing one hundred eighty pounds and standing six feet four barefooted, I'd just as soon not take on that chore . . ."

"Lord!" Anne breathed. "And how is a school*mistress* supposed to manage?"

"No problem," Ethan told her; "All the bigger boys immediately fall head over heels in love with the schoolmarm. So they'll bury you under mountains of eggs and chickens brought as gifts, and smother you with prairie wild flowers. Behave themselves too, I'm told. . . . What they won't do, Phil tells me, is *learn* anything, because he swears their heads are of solid bone!"

"Wait until I get through rapping a few knuckles, and keeping them in after school, and—"

"Aha!" Ethan said.

"You know," she said primly, "I just don't like the sound of that!"

"You shouldn't," Ethan drawled; "Catching herself a husband by keeping an outsize schoolboy in after school is an old Western school-marm's tradition . . ."

She smiled at him, then said:

"But I've already caught *you,* haven't I?"

"That you have," Ethan said, "and what's more, you're stuck with me for the rest of your life." He bent to kiss her, but she pushed him away.

"Not now," she whispered.

"Why not?" Ethan said. "We're properly engaged, aren't we? And that carries some privileges with it, or it ought to . . ."

"The reason why not," she said, "is that the Bellamys just walked into this Salon. Oh, Kane—isn't there *anywhere* we can be all by ourselves for a little while?"

"Your cabin—or mine?" he suggested solemnly.

"Why, Kane Lovejoy!" she gasped.

"Wal now," he quipped in an outrageously bad imitation of a West-ern accent, "puttin' in a crop afore you've built a fence ain't all that sinful, once a firm declaration of intention has been made. . . . Oh, all right, all right! What do you say to the Hurricane Deck—just behind the pilot-house? Since the captain and the chief pilot will out of sheer necessity be staring straight ahead, it will be private enough, as long as the pilot keeps this tub in midstream anyhow . . ."

By then the Bellamys were upon them.

"So you two dear children have gone and made up?" Cora cooed.

"Who said we ever had a falling-out?" Anne snapped. "Come on, Kane!"

"Come on—where?" Ethan teased her.

"To—where you said," Anne said, her eyes alight with both tenderness and mischief; "I mean to follow Tom's advice to the letter . . ."

"*My* advice?" Tom Bellamy said in a baffled tone of voice; "Just what advice was that, honey?"

"To turn Kane, here, every whichaway but loose! *Now*, will you come on, Kane, darling?" Anne said.

The Hurricane Deck of a river steamer is actually the roof of the Cabin Deck. Standing amidships on it, Ethan, with one arm around Anne's slender waist, was as perfect a portrait of elongated, mesmerized euphoria as it is possible to imagine. A state out of which—quite accidentally, of course—Anne almost immediately jerked him.

"Mrs. Kane Lovejoy," she murmured; "Oh, Kane, darling—how wonderful that sounds!"

Hearing her say that, he stopped in his tracks as though he had run up against an invisible wall. His pale blue eyes opened wide, absorbing the misty morning light. But, along with it, something else had got into them, too; something that hadn't any name, because thinking about it, contemplating it, was already too much, so putting a name to it was beyond him.

'What made me say to her: "My name is Lovejoy. *Cain* Lovejoy, at your service, my Dear!" I don't know. I'll never know. Hawthorne's sinful —and cowardly—preacher branded the scarlet letter into his living flesh, but I bear the mark of Cain, not upon my forehead, but burnt into my identity, my—essence—even into my soul, if I haven't been bereft of a soul by now. Oh, God, I—'

But, by then, she had half turned, and was staring up at him.

"Oh, Kane—you look so—so *awful!*" she breathed. "You—you're sick! Come on, let's go back downstairs. You'd better lie down. Is your old wound—troubling you again?"

"A little," he said ruefully, not lying at all, because, already, in so brief an interval of elapsed time, his gut had started in to ache dully, as it always did when things got to him, broke through his outer armor of pretended calm to reach the appalling plane of quiet desperation on which he now forever lived. "But not enough to make me go back downstairs, my dear. Hot as my cabin is, I'd only feel worse down there. Good Lord, Anne! Don't look so worried! I'm not really an invalid; I'll be able to feed and clothe you, and our children, too, for that matter . . ."

"That is, if you can even give me children, my poor old shot-up wreck!" she teased him solemnly.

Which touched him in his deepest wound, raw and bleeding still, in a secret place not really of his flesh, which was his hidden, anguished fear that his potency as a man, as a male, had been a permanent victim of that rebel's lead ball. Of course, afterward there had been Edith, but. . . .

He clawed her into his arms and almost broke her mouth.

She didn't fight. She kissed him back, arrogantly, fiercely, demandingly. Then abruptly, and as always, her conscious mind, hag-ridden by its legion of Victorian "Thou shalt nots" took over.

She drew back, whispering brokenly, "No—please, no. Don't kiss me any more, Kane . . ."

He growled, "Why not?"

She said very simply, her voice humid with choked back tears:

"You *know* why not. Are you going to force me to say it?"

"Yes," he said angrily, "because, so help me, I don't see—"

"You do see. And I can't tell you why not, because I don't even know the words." She added slowly, sadly: "If there *are* any words—for the way you make me feel . . ."

He stared at her and said, his voice slow, grave, tender:

"Like a woman—like a wife. Or even—female, as in those majestic words from the Holy Writ: 'And male and female created He them . . . To be fruitful, and multiply, and replenish the earth . . .' To bring forth children, in His image, and dedicated to His worship. . . . Lord, Anne, are you going to go against human nature, and even the teachings of our religion, because dirty-minded people have made you believe that fleshly passion—big, fine, warm, *normal* fleshly passion!—is somehow—base?"

"Not—dirty-minded people," she said bitterly; "I *saw* what happened to—my mother . . ."

"But, even so, in her case wasn't the sin promiscuity, and not the passion in itself? As long as we abide by that 'forsaking all others' and 'cleave only to one another,' what's wrong with it? I, for one, don't want a wife who'll give me gooseflesh and chilblains in bed. And since I'm going to be your husband, and the father of the children you say you want, would you rather that I gave you the horrors?"

She grinned at him then, with sad self-mockery.

"For the time being, yes!" she said.

"Oh, God, Anne!" he groaned.

"Kane," she said quietly, "I want to marry you in a church. Wearing white—and having the *right* to wear it. I want to bring forth our children decently and honorably in God's sight, and in man's. But now you've found out, you *know*"—she was already crying by then, bitterly, terribly—"that I naturally am the way no decent woman is supposed to be. I'm at least as passionate, as wanton, as my mother was, and probably even more so. *You* taught me those things about myself. I didn't even know them before I met you. So, since you could—crook your little finger—and lead me off to bed—this very instant—"

"Anne!" he moaned.

"Hear me out! And, what's more, since you have a year of backbreaking work in front of you before we'll have even the beginnings of the wherewithal to start our lives together; and I, a year of fasting and prayer and the mortification of my much-too-eager flesh, I ask you to lend me the strength I haven't got. Don't put more temptation in my way than I can resist, my love. The way I love you is—is holy, Kane. Don't make—let me—dirty it. I ask you, I beg you that. Let's not spoil a lifetime—in an hour—no matter how—glorious—that hour may seem. Do you—promise me?"

In answer he bent and touched her mouth, but as a worshiper might kiss the chalice of the Holy Grail. And they were almost perfectly happy, until the *Prairie Belle* came butting up to the docks at Atchison just at the edge of night.

But any kind of happiness is a fragile thing, and perfect happiness even more so. 'It is,' Ethan thought afterward, 'like the finest kind of crystalware that one long-held note can shatter . . .'

Not to mention the joyous bull-bellow of Phil Harris's voice as he stormed up the stageplank toward where they stood, roaring:

"Ethan! Ethan Lovejoy! By God, Old Hoss, you look great!"

3

The minute he got to the deck, Phil Harris grabbed Ethan in a ribcracking bear hug, pounding him on the back all the time.

"Lord God, Eth!" he boomed. "If you ain't ever a sight for sore eyes! Done filled out a mighty heap, put some meat on them long bones and—"

Then he became aware of Anne. He turned Ethan loose, swept his black Western slouch hat off his head, made her a positively theatrical bow, then put out his sadly withered right hand to her.

"And you're—Edith!" he breathed. "Plumb got to be! A ravishin' beauty jes' like ol' Eth here said and—"

"Only I'm not," Anne said a little sadly, "either a ravishing beauty, or even—Edith. Kane, you'd better explain matters to your friend Mister Harris. Starting with who I am. And after that, when you get around to it, you might try explaining to me what your Christian name really is— Kane or Ethan . . ."

"It's Ethan," Ethan sighed. "That Cain business is a kind of nickname I sort of hung onto myself because—Oh, Lord, Anne! Let me explain that to you some other time. Privately. When we've both got a couple of hours to waste, because—"

But Phil Harris was staring at him, his own ruggedly handsome face grave and sorrowing.

"Cain, eh?" he said. "Spelt C-A-I-N, like in the Good Book, right?"

"Right," Ethan sighed. "But the reason for that is rightly kind of complicated, Phil, so I vote we put the whole thing off until—"

"I *know* the reason for it," Phil said grimly. "Your brother Jonathan. And you're wrong, Old Hoss; dead damned wrong. What you did for your brother was—morally right, Eth. A mercy and a kindness. And you ain't got no goddamned reason to blame yourself for it none a-tall!"

Ethan's pale blue eyes opened very wide.

"Who the ever-loving hell ever told you—" he began.

"*You* did, Eth," Phil said quietly; "Not that you meant to, of course. Remember I was already in that pesthole of a ward when they brought you in. And you was out of your pore old Yankee head, and—raving. I sorta sat by your bedside and held your hand for you, and let you spill your guts up for five nights in a row. Thought I'd done you a sight o' good, let you bring all the pizen up, all th wormwood 'n th gall. But I see I failed you there, Old Hoss, and I'm mighty, mighty sorry . . ."

"Kane," Anne whispered; "I mean—Ethan—what—what happened to—your brother?"

He held her with those Viking eyes of his, and all the blue drained very slowly out of their irises, leaving them gray. Hoarfrost gray. Bleak. Wintery. The color of grave moss. With death in them. Hell.

"Exactly what you think happened," he said harshly. "I killed him."

She hung there. Said too quietly:

"Because of—her?"

"Because of her," Ethan said.

"Now look, Old Hoss!" Phil put in angrily; "You ain't a-tellin' the truth now. You was outta yore mind when you told it to me, and a fella plain don't lie when he's a-ravin!"

"But he might leave something out," Ethan said flatly. "Did I tell you what happened the night *before* my brother—died?"

"Nope. Can't say you did, but all the same . . ."

"All the same, it's motive that counts, doesn't it? Determines in a court of law the *degree* of a man's guilt: whether the crime is manslaughter, say, or—murder . . ."

"In this case it wasn't neither!" Phil said hotly. "He was real bad off, so you—"

"Ka—Ethan," Anne said with that dead stopped quiet more shocking than a scream; "She—wrote you a letter. Confessing that she—that she and your brother—"

"No," Ethan said grimly; "Edith wasn't the confessing kind, my dear. I came back to the campfire. And overheard, accidentally, my brother— boasting of another of his exploits. Naming names. Giving a no-holds-barred account of exactly what went on. Regaling his comrades-in-arms with the details. With the very dirty details. Skirting the borders of— perversity. Crossing them, maybe . . ."

"You mean he actually told the other soldiers—*whom* he'd—he'd—"

"Pushed over? Yes. As always. He felt no compunction against ruining a woman's good name after he'd already bereft her of what the authors of those plays you appeared in as a child were pleased to call her sacred honor . . ."

"And the next day—in the heat of battle," Anne whispered, "when you got a chance to, you—"

"Yes," Ethan said; "I killed him."

"Why, goddamn!" Phil Harris howled; "That wasn't the way it was done a-tall!"

"Then how was it, Mister Harris?" Anne said.

"Can't tell you that, ma'am," Phil said; "You're a decent girl—a lady. And that just ain't the kind of a thing a fella feels comfortable tellin' to a lady. Ask Eth. *Make* him tell you. 'Cause you ain't bein' fair to ol' Eth here. That you ain't, Miss—"

"Jeffreys. Anne Jeffreys," she supplied. "But don't you see, I have only his own words to go on, and he—"

"Ain't bein' fair to his own self. Even less than you are, Miss Anne," Phil said.

She looked at Ethan then. Smiled at him. It was the bleakest, saddest smile that either of the two men had ever seen.

"At least you've saved yourself the price of a ring—no, of the two rings, isn't it?—that you'll never have to buy for me," she said. Then she put out one slim, wildly trembling hand to him. Whispered: "Good-bye —Ethan. That's a nice name—Ethan. I like it. Far, far better than I liked the name of Cain . . ."

Ethan took her hand, said with grave dignity:

"I'm sorry, Anne. Far sorrier than you'll ever know . . ."

She stared at him, and her tears were a jeweled wash upon her cheeks in the steamer's lights.

"Then tell me the truth!" she stormed; "Don't just stand there— accusing yourself of murder—no—worse—of fratricide. I don't believe the things you said. My heart tells me not to believe them. You see—I—I *still* love you. And I'm going to go on loving you until the hour I die, so don't —kill me like this! Don't torture me to death, don't—"

By then he had her in his arms.

"Tell her, Old Hoss," Phil Harris said.

"All right," Ethan sighed; "but telling it will take some doing. Look, Anne, it was the second day at Gettysburg. At a place called precisely Culp's Hill, a little south of Cemetery Ridge. General Geary's division, of Slocum's Twelfth Corps, were dug in on the north peak of it. So Rebel General Ewell sent in two whole divisions to smoke 'em out. Our artillery made mincemeat of the first one, but old Ewell sent in the second and they just about had that damned hill, the southern peak of it, anyhow, when our commanding officer, General Gregg, sent us in—"

"The cavalry?" Anne said.

"Yes. But not as such. Dismounted, and fighting as infantry. That kind of terrain would have been suicide for horsemen. Even so, we had the advantage: we were equipped with Sharps—"

"With what?" Anne said.

"Sharps. A carbine. But a breech loader. And that made all the difference—"

"Why?" she said.

"Speed of fire," Ethan said; "we could shoot at least three times to their once, so when the Reb Foot came up against us, they got murdered. . . . It used to make my sore gut ache, watching those poor brave devils die. Lots of times I shot high, over their heads, wasted ammunition. I didn't enjoy killing men the way Jonathan did. . . ."

She stared at him; said sharply: "Ethan!"

"He did," Ethan said grimly; "that was *why* he got killed. Seeing that we'd wiped out the whole front line of the ones who were charging us, Jonathan stood up like a damned fool and ripped out a cheer. So a crackshot Reb got him . . ."

Her eyes made brands, burnt his face.

"But you said that you—"

"Killed him. I did. Afterwards. You see that Reb had his musket loaded buck and ball—all right, all right! That means he'd poured two cartridge loads of black powder down the barrel, then a double charge— twenty four buckshots—on top of the powder, then rammed a sixty-calibre ball home on top of all that. What a load like that did to the man it hit wasn't pretty. I puked my guts up when I looked at poor Jon. . . ."

She wailed: "Ohhhhh!" the sound utter desolation's self.

He went on bleakly: "The truth was, he could have survived that wound, Anne. Other men have. Only he didn't want to. He—asked me to kill him. I refused. Then Captain Bainbridge came over and saw how and *where* he was hit, drew his own service revolver, handed it to me, and ordered me to shoot him. Said: "It's his right, Eth. I'd ask the same thing of my brother, if I'd got hit down there . . ."

"Down there?" she said blankly; then her eyes flared into recognition. She said, slowly, softly, "Oh." Then: "Oh, my God!"

"Exactly," Ethan said. "He couldn't live with the thought that he wasn't going to be able to tumble some poor little dimwitted cluck of a factory girl every other night as long as he lived. That he'd never be able to bed *any* woman again, not even—"

Anne held him with eyes become blue ice, and said it then.

"Not even—your girl."

"Not even—my wife," Ethan said sorrowfully, "if I had been fool enough to make her my wife. But the thing I can't quite forgive Jonathan for, was not being merely the skunk he was, but a windy skunk on top of it. There're a hell of a lot of things that even if a man *does*, he has no business talking about 'em . . ."

"You didn't have to listen to him," Anne pointed out tartly.

"I *didn't* listen to him. I'd get up and leave the campfire every time he started in on that subject, even when it was freezing cold. Only *that* night, I came back too soon. Strange how inevitable such things are, aren't they? And heard—what I'd have given my life not to have ever heard— the one thing I can never forgive him for."

She said acridly: "Why? The matter required *her* cooperation, didn't it?"

He stared at her. "Not for that. But for leaving me to go through the rest of my life wondering whether I—killed him out of pity—or murdered him out of hate!"

She said harshly: "Which was it?"

"I don't know," he said quietly; "I honestly don't know. I only know that I'll never be able to sleep a night through again as long as I live . . ."

He looked past her, above her head. Said, slowly, calmly, flatly, not talking to her anymore, nor to himself, just saying it, that was all, out of some obscure inner necessity, the thing, itself, how it was:

"My hand shook. So the first time, I missed him completely. The ball ploughed earth, threw dirt all over him. He looked at me and groaned out: 'Please, Eth; please!' So I fired again. So close I powder-burned him. But even so I was crying and shaking and puking, and that shot only took off most of his lower jaw . . ."

If he had been looking at her, he would have seen that she was as close to fainting as it was possible to get without toppling over, so much so that Phil Harris stepped up close to her and very gently took her by the arm. But Ethan wasn't looking at her, so he didn't see that, and she must have clawed the strength to hold herself not only upright, but ramrod straight from somewhere inside herself, her womb, maybe, because she went on standing there between him and Phil Harris, petrified, frozen, listening to him, hearing it.

"I could see his tongue fluttering around like a thick red rag in what was left of his mouth. And my bones sort of melted inside my legs, and then I was right down there in the dirt beside him, and the captain said:

'Put it against his left temple, you goddamned fool!' So I did that. And killed him. But what I can't figure out is this: Why didn't I just refuse to do it? For fear of a court-martial for disobeying orders? Or did I—maybe, deep down wherever a man keeps his envy, his jealousy, his bile until they go rancid, sour into hate—*want* to kill my brother?"

She said: "You don't expect me to make up your mind for you about that, do you?"

He became aware of her again. Grinned at her, though it was far more a grimace than a grin.

"Do I buy those rings?"

She smiled at him then, softly, tenderly.

"Yes, Ethan. Oh, I do so like that name! Kane sounded like a tinhorn gambler's or something. You—you've had a bad time of it. You deserve a little happiness. And Phil—Mister Harris—is right—"

"Call me, Phil, honey. By taking on ol' Eth, here, you've just become my best friend's bride. Or, anyhow, bride-to-be. Which makes you my best friend too, and Martha's—among th ladies, that is . . ."

"Thank you, Phil," Anne said; "You were, and are, right. I wasn't being fair to—Ethan. And he wasn't being fair to himself. Now tell me a few things, will you? First of all, where is your wife? Didn't she come with you?"

"Sure Lord did!" Phil laughed. "The li'l woman don't trust me too far outta her sight, nor outta rollin' pin throwin' range, not neither one. Only she's over at Anderson's Hotel, lyin' down. Don't feel too pert at the moment. You see, we've got another little sinner on the way, so she's restin' up so she can bend your ears into corkscrew shapes tonight. Saaay! That reminds me! We'd better get your trunks and such like ashore and make tracks over to the hotel right away. Course I've already reserved a room for you, Old Hoss; but you didn't tell me you was bringin' your lady friend along, so we'd better rush before all the rooms are taken . . ."

"He didn't bring me," Anne said mischievously; "I caught him en route. My bags are all packed and ready; so, Ethan, dearest, please find a roustabout and have them taken ashore. But the two of you will just have to give me five minutes more. You see, I have to say good-bye to a fine and handsome gentleman . . ."

"Who is?" Ethan thundered in a wrath not entirely feigned.

"Why, Captain Easkins, of course!" Anne laughed; "I promised him I would. Don't worry, love; he's close to sixty and has ten grandchildren. But if it weren't for *that,* and the unfortunate fact that he already has a wife, I might be tempted. He *is* awfully good-looking, y'know, and he wears his years well . . ."

"Spirited li'l critter, that'un," Phil Harris said when Anne had marched away. "But, Eth, Old Hoss, you've got to bring me up to date. When they let you outta that pesthole, you was all set to take a train up to Pittsfield 'n marry that there Edith o' yourn . . ."

"I did—take the train, anyhow. But she hadn't waited for me, boy. Found her already wedded and bedded, as it were. So I reenlisted. Got back to my old outfit just in time to raid south along the Weldon Railroad with my old commander, Gregg. Then winter holed us up 'til the spring of 'sixty-five, when we were transferred to Phil Sheridan's command. After that we were all over hell: at Five Forks, at Dinwiddie Courthouse, then waltzing our mounts through the streets of Richmond to the tune of 'Garry Owen' and finally at Appomattox itself. And I tell you one thing, Phil, boy, the first thing I'm going to treat myself to after I get my first paying crop in is going to be a well-sprung *buggy.* 'Cause nobody, but *nobody,* is ever going to get my poor sore tailbone up on a horse again!"

"Done bought me one already," Phil sighed; "mounting a nag is too much of a chore with this buzzard's claw hand 'n arm they left me with. But to heck with that squabble! Tell me about Edith. What made her go 'n throw you over thataway? Thought y'all was formally engaged . . ."

"We were," Ethan said drily; "Only the War Department was being extra brilliant that year. Sent the report of my brother's death home to my parents with *my* name on it. And Edith decided that six months was plenty long enough to mourn over the *pièce de résistance* at a worms' banquet, due consideration being given to the fact that it was Jon and not me she was in love with anyhow. So she married a good friend of mine, who managed my old man's shoe factory and had become by then the richest man in town . . ."

"Lord God! But when you showed up big as life 'n twicet as ugly, what then, Old Hoss?"

"That's a long story, Phil—and one that'll have to keep, because here comes my darling Anne."

"The problem of my lodging for tonight has been solved, Phil," Anne said brightly as she joined them; "That is, if there isn't any room in that hotel you mentioned. Captain Easkins has kindly offered to allow me to remain on board tonight, as the *Prairie Belle* doesn't leave Atchison until eight o'clock tomorrow morning. He says that both the currents and the shifting sandbars upriver are much too treacherous for him to risk making the run up to St. Joseph and Nebraska City at night."

"And just where," Ethan inquired grimly, "does the old goat plan to let you stay? In *his* cabin?"

Anne laughed merrily at that.

"Of course not!" she sniffed. "He'll let me keep my old stateroom. There are very few travelers bound for Nebraska so far. Oh, come now, Ethan Lovejoy! You don't mean to tell me that you're going to be a jealous husband?"

"And a wife-beater, if necessary!" Ethan said.

"Exactly what I told my Martha," Phil Harris quipped, "but it turned out to be the other way around. Swear to God that li'l woman's aim with a piece of crockery at any distance up to fifty yards is downright miraculous! But, come to think of it, there really ain't any problem. They don't have an extra room, you kin bunk with Martha, Miss Anne, and th two o' you kin talk wimmenfolk's talk all night, while me 'n th Old Hoss will bed down together 'n chew the rag about th War 'n our future plans . . ."

"Fair enough," Anne said; "But Phil, since this elongated species of a New England codfish has first got to find his land, claim it, farm it for at least a year, and build a house on it before we can be wed, is there any chance of my finding a job in Marthasville so that I can keep an eye on *him* during all that time? I'm a qualified schoolteacher and—"

"Praise God from whom all blessing flow!" Phil roared. "Honey, for the last two years we've done left word with every hotelkeeper in Atchison, and in Wyandotte, too, that if any smart-lookin' young lady or educated-talkin' young fellow gets off a boat 'n even *mentions* teachin' school, they was to send us a telegram collect. Send it, that is, as far as you can send one so far, and that's just to Topeka, so th Pony Express would have to bring it to us. So far, no luck. Wyandotte and Atchison grabs every schoolmarm or schoolmaster passin' through for themselves, and if they start out West in our direction, Topeka grabs 'em. What with all our towns growin' like prairie grass, schoolteachers are in great demand, Anne, honey. 'N to make matters even worse, the one time a young lady did get out to Marthasville, she was laid seige to night 'n day by two hundred caterwaulin' lonesome polecats, and was married to one of 'em—I swear to God it was to be able to get a little sleep!—within the first two weeks . . ."

"I had to save Anne here from at least twenty of that breed aboard the *Prairie Belle,*" Ethan chuckled. "And, seeing how desperate they were, I decided I'd better keep her for myself . . ."

"*You* decided!" Anne said; "Now isn't that just like a man! Ethan, darling, from the minute I laid eyes on you, you hadn't a ghost of a chance of escaping *me*. But seriously, Phil, you don't mean to tell me that in Marthasville a girl as homely as I am would be the belle of the ball?"

"Homely!" Phil exploded. "Anne, honey, you're a real, honest-to-God, fem-eee-nine female woman, ain't you? You pokes out at the right places, and nips in at the others. Which is why I'm gonna take this heah Old Hoss to visit my gunsmith t'morrow. Le's see if old Heintz can't fix you up with a Gatling gun, because with the second prettiest woman in the whole state o' Kansas—you'll forgive me for being a mite prejudiced in Martha's favor, won't you, honey?—as your promised, Eth, boy, you're damned sure gonna need one!"

"I thank you for the flattery," Anne said solemnly, "but I'd thank you even more if you'd recommend me for the job, Phil . . ."

"Recommend! Lord God, honey, I'm the mayor of Marthasville, 'n you are hereby hired—if I kin get you by Martha, that is. You're so pert 'n perky that you just might scare her . . ."

"Don't worry, I'm going to be the most demure little girl in her company you ever saw," Anne said, laughing. "Now tell me, how do we get over to the hotel?"

"Shank's mare, honey. Atchison ain't that big, y'know. Th roustabouts will gladly cart yore stuff over there for an extra dollar. Speakin' o' which, we'd really better get a move on . . ."

But they hadn't walked more than a few yards away from the docks when Anne turned loose Ethan's arm—to which, up to that moment, she had been clinging most lovingly—caught hold of her skirt on both sides a little below the level of her hips, and lifted it ankle high.

"Ugh!" she shuddered; "I have never seen such a filthy place in all my life!"

"You're making an exhibition of yourself, my dear," Ethan pointed out to her gravely.

She was. By then it was fully night, and although, by the feeble light the street lanterns gave—fueled by kerosene, Anne guessed—she wondered how the passersby could even distinguish the fact that she was a woman, much less observe where her skirt's hemline now was, every man on that street had halted in his tracks and was staring in thunderstruck admiration at her slim ankles.

"Honey," Phil Harris groaned, "let that there skirt drop, will you please, huh? Or more'n one o' these here hard up 'n horny lonesome polecats will plumb fergit hisself, 'n I'll just have to shoot somebody. Or Eth will. That is, if you're packin' a shootin' iron. Are you, boy?"

"No," Ethan said.

"Buy you one tomorrow," Phil said. "Anne, honey, please! I'm a married man, 'n I see a pair o' ankles—'n a damnsight more—every livin' night. But there must be five hundred to a thousand men to every woman in the state o' Kansas so far, 'n you're plumb drivin' th pore critters crazy!"

"I'm sorry, Phil," Anne said firmly, "but I will not trail my skirt down a sidewalk that is inches deep in the—the excrement of animals. So they can jolly well look at my ankles, and enjoy the sight for all I care!"

"They're enjoyin' it, all right," Phil said with a rueful chuckle, "'n so am I, to tell the truth about it. But jes' explain me one thing, honey: When we get down to the corner—tha's where Anderson's is—'n you have to cross the street, whatcha gonna do? Lift yore skirt 'n yore petticoats up above yore *knees?*"

Ethan stared out over the expanse of the street he could see by the street lanterns and, better still, by the warm yellow glow stealing out from above and below the swinging doors of a barroom. Phil was exaggerating, of course, but not by very much.

"Lord God, boy!" Ethan said; "Is this a town or a stock breeding farm?"

"A little o' both," Phil said. "Atchison is th' freighting capital o' Kansas. But we're gonna get some relief from all the—fertilizer any day now. The Atchison, Topeka and Santa Fe Railroad was organized as far back as 'fifty-nine, 'n a bond issue of half a million dollars was voted to start th construction. That there small-size squabble you 'n me got mixed-up in, Old Hoss, sort o' put a stop to things. But since we got th news that the Kansas Pacific has gone and built a line outta Wyandotte to Topeka, everybody is up and rearing here in Atchison. Stands to reason they can't let Wyandotte beat 'em out that way, so the track layin' has started out in earnest now. . . . And that means that all this mule- 'n ox-hauled freightin' is plumb goin' to disappear . . ."

"Can't do it soon enough to suit me," Anne said. "Oh, Ethan, how on earth am I going to get across this street? Phil's right: I'd have to expose a goodly part of—of my netherlimbs—and my shoes will get absolutely *ruined* if I have to walk through *that!*"

"I'll carry you across, Anne, dearest," Ethan said.

"No, you won't!" Anne said fiercely. "Why, only this afternoon, you were positively sick from your old wound, and—"

"I was sick because I'd suddenly remembered my brother Jonathan, and the way he died," Ethan said; "Pure nerves and nothing more, my dear. For God's sake, Anne! If I couldn't carry a tiny package like you across the street, how the devil d'you think I'll ever be able to farm?"

"That's exactly what I was wondering," Anne said with wicked judiciousness, "apart from why you said 'package' when what you meant was 'baggage,' anyhow . . ."

"Sugar," Phil said with a grin, "I'm gonna let you in on a secret: woman what *ain't* a bit of a baggage ain't no woman a-tall 'n tha's a livin' fact! Tell you what, Old Hoss, le's both of us carry her across. You catch her by one arm, 'n me by th other. Long as we fix it so it's my left hand I use to boost her up, I can manage all right. . . . And that way, we won't put too much of a strain on yore busted gut nor my wasted right arm not neither one . . ."

"Agreed," Ethan said. "Here goes, Phil—up with her!"

They boosted Anne by her elbows high into the air and carried her across that street—at least a foot deep in animal dung by the most conservative possible estimate—like that. At the sight of which, from the sidewalks, all the Lonesome Polecats set up a lusty cheer.

At Anderson's, however, their luck proved to be good in one way. In another, it turned out to be dismal. The way their luck was good was very simple: a group of travelers, bound upriver for Omaha, Nebraska, suddenly decided to check out and go aboard the *Prairie Belle* that night instead of waiting for her departure time the following morning, so several rooms were unexpectedly left available.

"Played it smart, them fellers," Phil explained; "This way they won't have to get up afore dawn to get themselves and their gear aboard by sailin' time. But most of all, they won't have to put up with Andy Anderson's grub for not even one night more. The food here, friends, ain't too bad as Western hotel food goes. By that I mean it's just plain awful, instead o' Lordawful the way it is most places. . . . Don't y'all go 'n order steak. It's sure to have been hacked off the carcass of a mule what died o' old age two years agone. Chicken is always safe. 'N prairie chicken can be downright good . . ."

"What's the difference?" Ethan asked; "It's still chicken, isn't it?"

"Nope. Prairie chicken is a kind of grouse, so it tastes more like pheasant. . . . Lord God, Old Hoss, howcome that there couple over there are lookin' at you so hard? The woman, anyhow. Mighty heap o' woman, that one. Looks like she could turn a feller every whichaway but loose. 'N if I didn't have my Martha along, and she wasn't tied up with that sawed-off, square-built hunk o' *nothing* she's got with her, I'd sure Lord give her a try at me!"

And that, of course, was how, and when their luck turned dismal, for the couple sitting in the lobby of Anderson's Hotel were the Bellamys.

"Oh, God!" Ethan groaned; but before he got a chance to explain to Phil exactly where and how matters stood between him and the Bellamys, Martha Harris came down the stairs.

Ethan was shocked at the sight of her, for this thin, sunburnt, wrinkled woman, with her current pregnancy just beginning to show a little, was anything but the beauty that her husband had fondly—and sincerely, Ethan was sure—described to him. She looked much older than Phil, and yet, Ethan knew, she was actually two years younger. But, as she came closer, Ethan saw—in the sense of perceived—the truth: Martha Harris had been beautiful once—in the first flowering of her youth, almost surely. Not that she was old, even yet. Phil, Ethan recalled, was now, in 1866, twenty-six years old, which meant that Martha was only twenty-four. But she looked forty-four—or even fifty. Turning to Phil to say what polite inanity he could muster up, Ethan's gaze swept over the faces of all the women in the lobby. One and all they were farmwives, come into Atchison with their husbands to do a little shopping. And one thing became blindingly clear to him: beauty lies in the eye of the beholder. For, in comparison with the women of Kansas, Anne—plain Anne, homely Anne with her fresh, high coloring and her dewy, unfaded skin—was not only a beauty but a radiant one. Even then he began to realize what he very shortly would become certain of: Western life, prairie life, frontier life, was utterly destructive to feminine beauty; destructive, in fact, to women themselves. Later on, he would recall the bitter fact that in his prairie years, *every* woman over eighteen looked like well-used hell, so that a man had to hold hard onto the memory of how she'd looked at first, before time and endless hardships ruined her.

"Martha?" he said to Phil.

"Th same," Phil beamed proudly; then he saw Ethan's look. "Course she's a mite peaky 'n off her feed what with the kid on the way," he went on apologetically.

"That's natural enough," Ethan said gravely; "but even so, she looks just great to me. You've done yourself proud, Phil, boy . . ."

He managed to put enough sincerity into his tone to bring an uncertain smile back onto Phil's face. Then Phil rushed away to the foot of the stairs, clasped Martha in his arms, and kissed her as though he hadn't seen her in twenty years.

'Poor devil,' Ethan thought sadly. 'Now he's trying to convince himself that what I inadvertently made him see, just isn't so.' Then he added, even more sadly, somewhere in the echoing darkness of his mind: 'I wonder how long it will be before my poor Anne begins to look like that?'

Phil brought Martha over to where Ethan and Anne waited. When she was close enough, Martha put out a scrawny hand, burnt raw, and peeling—from an overdose of sun, Ethan guessed—to him and said:

"Howdy, Ethan . . ."

Ethan bowed grandly over her hand with a grace that matched his late lady-killer of a twin's, and perhaps even exceeded it. As he straightened up, Martha stared up at him in awe.

"Phil's right," she said fervently, "you are a gentleman to the manor born, ain't you, Ethan? No—more'n that: a prince right outta th story books, like all us pore silly females dream about when we be young'uns. Who's this prutty li'l she-critter? Your missus?"

"Not yet," Ethan said easily, "but, God willing, soon. This pretty little she-creature is my promised, Miss Anne Jeffreys."

"Howdy, Anne," Martha said, and smiled. "Mind if I buss you one? 'Cause you 'n me are gonna be mighty good friends, I hope . . ."

"We are, already, as far as I'm concerned," Anne said, and kissed that withered, sunburnt cheek. "Tell me, how many children do you two have?"

"This'un will make five," Martha said wearily. "Swear to Gawd there're times I get really tempted to give this horny critter two dollars 'n send him over to Gashouse Gertie's so's I kin get a li'l rest!"

At once Phil's withered hand shot out, palm upward.

"Hand 'em over, sugar-pie!" he chortled; "Gertie's right across the street. Say, Eth, what about you? I could do with a little change o' luck —'n you, Old Hoss, to judge by that prim expression on li'l Annie's pretty face, could use some luck of *any* kind!"

"Over my dead body!" Anne said; and Ethan had the blissful certainty that she wasn't joking, not even a little.

"Anne, honey," Martha said, "my weddin' gift to you is gonna be a rollin' pin, with lessons as to how to use it thrown in. Show you how to part his hair right down the middle at any distance up to fifty yards. Men! Swear to Gawd they're all alike, th miserable, horny critters!"

"You two," Ethan laughed, "must have invented a new method! Because, considering the fact that I know how old the two of you are— and subtracting four long years from that—you simply haven't had time to produce five kids . . ."

"Tha's what you think, Old Hoss," Phil said; "Me 'n' Martha got hitched in 1858 when I was eighteen years old, and she was all o' sweet sixteen. Had the first two before the War, the third one got started on Christmas leave when me darlin' was powerful glad to see me. An' the fourth came along in the spring of 'sixty-five, a little before Appomattox. Remember I was invalided out in the summer of 'sixty-four . . ."

"Only they didn't invalid you enough," Martha sniffed. "Should've left you plumb paralyzed. Say, le's all sit down. We kin have a nice cozy cup o' tea here in the lobby, or even a glass o' sweet wine, if you likes that, Anne, honey. No hard stuff, though, 'cept in th bar, and tha's supposed to be reserved for gentlemen, the one kind o' men that don't *never* enter it . . ."

"What do you call me, honey?" Phil said with an air of exaggerated innocence; "I like to take a snort o' two upon occasion, so what does that make me?"

"A likker-swillin' hawg, just like all the rest," Martha said grimly; "You don't drink, do you, Ethan?"

"Sorry to disappoint you, but I take a dram now and then, though very, very rarely," Ethan said; "Any of the kids of school age, Martha?"

"The first two gettin' past it, if anything," Martha sighed; "But since no schoolmarm in her right mind ever gets as far out as the back end o' nowhere that this here critter drug me off to, they're growin' up well nigh as ignorant as their pa 'n ma before 'em . . ."

"Honey," Phil crowed, "we plumb done struck it rich! Anne here is a qualified schoolteacher, an' since she 'n this longtall Yankee can't get hitched 'til he stakes his claim to a homestead an' farms it for at least a year, or maybe even two, we've got ourselves a schoolmarm at last!"

"Tha's so, Anne?" Martha said; "Why, do tell 'n praise th Good Lawd, sez I! You kin bunk with us, and I'll stand guard over you with a shotgun, 'cause even if yore Ethan looks just like a prince, I knows better than to trust any man that far . . ."

Anne's cheeks suddenly became a sunburst. She was remembering, Ethan was sure, the way she had kissed him on the boat.

But she had no opportunity to say—or evade!—whatever it was she thought, for, at that moment, obviously unable to resist temptation one second longer, the Bellamys descended upon them.

"I do declare!" Cora cooed; "You're being mighty unfriendly tonight, Mister Kane Lovejoy! Aren't you gonna introduce us to your friends?"

Ethan stood up. The impulse to say something cutting and cruel to the Bellamys was almost overwhelming, but he resisted it for two reasons: no remark, however pointed, was going to start to penetrate their rhinoceroslike hides; and he had been, quite literally, born in an old New England manor house, so that, in his case, Martha Harris's statement that he was "to the Manor born" was the strict and simple truth. He'd made a brave and gallant cavalry officer; his physical courage was beyond all question; but what it took to engage in a vulgar slinging match he lacked completely, though he sometimes regretted that fact, as now.

"Phil and Martha—" he began, then added "Harris" for the Bellamys' benefit, "may I present the Bellamys, Cora, and Tom?"

Tom's big paw shot out.

"Howdy, Phil!" he boomed; "Y'all's local folks, ain't you?"

"That we be," Phil said pleasantly. "Tell me: What brings you 'n Missus Bellamy way out here on Lonesome Prairie?"

Tom looked around for a bellhop and signaled him to bring up chairs. Ethan's heart sank down below his plentifully besmeared shoe tops. There would be no getting rid of the Bellamys for the rest of the evening now; he was dismally sure of that.

"Wal now," Tom said; "We're planning to homestead, we kin find a likely spread. I'm a real clodhopper, myself—born on a farm. 'N so was Cora, for all that she looks like sich a fine city lady . . ."

"Speaking of which, Mr. Harris," Cora said in the grammatically correct, slightly stilted, citified English she used whenever she wanted to impress someone, though she fell back into a country drawl soon enough, Ethan reflected with wry amusement, "we'd be mighty obliged if you'd suggest to us where we ought to try first, seeing as how you're native Kansans, that is . . ."

"Out near us!" Phil said fervently; "In or near Marthasville—named it after my missus, here. Pruttiest spot this side o' heaven! On Turkey Creek, twelve miles north o' the Smokey Hill River. Why, we've even got timber for building and—"

Anne caught Ethan's attention and rolled her blue eyes heavenward in so perfect an expression of pure despair that only a well-trained and professional comedienne could have managed it. Suppressing a wild desire to laugh, Ethan broke into his friend's panegyric as smoothly as he could manage.

"But, Phil," he said, "the Bellamys may not want to move that far out West. Cora, anyhow, is a city-bred girl, for all that she was born on a farm. And from what you've told me about Marthasville, conditions are still somewhat—well—primitive out there, aren't they?"

"Primitive ain't th word for it, Ethan," Martha Harris sighed; "What they are is Lordawful, so far. Of course they're getting a mite better with every passing year, but we got an awful hard row to hoe afore we start to be anything like civilized. Phil's drawing th longbow, for a fact . . ."

"Conditions are primitive *anywhere* in Kansas," Phil shot back hotly. "Does that street outside this hotel look like Fifth Avenue to you, boy? Lord God, Eth! What we need is *people.* Specially in Marthasville, so don't you go 'n start in to turnin' 'em away!"

"Tha's the truth," Martha said sadly. "I remember when us first got wedded, 'n Phil hauled me way out there in a covered wagon. I'm from Missouri—St. Joe—and though that ain't civilized, neither, it's a heck of a lot better than Kansas. This place wasn't a state, then, just a territory. Phil used to leave me two pounds o' sugar in a special tin—all mixed with strychnine—whenever he had to go away for a day o' two, just in case that Injuns showed up. Injuns jes' love sweetenings, y'know . . ."

"You mean," Anne said, her voice a-shudder with horror, "you mean you were actually prepared to *poison* a whole tribe of Indians? How— awful!"

"A danged sight less awful than what they'd've done to me," Martha said quietly. " 'Sides, it wouldn't have been a whole tribe, jes' a war party. Course, by now, they've gone and moved most o' th Injuns further West, so we don't have them kind of scares much, nowadays."

"Mrs. Harris—Martha," Cora Bellamy said with almost breathless avidity, "you're saying those redskins would have—raped you? All of them?"

"Lord, no!" Martha laughed; "Them fool savages hadn't found out that a white woman is built jes' like a red one in them days. Nowadays, they forces some pore white gal, oncet in a while. But white wimmen don't appeal to 'em much, that way. What they'd've done would have been to scalp me, first, then stake me out spread-eagle, stark nekkid on the prairie, and built a slow burnin' fire, with prairie grass and green wood mixed in, on my bare belly. Rightly kind o' unpleasant way to die, that is. Or if they was feelin' kind o' kind-hearted they'd've used me for target practice with bows and arrows. Flint arrowheads. Hurtful, too, but better than the other . . ."

"Lord Jesus!" Ethan breathed.

"Injuns got a funny way o' lookin' at things," Martha went on. "They don't mean to be so rotten cruel, it's jes' that they purely admires bravery above everything else. So they tests their own boys in the cruelest ways anybody kin imagine—like holdin' a hot coal under his armpit without cryin' out for a whole minute, say. And settin' a fire on a body's nekkid belly is their way o' seein' if a captive—man or woman, is worth savin'. German girl, out Salina way, got past 'em oncet. You see, she was deef 'n dumb, so she *couldn't* scream, 'n them wild Injuns thought she was bein' extra brave. So they brushed the fire off her belly, took her home with 'em, cured her hurts 'n married her off to their big chief's son. Soldiers rescued her ten months later. 'N d'you know what? First chance she got, she snuck off 'n went back to her Injun hubby. 'Pears she was plumb happy with that redskin . . ."

"Martha," Phil said sternly, "you're plumb downright discouraging our visitors!"

"Don't mean to. Y'all are mighty welcome, I tell you that. Jes' like Phil says, we *need* people—I need 'em 'cause the lonesomeness is plain awful, 'n he needs 'em cause he's scairt that the Union Pacific is gonna bypass us 'n build through Abilene, a li'l town twelve miles south o' us. We're about even with them in population so far, but the town with the most folks in it is gonna get that railroad station—and th other one is gonna—die . . ."

Ethan stared at Phil.

"Well, Phil?" he said.

"Much as I hate to admit it, Martha's right. That railroad run through Abilene, we'uns are gonna have to pack up 'n move down there 'n join 'em. Town without a railroad running to or through it don't amount to a hill o' beans these days. What difference do it make how good your own spread is if you gotta haul your produce forty miles by wagon to get to a railroad station to ship it out? But even takin' all that into consideration, Old Hoss, out our way is the place to go. Back here in the eastern part o' Kansas, all the *good* land is already taken. You have to go too far from runnin' water—creek or river—to find a hundred sixty acres all in a piece. Which means you'd have to dig a well. And that there's a chore I don't recommend. Most places in Kansas, the water table lies sixty to a hundred feet below ground level. While out our way, we got Turkey Creek, and the Smokey Hill River, 'n one branch o' th Solomon, so findin' a decently watered spread ain't too hard . . ."

"Even—three-twenty?" Ethan said; "I mean to homestead *and* preëmp, Phil . . ."

Phil stared at him.

"Greedy li'l fellow, ain't you, Old Hoss?" he said. "Look, Eth, I can't guarantee you *that* much. Not lyin' right together like you'd be needin' in such a case. For a spread that big, you just might have to go a site too far from runnin' water, even out our way. When you get out there, we'll have to look around 'n see . . ."

The evening wore on, pleasantly enough, despite the Bellamys' presence. Ethan was surprised at first at the fact that Phil and Martha showed not the slightest desire to go upstairs to what was evidently, in Martha's case, a much needed rest. As he knew from his own experience while helping his Grandpa Daniel run the farm near Pittsfield, farm folk generally go to bed with the chickens, but here it was well after nine o'clock, and Martha was still talking in her slow, flat, prairie drawl. Then he understood why: Frontier people were starved for human company, literally dying to hear talk, news of older, more agreeable climes, what was happening beyond the prairie's vast rim. They were also almost equally obsessed with a desire to unburden themselves, pour their hardships, griefs, troubles into a sympathetic ear. . . .

"Martha," Phil said; "don't you reckon you done spouted off enough for one night? 'Pears to me you oughta give somebody else a chance to git a word in edgewise!"

"Tha's purely th truth!" Martha sighed; "I beg y'all's pardons humble like. Hit's jes that I don't git a chance to talk to folks oncet in a blue moon 'n—so—enyhow, I'm all set to do some listenin now. The first thing I want to listen to is how come a man like yore friend Ethan, here—a gentleman 'n a scholar what even talks jes' like a pretty picture book—*ever* decided he wanted to farm!"

"Ethan?" Cora Bellamy said; "That's the fourth or fifth time your Kansas friends have called you that, Kane. And even Anne has once or twice . . ."

"Ethan's my name," Ethan said gravely; "Cain's a nickname I got stuck with during the War. Doesn't mean anything, so—"

"It means—far too much!" Anne said sharply; "And I, for one, don't like it—not at *all!* Ethan, promise me you're not going to use it anymore, not *ever.* I haven't asked anything of you, so far. But that I do ask you: I don't want to hear that ugly name from your lips as long as the two of us shall live. Do you promise me that, my dearest?"

"Done," Ethan said.

"Wal now, Ethan it is!" Tom Bellamy chuckled; "One handle's good as another, seems to me. But yore friend Missus Harris has got herself a point Ka—Eth, boy. You's just about the most unlikely-lookin' son o' th sod I ever did see!"

"Unlikely or not, farming is what I want to do," Ethan said; "And, according to my grandfather who's been a professional farmer all his eighty years of life, I'm even good at it. So the why's don't matter, really, do they? I vote we skip 'em, and talk about something else . . ."

Anne got up from her chair and stood before him, staring long and deeply into his eyes.

"But *I* want to know that, too," she said quietly; "I want to know everything about you, my love. You—you're interesting. You stand out. So it's normal for people to want to know more about you. What's not normal is the way you clam up and refuse to talk about yourself. Gives the impression that there are more dark secrets in your life. Are there? As your—promised—I have some right to know them, and it'll be at least a year before we can even—pillow-talk—as the saying goes. Are there still more things you're hiding from me? Are there, Ethan?"

He held her with those eyes of his, gone bleak as winter again, as cold. Said quietly, soberly, the bitter truth:

"Yes, Anne; yes, there are . . ."

She bent then, before all the assembled company, and kissed his mouth. Straightened up, let her own morning sky eyes fill up, brim, spill.

"Then—tell me. Tell me all of them," she said.

"No," he said harshly, a little shake getting into his voice. "Not here, anyhow. Not—now."

She studied his craggy face with almost painful care. Sighed, measuring her breath out upon the still night air. Whispered:

"Forgive me. You're right. You're very right. I'll have to wait. . . ."

Put her hand down on his shoulder, let it rest there, sorrowing.

The silence after Anne said that was heavy. It crawled along nerves even as controlled as Ethan Lovejoy had trained his to be.

"Look, Old Hoss," Phil said uneasily; "reckon I'd better take this here pore gravid she-critter o' mine up to bed, and—"

"No, don't," Ethan said; "because that part of the question that Martha asked me in the first place, I can answer, and I will. Why I decided to become something so unlikely for a man of my background and my training as farmer. The truth is, Martha, I didn't simply decide to take up agriculture as a way of life; I had that decision forced upon me . . ."

"How come, Ethan?" Martha said.

"About three years before the War, my august sire disowned me and kicked me out of the house without a cent. So, out of sheer necessity, I went to live with my grandfather, Daniel Lovejoy, on his farm seven miles south of Pittsfield and . . ."

All the time he was talking he was also watching Anne out of the corner of his eyes, waiting for the explosion. It came.

"Eeee—th—aaan!" she said.

He turned a face of boyish innocence all compact upon her, opened his pale eyes very wide in an expression of childlike perplexity and said:

"Yes, Anne?"

"Why did your father disown you and kick you out of the house? What had you done? What thing so awful that—"

"Tumbled the wrong filly likely!" Tom Bellamy laughed.

"Something very awful indeed," Ethan said ruefully. "You see, my father's factory hands had gone out on strike, asking for wage increases. I took the position that the pay, and the hours, at Lovejoy and Sons were offenses in the nostrils of God. Criminal offenses, because it's a demonstrable fact that every winter our workers die like frozen flies from respiratory diseases brought on by malnutrition. No, by sheer starvation. I threw the facts into my old pirate of a father's face, and the quarrel between us got out of hand. He damned me for a radical and a labor agitator and few other such endearments in his own inimitable style. So to get back at him, I

marched with the workers in their parade down West Street, bearing a sign
—I'd painted it myself, by Jove!—that read 'Lovejoy is Unfair to Labor'!"

"And thereby prevented a gang of hired thugs from beating the
workers up," Anne said bitterly. "That's the way the factory owners used
to do it in my native town of Lynn!"

"And in Pittsfield," Ethan sighed. "But, aside from saving them a few
broken heads, fat lot of good I did the strikers. Simply added one more
name to the list of the unemployed—mine. And in those days, I hadn't
lost my appetite. Fasting came damned hard to me. So I hiked the seven
miles out to my grandpa's place and he took me in. . . ."

"And once out there with the old man on his spread," Tom Bellamy
said, "you found out that you jes' plain loved farmin', that hard as the
work is you took to it like a duck takes to water, and—"

"Something like that, Tom—only much more slowly," Ethan said. "I
confess I hated it at first. You see, what I still wanted to be was an invent-
or . . ."

"And your father was opposed?" Anne said.

"Lord, no! He was delighted. He'd already reaped an awful lot of
profit out of my mechanical bent by then—"

"Like them finger-loppin' shears you'd done gone 'n made for him,
eh, Old Hoss?" Phil chuckled.

"Finger-lopping shears?" Anne said. "How awful! Besides, I don't see
what even an ogre like your father would have wanted with a machine that
cut people's fingers off!"

"Whacking off fingers wasn't what I'd designed them for, dear
heart," Ethan said, "though I have to admit—very sadly—that they did
maim three good men before I got 'em right. But in self-defense, and to
put the matter in its proper perspective, Anne, in our industry, anyhow,
machines had to cripple fifty or a hundred workers before anybody
would even dream of shutting that section of the factory down in order
to correct their dangerous faults. My father grumbled like mad when I
insisted on that, and even more so when he found out that the guards I'd
placed over those flying blades so the operators *couldn't* feed more than
one thickness of leather into my mechanical shears at the time—and
therefore not their fingers either—had cut the number of tops, vamps,
caps, pull straps, backstays, counters, shanks, toe boxes, and the like
that a worker could produce in a day down considerably. I had to point
out to him that one man was still producing more than twenty *before* I
put in my flywheel- and belt-driven, eccentric cam conversion of rotary

to reciprocating motion, bench-mounted mechanical shears, which calmed him down considerably until he found out—through Horace Willoughby, to whom I'd let slip the information in a careless conversation—that I'd also thought out the details of another machine capable of doing what my flying shears couldn't, that is, cut out in one whack those parts of shoes normally made of several thicknesses of leather such as heels, insoles, slipsoles, and outers . . ."

"Greek!" Anne sighed; "Classic, Attic, and pure!"

"Anne, dear," Ethan drawled; "it's not necessary that you understand the technical details. They don't matter. They didn't, even between father and me. My father was quite a good, if self-taught, mechanic; he was immensely proud of my skills in that field. He used to boast about them all over town, especially in the Manufacturers' Club, with the result that several other factory owners, knowing—as in a town the size of Pittsfield they had to—how badly Father and I got along, tried to lure me away from the Old Monster by offering me double what he was paying me . . ."

"And yet, you didn't go," Phil said; "How come, Old Hoss?"

"Phil, that's the hardest question to answer anyone has ever put to me yet," Ethan said soberly. "Put it this way: Ever noticed that it's very often the married couples who love each other the most who have the worst fights? The same thing holds true between fathers and sons, I suppose. My father loved me. I look like him physically; I inherited my mechanical bent from him. Therefore, to him, I became the extension of himself, destined to carry out all the great projects—leading toward the ever greater wealth and fame of Clan Lovejoy!—that he hadn't been able to accomplish in his own youth. And I cheerfully admit that I was—and am—fond of the Old Monster. I always realized that he could no more help being the horny-handed old pirate he is than I can help being—well—the altruistic sentimentalist that I am. But that difference in temperaments made us both see hell, precisely *because* we did, and do, care for each other . . ."

"Your brother Jonathan must have been a sore trial to him," Anne said then.

"Strange as it sounds, he wasn't," Ethan said. "Not at all. My father loved me, but he *adored* Jonathan. He let him get away—if not with murder—at least with fornication, adultery, drunkenness and riot, and chuckled complacently over 'the scrapes that boy is forever getting into!' In part that was because Jonathan looked like mother, and inherited—

much exaggerated, of course—a certain frivolity of temperament from her. In larger part it was because Jonathan was simply lovable. Everyone loved him, even the most straightlaced of puritans . . ."

"Even—you?" Anne said. "You've made him seem a blackguard and a scoundrel, to me . . ."

"Even I," Ethan said. "And he was neither a blackguard nor a scoundrel, because to be either or both, a man has to be conscious of the difference between right and wrong. Jonathan wasn't. He was amoral, not immoral, Anne. The distinction is important. He really was an innocent savage, laughing his way through life, aware of only what things made him feel good, and what made him feel bad. But I was held to the strictest standards of good deportment, and punished with implacable severity for the slightest fault, while nobody ever punished Jonathan for anything at all . . ."

"That must've been mighty rough to take," Tom Bellamy observed. "Seems mighty unfair to me . . ."

"Yet it wasn't, Tom. My father explained the matter very convincingly to me when he was trying to persuade me to stay home and manage the factory for him, marry the socially acceptable little creature he'd picked out for me since dear Edith was no longer available. . . . He admitted he'd given my twin up as hopeless early in our boyhood, and concentrated on shaping me for my destined role as future head of the Lovejoy clan. I'm only sorry he didn't explain it to me earlier. I never realized that having blisters raised on my seat with his razor strop meant I was the favored one. So I spent my whole life envying my brother and picking up, out of pity, the female wreckage he left behind him. Nearly all of my few—and miserably unhappy and inept—love affairs grew out of my morbid and stupid attempts to console some heartbroken ex-maiden that the 'Norse God,' the 'Young Sigurd'—I'm quoting the poor, dreary dears themselves, of course!—had seduced and abandoned without a backward glance. Yet let my father get wind of even one such straying on my part from 'the straight and narrow paths of virtue,' and you could hear him yelling all over town . . ."

"So, after the War, he wanted to call you back from your rustic exile, marry you off, and seat you upon the very throne of power," Anne said with wicked demureness; "but you'd become so much enamored of the noble task of tilling the soil that you refused?"

"I didn't refuse. Though I had come to love the life on Grandpa Daniel's farm—especially the fact that it was a way of earning my daily bread that was totally honest, my dear, that I could engage in it without hurting, abusing, or exploiting *anybody*. What I did was to put certain conditions on my accepting—"

"Like say you didn't have to put on double harness with your pa's handpicked li'l filly, eh, Old Hoss?" Phil Harris chuckled.

"That, among others," Ethan said; "Which wasn't important. The Old Monster accepted that one readily enough. What brought on the Second Civil War was my insistence that I be given full control over the hiring and firing of the factory hands, and carte blanche as far as wages and working conditions—including the hours of a daily stint—were concerned. That started a shouting match between us during which he damned me for a radical and an agitator, and a fool. He called me all that because I flatly refused to make, or even give him, a working drawing of my second invention, a sort of jigsaw, or rather sabre saw, that could cut through a pile of leather several feet high, thus producing hundreds of the heavier parts of shoes in one operation. You see, by then I'd seen the results of my first invention—"

"Lopping off fingers?" Tom Bellamy said.

"That, too, though I'd put a stop to the maimings by the guards I'd installed. What it lopped off was jobs, Tom. My august sire, seeing that one worker could produce in a day what it had formerly taken twenty to do, laid off nineteen cutters. His contention was that the market just couldn't absorb the overproduction my mechanical shears were forcing him into, and mine was that I just couldn't bear the sound of the laid off workers' hungry children crying. He was particularly outraged when he found out that I'd distributed my own salary—split nineteen ways, which helped practically not at all—to the workers he'd dismissed. So when the strike took place he used both incidents to teach me a lesson by kicking me—temporarily, he now says—off the place . . ."

"Anne, honey," Martha Harris said, "marry him. Soon as you kin. 'Cause a good-hearted man is mighty hard to find. So don't hold back 'n let some spraddle-legged she-critter grab him. Ethan, I thanks you for what you done . . ."

"*You* thank me?" Ethan said; "Lord God, Martha, why?" Then, looking at her, he saw to his astonishment how bitterly she was crying. "Forgive me, my dear," he added sadly; "I truly didn't mean to upset you . . ."

"You didn't," Martha said; "Hit was the rememberin' what done that, Ethan, honey. How hit feels to go hongry. My pore ma a-cryin' as she b'iled cornshucks a-tryin' to fill we'uns empty l'il bellies. My pa—gone away down to St. Louis a-huntin' work, 'n hit was months afore he found it. So you's done got to be somethin' mighty special, far as I'm concerned: a bossman's son what cared about pore folks like we'uns was . . ."

"You know, Ethan," Anne whispered; "I *knew* you'd be like this— the kind of a man I was beginning to doubt existed . . ."

Phil Harris grinned at the two of them with the married man's wry amusement at the spectacle of a young couple's diving headlong into a state they were certain-sure to regret a little later on.

"Oh, heck, let's go git a little sleep," he drawled. "Eth, 'n Anne, y'all don't have to git up early tomorrow. We don't aim to start back to Marthasville 'til day after. Y'see, th li'l woman ain't been into town in a coon's age, so she's got some shoppin' to do . . ."

"I'd purely admire for you to come along with me, Anne, honey," Martha said; "I means to splurge a little 'n buy myself some clothes. 'N that there frock you's got on is so prutty! You come along too, Missus Bellamy," she added. It was out of politeness, Ethan was sure, for it was abundantly clear that the Bellamys hadn't met with her approval, either. "You Eastern ladies got such good taste . . ."

"Call me Cora, won't you, Martha?" Cora said cheerfully; " 'Cause I ain't no more an Easterner than you are, dearie. I was born in Iowa— on a farm, at that. And the big city I was brung up in was Chicago, and tha's a long way from being East . . ."

"Wal now, boys, we've done had our Emancipation Proclamation signed—for one day, anyhow," Phil said; "So I reckon the two of you had better come with me and get yourselves outfitted right. Starting with some good stout boots, 'cause them citified shoes you're both wearin' plain won't do out here. Then we'd better stop off at Karl Heintz's gun shop . . ."

"A gun shop!" Anne said sharply, the revulsion in her tone clear. "Why, Phil?"

"To buy *you* a li'l lady's pistol, for one thing," Phil said quietly. "Double-barreled derringer, forty-one-caliber, over 'n under. You see, honey, the only place we got left to build the schoolhouse for you is a vacant lot way out on the edge o' town. 'N girls like you, fresh as a rosebud 'n twicet as prutty, is jes' about as frequent as hen's teeth in Kansas. You jes' might need that there li'l stingy gun to discourage some drunken tramp or outlaw, or even a redskin, though th Injun scares is about over by now . . ."

"You mean," Anne faltered, "that I might have to—to shoot some man to keep him from—from—"

"Yep," Cora said with a grim chuckle. "Either that, baby girl, or just lie back 'n plumb enjoy th occasion! The choice, after all, is up to you . . ."

"Cora, for Gawd's sake!" Tom Bellamy groaned.

"Eth—'n you too, Tom—we better pick up a six-shooter apiece for you boys . . ."

"Already got me one," Tom said complacently; "Navy Colt, 1851 model. 'N that there's one handsome sidearm, Phil. Throws all th lead a body could want to—"

"Cap 'n ball?" Phil asked.

"Sure, Phil," Tom said. "But then all revolvers is, ain't they?"

"Not anymore, they ain't," Phil said. " 'N if you'll take my advice, Tom, you'll take your personal artillery over to Karl Heintz's tomorrow 'n leave it with him. Have the cylinder bored straight through to take the new brass-cased cartridges. You seen some, ain't you? The Spencer 'n th Henry repeatin' carbines both used 'em during th War . . ."

"Phil," Anne said sweetly; "I don't understand one word you've said. And I'm glad I don't. I know you men *love* guns—love them far more than you do *us,* for instance!—but don't sound quite so enthusiastic about the ugly, oily, smelly things, will you? They *kill* people, my friend. They really do . . ."

" 'N they changes many the ornery critter's mind about how good his chances o' killin' *me* 'n gettin' away with it is, Anne, honey," Phil drawled. "Lord, girl baby, out here there ain't no law to speak of, 'n a man whut can't—or won't—defend his ownself is purely lost . . ."

"Then I'm lost," Ethan said quietly, "for I have taken my most sacred oath never to kill another human being again. Not for any reason, Phil. Not even in self-defense."

They all stared at him. Phil recovered first.

"That business about your twin brother ag'in?" he said. "Tha's a mighty heavy burden to have to live with; I'll allow you that, Eth. But you're wrong. You're plumb fergittin' th question of who's worth more: you—or the fella you's up ag'inst. You'd leave pore Annie a widow 'n yore kids defenseless orphans cause you's got scruples about blastin' some ratbastid the world is plumb better off without. 'N you'd cheat Marthasville, the county, th state o' Kansas 'n th nation—'cause you's plumb gonna be sittin' in th White House one day, Eth Lovejoy; I got money already laid on that!"

"That's one bet you're going to win, Phil!" Anne said fervently; "I'm going to see to it!"

"See that you do, honey, see that you do," Phil said. "Like I wuz sayin', Old Hoss, you'd cheat us all—yore friends 'n yore fellow citizens —of the services of an unusual 'n outstandin' man, 'n go down at the hands of some gun-totin' sonuva—son o' his two-bucks-a-tumble li'l mama— who ain't never done nobody no good 'n never will. That don't make no sense a-tall . . ."

"I know it doesn't," Ethan said. "Sense has nothing to do with this, Phil; if I had to kill again, I'd crack up. Go mad. It's as simple as that . . ."

"No, it's not," Cora Bellamy said. "Suppose Anne's life was in danger? Her—person? Oh, heck, I mean her—honor. What then, Ethan Love-joy?"

Ethan considered that.

"I don't know," he said soberly; "I honestly don't know. It's impossible for most people to understand just how deep my repugnance at the very idea of killing is, Cora. I suppose I'd try to defend her without using a deadly weapon and—"

"Git yore own damnfool self kilt, sure as shootin'," Phil drawled, " 'n leave th horny bastid to go right ahead with what he'd started out to do 'n takin' his own sweet time about it, since yore pore bloody corpse sure Lawd wouldn't be much of a hindrance. A man, Old Hoss, kin mebbe decide whether or not to defend his own self; but as far as his woman 'n his helpless kids is concerned, he plain ain't got no such choice. What's more, a married man, with a family, can't even make up his mind on th basis of some crazy principle to lay down 'n die. His life ain't his own no more; hit's plumb pledged to the future. So, tomorrow, you's a-gonna come with me to Karl Heintz's gun shop; you's gonna buy yoreself a shootin' iron, or leastwise allow me to make you a gift of one—"

"No," Ethan said. "If by a shooting iron you mean a revolver, no thanks, Phil. I'll buy a shotgun. That'll be useful for bringing down prairie chickens, won't it?"

" 'N loaded with buckshot—or better still buck 'n ball—it kin calm a hot-tempered fella who's snortin' fire down into a peaceful li'l lamb quick enough," Phil conceded. "Only trouble with a scatter-gun is they is mighty unhandy to carry around with you all the time, 'n yours just might be hangin' over th fireplace at home when the trouble starts . . ."

"A chance I'll have to take," Ethan said quietly. "And I much prefer that chance to the other of being crowded into killing a man because I had the wherewithal to terminate all his dreams, his hopes, ready and waiting in my pocket . . ."

Anne stared at him.

"And thereby allow him to—terminate *yours,*" she whispered; "Not to mention mine. Oh, Ethan—you're a good man, the best I've ever met, but don't try to be too good, too noble, for the world we're going to have to live in. Promise me that, my love—"

"It's not goodness but cowardice, to tell the truth about it," Ethan sighed; "But I do promise. In *your* defense, my dearest, I'll use all the force that's needful, so don't worry your pretty head about it, at all . . ."

After that, on that troublesome and troubling note, they all finally did go up to bed. But once abed, Ethan found he couldn't sleep. And it wasn't the bedbugs—of which, like any self-respecting Western hostelry, Anderson's had its due and full supply—that kept him awake. To an ex-cavalryman, bedbugs were an almost imperceptibly minor irritant in comparison to the horsefly and body lice bites he had had for so long to endure. Rather it was the fact that he had been forced to think about his twin brother's death and the manner of it, a matter against which he normally armed even the subconscious thresholds of his mind, knowing that to dwell upon that subject was an open and cordial invitation to madness.

By an effort of will, Ethan removed himself bodily from the center of that memory more vivid than any scene witnessed upon a theater's stage. Hurled his mind, his psyche, back over space and time through brooding night to Atchison, Kansas, to his dingy hotel room. Lay there upon his narrow bed, fighting the nausea crawling vilely up his throat, and wept and shuddered and shook, until finally, in the darkest of the predawn hours, he slept.

And then, of course, Jonathan came strolling through his bedroom's outer wall, with that blithe disregard for physical laws that is the special province of the dead. He was covered all over with clods of earth, with clots of blood, and little green flies were feasting upon his eyes. He had no lower jaw, and his tongue fluttered in the wreckage of his mouth like a thick red rag, making incomprehensible sounds. Which, in the dream-world's easy suspension of the way things actually work in bleak reality, became now flawlessly clear, resolved themselves into one of Jonathan's characteristically cheerful obscenities:

"It's got red hair on it, just like on her head. No, lighter—almost blond. That's what you wanted to know, didn't you? And she's got freckles on her lovely ass, just like the ones on her face. Bet you never thought of that, did you?"

Ethan lay there, staring at that apparition, his eyes stretched so wide they hurt.

"So you're in luck, Eth, boy. Thought it was going to take me time to thaw her out, what with her being frozen to the marrow of her bones the way I thought she was. But that there ice was mighty, mighty thin, and down there beneath the bushes at the fork, she's a-boiling, twin brother! Damned nigh scalded it off me before that Reb sharpshooter ever took aim and let fly. Wasn't much left, anyhow. *Our* darlin' Edith had worn it clean down to a nub and—"

"Shut up, Jonathan," Ethan whispered then. "Don't talk like that. Don't say those things. I don't want to hear them. Not about Edith. So stop it. Stop it, please!"

"You ought to thank me," the dream image chuckled. "Taught her all the tricks—just for you, twin brother! Even to toot on th old skin whistle. And, brother, can she ever toot!"

He, it, Jonathan, that dream image, that aberration emanating from Ethan's own tortured brain, that nothing at all, began to skip wildly around the room, spraying the walls, the floor, the ceiling with splatters of blood, making utterly revolting gestures toward its empty crotch, toward the shot-butchered remains of its genitalia, singing in a hoarse baritone:

> *"Go easy with the teeth, Edith, darling!*
> *Wanna keep li'l brother safe 'n sound;*
> *Course he's turkey-red 'n tastes a little salty,*
> *But don't bite him when you feel me coming round!"*

Ethan threw back his head and screamed then, rattling all the windows, his voice a trumpet of brass, a clashing cymbal:

"Get out of here, you swine! Go back to hell where you belong! Even dead you're no damned good, and I—"

Then it was dark again, and still. Very dark and very still and Jonathan wasn't there anymore. Nothing was, not even Ethan's conscious mind. Then that face came floating toward him in a little pool of light. Her face. Anne's.

"Oh, Ethan!" she breathed; "What's wrong?"

"A—dream," he muttered; "A nightmare—Jonathan—"

His sleep-drugged brain abruptly cleared. He jackknifed up to a sitting position in the bed. Then he remembered that he was stark naked and clawed the covers up around his bony hips and snarled at her:

"You get out of here, Anne!"

She smiled at him a little sadly, put the lamp she was carrying down on the night table beside the bed, and dropped into the lone chair.

"Sorry," she whispered, "but I can't. I *think* I got through your door before all the rest of them on this hall popped open to see where all the yelling was coming from. I leave here right now, and both my reputation and your manly honor will be gone!"

She stopped short and chuckled with pure mischievous delight.

"Don't worry, Ethan, dearest, I'll tell everybody that you put up one heck of a fight before you gave in and lost your boyish laughter!"

He sat there looking at her. Wrapped in a chaste and voluminous light cotton robe, with her hair in paper curlers, she wasn't really very appealing. But he suddenly visualized how she'd look out of that robe, and the nightgown beneath it, with her hair loose and foaming like soft brown smoke about her slender, milky shoulders, and a tiny flame appeared, then leaped, and flared in the depths of his pale blue eyes.

"Ethan—" she whispered, "don't—"

"Don't what?" he said.

"Look at me—like that . . . "

"And how am I looking at you, my dear?" he said.

"Like—like Cora Bellamy looks at *you*. As though my clothes—this robe and my nightgown—had suddenly vanished—"

"They *have*," he chuckled; "And the sight is awfully fetching, Anne, darling . . ."

"Eeee—tha—aaan!" she said.

"Don't you want to be attractive to your husband?" he went on solemnly. "We've agreed to have a large family, haven't we? D'you know any other way of going about it? *I* don't . . ."

"Ethan," she wept; "don't—please don't . . ."

"Please don't what?" he said.

"Start something—you couldn't—stop. And that I—I couldn't stop, either. You—or myself. Don't, Ethan—please . . ."

"Not even a little practice session to see if we've got the hang of it?" he said.

"Oh!" she laughed reedily. "That's a relief!"

"What's a relief?" he said.

"That you're only teasing now. I can hear the difference in your voice. Ethan, talk to me!"

"Talk to you? About what?" he said.

"Don't know. About anything. Anything at all that will get me past the—danger—I'm in, right now . . ."

"You're in no danger from me, my dearest," he said gently; "You have my word . . ."

"I know *that*. The real danger consists in this—this awful longing I have to reach out and touch you—stroke your face, even—"

"Climb in here beside me where you belong?" he said.

"Even—that," she said bitterly; "and we can't. You *know* we can't, Ethan. So talk to me. Say—"

"I love you, Anne, with all my heart. With every fiber of my being. With this body of mine that's fairly aching with desire—"

"Ethan—no!" she said. "Talk—about—Oh, I know! Tell me the reason why you left Pittsfield. The *real* reason. Not because you'd quarreled with your father again. Not because of your burning desire to become a gentleman farmer—"

"Then what was it?" he said.

She stared at him. Whispered, almost tonelessly:

"I think it was—because of *her*. Because of your—Edith. Because you couldn't bear the sight of her—married to another man, apparently happy, and—"

He shook his head, seriously, soberly.

"No," he said, "it wasn't that. Because I could have stood it, Anne. It would have been—hard. I don't deny that. I didn't know you, then; and I was in love with her. Still, I'd have got over that, settled down with the sweet little creature my father had chosen for me, been—who knows?— even reasonably happy. But, to repeat, the reason I left wasn't that. It was something far, far worse . . ."

"Worse?" she said, or tried to. At least her lips shaped the word, but no breath came to force it into sound.

"Yes. Two days before I left, Edith admitted to me that she didn't love Horace, that, in fact, she rather despised him, and had only married him because she believed that both Jonathan and I were dead—"

"So," Anne said.

"So I suggested that we both go to poor Horace, and put the matter to him fairly, and ask him to release her, allow her to come to Kansas with me, obtain a Bill of Divorcement from him out here. In Massachusetts, as you know, such a bill is practically impossible to procure. . . ."

"And he—refused?" Anne whispered.

"We never got to ask him," Ethan said drily. "*She* refused. She was not, she informed me, mad enough to leave the civilized city of Pittsfield, Massachusetts, to go live with an idiot on the prairie in a log house. Farms, she informed me, were not for the likes of her. A certain degree of comfort, she further informed me, was an absolute necessity to her . . ."

"Damn her!" Anne said savagely.

"Amen!" Ethan chuckled. "On the other hand, she saw no reason why we—she and I—couldn't make a cozy and satisfactory little arrangement, to be maintained—with the greatest of ease, she insisted—for the rest of our natural lives. I was to return to the management of Lovejoy and Sons, marry—for appearances' sweet sake!—the darling little creature my father had picked out for me, and we'd go on deceiving my wife and her husband for as long as the two of us should live. I was to father the children that Horace obviously couldn't sire, stand complacently by and see them given his name and inherit the fortune that I, with my softheartedness and mooncalf sentimentality would be absolutely incapable of accumulating myself. Neat scheme, what? Admirable in its completeness, come to think of it . . ."

"She should be horsewhipped!" Anne said.

"She should be left. Which is what, to her genuine astonishment, I did do. I even managed the manner rather gracefully. In reference to Horace, I quoted Shakespeare to her, *Julius Caesar,* Act Three, Scene Two: 'He was my friend, faithful and just to me . . . .' Then I turned and left her there, weeping bitterly out of disappointment and rage. But not out of love. She doesn't even understand what the word means . . ."

"Ethan—" Anne breathed.

"Yes, Anne?"

"I—I'm going to kiss you. I've got to. I must. And when I do, will you promise to—to behave yourself?"

He lifted one eyebrow—as blond as his dead brother's had been, far, far lighter than his dark brown hair—in a quizzical expression.

"Of course. Do you?"

"Oh, Lord!" she said. Then "No, I don't. You've got to behave for both of us, my love!"

"Now that there might turn out to be quite a chore!" he quipped, and put out his sinewy arms to her.

She slipped into them, bent, and kissed his mouth, softly, sweetly, tenderly, then put down her hands to break his grip.

He held her.

"Ethan, please!" she moaned.

He turned her loose.

" 'Good night, good night!' " she quoted impishly; " 'Parting is such sweet sorrow / That I shall say good night till it be morrow.' Oh, Lord! It already is, isn't it? Or almost. Anyhow, I'm going back to my room right now. Before you or I—or both of us—ruin matters beyond repair!"

"Anne—" he said, his tone deep, drawn out, dark.

She gave a little snort of bitter laughter and skipped through that door. Just outside it, she stopped. Hung there. Groping behind her, she found the knob, closed the door slowly and carefully behind her, knowing she was too late. She leaned back against it trembling, staring helplessly, hopelessly into that well-known face, into the delighted and yet contemptuous mockery of those eyes.

"Oh, God—please!" she wept.

The woman in the half-opened door directly across from Ethan's gave a snort of deep-toned, contralto laughter. The sound of it was curiously leonine.

"Of all the brazen little hussies!" she said.

Ethan Lovejoy took the letter from the hand of the desk clerk and stared at it in pure dumbfounded amazement. He was absolutely certain of one thing: he had told no one, not even his Grandpa Daniel Lovejoy, that his first stop in Kansas would be the city of Atchison. He hadn't because he only planned to stop there overnight before heading westward for the prairie lands around Marthasville. If he had wanted to leave an address to which his family and friends could write him, he would have left Marthasville itself; but a strong and bitter desire to cut all ties with his past had made him decide against even that.

And now, wonder of wonders, on the morning after his very first night in Kansas, as he was passing through the lobby, the desk clerk had called out to him by name, saying: "Mr. Lovejoy! Got a letter for you, sir." And handed him this missive penned on a delicate sky blue stationery in the most exquisitely feminine script imaginable. Then he saw two things: the handwriting was neither Edith's nor his mother's, and the envelope had no stamp on it. So he realized that the letter had to be from Anne. But why the devil should Anne write him a letter when all she had to do was to come downstairs and tell him whatever she wanted to in person?

He raised his eyes to the desk clerk's face, but the man shook his head.

"Sorry, sir," he said; "I know nothing about this here letter. Night clerk give it to me when I come on at eight o'clock this morning . . ."

Fishing in his waistcoat pocket, Ethan came out with his pocketknife and slit open the envelope. Out tumbled a lock of Anne's mousey brown hair, bound in a blue silk ribbon. Reverently Ethan raised this tender keepsake to his lips. Then he stuffed it into his left-hand waistcoat pocket along with his big key-winder watch, and began to read the letter:

"My Own," Anne had written, "My Heart's Own Dearest, when you get this heartbroken missive—oh, well, half-heartbroken, anyhow!—I shall be once more aboard the *Prairie Belle,* bound upstream for the town of Omaha, Nebraska. Why Omaha, you ask? Very simply because the time I talked with Captain Easkins, trying to find out where the no-longer-existing town of Tiltson was, I mentioned to him that I was a schoolteacher, and he informed me that he had been commissioned by the Mayor, the City Council, and the Board of Education of that city to steer as many members of my profession in their direction as he could.

"I know, I know! By now you are probably tearing your hair out by the roots, foaming at the mouth, and rolling on the floor—Oh, how well I could show you just how to do a mad scene!—over the question of just why I sneaked away like a thief in the night from your strong and loving arms. Ethan, Dear Heart, I had to, for when I left your room last night, or rather this morning—about three o'clock, wasn't it?—there stood *Cora Bellamy,* waiting for me to emerge from our 'Unhallowed Bower,' 'Den of Iniquity,' 'Sinful Love Nest'—Oh, heck! I can't think of any more Yellow Journalistic or 'Penny Dreadful' terms for it. Can you?"

'That big, broad-assed bitch!' Ethan raged inside his mind; 'Let her open her filthy mouth about my Anne, and I'll—' He went back to reading Anne's letter, but his hands shook so that the paper rattled.

"Ethan, Dearest One, listen to me, please! Of no other profession, except perhaps Ministers of the Church, is a sterner standard of moral behavior demanded than of schoolteachers—and quite justly so, for we have the world's greatest treasure—the hearts and minds of its future leaders—in our keeping to be shaped to the highest ideals of probity and honor! That you and I are innocent of what Dear Cora thinks we did (Or are we? The Bible says 'As a man thinketh in his heart, so is he . . .' And by that token I am the World's Original Scarlet Woman as far as *you* are concerned, my Love!) is totally irrelevant. We cannot *prove* that innocence, and therefore, in Marthasville I cannot teach.

"You don't imagine she'll keep silent about the whole thing, do you? By now, even you—as sweetly innocent as you seem to me—know women better than that!

"So I beg you to be sensible, My Poor Darling; Don't, please don't, come rushing up here after me like a madman. We cannot be married until you have established yourself a little, and I cannot live in Marthasville without work, and face the slander that, as a sinful spinster, would be hurled at my poor, defenseless head. Once you have our farm started, and I come down there as your wife, most people will dismiss her accusations as baseless gossip, particularly after they've counted on their fingers—and, I hope, on their toes!—how long I'm going to take to present you with an heir. Even those who believe her will still be inclined to be indulgent toward us for having decently and quietly remedied our supposed sin.

"In one way, I'm even grateful to her a little. Since we do have to wait, our courtship will be ever so much *safer* conducted by mail than it would be if you were within reaching distance of my eager, longing arms! Unwittingly she has helped surely me—and probably you—to carry out our union with dignity and decency, at the proper time and place.

"Ethan, I love you, and the knowledge that I cannot even see you for at least a year stops my heart, my breath, makes me feel as though I were going to die. But it is better so, and we two, and our children, born in honor, and reared to fear God and respect themselves, will be all the better for it.

"Tearfully, Your Forlorn, Heartbroken,
Anne"

She had added a postscript, which read:

"P.S. Dear Heart, since, as a *mere man* you are a Babe in Arms when dealing with the *absolutely ferocious* members of my sex, I beg you not to in any way enter into a controversy with Cora Bellamy about this matter. The perfect way to turn aside the sly innuendos she is sure to deluge you with is to stare at her with icy contempt and not open your lips. That tactic, my Love, will disconcert any member of my much too voluble sex whomsoever. Martha Harris, however, is another matter. Martha surely likes me; but she, too, is a woman. Ethan, no woman on the face of God's green earth is going to believe that another woman spent the better part of an hour in a man's bedroom, alone with that man, without falling into carnal sin. I wouldn't believe it myself if I didn't know it was so. Therefore I leave it up to you as to what excuse you may use to explain my disappearance to the Harrises. Would they believe we had a sudden and bitter lovers' quarrel, and that I have, temporarily, anyhow, thrown you over? Oh, no! Both Phil and Martha are anything but fools, and since, as the saying goes, 'Every couple consists of one who loves, and one who allows himself to be loved,' they have surely discerned who is the lover and who is the achingly, unbearably beloved in our particular case! Forgive me: I must close this. I have already asked the nightclerk to find me a hack to transport me to the docks, my bags are packed, my heart is broken, but hope lives on in me. Believe me, I love you,

"Anne"

He thought: 'How wise she is! How almost unnaturally wise. . . . The results of a hard childhood surely.' Then he put his mind to the problem of how to explain Anne's departure to the Harrises. Being himself, the product of seven generations of stern Puritan forebears, he decided to tell them the truth, however unlikely that truth might seem to them.

So thinking, he strode into the hotel's dining room to find, much to his disgust, that Phil Harris was not alone: Tom Bellamy was there with him. Tom had, Ethan saw, a marvelously evil grin upon his ugly face, while poor Phil's expression was badly troubled. 'I've come too late,' Ethan realized; 'This gelded boar hog has already spewed up his filth.'

He crossed to the table where the two men waited. Above the mountain of flapjacks he was wolfing down, Tom's evil grin broadened.

Ethan stood there looking at him.

"Tom," he said easily, pleasantly, "do you want to live to a ripe old age?"

"Why, why—I never said a mumbling word about you 'n yore—" Tom stopped, swallowed that "your little dilly" that was trembling on his lips, substituted prudently, "'n yore li'l lady . . ."

"You're right," Ethan said quietly. "That's the way to go about it. Keeping your trap shut is mighty—healthy, Tom. Phil, will you come with me out to the lobby a minute? The matter I have to discuss with you is private, and I'm sure you've found out by now that talking about anything before the Bellamys is exactly the same as publishing it on the front page of the local newspaper . . ."

"That I have," Phil said grimly. "Except maybe our hometown

rag wouldn't dare publish their kind o' news. All right, Old Hoss, c'mon . . ."

"So," Phil said, "that was it! I thought I heard somebody let out a war whoop, but when I didn't hear anything else, I sort o' turned over 'n went back to sleep. A nightmare—like the ones you've done had right pert frequent since yore pore brother's death. . . . Yep, stands to reason you would. 'N her—the pore li'l thing—that's just what she would do, fly to yore side without a second thought. . . . But, Old Hoss, you know how wimmenfolks is; gonna be harder'n old hell to convince Martha 'n the good ladies o' Bethlehem Methodist Church that didn't nothin' happen 'twixt the two o' y'all, given that y'all had both the opportunity 'n the privacy, both . . ."

"Still nothing did," Ethan said quietly; "You believe me, don't you, Phil?"

"Wal now," Phil grinned, "*I* wuz to be left alone with a she-critter as pert 'n perky as yore li'l Anne, I wouldn't lay a plugged lead nickel on my willpower, 'n that's a livin' fact! 'N not me nor any other man with blood 'n breath left in him is gonna blame you for partakin' of what is purely yours a li'l ahead o' time. That there pretty piece o' paper with all them seals 'n ribbons on it, 'n a few mumbled words afore a long-faced parson don't make all that much difference, Eth, Old Hoss . . . "

"The only trouble with that," Ethan sighed, "is that the women, and not the men, determine what's acceptable behavior in any town. All right, I'll admit I was tempted, more tempted than I've ever been in all my life, except once, and that time I gave in to the temptation, a fact that I'm going to regret as long as I live . . ."

"Why?" Phil said.

"The woman involved was married—and to one of my best friends. But to get back to last night, or rather this morning. Since the War, Phil, boy, I've had a mighty powerful dragbrake as far as temptation is concerned—"

" 'N that is?" Phil asked.

"My shredded gut. I just don't take fire like dry prairie grass anymore. Which means I generally have time to think my second thoughts first. And last night I did think them—such as the fact that we can't marry before at least a year is out and maybe even two, that the risk of putting in a crop before building a fence was a little too great. We mean to live in your little community the rest of our lives, Phil, and to do that in any comfort we've got to be accepted and respected both. So when she asked me to turn her loose, I did, with the reflection that we were going to have a lifetime of slow, sweet nights before us . . ."

"All right, I believe you," Phil said; "but that ain't the trouble. The fact is, Eth, I just don't see how I kin give Anne that teachin' job with every damn woman in town—including *mine*—whisperin' about her behind her back. Most of 'em will sure as hell keep their kids home from school rather than let a woman with a damaged reputation teach 'em. That the woman in question don't deserve that reputation ain't got one goddamned thing to do with it, as you know mighty well. You kin shut Tom Bellamy up, but short o' shootin her, you can't shut up Cora. 'N bein' hanged for killin' that big bitch wouldn't solve nothin' neither. . . ."

"There, you're right," Ethan said; "But that problem no longer exists; it's already been solved, Phil. Here—read this . . ."

He handed Phil Anne's letter.

After mumbling over it with pursed lips, and turning the pages with a wetted fingertip, Phil looked up at Ethan with troubled eyes.

"I oughta be plumb, downright relieved," he sighed; "but I ain't. I'll admit yore li'l Anne's reasonin' was first-class. She's done cut the ground clean out from under Cora Bellamy's 'n our homegrown witches' feet. Now they can't watch her like a flock o' hen buzzards 'n put a dirty twist to everything her 'n you, Old Hoss, might do, innercent though it be. But Lord God, boy—our pore kids is growin' up as ignorant as prairie shoats, 'n I wuz really happy at the thought that a girl as smart as yore Anne was gonna beat a little learnin'—the three R's anyhow—into their thick heads. But now . . ."

He stopped short and stared up at Ethan with what was surely a glow of inspiration in his eyes.

"You!" he roared; "You're a college eddicated man! 'N 'twuz all yore fault enyhow—what with you not havin' even the hoss sense to fergit that you plainly done yore lovin' duty by yore pore brother, 'n a broodin' over it 'n havin' nightmares. So since you've done gone and purely donated the first good schoolmarm we ever had a chance at to Omaha, Nebraska, I, as mayor of Marthasville, and by virtue of th authority vested in me by the City Council, hereby appoint you schoolmaster o' th Marthasville 'n environs district. Pay is thirty dollars a month, 'n that ain't bad, you gotta admit. 'N by Gawd you're gonna take the job!"

"Phil," Ethan said, "I came out here to farm—"

"Ain't nobody stoppin' you. You've got from now 'til September fifteenth to find your spread 'n file yore claim. 'N since the only damn thing you kin plant is a little winter wheat—'cause corn plantin' is done in *April* out here, Old Hoss, so you're too blamed late for that—me 'n all the other farmers will help you bust th sod to get your wheat in. You don't have to harvest it 'til next spring, so whatcha gonna do? Sit in yore dugout or yore log shanty 'n brood over Anne? Tell you another thing, too—as schoolmaster you'll start out big in any town. Western folks plumb respects book learnin'. 'N if you can throw th fear o' God, 'n stuff a li'l readin', writin', 'n figgerin' into our young hellions' heads, you'll make things a damn sight easier for Anne when you bring her home—in spite of how much pizen Cora will've spread around about her by then. C'mon, Old Hoss, what do you say?"

Ethan thought about that.

"Done!" he said; "And here's my hand on it."

"Whooopeee!" Phil yelled; "Thank you, Eth, boy. And beyond that, thank the Lawd!"

The three of them, Ethan, Phil, and Tom—from whose countenance the evil grin had totally vanished in the interest of protecting his evil hide—stood in Karl Heintz's gunsmithery and looked over the amazing collection of lethal firearms the Pennsylvania Dutchman had there. What struck Ethan was how utterly beautiful many of them were, especially a long, slim frontier flintlock rifle—the so-called "Kentucky Rifle" nearly all of which had been made in Pennsylvania and by Pennsylvania Dutchmen at that—that had been crafted by Karl's grandfather for—the story went!—Daniel Boone.

He stood there watching with wry amusement as, with almost boyish glee, Phil demonstrated to Tom Bellamy the advantages of a revolver whose cylinder had been bored straight through for metal-cased rimfire cartridges, over Tom's old percussion cap, powder, and ball Navy Colt. He did this by staging a race with Tom to see which of them could load his sidearm faster. Naturally, since he had only to slip six brass-cased cartridges—containing, as he'd already pointed out to Ethan, powder, fulminate, and ball in one compact unit—into the chambers of the cylinder of his own big 1860 Army Colt that Karl had just finished altering for him, Phil won hands down. In fact, since Tom had to pour loose black gunpowder from a little powder horn into each of the chambers of his six-gun, patch a separate ball with linen cloth, ram it home with a loading lever that was actually a miniature ramrod, and then fit separate brass percussion caps to the nipples at the back of each chamber, Phil had his weapon completely loaded before Tom had charged one round.

Tom immediately handed his Navy Colt over to Karl Heintz.

"Fix mine up for this here newfangled ammunition, too," he growled. "How soon kin you have it done, Mr. Heintz?"

"Two weeks from today," Heintz said; "The charge is five dollars. You can pay when you pick up your gun, but if you pay me in advance, I'll put it on the stagecoach to Marthasville in care of Mayor Harris, here, at no extra charge. Save yourself a trip all the way back here to Atchison, but it's up to you, sir . . ."

"Done!" Tom said proudly, and handed Karl Heintz a five dollar bill. Karl stuffed it into his unlocked cash drawer that had, Ethan saw, an amazing amount of money in it. And that money was perfectly safe, he realized, for Karl Heintz, along with being a gunsmith, was one of the fastest and best shots in Kansas.

"What about you, sir?" Karl said to Ethan then; "You got a sidearm you want bored through?"

"No, thank you, Mr. Heintz," Ethan said politely; "it so happens that I don't even own a revolver . . ."

"Perhaps I can sell you one, then?" Heintz said.

"No, thanks again," Ethan said quietly.

Karl Heintz stared at him.

"Preacher?" he said.

"No. Just don't like the idea of killing people, sir," Ethan said; "Had to kill one man too many during the Late Unpleasantness, so I've sort of sworn off the habit. What you can sell me, sir, is a shotgun. A light fowling piece good for game birds . . ."

"What do you aim to bag with it, young fellow?" Karl Heintz asked.

"Prairie chickens. Wild turkeys if there are any left," Ethan said.

"There aren't," Karl Heintz said, "and precious few prairie chickens either. Homesteaders have mostly killed 'em all off, and plowed up their nesting grounds. What I'd like to sell you, Mister—"

"Lovejoy, Ethan Lovejoy, at your service, sir," Ethan said.

"—Mr. Lovejoy, is a practical weapon. A rifle that can bring down a buffalo—and that'll supply you with a whole winter's fare out on the prairie. And one that will discourage folks who don't hold to as lofty ideals as you do. Incidentally, I agree with you. I don't hold with killing, either. Since I was working in an arms factory in Connecticut, I didn't see service, and I'm proud to say I've never killed a fellow human being in all my life. And one of the reasons I haven't had to, Mr. Lovejoy, is that fellows who've seen me shoot don't try to kill me. Out here, only a strong man can live peacefully. Here, let me show you this one. Just came in from the factory I used to work at. This here is the latest model Henry carbine, though now it's called a Winchester, after Governor Oliver Winchester of Connecticut, who's president of the company. Designed by B. Tyler Henry, though, who's a real genius if there ever was one . . .''

Ethan stood there holding that rifle. It was slim and deadly-looking, but as seductive to a man who loves beautifully made things as the wrong kind of woman had been and always would be to gentle male creatures like Ethan. It was a repeater, holding fifteen shots in its magazine, but it had a loading port that allowed the rifleman to stuff shells in almost as fast as he fired, so that a man with enough ammunition could stand off an army. He didn't know what the hell he needed a weapon like that for, but the skilled mechanic in him couldn't resist it.

"All right, I'll take it," he said. And thereby, long after, saved his life.

Ethan sat in the buggy with Phil Harris and looked out over that sweep of prairie. And from every direction the prairie looked back at him as though he were a mote in its great golden eye. Those winds that never stop blowing all day and all night long rustled the prairie grasses—buffalo, blue grama, and hairy grama mostly—burnt white blond by that pitiless prairie sun. What came over Ethan Lovejoy then was a feeling of profound peace, and even profounder recognition. 'This is it,' he thought; 'I've found it. I've come home . . .'

"Damned if I see what th hell you wanted to come this far south for," Phil said querulously; "we gotta be 'bout three miles below Abilene by now—'n as any fool kin plainly see, there ain't a drap o' runnin' water in sight. Nary a tree. . . . And after all the first-class spots I done gone 'n showed you on Turkey Creek, 'n on th Solomon River to boot . . ."

"But I didn't like 'em," Ethan said solemnly; "And I do like this . . ."

"Why?" Phil said.

Ethan considered how to answer that question without offending or upsetting Phil. In the first place, one glance at the grimy, dog-eared map of the state that Phil had procured years ago from the State Land Office at Topeka had shown him that the chances of the Kansas Pacific's passing through Marthasville were remote indeed. Phil's little town was too far north, located on Turkey Creek, instead of on one of the three rivers that flowed through the prairie in that part of the state.

So Phil had had to be stone blind to have failed to see what was topographically obvious: the Kansas Pacific, which was supposed to run from Wyandotte to Denver, Colorado, before looping north to join the Union Pacific at Cheyenne, was going to run through Junction City—so named because it was located at the junction of the Republican and the Kansas Rivers—and Abilene, which lay on that part of the Smokey Hill River that ran into both. From there on, Ethan shrewdly guessed, it would follow either the Saline or the Smokey Hill river valleys to the town of Salina, and very probably the valley between the two rivers westward to the Colorado line. It would do this, he knew, because it is several thousand times cheaper, and easier to lay tracks along a valley's level floor than to build a railroad up over mountains with all the grading, bridge building, and blasting tunnels that entails. No other route made sense, especially not one that passed through Marthasville, way up on Turkey Creek, for no other reason than the fact that Phil Harris and his fellow townsmen ardently desired that it do so!

Even Phil's argument about the comparative populations of Marthasville and Abilene wasn't valid. In the first place, neither town *knew* what its actual population was. Both tended to count drifters and the occupants of the farms that lay between the two towns. In the second, the railroads didn't give a damn about the size of the towns they chose as stations on their lines; if a town lay on the logical route to the place they were ultimately going to, they'd lay tracks down its main street if necessary, and that was that. The question of population would then take care of itself. Every town the Kansas Pacific had already incorporated—even as a whistle-stop—in its system had doubled, tripled, or, in some cases, quadrupled its population in a matter of months thereafter.

Therefore, the place where he was now, sitting with Phil Harris in his buggy under the awful immensity of a Kansas sky, was just about perfect. To procure a water supply meant digging a well. And that well, out here on the prairie itself, was going to have to be dug to a depth of anywhere from sixty to two hundred feet to have even a ghost of a chance of striking water. That one item alone was enough to discourage settlers from flocking in. Therefore, the lands around his claims, a homestead of one hundred sixty acres, and a preëmption of the same size, were going to continue to be available for a good many years. Long enough, he was sure, for him to earn the money to buy them from the railroad, or from the government, until, finally, he would have his golden empire of wheat and corn, his pens full of fat, sassy hogs, his flocks of chickens, his herds of both beef and dairy cattle. . . .

He tried explaining some of that to Phil, carefully not mentioning his belief that the Kansas Pacific was going to leave Marthasville "up the creek" both figuratively and literally.

"All right," Phil said grudgingly; "as far as th business o' not gittin' yoreself hemmed in is concerned, you're right. But mebbe you better explain me a few things, Old Hoss: Like say how th livin' hell a fellow what's done had a hole blown through his gut big enough to shove a doubled fist through ever expects to git to be strong enough to dig th kind o' well he's gonna need way out here?"

"By taking it easy," Ethan said; "I've got all winter, haven't I?"

"That you ain't," Phil said. "You's got from now to say mid-November—or with a li'l luck even into December. After that, the ground out here freezes so solid that th only way to bust through it would be to use blastin' powder. You got that kind o' money, Eth?"

"No," Ethan said sadly. He had, at that moment, five hundred dollars to his name, a gift from his Grandpa Daniel, and two hundred dollars of that had to be reserved to buy his preëmption acreage, leaving him three hundred dollars to meet all of his expenses for at least a year. He didn't realize that on the frontier the possession of that much hard cash made him rich beyond the dreams of avarice. Phil, for instance, had done the same thing, and founded the town of Marthasville to boot, on an initial outlay of exactly twelve dollars. Many, if not most of the settlers didn't have a red copper in their jeans, not to mention a dime.

"All right, fergit that," Phil said; "I'll send a stout fellow what owes me money to help you git it down to water afore th first freeze sets in. But you gonna need a house to put yore sweet li'l Annie in. Out here on the lone prairie that means a *sod* house, Old Hoss. You seen any forests hereabouts?"

"God, no!" Ethan got out, and his heart sank through the prairie's floor deeper than the well he proposed to dig. He had seen several sod houses by then, even examined one of them—out of curiosity—with some care. And his convinced opinion of that primitive structure was that no self-respecting swineherd back East would even keep his pigs in one. But now, he was up against one of the hard facts of Kansas life: the extreme scarcity of timber, that is, when trees existed at all where the settler was. More often than not, they didn't. Back in the fifties, when the Territory had first been settled, there had been a fairish number of trees clustered along the streams. But the earlier settlers had largely cut most of them down to make their log cabins, and burnt up a goodly part of the rest for fuel to keep from freezing in the winter. For in Kansas a man went from an Eskimo's to a Christian's hell within the space of a couple of months. Even before them, the Indians had burnt over the sparse woodlands in their game drives. So now most of Kansas was a treeless prairie that both the Spanish and the French explorers of two centuries before had declared unfit for human habitation. In his long life, Ethan Lovejoy was going to be driven to declare—at least ten thousand times—that both were right.

"So all right," Phil said with sardonic glee, "nacherly a smart, ed-dicated Eastern fellow like you, Old Hoss, knows exactly how to build a sod house? Where to find even one piece o' timber long enough 'n stout enough to make a decent ridgepole for yore roof? How 'n where to collect enough buffalo chips 'n prairie hay to cook with 'n to keep from freezin'?"

"Phil, lay off," Ethan said; "I'm as green as grass and you know it. Still—look at it this way: Isn't it better to endure hardships the first few years in order to insure a good life for your family later on?"

"If yore family even gits through them first few years alive," Phil said sadly, "or leastwise with all their wits still in their pore prairie-locoed heads. Many's th gentle, Eastern-bred filly what's done sat 'n gazed out over th lone prairie 'til one day th prairie gits to gazin' back at her like one great big cruel yellow eye. . . . I personally done knowed three mighty good 'n sweet li'l critters from back East what just couldn't take this awful loneliness. One of 'em cut her wrists 'n throat with her old man's razor, 'nother one drunk potash lye—didn't kill her, but left her throat so burnt she never talked ag'in—'n th third throwed herself down th well. You real shore that li'l Anne is built to live out here?"

"No," Ethan said honestly, "I'm not sure. But I kind of think she is. She had a rough childhood, Phil—wandering all over with her mother who was the leading lady in a traveling theatrical troupe—so she's a lot tougher than she looks. However, when I go up to visit her at Omaha at Christmastime, I'm going to put it to her fairly. If she thinks the life out here will be too rough, I'll still marry her, but I'll take her back to the eastern part of Kansas, say—or even to some more settled state like Iowa or Missouri. . . . I'd rather stay out here and grow with this country, but if she thinks she can't, I won't sacrifice her to my ambitions . . ."

"Good for you, Old Hoss!" Phil said. "I take it, then, that you're plumb set on claimin' this heah quarter section?"

"And the one next to it," Ethan said.

"All right. Hate to have you so damn far from Marthasville, but even so you're less than two days hard ridin' distance. So le's git you started.

Gonna send th Old Timer to help you find yore water—th right place to dig, that is, 'n to show you how to build a sod house, not to mention help you build it. That'll cost you a couple o' bottles o' whiskey—what's all th Old Timer lives on, anyhow . . ."

"The Old Timer?" Ethan said.

"Yep. Old ex-mountain man, ex-guide on th Oregon Trail, ex-Injun fighter, ex-squawman. Ex every damn thing you kin name—includin' hoss thief, 'n cattle rustler, though he don't exactly own up to them last two. 'Pears like he's tellin th truth 'bout bein' a scout 'n guide on th Oregon trail. Lots of old folks hereabouts remembers that. 'N he smells like a mountain man—stinkinest critters you ever run across, th mountain men . . ."

"Why?" Ethan said.

"Wal, first off, they used to live by trappin' beaver, 'n th stink o' beaver oil 'n fat—'n half-rotten beaver flesh, too—sort of worked they-selves into th pores o' the trappers' own skins 'til wasn't no way o' gittin it out. Not that they ever tried. Th Old Timer swears he knew a mountain man oncet who lived to ninety-three without ever lettin' a drap o' water tech his hide. Then the good Christian folks of the town he lived in—I mean *near,* ain't nobody even startin' to let no mountain man live *in* no town 'cause the wimmen, anyhow, would faint dead away ev'ry time he passed by—caught th old bugger 'n put him in a old folks' home. Nacherly they had to bathe th old coot, or the rest of them pore old people would-n't 've been able to stay in th home. He died two hours later of double pneumonia, the death certificate read. What he died of really, Old Hoss, was shock, disgust, and a broken heart. Mountain men just don't take kindly to cleanliness . . ."

"Hope I'll be able to stand him 'til I get my own shack built," Ethan sighed.

"Just don't let him get to th windward of you," Phil grinned. "Now, c'mon, we better make tracks. We got a lot to do. First we got to stake out yore claim. You figger th spot we're sittin' on is th center, or one corner of it?"

"Don't know," Ethan said; "What difference does it make?"

"Be a helluva lot easier to measure off if you calls it th corner. See this?"

"Yes," Ethan said; "it's a rawhide rope . . ."

"Wal now, tha's one way o' lookin' at it," Phil conceded; "but I calls it my measurement ruler. Laid it out plumb careful-like, 'cause them surveyors that comes out from the Land Office at Junction City can be mighty strict. It's exactly ten yards long. Each one of them knots I got tied into it is one yard from the next. Now this short one"—he drew out another rawhide throng from under the buggy's seat—"is one yard long, each o' th three knots indicatin' one foot. For inches, I got me a ordinary store-bought wooden ruler. Here 'tis . . ."

"Lord God!" Ethan laughed; "In three hundred twenty acres, they're going to quibble about inches?"

"They ain't—*we* is," Phil said seriously. "Out here on th lone prairie, stands to reason not havin' no neighbors yet to cramp your style, you goin' to make your spread a perfect square, ain't you?"

"Hadn't thought about it," Ethan said; "but that ought to be the easiest shape to measure, oughtn't it?"

"Wal now, that plumb depends. In a hundred-sixty-acre spread it purely is. You drive in a stake, measure off eight hundred and eighty yards in a straight line, and drives in another one. On the second stake you lays down a try square to make sure you's got a right angle. Run yoreself another line eight hundred eighty more yards from yore second stake, 'n pounds in a third. From that'un you measures off another eight hundred eighty, at right angles from the second line, back in th direction you started from, so that the first line 'n th third will be absolutely parallel to each other. Another right angle, done careful, so that your fourth eight hundred eighty will run parallel to your second. Get hit right, 'n it proves its own self. 'Cause that last eight hundred eighty, you been careful 'n got all four o' yore corners plumb square, is plain got to end up exactly at th stake you started out from!"

"I see that," Ethan said. "Heck, it stands to reason. Now all we've got to do is figure out how many yards each leg of a three-hundred-and-twenty-acre spread has got to be for the whole thing to come out as a perfect square . . ."

"Gonna tell you that 'un, 'n save you a headache," Phil said triumphantly; "each side of a three-hundred-twenty-acre square's got to be exactly twelve hundred forty-four yards, one foot six 'n a quarter inches. And that, Old Hoss, makes layin' out a three-twenty spread in th form of a perfect square a pain in th ass tha's a helluva lot more perfect than you'll ever get th square!"

Ethan checked Phil's figures, found that his friend was right again. It could be done, he supposed: all you had to do was to count off one thousand two hundred forty-four yards in a straight line, then measure off

—with Phil's schoolchild's wooden ruler—eighteen and a quarter inches. Only, he was certain that you'd get a built-in accumulation of error that would throw the whole thing off by several feet, if not by a whole yard or more by the time you got through. In a measurement of that size, you simply couldn't afford to play around with dimensions that worked out to a quarter of an inch. In fact, they had better not pull on Phil's rawhide measuring rod too hard, or the stretch would falsify their figures enough to make the government surveyors who'd come out to check at "proving up" time reject the whole filed application.

"You're right, Phil," he sighed; "that's a dimension that is practically impossible to measure with any degree of accuracy. We need one that works out to the yard exactly."

"Give you one," Phil said complacently; "Only you hafta give up yore perfect square. Be a rectangle, but 'bout as close to a square as you kin git without goin' plumb crazy tryin' to measure it. You done figgered out what th area of a three-hundred-twenty-acre spread is, ain't you? In square yards, I mean?"

Ethan glanced at his page full of scribbled figures.

"Yes. It's one million five hundred forty-eight thousand, eight hundred square yards," he said.

"All right," Phil said. "So now we makes th short sides o' yore spread eleven hundred yards long, 'n th long sides fourteen hundred 'n eight yards exactly. What do them two lengths multiplied by each other give you, Old Hoss?"

Ethan multiplied rapidly.

"Lord God!" he laughed; "You're a mathematical genius, Phil! How on earth did you ever figure that one out?"

"Stayin' up all night three nights in a row," Phil said solemnly. "'N when I ran outta paper, I scribbled on th walls 'n th floor. Martha was plumb fit to be tied when she saw them numbers all over everything, I kin tell you that. You see, my spread's three-twenty, too, only I had more trouble provin' up than you're going to, 'cause I laid one corner out from the outside bank o' Turkey Creek to make damn sure I had runnin' water on my place. Fact is, this here's a plain o' glory, or it would be, if you didn't have to dig that gawddamn well . . ."

"That sod house doesn't sit too well with me, either," Ethan said sadly; "I sure hate like hell to put Anne in one of those things. There doesn't seem to be any way to keep one clean . . ."

"There ain't," Phil said mockingly; "on top o' which she's a-gonna have to heat th place 'n cook your meals, Old Hoss, on a fire made outta dried buffalo shit, thrown on with her own two lily white hands. *You* wanted to come way th hell out here, so on yore head be it!"

"You're right," Ethan sighed; "Maybe I'd better change my mind and choose my spreads nearer to where there's water . . ."

"No, don't," Phil said seriously; "Not if you's plannin' on goin' from three-twenty to four-eighty, and from that to six-forty 'n beyond. For a place that gits as little rainfall as we do out here, you done chose well, Eth —for dry farmin' you needs acreage. 'N you'll never be able to accumulate a spread like that 'longside no stream, not if you ain't got the wherewithal to buy yore whole farm right now, this minute. 'Cause folks is gonna flock into them river valleys. Stands to reason you won't be able to raise th cash afore a passel o' homesteaders have done gone 'n hemmed you in. 'Sides, you's fergittin' another thing: In a mighty few years th Central Pacific 'n th Union Pacific is gonna meet. 'N that means we's gonna have a railroad plumb from the Missouri River at Wyandotte—cause th Kansas Pacific is a branch o' th Union Pacific, y'know—to th Pacific Ocean. 'N all them forests they got out in Oregon 'n Californy is gonna come through here on flatcars already cut into planks. Build yore li'l Anne a mighty fine frame house, she willin' to wait. 'N I kinda think she won't even mind a sod house; she kin snuggle up next to *you* in it, Old Hoss. Spunky li'l critter that'un, 'n she shore Lawd dotes on you. . . . Now c'mon. Let's git along with the measurin' . . ."

It took them all day, and night fell before they could finish it. Ethan hadn't anticipated any difficulties measuring a few thousand yards off in straight lines across a prairie that looked as level as a billiard table. Only, as the inexperienced nearly always are, it turned out that he had been wildly optimistic. *No* prairie is absolutely flat; even the best of them—and the prairies of central Kansas are among the world's best—are gently rolling. Laying that first eleven hundred yards out was as easy as eating apple pie, but once they had that second stake—or rather pole, because a stake wouldn't have showed above the prairie grasses—in, to keep the second line dead straight and at right angles to the first over a distance of one thousand four hundred and eight yards turned out to be a nightmare. They did it finally, after endless corrections, but by then the stars were out.

"I vote we camp out 'n git a early start tomorrow," Phil said. "Fact is, I had th li'l woman fix us up some grub just in case. Bottle o' her homemade dandelion wine, you kin stand th stuff. *I* can't. Tha's howcome

I snuck along a bottle o' some mighty fine drinkin' whiskey. Have a snort, Old Hoss?"

"Don't mind if I do," Ethan said; "As long as you've got some rations to put on top of it. My busted gut doesn't take kindly to firewater when its empty, Phil. Gets to churning and reminding itself—and me—how torn up it was. Lord, what a dunce I am! Never occurred to me to bring along anything to eat . . ."

"You ain't dumb, Eth; what you is, is green—and tha's curable. Dumbness ain't. Look at hit thisaway. Every livin' white man in Kansas wuz a greenhorn oncet. Only they learnt, most of 'em, 'cause they plumb had to. The ones what couldn't learn drifted back East, or cashed in their chips. The West is mighty hard on them what ain't got th makin's of a man in 'em. 'N you's already got yore growth in every way that counts. Proved that in th War . . ."

"Thanks, Phil; and you're all wool and a yard wide yourself," Ethan said, "as we say back home in New England. Anything I can do to help?"

"Yep. Take this here box o' matches 'n set a little clump o' prairie grass afire," Phil said.

"Lord God, Phil, why?" Ethan asked him.

"To have ourselves a safe place to camp 'n make a campfire," Phil explained. "Out here you always burns yourself a little patch o' ground clear. You waits 'til th patch you's done set burns down, 'n then you beats 'n stamps it out. Hit cools off, you got a place you can make a campfire to bake flapjacks 'n b'ile coffee over without th risk o' sendin' th whole damn prairie up in smoke. Prairie fires is plumb awful. Here's a tip—you sees one a-ragin' toward you, you stops where you is, 'n burns yoreself off a little clearin'. Wets yore clothes all you kin from th canteen you damn well oughta carry every time you sets off 'cross th prairie in the summertime. But you saves enough water to git your bandanna kerchief soppin' wet 'n puts it over yore mouth 'n nose. Then you stands stock-still 'n let th prairie fire burn on past you. You've done robbed it o' the fuel it would've used to burn you up, by making yore li'l one-man firebreak in th first place. Course you'll git a few blisters from sparks 'n cinders; but 'sides from that, you'll be as safe as in church right in the middle o' th hottest prairie fire anybody ever did see . . ."

"Phil—" Ethan said.

"Yep, Old Hoss?"

"My father spent a young fortune sending my brother Jonathan and me to the fanciest boys' school he could find. College, too, though they kicked Jon out for misbehavior—she was our math prof's *wife,* so they *had* to send him down—in his second year. But I finished. And now I come out here and find out that I don't know one thing that counts. Not one single thing . . ."

"You's too hard on yore own self, Eth," Phil grinned. "My old man sent me to th University o' Hard Knocks. Eddicated me through the seat o' my pants. And since tha's where my brains is located anyhow, I learnt a thing o' two. C'mon, Old Hoss, git our li'l firebreak burnt off whilest I unpack this gear . . ."

First in the morning, they started the measuring up again, and found it came easier and easier as they got the hang of it. A little past noon they had it all done, and Ethan was scribbling busily:

"Commencing at a stake in the prairie, three and one quarter miles southwest of the town of Abilene, thence due north for a distance of two hundred rods, to another stake, thence due east for two hundred fifty-six rods to another stake, then due south for two hundred rods, thence due West for two hundred fifty-six rods to beginning of claim. Containing exactly three hundred and twenty acres, half to be taken as a homestead, half as a preëmption. Signed this thirty-first day of August, 1866, Ethan Bayard Lovejoy . . ."

When he had finished this rough draft of the claim he was going to file at the Land Office at Junction City, he read it aloud to Phil Harris.

"Hmmmn," Phil said, "hit'll do, Eth, 'ceptin' for one thing: that there *exactly* three hundred 'n twenty acres. Tha's plumb gonna stick in th Land Office surveyors' craw. Sounds like you, a ordinary fella, is presuming on th kind o' professional knowledge what only they is s'posed to have. I wuz you, I'd put it more humble-like, fer instance: 'Containin' three hundred twenty acres more o' less, or what I suppose to be . . .' That way, they won't jump down on you with both feet, they finds you've done gone 'n made a honest mistake. 'Sides, it *ain't* exactly three-twenty. We done measured yore half section out with rawhide, 'n rawhide stretches. We could be up to a yard long on any one leg . . ."

"All right, Phil," Ethan said mildly; "This is your country out here, so I'm sure you know the ropes. Lord God!"

At his exclamation, Phil turned and looked north in the direction he was staring at; saw at once the reason for the acute disgust mirrored on Ethan's face. For there, some yards off, in a hired livery stable buggy, the Bellamys sat, grinning complacently at the two of them.

"Howdy, Eth, boy—howdy Phil," Tom Bellamy said; "I take it this here stake marks th corner o' Eth's claim. Whichaway do it run, Eth— north o' south? I mean do your spread lie north o' this here stake, o' south o' it?"

"North," Ethan said grimly.

"Then I'll jes' lay mine out south of it," Tom said. "Half section, three-twenty acres, right?"

"Right," Ethan said.

"Then all I gotta do is drive in my stakes 'longside o' yours 'n head th outside legs south in th opposite direction. You done figgered out how long them outside legs got to be?"

"Yes," Ethan said; "two hundred rods, or eleven hundred yards, or thirty-three hundred feet, depending on what measure you're going to use, Tom."

"Oh, rods is good enough. Got me a surveyor's reel tape right here. C'mon, Cora, git down 'n hold this end ag'inst Ethan's stake, so we kin start our measurin'—"

"Now wait a minute, Tom!" Ethan exploded; "Why the hell do you have to lay out your spread right next to mine? Trying to hem me in or something?"

"Lord, no, Eth, boy!" Tom chuckled; "Jes' 'pears to me out here a man kin do with neighbors. Could be a matter o' life 'n death at times, y'know . . ."

That, Ethan reflected, was perfectly true. An Indian attack, a buffalo stampede, a slip of the ax while cutting rails, could all get to be quickly fatal for a lone settler. But, despite that, he was certain he'd rather risk anything, even death, than to have the Bellamys as neighbors. But as soon as he'd thought of that, he realized what the alternatives were. As far as telling Tom Bellamy he couldn't locate his farm alongside his own was concerned, the possibility didn't even exist. As long as both farms lay within one of the government's alternative sections, as they did—Ethan had made sure of that—legally there was no way on earth he could force Tom Bellamy not to take his two possible quarter sections there. That was as much his right as it was Ethan's. Both were over twenty-one years of age, citizens of the United States, and Civil War veterans, to boot.

The only alternative Ethan had, he realized sadly, was to keep his mouth shut, let Tom lay out his three hundred twenty acres, file his claim at the Land Office, and then go lay his own out somewhere else—at least ten miles away. But he looked out over that luminous sweep of space, heard again the ceaseless prairie wind sweet sighing through the grass. And he couldn't. He literally couldn't. That feeling of recognition was in him again, and it was much too strong. He had crossed half the continent to find this place; he had dreamed it into being long before he ever saw it. It was his—his! And no boar hog gelding like Tom Bellamy, nor a big, dray horse mare like Cora, was going to drive him away from it. Besides, he suspected, they wouldn't last long out here. The kind of work it took to make a square mile of virgin earth like this one—for between them, the two farms, his and Tom's, made up a full section, six hundred and forty acres, one full square mile—bloom and flower, Tom Bellamy simply didn't have in him. He was a whiner, a quitter, and this was a place for men. . . .

He was thinking all that when Cora Bellamy spoke up for the first time.

"Heard from Anne yet, Ethan?" she said.

"No," Ethan said shortly; "there's hardly been time . . ."

"Strange she ups 'n runs off like that, isn't it?" Cora said.

"I suspect she had her reasons," Ethan said.

" 'N you, of course, lover boy, don't know what those reasons were?" Cora said.

Ethan stared at her, his eyes blue ice.

"I *know* what those reasons were," he said quietly; "And so do you, Cora. I simply see no reason for discussing them with you, or with anybody for that matter. No, don't get down. I'll help Tom with his measuring . . ."

Phil Harris was staring at Tom Bellamy with a strange expression on his face. That expression, to Ethan, looked remarkably like grim suspicion. And now, when Phil turned and looked at Ethan, his expression didn't change. Rather, the suspicious look on his weatherbeaten countenance deepened, if anything.

"Tom," he said, "'n you, too, Eth, I'm gonna put it to y'all fairly: I done showed both o' you boys green, well-watered spreads up near Marthasville on Turkey Creek. 'N on both th Solomon 'n th Republican rivers. Yet both o' you done chose to leave good spreads like them there 'n come way down here on this Gawdamned prairie. Why? Eth says it's cause he aims to own a two- o' three-section spread afore he cashes in his chips, 'n up there on th rivers or the creek, he's certain shore to git hemmed in afore he can raise th cash to expand his holdin's. I'll accept that. But y'all gotta admit it do look mighty funny you's both decided to locate this close to Abilene. Why, ag'in? Y'all know somethin' that I don't—about whicha-way that damn railroad's gonna run?"

"Wal now, Phil," Tom said uneasily; "I didn't have th heart to tell you afore now, but last week, me 'n the missus took us a long drive back in th direction o' Junction City 'n Manhattan. In Manhattan we run into an old friend o' mine from Chicago. Irish fella, name o' Tim O'Mallory. Done come up in life, Tim has. Right now he's section boss o' one o' th construction gangs what's building th Kansas Pacific. So I put it to him fairly: 'Tim,' sez I, 'this line gonna run through Marthasville? I got a interest in knowin' 'cause I'm kind o' thinkin' o' settlin' near there.' 'N he sez to me: 'Fergit it, Tom, 'n settle in Abilene o' Salina, 'cause them's th burgs we'll be building through . . .' "

Phil whirled upon Ethan, and his eyes were sick with actual hurt.

"Why, Gawdamn you, Eth Lovejoy," he said; "You knowed it, too! Tom wuz in his rights to keep his trap shut 'cause we jes' met 'n he ain't no special friend o' mine, but you—"

"Now, hold on, Phil," Ethan said quietly; "I didn't know it in the same sense that Tom did. That is, I didn't have a confirmed statement from an employee of the line about which way the Kansas Pacific was going to run. But, in another way, I did know it. And the reason I didn't say anything to you was because I didn't want to hurt your feelings since the man who gave me the information that made me practically certain that the railroad was going to run this far south, was *you,* my friend . . ."

"Me!" Phil exploded; "How th ever livin' hell could I ever have give you some info that made you think—"

"Nevertheless you did," Ethan said; "You showed me a copy of the official state map of Kansas. All I had to do was to study it for five minutes to see the line couldn't run through Marthasville . . ."

"I don't see why th hell not!" Phil fumed; "You knows where Denver, Colorado, *is,* Eth Lovejoy? Not to mention Cheyenne, Wyoming?"

"Yes. Both considerably north of here, as the crow flies, Phil, old friend. But who the hell ever told you a locomotive was a crow? Look, Phil, I studied engineering in college, and though that wasn't my specific line, several of my classmates were specializing in railroad construction, grading, track building, and the like. So I know that while a straight line is always the shortest distance between two points, it's not always the cheapest. Phil, it costs from ten up to fifty times as much to build a railroad up over even the foothills of mountains as it does to run it through a river valley. And what river valley runs in the right direction? Not the Blue, or the Republican, because both go almost straight north into Nebraska, and that's the Union Pacific's territory by agreement. And not either fork of the Solomon, though they both run in the right direction, because they simply don't extend far enough west. The same thing's true of the Saline, but the Smokey Hill River runs clear out to the Colorado line. And the reason that the Kansas Pacific is going to loop straight north over high but damned near flat tablelands to join the UP at Cheyenne, is that if it didn't it would have built straight across the highest part of the Rocky Mountains, which is not only an engineering nightmare but would cost more money than this whole country's got. So forget that ruler you've got laid across the map from Manhattan to Denver. That route would work only if the country were perfectly flat. But it's not flat, Phil; it's got mountains in it. Big mountains, old buddy . . ."

"And you never said a word!" Phil groaned.

"Why should I have? If I'd got here *before* you founded Marthasville, I'd have gladly pointed out to you that it was way the hell off any possible railroad route. In fact, if you just had to found a town, I'd have told you to put it on the Smokey Hill or the Saline. But I was too late for making those kinds of suggestions, so why should I upset you by showing you that you were up the creek all right, and without even a paddle to save you? Incidentally, Phil, I hereby—with great relief—resign from my schoolmaster's job. Marthasville won't be needing a schoolmaster—or a mayor, for that matter. If it follows the rule of towns bypassed by the only available railroad, by this time next year it won't even have a population . . ."

"There you's right, Old Hoss; but I ain't a-gonna accept your resignation. What I'm a-gonna do is transfer you to Abilene. You see, me 'n ol' Ned Tyler, who's mayor o' Abilene, has got ourselves a gentleman's agreement—along with a ten dollar bet what I done already lost, dagnab it!—to wit: whichever one o' th two towns what gits the KP line through it, with the corresponding freight 'n passenger stations, has agreed to provide free town lots to th citizens o' th one what loses . . ."

"Sounds mighty generous to me," Tom Bellamy said. "But what I don't see, Phil, is why Abilene would ever agree to a thing like that . . ."

" 'Cause they *need* population, Tom," Phil said. "Right now they ain't got nobody but a few drifters. And the more fine, upstanding citizens they's got, the more concessions they can bludgeon outta th railroad—cheaper rates, more frequent stops, a telegraph office, th works. We always did have 'em beat that way, 'cause Marthasville's sich a pretty li'l place. Only hit's plumb gone now. We're a-gonna start takin' our houses down, or even puttin' 'em on rollers 'n transportin' 'em down to Abilene with ox teams. Gonna break Martha's heart, but there ain't no help for it—"

"But, Phil, how do you know that Mr. Tyler wants me to teach there?" Ethan said.

"Ain't got no choice in th matter. We's bringin' th kids, so we brings th schoolmaster. There ain't five young'uns in Abilene right now 'n we's got close to sixty young hellions in Marthasville. C'mon, le's help ol' Tom finish his measurin' up, so we kin all light out for th Land Office at Junction City. 'Cause I'm a-gonna give up my claim and take out a new one—but farther east. On the river, but between Abilene and Junction City . . ."

"Why there, Phil?" Ethan said.

"The old-timers claim that Salina is on the exact border o' th rain belt. West o' Salina hit don't hardly rain none a-tall. East o' it, th rainfall is damn nigh normal for th state o' Kansas. Some old-timers swear that none o' the good ladies o' Salina who lives on th west side o' town ever managed to raise a decent flower garden yet, and th ladies on th east side o' town less than a hundred yards away is always braggin' 'bout their roses. Some of 'em tells how you kin stand on th sidewalk in certain parts o' Salina 'n stay dry as a chip while you's watchin' folks a-scurryin' to git into their houses on th other side o' th street, afore they gits soaked to th skin. But I reckon tha's drawin' th longbow more'n a mite . . ."

"But *here*," Ethan said a little worriedly; "Will I get enough rain here, Phil?"

"You's east o' Salina, so you might," Phil said judiciously. "But th truth o' th matter is, Eth, can't nobody depend on th rainfall in central Kansas. Some years you'll git too much, 'n you kin run into a two-, three-year stretch with hardly a drap. East Kansas's got a sight better luck as far as rain is concerned. West Kansas you don't worry about it—out there a child kin grow to man's estate without ever havin' seen a good hard rainstorm in his whole life. C'mon, we better git on with Tom's measurin', we want to git to Junction City afore nightfall tomorrow . . ."

"But there are people in West Kansas, aren't there?" Ethan asked, as they were unreeling Tom's fancy store-bought measuring tape southward from one of his stakes. "If so, how do they live if it doesn't ever rain?"

"Ranchin'. Tha's cow country out there. Reason I didn't go no further west to settle. 'N I tell you one thing, Eth, one o' my gal children takes up with one of them cow-chasin' varmints, I'm gonna stripe her li'l sitdown bloody with my buggy whip 'n then ship her East. Swear t' Gawd I'd jes' as soon see one o' my daughters in th line at Gashouse Gertie's parlor house as married to a cowboy . . ."

"Why?" Ethan said.

"Ain't nothin' worse. Not even a Injun o' a mountain man. Them runty li'l varmints is brought up on panther pee 'n locoweed, 'n they's all wilder than a grizzly bear 'n twicet as crazy. Wait 'til you meet some of 'em 'n you'll see . . ."

"Runty little varmints?" Ethan said; "Aren't cowboys built like anybody else?"

"Naw. Though I reckon they wuz, oncet. Hit's a matter o' selection: ranchers won't hire big fellas to trail drive 'cause their weight would wear down th hosses. So most cowhands is miserable li'l critters like jockeys back East. Even when you sees a tall one, he's a walkin' skeleton, not a foot wide 'cross th shoulders. But hit's th difference twixt ranchin' 'n farmin' that makes them pore bastids wild. You can't run no farm without wimmenfolks on it, so in farmin' country the number o' males 'n females gits to be danged nigh equal pretty quick. On a ranch it don't work out that way: you have th rancher, his wife, 'n maybe a daughter o' two, 'n two hundred hard-up 'n horny cowboys. Ridin' th range is th lonesomest work there is, Eth—worse even than seafarin'. 'Cause sailors is in a bunch in th same boat, but a cowboy don't have no company but a bunch o' cows for weeks on end 'til roundup time. I feels sorry for 'em; I even understands what makes 'em so wild; but I jes' don't want to put up with 'em, tha's all. Stretch it a little tighter, Tom! Or else we'll be way off on our numbers . . ."

Junction City was twenty-five miles from where they were, or nearly two days' journey in a buggy. Of course, there were "Lightning Stages" that could make all of thirty-five miles in a single day, but they accomplished that miraculous feat by changing their worn-out teams of horses every ten miles for fresh ones, and by reducing their passengers, Ethan swore, into almost permanent cripples. In a buggy you had to take it easy, or else you'd kill your horse. Still, they made it finally, filed their claims, including the new one Phil had hastily—and inaccurately, Ethan was sure —staked out about three miles east of Abilene on the Smokey Hill River. They paid their fourteen dollar filing fees, registered their claims at the Land Office, and Phil renounced his old one, promising to be off it by the early spring of 1867.

In one way they were lucky. They were able to transact this vital business in a matter of hours. A few years later, in 1871 or '72, say, it would have taken them days, for by then the lines of prospective homesteaders before the Land Offices of Kansas would be up to more than a mile long. In 1866, the land rush hadn't really started yet; by 1876 it would be a flood. Again, even in this Ethan proved how thoroughly he was a Lovejoy despite all his efforts to appear, and be, different from his kindred: he acted, once the main chance had been seen, as promptly and decisively as his Yankee forebears always had. That this trait would insure him fortune, and per-haps even fame, was a foregone conclusion.

But not—happiness. Happiness is another thing.

6

To his vast astonishment, Ethan found that in the first weeks on his claims, he seldom—and then only briefly—thought of Anne. The sad truth of the matter was that in September 1866, he was much too busy—and worn-out —to even speculate upon either the depth or the extent of his feelings for his bride-to-be.

During those first weeks, Ethan was almost crushed under the burden of the nearly backbreaking work he had to do. But what was even worse was the hellish business of constantly having to make decisions that he lacked both the experience and the knowledge to make wisely, if at all. The decisions revolved forever around the question of priorities: should he build a dugout first, to be used as a barn for his team once the cold weather came, or a house for himself and, eventually, Anne? Shouldn't he perhaps set about digging that all-important well before doing anything else? His place was located slightly more than three miles south of the Smokey Hill

River, and hauling water out to it quickly got to be a time-consuming chore, especially since every time he started in the direction of the river Tom Bellamy waylaid him with a couple of empty barrels of his own.

Yet Ethan couldn't blame Tom for that. Wagons were hellishly expensive. His own, bought secondhand, was a factory-made Moline farm wagon, and he had paid all of fifty dollars for it. New, it would have cost him three times that much. He had obtained the sturdy vehicle from a Marthasville citizen who had become so discouraged at the news that the Kansas Pacific had doomed their little town by choosing to lay its rails through their arch rival, Abilene, and leaving them high and dry, that he had given up and was moving his family back to Missouri, which had had its influence on the asking price. For the wagon was in excellent shape. In fact, it was practically new.

Ethan didn't buy a team of horses for his wagon, having been warned against that mistake by Phil Harris. Instead he bought oxen, not because they were cheaper—as they were—but because no horses then available were strong enough to break a Kansas prairie with a plow. But what really saved him from failure as a prairie farmer was the appearance of the Old Timer at his place.

Ethan's first impulse was to send the old man away, because the Old Timer's stench would have floored a turkey buzzard. He appeared at Ethan's spread early in September, and, at the first whiff of him, Ethan had all he could do to keep his breakfast down. The old man was clad in a typical Old Scout's costume: beaverskin cap, buckskin hunting shirt, leggings, breechclout, and moccasins, all of which were black and stiff with beaver grease, campfire soot, and plain dirt, as were his shoulder-length hair, and his belly button-length beard. Neither soap nor water, Ethan was sure, had touched his grimy hide since the day he was born. He bore a Golcher plains rifle, a later development of the famous, and misnamed, Kentucky rifle, shorter, and of a much heavier bore than that famous arm, caplock instead of flintlock, and cleaned, oiled and polished until it shone —which demonstrated where his priorities were, Ethan thought grimly— with a powder horn and bullet pouch slung over his emaciated shoulder, and a smaller pouch holding, Ethan later found out, a tin box containing his copper percussion caps at his belt. In that belt, too, he wore the scabbard of a hunting knife so big that it was practically a sabre.

"Howdy, young Eth," he cackled and stuck out an unbelievably filthy paw in Ethan's direction.

Shuddering, compelled by the politeness his mother had ground into his very nerve ends, Ethan took that paw. He hadn't then witnessed the

Old Timer's custom—shared with all mountain men, Ethan soon discovered—of wiping his anus with his bare fingers after defecating. After he did witness it, he never shook hands with the Old Timer again.

"Howdy, Old Timer," he said. "Mind telling me your name?"

"Be happy to, son, I could remember it," the Old Timer said, flashing Ethan a grin that was completely toothless except for two widely separated yellow fangs that had the shape and the length of a cougar's; "But since them Sioux scalped me on th Oregon Trail, I plumb disremembers my past life, mostly. Sometime hit comes back to me in flashes, but mostly I plain disremembers . . ."

"Sure it's not because that name is featured prominently on some sheriff's Wanted, Dead or Alive notice?" Ethan said.

"Could be, young Eth, could be!" the Old Timer cackled happily; "But effen hit is, tain't fer nothin' more serious-like than chawin' out some hot-tempered fella's liver 'n his lights when he come gunnin' fer me—not never sumpin' reel bad like hoss thievin' o' cattle rustlin'. . . . Wal, here I be. Whatcha wanta git started at fust?"

"Don't know," Ethan sighed; "I've got to build a sod house, but that can wait, I guess. What I really need is some sort of temporary shelter like a dugout, say—and a well. And I really can't say which comes first . . ."

"Th dugout, son," the Old Timer said. "Hit's plumb September now, 'n long about th middle o' this here month, you jes' might get rain. C'mon, le's git them dumb beasties o' yourn hitched up to the plow . . ."

"But," Ethan said, "if we're going to build a dugout, what do we want to start plowing for?"

"Woooopie!" the Old Timer roared; "Green as grass, 'n plumb bored fer th hollow horn! Dumber'n a li'l nigger wit a big belly button! Whoooopie!"

"All right, all right, I'll admit I'm a tenderfoot, but that's what you're here for, Old Timer, to set me right. Come on, why do we have to plow in order to build a dugout?"

"Cause we needs sod bricks for th front wall, tha's why," the Old Timer said, "'n sod bricks you lays out with a plow 'n then you spades 'em up. C'mon, le's git these here critters hitched 'n yoked 'n I'll show you how . . ."

That was the first time that Ethan had attempted to break the prairie, and he caught pure, undiluted hell. Breaking, of course, *was* plowing, but with one major difference: it meant turning virgin soil, grass root-anchored earth that never, in its millions of years of existence, had been broken by any man-made implement, hence the pioneer farmers' distinctive name for the process. After the prairie sod had once been broken, plowing it in subsequent seasons became fairly easy, and was referred to by the settlers as just that: plowing, not breaking. Breaking you did just once, and it was so difficult to do that the new farmers went from farm to farm helping each other do it, for the very simple reason that while you could *plow* with the single yoke of oxen most of them owned, to *break* an untouched claim you needed a minimum of six yokes—twelve muscular and powerful draft animals—hitched to a single John Deere plow. Even so, you usually needed three men to accomplish it properly: one to drive the teams, another to guide the plow, and a third, usually the biggest and heaviest man in that cooperative group of neighbors, to sit on the beam and thus help force the plow into that almost unbelievably tough ground.

That, actually, was the reason Ethan hadn't yet attempted to put in his crop of winter wheat on the ten acres he was required to by the Land Office to prove the seriousness of his intention to homestead, before said Office would give him a title deed to the lands he'd claimed. He was waiting for the fathers of the children he was supposed to teach that winter to come with their yokes of oxen and help him get started, in part payment of their offsprings' tuition. . . .

But now, there was no help for it. He wondered whether it was even possible to break that tough, grass root-matted soil with only two oxen. But when he said that to the Old Timer, that living piece of plains history answered:

"Us ain't got to break as deep as is needful fur plantin', young Eth, jes' six inches o' so. 'N that we'uns kin do, effen you'll jes' lift yore feet clear off th ground 'n put yore whole weight on th plow handles . . ."

By following the Old Timer's advice, Ethan managed to break two parallel rows, some eight inches deep and several hundred yards long, straight out into the prairie.

That having been done, Ethan went on about the second step, which was to cut out, with a spade, huge slabs of sod, a yard square, from between the two furrows, and load them on the wagon. Unyoking the oxen from the plow, and hitching them to the wagon, they transported their sod bricks to the proposed dugout site, a hill—or rather the nearest thing they could find to a hill, a sloping rise in the prairie. Into the side of that rise, they dug a square-shaped hole some ten by twelve feet, and leveled off the bottom of it to make the dirt floor. On the front, or open end of it, they began to lay their huge sod bricks, leaving of course, openings for a window and the door. The work went fast, especially after Tom became ashamed of himself and pitched in and helped them out. In fact, they would have had the whole thing finished long before night except that they ran up against the prairie's eternal problem: the total lack of timber.

Ethan shook his head.

"I'll just have to drive up to the river tomorrow and cut some," he said; "A pity I didn't think of it the last time I went after water . . ."

"Tell you what, Eth, boy," Tom Bellamy said; "le's all drive up there in your rig right now. Course with oxen we'll git there way after dark, but we kin bring my fly tent along 'n sleep in that. Then first in th morning we'll cut all th poles we'll both need, 'cause I'm damn sure gonna build me a snug shelter like that 'un. From what folks tells me, gits too damn cold for a tent in th wintertime . . ."

"Freeze yer balls blue, Mister Bellamy!" the Old Timer cackled; "'n after that they'll drap plumb off you 'n leave you with a voice like a choirboy's, 'n you kin throw away yore razor 'n tha's a nach'l fact!"

"Shut up, Old Timer," Ethan said. "All right, Tom, that's a good idea. Go get your ax and come along . . ."

When they reached the river, the Old Timer immediately crawled into the tent with Tom the moment Tom had it pitched. Ethan, of course, slept in the open that night, not wanting to hurt the old man's feelings. 'But,' he decided, 'when it comes to letting him into my dugout, he's going to have to bathe in the river first, before he can bunk with me—on that point I'll lay down the law!'

Both Tom and the Old Timer were first astonished, then impressed by Ethan's dexterity with a woodsman's broadax. On his grandfather's farm in the well-wooded Berkshires, he had learned, as a boy in his teens, to use that kind of logging tool with almost professional skill. For now, not only did he cut poles and brush for his dugout's roof, but a sizable pile of good-size logs, which he then proceeded to split into planks with no implements other than his ax and the kind of a wedge that woodsmen call a froe. Ordinarily, he would have built a sawhorse and whipsawed them lengthwise, but he hadn't thought to buy a whipsaw. It hadn't occurred to him he would need one out on the prairie.

But now he realized he was going to have to take a full four days off —in a rented buggy, since oxen were far too slow—and make the eighty-two-mile round trip to Manhattan. Since rumor had it that the KP had already got to, or soon would reach that town, he'd very likely be able to buy things like window sashes and window glass there, and maybe even a whipsaw, though he doubted that. A whipsaw would have to be ordered from St. Louis, though now he wouldn't have to go any farther than Manhattan to pick it up, and that was a hundred and twenty-eight miles closer than Wyandotte was. . . .

He reflected with profound gratitude upon the miracle of the railroads, which with their blinding speeds reduced a day's journey to a single hour. Twenty-five miles in sixty minutes! That was traveling, all right. No wonder many people still hesitated to take the steamcars for fear that the human constitution just wasn't built to take velocities like that, and that they'd die from a lack of breath. . . .

"Whatcha cuttin' planks for, Eth?" Tom asked him.

"To make the door, and shutters for the window. That's all it's going to have, shutters," Ethan said; "at least until I can get into Manhattan and buy some window glass—"

"Speakin' o' window glass," Tom laughed; "That time me 'n th missus drove back to Junction City 'n Manhattan we passed by a place that a fella had done left to go into th Land Office 'n prove up. You know what th requirements is, don't you, Eth?"

"Yes. Ten acres under cultivation, a well, and a dwelling house twelve by fourteen feet. Easy enough requirements to fulfill it seems to me . . ."

"Wal now, this here bunco artist had done fulfilled 'em, all right," Tom chuckled. "He'd gone 'n laid four logs on th ground, but them logs sure Lord wuz twelve by fourteen feet. 'N he'd done put a piece o' glass off a broken whiskey bottle in a forked stick at one corner o' them logs, 'n that there wuz his glass window. His well was all o' two foot deep, mebbe two 'n a half, but that wuz good enough, 'cause th law don't say a damn thing but you havin' to have struck water. 'N he'd sure as hell got two other smart fellas like him to come in with him and swear that he'd fulfilled th requirements. They'd do it with straight faces, too, knowing he'll do th same for them when they prove up . . ."

"Doesn't the Land Office send inspectors out?" Ethan asked.

"Yep. But them poor fellas is purely overworked. By the time they gits to a smart crook's spread he's done worked another dodge. There's a carpenter outside o' Junction City what's done built the sweetest li'l frame house you ever laid eyes on. Fullfills th government's requirements to th letter, Eth. Twelve by fourteen feet, *four* glass windows, shingled roof, roses in flower pots on the front porch. But along with that there mighty prutty li'l white-painted house that would make even my Cora weep for joy, he's done gone and built a outsize flatbed wagon to accommodate it 'n he's makin' hisself a fortune haulin' it out to smart fellas' spreads th day before th inspector's s'posed to git there. Natcherly, after th inspector leaves, he hauls it th hell away 'n rents it to another fella for provin' up purposes!"

"Aren't there any honest people in Kansas?" Ethan groaned.

"Two thet I knows of," the Old Timer cackled; "You 'n Phil Harris —'n I got hopes fer th two o' you. Y'all's real bright young fellas, so I'm sartin shore you'll smarten up, given time!"

"Wait!" Tom said. "There's one more dodge, 'n in some way hit's plumb the cutest one of all. Fella right next to th Land Office is got hisself a toy store. 'N th main thing he sells in that there store is doll houses— exactly twelve by fourteen inches. Doin' a land office business hisself, that fella—cause if you ever read th law, Eth, you'll know it says a twelve-by-fourteen dwelling house, leaving that business o' feet to be understood. So all the wiseacres buys theyselves a doll house, takes it out to their spreads, sits it down in a cornfield and calls in their witnesses to take their Bible oaths that they done seen a twelve-by-fourteen dwelling there. Which, by Gawd, they have! Neat, ain't it?"

"No," Ethan said soberly; "Kansas is headed for hell in a handcart if that's the kind of people who've settled here. Come on, we'd better be getting along back now . . ."

"Wait," the Old Timer said; "Cut yoreself a good stout ridgepole for th sod house you's gwine to built for your new missus, young Eth. Because I'm a bettin' that come springtime when th sap is up, you's a-gwine to start buildin' on thet there house like crazy. Be a good idee to have yore ridgepole dried 'n seasoned by then . . ."

Ethan conceded in his mind that the Old Timer was probably right. Once he had the dugout finished, he'd start in on his well. Thereafter, the sowing of his ten acres to winter wheat wouldn't take him long after the fathers of his prospective pupils had broken the ground for him. By then the cold weather would have set in, and time would hang heavy on his hands. He'd begin to miss Anne then, very surely. He only hoped that he could keep the memories of Jonathan's death from running like fire and silent screaming through his mind. A few more nightmares like the ones he had already had could—out here on this lonely prairie—shake his reason, perhaps even break it. But even admitting that thought to mind was no good.

"Come on now," he said.

The next day, they built the roof by stretching the new cut poles across the top of the dugout to meet the sod brick front wall. Then they covered them with brush, and after that with prairie grass cut with a scythe and finished with a layer of spade-tamped earth. Under the Old Timer's skillful guidance they gave the roof a reversed slant toward the rise, dug drainage ditches on both sides of the dugout and past it up the rise to keep as much water as possible away from a structure anything but waterproof.

The Old Timer came inside the dugout to show Ethan how to make the beds—Ethan was quick to note that the mountain man used the plural —the fireplace, and the chimney. But staying inside a ten-by-twelve-foot dugout with the Old Timer was, for Ethan anyhow, a physical impossibility. One second more, and he was going to throw up or faint, or both. It seemed to him incredible that a human being could stink worse than a billy goat and a skunk combined. But the Old Timer did—far worse. Ethan made a dash for the door opening, for he hadn't had time to make or hang the door yet, which was just as well. Inside that dugout with the Old Timer, and with the door closed, Ethan was quite sure he would have died of sheer asphyxiation.

"Wha's th matter, young Ethan?" the old man said with real concern. "You off yore feed o' sumpin'?"

Ethan decided to have it out with the Old Timer then and there. By then he had grown genuinely fond of the ancient manure pile. But putting up with the close physical presence of a man whose personal habits were as unbelievably filthy as he now knew the Old Timer's were, was another matter altogether.

"Look, Old Timer," he said; "I'm planning to keep you on until winter comes, but for me to do that I need some cooperation out of you . . ."

"Hell, son, I'm a-helpin' you all I kin, ain't I?" the Old Timer said.

"Yes, you are," Ethan sighed; "That's not what I mean. Put it this way; for me to let you bunk in here with me, you've got to bathe in the river at least once a week—"

"Bathe?" the Old Timer said in thunderstruck tones; "You means strip buck nekkid 'n wash myself all over?"

"Exactly that," Ethan said sternly; "And what's more, when you go out on the prairie to relieve yourself, use some dry grass, not your bare fingers, damnit!"

The Old Timer looked at Ethan then, and his sad old eyes were misty with sudden hurt. He pushed his beaverskin cap to one side on his head, picked up his magnificent—and clean—plains rifle, his powder horn, his bullet and percussion cap pouches, and shouldered them all.

"Good-bye, young Ethan," he said. "Daggum my stupid hide! I should of knowed better, lettin' myself take a shine to a city fella . . ."

"Now hold on, Old Timer!" Ethan said; "I didn't mean to hurt your feelings. I need you here. God knows you've forgot more than I'll ever learn. But the truth of the matter is that I've got a big nose and a weak stomach, and the way you stink would make a polecat run for cover. Would it really be too much of a chore for you to wash your filthy hide?"

"Yep. Shore would. Look at hit thisaway, young Ethan—effen I wuz to tell you to put that mighty prutty rapid-firin' rifle o' yourn upside yore haid 'n pull th trigger, would you do it?"

"No. Of course not! But I don't see—"

"Whut I means? Thet's whut yo's axin' me to do, more o' less. Nearly every mountain man I ever run across done lived to be ninety o' a hundred years old. 'N you know why, young Eth? 'Cause we don't have no truck with water. Water is plumb pizen. We don't drink hit 'n we don't never let a drap o' th stuff tech our hides, tha's howcome we most in generally lives so long. City folks is purely pullin' weaklin's 'cause they's always washin' th honest dirt off theyselves. Hell, son, dirt is plumb healthy! Keeps th buffalo flies 'n th fleas from borin' through to yore meat, keeps th cold out, 'n pertects a fella from gallopin' consumption 'n—"

"Look, Old Timer, you've seen me work. Do I look like a weakling to you?"

"Naw, you's mighty strong, 'n that's a livin' fact . . ."

"Well," Ethan said, "until I came out here, I had an all-over bath every single day in my whole life. Even out here I manage to bathe in the river every week—"

"Thet's cause you done gone 'n trained yoreself thetaway," the Old Timer said judiciously; "Like folks what takes a drap o' pizen every day 'til they enemies kin sneak a whole bottle o' hit into they whiskey 'n they won't turn a hair. Put me in a river nekkid, make me wash my hide, 'n I wouldn't last a whole hour. Th shock would plain kill me 'n I do mean *daid* . . ."

"And your stink, shut up inside that dugout with me, will kill *me*, Old Timer," Ethan said; "Oh, Lord! I guess we'll just have to build a separate dugout for you . . ."

"Naw, don't. Hit ain't cold yet, 'n I kin sleep out on th prairie. I kin damn nigh sleep standin' up, I has to. Tell you whut, next time you o' Phil goes to Junction City, ride on past hit fer a little ways 'n see effen you cain't buy me some buffalo robes from them there hunters whuts killin' off all th buffaloes to feed them railroad workers. Don't let 'em sell you no flint hides, though. Try'n git me a pair o' fresh kilt hides, roll 'em up, 'n bring 'em back here still soft 'n bloody 'n I'll scrape 'n tan 'em meself . . ."

"All right," Ethan said. "But you will use the grass, won't you?"

"Hell, young fella, grass meks a fella's arsehole itch like th dickens, but effen that will mek you happy, I'll try it," the Old Timer said.

"It will make me very happy," Ethan said solemnly. "Now tell me how to make that chimney and the bed . . ."

The chimney was made by digging a fireplace into the back wall of the dugout, making a hole in the roof, and erecting a little square box of mud-daubed sticks on top of that, on the inside of the dugout; the upper part of the fireplace and chimney was also made of mud-covered split sticks—"cat 'n clay chimney," the Old Timer called it.

The bed consisted of a pair of forked sticks—stout ones—driven into the floor with a hammer, side by side, with their forks at right angles to one another. Then long poles were driven into the walls in such a position that their free ends rested in the forks, and the whole thing was completed by a rectangular wooden frame, into which a handwoven netting of strong rawhide thongs had been bound to serve as bedsprings. This surprisingly comfortable apparatus rested on the poles on its two outer sides, and upon heavy stakes driven horizontally into the thick sod walls on the inner ones. On top of that Ethan piled dried prairie grass—which was all right until mid-October, maybe. But before November rolled around, he was going to have to buy himself some buffalo robes to keep from freezing at night.

Then he went to work on his door and the wooden shutters that would have to serve him until he could get into Junction City to buy his window glass—you couldn't buy anything in Abilene except whiskey yet —and found that they were going to take him longer than he had figured on. The trouble was, he had forgot to buy nails—by 1866 nails were already machine-made and were cheap enough, he could have bought three pounds of them for twenty cents—so he had to put his door and shutter together by boring holes in the planks and ramming in pegs of wood. Actually, this made a better and longer-lasting structure than nails would have, since the pegs, being of wood themselves, expanded and contracted with temperature and moisture changes at the same rate that the planks did, so that the whole thing had no tendency to loosen up as nailed carpentry always does. But it was hellishly inconvenient and slow, so that by the time he'd finished it, the well-digger that Phil had promised to send him was already there.

The well-digger was a professional who made his living digging wells for the prairie farmers, and though his fee for a well was usually ten dollars, he offered to dig Ethan's for five, since he owed Phil Harris that much money, and Phil had promised to consider the debt paid if Henry Atkins would do this chore for his friend Eth Lovejoy. . . .

Henry Atkins was a solemn man over six feet tall but as skinny as a rail fence, which was an advantage when it came to digging wells. "Fat fellas gits stuck in 'em," he explained.

Prior to getting started, he helped Ethan hang the door and the shutter on the wooden hinges with dowel pin connections that Ethan had made. He greatly admired Ethan's workmanship. "Helluva lot better than th rawhide hinges most folks use out here," he said.

But before they could begin to dig—for Ethan and the Old Timer were going to spell him at that murderously backbreaking work, and haul the loose dirt up for him in buckets when they weren't digging themselves —they had to decide upon the most likely spot beneath which water might be found. Henry Atkins refused to venture an opinion on the subject.

"Mister Lovejoy," he said honestly, "I've done dug more'n five o' ten miles straight down, effen you adds up all th eighty-'n hundred-footers I've done punched into this here prairie, 'n after more'n twenty years at it, I kin tell you this: any man who sez he knows exactly where the water's gonna be found is plumb a liar. I oughta know where you'd be likely to find it by now, but since I'm a Christian and a truth-telling man, I hafta admit I don't . . ."

"*I* does," the Old Timer said.

"And jes' how th hellfire 'n tarnation do you, Old Timer?" Henry Atkins said.

"Injun taught me. He wuz th medicine man o' a tribe o' Choctaws I was—well—kinda livin' wit oncet . . ."

"'N bigging all th squaws," Henry Atkins said with evident disgust. "No wonder them Sioux scalped you finally. Heard tell you didn't leave a single pore li'l Injun gal over twelve years old unbusted . . ."

"Wal now, tha's drawin' on th longbow a mite, Hank," the Old Timer cackled; "But squaw pussy is moughty good I hafta admit . . ."

"You ain't never had no other kind, squawman," Henry Atkins growled. "Aw heck, fergit it. So now you're claiming to be a water witch?"

"Naw. All I claim is I knows where to find water, 'cause a redskin medicine man showed me how. 'N he didn't never miss, that there Injun. Jes' y'all wait a minute 'til I goes git my dowsin' rod 'n I'll prove it to you!"

He scurried over to the wagon and took out of it a buckskin pouch in which he kept all the junk he called his "possibles." Out of it he drew a slender fork of weeping willow wood. Then he began to prance over the prairie like an ancient monkey with two branches of the fork in his two hands, and the third one free. Not a hundred yards from them the mountain man stopped.

"C'mon, y'all!" he bellowed; "I done found it!"

Ethan and Hank ran over to where the Old Timer was. In his hands the dowsing rod was jerking, the free end bending toward the ground as though drawn by some invisible force. Ethan was surer than old hell the old coot was faking it, but for the life of him he couldn't see how. He turned to Henry Atkins.

"Well, Mister Atkins?" he said.

The well digger shrugged.

"Don't make no nevermind, sir," he drawled; "Out here on the prairie anyplace you dig you're likely to find water—or you ain't. It's pure accident ninety percent o' th time. Who knows, this here stinkin' old billy goat just might be lucky . . ."

"We'll dig here, then," Ethan said.

It turned out that the Old Timer's dowsing rod was in fine working order, except that its sense of the chemical composition of the liquids it indicated existed in a state of urinal poverty.

A scant fifteen feet below that spot they struck oil.

Ethan stood there looking at that black muck oozing up at the bottom of that well, cursing with heartfelt profanity.

"Wal now," the Old Timer cackled, "don't take on over it so, young Ethan. After all, you kin use it t' grease wagon axles . . ."

"Ain't this here th stuff they make coal oil outta back in Pennsylvania?" Hank said dubiously. "For lamps, I mean?"

"Yes," Ethan groaned; "you can distill it—or rather refine it into benzine for cleaning spots off clothes, or kerosene—the stuff you call coal oil—for lamps. Only they haven't got the process to the place it ought to be, Hank; that's why you're always hearing about kerosene lamps blowing up in people's face and blinding them. Apart from that, this black gook is just a goddamned nuisance. C'mon, let's fill this filthy stink hole in . . ."

Henry Atkins stared at him thoughtfully for some little time. Then he shrugged his lean shoulders.

"You're the boss, Mr. Lovejoy!" he said.

But when the Old Timer started capering over the prairie again, dowsing rod in hand, Hank Atkins said gravely:

"Pay him no mind, Mr. Lovejoy. Wouldn't be safe to dig no well too close to where there's oil . . ."

"Why not?" Ethan said.

"Well, th same acre you've struck oil in is sure to have Black Damp at the bottom of it. Tha's a kind o' marsh gas, Mr. Lovejoy, 'n it's done killed more well diggers out here in Kansas than I like to think about. You've got a lot o' land here, a half section 'pears to me, so I vote we move about as far from this here oil well as we can git . . ."

Ethan looked out to where Tom Bellamy's tent stood in the exact middle of his acreage. 'And from *that*,' he thought. He said:

"All right then, come on . . ."

They found water, finally, sixty-two feet down, in the corner of Ethan's farm closest to the river. But finding it almost cost Ethan his life. He was manfully taking his turn, digging near the bottom of that well, when something, the instinct for danger developed in four long years of war, made him look up. The rope that Hank and the Old Timer were using to haul buckets of dirt up out of that well had gradually frayed as they drew it up against the edge of the hole, because Kansas settlers were so poor that not even a well digger could afford a block and tackle. It chose that moment to break. Ethan flattened himself against the side of the well. That bucket took the tip off his long, Yankee nose, all the buttons off his shirt, a strip of skin off his bony chest, and buried itself up to the handle in the mud between his feet.

"You shore wuz lucky," the Old Timer said, when they had drawn him up and were attending to his cuts and bruises, " 'n not jes' 'cause that there bucket didn't brain you. You'd've had sumpin' else pokin' out, thet there li'l lady Phil says you's gwine to wed next harvest time would've been a mighty disppointed li'l gal come yore weddin' night!"

"Mr. Lovejoy," Henry Atkins said, "I vote we shoot him 'n b'ile him down for skunk oil. Git enough to light yore place all winter, 'n tha's a living fact . . ."

But, once they had found water, it turned out that Ethan was lucky in another way, though the well digger had to point that out to him.

"Good thing you ain't built nothin' more than a dugout," Hank Atkins said; " 'Cause now you know where you gotta build yore house. Right here, next to yore well. 'Cause it's real onkind to ask a pore frail female critter to lug a heavy bucket o' water half a mile 'cross th lone prairie . . ."

"Lord God, you're right!" Ethan said; "I hadn't thought of that . . ."

"Well, think about it now, Mr. Lovejoy," Hank said. "That 'n one more thing: Where d'you plan to put yore outhouse, sir?"

Ethan stared at him. Up to that moment, he hadn't thought about the obvious necessity of building an outhouse at all. The prairie with its luxuriant grasses provided all the privacy that a lone man—or two men, counting the Old Timer—needed. But within a year or two he was going to be wed, and you just couldn't ask a gently bred, modest woman to put up with what a man could. . . .

"Not only that," Hank said when he had expressed his thought, "but it's gonna be winter pretty soon, now. 'N gittin' chilblains in th hams ain't rightly smart. But th reason I asked you that, sir, was to give you a li'l professional advice: an outhouse has plumb got to be built at least twenty yards from yore well, or else you'll foul yore own drinkin' water . . ."

And again Ethan reflected sadly about how many things there were about farm life he simply didn't know. . . .

Ethan had thought—though God knows why!—that having relieved himself of the necessity of making daily trips up to the Smokey Hill River to fetch barrels of water, he had also rid Tom Bellamy of his excuse for daily visits. It turned out, however, that when Tom discovered Ethan had a well, he appeared three and four times a day, bucket in hand, or even oftener than that sometimes, simply because he was lonesome and wanted, as he put it, "To set 'n chew th fat . . ."

Ethan wondered how Tom could be so unconscious of how much he disliked him. But, Ethan supposed, a lifetime of having most people dislike him had caused Tom to grow a hide four inches thick and armored on top with horn.

What enabled Ethan to escape Tom's unwanted company for a couple of weeks, anyhow, was the appearance of the fathers of the children Ethan was supposed to teach, with their oxen to break ten acres of prairie sod for him so that he could put in his crop of winter wheat. Tom, with his marked distaste for anything having the remotest resemblance to hard work, disappeared completely the whole time they were on Ethan's place. Ethan wondered what he used for water during that fall plowing. Whiskey, he guessed, because Tom wasn't much more fond of washing himself than the Old Timer was.

Ethan learned a great deal from those prairie farmers who, sadly enough, weren't neighbors of his, since most of them had been seduced by Phil Harris's incessant preaching of his honest but completely erroneous belief that the Kansas Pacific was going to lay its tracks through, or near, Marthasville and had holdings near that pretty but now doomed town. As a matter of fact, almost none of them had farmhouses on their land, having, on Phil's suggestion, followed the European custom of clustering their homes in the town and laying out their farms all around it, always within easy walking distance of where they lived. It was, Ethan conceded, an excellent idea, especially for their womenfolk, who had the company and the sometimes desperately needed help of other women there at hand. Ethan was already beginning to learn what a terrible thing the loneliness of the prairie was. . . .

But now he asked endless questions of these experienced farmers, and profited greatly from their answers, once they had got so they could even understand his crisp New England accent. In fact, he actually got more benefit out of their experience than they had been able to obtain themselves. The reason for this was very simple: Ethan had an essentially inventive, innovative mind; he saw at once the changes that should be made, departures from routine and custom the deep-seated conservatism of agricultural people largely blinded them to.

Yet what actually gave him his head start as a farmer, he afterward realized, was the fact that he had, along with his inventive turn of mind, an advantage that almost none of the other homesteaders had, and that was a little cash to carry his ideas out. In terms of the purchasing power of a dollar in 1866, he was quite well off. He had close to two hundred dollars left, even after having paid for his preëmption acreage, and bought the supplies, the seed, and the equipment that he needed, so now he decided to risk a sizable portion of his money to break free from the one handicap that kept most prairie farmers dirt poor for years. That handicap was, as Rad Stevens, perhaps the best farmer in the lot, put it:

"Takes a man too damn long to git enough ground broke to put in a crop tha's worth anything, Professor Lovejoy. We's all got land—from a quarter to a half section, most of us. But it's danged nigh impossible to break more'n ten acres a year, 'n that means more'n thirty years to git yore whole spread into production . . ."

So what Ethan did, without saying anything to anyone, was to go out and buy four more yoke of oxen. Draft animals didn't cost anything to keep: the prairie lands had been supporting something like a hundred million buffaloes for several thousand years, therefore the only expense involved was in their purchase price. After that he set his mind to the other problem involved in breaking prairie sod, the fact that no one man weighed enough, or was strong enough, to force a plowshare to the required depth in that tough, grass-matted sod. Going up to the river for more timber—and noting with a certain sadness that his depredation of the not all that abundant riverside groves was beginning to show—he cut logs and hewed them into planks with his ax and his froe. Out of these green planks he made an oblong box. This box he fastened to the beam of the plow, above and a little ahead of the plowshare and the moldboard. Hitching his six yokes of oxen to this modified plow, he filled the empty box with dirt, shovelful by careful shovelful, from opposite sides of the box to make sure it would balance over the exact center of gravity of the beam. When he tried it, it worked like a charm: the tremendous weight of the dirt in that box drove his plowshare far deeper into the sod than his neighbors had ever been able to reach with the makeshift method of having the heaviest man in the group sit on the beam. What was more, it freed the proud and canny Yankee newcomer—along with, of course, his having been able to buy enough oxen to do the job—from any dependence upon the other farmers when it came to breaking. Since the winter of 1866–67 turned out to be a mild one, so that the sod only froze for a couple of weeks in January, it was very likely that had he been able to keep at it, he might well have broken at least half his acreage to the plow that winter.

But he couldn't keep at it. The first week in October, he had to keep his promise and begin to teach school.

Looking up from the plow handles over which his lean body was bent in one long, fatigue-drunk, quivering ache, Ethan saw Phil Harris's buggy coming toward him over the prairie. By then it was the last week in September, so it came to him that Phil had probably come to remind him of his promise; but when the buggy drew closer and he saw the troubled expression on Phil's face, he realized that his oldest friend in Kansas probably had other—and graver—things on his mind.

"Brung you these," Phil said gruffly, and handed him a shoebox absolutely full of letters. "They come on th last stage. They've been piling up in Manhattan or wherever th hell that damn railroad has got to by now..."

One glance at the letters showed Ethan they were all from Anne.

"Lord God!" he breathed. "And I haven't written her a line!"

"You better write her one right now," Phil said sternly. "Or better still, send her a telegram. Say somethin' like: 'Your letters received; answer follows, Love, Ethan.' That there will purely relieve her pore li'l left lonesome mind . . ."

"But where the devil is there a telegraph office to send it from?"

"Wherever the KP has done got to by now," Phil sighed. "They're stringing wires atop th poles they're settin' in alongside th tracks. Can't run no railroad, you know, without a telegraph to keep the tracks clear. Be too many head-on collisions, they couldn't wire on ahead to put one locomotive o' another on a sidin', 'n let th other highball on through. C'mon, le's go back to that there dugout o' yourn, so's you kin write it out. I'll take it in to the telegraph office. I got to drive into Manhattan a couple of days, anyhow . . ."

"Why?" Ethan asked.

"Money troubles," Phil said sadly; "Got to ax th bank there for a loan. All us Marthasville folks is havin' problems, Eth, boy—what with us havin' to move our houses down to Abilene, or build new ones in it. 'N we got to rush. All of us—'ceptin' the ones who already have, like me —has got to file new homestead claims down thisaway. 'N we got to do it in a helluva hurry. You see, th government has granted th Kansas Pacific twelve thousand eight hundred acres 'n sixteen thousand dollars in government bonds for every mile o' track they lays down. Now it stands to reason that all th land alongside th river is gonna be included in them twelve thousand eight hundred acres per mile. But there's a clause that says that if a fella's already settled on th land that would've been granted to the railroad, long as that claim is bona fide 'n he's done filed it with th nearest Land Office, the railroad's got to respect it 'n take their own grant someplace farther west. So I've got all the Marthasville—ex-Marthasville now, daggum it!—folks busy at layin' out new claims as near to Abilene as we kin get. But filin' a claim costs fourteen dollars 'n practically nobody's got that much hard cash. So, since I got 'em into this here pickle by convincin' 'em the railroad wuz gonna come through Marthasville, I done promised to raise th cash for everybody, 'n tha's all of five hundred 'n sixty dollars, for th forty families that has done agreed to relinquish their Marthasville claims 'n take new ones down this way. Course they'll pay me back when they git th money, that is if they ever do. But it was all my fault for bein' a blind, pig-headed fool, so I got to help 'em all I kin . . ."

"I suppose you're right, morally speaking, anyhow," Ethan said; "but Jesus, Phil, to go that far into debt! What are the interest rates on a loan out here, anyhow?"

"Twelve percent per annum," Phil sighed; "but then, the folks have agreed to keep the interest payments up, so I'll make out all right. That ain't what I come to see you about, Eth, Old Hoss. The sad truth is that we jes' don't see how we kin pay you them thirty dollars a month we done gone 'n promised you for teachin' school. So the folks done delegated me to come down here 'n ax you if you won't take your dollar a day in room 'n board. That is, you lives 'n eats with each family in th school district accordin' to how many school age kids they's got. That way, we kin pay you. Otherwise we can't. 'N I'm appealin' to your better nature mighty humble-like, Eth Lovejoy, 'cause effen you don't accept, our children is gonna have to go without book learnin' another year . . ."

Ethan thought about that. He knew only too well what it meant: sleeping in crowded sod houses and eating absolutely atrocious food. What's more, since by an unwritten law of nature, the poorest couples always had the most children, he'd be compelled to stay longest with the families who could least afford to feed another mouth. Washing and toilet facilities would be at a health-threatening level wherever he boarded. The whole proposition was unattractive to a truly distressing extreme. And yet —and yet—

He had given his word. And having come from that section of the country where, at that very period, the nation's greatest fortunes were being piled up through sheer chicanery and fraud, he had resolved—stern puritan that he was!—never to give any human being cause to doubt him by his failing to keep the slightest verbal promise that he had made.

"No, Phil," he said quietly, "I won't board with your friends, because, as you know damned well, quite a few of them really can't afford to keep me. I will, however, teach your school for one full year, accepting a salary cut to fifteen dollars a month—said salary to be paid to me whenever the families of the school district can rake it up—and with no interest charges added . . ."

Phil jumped down from the buggy and hugged him then. When the young Kansan spoke, he had tears in his eyes.

"I done knowed some decent fellas in my time," he husked, "but damned if you ain't th whitest white man I ever met, Old Hoss! And I thank you on behalf of the whole Abilene School District. You won't regret what you've gone 'n done!"

But Ethan was going to regret it—and bitterly. Shortly after Phil had driven off, he saw the Old Timer loping toward him over the prairie like a gray-bearded wolf. The old man came and went as he saw fit, and Ethan was always glad to see him despite his monstrous stink, because when it came to a practical knowledge of frontier life, the Old Timer was a walking encyclopedia. From afar, Ethan saw that the Old Timer had something that looked like a thick rope wrapped around his free shoulder, that is, the one unencumbered with his Plains rifle, powder horn and bag of "possibles." But now, as the mountain man came closer, Ethan discovered that the coil wasn't a rope, but rather a mule skinner's or a bullwhacker's rawhide whip. For the life of him, Ethan couldn't imagine what that ancient, ambulating manure pile needed a whip for, since he didn't even own a riding horse, not to mention a team.

"Here," the Old Timer said, slipping the coiled whip off his shoulder; "I brung you this. Made it meself. Took me th whole o' yestiddy, but I figgered you wuz gwine t'need hit . . ."

"I'm going to need a bullwhip? Lord God, Old Timer, why?" Ethan said.

"Them boys. Young rapscallions you's s'posed to git some book larnin' through their solid bone heads. Not th kids from Marthasville, 'cause their own folks has done throwed th fear o' God in 'em long time ago. But these here young hellions from round 'bout Abilene, itself. Ain't but five o' 'em, but three o' them five is bigger'n you is, young Eth. 'N they don't want to have no truck wit book larnin'. Their folks is makin' 'em come to yore schoolhouse mainly 'cause they cain't do nothin' wit 'em overgown young'uns they ownselves 'n is hopin' 'n a prayin' you'll be able to straighten 'em out . . ."

"And you think they're so tough I'll need to use a bullwhip on 'em?" Ethan said.

"Oh, I don't recommends that you lift a square yard o' hide off'n their stubborn young asses, 'cause that would git their maws too riled, I reckons. . . . This here is fur you to discourage 'em from runnin' you plumb outta th state o' Kansas, young Eth, 'cause tha's whut they's aimin' t'do. Heard 'em talkin' 'bout hit day afore yestiddy out back o' Hawken's Saloon. Tha's howcome I done made you this here cute li'l toy. You knows how to use one?"

"No," Ethan said; "No, of course not! And what's more I don't mean to—"

"Whup them young hellions? That ain't what I'm a-tellin' you to do, young Eth. Jes'—discourage 'em a li'l. You sees that there fly on yore lead ox's ear?"

Ethan looked. There was a large black fly on the ear of the ox on the right side of his lead yoke. Try as the poor beast would, he couldn't seem to twitch the biting, stinging insect off.

The Old Timer uncoiled that twelve-foot-long length of plaited rawhide with a smoothly sinuous flip. Made the slightest, most insignificant motion imaginable with his own bony wrist. The whip snaked out like a rattlesnake striking, cracked like a pistol shot, and the fly was a little smudge of blood and pulp against the ox's no longer twitching ear.

"Old Timer," Ethan said solemnly, "you know damned well I'd never learn to handle a bullwhip like that anytime in the next ten years."

"Danged right you wouldn't," the Old Timer said complacently. "Took me a sight longer than thet to git th hang o' hit 'n I wuz plumb born wit th knack. But then, you ain't got to, young Eth. All you's got to do is to larn how to crack it real smart-like so's hit'll sound like a volley o' musket fire. 'N to be on th safe side, to be able to hit what you aim at with it, inside o' a foot square, anyhow. You see, all you wants to do is scare off them li'l rapscallions, they take it in their heads to rush you—not leave one o' 'em stone blind. Any good whip handler kin do thet, y' know—slash the eyes right outta some ornery fella's face furst crack—'n from twenty foot away. Good whip hand kin beat a hombre with a knife ten times outta ten. He kin even beat a man with a six-gun, th gunslinger bein' nervous 'n not too good a shot. 'N truth to tell, most fellas whut goes around reachin' 'n slappin' leather wit a shootin' iron couldn't shoot shit off a outhouse floor, when th goin' gits really rough. Every barroom killin' I ever seen, them six-gun artists wuz close enough to powder burn each other. 'N even at that, they misses a mighty heap o' times. I 'members oncet, down Texas way, this gamblin' dude 'n a cowboy shot it out 'cross a card table. Both of 'em missed each other six times. . . . Kilt three pore innercent rangehands standin' at th bar, though, whut didn't have one damn thing to do with th argument . . ."

"Old Timer, for God's sake!" Ethan groaned.

"C'mon now, lemme show you how to use this here bullwhacker. In half a hour I kin larn you all you need to know for now. But be a durned good idee fur you to keep yore hand in, young Eth! You's gittin' married soon, ain't you? 'N ain't nothin' like rawhide fur keepin' a sassy filly in th traces, let alone coolin' off all th horny bastids whuts shore to come flockin' round yore door every time you ain't to home!"

"You know, Old Timer," Ethan said solemnly, "that's what I like most about you: you may smell like what a polecat left behind him after a bad night, but you've got such a nice, clean mind!"

Ethan was blessed with a high degree of manual dexterity. Well within a single hour, he showed a surprising mastery of the terrible weapon that a bullwhip actually is. But, then, being himself, he decided not to use it, though he didn't tell the Old Timer that. There were, after all, other ways of defeating bullies than the primitive descent into naked force. Facing a man who is calmly and quietly unafraid was the one thing a gang of teen-aged oafs were simply not equipped to do. He'd see that they learned that lesson very soon. In fact, he was actually looking forward to it. But, even so, he put that bullwhip under the driver's seat of his wagon, just in case. . . .

That night he read all of Anne's letters. They made him almost physically sick from shame. They were so candid, so filled with what was so clearly adoration, that they made him feel he'd been a callous, unfeeling cad. Being anything but a fool, he recognized the grave danger to their mutual future those letters exhibited. The portrait of him that Anne painted in swift, well-chosen, even vibrant words, was totally unrecognizable. Out of her loneliness, her need for love, out of her sad experiences with other members of his sex, she had fallen into the facile trap of actually idolizing him for the slight, perhaps even nonexistent differences from other men's behavior and their ways she believed she saw in him.

Her most recent letter was heartbreaking: she feared, and was candid enough, unsophisticated enough, to express those fears in tearspotted words, that he had found a newer love; for if not, why, in all these weeks of absence, had he failed to write?

"No," he wrote upon finishing all her letters, "I've found no newer love, though perhaps a more demanding mistress, and her name is the land. Night after night I have picked up pen and paper, settled myself down upon my homemade chair—'tis made of cottonwood, Dear Heart, and already so badly warped that keeping it upright, and my worn-out carcass perched upon it, is providing me with the training for a new profession, that of circus acrobat!—only to have gentle Morpheus quickly woo me; no, only to have sheer weariness hit me over the head with a single tree! I wake, with the morning sunlight in my eyes, to find my head pillowed on my arms upon the table (as warped and rickety as the chair!), pen and paper on the floor, and the ink, which I make myself of pokeberries, adding one more interesting stain to the variety on my shirt. . . .

"I will make a go of farming, Dearest Anne, I will! For all our future depends upon it, but I must confess that I had vastly underestimated the difficulties involved in tilling virgin soil, and even more vastly overestimated my willpower, my patience, my courage, and my strength. I could fill pages with the trials I've had to undergo, the burdens and problems

I've overcome, but why bore—or perhaps even distress?—your tender heart with these unimportant things? Vanquish them I must and will, for they, and only they stand in our path, postpone our bliss. And now while my Old Hussy still holds out to light this page, I solemnly swear to write you a long letter every week, which will, as the track laying crews of the Kansas Pacific move ever closer to Abilene, the town nearest to my—*our* —farm, reach you ever faster. More than that I can not promise, because now I know the limits of my strength. What has no limits, Dearest One, nor frontiers, boundaries nor end, since it fills all the mighty sweep of space, and, in time, extends beyond eternity, is my love for you. Having written that, I can only repeat it: believe me,

"I love you,
"Ethan

"P.S. In case you're wondering, my Old Hussy is a lamp—homemade like nearly all my possessions. She's a hollowed-out bowl of wood, filled with sand, with a rag-wrapped stick in the middle of the sand to make a wick. Over the sand I pour two or three cupfuls of *skunk* oil, which, believe it or not, is practically odorless. A wonderful old character of a frontiersman called the Old Timer provides the skunks. My theory is that they swoon outright at his approach, overcome by his aroma, which is far worse than theirs! But to the Old Timer and other colorful denizens of this region, I shall devote an entire letter. Keep well, be patient, and wait for me; I promise I shall not tarry overlong.

"All my Love, E."

He gazed at his letter with sleep-blurred eyes. Had he achieved the light, playful, yet reassuring tone he'd wanted to? He didn't know. He was far too sleepy to tell, and what was worse, he couldn't even go to bed. Phil Harris was going to set out for Manhattan early in the morning, and that meant Ethan had to walk into Abilene that very night. Phil had already moved his family to Abilene. His family and his house, having placed that well-built frame structure on a huge flatbed wagon, made for that very purpose, and transported it behind six yokes of oxen across the gently rolling prairie the twelve full miles from Marthasville to Abilene. All the Marthasville people were doing that, having constructed three huge flatbed transport wagons among them for that special purpose. By sharing their oxen they were gradually moving the whole town from its original site and joining it to Abilene.

Ethan thought sadly, too, on that weary hike across the prairie to the town, of the ugly fact that he had no other recourse but to build a sod house for Anne. Even if he hauled timber down from the river to his place, that timber would be nearly all cottonwood. And a frame house built of cottonwood was a damned sight worse, over the long haul, than even a sod house was. If you sawed the stuff into planks, they cracked and warped so badly that you had to push so much grass and mud into the gaps that in a year or two your frame house became practically indistinguishable from a sod house anyhow. What's more, they were hideously inflammable, and therefore deathtraps whenever one of the all too frequent prairie fires swept across a man's holdings. Nor could he build her a brick house, for although there was a goodly supply of clay on his spread, the fuel for firing it into bricks was almost nonexistent.

It came to him then that he could put his weekly letters to Anne to far better use than the mere exchange of tender vows and dulcet words. Wisely and subtly written, they could serve as a course of indoctrination into the harsh realities of prairie life, as well as—more importantly, perhaps—giving her the emotional anchor of the near certainty of a better future.

Here Ethan—though, of course, he didn't know it—was making the literate man's classic mistake of not realizing how little mere words ever mean.

Walking back toward his farm in the early light of morning, after having spent the night in Phil Harris's hayloft—a custom so universal in the prairie states that the word "hayseed," derived from the fact that their hair was always full of it, would come to be a derisive nickname for the dwellers of that whole vast region—Ethan was overtaken by the Bellamys, who were driving home from Abilene in a rented jump seat wagon, with all Cora's luggage piled up in the back of it.

Ethan wasn't surprised that Tom had finally gone into town to fetch his wife home to the much bigger dugout than Ethan's that he—aided by both Ethan and the Old Timer—had built on his place. In Abilene, according to Martha, rumor had it that Cora was "carrying on" with Henry Atkins, the well digger, who was both a widower and childless.

When Tom said jovially, "Shove some o' Cora's plunder aside 'n hop in, Eth—mighty far way out to our diggin's still!" he accepted at once, because he knew by then how badly he needed to husband his strength.

To avoid having to walk another two miles or so made even putting up with the Bellamys' company endurable.

"Thank you, Tom," he sighed; "that's mighty kind of you. Cora, I must say you're looking great . . ."

"You're not," she shot back at him; "You look like death lightly warmed over, Eth Lovejoy. Men! Without having a woman to fuss over and take care of you, you go plain to seed, and mighty fast at that. . . . Tell me, when have you heard from your darlin' Anne?"

"Yesterday," Ethan said; "that's what I was doing in town, mailing off an answer to her letters. Batch of 'em finally caught up with me. You know how slow the mail is . . ."

"Gittin' faster all th time," Tom said complacently. "Didya know the KP's tracks ain't no more than a mile o' two outside o' Junction City now? Course winter is gonna slow 'em down a heap, but my friend Tim O'Mallory swears they's a-gonna git through Abilene and Salina both by March o' April o' next year. At the latest, May . . ."

"Ethan," Cora said, "you come over to our place tonight. Let me fix you up a good, hot, homecooked supper. You've done got so blamed thin that I bet you have to carry rocks in your pockets to keep this prairie wind from blowin' you away . . ."

"No, thank you, Cora," Ethan said.

"Why not?" Cora demanded.

"Matter of principle," Ethan said drily; "When I've got my own wife on my place, and we can reciprocate such kind invitations, all right. But now, no. What I haven't got, I'll do without, and favors I can't return, I won't accept. In other words, Cora, I'm dead set against accumulating debts—not even moral ones . . ."

"Aw, Eth, you's bein' too damn tetchy," Tom Bellamy said, but Ethan could hear the relief moving through his voice.

"Perhaps, but that's the way I feel about it. Thanks, just the same, Cora," Ethan said.

"Heard tell you're going to teach school this winter," Cora said to Ethan then, much to his relief, because it indicated that she wasn't disposed to pursue that matter of inviting him to supper any further. "That's so?"

"Yes," Ethan said drily, "it is . . ."

She looked at him in a new way, now; a way he couldn't fathom. With —sadness in her eyes? Acknowledged defeat? Resignation? He didn't, couldn't, know. . . .

"You'll be good at it," she said quietly; "You'll be good at anything you do . . ."

"Thank you, Cora," Ethan said. But if there were anything on earth he doubted, it was precisely that. In fact, he doubted it profoundly.

7

There was one good thing that could be said of oxen: given their heads, they travel, with little or no meandering, in a straight line. Therefore, in spite of the fact that due to their ponderous slowness—from two to two and a half miles an hour at their absolute best—Ethan was forced to get up while the stars were still jeweling the vast sweep of the prairie sky, he could stretch out comfortably in the wagon bed and sleep the sleep of the worn-out for another full hour and a half. By the time the morning sunlight, falling on the closed lids of his eyes and making them blaze blood-red, had waked him up, to his left, to his right, or sometimes even straight ahead, the schoolhouse was always in sight.

But, on that first day of school, he hadn't yet realized that soul-and-body-saving fact, so he dozed uncomfortably upon the wagon's high seat and arrived with his long body reduced to one scythe-shaped ache, his neck board stiff, and a legion of invisible and presumably tiny fiends reducing the gray matter beneath his skull to cornmeal mush with sledge-hammers, none of which contributed any notable degree of sweetness and light to his temper, or elevated his generally dismal view of human nature in the slightest. In short, he arrived at the log cabin schoolhouse—built by the fathers, older brothers, and uncles of his pupils—angry with the world, with fate, and with himself for having been a blind, spavined, swayback, windbroken jackass, the only creature extant stupid enough to take the miserable job of teaching a prairie school.

As it turned out, given what he found upon getting there, that was an excellent frame of mind in which to arrive.

The younger children, little boys and girls, were standing in a compact group and bawling their utterly terrified little heads off. Their clothes were in rags, and those rags, along with their faces and their hair, were thickly plastered with mud from the riverbank a few yards away. The books that some of them had proudly brought with them were blowing across the prairie in a white snowstorm of ripped out pages. And the authors of this gentle and courteous reception had by then turned their thoughtful and considerate attention to the schoolhouse itself.

There were five of them: the same five overgrown oafs about whom the Old Timer had warned him. They had cut stout poles from the groves beside the Smokey Hill River and were using them to pry the logs at one corner free of their notches, a process that once accomplished, would have brought the entire structure down in utter ruin. But they hadn't accomplished it yet.

Blessing the old man in his heart, Ethan put his hand under the seat and came out with that mule skinner's whip. Slowly and carefully he got down from the wagon and stole up behind them. Enwrapped in the berserker joy of the ancient Vandals they were racially descended from, drunk with the blind overconfidence of callow youth, they failed completely to see or hear him coming.

Ethan considered that inviting array of targets. Closest to him were the fatty buttocks of the biggest of the boys. That broad expanse of straining human flesh was clad in homespun, broken by a huge patch of floursacking. "Merton's Grist Mill" the words on that patch read. Ethan bisected those letters with all his lean and sinewy force. The bullwhip cut through the cloth like a knife, through the skin beneath it, drew blood.

The leader of that band of amateur house—or rather school—wreckers leaped a full yard and a half in the air. The screech he let out awoke echoes among the distant Smokey Hills. Then Newton's law and his own dismay overcame him. He returned to earth again, hung there, paralyzed, mouth and eyes stretched wide, both hands gripping his whip-torn seat.

The others whirled. One of them made what Ethan took to be a threatening backswing with the green sapling pole in his hands. It is likely that Ethan was mistaken, that the boy's gesture was involuntary, caused by the tightening of his muscles through surprise and fear. But, if so, it was probably the most costly motion, conscious or not, that idle and stupid young oaf had made so far in all his life. He was clad in a "wampus," as prairie dwellers called a loose hickory shirt, worn outside his belt over his blue jeans, a costume his descendants slightly more than a hundred years later would still consider smart, since the abysmal taste of oafdom remains a constant over the years. Ethan cut both it and a considerable portion of the hide beneath it to ribbons. The second member of that teen-aged bullies' cadre threw down his pole, raised both his hands and covered his face with them.

At that, the other three made a break for it.

"Halt!" Ethan cried out. "Stop where you are!" His voice, ripping out that command, was no louder than it had to be; but it was ice cold, calm, and sure, yet vibrant with the unmistakable authority of one accustomed to issuing orders, and to having those orders obeyed.

The three so far unstriped fugitives stopped as though they had run up against an invisible wall.

"Bend over," Ethan said quietly, "catch your ankles in your hands. Not you," he added to the boy in the tattered wampus, whose arms and shoulders were oozing blood. "I think you've had enough; haven't you?"

"Lord, yes, Prof Lovejoy!" the wampus wearer moaned.

"Me, too," the erstwhile leader got out; "Prof, I'm bleeding! You's done gone 'n cut my ass—my behind plumb in half!"

"Boar hogs and wild shoats have to be bled," Ethan said calmly, "to cool them down a mite. You heard me, bend over!"

Sniffling and groaning, the four rebels against "book larnin' " bent. Ethan cracked out four more whistling whiplashes across the leader's seat, and five each to the other three. But this time, he was careful not to bring blood. With that bleak sobriety that spent rage always leaves behind it, he realized that having five outraged fathers, shotguns in hand, descend upon him tomorrow, would be one hell of a way to commence his professorship.

That done, their punishment well and justly administered, he looked the culprits straight in the eye; and, with his voice as cold as the blue glacier of his gaze, said:

"Your parents sent you here to learn. So now you've had the first lesson: while I'm running this school, you obey the rules, or you take the consequences. I don't think I need to spell the matter out, but to make myself clear enough for even such utter dolts as you to understand, hear this: I don't scare. I don't back down. And I don't quit. You now, what's your name?"

"Cy—Cyrus Curtiss," the leader whispered. He had to lick bone-dry lips before he could even get his name out.

"And the rest of you?" Ethan said.

"Walter Thomas," one of them quavered. "Gordon—Lee," answered another. "Newton Purvis." "Tyler Burton." The names came out slowly from throats stiffened with actual anguish. For all unknowingly, Ethan had submitted them to the worst fate conceivable to the adolescent mind: he had punctured their pretenses to manhood and valor; he had shamed them before their peers.

"All right. Tell your fathers—*all* your fathers—that I want to see them tomorrow. Here, at this schoolhouse. Now, all of you fan out and gather up the pages you ripped out of these childrens' schoolbooks. Get going now!"

He turned to the tallest girl there, a winsome miss of at least sixteen, trying hard to maintain the professorial sternness of his tone, for that this one was going to be a real beauty was already evident.

"What's your name, young lady?"

She dropped her gaze, stared at her high-buttoned shoe tops, blushed like a peony, and whispered:

"Nora. Nora—Curtiss, sir . . ."

"*His* sister?" Ethan said with genuine astonishment, nodding his head in the direction of the Number One Oaf.

"Yessir," Nora breathed; "And Professor Lovejoy, sir, I begs yore pardon real humble-like for th *awful* way my brother done gone and acted! I'm gonna tell Pa"—by then the tears were already there, brimming on her lashes, penciling her cheeks—"to give him ten whacks for every one you give him. Oh, Lord, sir, I'm so 'shamed I could drap right down 'n die!"

"You're not responsible for your brother's behavior, Nora," Ethan said gravely. "All you have to do is to keep your own up to the mark. Now I want you and these two other young ladies—"

"Mary Sue Hollis," Nora said breathlessly, " 'n Billie Jean Caldwell, my best friends, sir . . ."

"—to take these kids down to the river and clean them up. After that, we'll have a try at what we came here for, which was to get a little useful knowledge through your heads . . ."

While four of the five fathers of the amateur schoolwreckers were essentially decent men, who, in an age when corporal punishment was the norm, accepted the chastisement their sons had received as just, two of them, in fact, going so far as to repeat it to emphasize the matter; the fifth, Barton Lee, arrived at the schoolhouse that next morning snorting fire, having declared en route that he "wouldn't've whupped a mule, a dawg, o' even a nigger th way this goldanged Yankee schoolmaster is done gone 'n cut up my boy!" and wearing a huge Colt Dragoon revolver in his belt to lend weight to his grave displeasure.

Barton Lee was actually a blusterer—a "blowhard," the prairie folk called him—and a coward, a small man with an outsize and well-justified feeling of inferiority that was poisoning his whole existence. At certain times, and under some fairly unusual conditions, that combination can get to be exceedingly dangerous. And on that Tuesday morning, the second day of school, it did.

In the first place, Barton Lee had an audience. His whiskey-inspired declaration that he was "gonna mek that sissy Yankee schoolmarm in pants eat turd 'til hit's plumb runnin' outta both ears!" caused a sizable number of Abilene's idlers, numbed by the almost unbelievable boredom of a tiny prairie town where nothing ever happened—a condition that the railroads and the cattle raising industry were very shortly going to change —to follow him out to the schoolhouse, which was situated one mile west of town on the banks of the Smokey Hill River. Word of the impending trouble reached the more respectable citizens, among them Mayor Ned Tyler and his good friend Phil Harris much more slowly. But they, too, scrambled into buckboards and buggies and pounded toward the scene with a view of, as Phil Harris put it, "Stoppin' that damnfool Bart Lee from doin' somethin' rash o' mebbe even fatal."

As it turned out, they got there too late. "General Lee" had already taken direct action. For the second condition that made that morning dangerous was the fact that Lee had screwed his always uncertain courage up to the sticking point by taking on an unusually heavy dose of rye whiskey, having gone so far as to even pay for it himself.

Now, inspired by the firewater and the respectful, even awed expressions on the faces of his cronies, Lee was standing outside the schoolhouse and bellowing:

"C'mon outta there, you chile-abusin' Yankee varmint! I've got a bone to pick wit you, 'n I means to pick it clean right now!"

Ethan looked up from behind his desk—it and his chair being so far the only two sticks of furniture in the schoolhouse—to meet young Gordon Lee's terrified eyes.

"Oh, Jesus!" the boy got out; "hit's my pa!"

Ethan smiled.

"Don't worry about it, Gordon," he said, and uncoiled his lean length out of that rickety chair. As he did so, and crossed to the door, he had the distinct impression—heartwarming to his male vanity but utterly confusing to a man already engaged to be wed!—that Nora Curtiss's cornflower eyes were very shortly going to eclipse her whole lovely face. The way she was gazing at Ethan at that moment spoke more volumes than then existed in the states of Kansas and Nebraska, with the Indian Territory of Oklahoma thrown in.

Ethan came out the schoolhouse door without pausing, walked quietly, calmly up to the little group of men. They found his evident lack of fear disconcerting. They fell back and left Barton Lee to face the young Yankee schoolmaster all alone. Ethan towered over Lee by a full head, and his every movement betrayed his easy strength.

"What can I do for you, friend?" he said.

Barton Lee stepped back a foot.

"You's no friend o' mine!" he spluttered; but by then, Ethan had seen that revolver tucked into his belt and weighing the small man down so much that he actually listed to port, in Ethan's nautical New England view of things.

Ethan nodded toward that piece of hand-held artillery.

"And what," he said with icy calm, "d'you propose to do with that?"

Despite all the whiskey blurring his brain, Bart Lee sensed that this wasn't going at all well. And a half-suppressed chuckle from one of his cronies confirmed his dismal estimation of the situation. So he playacted a little. He was good at playacting by then. He had spent his whole life doing it.

"Wal now," he drawled, "thet there all depends. You got a shootin' iron in yore pocket, you better reach fer it, Professer!"

"It so happens that I haven't," Ethan said in an easy, conversational tone. 'The way to handle drunks and madmen is to humor them,' he thought.

"Wal then," Bart said, "reckon I won't let no daylight through you, 'cause ain't no damyankee born worth gittin' hanged over. But 'pears to me a li'l pistolwhuppin' would improve this here pretty womanish face o' hisn, now wouldn't hit, boys?"

"Shore would!" his followers chorused, eager to see a little sporting action.

A quick glance backward over his shoulder showed Ethan that the older children had come out of the schoolhouse and were standing there behind him, gaping at the spectacle.

He put out his hand.

"Here," he said, his voice a whipcrack that snapped Barton Lee back into near sobriety, into the born coward's usually realistic view of things, "give me that six-gun!"

"Whutttt?" Bart got out, stupidly and stammering; "give *you* my shootin' iron?"

"Yes," Ethan said, his voice brimming with contempt; "You're drunk, Lee. You might hurt yourself. Or even one of these kids who haven't anything to do with our differences . . ."

"Why, lemme kiss my own elbow, 'n then y'all call me Susie!" one of Bart's followers sang out at hearing that. "Effen you takes thet, 'Robert E.,' you jes' plain ain't no man!"

At that taunt, which pierced to the very tendon of the small man's Achilles' heel—his pride—Barton Lee reached for his big Walker Colt Dragoon.

Ethan's motions, fast as they actually were, looked, because of the studied grace with which he made them, dreamlike and slow. His big right hand moved out—flowed out, it seemed to the petrified spectators—and clamped over Barton's wrist. He drew Barton Lee's right hand out with the big Walker Colt clamped in it. Then he shook the small man's hand and arm like a terrier shakes a rat, until Lee let the huge revolver fall. Stooping, Ethan picked the weapon up, then stood there holding it in his hand, gazing at it with evident distaste.

"I don't think you need this," he said quietly; "You're too hotheaded and too stupid to carry a six-gun. Get your fool self killed as sure as hell . . ."

Then arching his long, sinewy arm back, he threw that heavy revolver in a spinning curve far out into the Smokey Hill River. It made a small and sparkling splash going in. Ethan turned back to Lee with a pleasant smile, said, almost gently:

"Now, what can I do for you, little friend?"

"Nothing," Bart muttered, fighting to hold back the actual tears of shame and rage that were stinging his eyes. He was disgraced forever and he knew it; he was going to have to leave Abilene, drift someplace else unless—unless—

"That being so, I guess I'll get back to my charges—including your son, who, incidentally, seems quite bright," Ethan said, and turned away.

It was the sole mistake he made, and it almost proved fatal. For Barton Lee, in his own pitiful dreams, fancied himself to be a desperado, and carried with him not one gun, but two. The second weapon was his "stingy gun," a typical gambler's hideout pistol: a double-barreled, over and under Remington .41-caliber derringer, small and light enough for even undersized men to handle them effectively, though a number of strapping six-footers didn't scorn to carry them as a reserve life insurance policy, as it were, as well.

Ethan heard Nora Curtiss's scream tear the day apart, and he whirled a fraction of a second too late. The little derringer bucked and barked in Bart Lee's wildly shaking hand, and a sear of living flame raked upward from Ethan's craggy, rugged cheekbone almost to his ear. Shaking his head to clear it, Ethan bored in.

Bart fired again, but this time he missed Ethan completely. Which ended the matter, since the little Remington only held two shots, and by then Ethan's big fist had connected with Barton Lee's jaw so hard that the impact of the blow lifted the little man bodily into the air to send him sprawling a good five feet away. It took his so-called friends the better part of an hour to bring him to his senses again. In the confusion, one of them must have pocketed poor Bart's "stingy gun." For it is a part of the legend that grew out of that day that he never saw it, or his big Colt Dragoon, again.

Ethan turned back to his pupils, but the expression on Nora Curtiss's face, the utter horror in her eyes halted him. Raising his fingers to his cheek, following the lightlocked indication of her frozen gaze, he felt the thick, hot flooding of his blood. 'Little bastard actually shot me!' he thought in mild amazement; but when he looked in Nora's direction again, she wasn't there. Then he saw her: she was stretched out on the schoolyard in a dead faint, and all the other girls were bending over her and screaming their heads off. Which, Ethan decided, simply wouldn't do.

He dragged his handkerchief out of his breast pocket, pressed it to that ugly bullet scrape on his cheek. It was soaked and dripping within seconds, but Ethan paid no attention to that.

"Stand back and give her air," he said; "Come on, now, let me have a look at her . . ."

So it was, that when the better citizens of Abilene pounded into the schoolyard, they found Ethan bent over the second major difficulty of his teaching career and even—as it later turned out—of a large part of his life.

Now among those better citizens—to be sharply distinguished from the riffraff who had accompanied Bart Lee on his dismally failed punitive expedition—who were descending from buggies, buckboards, jump seat wagons, and surreys, and rushing toward Ethan and the children on foot, was Cyrus Curtiss, the saloonkeeper. Mr. Curtiss could quite legitimately claim to be numbered among the respectable people of Dickinson County —Abilene itself counted for little at that time—because he was a large man of grave mien, a regular churchgoer who didn't smoke, cuss, or chew tobacco, and what was more, to the astonished awe of Abileners, never touched a drop of the poison that he sold. The fact that he owned and ran a saloon was not held against him; in 1866, the antiliquor furor hadn't so much as started. To all these considerations must be added one more simple yet overwhelming fact: Cyrus Curtiss, saloonkeeper, father of Cyrus, Jr., would-be school wrecker, and of the winsome Nora, was, by long odds, the richest man in town.

Like all men blessed—or cursed—with an exceptionally pretty daughter, Cyrus doted on Nora, his tender feelings toward her being constantly deepened by the marked contrast between her and her loutish brother, for while Nora was dutiful, obedient, good, and as sweet as she was pretty—at least up until the moment that one Ethan Lovejoy came into view on a dead, though unintentional and unwilling, collision course with her life—Cyrus, Jr., was a sore trial for even so patient a man as his father to bear.

Pushing his way, with Phil Harris at his heels, through a little knot of fallen warrior Bart Lee's friends—who had rushed forward in the pious hope that Lee's second shot, the one that had missed Ethan entirely, had done at least a *little* damage to *somebody,* after all—Cyrus Curtiss was confronted with the lamentable spectacle of his daughter's still form stretched out on the ground, with several large blood splotches decorating her well-starched and crisply ironed blouse above the gentle swelling of her left breast, while the Yankee schoolmaster bent his long, lank form above her, doing what little he could to revive her.

Mr. Curtiss took a backward step. His heavy, beefy face turned a lovely shade of mauve. It is very likely that he would have fallen had not Phil Harris caught him by his left arm, and Ethan, seeing how it was with him, by his right.

"Easy does it, sir," Ethan said as reassuringly as he could manage; "there's nothing wrong with Nora. She's just fainted, that's all . . ."

"But—but—the blood?" Cyrus Curtiss muttered.

"Mine," Ethan said, and took away that bloodsoaked handkerchief.

"Jesus God!" Phil Harris roared; "what th hell happened to your face, Old Hoss?"

"The father of one of my pupils," Ethan said wearily, "objected to my disciplinary methods—and backed his objections up with a six-shooter. Or rather with both a six-shooter and some sort of a pocket pistol. It was the smaller weapon that did all the damage. I didn't give him a chance to use the big one. Oh, I say, looks like Nora's back with us. . . ." He turned Cyrus Curtiss's arm loose and dropped to one knee beside the girl.

"No, don't try to get up!" he said sharply. "Just lie there. That's a good girl." Then looking up, he added: "Do any of you gentleman have a pocket handkerchief handy?"

Half a dozen were produced. Ethan took them all, handed them to Mary Sue Hollis and Billie Jean Caldwell.

"Run down to the river," he said gravely, "and wet these. Don't wring them out. Bring 'em back as wet as you can manage . . ."

"Yessir!" the two girls chorused, and scampered off. Well within one minute they were back with the dripping handkerchiefs. Ethan took them, one by one, and bathed Nora's forehead, her eyes, her throat. She shivered with a pleasure that went beyond the sensuous into the sensual.

"Oh, Lord, sir," she murmured; "that feels so good!"

Phil, who knew women all too well, looked up from Nora's rapt face, her petal soft, adoring eyes, to the countenance of her father. It had changed color again, gone from mauve to beet red.

'Jee-sus!' Phil thought with an awe not unmixed with fear, ol' Cy's a-gonna bust in a minute!'

"Now, see here, Professor!" Curtiss growled; " 'Pears to me we hired you to git some book learning through our children's heads, not to git mixed-up in shooting scrapes and put their lives in danger!"

Ethan looked at him, then down at Nora. He said: "That does it, I think. . . ." Uncoiled his long, lean, Lincolnesque frame from a kneeling into a standing position, faced Cy Curtiss.

"Oh, I agree, sir," he said calmly; "In fact, I agree two hundred percent. And since I see Mayor Tyler and practically all of the City Council are present, I vote we hold a town meeting right now and pass an ordinance prohibiting the carrying of deadly weapons within the town limits, or anywhere closer than one mile in any direction from a school-house . . ."

"Mighty fine talk!" Cyrus said; "Yessir, mighty fine! But if you hadn't've got into a gun battle, with whoever it was . . ."

"Mr. Lee—over there," Ethan said. His face was aching him damnably by then, for no gunshot wound, however slight, is anybody's pleasant experience. He was thinking, bleakly, 'I'm going to be scarred for life—and what's worse, I'll have to explain this whole stupid business to Anne...'

But by then, dear Nora was on her feet. She pushed one slim arm through the crook of Ethan's elbow and clung to him fiercely.

'Every gal child,' Phil Harris groaned inside his mind, 'is plumb *born* knowing jes' how to git her pappy wild!'

"Pa—Paw!" she shrilled; "You ain't bein' fair! In fact you's bein' mean, 'n you's makin' me purely 'shamed o' you! What kind of gun battle is it, when only one man's got a gun? Professor Lovejoy is the bravest man I ever seen, 'n the best! Better'n you, anyhow! Here you go low-ratin' him, when that li'l old pizen-mean Bart Lee come out here a-gunnin' for him jes' 'cause he tanned Gordon's hide. 'N you *knows* whut Gordon done— 'cause yore own son 'n my precious brother wuz the ringleader of that gang what tried to tear down th schoolhouse, 'n tore up th books, and messed up all th li'l kids and—"

"Nora," Ethan said sternly, "that's quite enough, my dear!"

Nora halted in midflight.

"You're supposed to respect your elders," Ethan said; "Including your father, who, from everything I've heard, has been an excellent parent to you. Incidentally, sir, your daughter saved my life. If she hadn't cried out and warned me when she did, I should probably be the late, unlamented Ethan Lovejoy by now . . ."

"Jesus, Old Hoss, what *did* happen, anyhow?" Phil said.

Ethan told them, clearly, succinctly, drily, without any emphasis at all.

"Lord God," Phil said; "Lord God! You mean that with *nothing* in yore hands you took on a fella what was totin' *two* guns?"

"Didn't see but one," Ethan said; "but something like that, anyhow. Couldn't risk his accidentally killing one of the children, you know . . ."

Ned Tyler, mayor of Abilene, whirled with military precision.

"Go tie Bart Lee up!" he barked. "Course we ain't got no jail yet, but we kin keep him in th livery stable 'til we kin try him. Assault with a deadly weapon with the intention to kill is a mighty serious matter in this here state!"

"Mayor," Ethan said with a crooked, sidewise grin that was all he could manage, and that hurt like hell at that, "don't. The minimum sentence on that charge is all of seven years. So you'd have to put the good citizens of Abilene to the expense of building a jail for Bart Lee's special benefit, and you'd have to feed and clothe the little blowhard for all that time. Don't think it's worth it. Let him go free, or, better still, make him county sheriff. After all, he did ride with Quantrill, didn't he? And seeing how handy he is with a gun . . ."

The roars of laughter that went up at that made the schoolyard ring.

Only Nora didn't laugh. She was crying very quietly, the tears chasing one another in steady progression down her cheeks. *Ethan* had rebuked her in public. *Ethan* had spoken harshly to her, and her heart was broken.

"Look, Eth," Phil Harris said worriedly, "you better come home with me 'n let Martha patch you up. We ain't got no sawbones nearer than Manhattan, 'n that's too blamed far. That there don't look good to me, none a-tall. It's still a-bleedin' 'n—"

"Oh, Phil, for God's sake," Ethan said; "You don't expect me to make my pupils lose a whole day over this scratch, do you?"

"That there ain't no scratch," Cyrus Curtiss said. "That's a bullet scrape 'n a bad one, Professor. Hardest wound there is to fix up properly. Too wide to stitch, so all you kin do is wash 'em out with whiskey, pack 'em with lint, 'n hope for the best. Hope your wife, if you've got one, ain't too finicky, 'cause that's gonna leave you with a mighty ugly scar . . ."

"I haven't a wife—yet," Ethan said. ('Praise the Good Lord!' Nora exulted.) "And since my fiancée was made of stern enough stuff to accept me as I am in the first place, I don't think a scar will make that much difference. Improve my looks, likely." ('I'll kill her!' Nora resolved with unbridled fury; 'Daid!')

"I agree with Phil, Prof Lovejoy," Mayor Tyler said. "The kids can do without one more day's schoolin'. That could give you blood poisonin', it ain't cleaned out good 'n patched up jest right. C'mon, turn th kids out 'n let's git back into town so Mrs. Harris kin fix you up. Best self-taught practical nurse I ever did see, Martha is . . ."

"All right," Ethan said wearily. He felt weak and sick, and the after-battle reaction that every combat veteran knows only too well had him in its grip. He felt the green tides of nausea crawling vilely up the back of his throat, and his head, quite apart from his torn cheek, ached dully. The whole left side of his face had stiffened up into what felt like a piece of burning stone, and the only thing he could make out clearly was the expression on Nora's face.

'Don't, child,' he thought sadly. 'Please don't. It's no good—not for either of us. It really isn't . . .'

He shook his head to clear it, said:

"Very well, school's dismissed for today. But before I go, I'd like you, Mr. Curtiss, and the fathers of Walter Thomas, Newton Purvis, Tyler Burton, and even my recent adversary, Mr. Lee, if he'll be so kind, to send me their sons, here to the school, every Saturday while the warm weather lasts. Not as an additional penalty for their outrages against the smaller children and the school, for they've been punished enough, I think. But rather to try an educational experiment. Your sons, gentlemen, with the possible exception of young Lee, oddly enough, simply don't seem to me equipped to get much profit out of formal studies. So I propose to give them a little manual training that will stand them in good stead in the future. Starting with carpentry. As you may have seen, my pupils have had to sit on the floor—after we'd lost a whole hour covering it with hay— because the powers that be failed—or forgot—to provide us with benches. Also, a blackboard's a mighty handy thing to have in a schoolhouse, friends—"

"Lord, God, Ned!" Phil Harris said to the mayor, "he's right, we plumb forgot!"

"Not to mention," Ethan went on slowly, trying to hide the effort that every word was costing him by then; "that *one* outhouse for both the girls and the boys isn't exactly a good idea, because it's sure to cost me unnecessary problems from the standpoint of discipline. I can handle all such problems, as I think I've demonstrated; but I shouldn't like to have to waste time much better employed in teaching your children to read, write, and figure, than on things like that. So, on Saturdays, I'll teach your boys to handle an ax, a hammer, and a saw—which will cool their excessive energies down a mite—and the products of their lessons—benches, writing desks, and a blackboard—will benefit our school. All right, gentlemen, what do you say?"

The fathers of the five would-be school wreckers looked at each other. They were at a grave disadvantage, and they knew it, because they were surrounded by the fathers of the smaller children, whose clothes their loutish sons had torn, whose hair they'd plastered with mud, and whose schoolbooks they'd ripped to pieces. Besides, four of the five men were genuinely distressed by their sons' behavior. They nodded gravely among themselves, then looked expectantly at Cyrus Curtiss, conceding the saloonkeeper, as the richest man in town and, after Mayor Tyler, the most important, his due right, because of those things, to act as their spokesman.

Mr. Curtiss cleared his throat.

"Strikes me as fair," he said solemnly; "the only reservation I've got is this one: D'you, Professor, know enough about carpentry to teach it? Oh, I know you're a college man, but sawin' 'n hammerin' 'n nailin' ain't what they generally teaches in college."

"I was taught carpentry, Mr. Curtiss, by my grandfather, who, in his youth, was head carpenter in a shipbuilding yard at Salem, Massachusetts," Ethan said; "And if you know what New England shipbuilding carpentry is like, you'll know I was taught by an expert. Incidentally, after he married my grandmother, my grandfather became a farmer. Still is, in fact. And he taught me all I know about that, too. So maybe what I'm *least* fitted for is teaching school, because my grandpa was a lot smarter than any long-headed college professor I ever met . . ."

That sly piece of diplomacy won an approving chuckle from his ninety-nine percent uneducated audience.

"But," Ethan went on, "you'll have ample time to judge my qualifications, or the lack of them, before this term is out. I take it then, you all agree to send me your boys on Saturdays to learn something useful, and to help out the school?"

"Yes, Professor, we do," Cyrus Curtiss began; but the shrill-with-rage voice of Barton Lee cut him off. Lee was fully recovered from Ethan's knockout blow by then, and his despairing fury at having being shown up before his cronies lent him the momentary courage to try to regain his loss of face.

"I don't!" he got out; "I'll see my boy daid 'n in hell afore I'll have no damyankee he-schoolmarm a-messin' up his haid! Gordon, you's comin' home wit me right now, t'stay! Never did hold wit book larnin' nohows, not fur boys, enyhow! Makes 'em weak 'n sissified 'n—"

" 'N bein' as ignerant as a woods shoat is what makes you so all-fired brave that you ups and tries to shoot an unarmed fella in the back?" Mayor Tyler said. "Don't try my patience too far, Bart. 'Twas left with me, you'd be tied up in the livery stable by now. That boy o' yourn wants to go to school, you let him, you hear me?"

"Aw, Ned," Bart Lee, completely deflated once more, whined; "I jes' ain't got th wherewithal to give my kid no eddication, nohows, 'n you knows it . . ."

"Send him, anyhow," Ethan said crisply; "And if he's as bright as he seems to be, I'll teach him for nothing. Fair enough, Mr. Lee?"

"Wal, now," Bart Lee muttered; "I hafta think about it. Right now I'm plumb confused . . ."

'And have been all your life,' Ethan thought with real pity; 'And will be until you die. But that's the fate of most of humanity, I guess. . . .' He said:

"It's up to you." Then: "Phil, give me a ride to your place? With this ox team of mine, it would take me 'til day after tomorrow . . ."

After that, Ethan's life, and his career as a teacher, settled down into something approaching normalcy. The teaching itself went better and better with the passing days. Ethan's skill with the broadax and the wedge, not to mention with the complete set of brand-new carpenter tools that Mr. Curtiss sent along with Cyrus, Jr., on that first Saturday, won the at first reluctant, then wholehearted respect and even the admiration of his four refractory charges. Four, not five, because from young Gordon Lee he quickly gained a near worship disturbingly similar to the adoration that Nora showered visibly upon him, so that his two star pupils, as Gordon and Nora indisputably were, became the sources of a hidden, gnawing nervous tension that robbed him of much of the satisfaction he otherwise legitimately could have drawn from his success as a teacher, and from the two of them as the primary examples of it.

Gordon's devotion to him was so marked that Ethan began to wonder if Barton Lee hadn't been right: whether he, by introducing the boy to the joys of the intellect, was not seriously interfering with young Lee's growth into normal manhood. Seventeen-year-old Gordon Lee was apparently just as much in love with him as Nora Curtiss obviously was. But, simply because he was totally at a loss as to what to do about either case, Ethan accidentally did the wisest thing he could have: that is, he did nothing at all. And, better still, because his own intelligence was of a decidedly subtle kind, he didn't even make the mistake, so often fallen into by beginning teachers, of bending over backward and being unusually and unnecessarily severe toward his two best students in an effort to avoid the very appearance of favoritism. They were his favorites, of course, but only because they deserved to be. Both of them worked terribly hard over their studies, and though he suspected that their motives for doing so would not have withstood public scrutiny, teaching them both was an unfailing joy. The only drawback that instructing them had was the fact that Gordon was visibly crushed, and Nora reduced to unashamed tears, by his lightest rebuke, which, being human, both of them occasionally earned.

With the rest of his pupils, he got along well enough, especially since he had a sufficiently Machiavellian turn of mind to take deliberate advantage of their small vanities and follies. For instance, he allowed his beginning carpenters and cabinetmakers to burn their initials into the benches, stools, and desks that they made, but only if, in the judgment of all five of the boys, put to a voice vote, that particular piece of work was noticeably superior. That one stratagem alone made a marked difference in the quality of their work, so that Cy Curtiss, taking, for the first time in his life, an actual constructive interest in something that he did, began to turn out pieces that had an almost professional finish. And the result of this was the little schoolhouse was shortly very well equipped indeed, with benches, desks, and even a blackboard made of buttjointed planks, smoothed with a drawknife and an adz, then covered with plaster and painted black. One thing Ethan soon learned to do was to praise his slower students as much as he could whenever they did something even moderately well, and to rebuke them as mildly as possible over their failures, even—when the failure revealed an honest effort—not to rebuke them at all.

There was, he sadly realized, a core component of anti-intellectualism in American life that made teaching prairie children unusually difficult. Many of his pupils were far brighter than they appeared to be, because, held in that cruelest of all tyrannies—their youthful need for the approval of their peers—they dared not display their wit and talent for fear of being labeled "Smarty" or "Highfalutin'" or, worst of all, "Teacher's Pet." And, comical to relate—or saddest of all—after Thanksgiving Day, Ethan had the wholehearted respect of every boy in the school, not because he was the really brilliant man he was, but because on that day, during the games indulged in on the frontier upon that occasion, he had won the turkey shoot with his new Winchester, and knocked the ball clear across the river beyond the grounds while playing on the farmers' team against the town dwellers at the game of "Four Old Cat" which not long afterward would develop into baseball.

But his problems and worries persisted, and some were morally troubling. Why, above all, had he never so much as mentioned Nora Curtiss's name in the letters he wrote weekly to his Anne? He'd told her many a jolly tale of other pupils, especially of their gaucheries and stupidities. He had candidly singled Gordon Lee out for high praise. But of Nora— nothing. Not one word. Even to him that seemed highly suspicious. And when, at the end of his first month of teaching, Mayor Tyler drove out to the school to give him his first pay envelope, Ethan began to realize that his troubles, as far as Nora Curtiss was concerned, were even more profound than he had believed they were. He had agreed to a cut of fifteen dollars a month and to waiving the receipt of any pay at all until the townspeople of Abilene felt that they could afford it, yet here Ned Tyler was giving him an envelope that proved to have, once he had opened it, thirty crisp new dollar bills in it!

"Now, look, Ned," Ethan said then, "don't know whether you got lucky 'Bucking the Tiger' in that gambling joint in Junction City, but I agreed to serve without pay until you folks could afford to pay me. Well, I see as many patched pants and faded calicos in town as ever. Nary a sign of any sudden wealth. So maybe you'd better explain to me the source of this, Your Honor!"

"Well, Eth," Ned said uneasily, "it's like this: Last Town Council meetin' we had, th subject o' yore pay come up. Folks feel real bad over not payin' you, 'cause one 'n all they's plumb dee-lighted with th progress their brats are makin'. Little buggers actually *like* to go to school since you took over. Beginnin' to read right smart good 'n figger 'n scribble to beat th band. Th Lee boy, now, stood up to Bart 'n threatened to leave home if that drunken old blowhard wouldn't let him attend—"

"I've heard all that," Ethan said; "and some of it may even be true to an extent. But that's not the question, Ned: the thing I'm asking you is, where in a town whose treasury is empty, and the average citizen doesn't see ten dollars hard cash in a whole year, did these thirty dollars come from?"

"Cy Curtiss," Mayor Tyler said; "volunteered to pay your salary all by hisself. Said it plain wasn't right for a pore young fella like you, who was doin' th community as much good as you was, to hafta suffer want and—"

"Jesus God!" Ethan said.

"All right, Prof, tek it easy," Mayor Tyler said; "As man to man, and as yore friend, reckon you have got cause to worry over this. Ain't a soul in town what ain't deef, dumb, 'n blind what don't know that that there pretty child is plumb daft over you. 'N could be that ol' Cy—who dotes on his darlin' daughter—is kind o' figgerin' he'll be able to buy you for his son-in-law like he's already done bought everything else in town what ain't nailed down or could be pried loose. But, still, all things considered, you's still got th whip hand . . ."

"*I've* got the whip hand?" Ethan groaned; "Damned if I see how . . ."

"You has," Ned Tyler said, "because o' your comportment 'n behavior. Every homegrown witch we've got in town—'n tha's one hundred percent o' th female population, includin' my own darlin' Nellie!—has been watchin' you like a flock o' hen buzzards to see if you'd make th slightest slip in li'l Nora's direction. 'N with yore good friend Cory Bellamy hintin' that your promised had to leave Atchison in a hurry afore her front end started poking clear across th Missouri—"

"Goddamn Cora Bellamy anyhow!" Ethan grated.

"Amen. Goddamn her twice. That there woman is jes' plain *evil* for my money. But what I'm sayin', Eth, my friend, is that even with every ma in town questioning their female young'uns like a bunch o' backcountry lawyers at courthouse time, ain't nobody kin say you ever touched her hand after th time you went 'n washed her face in public, when she swooned in front o' everybody 'cause you'd been shot. So you has got the whip hand, Prof—long as you don't never find yoreself all by yore lonesome with li'l Nora so much as by accident. 'Cause if you do, even if the both of you spends the time quotin' Bible verses to each other, th fat's plumb gonna be in th fire. Be you both as innocent as newborn lambs, folks'll talk so damn much that ol' Cy will hafta arrange hisself a shotgun weddin' for his daughter. 'N th bad part about thet is that Cy purely admires you as a person and a man 'n sez so . . ."

"Ned, Your Honor, drive me into town with you, will you?"

"All right," Ned said; "but I'd purely admire to know what you plan to do . . ."

"Have it out with Cy. Give him his money back. Explain to him *again* that I'm already engaged and—"

"Saaay! That gives me an idee, Prof! You're plannin' to go up to Omaha come Christmastime to spend th holidays with yore promised, ain't you?"

"Yes. Even though I can't really afford the railroad and steamboat fares, that's what I'm planning to do."

"Don't," Ned said solemnly, "send for her to come down *here* to spend th festivities with you. That way you'll kill a whole flock o' noisy flyin' critters with one well-chunked rock. Look at it, Eth: first o' all you'll demonstrate to all 'n sundry that Cora Bellamy is a liar, 'cause yore li'l lady's waistline will still be—I piously hopes and devoutly prays!—as slim as ever."

"Me, too," Ethan said with the crooked grin Bart Lee's wild shot had made a permanent feature of his face, "because if it isn't, she's sure Lord done me dirt!"

"Oh, I doubts that," Ned chuckled; "You brings yore li'l Annie down here to stay at *my* place as the invited guest o' Mayor 'n Missus Tyler, 'n you've purely done gone 'n crossed up everybody—"

"Look, Ned," Ethan said, "I wouldn't want to put you and Nellie to that much trouble . . ."

"No trouble a-tall. What's more, it's plumb strategy. Th wimmen-folks know my Nellie. When it comes to guardin' the public's morals, my darlin' Nellie is Number One. So can't nary a breath o' scandal attach itself to yore Annie's name while she's a-stayin' at our house. You don't ride her too far out on th lone prairie in a livery stable buggy, you-all will be just fine, Prof!"

Ethan stared at him.

"Then you think I shouldn't call on Cy Curtiss, Mayor?" he said.

"Lord, no! That there would be a tomfool thing to do, Eth. You'd be crowdin' ol' Cy more'n somewhat, then. Just you go on playin' th young, serious schoolmaster, what just can't see a damn thing what ain't writ down in a book. Cy ain't no fool, he can take a hint. 'N your li'l Annie, draped over your sturdy arm, is one helluva hint, right? As for the money, he kin afford it. And he owes th community some recompense for all th harm that rotgut pizen swill he sells has done. In a way it's plumb blood guilt money, 'cause ain't been a shootin', a cuttin', o' a pore women kicked in th belly by her drunken old man 'n caused to lose th kid she was carryin' that Cy Curtiss's likker wasn't a prime cause of, these last five years, anyhow . . ."

"You sound like a temperance reformer," Ethan said.

"Well, I ain't. Gits th yen to soothe my tonsils with th cup that cheers a mite too frequent for that. It's Nellie what's the temperance reformer in my house . . ."

"And Martha in Phil's—"

" 'N li'l Annie in yourn," Ned Tyler laughed, "after you've done gone 'n boosted her over yore doorjamb, that is. That's the very nature o' th female o' th species, Prof: anything, and I do mean *anything* a man plumb enjoys, th li'l woman is ag'in, or she soon gits to be . . ."

"You're probably right," Ethan sighed, and put out his hand to him. "Thank Cy for the money, will you? Truth to tell, I was fairly hurting for some extra cash . . ."

"Can't thank him. That he's paying you all by hisself is a secret agreed to twixt him 'n th whole Town Council. So don't you go 'n let slip, Eth, boy . . ."

"I won't. But then Cy's a man I almost never see, since hanging out in saloons is one of the many things I just plain can't afford," Ethan said.

The day after his conversation with the mayor of Abilene was a Sunday, the one day Ethan had left to go on with the slow breaking of his virgin acreage, since Saturdays he still dedicated to the boys he considered his difficult students. Ethan was sitting beside his plow, eating his frugal noon meal, not because he had any appetite but out of the simple need to maintain his strength. And, although he kept well upwind of the Old Timer, who came out every Sunday to help him with that all-important task, the mountain man's aroma wasn't helping his always slight appetite at all.

"Minds me o' my old friend Lem Blanchard," the Old Timer said; "Now thet there wuz a farmer, yessireebobtail! Did I ever tell you about Lem?"

"Repeatedly," Ethan groaned.

"Tha's so? Wal now, I do be gittin' ol' 'n fergetful. What did I tell you, young Eth?"

"That," Ethan sighed, "his farm was so big that his hired hand and the milk maid set out one day to milk the cows on the west side of it, and by the time they got back to the house they had a child one year old. That he never had to build a house, because the pumpkins he grew were so enormous that he could scoop 'em out and live in 'em come wintertime. That the wind blew so hard on his place that it turned the well end over end and left it sticking eighty feet straight up into the air, so poor Lem had to buy himself a pump, because having to throw a bucket that high to pull the water down was more blamed work than he was aiming to put up with. That he had the most peculiar-looking dog in the state of Kansas, because the stupid mutt took it upon himself to bark at a twister and the wind turned him inside out. That he lost his whole flock of chickens because that same twister blew all the feathers off them and onto his ducks, and all the feathers off the ducks onto the chickens, and while that didn't do the ducks any harm, those fool chickens got confused and thought they were ducks, so they all drowned trying to swim in Lem's pond, which, I take it, was about the size of the Atlantic Ocean . . ."

"Half," the Old Timer cackled, "jes' half, young Eth—hit don't do t'eggsagerate, y'know. Why damn me fer a sinner! I tol' you all thet? Then I reckon th only thing I got left to tell you is how pore ol' Lem died—"

"Then he's dead? Praise God from whom all blessings flow!" Ethan said fervently.

"Yep, shore is, pore fella. Took th notion in his haid to climb up a cornstalk on his place in th Republic River valley 'n look out over th whole state o' Kansas. By the time he got to th top, that there stalk had done growed so high, he could see clear 'cross Nebrasky to th Black Hills o' th Dakotas, 'n lookin south, all th way to Texas. But th trouble wuz, when he started t'git back to work, he found out that blamed stalk wuz growin' *up* a heap faster than he could scramble *down*. Starved plumb t' death, th pore ol' critter. 'Twasn't 'til his neighbors noticed they wuz a sight too many crows 'n buzzards flockin' around pore Lem's cornfield that they come over to see whut wuz wrong. Found thet fool dawg runnin' round'n 'round a certain cornstalk 'n trippin' over his own guts 'n draggin' his liver 'n his lights on th ground 'n barkin' his stupid haid off. Only you's gotta remember he'd done had his woolly hide on th *inside* ever since that damn twister had done gone 'n turned him wrongside out, so he couldn't bark loud worth a damn, 'cause all thet hair plumb muffled him. But, enyhow, Lem's neighbors got th idee 'n started to chop thet cornstalk down. Took 'em two whole weeks to do it, 'n another three to find pore Lem. You see, young Eth, by then thet damn stalk had done growed so high thet when hit fell, th top 'n tassels wit pore Lem's stinkin' corpse in 'em landed clean across th Colorado line. Pore ol' fella. He wuz onrecognizeeble by then, as th newspapers say. Them crows 'n buzzards had done messed him up for fair!"

"And all that, I suppose, is strict, literal truth, and you'd take your Bible oath on it?" Ethan said.

"Wal, goin' so fur as to swear on th Good Book, mebbe not," the Old Timer said. "But hit's mostly th truth, young Eth. Same thing happened to me. Only I wuz luckier'n ol' Lem; by th time I got to th top, th corn wuz ripe. My neighbors 'lows they found all o' forty bushels o' corncobs round th bottom o' thet stalk by th time thet balloon ascension fella drifted by 'n lifted me off of thet there stalk . . ."

"A balloonist lifted you off? Oh, come off it, Old Timer!"

"Shore did. Tha's howcome I got to visit Paris, France. They wuz havin' a fair down Topeka way, 'n th main attraction wuz this here balloon ascension. But you knows how Kansas winds is by now. Wal, thet great big gas bag got blowed clear up to my place on th Big Blue River, 'n thet there balloon driver seen me clingin' to thet cornstalk 'n munchin' on a ear o' corn 'n lookin' mournful. So he let out a li'l gas, drapped down low 'n let me scramble into thet there wicker basket wit him. Then he throwed out a couple o' sandbags, 'n up 'n off we went! Only by then thet damn wind wuz blowin' so hard thet hit blowed us clean across th Atlantic

Ocean to Gay Pa-ree. 'N you knows whut, young Eth? Them French gals not only washes theirs in a li'l footbath tub, they perfumes it, to boot! Shore did smell good. Them Frenchies swears hit tastes good, too, 'cause they's got some mighty peculiar notions as to whut a fella's s'posed to do wit it, 'n—"

"Oh, Gawd!" Ethan groaned.

"Gawd's own truth! Saaay, looks like we's got company . . ."

"Not the Bellamys *again,*" Ethan said.

"Nope. Though one o' these fine nights thet there big woman is gonna sneak some knockout drops in her ol' man's likker, 'n then come over here 'n rope 'n hawgtie you, young Eth. Tek hit right outta yore pants wit her own lily white fingers 'n—"

"Will you shut up, you filthy-minded old coot? Hmmmn, you're right, that is some kind of a light rig coming this way. Only it's too far away to make out who's driving it . . ."

"Swear t' Gawd you young fellas is blinder than bats. Hit's yore pappy-in-Law, young Eth . . ."

"My father-in-law? You'd better change whatever brand of rotgut you're drinking these days, Old Timer. When the hell did I ever acquire a father-in-law?"

"Mebbe you ain't—*yet,*" the Old Timer said judiciously. "But you's purely gonna, mighty damn soon. You don't mean to set thar wit yore bare face hangin' out 'n tell me you actually thunk you could git into a sixteen-year-ol' schoolgal's drawers 'n not have her pappy go fur his scatter-gun, d'you?"

"Oh, Lord! Is that what the Abilene Association of Female Carrion Crows and Hen Buzzards are saying now, Old Timer?"

"Shore is," the Old Timer cackled; "Every ol' Broomstick Wrangler in town is watchin' thet there pore sweet li'l chile's cinch ring to see whether her middle's done gone 'n swole up a sixty-fourth o' a inch, mebbe. But you's got them scandal-lovin' females buffaloed, young Prof Ethan, thet you is . . ."

"Buffaloed how?" Ethan said.

"Cain't nary a one o' 'em figger out jes' when 'n whar 'twas you pulled her faradiddles 'n her furbelows down off'n her battleground . . ."

"That's cowboy talk. Texas cowboy at that," Ethan said; "And it's Greek to me. Explain yourself, will you?"

"Aw heck, I allus fergits whut a Mister Pilgrim you is!" the Old Timer sighed. "Wal, to put it plain 'n outspoken-like, them ornery female critters would like to know when 'n whar 'twuz you ripped her frilly li'l onmentionables right off her cute li'l Manassas. O' when 'twuz she took 'em off her ownself, not to put you to no trouble, 'n thet's whut most of 'em is a-sayin', 'cause thet thar li'l angel-baby sugar-pie is purely long gone over you 'n don't mek no bones about hit. Fact is, you's even got *me* boogered on thet p'int. C'mon, fess up, young Eth: when 'n whar did you, now?"

"The answer to that one is simple, Old Timer," Ethan said solemnly. "Never and nowhere. All right?"

"Aw heck! Wal, stand t' reason you ain't gonna admit a thing like thet out loud. Now, kin you see thet I wuz right? Hit's yore pappy-in-law-to-be, shore as shootin'! Course I caint mek out whether he's a-totin' his scatter-gun o' no, but he shore looks madder'n ol' hell, Perffessor!"

By then the smart little buckboard had come much closer, but Ethan still found the distance too great for anyone who didn't have the eyesight of a bald eagle to make out who the driver was. On the vast sweep of a prairie's horizon that fact was not unusual: since the gently rolling grasslands were free of woods, hills, or any natural obstacles whatsoever, you could clearly see a horse-drawn vehicle approaching from well over a mile away. Then the sole peculiarity of this one struck him: it was drawn, not by the one horse that was really all a rig as light as a buckboard needed, but by a splendid, high-stepping pair. So now he knew how the Old Timer had been able to determine who their visitor was: several times, in Abilene, he had heard sour—and envious—remarks to the effect that "ol' Cy is gittin' too big fur his britches, drivin a showy pair like them there prutty hosses o' hisn . . ."

But the realization that the Old Timer had been pulling off a fast one again, with his pretense of being able to see who a man was from a mile and a half away, didn't help Ethan's peace of mind at all. That his name was being bandied about Abilene in connection with little Nora's was enough to bring down more trouble than he was prepared to handle upon his all but defenseless head. And, even granting his star pupil a highly unusual degree of veracity, which reinforced the probability that she had told her father how circumspect his behavior toward her had been, one question remained: Had Cy believed her? A suspicious, jealous, doting father was a difficult problem for any man to manage, and whether the man in question were guilty or innocent of the accusations raised against him was a very nearly total irrelevancy. To prove one's innocence, Ethan sadly realized, was always close to an impossibility when you considered the degree of secrecy with which any such socially disapproved of love affair would normally be carried out. . . .

But thinking about the matter didn't do any good at all, and preparing arguments to meet the accusations that Cyrus Curtiss hadn't yet even made was worse than useless. Better to wait, let the saloonkeeper have his say, then, if necessary, defend himself with the calm conviction of the truth. . . . The only trouble, in this case, lay in the prickly fact that he wasn't all that sure exactly what the truth was.

What, really, did he feel for Nora Curtiss? He was curiously reluctant to go into that delicate question. Thinking about it now, as he watched her father turn his showy pair into the very field where he waited beside his plow, the only conclusion that he came to was that he was fond of Nora, much too fond. That the only reason he was not—quite!—in love with her was that he had given his pledged word to a good and blameless woman, so he couldn't afford to let himself be. A man who broke his vow to a woman like Anne to take up with a schoolgirl was at least a fool, and probably something a good bit worse. Of that, stern puritan that he was, Ethan had no doubt at all.

"Howdy, Professor," Cyrus Curtiss said.

"A very good day to you, Mr. Curtiss," Ethan said, and added, deliberately seizing the psychological advantage: "What brings you way down here this fine Sunday morning?"

"Two things: One of 'em a mission given to me by Reverend Brownley," Cyrus said gravely. "He asked me to find out why you don't show up for services no more. Reckon I see why, now. Want to get yore whole spread under cultivation as fast as possible, eh? Still, working on th Lord's Day is a serious sin, young fella. You *are* a believer, ain't you?"

'Your round!' Ethan conceded mockingly inside his mind. "Yes, sir," he answered calmly, "that I am. In fact, appears to me I have a higher opinion of the Almighty than most people do. I believe in His loving kindness, His mercy, and His understanding. . . . But why don't you get down, sir, and stretch your limbs? Mighty long drive from Abilene to down here . . ."

"That it is," Cyrus Curtiss sighed; "but I purely needed to have a talk with you, Professor—over a matter tha's kind o' preying on my mind . . ."

With an agility surprising in a man of his bulk, he hopped down from the buckboard as he said that, and he put out his hand to Ethan.

'So,' Ethan thought wryly as he took it, 'our battle is to be fought on a reasonably civilized plane? God knows I'm glad of that. . . .' He said:

"I suppose Cy, Jr., told you I had to wallop him again?"

"No, sir, he didn't; but Nora did—and why. 'Pears to me you was a sight too lenient with the young rapscallion. You only gave him one whack, my daughter says, 'n—for what he done—you ought to have give him ten!"

"I don't really hold with corporal punishment, Mr. Curtiss," Ethan said slowly; "I only gave Cy one whack across the seat of his pants because I had to, as a warning to the others. But, as far as your son was concerned, it was already unnecessary. He was much repented of his offense by then. In fact he had tears in his eyes, after the talking-to—privately, and man-to-man—I'd already given him. With all due modesty, I think I can boast of having a keen understanding of the psychology of the human male animal, sir, especially when said animal is young!"

"That you do," Cy Curtiss conceded gravely, "likely drawn from the fact that you ain't exactly decrepit yourself, Professor. By th way, how old d'you be, anyhow?"

"Twenty-seven," Ethan said and, seeing Cy Curtiss brighten at that, marked that round a draw.

"Look, Prof," the saloonkeeper said; "Couldn't you send this here walking manure pile on some sort of an errand? What I've got to talk to you about is rightly kind o' personal. 'N this here old polecat's got a tongue that's hinged in the middle so it flaps away like crazy on both ends!"

"Ol' Polecat!" the Old Timer snorted; "Mebbe I don't smell so good, Cy Curtiss, but I ain't never done a livin' soul th harm thet you is, you widder-maker, you! Drivin' folks crazy 'n turnin' 'em stone blind wit that thar coffin varnish thet you sells in thet den o' iniquity o' yourn! Why, every bottle's got a guaranteed pink elephant in it, thet is when it ain't got a purple snake!"

"You oughta know, Old Timer," Cy said imperturbably, "considering the amount of it you gargles whenever you can find a greener dumb enough to buy you the stuff 'n listen to your lies. C'mon now, be a good ol' fella 'n run along, will you? Didn't mean to hurt yore feelings, 'n here's a token of my goodwill to prove it . . ."

At that Cyrus Curtiss brought out a half pint bottle and handed it to the mountain man.

"Why, thank you, Cy!" the old man cackled; "Thank you mighty kindly! Reckon you's still got th mekins o' a white man in you yet!"

And with that he loped off across the prairie like a gray-bearded wolf.

"Well, sir, what can I do for you?" Ethan said.

"Dunno," Cyrus sighed. "That's likely up to you, young fella. But lemme take one thing at a time: you really feel you've got to break sod on Sunday, so you jest can't get to church?"

"It's the old question of faith as against works, isn't it, sir?" Ethan said sadly; "I gave up my Saturdays to do a good work, which was straightening out five youngsters who were headed for hell in a handcart, in spite of their parents' best efforts. And I honestly believe I've done them some good. Am I wrong about that, Mr. Curtiss?"

"No," the saloonkeeper said sadly, "that you ain't. You've straightened that boy o' mine out a heap more than I was ever able to. I freely admit that, and thank you for it, too. But before we git any further along on th subject o' my kids, what am I to tell Reverend Brownley: that you don't aim to come to church anymore this year?"

"That I *can't.* Tell him that fact grieves me, and that I've frequently taken it up with the Good Lord in prayer. But there are sins and sins, it seems to me. I gave Phil Harris and Mayor Tyler my word that I'd teach their school this winter, and that cost me several weeks of the time I ordinarily would have devoted to my plowing, and, not to rub it in, sir, sacrificing my Saturdays to my mixed-up boys has cost me the one day I still might have used for that. So I asked the Almighty to lend me Sundays this year, promising to pay Him back when I could. Look at it, sir! Every farmer who has failed out here lost his fight to succeed and his land for the same reason: it took him too long to get enough acreage under cultivation to provide him with enough cash for running expenses and improvements of the kind that every well-run farm has got to have. So he went into debt, took a mortgage on his place—and ultimately lost it when he couldn't pay. I don't mean to let that happen to me. I won't go into debt. I'll never mortgage my place. I love it too much. A man like you, who's never been cooped up in a city, choked half to death on factory smoke, maybe can't understand how much this spread of prairie earth, this sweep of sky the Lord has given temporarily into my keeping, means to me. Only one thing means more: treating people honorably and decently and justly, and keeping my pledged word. So I'm hoping that God will forgive me for not keeping the Sabbath. But, if He won't, on my head be the punishment. There are worse sins, you know . . ."

"You're damned right, son," Cy Curtiss declared sorrowfully; " 'N keeping a saloon is likely one of 'em. That I don't drink th stuff myself, and refuse another dram to a fella what I can see has already had too much, don't really excuse it, none a-tall. But I've got two kids 'n don't know no other way of making a living. . . . But, to heck with that! Wasn't what I come out here to talk with you about, anyhow. Nora tells me you whalloped my son ag'in, 'cause the randy young fool bored a hole through th partition twixt th boys' 'n th girls' outhouses, so he could gaze upon th fillies' cute li'l bare bottoms when they pulled down their drawers to sit on th throne. Is that right, Prof?"

"It is. But, as I've already told you, that one whack of my paddle—which, incidentally, young Cy made for me; he's fast becoming an expert carpenter, y'know—was for form's sake only. I'd already got next to Cy—"

"How?" Cy, Sr., asked.

"By pointing out to him what a *man* was, as opposed to a boar hog, or a randy billy goat, or even a seed bull. A creature created by Almighty God, in His own image, but little lower than the angels, crowned with glory and honor. Who protects the weak and the helpless, never abuses them. Who respects his womenfolk, instead of degrading them. I ended up the lecture by asking him what, since he had bored that convenient hole, was to prevent the other boys, especially his four cronies, from taking advantage of it to gaze upon his own sister's dainty anatomy, just as he'd looked at the other girls'? That hadn't occurred to him. He was appalled. I'm sure I have never seen a youngster more ashamed in all my life . . ."

"You done well, Prof," Cyrus Curtiss said; " 'N like I said, you've come closer to straightenin' that boy o' mine out than anybody else ever has, even me. Fact is, I ain't much worried 'bout Cy anymore; it's that girl o' mine who's got me plumb buffaloed, and that's a living fact . . ."

"Nora?" Ethan said with well-feigned astonishment. "Why, sir, she's by far the best student that I've got! She's smart, dutiful, obedient, and never gives the slightest trouble. If I had a roomful of kids like her, Mr. Curtiss, teaching would be an actual joy . . ."

"Son, you're making this plumb hard for me. Oh, well, put it this way: Before *you* come here, Nora was all them things you said. At home, too. As a daughter, no man could ask for better. But now she's plumb done changed. Snaps my head off if I say a word to her, is ruining her pretty eyes crying herself to sleep every night, don't eat enough to keep a jaybird alive. . . . Prof, you real sure you ain't never give her any encouragement a-tall?"

Ethan stared at the big man's troubled face. He felt quite honestly sorry for Cy Curtiss then. Being the father of a pretty daughter was a hard row to hoe, everyone said that. And it was a problem he might well be confronted with himself one day.

"Sir," he said gently, "I take it you're referring to the fact that little Nora is growing up a little faster than she knows how to cope with. . . . And that she has—as schoolgirls will—fixed her attention on the one outlandish and different creature she's run across, namely me. That, Mr. Curtiss, is a great compliment, and I'd value it much higher than I do if I didn't know it is born of inexperience—and innocence, both. Give her time, sir. She'll meet some handsome young fellow, much nearer her own age, and then she'll realize that I'm as homely as a hog in a fence, and a dull dog to boot . . ."

"Done told her all that," Cy Curtiss sighed; "But then she comes back with the fact that you ain't but ten o' eleven years older than her, and that her ma was twenty younger than me when we was wed. As for your looks, she claims you're something far better than handsome, you're interesting 'n exciting, both. She even claims that ugly scar ol' Bart went 'n burnt clear cross yore face with a bullet makes you more attractive than ever. *Dashin'* is th word she uses, I do believe. Son, you've got to help me out. You told me you was engaged, didn't you?"

"I did," Ethan said.

"How serious is that there engagement, Prof?"

"You haven't been listening to me very carefully, Mr. Curtiss," Ethan said quietly; "I gave a woman—of spotless reputation and blameless life —my pledged word. I just can't think of anything more serious than that . . ."

"You're right. I stand rebuked. But, O Lord, if I could only think up some way to cool that pore lovelorn child o' mine off a mite!"

"Leave it to me, sir," Ethan said. "I've two excellent ideas. And one of them ought to accomplish just that. First of all, at Christmas closing time I mean to stage a school play—a shortened version of Shakespeare's *Romeo and Juliet.* I mean to cast Nora and young Lee in the principal roles, both because as my best students, they deserve the honor, and with malice aforethought. And you'll have to admit that Gordon's a very handsome lad."

"Lord God, Prof!" Cy Curtiss exploded; "I damn sure don't want my child to get mixed up with Bart Lee's sprout!"

Ethan looked at him.

"Now you're visiting the sins of the father upon the head of the son, sir," he said quietly, "which is one of the few concepts in the Bible I've never been able to swallow. Gordon is nothing like his father. I suspect he takes after his dead mother, who, I'm told, was far above the man she mistakenly chose to marry in almost every way. Next to your Nora, he's the brightest student that I have. I see a great future for him if he persists in his studies. But forget that. Let it go. I'm saying that a harmless classroom romance between schoolmates, which will burn itself out before a year is out, is preferable to letting Nora go on fixing her girlish dreams on a poor schoolmaster who is going to change into an even poorer farmer before too long. So I'd like to try the strategem of the play, sir; and I hope it works, because if it doesn't the only alternative I'll have left will be— harsher. I don't much like the idea of hurting your daughter's feelings, sir, but—"

"What's the second thing you've done thought of, Prof?" the saloon-keeper said.

"That instead of going up to Omaha, Nebraska, to visit my fiancée at Christmastime, I'll bring Anne down here. Mayor and Mrs. Tyler have already agreed to put her up. In the first place, having the townspeople meet Anne ought to put a stop to the lies that Cora Bellamy, for reasons of her own, has been busily spreading about her—"

"Them reasons being you refused to oblige Cora, or I miss my guess!" Cy Curtiss snorted. "But let's get back to my Nora and the awful shine she seems to have taken to you, Prof. You think that seein' yore promised in the flesh would kind of change my pore child's mind?"

"Don't know, sir. Who, short of the Good Lord Himself, can ever predict how any woman—and Nora is already a woman in some ways— will react to any particular set of circumstances? I'd much rather try my first tactic of diverting her attention in the direction of a boy her own age, and only if that doesn't work, I'd fall back upon sending for Anne. I'm going to have enough of a problem explaining this scarred-up mug of mine to her without having to defend myself against all the sly innuendos concerning Nora and me the town's gossips are going to pour into her ears."

"Bring yore lady here, Prof," Cyrus Curtiss said heavily. "Be the best thing. It'll convince my pore lovelorn child that there ain't no hope as far as you're concerned. Oh, she'll cry her eyes out, but she'll git over it. And by hurtin' her a little, you'll have done her a kindness in the end. . . . As for yore sweetheart, if she won't believe in yore innocence, bring her to me, 'n I'll straighten her out on that point. I know my daughter. I ain't a-saying that she couldn't stray from th straight 'n narrow, but what I am saying is that if she ever did, she'd come home, hand me my razor strop, 'n say: 'Papa, I done wrong—really wrong. So take this 'n beat me t' death, if you wants to . . .' "

"Good God!" Ethan whispered.

"That's just what she would do, Prof. And that's exactly why I believed her when, after I'd asked her about you 'n her, she said: 'Papa, there ain't nothing. Nothing at all. 'N th reason there ain't is 'cause Prof Lovejoy is a gentleman 'n a scholar, not because o' me. He was to crook his little finger, I'd jump into his arms so fast it would make his head swim. But he hasn't never crooked that finger, 'cause to him I'm jes' a silly schoolgirl that he don't care about none a-tall . . .' "

"That's where she's wrong," Ethan said honestly; "I *do* care for—and about—Nora. If she weren't so young, and I hadn't met Anne first, who knows? But matters are as they are, and there's no way—no decent and honorable way, anyhow—of changing them. I don't think I need add that you have my word—the word of a gentleman, anyhow, if something less than a scholar!—that I'll never, by word or deed, take advantage of Nora's inexplicable fondness for me, do I?"

"No, you don't. Reckon you've plumb proved you can be trusted by now. And the way my daughter feels about you ain't unexplainable; you stand head 'n shoulders above all th younger fellows hereabouts. It's purely a pity that things are like they are, but that's life, I guess . . ."

He put out his hand to Ethan. Ethan took it, gripping hard.

"Get on with your plowing, Prof. That there box loaded down with dirt above the beam to make it dig in, don't reckon I've ever seen nothing like that, before—and it's proof positive that you're mighty smart. Hope you and yore new missus will be happy, here, 'cause town and county both plumb need younger folks of yore stature," Cyrus Curtiss said.

"Thank you, sir," Ethan said; "Good-bye, now . . ."

Watching the saloonkeeper driving away, what came to Ethan's mind was a quotation from one of the better New England poets, John Greenleaf Whittier:

For of all sad words of tongue or pen,
The saddest are these: "It might have been."

That very next day Ethan put his first plan in action only to have it fail completely from the outset. For sweet Nora, demure Nora, obedient Nora, faced him with quiet defiance and said:

"Can I say no, Professor Lovejoy? I mean, do I have any choice in the matter?"

"If you'll amend that first sentence of yours into 'May I say no,' which is much better grammar, my answer is, 'Yes, of course, you may, Nora,' " Ethan said. "The school play is an extracurricular activity and, as such, is entirely voluntary. Though I must say I'm both surprised and disappointed at your rejection of the part. I offered it to you as a reward for the excellent work you've been doing so far . . ."

"I know that, sir, and I thank you," Nora whispered; "And I don't mind being in your play—"

"Not mine, child!" Ethan laughed; "It's Shakespeare's! But go on. You were saying?"

"I don't mind being in the play, long as I don't have to be Juliet. Couldn't I be the old nurse, or even Juliet's mama? Then you could make Mary Sue, Juliet. Being so much taller than her—"

"Than she is," Ethan corrected patiently.

"Oh, Lord! Will I never learn to talk fair? Since I'm so much taller than Mary Sue, it would even look right . . ."

"Of course, Nora," Ethan said gravely. Then temptation overcame him: he asked the wrong question, the one he knew damned well he had no business asking at all. "But I should like to know," he said, "why you don't want to play Juliet. It's by far the best female part, and most girls would jump at the chance. Why don't you, my dear?"

"Because, sir," Nora said, looking him straight in the eye, "I'd have to playact like I was in love with another fellow. Besides the—the person —I am in love with, sir. And I couldn't do it. The way I feel about him —is holy, sort of. I couldn't even make like I was in love with somebody else. It would—kill me to even try it. Just like being without him is killing me little by little now. But I reckon being dead can be rightly kind of peaceful. Better than living is, when a body has done lost all hope . . ."

Ethan was intelligent enough to know when to let a thing drop. As now, for instance.

"Very well," he said gravely. "I'm not prepared to argue the question, Nora. I'm neither old enough nor wise enough to advise you about such things. Let's put the whole discussion aside for two years, say. Until you're eighteen. Then we'll see how you feel . . ."

"Eighteen or ninety, won't make no—any—difference, sir. I'm going to love y—him—'til I die," sweet Nora said.

That very day, after school was out, Ethan wrote Anne a letter. He walked into Abilene and put in on the stage that didn't have to go any further than Junction City, now, because the KP had already reached that point, only twenty-three miles from Abilene itself by then. In that letter, of course, he invited his fiancée to spend the Christmas holidays in Kansas with him, instead of his going to Omaha, Nebraska, to spend them with her. He gave several reasons for this request: the necessity of shutting Cora Bellamy up once and for all; the advantages of getting to know and becoming friends with the leading women of the town near which they were going to live, et cetera, so forth, and so on. . . . But in the end he was guilty of a certain degree of moral cowardice even though he knew it was going to cost him dearly.

He still failed to write a single line about Nora Curtiss. Which was, perhaps, just as well, for he would have needed to write a book.

8

"You," Ethan's twin brother Jonathan said, "can't pick your women worth a good goddamn!"

Ethan peered unblinkingly into his brother's face. Jonathan had no lower jaw. There was a little round bluish hole in his left temple. His right temple didn't exist. That .44-caliber ball had mushroomed and lifted a fist-sized mass of bone, gray matter, and flesh from that side, coming out. Little bottle green flies were feasting on his eyes. The sight wasn't pleasant. Ethan looked away.

Which did him no good. In whatever direction he turned his gaze inside that damp, ill-smelling dugout on a Kansas prairie that God had not only forsaken but whose very existence He had forgot—that is, if the Almighty had ever held that empty sweep of desolation and loneliness in mind—Jonathan's ruined face, his shot-castrated body, floated before Ethan on the freezing dark.

'I can't break sod any more,' he reasoned slowly; 'It's the last of November now and too damned cold. So I'm not three-quarters dead from sheer exhaustion any longer when I hit the hay. *Ergo* I can dream. And what do I dream about? My windy polecat of a brother. All I need to make my cup of joy run over. This is no good. No damned good at all. I must wake up. I must!'

He said: "Go away, Jonathan. You're dead, you know. There's nothing you can do to, or for me, now . . ."

"I can help you out," Jonathan chuckled. "Keep you from fucking up, as usual. The young one, Eth. That sixteen-year-old unbusted piece. What's her name? Oh, yeah—Nora, right? Take her. She'll last you a while. Your tent show ingenue *cum* schoolmarm won't. 'Sides, since one of my jobs down here is to help the Devil concoct the unholy messes that poor bastards like you, twin brother, either dive into headfirst or fall into ass-backward, I tell you this: you're gonna end up with little Nora, anyhow. So take her now while she's still all yours, before all and sundry have partaken of what she's fairly panting to push off on you. Later on, my stewbook says she'll still be yours, but only after she's laid down and spread wide for every horny son of the sod in Kansas. The ones who've got two dollars, anyhow. And between fresh and worn-out tail, the difference is vast, me boy!"

'This is—wrong,' Ethan thought. 'He didn't know Nora. Nor—Anne. He died—I killed him—three years before I met either of them. So what am I doing with this dream? Putting the thoughts I can't acknowledge, that are too dirty, twisted, vile, for me to face, into his mouth. Into his shattered mouth that I blew the lower jaw clear off of. That couldn't talk even if he were alive, and since he's dead, dead, dead—dead and rotten!—I—

'There's only one way to stop this,' Ethan told himself; 'Come on, Ethan Lovejoy, throw your buffalo robes back. Let the cold air hit you in the face. It'll still stink, though. Everything in this prairie mudhole does —including me. Me, more than anything else, I suspect. But the freezing cold will wake you up. It—will—wake—you—up . . .'

He made a sudden, convulsive lurch. Hurled the buffalo robes back. The icy but still fetid air poured over his long johns-clad form. The pupils of his pale eyes contracted, the irises cleared. The inside of his dugout took on mass and weight. Things grew edges, achieved form.

And his brother Jonathan vanished, faded very slowly out of the man-made concepts of space and time.

But when Ethan tried to stand up, the whole dugout began to revolve, all the more sickeningly for its ponderous slowness, about his defenseless head.

'I'm—sick,' he realized; 'Sick. . . . That Irish thug—in Junction City.

Tore my shot-up gut all to hell again. Oh, well—it's early yet. I'll just stretch out for a while longer. Get some strength back, and—'

Now, in spite of the ungodly hour it was, he could see around the dismal little room much too well. The sight wasn't cheering. For a moment, he regretted having finally installed a glass window, because, even in the pale, watery dawn light stealing through it, it was evident how Lordawful his primitive dwelling was. He had bought the window glass in Junction City, for now that the Kansas Pacific had reached that town, it was the logical place to go to buy all the things that still weren't available locally. But now, looking about his—he hoped!—temporary shelter and conceding that, granted choice, no self-respecting pig would live in it, not to mention a human being, among all the other totally disheartening things he perceived was the sad fact that there weren't any buffalo chips left in the box he kept them in. He swore feelingly. Day after day he had to wander farther west and north in search of buffalo chips to make the fire that barely kept him from freezing and that converted the chore of cooking his sparse and frugal meals into an unmitigated hell. Because Ethan had resolved not to use the thin strands of timber bordering on that part of the Smokey Hill River closest to his farm for anything so devastatingly destructive to those scant groves' chances for survival as employing them for fuel would have been, he had to depend mostly upon buffalo chips, and bring them in from ever farther away. The hunters were already decimating the still vast herds by then, driving the magnificent beasts before them.

Ethan looked at the other box beside his fireplace. To cook his breakfast he needed at least a boxful of hay logs, and he had only three left.

Groaning, he made another halfhearted attempt to get up, but as he moved, a drop of icy water fell onto his face. Then he remembered: it had rained long and hard last night. And despite the fact that the downpour had stopped several hours ago, his dugout's earthen roof, sodden through, would go on dripping for another two days at least, soaking the prized and expensive buffalo robes he used for blankets, and converting the floor of the dugout into one big mud puddle. So, gathering more hay to twist into imitation logs was out of the question. Wet by last night's rain, it wouldn't burn at all, and what was even worse, would only fill his dugout with asphyxiating clouds of smoke.

Then the absolute nadir of the plight he found himself in hit him like a blow to his shrapnel-shredded gut: even if, despite his being dogsick and weak as dishwater, he succeeded in making a fire, he *couldn't* cook his breakfast anyhow, for the very simple reason that there wasn't a damned thing to eat in that miserable hole in the ground he lived in.

He lay there and considered that, reflecting sadly upon the reasons for that curious and complicated state of affairs. It grew out of several circumstances that might have happened to any man, but also out of one last, unique one that could only have happened to Ethan Lovejoy.

First, since he had arrived in Kansas far too late to plant garden crops, he had to depend almost exclusively upon store-bought food. Thanks to his would-be father-in-law, Cyrus Curtiss, he had money enough and to spare to buy the scant amounts of it he needed. The only trouble was finding food to be bought, because there was little, if any, to speak of to be had in Abilene.

There was, of course, a general store that sold, among other things, groceries. But those groceries consisted of baking soda, flour, salt, coffee, tobacco—plug for chewing, cigars for smoking, and some loose, shredded leaf for those who favored a corncob pipe—and whiskey. Period. To buy even dried vegetables and dried fruit—fresh produce was, of course, out of the question in the wintertime, and the canning industry with its production of "airtights," as Westerners called canned goods, lay still a decade or more in the future—he had to go to Junction City. With a rented horse and buggy, and starting out immediately after school on Friday, he could have all of Saturday in what was now actually, if only temporarily, the city it had always called itself and Sunday to come home in, so he didn't have to miss even a day at the schoolhouse.

But to date he had indulged himself in the luxury of such a trip only once, for two reasons. First of all, it cost too much. For though Luke Prevost, the livery stable keeper, cut his usual fee for renting a horse and buggy, five dollars a day, down to three out of his shame at not paying Ethan anything at all for his two children who were attending Ethan's classes, to take the long ride into Junction City cost the frugal Yankee six dollars that he could ill afford to spare for the transportation alone.

But beyond the cost, Ethan had come to the conclusion—or, more accurately, had it forced upon him—that in the future, if he could possibly avoid going there, he'd stay the hell out of Junction City entirely. Before the Kansas Pacific had got there, the town had had a population that Ethan had estimated at some four hundred people. Now, almost overnight, it had close to seven thousand. Nearly all the newcomers were members of the railroad's construction gangs, and as far as Ethan could judge, ninety-seven percent of them were Irish. And, as such, they had a truly Hibernian love for the cup that cheers, combined, after a few such cups had been tossed down their roaring gullets, with a berserker delight in sheer mayhem.

Ethan had gone down into the new section of Junction City, where the Kansas Pacific's huge new warehouses were. There, he was sure, he could find window glass. When a town became the temporary terminus of a railroad line—as Junction City was now—you could find damned near anything imaginable in it, even, if Ethan had been so inclined—or had the price!—fresh oysters shipped in from the East Coast, packed in ice, as well as caviar and champagne.

But what hadn't occurred to the sober and temperate soul that Ethan was, were the kinds of establishments that always sprang up—as though called into being by a sorcerer's magic wand—around the warehouses of the road and the barracks of the construction crews. The establishments were generally housed in tents, forming a sort of supplementary canvas city. And that flimsy city was both a reasonable facsimile and an unbridled outpost of hell itself. Under those tents there were, of course, legitimate businesses: stores, banks, brokerage houses, auction rooms, restaurants. But they were outnumbered. Every other tent housed a saloon, a gambling den, a taxi dance hall, or a whorehouse, though the taxi dance halls and the saloons often offered the services of the "fallen doves," as they were known on the frontier, in curtained-off alcoves in their corners.

Now Ethan had to pass through this brand-new tenderloin of Junction City to even get to the warehouse where they had the window glass he wanted to buy. He almost made it, weaving his way cautiously through the two dozen simultaneous bloody brawls that the Sons of the Auld Sod delightedly engaged in—making use of their brawny fists, broken bottles, knives, brass knuckles, blackjacks, fence posts, iron bars, and even, tragically enough, for their use provoked most of the fatalities, an occasional six-shooter or two—at any hour of the day or night that enough of them were off from work. But, in the end, he had bad luck. One huge Irishman noted that alone among all the happy participants in that glorious slugging match, the tall Yankee schoolmaster was neither bruised nor bloody, and that his clothes were not plentifully besmeared with horse dung or so much as even torn.

"Here's wan fur ye sainted mither!" the big Hibernian roared and sank his hairy fist into the mass of scar tissue and postoperative adhesions that served poor Ethan for a middle. Fire exploded inside Ethan's shredded gut; sixteen tons of rock solid midnight crashed down on his head.

When Ethan came to, he was alone. The glorious brawl had raged on down the street and was now wrecking everything in sight two blocks away. Ethan came up on his hands and knees, hung there, shaking his head to clear it. Then he started to vomit. And what came up was blood.

He continued to bring up blood—though, fortunately, in ever diminishing quantities—for two days after he'd come back to his claim. But proud and stubborn New England Yankee that he was, he didn't mention his injury to anyone. Dog sick and reeling, he didn't miss a single day at the school and taught his classes, if with something less than his usual verve, at least acceptably enough. Only Nora, attuned by then to the slightest change in the rhythm of his breathing, lingered, with what was for her nerve-twanging daring, a moment after school was out to ask:

"Sir, you—you're sick, aren't you?"

To which Ethan had replied:

"It's nothing much, my dear; I'm just a bit off my feed, that's all . . ."

Ethan endured gut-gripping abdominal pains in stony silence, knowing that to find a doctor, he'd have to go back to Junction City. But he had an understandable reluctance to revisit so soon a town where people punched your guts in for the sheer hell of it; so he lived for a week or two on the broths he made from the flesh of the prairie chickens he caught in a figure-four box trap—shooting those wily game birds with a rifle was a pure impossibility—and his torn gut apparently healed on its own.

Now, lying there, he thought, with what was far more wry amusement than any bitterness, of how he had managed to run completely out of even the last grain of coffee that, expensive as it was, he practically lived on, sacrificing the purchase of much more nourishing fare to his love of it, as well as the last of the flour for the flapjacks, which, because they were so easy to make, were a staple of his daily diet. The truth of the matter was that though he had fully intended to drive into Abilene after school was out and buy enough of the scanty supplies to be obtained there to tide him over until he could make the no-longer-to-be-put-off trip into Junction City, by the time that classes were over on each of the past three days, the whole thing had simply slipped from his mind.

The spreading mass of scrap iron the Rebel sharpshooter had pumped into his middle the day after his brother's death at Gettysburg had destroyed so many of the nerves that cause the contractions and the pangs by which the stomach signals its need for food, that Ethan almost never got hungry at all. He had to make a deliberate, intellectual effort to remind

himself to eat; and, immersed in the routine of his teaching, troubled by
the sight of Nora's growing ever thinner and paler with each week that
passed until her truly lovely eyes seemed bigger than what self-inflicted
famine had left of her face—since starving herself to death seemed to that
poor, sweet child a perfectly reasonable means for dealing with a hopelessly unrequited love—busy with his grandiose plans for what he fully
intended to make an agricultural empire, he often forgot the whole boring
and burdensome business of preparing his meals and then eating them.
And when to that was added the circumstance that he was anything but
a *cordon bleu* chef, the fact that he was frequently in real danger of falling
ill through malnutrition if not from actual inanition becomes understandable.

It was now about an hour before the time he ordinarily had to get
up, light his fire, prepare his breakfast, wash, shave, comb his long brown
hair, and set out for school, yet he still lay under his buffalo skin blankets,
wondering with real fear whether he was going to be able to get up at all.
He was shivering like a man with a chill, though, thanks to those beautiful
squaw-tanned robes, he should have been plenty warm enough. He had
bought the buffalo robes in Salina, hesitating long minutes over their price
of four dollars each. But finally he bowed to the bitter recognition that to
a man who had frozen to death during the night, or died of pneumonia
in the morning, everything on earth became superfluous, including his
magnificent three-hundred-twenty-acre spread, so he had doled out eight
dollars of his scanty cash. So now he doubled his long body up until his
bony knees touched his chin, in order to conserve what little warmth there
was left in him, and thought about what it meant for a lone man to get
sick out on the prairie in a damp, ill-smelling dugout.

In one way, he was lucky. More than one prairie farmer, even, at
times, a whole farming family, had died of hunger and cold when illness
had left them too weak to fend for themselves, for by the time their nearly
always distant neighbors became aware that something was wrong, they
were either dead or too far gone to be saved. That extreme couldn't happen
to him, he knew, because first of all, if a couple of nosey parkers like the
Bellamys didn't see his big wagon, drawn by a plodding pair of oxen, start
off across the fields in the general direction of Abilene on a school day,
they'd come over at once to investigate. And secondly, although it was
true that, being normal children, the vast majority of his pupils would
greet the absence of the schoolmaster with whoops of joy and rush out to
play "Drop the Handkerchief," "Hide and Seek," "Black Man," "King

William," or one of the bat and ball games—"One, Two, Three" or "Four Old Cat"—at least two of them, Gordon Lee and Nora Curtiss, would immediately set out for town to report his nonappearance.

Lying there, he went over in his mind how little he could afford to get sick at this particular juncture. Less than a month from now, Anne would come down from Omaha. And he couldn't face her looking like—what was that apt phrase of Cora's?—oh, yes: "death lightly warmed over." He had to pull himself together, and regain, within the next month, whatever he could of his health and strength.

The easiest and most immediate solution to his problem was, of course, to force himself to get up, get dressed, and then totter over to the Bellamys', whose dugout was less than a quarter of a mile from his own. Cora would feed him gladly. But then she would also flatly refuse his offer to pay for the meal, and he'd find himself under heavy obligation to his neighbors. And the same thing was just as true of Phil and Martha Harris, and Ned and Nellie Tyler, with the additional drawback that he'd have to make his way over three miles of prairie without fainting outright from hunger in order to ask the aid of either of his best friends.

In any event, first things first. And step number one was to get up. But it was so hard to do. His bed was seductively comfortable, and, despite the chill that his starved-out body manufactured for itself, warm. The dugout was as cold as the tomb, and as damp. The mere thought of dragging his long johns-clad form out from under those buffalo robes made him shiver harder than ever.

'Hell!' he thought; 'I'll just lie here 'til some of the kids—Nora and Gordon, surely!—give the alarm. Then either Phil or Ned will drive out here to see what's wrong, and—'

But the thought of his pupils sent a sudden danger signal crashing through his mind like a fireball in the night. He knew damned well that the children would swarm out into the prairie to play, which would have been perfectly all right except for one thing: the *first* game that would come to the minds of his supposedly and surely imperfectly reformed bullies to browbeat and threaten the younger and smaller children into joining them in, would be "Crack the Whip." They would choose that particular game, Ethan was sadly sure, *because* he had forbidden his pupils to play it at all. This prohibition had the wholehearted approval of all the parents, if not of the entire student body, since "Cracking the Whip" consisted of having a dozen or more boys and girls join hands, always with the smallest and lightest children at the tail end of the line, and then race across the prairie as fast as they could run. At a signal, secretly agreed to among themselves beforehand, the biggest and heaviest boys, notably Cy Curtiss, Jr., and his cronies Walter Thomas, Newton Purvis, and Tyler Burton, who always made up the beginning or head of the line, would stop dead, digging in their heels, with the inevitable result that the whole line of children, pivoting around this suddenly man-made axis, would whirl out and away with such terrific force that the small boy or girl on the end of the line would be torn free of the next child's clasp and sent hurtling bodily through the air to land as much as—at times— a dozen yards away.

Up to the day that Ethan had put a stop to it, the consequences of the game had been four sprained ankles, three dislocated wrists, and one broken leg. It was, of course, the broken leg that had forced Ethan to forbid the game. But, as he lay there now, weak and ill beneath his buffalo robes, it came to the young schoolmaster that in his absence there was nothing to prevent the game's being carried to such extremes as to end in some child's death through a broken neck, or what was to Ethan's mind even worse, in a lifelong paralysis caused by a fractured spine.

So now there was no help for it: he had to get up and go to the school no matter how Godawful he felt. Groaning, he forced himself from his bed.

As he hung there, waiting for another attack of dizziness to pass and hoping that it would, his head brushed against something light and dry, suspended from the ceiling of his dugout on a rawhide thong. Reaching up his bony hand, he caught the object, so dark in color as to be almost invisible in the gloom, and bringing it close to his eyes, saw that it was the breast of a prairie chicken, one of the two dozen he had smoked and dried, Indian fashion, as the Old Timer had taught him to, and hung up on buffalo skin strips, the universal substitute for manufactured twine on the frontier, to serve him as emergency rations.

Standing there, staring at it, Ethan threw back his head and laughed aloud. He had been starving to death for the last three days with the makings of at least two reasonably solid meals dangling from the ceiling in plain sight above his head. Only he had forgot that they were there. And when he had gazed in their direction, as he had to, innumerable times, his mind had been too far away, too busy with his problems and his plans to permit the optical centers of his brain to even identify what he was looking at.

Cheerfully labeling himself a windbroken, blind, and spavined fool— for he had the rare grace of being able to laugh at himself, which was one of the things that made him the likable young man he was—Ethan took down six of the smoked grouse breasts and, masticating slowly and carefully, ate five of them. The sixth was more than he could manage, so he hung it back up again. Thereafter, he felt much better. By the time he had washed and shaved, and got into his worn, wrinkled, and baggy suit, absolutely normal dress in the prairie states, where a crisply pressed one would have earned him the not exactly complimentary epithet of "Sharpie," he felt almost human again.

On his way to school he considered what he had better do—beyond driving into Abilene that evening and buying coffee, flour, salt, lard, and sugar, if it were available, as it occasionally was now that the KP's terminus was only twenty-three miles away, or molasses, if no sugar was to be had—to solve the problem of eating both enough and with sufficient frequency so that poor Anne wouldn't scream and faint at being embraced by a walking skeleton upon her arrival at Christmastime. Complicating his problem was a prudent desire to procure his rations without having to drive into Junction City and run the ever present risk of having his jaw fractured or his gut punched in again by some drunken and belligerent Irishman.

He wasn't ashamed of that prudence, because four years of war had amply demonstrated to everyone who knew him that it wasn't cowardice.

He wasn't afraid of the KP's bellicose Hibernian construction crews. In college, he had taken up boxing as a sport and had got to be good enough at it to have whipped any one of them right handily. But he couldn't whip twenty-five or fifty, which were what the odds usually were in Junction City nowadays. And to get himself beaten into bloody insensibility to prove how clinking brave he was seemed to him the act of a fool.

He decided to stop at Matthew Hendricks's place. Matt was an experienced farmer who had a spread about a mile out from Abilene and half a mile north of the school. There was a certain Machiavellian element in that decision. Sarah Hendricks, Matt's wife, was Gordon Lee's aunt and the sister of the gentle and highly cultured—for Kansas, anyhow—Sally Lee, whose early death had been caused, the majority of the townspeople believed, by Bart Lee's drunkenness and his improvident ways. Ethan knew, through Gordon, that his aunt had been delighted that he had taken her ex-brother-in-law down a peg. So, although he had never met Mrs. Hendricks, he was practically sure she'd be willing to sell him the dried or otherwise preserved vegetables he so badly needed, and put a reasonable price on them, too.

The next thing he thought of was the idea of going hunting this coming weekend and restocking his larder thereby with enough game to last him practically all winter. Which meant his best bet was to try to bring down a buffalo. Deer and elk had both existed in this region, but the coming of the wave of settlers in the preëmption days of the early and middle fifties had driven these wary animals so far north and west that he would have needed far more than a single weekend to reach the northwestern part of the state where—in sadly reduced numbers—they could still be found. The same thing was true of antelope. But in that winter of 1866–67, buffaloes still existed in large numbers. By then, of course, they were already being relentlessly hunted because every smart Easterner had to have a lap robe made of buffalo skins for his victoria or landau or barouche or gig, or whatever the fashionable open vehicle of the moment was, and more especially in the more northerly New England states, for his sleigh, as well as the ten thousand and one other articles that the leather goods industry, cashing in on what had suddenly become high fashion, soon realized could be made of the bisons' soft and spongey hides. Like everybody else at that time who had ever watched a herd of the great shaggy beasts take three full hours to pass a single spot, Ethan had no idea that, ten years later, they would be entirely gone from Kansas, and in twenty, practically extinct in the whole of North America.

So Ethan was sure he could find buffalo, and reasonably close to home at that. But now the question was: What would he shoot a buffalo with if he found him? Because he had already learned that buying that beautiful Winchester had been a mistake. Both the powder charge and bullets of the early model, .44-caliber, rimfire Winchester were far too light to bring down a beast as heavy and powerful as a buffalo. In fact, Ethan's original intention to buy a shotgun would have been, considering the small game he had to hunt in the region where he lived, by far the wiser choice. To kill jackrabbits, prairie chickens, and the few wild turkeys left by then with a rifle called for a marksmanship that only a few frontiersmen were capable of, and Eastern-bred Ethan Lovejoy—though he was good enough to hit the relatively stationary target that a turkey's head protruding through a hole cut in a wooden box provided and had proved it by winning the Thanksgiving turkey shoot—was definitely not among that few.

He considered for a long moment borrowing Phil Harris's double-barreled shotgun and laying in a supply of shells at the general store, but after reflection he rejected the idea. Even if he had almost unbelievable luck, he simply couldn't shoot enough small game to last him more than a week or two, while a buffalo, after he'd got the Old Timer in to help him smoke and dry the flesh, would see him through 'til spring planting time.

Then it came to him what to do. He'd have to follow a party of buffalo hunters and wait until they had shot out their stands, and their skinners had stripped the hides from the fallen animals. Then, after they'd gone, he'd help himself to as much buffalo meat as he needed. The hunters wouldn't give a damn. Except for a few tongues, or a hunk or two of meat off the hump, hacked out to provide themselves and their skinners with supper, they almost always simply left the huge carcasses to rot, a fact that drove the Plains Indians, who had lived upon the herds for hundreds of years, reverently and carefully killing no more than they needed for food and for the skins to make their teepees of, to an understandable blood madness.

It was already Friday, so, after having stayed after school long enough to run the cast of his abridged version of *Romeo and Juliet* through a rehearsal of the more important scenes, and noting with real relief that "Romeo" (Gordon Lee) and "Juliet" (Mary Sue Hollis) had definitely formed the custom of walking home from school together hand in hand, Ethan headed his oxen not southward toward his farm, but directly east toward Abilene.

As he did so, he called out to his pupils:

"All you kids who want to and can fit in, climb aboard. I'm driving into town . . ."

With whoops of joy, for any departure from the mind-numbing sameness of everyday prairie life was keenly welcomed by young and old alike, the youngsters scrambled into the bed of the big wagon. Cy Curtiss got into the seat beside Ethan. As they started off, Ethan noticed Nora, head bent and staring sadly at the ground, and keeping well apart from those children who hadn't been able to find space in the wagon, walking all by herself. That sight was too much for Ethan who, after all, was young, male, and human.

"Cy," he said to her brother, "hop down and let Nora ride. It's a long way into town, and, after all, she is a girl . . ."

"Aw, Prof!" Cy, Jr., who hadn't a chivalrous impulse to his name, protested.

But Nora had heard the exchange between Ethan and her brother.

"No, thank you, Professor Lovejoy," she said in her clear, sweet voice; "If you don't mind, I—I'd rather walk . . ."

"As you like, Nora," Ethan said, and flapped the reins across his oxen's backs. As he moved off with his wagonload of babbling, squealing, laughing children, he thought:

'Let Christmas come soon. O Lord, let it hurry up and get here!'

In Abilene he drove first to the Hotel D'Horse, as Luke Prevost, with a true Westerner's sense of humor, called his livery stable. There he made a deal with Luke: Prevost would stable and feed his oxen until Sunday night, and rent Ethan a team of mules for the same length of time but on a straight barter basis. Ethan promised to pay him one whole buffalo ham for both services. Luke accepted at once; actually, even at three cents a pound, the going rate for buffalo meat at the time, he was getting much the better of the bargain. Ethan realized this, but he didn't much care: to have to depend upon a yoke of oxen with their mile-and-a-half to two-mile-an-hour speed would make his meat gathering—he couldn't call it hunting, though in a way it was—expedition very nearly impossible.

After that, Ethan went to the general store and laid in the staples whose lack, caused by his own forgetfulness, had brought him to the brink of serious illness. That done, he sought out the Old Timer, which caused him no trouble at all, because the mountain man was in Cyrus Curtiss's saloon as usual, busily engaged in his semiperpetual attempt to cadge drinks off anybody who came into the place.

"C'mon, Old Timer," he said then; "You and I have a job to do . . ."

"What kind o' job, young Eth?" the Old Timer said; "Much as I hates to admit it, I be gittin old 'n more'n a mite stiff . . ."

Ethan told him.

"Heck, son!" the old man cackled happily, "thet thar ain't no job a-tall. Tha's purely a divertisement!"

In his wanderings the Old Timer, Ethan had found out, had spent two whole years in New Orleans. There he had been much impressed with the strange customs and stranger ways—to him!—of that city's still numerous French-Creoles. That fact of his personal history was, of course, the source of his pretense to having visited Paris and the reason he used an occasional French word like *divertissement.*

But as they came out into the ankle-deep mudhole and draft animal's cesspool that served Abilene as a main street, the Old Timer glared at Ethan a little scornfully.

"Hell, son," he said, "you doan mean t'tell me that you's aimin' to go out 'n butcher buffalo carcasses in *thet* outfit, d'you?"

Ethan looked down at himself. He had on his one good suit and although he had thought to bring along his broadax and his hunting knife for the expedition he proposed to engage in, it hadn't occurred to him to throw a change of clothes into the big wagon. Anything he wore, even his overalls and ragged hickory shirt, were sure to get ruined beyond repair by the bloody business of hacking a buffalo's carcass into manageable-size pieces and then loading those pieces into his wagon.

"Oh, Lord!" he groaned, "now I'm going to have drive all the way down to my place first, before we can even get started!"

"Naw, don't," the Old Timer said; "Le's stop by th Harrises 'n you kin borry some ol' wuk clos off'n Phil. You 'n him is 'bout the same size enyhow. . . . Say, you doan have thet thar tall stovepipe hat o' yourn in th wagon, do you?"

Ethan had long since given up wearing his tall silk hat except to church. It was too tempting a target for the mud and/or horse dung balls of some of his students. Ethan didn't blame them for this: in his own boyhood, tall hats had all too often provoked a hail of snowballs from both his twin and himself. But on Sunday it was safe to wear one; both Cy Curtiss and Mayor Tyler also did. On weekdays, like all the other men, Ethan wore the broad-brimmed Western slouch hat.

"No, of course not," he said; "Why, Old Timer?"

"Wuz talkin' to ol' No Nose th other day," the Old Timer said; " 'N thet thar Injun sho Lawd do purely admire thet lid o' yourn. Tol' me t'tell you he'd swap his youngest 'n prettiest squaw fur hit, you be willin' . . ."

"Lord God!" he said to the Old Timer; "You mean to tell me that old Indian would swap me his *wife* for that hat?"

"Naw—jes' *one* o' his wives. He's got six, y'know. 'N even ef White Antelope is the pruttiest 'n th youngest o' his squaws, she ain't worth as much as some o' th others. Got too much to learn yet—how to flesh 'n tan skins, porcupine quill embroidery, bead work, furst-class cookin', 'n all th million 'n one things a good squaw's got to know. 'Sides, she ain't even birthed him a papoose yet. Thet sly ol' bastid couldn't git more'n two hosses fur her, he wuz to trade her off to another Injun. But she *is* jes' th right age fur beddin'—'bout sixteen o' so, like yore li'l Nory. I wuz you, I'd shore Lawd mek thet swap . . ."

"But you're not me," Ethan said drily; "I mean to live in this community a good many years, Old Timer, so I'd just as soon not get labeled as a squawman from the outset. Tell Chief No Nose, no thanks, will you?"

"He gonna be plumb disappointed," the Old Timer sighed. "Funny thing, thet ol' Injun has taken quite a shine to you, young Eth—mainly 'cause th two o' you is got th same totem . . ."

"No Nose and I have the same totem? How the hell does he—or you —figure that?"

"Yore sniffer, young Eth. You done looked in a mirror enytime lately? Ever since thet bucket broke loose when you 'n me 'n Hank Atkins wuz diggin' yore well 'n took th tip right off yore nose, hit look jes' like hisn. Only 'twuz a Cheyenne what shortened his snoot fur him. Wit a tomahawk. Throwed hit from nigh onto thirty foot away. Enyhow, he calls you Young Cut Face-No Nose 'n swears thet you's a mighty brave warrior, countin' coup on Bart Lee wit nothin' in yore hands, while thet li'l blowhard wuz packin' two shootin' irons. Good thing, too. Be powerful Big Medicine to have ol' No Nose fur a friend, them Injuns go on th warpath, like they's sho to what wit them greedy bastids o' hide hunters killin' off th buffalo . . ."

"The trouble with that is you're probably right," Ethan said. "Now come on; I'd like to get close enough to one of the hide hunters' camps before it gets too far into night, and we still have to stop by Phil Harris's house so I can borrow some old clothes from him . . ."

They moved off down the street. But before they got to Phil's house, Ethan pulled up his team of four rented mules.

"Since when did we acquire a blacksmith's shop?" he asked.

"Las' week," the Old Timer said. "Stop a minute 'n say howdy to Will Trainer. He's our new blacksmith—'n a mighty fine fella young Will is . . ."

Ethan started to point out to the Old Timer that they really were pressed for time, but he thought the better of it. For if there ever were a man in a Western town it paid to know and even, if possible, to make friends with, that man was the local blacksmith. This was especially true, Ethan realized, in his own case. Since he had had to give up breaking his virgin acres because of the cold, Ethan had made half a dozen sketches for farm machinery, all of them considerable improvements over the Kirby Patent Harvester, or even the Self-Raker that had come into use just before the end of the War.

Ethan's determination to stay completely out of debt—a thing that, so far, almost none of the farmers in the wheat and corn lands of central Kansas had managed to do—was the reason he was planning to use his inventive turn of mind, and the high order of his skill as a carpenter, to build his own farm machinery himself. But to do that he needed to form a working partnership with two other men: a first-class blacksmith, to make the iron parts of the machines he'd already designed, and a patent attorney to make sure his idea wouldn't be stolen from him the minute the agents of some of the great farm machinery manufacturers already existing in Illinois got wind of it. Of the two partners he had to find, the blacksmith came first and was, at that stage of the shrewd young Yankee's plans, the more important.

And, of course, the smith in question had to be a first-class craftsman. In that regard, Ethan wasn't worried. Most Western blacksmiths were excellent general mechanics for the very simple reason that they had to be since the farmers called on them constantly not only to shoe their draft animals, but to repair anything made out of iron when it got broken, including the most intricate parts of the primitive farm machinery then in use.

As soon as he got down from the big wagon and entered the blacksmith's shop, Ethan realized that he had been exceptionally lucky. Will Trainer, a huge, muscular man with an enormous black beard covering his broad chest so that he looked exactly like the village blacksmith in the poem by Longfellow that Ethan had read before the War, was slowly and carefully assembling a farm wagon, the iron parts of which he had evidently made himself. At a glance, Ethan saw that his workmanship was superb; the finish of the simplest, least important fitting, including those that would go into places on the wagon where they wouldn't be seen anymore, was jewellike. That, Ethan knew, was the truest test of a craftsman. Most mechanics will work a piece that instantly meets the gaze of a prospective buyer to an acceptable appearance, qualitatively speaking; but only a true lover of his own art will grind and polish the components henceforth invisible to a state as closely approaching perfection as he can get them.

Looking at Will Trainer, meeting his steady gaze, Ethan realized that the big man had the calmest face, the most serene eyes, he'd ever seen in another human being. It was a characteristic that often went with unusual physical strength. 'Because big, strong men—especially when they're also handsome, as Trainer is—have so little to prove,' Ethan thought. He put out his hand to the blacksmith.

"Mr. Trainer," he said, "I'm Ethan Lovejoy. I just stopped by to make your acquaintance, though I'd like to have a good long talk with you when you can find the time. About a subject that ought to be of profit to us both, that is . . ."

"Now's as good a time as any, Professor," Will Trainer said, after having wiped his huge, grimy paw on his leather apron and taken Ethan's hand. "But first off, I got a couple o' young'uns—a boy 'n a girl—I'd like to enroll in yore school. Will a dollar a month per head suit you, sir?"

"I'm being paid by the City Council, so there's no charge at all," Ethan said. "But what I want to know from you, Mr. Trainer, is whether you can work from drawings. I mean make up an entirely new piece of machinery from some sketches I've drawn. Couple of ideas I've got for harvesters, threshers, separators, and the like, that ought to save me—and all the other farmers hereabouts—a heck of a lot of work, and increase our production to boot . . ."

"Got th drawings with you, sir?" Will Trainer said.

"No, I haven't. Thought I'd have to go into Junction City to find a blacksmith, so I left them at home today. I'll bring them by here Monday evening after school. You can work from drawings, can't you?"

"If they're good and clear, and have got the dimensions written on 'em, I can," Will Trainer said; "I can even work to scale, but I'd druther not. Means measuring each part of yore drawing 'n multiplying it up to size—o' reducing it as the case may be—'n that takes too blame long. Gimme clear sketches with point-to-point dimensions, and I'm yore man, Professor. I take it that yore ideas are new, so we won't have no patent lawyers breathing down th backs o' our necks?"

"New, and, I believe, original," Ethan said; "so, if my ideas prove workable, as I hope they will, I mean to have an attorney in from Atchison to file patent applications for me. Or rather, for us, because, if it turns out that my machines can do what I designed them for, I'd like you to consider coming in with me in a small manufactory as an equal partner. You'd run the factory, of course. I like inventing machinery and using it on the land, but manufacturing itself, no thank you!"

"Why not, Prof?" Will Trainer said.

"My father owns a shoe factory in Pittsfield, Massachusetts," Ethan said; "so I got a bellyful of factory management years ago. I invented two of the best machines in my father's place, but as a way of life, I much prefer the land. . . . Oh, heck, I'm wasting your time and my breath. Let me bring the drawings in, and then we'll talk . . ."

Will Trainer stared at Ethan Lovejoy. Studied him, really. Then, once again, his big hand shot out.

"You've got yourself a partner, Prof," he said.

"Look, Will, you're taking too big a chance. You haven't seen what I propose to do, so—"

"I ain't taking no chance at all," Will said quietly; "Your farm machinery will work, Prof. I know that, because I know *men*. Every honest-to-God first-class inventor I ever met—and I've done met quite a few, I kin tell you—wuz just like you. A little dreamy, a mite crazy—but, at bottom, smart. Smart and decent. Never knowed an inventor what was crooked—tha's th main reason most of 'em dies broke, 'cause they lets other fellas pick their brains 'n rob their ideas off 'em. Now tell me, how we gonna raise some working capital? Moving here from Junction City— that there town has done got too rough for a fella to raise a family in— took all my extra cash. 'N teaching school 'n farming ain't very likely to have made no John Jacob Astor outta you, Prof . . ."

"Well, there you've got a point, Will!" Ethan laughed. "But, if possible, I'd like to steer clear of borrowing. Let's make the machines between us, contributing labor and materials both, and then I'll use them on my place. In one good growing season with those machines to help me I should be able to make enough cash to get our little factory going. After that we ought to be able to keep going and build up our profits little by little. But no debts, Will. Debt is the curse of the prairie states. Everybody seems to be in hock to some Eastern banker . . ."

"Tha's purely th truth," Will said; " 'N you're dead, daggummed right on that point. Damned if I don't like yore way o' thinkin'! So, when you come in on Monday, come up t' th house, will you? This here old coyote will show you where it is. Meet th missus 'n th kids. Molly'll be pleased as punch to meet you. She's been after me for years to find some way to go up. But all I got is a strong back 'n weak brains—while with you, it's th other way around, ain't it? But hitched up together, we'll make one helluva team, Prof! I'm certain sure o' that!"

Ethan looked at the blacksmith, and in his own sober and cautious soul, hope blazed up, stood tall. Again he put out his hand to Will Trainer.

"So am I, Will; so am I," he said.

"Why, Gawdamn!" Phil Harris roared; "that there's a wonderful idea, Old Hoss! All them hide-peeling varmints ever do is to shuck th skins clean off the bulls 'n cows they've done gone 'n shot—'n leave th carcasses to the coyotes and th weather. Shore I've got some old duds you kin git into. 'N after that you kin burn 'em, 'cause they're so stiff with grease 'n dirt now, they kin stand up by themselves. Heck, I'm coming with y'all. I'll hitch up my team and—"

"Phil," the Old Timer said; "Don't. Come along with young Eth 'n me in the *same* wagon . . ."

Ethan and Phil both stared at the old man.

"Name o' God, Old Timer, why?" Phil said.

"Buffalo hunters is mighty peculiar folks," the Old Timer said gravely. "Now 'n ag'in you finds a decent fella 'mongst 'em, but hit's plumb downright rare. Mostly they's pukin' polecat puppies 'n a cross twixt a sidewinder 'n a turkey buzzard. Hafta be to do whut they does . . ."

"I don't follow you, Old Timer," Ethan said.

"Look young Eth, 'n you, too, Phil—reckon I done lived among redskins so long I thinks like a Injun. Put hit thisaway—the Great Spirit ain't ag'in hunting—'cause effen He wuz, howcome he done went 'n made so many critters whut's purely got to kill to stay alive? But them buffalo hunters, they's pure murderers, not hunters. They kills 'n kills 'n kills— 'n leaves the carcasses to rot. Heap o' times they don't even take the skin when their hired knife artists looks it over 'n finds out hits a li'l mangy, say. 'N because they's killers not hunters, miserable varmints without a noble bone in they bodies, you gotta handle 'em real careful . . ."

"You mean they'd object to our taking the meat from the buffalo they've killed and skinned?" Ethan asked.

"Naw—but they'd object t' *two* wagonloads o' fellas doin' it. One wagon, they'll say 'Aw, what th hell!' 'n pay hit no nevermind. But two —'n they'll get up on they hind legs 'n start growling jes' like that dawg in th cow barn. He couldn't eat hay worth a damn, but hit purely made th miserable critter mean mad 'n downright hateful to see them pore cows a-eatin' hit . . ."

"He's right, Eth," Phil said. "I've done met more'n a few buffalo hunters by now. 'N you know whut? Ain't never met even *one* whut was a regular Army man—either Cornfed o' Yank. They gits drunk 'n the truth comes out: deserters by th score. Bushwhackers, skulkers, renegades, robbers o' th dead on both sides . . ."

"What do you think we ought to do then, Phil?" Ethan said; "Give up our carcass butchering expedition altogether?"

"Nope. I vote we do a li'l skulkin' on our own. Wait, keepin' out of sight until they've shot out a stand—and peeled the bodies, too. Then they'll either move on, followin' the herd, or they'll go back to camp.

Either way they'll leave anywhere up to fifty fresh-killed buffalo that we kin hack enough meat off of to keep not only ourselves, and our families —my family, anyhow—but th whole damn town o' Abilene eatin' good clear through 'til spring . . ."

Ethan gave a little shudder of disgust.

"Why don't we just shoot ourselves a buffalo or two, and not have to be obliged to the bastards?" he said.

"Number one, we ain't got the guns what can do it," Phil said. "A rifle like your Winchester, or my Spencer, will only tickle a buffalo 'n make him laugh. Or git him mad enough to charge us. 'N since a forty-four rimfire won't stop a chargin' bull, we'd most likely wind up dead. Messed-up dead at that. Besides which, we just ain't equipped to skin a buffalo out. 'Twould take us all night, 'n even then we'd make an awful hash outta th proceedings. . . ."

As he was talking, Martha came into the room and stood there listening very quietly. She was great with child by then, although the little newcomer wasn't expected until late in February or early March according to Phil's somewhat imprecise reckonings. She looked very weak and tired, and more than a little sad, Ethan thought. But when Phil told her what they proposed to do, she cheered up at once.

"Phil," she said; "y'all had better take along a skillet 'n a coffeepot. Flapjack flour, too, jes' in case y'all don't even find no buffalo—"

"You see?" Phil groaned; "that's a woman for you, Old Hoss! Always so cheerful 'n hopeful!"

But they found the herds all right, though they had to go well west and north of Salina into the beginnings of the Smokey Hills to do it.

Lying on his belly between Phil and the Old Timer atop a low hill, Ethan watched the buffalo hunters in the Saline River's broad valley down below. There were only two of them, but each hunter was accompanied by three skinners, one of whom also served as driver of the huge wagons drawn by a team of four big, husky mules that the hunters and skinners used to haul the piles of bloody hides back to camp. Ethan could hear the booming of the big Sharps breechloaders, see the clouds of white smoke, shot through with sudden tongues of orange flame that burst from their muzzles each time the hunters fired. One of them was using a shooting stick—a sort of tall iron fork to rest the muzzle of his rifle on—and was shooting from a standing position. The other lay on his back on the ground and cradled the barrel of his Sharps Big Fifty between his own two feet to steady it as he pulled the trigger. They were astonishing marksmen. Every time they blasted off a round, a buffalo bucked, snorted, plunged, crashed to earth.

"They's doin' hit right," the Old Timer whispered; "Shootin' 'em through th lights—what you greeners call they lungs. Shoot a bull buffalo through th heart 'n he'll run two miles o' more afore he draps down daid. But put one o' them heavy balls through his lights 'n his own blood drowns him in half a minute. Them fellas is experts, all right. No damn offhand shootin' for them—a buffalo gun is too daggummed heavy for that. Even thet thar dude wit th shootin' stick is bein' a sight too fancy fur my money. Thet other fella lyin' flat on his ass is gonna git twicet as many . . ."

"But—but—" Ethan said wonderingly; "Why doesn't that herd stampede? Jesus! I make it a full three minutes between shots—and there're at least ten buffaloes already down—and yet the rest of them go right on grazing as though nothing were happening!"

"Buffaloes," the Old Timer said, "is jes' about th dumbest, stupidest critter they is. Injuns done been huntin' 'em over a thousand years, I reckon, so they finally done learned to haul ass when they gits a whiff o' a redskin's scent. But a white man's smell doan mean a damn thing to 'em. You could walk up to one 'n pat him on his tail—doan recommend *nobody* playin' round wit th front end o' a buffalo, nosireebobtail!—'n still he wouldn't spook. 'N th noise o' that thar artillery likely 'pears to be comin' from too far away for them pore dumb beasties to pay hit no neveryou-mind . . ."

That sickening slaughter went on and on. Ethan, who had never enjoyed hunting, for to him, killing a noble animal or a beautiful flying creature for mere sport had always seemed an obscenity if not an actual sickness, was losing what little appetite he might have had for buffalo steaks by the minute. He had come to accept the idea that hunting was a legitimate way to obtain the food a man needed to stay alive. But this wanton, brutal mass slaughter, this destruction of the very basis of the Plains Indians' way of life to fill an artificial, commercially created need —one that could more easily have been satisfied by articles woven of wool, or made from the hides of domestic animals constantly being replaced through breeding—struck him as unpardonable.

After each three shots, the hunters cleaned their rifles by thrusting a brush, wet with water from their canteens, down the long, heavy barrels.

"A Fisher brush," Phil explained, "made out o' rubber washers 'n hawg bristles. Don't do that, 'n a charge of black powder as heavy as a big Sharps uses will foul th inside o' them barrels up so that they'll bust in yore face before you kin get off five rounds, sure as old hell . . ."

"Not in *my* face," Ethan said grimly; "Those long-distance butchers are curing me of what little desire I ever had to go hunting. Lord God, what a way to make a living!"

"We wuz—soldiers, Old Hoss," Phil pointed out to him, " 'n th half-starved, louse-infested critters we got paid fur shootin' wasn't even good fur eatin' . . ."

"True. And I plan to be a conscientious objector if another such piece of criminal stupidity breaks out in my lifetime," Ethan said. "Good Lord! Why *won't* that herd stampede? Those butchers keep creeping up on the poor beasts, closer and closer and still—"

"Them fellas is smart," the Old Timer said. "Effen you'll pay some 'tention, young Eth, you'll see that they always shoots *next* th bull o' th cow what's lifted its haid 'n is peerin' round kinda oneasy-like. Thet means thet particular buffalo has caught the blood scent 'n is gittin' set to bellow out th alarm. But they won't be able to keep hit up much longer, 'cause effen they moves in eny closer than they is right now, the noise them cannons o' theirs meks is gonna spook thet herd . . ."

The Old Timer was right. Out of their sick bloodlust and their greed, the hunters finally moved in too close. A big bull raised his head at the sound of the booming guns, snorted, pawed the earth, and was off, tearing across the low, rolling hills at express train speeds. Much to Ethan's relief, the whole herd followed him. Ethan started to stand up, but Phil laid a cautioning hand on his arm.

"Wait," Phil said; "we got to let them skin them beasties out 'n leave before we can carve ourselves some mighty good winter eatin's . . ."

"Which means we'll be here all night," Ethan said; "there must be at least twenty-five dead buffaloes down there . . ."

"No, we won't," Phil said. "A good skinner can peel fifty buffaloes a day all by hisself, 'n there're *six* skinners down there. We won't have to wait more than an hour—hour 'n a half; you'll see . . ."

The way those skinners worked, Ethan realized that Phil's estimation was conservative, if anything. They swarmed all over the fallen buffalo, ripping the hide down the belly from throat to tail, then down the inside of each leg, and around the tops of the hooves. The head, they didn't touch; they simply ringed the neck with deep cuts. After that, they yanked the hide back for about a foot or two, and tied a rope about the resulting neck flap. Then the drivers brought up the mule teams, unhitched from the wagons, and tied the other end of the rope to the team's harness. A volley of whip cracks that sounded like revolver fire, and the mules dug in their hooves, straining, straining. In about one minute, and sometimes even less, the hide was torn free by main force from the fallen buffalo. The total elapsed time, Ethan estimated, from the moment the skinner began his fancy knife work until the mule team dragged the bloody skin off the dead bull or cow was about ten minutes to a quarter of an hour.

The skinners left the hides where they lay, next to the flayed carcasses of the buffaloes, until they had finished skinning all the dead animals. Then, rehitching the mules to the wagons, they drove about the rolling, hilly ground, loading the skins onto the flatbeds of the vehicles. Ethan was surprised to note that it took four skinners, one on each corner, to heave the wet and bloody hides up into the wagons.

"A green hide," the Old Timer explained, "weighs anywhar from sixty to a hundred pounds, 'n 'sides, they wants to stack 'em nice 'n flat. Thet's why hit teks four fellas to load. After thet, they'll haul 'em back to camp 'n stake 'em out to dry. Teks about five days to do hit, but hit's worth hit, 'cause a flint hide only weighs 'bout thirty pounds . . ."

"A *flint* hide?" Ethan said.

"'Cause thet's how hard they gits, once dry. Have patience, young Eth. 'Twon't be long now . . ."

After the buffalo hunters and their skinners had gone, taking with them—besides the skins, of course—nothing more than three or four tongues and some thick slices of meat off the humps of a couple of the buffaloes, leaving the huge carcasses to rot, as usual, the Old Timer, Phil, and Ethan, using their axes and hunting knives, began to butcher as many buffalo carcasses as they thought Ethan's wagon, with his rented team of four mules, could haul back to Abilene. Phil guessed that they could bring back six, if they hacked them up into manageable-size pieces, not including, of course, the huge, unskinned heads or the forelegs, which, in the face of such a surplus as they had, were judged too stringy and tough to bother with. But the Old Timer, wise in the ways of mules, thought that five would be all they dared load on; and Ethan—not because he knew anything about mules, but because he didn't want to risk laming one or more of Luke Prevost's animals—agreed with him. Phil argued a while, then gave in, good-naturedly enough.

It was hard, bloody work, but Ethan, out of pride, bore it well. Finally they had it done, and the wagon loaded. Thereafter, since night had fallen by then, they sat down to a supper cooked over their campfire that was something of a royal feast.

The main dish was buffalo tongues, cut out through the lower jaw and roasted over the fire, and thick red slices off the hump, cooked the same way. But even so, Ethan wondered how a man as toothless as the Old Timer was would be able to manage meat as tough as any part of a buffalo was. He soon learned, to his sorrow.

The Old Timer plunged his hunting knife into the nearest carcass and came out with the buffalo's liver and his gall bladder. Then, sprinkling the gall from the gall bladder all over the liver, he proceeded to eat it—raw. After that, he went back to the fallen beast and dragged a yard or two of guts out of it, telling Ethan that they were called the *boudin,* as well as several huge chunks of back fat, announcing cheerfully:

"This heah's th *depouille,* young Eth—o' Injun bread—'cause that's whut them redskins uses hit fur. Mighty good. Wanna try some?"

"God, no!" Ethan shuddered.

"Doan know whut you's missin, son," the mountain man said. Then, after singeing the guts a little in the fire, he ate them without bothering to clean them first, wolfing down the green, slimy masses of the half-digested food inside those guts along with the buffalo tripes themselves.

"Lord Jesus!" Ethan said.

"Hell, son, the chyme inside th *boudin* is whut gives buffalo guts sich a fine flavor," the old mountain man cackled happily.

Then, after having ruined Ethan's all but nonexistent appetite for well past his coming Christmas supper with Anne, the Old Timer wrapped himself in his buffalo robes, lay down by the campfire and went blissfully off to sleep.

They had almost reached Salina by midmorning on Sunday, when they stopped to let the team drink their fill in the waters of the Saline River, which, despite its name, was reasonably fresh and sweet. About two dozen yards from that part of the bank where they'd pulled up the mules, they could make out what seemed to be a tumbledown log cabin, absolutely the poorest example of that primitive structure that Ethan had ever seen. And while they were watering the mules and eating some cold slices of buffalo tongue, a tall Black came out of the cabin and walked slowly up to the wagon.

Ethan wasn't surprised to see a Negro in Kansas because Phil had told him that, according to the census of 1865, there were twelve thousand five hundred and twenty-seven Blacks in the state. In fact, they had made up two of the state's five regiments and had fought with considerable bravery in the War.

But now this one was staring at all that buffalo meat with a mournful expression on his lean black face.

"Cap'ns," he said then, his very tone revealing how little hope of receiving an affirmative answer he had, "could y'all spare me one o' them buffalo hams? I come to wuk on y'alls places fur long a time as y'all wants to sot fur hit's price . . ."

"Why, hell no, nigger!" the Old Timer began. "You doan think we done gone 'n put ourselves t' th trouble of huntin' buffalo jes' to feed the meat to a bunch o' coons, d'you?"

"Shut up, Old Timer," Ethan said mildly; then, addressing himself to the Black: "You've got a family, friend?"

"Fo' kids. 'Nother one on th way, cap'n. 'N they's cryin' from hongry, suh. Didn't have no money fo' seed. Planted whut corn I could wit a hoe, my woman helpin' me; but all we'uns could raise done run clean out, now. One o' them hams see we'uns through 'til spring, cap'n—slicin' hit thin, 'n not eatin' too blamed frequent . . ."

"Take one, then," Ethan said. He felt Phil's disapproving gaze upon him. Kansas was a Free State, had joined the Union, fought against the Confederacy; but race prejudice was one of the iron facts of American life, Ethan realized. He said:

"It's mine, Phil. You and the Old Timer can deduct it from my share when we get back to town and divide up . . ."

" 'S all right, Old Hoss," Phil said, and Ethan could see that he was ashamed of his involuntary reaction.

"What's your name?" Ethan asked the Black.

"Randal Otis, suh; but folks most in general calls me Randy . . ."

"All right, Randy, take your pick," Ethan said.

"Thank yuh mighty kindly, suh," Randy said; "How many days o' weeks o' wuk you gonna charge me fur hit?"

"Not one," Ethan said; "Call it a Christmas present, Randy. But tell me something: is this land you're trying to farm yours?"

"Nossuh, hit ain't," Randy said sadly. "Hit oughta be, 'cause I'se a veteran, suh. I fit in that there War, jes' like you white folks. Second Kansas Cullud Regiment. Lost my onliest brother in hit, too. He wuz wounded 'n taken prisoner long wit eight other cullud soldier boys in that battle in front o' th Saline River in Arkansas. Th twenty-ninth o' April o' 'sixty-four that wuz, cap'n. We won that battle, took a whole Reb artillery battery wit a bayonet charge, tho hit cost us eighty dead to do hit. But them damn Rebs wuz pressin' us so hard that th next day we had to leave our wounded 'n retreat to Little Rock. 'N jes' as soon as we'uns pulled out—us 'n six mo' white Kansas regiments, that wuz—a Texas white man walked into that Reb field hospital jes' outside Princeton, Arkansas, 'n saw them nine po' wounded niggers lyin' there. Hauled out he sidearm 'n kilt all nine o' 'em, suh—daid. Took his own sweet time. Reloaded he six-gun to kill th las' three—my po' brother, Rad, 'mongst 'em. So I reckons I'se entitled to some land. Only I ain't got no fo'teen dollars fur filin' no claim. 'N 'sides, this heah hilly country ain't worth a damn fur farmin' nohows . . ."

Ethan stood there. He was a little ashamed of the idea that came to him then, because extracting a profit from what should have been disinterested charity struck him as being more than a little shabby, somehow. But the profit was at least mutual, because it would put food in this black family's stomachs—and insure that his whole three hundred twenty acres would be broken to the plow within the coming year of 1867.

"Randy," he said slowly, "my name is Ethan Lovejoy. I have a farm three miles south of Abilene. When the weather breaks—in February or March—you come down there, and bring your family. I'll assign you forty acres to feed your wife, your children, and yourself. Buy you a mule for your plowing. You'll work for me—not for wages, for I haven't any cash money to speak of, either—but on the basis of sharing the crops you help me sow, cultivate, and harvest. That way, nobody can put you off my place, because I won't let them. While up here, anybody can show up with a bona fide claim title, filed at the Land Office in Junction City, and kick you the heck off this land as a squatter, which legally is all you are. On the other hand, you come to work for—and *with*—me, and in a year or two you'll maybe have the cash to file a claim of your own. C'mon, Randy, what do you say?"

Hope wasn't an emotion that any Black was accustomed to entertaining anywhere in the United States in the 1860s. But looking into Ethan Lovejoy's calm, serious face, recognizing the absolute honesty, probity, even honor in those pale blue eyes, Randal Otis entertained it then, knowing that he could.

"I says done, suh! 'N heahs my hand on hit!" he said, fervor shaking his voice.

They shook hands, gripping hard.

9

When Anne Jeffreys stepped down off that train car in Junction City into Ethan's waiting arms, she said—after he finally gave her a chance to say anything at all—exactly what he had predicted to Ned and Nellie Tyler she was going to at the sight of him, in precisely the tone of appalled shock he'd also forseen, though—and this was his sole failure—not in the order that he had prophesied, for she proceeded from the general to the particular, and not the other way around as he had been sure she would.

"Ohhhh, Ethan!" she gasped; "How *awful* you look! You're so thin! You've been sick! Don't lie to me. Tell me the truth. You *have* been ill, haven't you?"

Ethan smiled. And his smile was one of real happiness, of almost blissful satisfaction, because the way Anne looked to him was anything but a disappointment. In fact, she was an almost total contradiction of all his gloomy forebodings—inspired, of course, unconsciously, even subconsciously by his growing, though valiantly resisted fondness for little Nora Curtiss—that she'd turn out to be the plain, mousey little creature he'd tried, ever since her abrupt departure, to convince himself she wasn't, and that, in sober truth, she was.

Only Ethan couldn't see that sober truth at the moment. His heart, racing at a breakneck gallop, was at least three furlongs ahead of his poor, slow-trotting head. And all the mindless little glands that make the continuation of the race a certainty by effortlessly overruling, negating, or plain annihilating human intelligence, were pouring their subtle poisons into his blood, so that his usually quite acute critical faculty was the first victim of what he—true romantic, truer Victorian!—would have been horrified to recognize as merely the age-old procreative urge.

'Why,' he thought; 'She has become—beautiful! Who would have ever believed—'

"Eeeeethaaaan!" Anne gasped, her dainty shoe tip making a drumroll on the train platform's rough hewn planking. "Who—cut up your face like that? And what—carnivorous little *female* canine bit the tip entirely off your nose?"

Ethan's grin broadened.

"Can't say I remember, Annie, me darlin'," he quipped. "All the girls hereabouts swear I'm sweet enough to eat, so which one it was who actually tried a little plain and fancy cannibalism, I can't quite call to mind . . ."

"Ethan Lovejoy!" Anne began; but he stopped her with a lifted hand.

"Love of my life," he chuckled; "let's postpone the battle until later, when it's closer to the appropriate time for making up. Who knows, with any luck, we might even have a moon tonight. So will you stop being— or at least looking—so adorably furious, and meet my friends, the Tylers? Ned, here, is mayor of Abilene, while Nellie actually runs it, starting with *him,* of course. . . ."

"Howdy, Anne, honey," Ned said, and put out his big paw to her. "I hafta admit right now that this here longtall Yankee walking encyclopedia ain't never forgot his bumbershoot before going out in no rainstorm. Lord, but you kin pick 'em, Eth!"

"*Them,* plural," Anne said with wicked calm. "The point's—interesting, Mayor. I trust you'll be able to supply me with a list?"

"I could," Ned chuckled; "but I'll be daggummed if I'm going to, honey! As mayor o' Abilene, I'm interested in keepin' th peace in my town. 'N startin' two dozen screechin' catfights 'n hairpullin' contests jes' ain't th way to do it, 'pears to me!"

"Two dozen?" Anne retorted. "So now I know what I'm up against. Instead of my dainty little lady's pistol, it seems I should have brought along a Gatling gun!"

"Howdy, Anne!" Nellie Tyler laughed; "You're all wool 'n a yard wide, ain't you? I purely do admire a female critter with spunk, 'n you've got more than yore share. Come here 'n let me buss you one. Martha Harris told me you was one great li'l gal; 'n I see now she was right!"

She bent and kissed Anne, straightened up, holding the younger, and much, much smaller and shorter woman by her shoulders.

"You ain't pretty," she said candidly; "but that don't make no nevermind. You're pert 'n perky enough to drive any pants-wearin' critter right outta his pore thick haid. 'N you're plumb a fashion plate, ain't you? Purely a page from *Godey's Ladies Book!* Yore clothes are a marvel, honey. Gonna have every young female critter in town turnin' jade green 'n foamin' at th mouth!"

It was this simple circumstance that had given Ethan—poor backward, lovelorn male!—the impression that Anne had become beautiful.

She was exactly the sort of thin, pale, insignificant-looking young woman who wear clothes supremely well, a fact that she was perfectly aware of. She had saved a considerable part of her salary and used those savings to buy a complete and modish wardrobe to wear during her visit. The sad truth was she had deliberately misled Ethan as to the exact date that her holidays would begin, thus robbing him of three whole days of her company. She had spent those three days in St. Louis, engaging in a shopping spree. That the results had been worth the trouble she was now completely sure. She could tell that from the warmth of Ethan's gaze, the discernible joy that glowed in his eyes every time he looked at her.

It was a heady feeling; but what—oh, what!—had happened to his nose, his face? Those scars didn't seem to her to be the products of an accident. Rather, a man who had engaged in a terrible fight might get marked up that way. And what did men ever fight over except money—and women?

"Anne," Ethan said then, staring at her with real concern; "what's wrong, my dearest?"

"Your—your face," she whispered; "Oh, no! It's not—repugnant. Rather—dashing, in fact. Makes you look like some sort of romantic buccaneer. Only—I keep wondering *who* cut you up like that. And—why?"

"A man," he said gravely. "Windy little polecat who doesn't come up to my chin. And he didn't cut me; he shot me—"

"Oh, my God!" Anne said.

"There wasn't anything to it. He was drunk and his hands were shaking so that he oughtn't to have been able to hit the side of a bright red barn at ten feet. Only, as luck would have it, he didn't quite miss. Bullet plowed along my face and made this mess. Look, Anne, tell me the truth. It isn't going to bother you, is it?"

"It—no," she murmured; "*Why* he did it, might."

"Well," Ethan said with sardonic humor; "the little hotshot is a widower, and he hasn't a daughter to his name, which ought to relieve your mind. So let's drop this whole somewhat less than inspiring subject, shall we?"

"I will not!" Anne said; "You tell me *all* about it, Ethan!"

With a sigh, Ethan did, making of the whole opening day attempt at school demolition a masterpiece of understatement, playing down his part in it to an almost ridiculously unimportant level—and, of course, not mentioning Nora Curtiss's stellar role in the whole absurd near tragicomedy at all. "What it turned on really, my dear," he said finally, "is the fact that Bart Lee is a Southerner, an ex-rebel, and a pro-slavery man. And I—every time I open my mouth—brand myself as a Yankee.' 'N no gol-durned damyankee is a-gonna whup *mah* young'un!' Oh, heck, Anne, you know how it goes . . ."

"I suppose I do, come to think of it. Southerners can be awfully tiresome, can't they? So, after—as I gather from all the things you *haven't* said—you took his revolver from him—"

"His *two* shootin' irons, Anne," Ned chuckled; "that li'l bastid— 'scuse me, honey!—that li'l skunk came to the schoolhouse loaded for bear that morning . . ."

"Oh, Ethan!" Anne wailed.

"It really wasn't anything, dearest," Ethan sighed. "Please, let's drop the whole thing, shall we?"

"No. After you'd knocked this Lee person out, and disarmed him, I take it he revived and bit off the end of your nose? Or was it—his sister? You've said his wife was dead and he had no daughter, but what about—"

"His sister? Doesn't have one either. Nor any female relatives of any sort. And he didn't chew off my snoot. You can rest assured of that . . ."

"Now that there mangled sniffer of th Prof's is a thing that purely intrigues me, Anne, baby," Nellie Tyler said; " 'N it's had my femeenine curiosity exercised for quite a spell back. 'Cause I happen to know from my sister's young'uns that when Prof Lovejoy showed up to teach school that first day, he *already* had that chewed-off nose—so it dates back to before Bart Lee tried to let some daylight through him for tanning Gordon's hide. 'N granted the fact that *all* his girl students are head over heels in love with him, plus the two o' three spinsters in town who haven't managed to catch themselves husbands yet, not to mention quite a few married women whose names I'll keep to myself for prudence's sweet sake, I'll admit I'd purely admire to find out what li'l dilly it was who put to positive proof th question o' whether he tastes as good as he looks! C'mon, Prof, 'fess up. It wasn't li'l Nora Curtiss, was it?"

"And *who*, may I ask, is Nora Curtiss?" Anne demanded, trying unsuccessfully to keep the frost and flint out of her voice.

"My best girl student," Ethan said. "Heck, she's my best student of either sex. And the prettiest. But she didn't bite the end off my nose. She's much too shy—worse luck! If she'd wanted to dine off my carcass, when she'd finished with my snoot, I'd have served her up my ear—on a silver platter, at that . . ."

"You know, Ethan, dearest," Anne observed; "I'm not all that sure you're really joking now . . ."

"Me, neither!" Nellie laughed. "All right, Prof; if it wasn't little Nora, who was it?"

"Well now," Ethan drawled; "I don't exactly remember, but I kind of think it must have been White Antelope . . ."

"White Antelope?" Anne gasped; "An *Indian* girl?"

"Yep. Old No Nose's youngest squaw. Chief No Nose saw me wearing my stovepipe hat to church one Sunday, and offered to swap me White Antelope for it. So I told him to bring her over because I wasn't even starting to buy a pig in a poke; and, when he did, I saw how cute she was, so I handed him over my lid, and he passed that little doe-child over to me. Was she ever wild! Biting the tip off my nose was just her way of demonstrating her enthusiasm for the proceedings, or her tender love and affection for me, or—"

"Ethan Lovejoy!" Anne said severely; "That's quite enough of outrageous lies, Western-style! Come on, tell me: What *did* happen to your nose?"

"The truth is as dull as dishwater," Ethan sighed. "The Old Timer, or Hank Atkins, or both of them, dropped a bucketful of dirt on it . . ."

"A bucket o' dirt?" Ned said. "Unlike yore sweet li'l promised here, I'm perfectly willing to believe that yarn about White Antelope, 'cause I've done seen that pretty redskin filly; but a bucket o' dirt is a mite farfetched, 'pears to me . . ."

"No, it isn't," Ethan said. Then he explained the well digging accident: the fraying of the rope, the heavy bucket—full of the earth he had shoveled up from the well's bottom—crashing murderously down, how narrow his escape had been. . . .

"You wuz plumb lucky," Ned sighed.

"I was," Ethan said solemnly, but his pale eyes were alight with mischief, for he had suddenly remembered the Old Timer's wry comment on that occasion; "In fact, I was lucky twice. For not only did that damned bucket take the tip off my nose, all the buttons off my shirt, and a strip of hide off my chest, but it also tore my big cavalryman's brass buckle right off the front of my belt. And it was that buckle that saved me from the fate worse than death . . ."

"The fate worse than death?" Anne began uncomprehendingly. Then she clapped both hands to cheeks gone fiery red. "Why, Ethan Lovejoy!" she gasped.

"Yep," Ethan chuckled; "hadn't been for that buckle, you'd have very likely been a wife in name only, Annie, me darlin'. And Clan Lovejoy would have ceased to exist upon my departure for a better world. Gloomy thought, isn't it?"

"It is. And also—indecent," Anne said primly. "Haven't you any respect for me at all, Ethan Lovejoy?"

"No'm; nary a bit. I only respect women I don't love," Ethan said.

All in all, Anne's visit to Abilene during the Christmas holidays was a great success. She and Ethan were wined and dined by all the town's leading lights. That said prominent citizens, in the overwhelming majority of the cases, really couldn't afford to entertain anybody detracted not at all from Anne's pleasure at this convincingly sincere evidence of how greatly her fiancé was respected, even admired in the township and the county, because she was completely unaware how dreadfully poor most prairie dwellers were. Ethan, who knew very well that except for the Curtisses, every family in town hovered forever on the borderline of actual want, kept his mouth shut about this sad fact—although he was badly troubled by it—and for two reasons: he didn't want to spoil Anne's joy at the warm hospitality they were extended almost everywhere; and he was aware that the people who invited them to dine would have been seriously offended had he so much as attempted to refuse their invitations. More, given the prickly nature of Western pride, the people least able to afford entertaining them would have been precisely the ones most offended by any refusal on his part to accept.

He was, however, not at all surprised that they were *not* invited to dine at saloonkeeper Cyrus Curtiss's neat frame house—at that date the only such imposing structure in a town of log cabins and sod houses, and built of lumber brought all the way from well-wooded Missouri by train to Junction City and by freight wagon from there to Abilene—because he was absolutely sure that Nora must have objected with quiet and stubborn violence to welcoming in the home that she, herself, practically ran, young as she was, with, of course, the able assistance of a half-breed woman from the highly civilized Wyandot tribe, the female stranger who, in her wildly romantic view, had practically wrecked her life. Otherwise, Ethan was certain, Cy Curtiss, whom he had no hesitation about listing among his friends, would have gladly extended such an invitation. But for all her—

seemingly!—shy and gentle ways, Nora had considerable force of character. And the facts that she was well behaved, an excellent student, a dutiful daughter, and that her virtue wasn't seriously questioned by even the town's worst gossips, made it difficult—especially when the circumstance that her father literally adored her was added to the rest—for Cy to gainsay her in a matter that was causing her so much visible, terrible pain.

Nor was Ethan anything more than relieved that no invitation came from his neighbors, the Bellamys. Living in a dugout himself, he shrewdly guessed that Cora was ashamed for Anne to see the squalor and the filth in which they lived. But for that, the Bellamys, too, would have surely had them in to dine, for, strangely enough, they seemed to have plenty of money. It wasn't until almost a year later that Ethan learned the source of it: an inveterate gambler—and an exceptionally unskillful one—Tom had bet a full one hundred dollars on a twenty-five-to-one longshot in a horse race in Chicago. The favorite took a header; the horses seeded to place and show piled into him. Within seconds, the track was a mound of thrashing, screaming, fallen horseflesh, with not a few unfortunate jockeys crushed beneath the pile. Only Tom's choice and three other horses escaped. And the jockeys of the other three, appalled by the carnage, pulled up their mounts. The jockey of the ancient, wheezing rack of bones Tom Bellamy had bet on, didn't. That living disgrace to the equine species came in all alone, and Tom was in twenty-five hundred dollars. Which Cora, who had accompanied him to the track that day, for want of something better to do, promptly confiscated with the happy result that, a full year after that memorable day, they still had over two thousand left, so shrewdly had Cora managed it.

In fact, as the holidays passed, Ethan was beginning to allow himself to hope that he'd be able to put Anne on the train for her return trip to Omaha without any direct confrontation having taken place between her and Nora Curtiss at all. To even permit a hope that impossibly vain to so much as enter his head was purely tempting fate. So, naturally, he paid for it.

By then they had dined—or had at least taken "coffee 'n cake"—with practically every family in town. The last two occasions had been especially notable ones, for they had sat down to an absolutely stupendous dinner that included everything from roast turkey stuffed with chestnuts to pumpkin pie—made, as always on the frontier in the winter season, with dried pumpkins so that the result left a great deal to be desired—cooked by Molly Trainer, blacksmith Will Trainer's plump and merry Irish wife. Ethan had brought along the drawings for his proposed harvester-binder, which, instead of sweeping the cut grain off the platform with an articulated rake—hence the name "self-raker" given to this widely used type of machine—delivered the harvested wheat, by means of a series of slatted canvas aprons attached to the bull wheel, to a platform on the machine itself, beside the driver and opposite the slow-turning slatlike reel—oddly resembling the paddlewheel of a river steamboat—which did the actual reaping after the multiple scissors mower had cut the stalks.

"Don't see th sense o' that, Prof," Will Trainer said.

"Look at it, Will!" Ethan said, his voice vibrant with the enthusiasm that all things mechanical always awoke in him; "we put a little table *here.* Right here beside the driver and two men *riding along*—under this canvas awning, see? Then the two riders bind—while a kid drives—and one man following the machine on foot shocks the bound sheaves immediately, instead of waiting until the cutting and the binding of the loose gavels into sheaves are over, and having all hands pitch in to shock it late in the evening the way it's done now. So we won't have eight or ten borrowed or hired hands scrambling along behind the harvester, binding 'on station' in the fields, and being 'doubled,' as you call it out here, when the self-raking harvester finishes cutting a row before they bind up the gavels under that Lordawful prairie sun. The awning will keep the sun off the binders, and the reaping reel will stir up quite a breeze even on the hottest day—"

"So you've got yoreself two happy 'n comfortable hands, riding along like they was goin' to church," Will chuckled; "but since the object of all this here pretty machinery is to harvest yore wheat, oats, rye, o' suchlike, not to make yore hands fat 'n lazy, I don't see—"

"I know you don't. But binding on the machine itself, and shocking at once, will be so much faster that I'm betting that my three binders— and shockers, because, of course, the three of them will have to take turns at the two chores during the day or else the briars and the rust spores will leave their hands looking like chopped meat—should be able to outdo a whole crew of harvest hands afoot. I estimate that, pulled by two *good* horses, like those Morgan-Percheron crosses they're breeding back in Missouri right now, my rig will harvest—completely harvest, Will!—a good *ten* acres every day . . ."

Will Trainer studied the drawing. As he did so, Anne got up from where she sat beside Molly, giving the blacksmith's wife back their youngest child, whom she had been holding with evident maternal longing in her arms, and looked over Will's shoulder at Ethan's neatly inked-in brainchild, her small, square face serious and intent.

"D'you understand what you're looking at, Annie, me darlin'?" Ethan teased her solemnly.

"Of course," Anne said sharply. "At the risk of repeating myself, the wearing of skirts is no proof of idiocy, nor of pants, of high intelligence. Rather the other way around, most of the time, it seems to me . . ."

"Prove it!" Ethan said.

"Well, this sort of gang clippers cuts the grain, doesn't it? And then this paddlewheel knocks the cut stalks into these canvas bags. But, since they're attached to this spiked wheel—"

"The bull wheel," Will Trainer put in; "Go on, ma'am—I mean miss—"

"Since they're attached to the bull wheel at three places each, they can't twist. Therefore, as they get to the top of it, revolving along with it, they're upside down, so the grain falls out of them by its own weight onto this platform, or table. Am I right, Mr. Brilliant Inventor Lovejoy?"

"Perfectly!" Ethan laughed. "And all our kids are going to be little geniuses! How can they help it, having such a smart mama?"

"With *you* for a father, I suspect they'll manage to escape that dire fate quite handily," Anne shot back at him. "But what happens to the loose grain after you've got it atop this little table? Your drawing only gets it *that* far, Ethan—and there's a lot more to harvesting than that . . ."

"The strong backs, willing hands, and weak minds of *mere* men take over, Anne o' my heart," Ethan sighed, "to bind the loose grain—what we call gavels—into bundles, called sheaves, which a poor devil walking behind my harvester then sets up in piles called shocks . . ."

"Then why don't you invent some more machinery to do all that automatically?" Anne asked. "It wouldn't throw people out of work the way your shoe manufacturing automatic shears and sabre saw did. Martha Harris told me that the farmers out here are so shorthanded that they have to go around from farm to farm at harvest time helping each other out, with the result that they always get to the last farms so late that the grain has become too dry to bind properly, or the first fall rains catch them and rot it. Isn't that true?"

"Prof," Will Trainer said, "you've done gone 'n found yoreself a livin' treasure! This here is th smartest li'l girl I ever did see! 'Cause she's right! S'posing we was to make some sort of a endless belt like a treadmill, druv by cogwheels, o' gears taken off th bull wheel, instead o' yore li'l table, 'n feed th gavels into a hopper, 'n—"

"For God's sake, give me one of the kids' pencils, Molly!" Ethan said.

But they didn't work out the self-binding harvester that made both of them famous in the prairie states, and ultimately even rich, that night. In fact, they didn't really perfect it until the spring of 1874. For it turned out to be a far more complicated and trouble-ridden piece of machinery than either of them had ever dreamed it would be. . . .

The next night they dined with Matthew and Sarah Hendricks, to whom Ethan owed a debt of gratitude, for Sarah's excellent tomatoes, preserved in brine, her pickled cucumbers, her cabbage rendered into sauerkraut, a bushel or two of her old potatoes buried in the straw, and occasional dozen of eggs had—when added to his daily diet of smoke-cured buffalo ham and strips of "jerky," buffalo hump meat sliced into yard-long ribbons and dried over a hay fire until it looked, and tasted, like pieces of old boots—kept Ethan in remarkably good health for the whole of December and would, with luck, see him through 'til spring. Of course, Sarah Hendricks had accepted his hard-earned cash for these essential foods, but she had set her prices so low that they were practically gifts from her well-stocked larder. But when Ethan had protested that she was being too generous, actually cheating herself, she had laughed with real satisfaction.

"Consider it a bonus for taking that miserable polecat Bart Lee, who all but murdered my poor sister, down a peg, Prof!" she had said.

The night that Anne and Ethan had supper, rather than dinner, with the Hendrickses, Sarah's nephew, Gordon Lee, was also there. Anne found the boy—with his almost extravagant good looks, for, at that age, Gordon was more nearly pretty in the feminine sense than handsome in the male one, and his ready and obvious intelligence—enchanting. So she spent a large part of the evening chatting with him to his noticeable delight and Ethan's complacent pleasure, for he regarded both Gordon and Nora as perfect demonstrations of his own teaching skills. But when Anne said:

"Well, I'm quite sure you're going to win all the prizes for scholarship this year, Gordon!" the youngster shook his head, and said a little sadly:

"No'm, Nora will. She's a heap smarter than I am, ma'am, at everything but English Composition. 'N I'm only a little ahead of her there. So she's sure to win all the prizes—that is, if she comes back to school a-tall . . ."

Ethan stared at Gordon then; and the expression of concern on his face was very clear.

"Why shouldn't she, Gordon?" he demanded. "Don't tell me she plans to drop her studies?"

"She wants to, yessir, Prof. Only her pa won't let her," Gordon said earnestly; "That ain't the main trouble. You know she and my girl Mary Sue are friends, don't you? Well, Mary Sue swears that if Nora don't start eatin' ag'in mighty soon, th wind is gonna blow her away. She's so weak 'n sick by now that she can't hardly get outta bed a-tall . . ."

"I take it that this Nora is the lovely Nora Curtiss I've heard so much about during my stay here," Anne said, the tiniest edge creeping into her voice; "is that right, Gordon?"

"Yes'm. Nora's the prettiest girl in town, or she was; but giving up eating altogether cause she's in love with a—fellow—who doesn't—well —correspond to her sentiments, ain't likely to improve anybody's looks, Miss Jeffreys," Gordon said.

Anne was staring at Ethan. Her eyes were making a very nearly successful attempt to bore, or burn, twin blue holes straight through his head.

"Ethan," she said, very, very quietly; "I think you'd better say something, now. Something—believable . . ."

Ethan grinned at her with solemn mockery.

"Such as?" he said.

"Oh, Lord! Such as there's no *reason* for your Underage Light of Love's starving herself to death over you, Mister Lady-killer Lovejoy! That you've never, never—"

"I've never *what?*" Ethan said even more solemnly.

"Why, Ethan Lovejoy!" Anne gasped; and burst into tears.

"Oh, come off of it, Anne," Ethan said wearily. "Nora has some right to behave childishly, because that's just what she is: a child. But you haven't. So stop this nonsense, will you? For a youngish schoolmaster to be on the receiving end of a schoolgirl's crush is hardly the rarest thing in the world. Just a bit uncomfortable, from my point of view. All it adds up to is a girl child caught up in a not unusual romantic fantasy, caused and occasioned, I verily believe, by her having been an eyewitness to the horrendously bad melodrama of Gordon's father's pistoling me. . . ."

"It was *Gordon's* father?" Anne said.

"Yes'm," Gordon sighed; "my Pa is a drunk and a ne'er-do-well, Miss Anne. And I've made up my mind to be nothing like him. But Prof Lovejoy's right. That's why Nora fell for him—him being so brave 'n all, taking Pa's six-gun away from him with his bare hands. But Prof didn't know Pa had that little hideout pistol in his pocket, 'n if Nora hadn't screamed 'n warned him, he'd have been dead two months by now. So you oughta be kind o' grateful to her, ma'am—after all she saved your promised's life . . ."

"Well, Gordon," Anne said in a wickedly demure tone of voice, "the point's rather moot, isn't it? In a year or two from now, I'll *know* whether I should be grateful to little Miss Curtiss for preventing your father from sending this *rara avis* to his reward in heaven, or his just deserts down below. But now, I don't. Perhaps my marrying him might well turn out to be another of those fates one might legitimately label 'worse than death'!"

"That being so," Ethan drawled, "why don't you loose my tether, Anne, honey? So I can mosey on over to Cy Curtiss's house and feed little Nora a bowl of soup, say . . ."

Anne stared at him then, and all of her was suddenly very still: her eyes, her voice, her breath.

"Ethan," she whispered; "is that what you *want?*"

"And if it were?" he said almost as quietly.

"I'd grant you—your wish" Anne got out on an ebb tide of breath almost too slow and still for sound; "thereby merely—replacing—one sacrificial victim—for another. The choice is up to you, Ethan."

"Anne, dear," Ethan said gravely, "one of the most fondly held of all human illusions is that we have choice at all—about anything in this world. And next to it is the self-centered idea that what we *want* matters a good goddamn, ever, in all our existence. But, all right: My choice—my rational as well as emotional choice for wife, helpmeet, mother of my sons —is you. What I want is to marry you as soon as it will be possible for me to support you under conditions you'll have some remote chance of bearing . . ."

"You think I'm a hothouse flower, Ethan?" Anne flared.

"I think you don't know how hard life on the frontier actually is," Ethan said gravely; "Therefore, tomorrow I'm going to take you out to my—our—place and let you see for yourself how I live. No, exist, for to call what I do living is a flagrant abuse of the Queen's English. I mean to improve those conditions at least two hundred percent before we're wed. But, even so, that might not be enough. You're—very small and slight, physically, Anne, darling. Being a farmer's wife might well be beyond your strength . . ."

"But not beyond dear little Nora's?" Anne said with icy quiet.

"Lord, yes!" Ethan said. "Beyond hers as well. She's at least as unsuited to the crippling work, the general hardships, the monotony, the unbelievable loneliness of that existence as you are, Anne—and perhaps even more so. If I had known what I was getting into, I'd have chosen my prospective bride by the yard—measured around the hips!—and by the pound. Somebody like Cora Bellamy, say . . ."

"'N you'd have still been wrong," Sarah Hendricks said grimly; "I'm a big cow myself, and there've been times when I've sat there lookin' out over that blasted prairie, listenin' to that blamed wind that don't never stop—not for a second, Anne, honey, day o' night—'n holdin' Matt's razor in my hand, wonderin' ifn to slit my throat from ear to ear would really hurt any worse than to put up with that Gawdawful way o' livin' one more day . . ."

"Sary!" Matt said, his big, deep voice going high and reedy with shock.

"Never told you that Matt, sugar," Sarah sighed. "'N mainly I got past that rock-bottom lowness o' th sperrit, 'cause it come to me that I jes' couldn't hurt a man as good 'n true as you be, that damn bad. But life out here is mighty hard, Anne. I don't know a woman, not *one* in th whole of Dickinson County, who won't allow, when you pin her right down to th truth, that there ain't been at least a dozen times in her life when she wasn't mighty close to killin' herself o' losin' her mind, o' *both*. When it ain't th heat, it's th cold. When it ain't th rain turnin' everything into a mudhole, it's th drought turnin' everything into dust 'n dirt. Back in Missouri, where I come from, a body could keep herself clean 'n smellin' good; but out here—ugh! 'N th bugs—Dear Lord—th bugs! They uses yore house for a parade ground; they gets into everything—into yore food, yore clothes, yore eyes, yore nose, yore hair. 'N *everything* is too hard to do. Well water jes' ain't fit for washin' so you's got to beg yore pore, tired, dead-beat-from-overwork hubby to drive you 'n th week's washin' miles 'n miles away to th nearest river o' th nearest crik. You know how to make tallow candles? Render skunk fat into oil for lamps? If you don't, you gonna hafta go to bed with th chickens—'n th result o' *that* generally is more kids than yore place can rightly feed . . ."

"Lord, Sarah!" Matt said; "You're sure painting th picture mighty black!"

"Not half as black as it *is,* " Sarah said. "You know how to make soap, Anne? You've got to, you know. Store-boughten soap comes in oncet in a blue moon—"

"That sort of thing is going to improve, Sarah," Ethan said. "After all, the Kansas Pacific is sure to get to Abilene early next spring . . ."

"All right. But are you, Eth Lovejoy, gonna have th hard *cash* to buy her th things she's gonna need? *Need,* not jes' want, Prof? What with what the freight rates are, added to the price of every store-boughten thing? 'N with th grain brokers robbin' you blind? You've done gone 'n put in winter wheat, Matt tells me. Well, Prof, you're a might smart man I'll allow; but ain't nobody ever been able to make winter wheat grow worth a cuss out here. Le's see how much o' it you harvests next spring. Ten bushels th acre? Two? When it ain't th rust what gits it, it's th rot; when it ain't th rot, it's th mildew. Eth, won't no kind o' wheat grow out here good enough to be worth botherin' about. Tha's why nearly everybody plants corn. Ain't that right, Matt?"

"It purely is," Matt sighed; "Corn is th only crop prairie sod lands is good fur, Prof . . ."

"Corn!" Sarah exploded. "A cousin o' mine up Nebrasky way sent me a clipping from their newspaper—*The Nebraska Farmer,* issue o' January 'sixty-two. 'N you know what, Anne, honey? It had *thirty-three* recipes for makin' things outta corn in it. Take our kids, now. I have to take Matt's belt o' his razor strop to 'em to get a bite o' cornbread down 'em anymore, they's so sick o' it. My oldest boy took our family Bible off th shelf t'other day, laid his hand on it 'n said real solemn-like: 'Mama, I swears by God, 'n on His Holy Words, that when I'm a grown-up man I ain't gonna let a crumb o' cornbread o' a drap o' molasses pass my lips no more as long as I live!' "

"Look, Sarah!" Ethan laughed, "I *want* to get married, you know! So please don't scare off the only girl foolish enough to have me!"

"Well, I like that!" Anne said. "Sarah, *you* stood it, didn't you?"

"Yep, I shore did, but only because I didn't know no better. Girl child o' mine can take up with a drummer, a carnival barker, a patent medicine salesman, a gambler, or any blamed kind o' crook you heard tell of—even, Lord love us!—a cowboy; and she's got my blessin'. But a prairie *farmer?* Swear to God I'll shoot her my ownself 'n put her outta her misery from th' start!"

"Sarah," Anne said quietly; "I'm glad you sounded off that way. And I've heard much the same sort of thing from Martha Harris. So now you, all of you, including young Gordon, here, listen to me—"

She turned then, abruptly, jerkily to Ethan, and he saw that her eyes were jeweled with sudden tears. "Give me your hand, Ethan!" she said.

He put out his hand to her. She took it. Sat there peering into his eyes.

"I swear by God, and upon my honor as a woman, that if *ever* you hear one word of complaint from me—ever in our life together—you have carte blanche to leave me, Ethan," she said.

He bent and kissed her then, before them all. And the knot in his throat was at least the size of one of the smaller of the Rocky Mountains. It was, he realized, one of those painfully awkward, solemn, and tender moments that are almost impossible to bear.

The next day he drove her out to the farm in Phil Harris's buggy, lent to him for the duration of her stay, since livery stable charges for an entire week would have wrecked his budget beyond repair, and showed her all of it. She was astonished at how big it was, since three hundred twenty acres are full half a square mile, and appalled at the evident difficulties of getting it all under cultivation within a single year. But when he told her of his intention to install a Black family as tenants on the place and to use their labor on a sharecropping basis to get the farm into full operation, he was surprised and a little shocked by the expression of fear—distaste?—that appeared in her clear blue eyes.

"Don't tell me you're a coreligionist of Bart Lee and the Bedsheet Boys, Anne?" he said a little angrily.

"No," she said; "I'm a New England Yankee just as you are, my love. I've always felt that slavery was an abomination, and that the colored people should be free. I hold they should have the same rights as anyone else, but—"

"But what, Anne?" he said.

"I'd—rather not live too close to them," she whispered. "Wait! I don't try to justify that attitude of mind, Ethan. It has no justification, really. It's—purely emotional. The truth is—they—they frighten me. They're so—so physical. So—ugly. And so—*black* . . ."

"Not all of 'em," Ethan said.

"I know. I heard Frederick Douglass speak before the War. He was a remarkably handsome man. But then he was mulatto, not Black. I also heard Sojourner Truth and Harriett Tubman address abolitionist meetings, and applauded what they said until my palms were sore. But if anyone had left me alone in a room with either of them, I'm quite sure I would have fainted, Ethan. Those two women were—absolutely hideous —ugh! That—frizzly hair, those sausage lips, those huge breasts, that inky skin—"

"Maybe *we* look hideous to *them,*" Ethan said gravely.

"I shouldn't doubt it. And, if so, they're perfectly within their rights. But, Ethan—isn't there any other way you could get our place under cultivation without making me so—so uncomfortable?"

"Yes," he said grimly; "I can take a mortgage on half, or all of it. Go into debt in order to hire a crew of farmhands and extra draft animals for a year or two. Maybe I could pull it off that way, but—"

"But the risks are too great, aren't they, love?"

"I think so, yes. Anne, there's not a farmer in this county who has his full acreage under cultivation, and some of them have been here since preëmption days, before the War. As a result, every single one of them is dirt poor, living on the borderline of actual want. All those dinners we've been to almost choked me because I knew—*knew, my dear!*—how those people could ill-afford to invite us. The only man in town who has any money is Cy Curtiss—Nora's father—and that's because he runs the local saloon . . ."

"Now *that* would be a solution, wouldn't it?" Anne said with studied calm; "You marry *her,* and your rich father-in-law then proportions you the wherewithal to get your—and dear little Nora's—farm started . . ."

"Done!" Ethan said with a mocking grin; "But on one condition, Annie, me darlin'!"

"And that condition is?" she whispered.

"That you agree from the outset to become my kept fancy woman on the side," he said. "Speaking of eating one's cake and having it, too, that—"

"Ethan," she sighed; "You always speak your deepest—and most bitter—truths in jest, don't you? All right, you win. Bring your Black slaves in . . ."

"They won't be slaves, Anne!" he said sharply.

"I know. I was only teasing. Now show me where you live . . ."

"Anne, baby, I'd rather not," he said sadly; "It's—absolutely abominable, and—"

She glared at him.

"Show it to me, Ethan!" she said.

But when she saw that dugout, she cried. Ethan felt like crying himself, seeing it anew through the unresigned clarity of her eyes.

"But you won't have to live in anything like this!" he said. "Before we're wed, I'll have built you a decent house. Halfway decent, anyhow, but still—"

"You don't have to," she said; "it's not really necessary. I'd live anywhere with *you,* my love. Anywhere—even in that!"

"Tha's 'cause you've never tried to," Cora Bellamy's voice came from just behind them, less than a couple of yards away. "Howdy, Anne, baby! Lord God, but you're smart! Your dress—I'd give my back eyeteeth to have one like that!"

"Then take a singletree to Tom and put him to work," Ethan said grimly.

"Aw, Eth," Tom groaned. "'N me thinkin' you wuz a friend o' mine!"

"I suppose I am, come to think of it," Ethan said. "But my advice to Cora stands. A friend is honor bound to tell his friend the hurtful truth, for his—in this case *your*—own good, Tom."

"Hello, Cora," Anne whispered; "I must say you're looking well . . ."

"'N so are you, Anne, baby!" Cora laughed, and stepping forward, kissed her cheek. "Eth, you old horse trooper, you! Always did hear that you cavalrymen couldn't hit a railroad's roundhouse at point-blank range! Figgers. If you hadn't been shooting wadded blanks that night at Anderson's, you'd have gone rushing up to Omaha long before now, to do right by our Li'l Nell, honorable as you are!"

"Cora," Ethan sighed; "you've got a dirty mind . . ."

"That I have!" Cora said cheerfully. "Tha's exactly why what I think turns out to be so, nine times out o' ten. C'mon over to our place 'n let me rustle you up some grub. By the time you get back to Abilene, it will be night, 'n there ain't no eating saloon in that one-horse burg yet, so far as I know . . ."

"No, thank you, Cora," Anne said; "I—we—really aren't hungry . . ."

"Aw, come off of that one, Anne," Cora hooted. "Whatcha tryin' to do, compete with Eth's schoolgirl sweetheart? Starving yourself to death is no way to keep a man inside th traces. Even li'l Nora has found that out by now!"

"Cora," Ethan said; "I wish you, and all and sundry, would leave poor little Nora in peace. There's absolutely nothing to those stories, and you know it!"

"Wal now, Eth, boy," Tom put in, "you can't deny that that pore li'l lovelorn critter has done took to her bed, vowin' that if she can't have you, she'll never git outta it ag'in—not alive, anyhows—"

"Tom," Anne said worriedly; "is that hearsay? Or do you know it for a fact?"

"That th li'l dilly has took to her bed is a fact, Anne, baby," Cora said; "But *why* she's gone 'n done it is a horse of another color altogether. My guess is that that business about her starving her pore li'l self to death because of un-ree-qui-ted love is so much hogwash. Five'll get you ten that she just can't afford having th general public measure her cute li'l waistline with th nekkid eye anymore . . ."

"Ethan!" Anne said furiously; "Come on! Take me back to town— right now!"

"I," Ethan said, as they rolled away from there, "have never touched that poor, sweet child with my little finger—"

"With your little finger, maybe not!" Anne said bitterly; "I am not so innocent, *Professor* Lovejoy, as to believe that that's the instrument you men generally use! Why—"

"Anne," Ethan said; "you *want* to give me away? And—especially to Nora, which wouldn't be hard to do?"

She turned, faced him.

"Ohhhh, Ethan!" she wailed.

"The truth is I *am* fond of that lovely child. Much too fond for my own good, or my peace of mind. But it so happens that I love you; not to mention the fact that, as a rational man, taking unto myself a child bride, however great her beauty or her charm, simply doesn't appeal to me at all. I want a woman, and a wife. You have no rival in sixteen-year-old Nora Curtiss, my dear. Your only rival—and your own worst enemy —is you yourself. These childish displays of jealousy—and bad temper!— are, or should be, far beneath you, Anne. Not to mention the obvious fact that they're also more than a little insulting to me as a man. I don't cheat, not only because cheating goes against my grain, and is, or would be, demeaning to the essential who and what I am, but because it's unintelligent behavior. What's more, it's unnecessary. If I wanted—seriously wanted—anyone else, I'd say simply and quietly: 'Sorry, my dear, but this isn't working anymore. So, since there's no hope for it, or us—good-bye!' "

"Ethan, you wouldn't!"

"I most certainly would; and I *will,* if you crowd me that far. So hear this: I have never touched Nora Curtiss's hand. I have never kissed her—"

"Have you—wanted to?" Anne whispered.

"Of course," he said at once without any hesitation at all; "I am both male and human, my dear! But I never have. And whether I ever will— or even proceed to blithely go on from there!—depends upon neither her nor me, but upon one Anne Jeffreys, who is either the most brilliant woman I've ever met or the biggest female fool extant. And more than half the time, I can't make up my mind as to which she is . . ."

"The—fool," Anne whispered, brokenly; "absolutely the fool—to take the awful risks—with my own life, the way I have today. Ethan, I won't say I'm sorry, although I do—with abject humility!—beg your forgiveness. The truth is, I'm *not* sorry. Why be sorry for having blue eyes or brown? I'm—jealous. It's—unintelligent, but that's the way I am. And I love you—totally—because I'm made that way, too. So pin the blame on God or the Devil, whichever of the two had the greater hand in creating me. A rotten job! Rank amateurism—unworthy of either of them! But there you have it—as you have me—now and forever—if you still want me . . ."

"Now and forever!" he said and kissed her; "World without end, amen!"

And they were at peace, almost happy. At least for another day.

But that next day was the last day of Anne's stay in Abilene; and, as they rolled along at a spanking trot behind Phil's high-stepping gelding, Anne's slim fingers suddenly became claws, biting into Ethan's arm.

"Stop the buggy, Ethan!" she said.

"Stop the buggy? Lord God, Anne; why? We're late now, and Phil and Martha have gone to a lot of trouble for your farewell spread . . ."

"Stop all the same. I'll only be a minute. Believe me, it's important. Pull up the horse, will you? Right *now,*" Anne said.

Ethan hauled back on the reins. In a flurry of skirts and petticoats, Anne jumped down into the dark, muddy, horse droppings-laden street without waiting for Ethan to help her, which considering the sheer volume of the clothes a woman wore in the 1860s involved a considerable risk of her spraining an ankle or even breaking a leg.

Wonderingly, Ethan got down after her, tied the horse to one of the ever present hitching rails, reached the wooden plank sidewalk just in time to see that Anne was clutching a small, slight, obviously female figure—who was struggling violently to get away from her—by the arm.

"Be still, will you?" Anne said sharply. "I won't hurt you, child. You're—Nora Curtiss, aren't you?"

"Yes'm," Nora whispered; "And I ain't—I mean I'm not scairt—afraid—of you hurting me. Nothing left to hurt. You's—you've—done gone and killed me already, Miss Jeffreys, ma'am . . ."

'Oh God!' Ethan groaned inside his heart. "Nora," he said sternly, "what on earth are you doing out alone this time of night?"

"Knowed—I knew"—Nora fought desperately to retain a grip on the grammar *he* had taught her—"that you-all was—*were*—going to the Harrises tonight. And I wanted—*had*—to see her. The woman—what's —*who's* done gone 'n busted my heart all to smithereens . . ."

"At least you have tried to teach her to talk properly, haven't you, Ethan?" Anne said. "Look, child, I haven't done anything to you. Certainly I haven't broken your heart. How could I? I've never seen you before this very minute . . ."

"Ohhhh, Lord!" Nora wailed; "Dressed like this, like a princess o' a queen—'n talking just like a grammar book! So—natural and so fine. And—and pretty, too!"

"There you're wrong," Anne sighed; "I'm not at all pretty. But you are, aren't you? Come over here, closer to the light. Let me have a look at you, will you?"

"No'm!" Nora gasped; "That there's my pa's place! It's a saloon, ma'am. 'N women—no kind of women, not even *bad* ones is—*are*— allowed in there . . ."

"Don't mean to go in. I just want to see my chief rival, just as you wanted to see me. Lord, but you're pretty! No—far more than merely pretty. You didn't tell me she was—beautiful, Ethan . . ."

"I didn't tell you anything about her, except maybe that she's my best and brightest pupil," Ethan drawled. "And if ever she were pretty once, not to mention beautiful, she's not now. A bag of bones. Skinny as a rail fence. And as ugly as a starved-out shoat caught in an Osage orange thornbush—"

"Ohhhhh, Eth—Professor Lovejoy!" Nora sobbed.

"Come on, my dear," Anne said; "Get up into the buggy and come with us to the Harrises'. They won't mind; and *I* mean to forcefeed you like a Christmas goose. Can't have you on my conscience, y'know—"

"Can't," Nora got out; "Papa would be hoppin' mad I was to sneak off like this. 'Sides—you're laughing at me! Poking fun at th pore silly schoolgirl who—"

"Has the good sense, and the excellent taste, to love the same man I do?" Anne said gently. "Hardly, child. From what I've seen of you, I like you very much. And as far as love is concerned, none of us women is very smart. It would be much nicer—and more civilized—if we were friends. Don't you agree?"

"Yes'm. Only tha's plumb—im-possible, ma'am. Every time I even hear about you 'n *him,* my insides *die.* 'N they die screaming, Miss Jeffreys . . ."

"I know. But you'll get over that. Time will cure that particular ill. It always does in girl children as young as you are, Nora. For it will bring your tall and handsome cavalier a-riding, the right age for you. And you'll forget all about this scarred-up, weatherbeaten old wreck . . ."

"Yes'm," Nora whispered; "Reckon I will forget Eth—Professor Lovejoy—one day—"

"Call him Ethan, child," Anne said; "We're not in school tonight, and I really don't mind . . ."

"All right. I reckon I will forget Ethan—*my* Ethan—th handsomest man alive 'n th bravest 'n th best—one day. But you know when that day will be, ma'am?"

"No. When will it, Nora?" Anne said—rather sadly, Ethan thought.

"The day they nail me up in a tight-fittin' cottonwood box," Nora whispered, "'N pick me up, carry me way out on th lone prairie, 'n—put me to bed with a shovel, ma'am . . ."

"Oh, Lord!" Anne said.

"Prof—Ethan," Nora said, her voice tight, high, breathless, "I—I love you. I ain't never—I haven't ever—said that to you before, straight out and plain. So now—you know . . ."

Even Anne had to admit that Ethan handled the situation—and himself—very well then. Well—and with immense dignity.

"And am honored far beyond my poor deserts," he said quietly. "But, that being so, it follows that you don't—or shouldn't—want to hurt or distress me, doesn't it, my dear?"

"Hurt *you?* Oh, Lord, I'd die first!"

"But you *are* hurting me. Terribly. This business of starving yourself practically to death. *That* distresses me no end, Nora . . ."

"Don't do it on purpose. I *can't* eat, Prof—Ethan—I purely *can't!* Get to thinking about you, 'n my stummick ties itself up in a million knots, 'n every spoonful o' anything a-tall I put into my mouth plain makes me want to vomit, and—"

"Still, you must promise me to try. Will you? But first, I'll go in there and ask your father to allow you to come with us to the Harrises'. We'd both be happy to have you along. And it would stop an awful lot of ugly talk that's been going around this town—mostly through *your* fault, my dear . . ."

"My fault? Ohh, Ethan! You don't mean folks have been saying—"

"Everything imaginable, child," Ethan sighed. "Now just you wait here until I—"

"No! Please, no! I—I'd rather not. I'd just spoil everything for everybody. And I wouldn't be—at ease or happy either one. I—I'm going to eat. And—and take care of myself. So—so *you* won't think I'm ugly anymore. And because I want you never to feel bad—and to be real happy and—"

"Which means you've got to accept the idea of Anne and me, child," Ethan said. "Do you?"

"Yessir. It's—'most killing me—but if *she's* what you want, I'll just have to take it. 'Cause you being happy comes first, even if I'm miserable," Nora whispered.

Leaning forward, Anne kissed her then. Straightened up, misty-eyed but smiling.

"Spoken not like a silly schoolgirl, but like a woman. A true one, Nora, dear," she said.

10

"Whom the gods would destroy, they first make mad." Ethan Lovejoy knew that very well, though perhaps not in those exact words; for Longfellow wouldn't get around to crystallizing that phrase into the form the world now quotes it until 1875, in his *The Masque of Pandora.* But the principle behind them, anyhow; he'd had enough trouble in his life to know damned well how exact the idea was. . . .

The curious part about this ancient truth is that the method that the hypothetical rulers of human destiny employ is nearly always the same: they permit their victims to become puffed up with unseemly and unwarranted hubris because of a series of deceptively easy successes before sending their perfumed and cowardly agent to slam the poisoned arrow into his heel from a totally unexpected direction. In that year, 1867, it could be argued that precisely such a fate fell upon Ethan Lovejoy.

Within the next five years, Ethan had the contention, firmly held by Matt Hendricks as well as by nearly every other prairie farmer whom he knew, that winter wheat wouldn't grow worth a good goddamn in Kansas, demonstrated to him as solid truth and beyond all possible doubt. But *his* did. That once, and inexplicably, it did. In the spring of 1867 he harvested one thousand two hundred bushels from the fifteen acres he had sown to it the previous fall, ten of them broken for him by his friendly and cooperative neighbors, and five more that he managed, by close to suicidal effort, to break himself. Neither rust spores, nor rot, nor mildew attacked it; and with the new harvester he had built with the able help of Cy Curtiss, Jr., fitting into the wooden parts that he and his best carpentry student or apprentice had made, the marvelously precise and beautifully finished iron pieces—the spiked bull wheel, the gang mower's scissor blades, the cogwheels, bevel gears, and belt-driven smaller flywheels—that Will Trainer had cast, tempered, welded, and ground to his specifications, Ethan cut, bound, and shocked his entire harvest in a single day.

He did this, of course, with voluntary labor and a borrowed team. Phil Harris and Matt Hendricks served, of their own free will, as riding binders, working on the moving machine itself, under its canvas awning in a comfort they'd never known before. They did this not only out of a friendly willingness to help Ethan out, but perhaps even more out of a keen desire to test the performance of the new machine.

Black Randy Otis's equally Black twelve-year-old son Tim, drove, with easy skill, the magnificent team of Morgan-Percheron crosses that Rad Stevens, the best and most prosperous farmer in the county had lent Ethan; and Randy himself walked behind the harvester, shocking the already bound sheaves as Phil and Matt kicked them off the platform. Again the loan of the team grew out of the same sincere friendship combined with shrewd self-interest that had caused Phil and Matt to volunteer their labor.

Rad, of course, had come along to drive his team; but he hadn't been able to, because Ethan had designed the seat of his machine, deliberately with a view of cutting down all unnecessary weight, to accommodate only a driver much slimmer and smaller than Rad Stevens was. Nonetheless, Rad remained on Ethan's farm and at his side all that one full day that the spring harvesting—the unique feature of winter wheat—lasted.

"Any suggestions, Rad?" Ethan asked him.

"Yep," Rad said solemnly; "git on a train, now, tonight, 'n put yore drawings in th hands of a patent lawyer in Atchison. 'Cause if you don't, one of them farm machinery manufacturers is gonna hear about this 'un. 'N one day, a nice, polite, soft-spoken stranger will show up 'n ax you a mighty heap o' innercent questions 'bout this here livin' miracle you've done gone 'n invented. Won't take down a note or mek a sketch. They're too smart for that, th damn robbers. He'll jest memorize every daggum new feature on yore harvester, 'n when he gits back to Chicago, o' Des Moines, o' Springfield, he'll sit up all night with a whole crew of them drafting fellas. 'N th next day, they'll have a patent claim into th Illinois branch office, 'n you won't mek a dime on a idea tha's worth Lord knows how much money . . ."

"Thought about that," Ethan said. "Will Trainer, who's my partner in this venture, is in Atchison right now, sitting in Merrick, Merrick, and Greenfield's offices, with a nice, new, clean set of drawings. What's your other suggestion, Rad?"

"You're downright smart, ain't you, Prof?" Rad said. "Reckon I've got two more ideas I'd like to pass along to you. Both of 'em grows outta th same thing yore harvester did: th need every pore bastid of a farmer has got to speed things up. 'N since you've got th kind o' head that plumb works, I'm axing two more inventions outta you, Prof: a *breaking* plow that a two-, or at worst, a four-hoss team could pull. Ordinary plows jes' ain't good enough, 'cept maybe the John Deere plow, what's made outta steel. 'N even it was designed with the conditions in Illinois in mind, not th kind o' tough prairie sod we've got out here. With oxen, we kin break, at most, an acre a day. 'N hit's breaking, not ordinary plowing, that's th trouble. Once you've got yore whole spread broke to the plow, most any iron plow will do to row it off for sowing. Now, if you was to come up with a plow that would slice through the matted roots of all that there prairie grass that makes breaking virgin sod so damn hard to do, who knows how much land we couldn't break every day—three acres? Five? Enough, anyhow, to bring in a crop that would be worth something, that would put some *cash* in our pore empty pockets, git us outta debt . . ."

Ethan stood there, transfixed. It hadn't so much as occurred to him to take a look at the plow itself. And now he didn't even need to, for by then he could visualize perfectly well how that homely implement of husbandry looks and works. The front edge of any plow whatsoever was sharp, of course, but only sharp enough to cut and turn earth, which meant, actually, that it was rather blunt. The trouble lay in the fact that plows imported from even no farther east than Illinois, fast becoming the leading farm machinery manufacturing state of the Union, simply weren't designed to do what they had to in Kansas, Nebraska, and the Dakotas, which was to cut not only the soil, but also through the toughest mass of interwoven prairie grass roots anybody ever saw. No good woodsman ever tried to cut wood with a dull axe; Ethan, who kept his broadax sharp enough to shave with, knew that very well. And grass roots were wood, or rather a woody fiber. At once the association of ideas, an ax sharp enough to shave with and the instrument ordinarily used for shaving, the straight razor—for safety razors hadn't been invented then—put something very close to the actual solution to the problem into Ethan's remarkably inventive head. It followed that the cutting edge of a plow designed to break the sod in the first place, and subsequently to plow it with ever increasing ease during the coming years, ought to look something like two hollow ground straight razor blades, fitted or rather welded together to make a curving V-shape, and then reground to hairsplitting sharpness. It shouldn't *plow* through the sod by the brute force of twelve maddeningly slow oxen; it should *slice* through the matted roots by reason of its own keen, finely tempered edge so easily that a single horse, or, at worst, a two-horse team could pull it with little effort. 'Five acres a day? Yes!' Ethan thought triumphantly; 'Yes!'

"All right," he said quietly; "I'll consult with Will about your idea, Rad. Designing a plow like that seems easy enough, but how well it will work, only Will can say. I could draw you a pretty picture right now of the finest cutting edge you ever saw; but whether the plow will hold that edge depends upon the tempering, and that's Will's department, not mine. What's your other idea, Rad?"

"Build us a thresher-separator. Right now we're still threshing our grain with flails 'n winnowing it by tossing it up into the air, jes' like they done in Biblical times. Or else we have our oxen tread it out, 'n that dates back to th pyramids o' Egypt, too. So we sure Lord could use a machine like that. A *good* one, not like them Lordawful pieces o' junk they're using back in East Kansas right now. Ever see one?"

"No. But now that the KP has got here at last, I'll take a trip back to Wyandotte or Atchison and have a look. What do they use for power: horses?"

"Yep. On a li'l treadmill, some of 'em. Others have th pore critters walking round and round in a circle with a pole attached to their harnesses 'n turning a central bevel gear system something like the ones that work them waterwheels you see on some irrigated farms. They takes the power off them central gears, but don't ask me how th threshing machine itself works, 'cause I don't know. Never bothered to find out since everybody who was fool enough to buy one when they first come out in th last year o' th War swears they mostly *don't* . . ."

"I'll take a look at one, then," Ethan said; "but I'm not promising you anything, Rad. That's mighty complicated machinery, you know . . ."

" 'N tha's a mighty complicated head you've got, Prof; but so far it's working great!" Rad Stevens said.

Ethan's importation of the Otis family to serve him as sharecropping hands cost him a certain degree of trouble, though only of an individual nature, for his friends and fellow farmers accepted them without too much grumbling. By then Randy and Cindy Otis already had five of the twelve children they were ultimately to bring into this world. So Ethan immediately surrendered his dugout to them and lived in Tom Bellamy's tent, now that the weather was becoming reasonably warm. He tried to buy the tent from Tom; but Tom, who genuinely liked and admired Ethan, and was curiously unaware how little his friendly sentiments were reciprocated, had given Ethan the tent outright. Ethan had wanted badly to refuse the gift; but, try as he would, he could think of no inoffensive way of doing so. He reconciled himself to accepting the tent, which he truly needed, with the thought that after all, he had done the Bellamys many favors in the past and would surely be called upon to do them even more in the future.

Meantime, his streak of misleading, hubris-breeding luck continued without a break, which, if he had thought about it at all, should have warned him. About a week after harvesting his phenomenal wheat crop, he was coming back from Merton's Grist Mill, which Dan Merton, after looking over the prairie country around Abilene and Salina, had shrewdly moved to a point on the Smokey Hill River midway between the two towns with a view toward serving them both, remarking to Ethan, "Corn be damned! This here is wheat-growing country out here, Prof—'n yore winter wheat crop proves it!" And as he was passing through Abilene where he meant to store the flour that Dan had ground from his wheat, a large, florid man, clad in a derby hat, a checkered waistcoat, hickory-striped pants, and a black broadcloth suit jacket of the kind worn by preachers, city officials, and other persons of note, waved him to a halt.

"Mister Farmer," the man said, thus proving he was a stranger, for any citizen of Abilene who had resided there any time at all would have called Ethan "Prof"; "What d'you aim to do with all that there flour you've got on your wagon?"

Ethan stared at the man. He didn't look like a grain broker, or even one of the wholesalers who went around the prairie country buying up whatever already milled and surplus flour the farmers might have on hand to sell for sorely needed cash. Rather, he looked like a railroad official. And, about anyone who worked for the Kansas Pacific, Ethan, like all the citizens of Abilene and the nearby farmers, had become, by then, of a distinctly reserved, if not downright hostile turn of mind. Three weeks ago, Abilene had become the temporary terminus of the railroad. As a result of that minor event in the history of American transportation, Abilene, exactly as Junction City had before it, exploded, practically overnight, from a town of some three to four hundred souls, into a city of over seven thousand. And, like its predecessors, the quiet little farming town immediately metamorphosed into a real "hell on wheels." Gambling joints, saloons, and whorehouses had sprouted like canvas—for most of them were housed in tents—and poisonous mushrooms, all around the already existing houses. No decent woman or girl was safe on the streets by night. The Irish construction crews staged their nightly and bloody drunken brawls; the fallen doves swayed down the plank sidewalks, red lanterns in hand, and every sober citizen, family head, and permanent male resident—including, to his total outrage, Reverend Milton Brownley, minister of the Methodist Church of which Ethan was a member— had been repeatedly accosted by the generally fat, usually ugly, always vile-smelling—considering what the sanitary arrangements in a town converted into a railroad construction camp within the space of seventy-two hours were, or rather *weren't*—harpies.

That Ethan and the good citizens of Abilene bore this situation with weary patience was due to the fact that they knew perfectly well it wouldn't last. Now that the warm weather was coming in, the line was going to sweep on down the Smokey Hill River's valley to arrive at Salina in a matter of a few more weeks. Then it would be Salina's turn to become "hell on wheels" and Abilene, as Junction City had before it, would sink back into the blissful peace and habitual boredom of an agricultural town on the vast prairie.

But, while the invasion lasted, it was no wonder that the townspeople had only such contacts as they couldn't possibly avoid with the railroad builders. In this case, however, it was obvious that the big man who had waved him down wasn't a mere construction worker, but rather someone much higher up in the KP's hierarchy. Both his dress and his speech displayed that fact.

"Well," Ethan said; "I mean to take my flour down to Henry Dingle's warehouse to store it, except for maybe a bushel I'll keep for my own use, until I can find a buyer for the lot . . ."

"You've found him!" the KP man said importantly. "How would a dollar a bushel suit you, friend?"

Ethan sat there, speechless with astonishment. Even after the agreed percentage of the resulting flour he'd had to pay Dan Merton for milling his winter wheat had been taken out, he had slightly over a thousand bushels piled up on his big wagon, so much, in fact, that he had had to hitch all six yokes of his oxen to the wagon, both to haul his wheat crop to the mill, and the bushel bags of flour from it on his return trip to the warehouse.

"All right!" the KP man snapped; "I'll go to a dollar and a half, but that's my top limit, friend!"

And Ethan sat there, hugging himself, having gained five hundred extra dollars because he'd been too thunderstruck to sing out "Done!" when the railroad man had offered him the—for those times—absolutely magnificent price of a dollar a bushel. But he said it now, quickly enough.

"Done, mister! That's cash, I hope?" he said.

"Naturally," the big man said; "Th handle's McGinnis, friend. I'm Food Commissioner of the Construction Department of the KP. Got to keep them wild Micks of ours fed, y'know, if only to keep the rotgut in their bellies from blowing the tops clean off their heads . . ."

"Where'll I deliver it, Mr. McGinnis?" Ethan asked.

"Just you move aside on your wagon seat 'n make room for me, and I'll show you," Food Commissioner McGinnis said.

Coming back from the KP's supply warehouses with one thousand five hundred dollars in crisp new greenbacks—wrapped up in a sheet of newspaper and carefully pinned up inside his woolen lumberjack's shirt with a huge safety pin—Ethan's first impulse was to rush down to Abilene's brand-new telegraph office—another advantage that becoming a station on a railroad line automatically conferred upon a town—and send Anne a wire to quit her job and join him at once. That he had absolutely no place to put her once she got there, except a frayed and leaky Army tent, didn't, at that moment, so much as enter his dizzily spinning head. It was spring. Ethan had eaten very well indeed that winter, to the extent that he had actually gained five whole pounds, which meant he was now acceptably lean instead of cadaverously skeletal and his health was far better than it had ever been at any time since the War.

As a result of having been constrained by his nose and his stomach —and, of course, his high morality!—to an abstemious, even monkish existence, Ethan's mind gently turned to thoughts of love. Or, to translate that high-sounding phrase into less euphonious truth, he was suffering from sexual starvation and was as hard up as old hell.

What caused him not to send that telegram—and, here, too, his luck was good, for considering the fact he had only an Army fly tent to put her in, summoning his darling to his manly bosom would have been a grave mistake—was nothing so respectable as rational thought, but rather a piece of female insanity that matched and overtopped his male one. For as he began the laborious business of turning twelve slow, stupid, and balky oxen a full one hundred eighty degrees in order to go back in the direction he was coming from, for he had already passed the railroad station and telegraph office, that soft, sweet voice called out to him:

"Prof—I mean—Ethan—can—may I speak to you a minute, please?"

"Of course, Nora!" Ethan said, trying vainly to stop all the songbirds there ever were under heaven from chanting hosannas through his voice. He set the brakes, huge curved blocks of wood that clamped themselves against the iron tires of the rear wheels, by pulling back on the heavy iron brake lever on the right side of the wagon beside the driver's seat. That way he was sure the oxen wouldn't wander off while he attended to the interesting and delicate matter at hand. Though they probably wouldn't have anyhow. Stopping comes naturally to oxen; it was getting them to go that was the problem.

"Well, my dear?" he said, acutely conscious of the mooncalf quaver that had got into his usually controlled and pleasant voice.

"Not—*here!*" Nora got out breathlessly; "Le's go—in there—a second—will you?"

"In there" was a narrow alley between Abilene's two new dry goods stores, neither of them more than a week old, that had sprung up, as though at the waving of a magician's magic wand, to compete with the already existing one. Ethan suspected that they'd be pulled down again and hauled away to Salina when that pleasant town succeeded Abilene as terminus of the line. But then, they might not. A town always grew considerably after a railroad ran through it. There might even be trade enough for them here. At the moment, all three establishments were doing a land-office business, so neither their owners nor their clients had time for the gazing about and lively speculation about every passerby's affairs usually so characteristic of a prairie town. That was one thing. Another was that the shedlike buildings that were knocked together by a crew of rough and ready carpenters in a matter of hours along the streets of a town the railroad had finally got to, nearly always had windows only in their front ends, i.e., that side opening on the street. The reason for that was very simple: window glass was both scarce and expensive, and tended to remain so until some months after the railroad's arrival, when the increasing store of it piling up in the warehouses began to outrun the demand and thereby brought the prices down. Therefore, in a new railroad town, the alleyway or passage between two commercial buildings usually provided a fairish amount of privacy if some nosy pedestrian didn't happen to gaze down the one you happened to be in at the exact moment that you were doing—or, as in Ethan's absolutely flabbergasted case, having done to you —what you damned well oughtn't to, such as being fervently, even ardently kissed by the prettiest girl in town.

Again Ethan's luck held: nobody was looking down that alley.

"Nora!" he gasped when she finally turned him loose. Then he saw how she was crying.

"I—I *had* to do that, Ethan!" she sobbed. "Kkkkiss yyyou, I mmmmean! I—I—I'mmmm ggggoin' away. To—Chicago. In abbbbout three wwwweeks. 'N I mmmmight not ever cccome bbback—ssso—"

"Then—I thank you for that kiss," Ethan said gravely, in control of both himself and—he thought—of the delicate and troublesome situation by then. Being human, he wanted to go right on kissing little Nora Curtiss and, he realized with a bitter surge of shame, even go on from there. But the shame did absolutely nothing about that feeling. It never does, at least not until far too late. What saved him, saved both of them, was the sheer difficulty, amounting in fact to near impossibility, of carrying out a seduction in a prairie town.

"Nora," he sighed, "let's go back out into the street and continue our conversation there. I assure you, dear girl, that the implications that this town's gossips would put upon our being seen hiding in an alley together this late in the evening, you wouldn't like at all—and your father, even less!"

"I don't care!" Nora said fiercely. "I love you, Ethan! I love you so bad I *hurt.* Tha's *why* I asked Papa to send me away—"

"Please, child," Ethan said sadly, "it's much smarter to talk about all this out in the open where everyone can see us. You're—or were—my pupil, so our talking is normal enough. But whispering together in an alley would—"

"Didn't come in here to whisper—or to talk either one!" little Nora hissed, and hurled herself upon him again.

Gently he broke the stranglehold she had around his neck, caught her by the arm, and propelled her with well-hidden force out into the street.

"*I* have to live here even after you've gone, child," he said. "You want to make that impossible? Or even wreck my friendship with your father?"

"No—" Nora said uncertainly. The truth was that she was beyond caring whether Ethan had to leave Abilene or not. 'And,' the hot and rebellious thought raced through her mind, 'if Papa was to take his shotgun down 'n *make* Ethan marry me, even by mistake, even believing what ain't so, *I* could stand it without bustin' out in tears!'

"Tell me," Ethan said; "Why—Chicago, Nora?"

"Because my Aunt Milly lives there. Mrs. Mildred James—Missus Wilbur James—Papa's only sister. They—she 'n her husband run a restaurant there. And they don't have no—*any*—children of their own, 'n they'd be deelighted to have me come 'n live with them. Aunt Milly has written that a dozen times in letters to Papa. Only—"

"Only what, Nora?" Ethan said, seeing the light of the afternoon sun turn gray suddenly, grow cold and sick, somehow, hearing the wing-clack and clatter of all those million-million songbirds as they beat upward and away from his poor sad heart, leaving it—and him—utterly desolate. . . .

"Papa wants me to stay home with him. Tha's natural, I reckon: mighty hard to give up a daughter when you ain't got but one. Fact is, he's only letting me go to spend just *this* summer with my auntie in th hopes that being away that little time will get me over *you*. Tha's what *he* thinks. I ain't never—I'm not ever coming back. Not to live down here 'n see you 'n *her* together every day. I'll run away first! But I don't *want* to go up there, to tell th honest truth about it. And I wouldn't, if you was to say *one thing* . . ."

"Which is?" Ethan murmured.

"That you love *me,* not her! That you ain't a-gonna—That you aren't going to marry her. That you'll wait until I'm eighteen 'n then—marry—*me* . . ."

Ethan hung there, realizing bitterly how close that first requirement of this lovely child's was to simple truth. And how—if honor existed and he were to uphold it—agonizingly impossible those last two conditions were.

"Nora," he said; "you're asking me to break my pledged and promised word, do a thing so shameful that I'd never be able to look at my face in the mirror again without cringing, as long as I should live . . ."

"All them—*those!*—highfalutin words mean is that you plain don't love me," Nora moaned.

"You're wrong," Ethan said; "I *do.* Far too much for my own good or my peace of mind. But I also"—'Do I?' he wondered, his heart pierced through with the icy arrows of doubt; 'Do I, really?'—"love Anne. And my pledge to her exists, child. Given in honor, and not to be broken. When you're older, you'll understand that . . ."

"Then I don't want to get a minute older!" Nora stormed; "Not one minute, Ethan!"

"Please, Nora; don't make a scene. Not here in public. Not in the street—"

"*You* wanted to come out into this old street; I didn't," Nora said sullenly. "Ethan—write my address in Chicago down. It's Ten North State Street, care of Mrs. Wilbur James. She—my auntie—wants to send me to a high-toned girl's school in Evanston, Illinois, to train me to be a real lady. But I don't want to go to school no—*any*more. I'd hate school without you there to learn—*teach!*—me. Not hearing your voice anymore —so deep, so like—like thunder echoes way out on th edges of th sky, and like hot coals and icicles crawling up 'n down my backbone—saying: 'Two of the fairest stars in all the heavens do entreat her eyes. . . .' Oh, Ethan! I can't live without you! I can't! I can't!"

"Nora, please!" Ethan groaned.

She stared at him. Saw, perceived, his distress. Whispered:

"All right. I'll be good. Ethan—if anything—anything at all happens to—to separate you 'n her, write me. Even if it's ten years from now, twenty, thirty—I'll be waitin'. 'Cause I'm not gonna marry anybody else but *you.* Not ever!"

She whirled then, and raced off down the street. Watching her go, Ethan had something like death in his heart. Or wasn't it rather a premonition of—of what? His coming punishment for hubris? Or of the bitter fact that he was going to learn—and soon—that the ancient Greeks were right in their belief that morality, decency, even honor, are concepts absolutely incomprehensible to the gods?

*   *   *

He had one more stop before he could drive back out to his farm; he had to visit the blacksmith shop to see how the four plows Will Trainer had cast to his design were coming along. Explicitly *cast,* because, taking fire from Ethan's towering ambition, Will had set up a little foundry behind his blacksmith's shop. The KP had made that possible by bringing in coking coal from the coal mines that had been put into production as early as 1863 at Leavenworth, Kansas—for Ethan had been dead, damned wrong in his honest belief that there wasn't any coal to speak of in the West, Kansas itself being so rich in that valuable mineral that homesteaders in the southeastern counties were already strip mining it for their own use, with ordinary picks and shovels, from a few inches below the earth's surface—as well as pig iron from as far east as Pittsburg. The KP did this, of course, not because there was a commercially viable market for either product in West Kansas as yet, but to use the iron and the coke in the portable foundry that accompanied its construction crews in order to cast on the spot any special, not normally manufactured iron part that might unexpectedly be needed.

So Will had cast four plows to Ethan's design for the simple reason that from a practical standpoint you could cast four almost as cheaply as you could one, and heat-treating that many could be done simultaneously at no additional expense. Will intended, of course, to sell the extra three, and thus recoup the money he'd put into the venture. For the past seventy-two hours, he had been cooking those plows in a sealed iron vessel with charcoal packed all around them.

"Case hardening," he explained. "Jes' like you do knives. Th charcoal soaks into th iron a li'l ways, turning th outside into th hardest steel you ever saw. But th middle stays soft 'n flexible. I git it right, these here plows oughta cut through rocks, let alone th roots of prairie grass . . ."

And he *had* got the heat treating and the tempering right. A blade of grass passed down those gleaming blades so lightly that it almost seemed not to touch them, divided effortlessly into halves that showed absolutely no fraying, both edges of the cut being as clean as though it had been made with surgical scissors.

"Wait!" Will said triumphantly, and yanked a long hair out of his own thick black beard. Touched to the edge, it parted as though that plow were a well-honed razor.

"Lord!" Ethan breathed. "But will it *hold* that edge, Will? Or am I going to have to sharpen it at the end of every row?"

"If it don't, I better get outta blacksmithin' 'n go into preachin'," Will chuckled. "Oh, it'll dull a little, Prof; but not enough to make no never-mind. My reckoning is you won't hafta lay a whetstone on it more'n oncet o' twicet in th whole spring plowing season . . ."

At the words "spring plowing season" a great light broke somewhere behind Ethan Lovejoy's eyes. If Anne or Nora had seen him at that moment, either of them would have been—with entire justice!—furious, for Ethan had forgot, completely forgot, that they existed or even that there were any such delectable creatures as women in this world.

In that moment, Ethan Lovejoy invented, or rather, far more likely, reinvented—since most worthwhile inventions are the products of dozens, if not hundreds of talented minds working independently of, and unknown to, one another, as the case of barbed wire was going to prove before another decade was out—the gang plow.

"Will," he breathed; "Let me have all four of 'em! It's an idea that I've got. New idea that just came to me. Heck, I'll pay you whatever you were going to sell the extra three for, anyhow, and—"

"No, don't, Prof," Will Trainer said then. "You can reimburse me for th outlay in materials, 'cause truth to tell I'm kinda short o' cash. But I won't sell 'em to you like you was a stranger. Tell you what: Why doncha cut me in on this idea, too—write it into our partnership? Plows is farm machinery, too, as much as a harvester is, ain't they?"

"Done!" Ethan laughed, and put out his hand to Will.

Within that same week, Ethan had built two wooden rigs, to each of which he attached two of the new, extra sharp, twenty-inch plows, instead of the one old, comparatively dull, sixteen-inch single one. Now he could plow two furrows at the same time, while Randy Otis turned still another two. But when they tried it behind oxen, they found the new gang plows made very little difference as far as the speed of the operation was concerned. To be sure, Ethan's invention, or rather improvement over the single plow, could be drawn quite easily by a single yoke of oxen instead of the six yokes he had had to use before. The trouble was the ponderous slowness of the oxen.

After the first day's trial racked up the miserable results of only one and a half acres for Randy and slightly over one for Ethan, despite those excellent new gang plows, the young ex-schoolmaster—for, God be praised!—the KP had already brought in a prim and forbidding spinster of forty odd, a Miss Helen Ellis, to take over the difficult task of getting some book learning into the prairie children's unwilling heads—knew what he had to do. He drove all six yokes of oxen into town and sold them —without a qualm, for oxen simply haven't enough individuality for a man to become fond of them—to the local slaughterhouse, receiving, at two and a half cents a pound and an average of eighteen hundred pounds each, five hundred and forty dollars for the twelve of them. Then, with Rad Stevens and Matt Hendricks both standing by to see that he didn't get cheated, Ethan bought two teams of really first-class draft horses, four animals in all, big-boned, heavy, powerful, standing over sixteen hands high, geldings, of course, since he didn't intend to go—as yet, anyhow— into the really specialized field of breeding horses, and brought them home, the return trip from Abilene taking him less than a third of the time it always had before behind his ox teams.

The next day, at dusk, both he and Randy whooped for joy and pounded each other on the back, for between them they had broken ten full new virgin acres. Ethan was sure then that he had his battle won, that even with time out for sowing his corn, wheat, and sorghum, he was going to be able to put his entire farm, except the twenty acres he meant to reserve for pasturelands and haying, into cultivation that summer. The minute he was certain that, even allowing for the unforeseen worst, he was going to be able to average five new acres broken to the plow every day, which meant sixty days for the whole three hundred, he sent for the Old Timer to help him build his sod house.

'This fall,' he exulted, 'I'm going to harvest the damnedest crops ever seen in Kansas. And with Cindy Otis tending a whole two-acre kitchen garden with the help of the bigger kids, plus the hogs and chickens I'm going to buy—and a seed bull and three milk cows, by God!—I'll be able to invite Anne down here again for the next Christmas holidays, but this time to stay! And it was that winter wheat—that blessed winter wheat that made it all possible! I don't care how many times Matt, Rad, and Phil tell me that it was a fluke, that I'll never get the stuff to grow again another winter within the next ten years, I'm going to put in forty acres of it this fall, and then—'

Hubris. To be paid for, implacably.

Ethan and the Old Timer were laying out the corners of the proposed sod house when they saw Tom Bellamy coming—or rather staggering— toward them. Since he moved in a widely meandering line, and at a snail's pace at that, they figured he was drunk. He often was these days, because Cora, incensed by the contrast between the unceasing drive and evident results with which Ethan was running his farm, and the all but nonexistent drive and no results at all on the part of her ne'er-do-well of a husband as he piddled about their holdings, pinned never ending hell on poor Tom in the vain effort to get him to do what he was morally if not physically incapable of: in a word, *work*. Since Tom maybe couldn't, and certainly wouldn't, have anything to do with any activity discernibly laborious, he had taken to drink to dull the pain inflicted upon his delicate psyche by the rough edges of Cora's tongue, which, he moaned, "Kin raise blisters on a boot!"

Knowing this, Ethan and the mountain man paid him no attention at all as he weaved his way toward them clearly dazed or even crazed by what they took to be the effects of indulging in an overdose of the cup that cheers, and went right on with what they were doing.

What they were doing was measuring off four lengths of rope, using the lengths of their own forearms from wrist to elbow as the unit of measure. It didn't matter how long or short those units were, the only essential being that they had to be identical to each other. The Old Timer's forearm was considerably shorter than Ethan's, so the two ropes he measured with it weren't the same lengths as the two Ethan measured, but that didn't matter, since all they were trying to do was to lay out the corners of the house they were going to build as perfect right angles so that the resulting structure would be a true rectangle. The method they were using was probably employed by the Egyptians to lay out the pyramids, or even by the first men to emerge from the caves to build the first loghouses. That is, they measured off three forearm lengths and tied a knot. From this knot they counted off four more of the same bodily units and tied another knot, then five more, and the job was done. Then they pegged the four ropes down as triangles at the places they meant the corners of the house to be, with a stake at each knot. Stretched tight, the angle at the stake between the three-knot length and the four-knot length is a perfect ninety degrees, as the ancient Egyptians and Babylonians had found out thousands of years ago.

The night before, at the Old Timer's superstitious insistence that "a man's dwellin' house is plumb got to set four square wit the compass, young Eth, 'n thet means yore walls is got to run true north 'n south, 'n due east 'n west; none o' thet nor'east by so'west business, nosireebobtail, o' you 'n th li'l woman won't never know no happiness in yore house," Ethan had staked out a rope dead straight in the direction of the Pole Star. He didn't believe the old man's damnfoolishness, but he was too troubled in mind to take a chance. Now, with that one wall and their four perfect right-angled corners laid out, they were ready to go to work at building the actual walls.

Only before they could begin to plow up an acre of virgin sod into parallel furrows from between which they would spade up the heavy squares of grass-matted earth to be used as building blocks for the walls of Ethan's sod house, Tom Bellamy got there.

And he wasn't drunk. Dazed, yes. For blood was trickling down his face from a deep and ugly gash above his left ear.

"Lord, Tom!" Ethan laughed; "What did she crown you with, the skillet? Hell's bells, old fellow; don't you think it would be cheaper to do a little work and get Cora off your tailbone?"

" 'Twasn't—Cora," Tom croaked. "Injuns done this, Eth. Flint arrowhead scraped 'longside my noggin jes' as I lit out for th tall grass . . ."

"Jesus!" Ethan whispered. Tom wasn't lying. He could see that.

"Howcome they didn't scalp you, then?" the Old Timer cackled. " 'Tain't but one o' you 'n thar's always eight o' ten braves in a war party . . ."

Tears burst, exploded from Tom's little piglike eyes.

"They wuz—too busy with—Cora," he whispered.

Ethan passed a tongue tip over lips gone suddenly bone-dry. He had never liked Cora Bellamy; but, in a way, he'd always respected, if not the woman she was—'a woman,' he realized again now, 'twisted into bitter meanness by being tied to this coagulated lump of polecat's puke!'—at least the woman she could surely get to be if given half a chance. But that required somebody's shooting or otherwise disposing of Tom Bellamy. By definition, murder, and a hanging matter. 'Not a feasible solution at all,' he thought bleakly.

"They haven't—?" he got out.

"Kilt her?" Tom groaned. "Naw—jes' raped her. One of 'em, anyhow. Th redskin she whupped. Then they tied her up, throwed her across a spotted Injun pony, 'n made off with her . . ."

"Cora—whipped an Indian brave?" Ethan said. By then, Easterner though he was, Ethan had learned enough about the Plains Tribes to realize the enormity of that offense. Indians had very definite ideas about the humble place of squaws in the general scheme of things; and the color of a squaw's hide wasn't likely to impress them a good goddamn. A squaw didn't strike a brave. Not ever. And to give the redskins their due, the Plains Tribesmen very seldom beat their wives. Only in cases of extreme necessity. Ethan, after his recent experiences with both Nora Curtiss and his darling Anne, was willing to concede that the red men had a very accurate idea of what was fitting as far as male female relations were concerned.

"Yep," Tom groaned. "They wuz drunk. They'd done bushwhacked a bunch o' Cheyenne someplace up north. 'Cross th Nebrasky line, likely. Them painted bastids make seventy or eighty miles a day without even tryin' hard. A hundred if they's pushed. 'N they'd took a heap o' scalps. So yesterday they wuz sellin' 'em on the streets o' Junction City, 'n using th money to buy likker with . . ."

"Jesus, Tom! How could *you* know about that?" Ethan demanded.

"Fella I was havin' a snort with in Cy Curtiss's saloon last night told me. He'd just come from there. Remember Junction City ain't but one hour from Abilene by train these days, Eth. 'N since them storekeepers back there done lost a mighty heap o' trade 'cause Junction City ain't th terminus of th KP no more, 'n Abilene is, reckon even redskins' money looked good to 'em. Anyhow, this bunch showed up at our place li'l while ago. Reckon you'd of seen 'em if you hadn't decided to put yore well way up here . . ."

"Didn't decide," Ethan said drily; "You dig a well where there're signs of water, Tom. Get on with it, will you?"

"Yore niggers seen 'em 'n lit out for parts unknown. But Injuns don't bother niggers much. Niggers generally ain't got nothin' worth stealin', 'n anyhow I reckons them Injuns think they're kind of kin. . . . Anyhow, they rode up to our place 'n started axin' fur chickens 'n 'hawgie meat,' as they calls pork. 'N you know Injuns. Start to feed 'em 'n they'll eat you plumb outta house 'n home 'fore they'll move on. So Cora cussed 'em 'n told 'em to git along. But like enybody what's ever had dealin's with 'em coulda told her, ain't no brave from even a dirty deegenerate tribe like th Kansa startin' to take no orders from no squaw, be she white o' no. 'N when they wouldn't, she took a blacksnake whip to their bare legs. I done told that fool woman 'n told her that Injuns 'n niggers is different breed o' dawgs altogether . . ."

"They were Kansa, then?" Ethan said.

"Yep. Seen some o' th same ugly beggars in town couple o' times before with their chief, ol' No Nose . . ."

Ethan turned to the mountain man.

"You know where that bunch of the Kansa is camping, Old Timer?" he asked.

"Nope, young Eth. Not eggs-zac'ly. But I kin find 'em right enough. You got eny saddles fur them outsize hosses o' yourn?"

"No," Ethan said.

"Never catch them Kansa in no wagon. Injun ponies is th fastest breed o' Cayuses they is, y'know."

"We'll throw blankets—buffalo robes—across their backs and ride 'em Indian fashion. Go get your six-shooter, Tom."

Tom's face turned even grayer than it was.

"Ain't got it no more," he groaned. "Them Injuns stole it. 'N my scatter-gun, too. All I got is a pocketknife in my jeans, 'n—Lord God, Eth —they's only three o' us, 'n they's *hundreds* o' them damn Injuns in that there camp, that is if we *ever* catch up with 'em!"

'With you along, we never will,' Ethan thought with real pity; 'In fact, you'd only be in the way . . . .' He said, gently enough: "Take one of my horses and ride into town. Tell Ned Tyler what's happened. Ask him to send me and the Old Timer reinforcements. Get along with you, Tom. C'mon, Old Timer, let's unhitch these horses . . ."

But Tom wasn't even out of sight in the direction of Abilene, and they, themselves, hadn't ridden even half a mile west and south, when the Old Timer pulled up his mount suddenly.

"Why, damn me fur a sinner, why didn't I think o' *that* before?" he cackled. "C'mon, young Eth, le's git back to yore dugout . . ."

"Lord God, Old Timer, why?" Ethan said.

"Stand to reason we cain't fight th whole damn tribe o' Kansa. There's still three o' four hundred of them crazy, drunken bastids, all told. So we's got to dicker wit 'em. 'N you's got one piece o' mighty Big Medicine in yore dugout, young fella!"

"I *have?* What kind of medicine, you crazy old coot?"

"Thet stovepipe lid o' yourn. Ol' No Nose wuz willin' to swap you a filly as prutty as li'l white Antelope fur hit, he sho' as hell will be deelighted to give us back a big buffalo cow like Cora Bellamy fur thet lid. Thet stands to reason, don't hit?"

Ethan sat there on that huge draft horse that was never meant for riding, anyhow, and stared at the Old Timer.

"Don't know," he said finally; "but anyhow, it's worth a try . . ."

They put the tall silk hat, carefully packed in hay, inside a duffle bag, which Ethan gingerly laid before him across his big mount's back. Then they set out again to track down the Kansa.

It took them four days of hard riding to catch up with the tribe, and they were able to do so even then because the pitiful remnants of that once proud people had turned northwest, and believing themselves beyond pursuit, had camped on the banks of the Saline River about eighty miles west of Salina.

At the Old Timer's suggestion, the two of them rode boldly into the Kansa camp, moving very slowly, with their rifles cradled in the crooks of their left arms and their right hands raised palm outward in the sign of peace. All the squaws ran squealing into the teepees, bearing the smaller children with them. Old No Nose came out of the biggest teepee and stood there like a statue of brown granite, staring at them. His Medicine Man, a mean-looking Indian with an ancient, frayed, and mangy wolf's skin that had long since lost most of its fur draped over his head, stood beside the chief. The two headmen of the tribe were flanked by fifty or sixty ominously painted braves, a few of them armed with Sharps single-shot carbines captured from the U.S. Cavalry, but most with wicked-looking bows and arrows, at that range plenty good enough, Ethan was dismally sure.

The chief motioned with immense dignity for them to dismount. But once they had done so, he suddenly grinned broadly, stretched out his hand, and touched the scarred and truncated tip of Ethan's nose. And Ethan saw that the old chief was right; for though one had been abbreviated by a Cheyenne tomahawk and the other by a falling bucket of earth, their cut-off noses looked remarkably alike. The chief then made a brief speech full of grave, booming music.

"He sez you's his sperrit's son, 'cause y'all's got th same totem," the Old Timer translated.

"How the devil d'*you* know what he said, Old Timer?" Ethan demanded.

"Kansa is a branch o' th Sioux language," the Old Timer said; "so hit's jes' like Osage, 'cause both th Kansa 'n th Osage belong to th Sioux fambly. 'N I speaks Osage. Long wit Caddoan, so I kin palaver wit th Pawnee 'n the Wichita. 'N I knows a fair amount o' Algonquian, so I kin talk wit th Arapaho 'n th Cheyenne effen I has to. But when hit comes to th Kiowa 'n th Comanche, I hafta use sign language. Th' Kiowa's got they own tongue what don't no other Injuns speak. 'N don't me nor eny other trader know Shoshonean, what th Comanches talk, 'cause ain't nobody ever stayed alive round no Comanches long enuf t'learn hit . . ."

"Tell him I'm honored to have the same totem as so great a chief,"

Ethan said; "And explain to him that Buffalo Cow Woman is the squaw of a friend of mine who wants her back. Remind him that we came in peace —only the two of us, without calling out the troopers. And after you've let that sink in, ask him what he'll take for her . . ."

The Old Timer burst out into a long harangue. Ethan realized at once that the mountain man was a born linguist, and a brilliant one. But when Chief No Nose answered, the Old Timer groaned.

"He says he'll take your Many Thunders Firestick for Cory, young Eth! So you better figger out a way t'turn him aside thar. Cain't let no Injun git his hands on a Winchester repeater. He'll go on th war path jes' to try hit out!"

"Tell him I offer him my Magic Hat," Ethan said gravely. "Tell him it's the greatest of all war bonnets and will make him ever victorious over his enemies the Cheyenne. And over the noisy Pawnee; you know, the tribe that live way out on the source waters of the Smokey Hill River. I've heard they and the Kansa don't exactly see eye to eye, either . . ."

"Them fool Injuns stop killin' each other, 'n jine together ag'inst *us,* we wouldn't never be able to take over this country," the Old Timer said. He turned back to No Nose and began another long and flowery speech.

While he was talking, Ethan turned to his horse, took down the duffle bag, opened it, fished out the tall silk hat, dusted the straw off it.

The minute he saw that long desired hat, No Nose's small black eyes took fire. He showered sonorous gutturals upon the mountain man.

"He wanted to know effen hit would ward off bullets," the Old Timer cackled happily after he'd replied to the chief's grandiloquence with a mighty oration of his own. "So natch'ly I told him 'twould—'n arrows 'n spears 'n tomahawks to boot. So he sez hit's a deal. They's gone to git Buffalo Cow Woman, I mean Cory Bellamy, right now . . ."

When Cora saw Ethan, she cried. She cried with great dignity but in a way that was intensely feminine despite her size and strength. Ethan found that sight unsettling and put out his hand and touched her cheek, gently, in a gesture meant to comfort her. But she shrank, shuddering, away from his hand.

"Don't touch me!" she said fiercely; "I ain't fit to be touched—not by a good man like you, Eth Lovejoy! Not me—a hunk of she-meat what's been *used* by these filthy redskin dogs!"

"Cora," Ethan said gently; "Don't say that to anybody else. You and Tom will have to leave Kansas if you do. You know how women are. Don't make of yourself an outcast, my dear. Try to forget it. I'll make

damn sure the Old Timer won't open his trap. And nobody in Abilene will
know for sure that—"

"Th hell you say! And me being in their greasy hands damn nigh a
week? Ugh! They smell just like dog-foxes in rut!"

Ethan stood there, thinking. Then, suddenly, the way out for Cora
came to him.

"Cora," he said slowly, "I beg your pardon in advance for mentioning
a subject that a man plain oughtn't to talk about to a woman who is not
his wife. But in this case, it seems to me I've got to. Look, my dear, you
can tell the women you—you were with your monthlies. No Indian will
touch a woman when, as they put it, the fountain of her moonblood is
upon her. It's the strongest of their taboos. Even after it's over, a squaw
has to make sacrifices and purify herself before she can return to her
husband's lodge. The Kansas women know Indian customs. They'll believe you if you say that . . ."

"Oh, Jesus!" Cora wept; "If I'd have known that, I'd have faked it,
somehow; but now . . ."

She peered at Ethan, said bitterly:

"How's my brave hero of a husband? You notice how fast *he* came
riding hell for leather across the prairie to save me!"

"Tom—was wounded, Cora," Ethan said quietly; "He took an arrow
in one side of his head and was bleeding like a pig. I sent him into town
for help. But it appears we won't need it now . . ."

They had to endure the peace pipe ceremony and an Indian feast
before leaving the Kansa camp. And due to the white man's wanton and
merciless slaughter of the game upon which the red man had lived for
thousands of years, the *pièce de résistance* of that feast was roast dog. It
was a tribute to the iron concept of courtesy bred into his nerves, his blood,
that Ethan managed to keep his portion down until he was out of sight
of the camp on their homeward journey. Then, of course, he vomited it
up, spewed it up, retching terribly.

"You's plumb, downright crazy. A nice fat puppydawg meks mighty
good eatin's," the Old Timer said.

They took Cora, riding behind Ethan on his big gelding, all the way
into Abilene. But before they got there, the Old Timer gave voice to a thing
that was troubling Ethan more than a little as well.

"They didn't come after us," the old man said; "Ain't a soul set foot on thet thar trail after we'd done gone 'n left yore place, young Eth. Plumb doan understand hit. Tracks these here elephant-sized hosses o' yourn left, a chile coulda followed us, let alone trackers as good as Matt Hendricks 'n Phil Harris . . ."

"Maybe," Cora said bitterly, "Tom didn't even tell them. Maybe he was so damned glad of the chance to get rid of me for good that he—"

"You don't believe that yourself, Cora," Ethan said. "Tom loves you, whatever his faults. When he left my place he was crying like a child . . ."

"Leaving a *man* to come and save me," Cora said softly, and tightened her grip around Ethan's waist.

'Oh, Jesus!' Ethan thought. He said:

"There must be some reason for it, Old Timer. Maybe the Pawnee or the Cheyenne attacked Abilene and they—"

"Naw. Hell, naw! Injuns is brave but they ain't fools. They doan attack no city wit all o' seven thousand people in it, 'n most o' them seven thousand young able-bodied menfolks, young Eth. On th other hand ain't neither Phil nor Matt nor Rad nor Ned nor eny o' our friends lily-livered cowards. They'd've knowed th danger we wuz in, they'd've come. But damned effen I kin think o' eny reason for Tom not to tell 'em. Lawd Gawd, you doan reckon he fell out 'n fainted 'n never did git thar?"

"No," Ethan said. He was thinking that perhaps there had been more than one Kansa war party out, and that poor Tom had run into a second group of braves before reaching Abilene, but he didn't want to say that out loud where Cora could hear it. "No," he repeated; "his wound wasn't *that* bad, Old Timer . . ."

"Then I plumb doan understand hit!" the Old Timer said.

They took Cora directly into Abilene without stopping at either farm so that Martha Harris could look her over. Martha was the nearest thing to a doctor the town had had up until now. At the moment, however, there were four temporarily in residence, all of them employees of the KP, and kept busy night and day patching up the mayhem the construction crews committed upon one another, upon any local citizen unwise or unlucky enough to get in their way, and even, occasionally, upon the whores. But Cora flatly refused to submit to the indignity of allowing one of the railroad's doctors to examine her, so Martha Harris it had to be.

Martha wouldn't talk. Not after Ethan asked her not to. Besides, being much more broad-minded than most of the women of the town, she sympathized with Cora's plight and didn't blame the big woman for it. Martha was all too aware that it could happen to *any* farmwife. Being kidnapped by the Indians was becoming, with terrifying frequency, a fate that had to be reckoned with by the white women on the Kansas and Nebraska frontiers. In 1867 and 1868 the tribes had in their power eighteen white female prisoners of various ages. By then the redskins had learned that the white men were crazy enough to value one of their pale-faced, straw-haired squaws more highly than even a first-class example of horseflesh. So they profited from such utter stupidity and began stealing more women than horses. After all, if a white were fool enough to pay more ransom for a mere woman than for a splendid Morgan stallion, why not take advantage? Women were far easier to steal.

But while Martha was working on Cora, cleaning and anointing with soothing salves the cuts, bruises, and abrasions she had all over her big, fine body, Ethan caught Phil by the elbow and propelled him out into the street.

"All right, Big Chief Whitefeather Yellow Belly," he growled with an anger that wasn't maybe as feigned as he thought it was, "speak up! And not with any forked tongue, either. Why the hell didn't you fellows come after us? Whatever the reason you, Ned, and the rest left me and a broken-down old coot of a mountain man to face three hundred Kansa all by ourselves, I'd 'purely admire' to hear it, as you say out here. Don't tell me that Tom Bellamy didn't even get here! Because if he didn't, we're going to have to put a scouting party out to look for him—or his scalped corpse, and I'm betting it would be the latter in such a case . . ."

"No, Tom got here all right. Only—Oh, Jesus, Eth, Old Hoss, I jes' don't know how the hell to tell you this. The fact was that we had ourselves a first-class shootin' war right here in Abilene for three whole nights in a row, 'n outnumbered like we was, didn't none o' us *dare* leave town to come after y'all . . ."

"A *war?*" Ethan said; "A real honest-to-God gunfight? Lord God, Phil, why—and with whom?"

"Th 'why' is th bad part, Old Hoss," Phil whispered; "It was all because o' yore little Nora—"

"But hasn't she gone to her aunt's place in Chicago?" Ethan said. "She should have by now. She told me she was going to . . ."

"Naw. She ain't. Mebbe she will later on. Right now she's in the hospital in St. Louis. Cy took her there hisownself on th train. Only place anywhere nigh she kin git decent medical care . . ."

"In the hospital!" Ethan said; "Lord God, Phil—why?"

"Brace yoreself, Old Hoss," Phil said sorrowfully. "It wuz them Micks. Them drunken bastids o' the KP's construction crews. She wuz wandering all by herself a mite too late. Thinkin about *you,* she told Martha. 'N they grabbed her. Four of 'em. Took all Martha could do to stop th bleedin'. 'N th worst part about it is that she begged her pa to take her away before you got back. Swears she's shamed to look you in the face."

Ethan stood there. That was all he did. He stood there, with his heart completely stopped. His breath. His mind.

"Me 'n Ned got her away from them slobbering dogs. Kilt one of 'em, I'm proud to say. 'N two more is bad hurt. Ned's good with a six-gun, y'know. 'N I ain't so bad myself, for all that I hafta shoot with my left hand now. So th rest of them Paddy's Pigs started in to wreck th town. But we stood 'em off. Had to call in all our friends from th nearby farms to help us out. . . . When them Micks found out that they wuz up ag'in men with daughters o' their own, and them men armed with Sharps 'n Spencers ag'inst their six-shooters 'n pocket pistols, they cooled off mighty fast. Only they started drinkin' 'n got their Irish up ag'in two more nights in a row. If some cool-headed railroad section bosses hadn't telegraphed th main office and brought th big bosses out here to settle things, Lord knows what mighta happened. . . . Jesus, how I hate to have to be th one who had to tell you about it. . . . Thet pore li'l thing. We—Martha 'n me, 'n Nellie 'n Ted—'n even Cy hisownself was afraid fur a while there that it had done gone and affected her mind . . ."

'That dream!' Ethan thought. 'Jonathan said—told me—that she— that she—'

He whispered: "And there I was riding all over hell looking for Cora Bellamy. For Buffalo Cow Woman! While Nora—*my* Nora—Oh God Oh Christ Oh Jesus I—"

He turned away from Phil Harris then. Walked quietly down that wooden plank sidewalk into the dark. And it seemed to Phil that darkness had a special quality to it. That it was more than the absence, it was the negation, the very annihilation of light. Not that the unlettered Kansan knew those words, of course. He reached for, and found, a Biblical phrase that served well enough. 'Th darkness on th deep,' he thought; 'Before th footsteps o' th Almighty had even gone 'n troubled th waters . . .'

"Eth!" he cried out into that air turned Stygian, that night crashed down from heaven like a sudden stone. "Wait, Ol' Hoss! Don't go! I—"

Ethan's voice floated back to him upon that thick blackness. It was curiously muffled. It sounded as though he were crying, but there was no way for his friend to tell.

"I'm all right, Phil," he said.

But he wasn't. And from that moment on, all the probabilities were that he would never be again. Not ever in this world.

11

"You can so leave!" Phil Harris said hotly; "Yore nig—cullud folks is doin' all right, 'pears to me . . ."

Ethan looked out over his freshly plowed fields. The Otis family—all of them who were big enough to work, anyhow, and even a couple of children that Ethan himself considered a shade too small—were planting corn by the method it was generally done on the frontier. Behind two of Ethan's big horses, Randy had already driven a sled that had four parallel wooden runners, set four feet apart, which his own weight, standing on the sled itself, caused to lightly furrow the earth lengthwise down the field. After he had finished that, Ethan's black tenant farmer had repeated the operation, but this time across the field, so now the acreage to be planted to corn looked like a big checkerboard. Four of Randy's children walked along, digging their bare toes into the cool, moist dirt at the intersections of the shallow furrows forming the corners of each individual checker square, and dropping three or four kernels into the little holes their toes had made. They were incredibly graceful doing this, converting the corn planting into a slow and stately dance. After them, Randy and Cindy—who had her newborn youngest strapped to her back in a highly decorative and colorful papoose's pack Ethan had bought in Salina from a Pawnee squaw—came, covering up the kernels with a quick downward and backward slash of their light, long-handled hoes. And one of the reasons that he loved farming so came over to Ethan again: it was so beautiful. So attuned with the natural order of the world.

"Besides," Phil went on, "you've got yore sod house all finished. Fine job. Best one I ever seen. Shingled roof *and* plank floor, so yore li'l Anne oughta be mighty satisfied with it. Now, damnit, Eth, come on!"

"Don't see why you need me," Ethan said gravely. "What with all our friends in town, and from the farms in walking distance, appears to me that you already have enough people on your side to outvote this— what's his name again?"

"McCoy. Joseph G. McCoy. Smart fella from Illinois. The trouble is, Old Hoss, that I ain't all that sure I *can* muster up enough votes to defeat the proposition Mr. McCoy has made th Town Council . . ."

Ethan looked out over the sweep of his fields. Looked back at his best friend.

"Explain it to me again, Phil," he sighed. "Guess I wasn't really listening—not carefully enough, anyhow. Kind of—woolgathering, I suppose. I often do, these days . . ."

"Oh, Lord!" Phil exploded; "Fergit li'l Nora, will you? She won't come back here. Not *never,* Eth. Sendin' her to her auntie's in Chicago was th best thing Cy could've done. There she kin live peaceful-like 'n find herself a good husband. While here, she's done fur. You know that, Old Hoss. 'N don't give me a lecture about how unfair it is. I know that as well as you do. But twisters 'n crop failures is unfair, too; yet we take 'em fur what they is: facts o' nature. So's this a fact o' human nature; female division. Besides, ain't a damn thing you can do about li'l Nora without doin' yore Annie dirt. Tha's so, ain't it?"

"It is. Only I keep thinking that if I hadn't ridden off like a jackass to do Tom Bellamy's job for him, getting Cora out of the hands of the Kansa, I might have been in Abilene that night, and—"

"And you jes' as well might *not.* More likely not 'cause you damn sho' ain't given to hangin' around town. Tha's one thing. Another is that yore Winchester would've been danglin' over yore fireplace jes' like it is right now, leavin' you no other out but to tackle them Micks with yore bare hands. 'N you'd've done it, too; I don't doubt that. But them horny bastids wasn't Bart Lee, nor anythin' like him. They'd've kilt you without turnin' a hair. Helluva lot o' good that woulda done pore li'l Nora, not to mention yore Anne. Oh, fur chrissakes, Eth; fergit that, will you?"

"I try, but I can't," Ethan said sadly. "You're right, of course. So let's get back to what we were talking about. You were saying that Mr. McCoy proposes to—?"

"Build cattle pens north 'n west of Abilene. He's already done got an agreement from the KP to ship the beasties back to Wyandotte. From there he was goin' to ship 'em via the Union Pacific's spur line to St. Louis; but th UP didn't want no part o' that . . ."

"Why not?" Ethan asked.

"Them Longhorn Texas cattle is sure death to any cows what ain't from down there," Phil said. "They's got a sickness that don't do *them* no harm a-tall. But let 'em pass within a mile o' where you've got yore cows, 'n everyone o' th pore things will start to sicken. Then they'll up 'n die on you, sometimes a month or more after them evil Texas steers is long gone from anywhere nigh yore place. Folks in Missouri don't let them Texas ranchers trail drive their herds through that state no more. Far back as 1855, they had a epidemic after Texas cattle passed through. Same thing happened in East Kansas in 1858. 'N ag'in, *last* year. Now our Great Legislative Minds, every one o' who is from th eastern part of this here state so far, 'cause we ain't got th population yet to send our own representatives to Topeka, have come up with a beaut: them long-horned four-footed devils kin be brought into Kansas any time during th year fur shippin' to th meat packin' houses, as long as they're druv in 'west of the sixth principal meridian.' And d'you know what towns, *lying on a railroad,* is west o' th sixth meridian in Kansas?"

"No," Ethan said.

"Salina, what's now the terminus of the KP, 'n thereby has set us free, thank God! o' Micks, whores, gamblers, and bunco artists, for th time bein', anyhow—and *us,* Abilene. Now th good citizens o' Salina ain't no fools. They doan want a bunch o' Texas cowhands turnin' their town upside-down 'n wrongside-out every livin' night. 'Sides, out that fur, quite a few o' th folks is stockbreeders, on a small scale, anyhow, 'n they've done heard what happens to northern-bred cattle when Texas Longhorns pass through. So they turned McCoy down flat. 'N now here he is in Abilene, sweet talkin' th folks about how much good makin' a cattle shipping capital outta our town will do everybody. And folks in 'n around Abilene is waverin'. First of all, mighty few of us homesteaders has been able to buy ourselves no cows yet, so my argument about that Texas cattle fever don't impress 'em none a-tall. 'Nother thing: McCoy points out that th trail herds would leave *tons* o' cowchips behind 'em to replace that there real good-smellin' dried buffalo flop—that's gettin' mighty scarce nowadays—fur us to use as fuel in a country where timber is a damn sight harder to come by than unbroke fillies. Wouldn't even smell any worse, since cattle 'n buffaloes both eat grass, don't they? Then, them trail drovers sells for practically nothin', or even gives away, th calves born to th cows in their herds every livin' night to th homesteaders what lets th Texans bed down their herds on th farmers' pasturelands a day o' two to rest 'em up 'n calm 'em down before drivin' 'em on to th railroad stockyards. Ditto with steers gone lame. Powerful arguments, 'n damned attractive ones to a pore sodbuster who's catchin' hell tryin' to make a go of a farm out here . . ."

"I can see that," Ethan said; "In fact you're even convincing me that McCoy may be right . . ."

"Lord God!" Phil exploded; "Ain't you got no brains in yore head, Eth Lovejoy?"

"There've been times when I've doubted it," Ethan said. "Go on, Phil; I'm perfectly willing to listen to your side of the argument . . ."

"Wait. Lemme finish with what we're up ag'inst, first. Do you know what th population of Abilene is right now?"

"No," Ethan said; "but I'd guess that the town has shrunk right back down to the size it was before the KP got here, now that we're no longer the end of the line."

"You're wrong. We've got a shade over half as many folks ag'in as we had before. We've got three new stores what actually have a decent line o' goods to sell in 'em. A molasses mill. A new grist mill. 'N there's talk o' startin' a newspaper. Not bein' a fool, I'll concede from the outset that there ain't no doubt that the town's businessmen will benefit by lettin' McCoy turn Abilene into a cowtown . . ."

"Phil, is McCoy paying you a salary?" Ethan gibed.

"Naw. But he would if I'd take it, 'cause he knows I'm the chief opposition he's got. Look, Old Hoss, ever since—that—happened to pore li'l Nora, you've been walkin' around with yore tailbone plumb draggin' in th dirt. You want to see our town changed into th kind o' place where every married man has got to lock his wife 'n daughters up, come dark, 'n stand guard all night long over 'em with a rifle 'n a brace o' six-shooters to make sure them trail-drivin' varmints don't bust down his front door to git at 'em?"

"Now you're exaggerating," Ethan said.

"Th hell I am! Them Texas cowboys has sat on their hosses months on end out on th range, lookin' up th assholes of a bunch o' cows—cows bein' th onliest female critter they ever see. So they's plumb ob-*sessed* with th very idea o' wimmen, th way a man who gits his fair share o' tail cain't never be . . . Turn Abilene into th shipping dee-po for every damn cow in Texas, 'n the whorehouses, the dance halls, the saloons, and the gambling joints won't be in no damn *tents.* They'll be wooden frame buildings built to *last.* 'N th drunken carousin', the shootin' scrapes, th plain *indecency* will go on day 'n night from here on in. I got girl children, Eth. 'N you jes' might father a daughter or two yoreownself. What I'm saying, Old Hoss, is that Joseph G. McCoy proposes to make Abilene th Queen o' th Cowtowns, 'n downright rich off th cattle shippin' business. I don't dispute that he may be right there. I jes' say there's other things besides money. More important things—like say, peace 'n quiet. 'N—Oh, hell—nach'l beauty—"

"Of the kind you had in Marthasville. And you're right. You're dead, damned right, Phil, boy . . ."

"Yep, reckon I am. I want to hear—church bells ringin', Old Hoss, not gunfire. I want to live in a place that may be slow 'n pokey, but tha's part o' th land. Of the—earth. The good earth th Lord give us for growin' things 'n livin' peaceful 'n bringin' up our famblies to fear Him—'n keep His Commandments . . ."

"Amen to that," Ethan said gravely; "I left a region obsessed with money-making to find that exact kind of peace and tranquility. So I'm with you, boy. Wait 'til I change my clothes, and we'll ride into town . . ."

But they hadn't a chance. Not a ghost of a chance, as—being anything but stupid men—they should have known. The good citizens of Abilene could easily see what the economic results of having several hundred Texans pouring into town with their pockets full of silver dollars after having been paid off at the end of the trail would surely be. But they couldn't see, or wouldn't believe, that Abilene, within the next five years, was going to come close to earning the self-applied and not exactly admirable title of "The Wickedest Town on Earth." That title was, of course, subjective, and hence impossible to verify; Newton and Dodge City would dispute it hotly a little later on. But that Abilene, Kansas, was—for at least three of those five years—the murder capital of the United States is indisputable. The statistics bear that sad fact out.

Phil Harris and Eth Lovejoy lost their battle to prevent the conversion of a pleasant little agricultural community into the Queen of the Cowtowns by a vote of over ninety percent in favor of permitting Joseph McCoy to build his stockyards just beyond the municipal limits, to less than ten percent against. On their side they had, notably, Reverend Milton Brownley of Christ Church, Methodist, and Cyrus Curtiss, who manfully voted against his own financial interests—since a flood of thirsty cowboys pouring into the town was sure to make him, as a saloonkeeper, super rich to put it mildly—out of the bitter memory of what had happened to his daughter. There were others, of course; but, as the vote was secret, Phil and Ethan didn't know who they were. Only the Methodist minister and the saloonkeeper had the moral courage—far greater, Ethan realized, by the very nature of things, on the part of the latter, than on that of the former—to speak out against the measure.

But they had lost by a fair vote, expressing the will of the majority of their neighbors and their friends, so they accepted their defeat with quiet dignity like the true men they were.

That spring and summer, Ethan brought his entire farm, except for forty acres, under cultivation. Those forty—twenty more than he had intended to, due to the impossibility of sowing so much land to wheat and corn in the time at his disposal—he reserved for haying and pasturing his animals. The results of his efforts were mixed: he didn't fail, but then neither did he succeed.

The kitchen garden, under Cindy Otis's experienced hand, was outstandingly successful. The corn crop was a marvel; the sorghum—Chinese sugar cane—was good. The spring wheat, however, gave a relatively poor yield of from ten to fifteen bushels to the acre, which wasn't total failure but had to be compared with the same crop's average of twenty-five to thirty in the Dakotas. The reason for this was very simple: west of Abilene the great plains slant upward to the Colorado line and beyond it to the Rocky Mountains, and on those high plains summer is often a blast furnace. So a sizable portion of Ethan's wheat burned up. And though he didn't know it, and wouldn't until the spring of '68, what he called his "winter wheat" and stubbornly sowed forty acres to that fall, was going to freeze. He had—to his sorrow—demonstrated to him one of the facts of Kansas farming: in East Kansas wheat—the kind of wheat they had in 1867—would grow. In West Kansas it wouldn't.

So Ethan sharply reduced the acreage he sowed to wheat, and his dependence upon it as a cash crop. But, being a stubborn New England Yankee, he didn't give up planting wheat altogether as many of his neighbors had. Instead, he set aside two acres sown to it for experimental purposes. Here he planned to save the seed of whatever few stalks survived the winter on one of the acres, and those that got through the heat of the summer on the other. One or the other, and maybe both, by natural selection, he reasoned, would finally provide him with enough seed to produce a strain of wheat suitable for the local climate. He was quite right, except that he didn't realize how many years that was going to take him.

But other aspects of his farming went well: he bought his bull and three milk cows, his chickens, and his pigs. The pigs, however, provided him with a problem he hadn't anticipated: penned, as they had to be on a farm totally lacking in timber, within walls of sod, they rooted those walls down with the greatest of ease. Ethan had to call on that walking encyclopedia of Western lore, the Old Timer, for help in this matter, too.

"Why shore, young Eth!" that ambulatory encyclopedia and/or manure pile cackled; "I knows how to stop them danged hawgs from rootin' their way outta yore pen. You digs a ditch—jes' wide enuf to keep th greedy cusses away from th wall, 'n jes' narrow enuf so they cain't fall into hit—all around th inside o' th pen. . . . How deep? Wal, say deep enough to scare th li'l grunters . . ."

And of course, like most of the mountain man's suggestions, it worked.

That fall, at harvest time, Ethan made a fair amount of cash and considerably more than that in barter by harvesting the crops on all the nearby farms, and even on some that weren't so near, with his new mechanical harvester. By then, he and his partner Will Trainer had seen what was wrong with their scheme to manufacture the harvester and sell it to the prairie dwellers: none of their neighbors had the money to pay what it would cost the blacksmith to even build the machine in the limited numbers local demand would call for, not to mention sell it at a profit. So they reluctantly dropped that particular venture, except for one more example of the machine they built for prosperous Rad Stevens.

Just as Rad had predicted, however, a representative of one of the great Illinois farm machinery manufacturers showed up during that harvest season and asked a good many questions about Ethan's harvester. Ethan answered him courteously enough; but when he showed the agent the patent pending numbers etched into the bull wheel of the harvester itself, the man went away, and that was that. Years later, to his sorrow, Ethan witnessed the fact that a good many of his friends and neighbors went deeply into debt—and some even lost their holdings because of the mortgages they had taken out to do so—to buy a machine practically identical to the one he had invented. But it had enough changes introduced into the mechanisms to make the winning of a patent infringement suit doubtful. And, besides, Ethan didn't want to risk paying sizable sums of money to the greedy tribe of lawyers with which the frontier was infested with no sure guarantee of the results. So it turned out Rad was right: Ethan never made a red copper on his invention.

His gang plows, however, were another matter. They could be made cheaply enough to sell. And they did sell throughout the region, providing Ethan and Will with a moderate but steady cash income. More importantly, they proved to be the difference between success and failure for nearly every farmer who bought them, since, because of the ease with which they broke the tough prairie sod, their users were able to put enough land into cultivation to insure at least the small profit necessary for survival. Everyone agreed on that point, and blessed Eth and Will not only for their brains and skill, but even more so for the reasonableness of their asking price.

All these things done, and counting the balance a little more on the side of success than on that of failure, Ethan found himself with a really troublesome problem on his hands: should he gamble on the modest amount of money he had in the bank, his reasonable prospects for success during the next two or three years—now that he had his whole farm broken to the plow—and marry Anne at Christmastime? His loneliness and his anguished need cried out a thunderous, "Yes!" But his native caution, and his acutely developed moral sense, presented him with a series of reasons for waiting at least until spring, if not for another entire year that were of considerable weight. And the first two of those reasons were anything but the *reductio ad absurdum* they sound like when stated baldly: in 1867 neither was to be taken lightly. Those reasons were cowboys and Indians.

Ethan considered the Indians first, because to him, a white man and a homesteader, the resolution of the Indian problem was *de facto* a matter of time. To his credit be it said that Ethan admired and respected the red men; he realized that they possessed a quality that his own race entirely lacked: the ability to live in and with the natural world. The whites, flooding into the West, lived upon and against the world of nature. And ended up converting the rivers into cesspools and the land into a dust bowl that the prairie winds blew away.

But Ethan Lovejoy, for all that he was greater of soul and broader of mind than his racial brothers and contemporaries, had to consider the dismal specifics of his time and place: in short, did he *dare* bring a bride to an outlying and exposed farm where she might be, as Cora Bellamy already had been, carried off by a war party to be held for ransom? That way of putting it was, of course, incomplete. In addition, he had to face the mentally disturbing and emotionally shattering question for a man who was both young and a lover: 'Can I submit her to the danger of a physical, sexual violation—actual rape?'

Essentially, the Indian danger reduced itself to a question of time. In that very year, 1867, treaties had been made by which the more peaceful and civilized tribes, the Sauk, the Fox, the Ottawa, and, notably, the Wyandot—far more cultured than most of the whites who opposed them, the establishers of the first free school in Kansas's history—agreed to be removed to Indian territory in Oklahoma. But what about the Cheyenne, the Arapaho, and the Kiowa? Those tribes were drowning all West Kansas in blood, sending it up in flame. Hardly a day passed that the KP's construction crews, well past Salina now, laying their gleaming rails across the open plains, didn't have to drop their picks and shovels, and take up their guns. And, in response to the fact that the Tribes, maddened by the wanton slaughter of the game that was their only source of food had gone on the warpath, the U. S. Cavalry, under General W.S. Hancock, had destroyed a Cheyenne Village of three hundred lodges on Pawnee Fork, while the Eighteenth Kansas Volunteer Cavalry had been raised to protect the frontier.

But *where* was the frontier now? Somewhere near the Colorado line, surely. The Kansa were gone from the neighborhood, living, if it could be called that, on a "Diminished Reservation"—how often in the long and shameful history of the endless perfidy of the United States Government toward its redskin charges were those two brutal words to appear!—nine miles wide and fourteen miles long near Council Grove, southeast of Junction City on the old Santa Fe trail. And it had already been noised abroad that the five great and warlike Plains Tribes—the Kiowa, the Comanche, the Arapaho, the Apache, and the Cheyenne—had agreed to meet with government commissioners at a spot on the Western Map called Medicine Lodge to draw up a treaty of peace, late in this very month of October 1867.

Therefore, logically speaking, Ethan could consider the Indian danger as largely over with. But what about the cowboys?

Try as he would to be fair-minded, Ethan had to concede that Phil Harris's deep and abiding prejudice against that bowlegged, runty, hog-wild subspecies of humanity was largely justified. By then, a good half of the thirty-five thousand head of Texas Longhorns that would reach Abilene's brand-new stockyards that year had already got there. And that section of Abilene that came to be known as "McCoy's Addition" or more accurately as "The Devil's Half Acre" was already being built. Before the year was out, it would consist of twenty-five to thirty single-story frame houses, each with anywhere from ten to twenty rooms, and gambling, drinking, whoring, and violent death went on in "Hell's Half Acre" all day and all night long.

In one sense the cowboys were worse, or at least more dangerous than the KP's construction crews had been. The drunken Irishmen had fought usually with their fists and only occasionally, when things really got out of hand, with knives or six-shooters. But cowboys *never* fought with their fists, and held any man who would condescend to do so as beneath contempt. "Good Lord meant a fella to fight like a dog, He'd've give us fangs 'n claws," they sneered. And: "Matter ain't worth reachin' 'n drawin' over, it ain't even worth discussin'." Already, in the brief time since the herds had come loping up the Chisholm Trail, five men had been shot to death in the saloons and streets of Abilene. And the worst part about that, to Ethan's mind, was the fact that surely two and probably three of the victims had been innocent bystanders. For a drunken cowboy to hit the man he was actually out to kill, with the Civil War six-shooters converted from cap and ball to brass-cased rimfire ammunition available in 1867, was a matter of pure luck. The accuracy of every handgun of the epoch ranged from pisspoor to Lordawful, and hammer fanning, slip shooting, and quick drawing, when combined with an eye blurred into near blindness by a bellyful of rotgut didn't help cowboy marksmanship much, if at all.

Other of Phil's dismal predictions were coming true as well. Only yesterday, Randy Otis had reported to Ethan:

"Prof Lovejoy, suh, 'pears t' me yo' seed bull 'n one o' them cows is lookin' mighty peaky . . ."

While as far as the cowtown doves were concerned, they were arriving in flocks on every train. In fact, sensing where the profits were to be found, Gashouse Gertie had moved her famed—or ill-famed—establishment from Atchison to Abilene and was presiding over the festivities in person.

So what was poor lovelorn—and starved for a little country comfort —Ethan to do? Wait another year and see if things wouldn't calm down to some extent in Abilene? The trouble with that was there were absolutely no indications that they were going to. The decent women of the town no longer dared stir forth from their houses even by *day* now, for fear of being accosted by drunken cowboys. And it made no difference how old or ill-favored the woman might be; if she were even slightly better-looking than the hindquarters of a mustang or a steer, to the Texans she was beautiful.

In their defense, and despite Phil Harris's dire predictions, be it said that the Southerners—boys in their late teens and early twenties, nearly all of them—seldom tried going any further than to steal a playful kiss. The sharp distinction between good women and bad, firmly held in those remote and backward times, had been ground deep into their very psyches by then.

But the restrictions upon her liberty to come and go as she pleased were sure to detract terribly from the sum total of his bride-to-be's personal happiness. And, out here, combined with the awful loneliness, the primitive conditions, the heat, the cold, the bugs, the endless drudgery of a farm woman's life, and above all the sound of those winds that never ceased by day or night, that one more burden might prove too much for her city-bred—and therefore fragile—equilibrium of mind.

So he couldn't decide. He couldn't at all. And after having woolgathered over the question all of a whole day, during which he put in the last of his so-called, and ill-fated, winter wheat, he went to bed determined "to sleep on it," not knowing that on that very morrow the question of whether he should marry his Anne at Christmas or wait another year was going to be taken completely out of his hands, and rudely and conclusively decided for him. . . .

But when he fell asleep—easily enough after a hard day's work—he dreamed. He was walking through a gray fog that had weight and texture and tactility so that it seemed to him it clung to him with cloudy, ice cold and slimy tentacles that restrained him, held him back physically, as he struggled against its unreal clasp to rush after—

A whore. A small and shapely whore with a crown of pale blond hair piled high upon that little head he knew just as he knew those maddeningly lissome and provocative legs encased in black net stockings he had never and could not ever by the very customs of his times have seen which moved below that knee-high scarlet skirt as she tiptoed along upon high heels making no sound against the wooden sidewalk—

And he reaching her and not reaching her at the same time was steamscalded with desire simultaneously frozen in utter horror as she—Nora! *his* Nora!—innocence itself, virtue personified—turned and smiled mockingly invitingly at—no not at him but at another being who defied the laws of physics by not only occupying the same space at the same time as he did but filled up his guts his belly his testicles his mind until with a jeering laugh saying "This is for *me,* twin brother!" Jonathan moved out of him away from him and took her in his arms and there on the plank sidewalk they—

Now the dream had shifted in that effortless way dreams do—upstairs in Gashouse Gertie's place they—

('How the hell,' Ethan wondered, 'do I know this is Gashouse Gertie's when I've never seen the place and have no idea where it is?')—they lay naked and close coupled on a narrow bed. Jonathan was on her, in her ('With *what?* He had every goddamned thing shot away!') and was pounding her to pieces bucking snorting slobbering gobs of blood from his shotaway jaw cursing her with an endless profane inventiveness that any mule skinner would have envied from a shattered mouth incapable of intelligible speech—

While she ('Nora! *My* Nora! Pure as an angel spotless as snow') moaned and twisted and urged him on begging him to do this (rotten filthy perverse obscenity) to her or that one (even worse) calling him by name the name she couldn't didn't know because she had never so much as heard of Jonathan Lovejoy was totally unaware that he Ethan had ever had a brother—

Until listening closely he heard her say:

"You'll never get rid of me throw me over cause even if you did spend four days fucking (did Nora, his Nora even *know* that horrid that unspeakable word?) Cora Bellamy in an Indian teepee you're mine, Ethan Lovejoy; mine!"

Ethan Lovejoy. Not—Jonathan.

He came back then, fought his way upward through layer after layer of ice cold, slimy sleep, sat up in his rude bed, his tears an acid scald upon his bony face. Then, as though hit in the gut by a wagon's tongue, he bent his head and vomited upon the floor.

He was sitting outside his barn, built of sod like his house, husking corn with Randy and Cindy helping him, and the Old Timer pretending to but actually entertaining them all with the most outrageous lies ever heard before on land or sea, which was a help of sorts, because it made the time seem to go by faster and thereby the task less onerous than it actually was.

"Had me this here spread down Texas way," the stinking old buzzard cackled, " 'n this here Mex filly name o' Petra to cook fur me—'n wal, tend to me sweet-like come night . . ."

"Huh!" Cindy snorted. "That musta been two hundred years ago, Cap'n Old Timer!"

"Wal now," the old reprobate chuckled, "hit wuz a right smart time back, come to think of hit, nigger-gal. But enyhow, my steers had th longest horns in livin' memory. Why one of them smart ol' critters—swear t' Gawd he could speak Latin 'n Greek!—had a pair thet spread so wide thet when my pet crow Whitey—called him that 'cause he wuz a shade o' two blacker than Ol' Randy here—took a notion to fly from th tip o' one horn to th tip o' th other, hit took him plumb from fall through th winter to spring ag'in to git thar. 'N to do hit he had to carry his own rations, 'cause thet ol' Mosshorn wuz so tough thet not even a tick would stay on his mangy hide, 'n—"

He stopped short. Looking up, Ethan saw Cora Bellamy coming toward them. He got up slowly, knowing in his bones—from her very posture, the way she moved—that something had happened. Something —terrible. He hadn't seen Cora since he had brought her to her own place from Abilene the night Martha had tended to her minor hurts, the results, he suspected, more of enthusiasm rather than any brutality on the part of the Kansa who had abducted her. These days she sent Tom, bent, grown thin, and utterly defeated by both life and the work she forced him to do, as a result of which they had corn enough, anyhow, to live on through the winter. Tom also obtained their daily ration of water from Ethan's well, so that Ethan no longer had the problem of having to deal with her and her undisguised inclination toward him.

And now, he saw why. She wasn't showing yet and, as is often the case with big, strapping women, wouldn't for a month or two more. But that she was with child he was abysmally certain; and what was worse— his generous heart went sick with pity at the thought—that child was surely a half-breed, and very probably was going to be visibly, discernibly, the offspring, of a Kansa brave.

That being so, his mind went off shudderingly on another ice-cold tangent: could not Nora—*his* Nora!—be likewise in the same—delicate? —horrible!—condition?

'I'll go to Cy!' he raged; 'I'll ask him outright! And if so, if so—'

"Ethan—" Cora whispered. She was crying. Again, and as always, that sight unmanned him. 'Goddamn!' he howled inside his mind. 'She keeps on crying the way she does—and I—*I'll* fall in love with her, too. With big Buffalo Cow Woman!'

"What's wrong, my dear?" he said as gently as he could manage.

"Tom," she moaned; "I—made him dig us a well, because I was sick and tired of us having to impose upon your kindness, Ethan. Cussed him, and threw things, and took a bullwhip to his tail. Now—he's down there in the bottom of it. Fainted from overwork—or lack of air, I reckon. Will you come and help me get him out? Worthless as he is, I don't want him to—die. Between you and your nigger, it seems to me that—"

"Of course, Cora," Ethan said. "Come on, Randy!"

"Now jes' you hold on thar, young Ethan!" the Old Timer said; "We'uns is gonna need ropes, 'n a beam to serve as tackle. 'Nother thing: Cindy, go kotch me a chicken. Doan kill it. I needs hit *live* . . ."

Ethan stared at the mountain man. By that time, his respect for the old man's wisdom was boundless.

"Do it, Cindy," he said.

Ethan peered down that well, amazed to see how deep it was, and saw Tom Bellamy lying in a crumpled heap at the bottom of it. Tom didn't move. Maybe he was breathing, but from a height of at least sixty feet above him, it was impossible for Ethan to tell. When he straightened up, he saw that the Old Timer was binding the live chicken by its feet to a long rope and weighing it down with a section of planking. Then he started to lower it down the well.

"Name of God, Old Timer!" Ethan exploded; "Tom's down there—badly hurt, maybe. This is no time for Indian Big Medicine! Why—"

"Not Big Medicine, *sense,*" the old man said. "I'm mighty afeered thet thet thar's the Black Damp down thar whut's done gone 'n laid pore Tom out. 'N effen hit is—"

"And if it is—what?" Cora whispered.

"This here bird will die," the Old Timer said sorrowfully. " 'N effen hit do, Miz Bellamy, ma'am, th sad truth o' th matter is thet yore pore hubby is already gone 'n has been ever since he fell out down thar. Black Damp is—quick, ma'am. Hank Atkins sez hit doan hurt none a-tall—bein' a well digger he's done been most overcome by hit oncet o' twicet. Reckon we kin be kinda grateful fur thet, enyhow . . ."

"Grateful!" Cora said.

"Gently, Cora," Ethan murmured, and put his arms around her. He stood there, holding her, letting her cry against his shoulder while the Old Timer lowered the chicken down the well. When he drew it up again, it was a limp bundle of feathers, its beak open, its tongue protruding sidewise from it.

"Oh, Jesus!" Cora wept; "We've got to get him out of there—give him a decent burial! Ethan! You go down there. Tie a couple of ropes to his poor, miserable carcass, and—"

"Effen he do," the Old Timer said grimly; "he'll stay down thar with pore Tom—forever, ma'am. Black Damp is heavy. Hit doan rise like other vapors do. So it ain't even fixin' t'go away. Hit'll stay down thar fur years, mebbe. 'N enybody what goes down thar is gonna die jes' like this here chicken did. Th onliest thing we kin do, ma'am, is—kiver him up, right thar whar he lays. Send for th preacher, hold th funeral service above thet thar damn' well. Put a headstone over hit. Hit's a decent enuf grave, as graves go, ain't hit?"

Cora peered at Ethan with wild eyes.

"He's right, Cora," Ethan said sadly; "Marsh gas—the stuff the Old Timer calls Black Damp—would kill me or any man long before he could tie the rope around poor Tom's body. I'm sorry, my dear, but that's the way it is . . ."

Cora bent her head and wept. A long time. But soundlessly and with —immense dignity, Ethan thought. But strangely enough, when she straightened up she was smiling, although her tears still rained down.

"Poor Tom," she whispered, her voice tender—and fond, Ethan realized; "He's got his wish at last . . ."

"His wish?" Ethan said.

"He always wanted to be—the best. The richest, the bravest, the smartest, the handsomest—the *most* of everything, you know. And he couldn't. He didn't have it in him. He was—a good man, but weak. So now one thing can be said for him at long, long last—"

"And that is?" Ethan asked her.

"He's got the deepest grave in Kansas," Cora said.

That night, after the funeral was over, after he had carved Tom's name and dates upon a wooden cross and set it up atop that sixty-odd-foot-deep grave, Ethan wrote Anne a letter, setting the time of their wedding for Christmas Day.

He had had his mind made up for him, his doubts and hesitations vanquished. The truth was he no longer had any choice about the matter.

Not with Cora Bellamy with child, a widow, and living less than half a mile away.

12

"Ethan," Cora Bellamy said; "you always buy whatever you need in Salina nowadays, don't you?"

Ethan took his knee off the plank he was working down to a satiny smoothness with a carpenter's plane. The plank lay across two sawhorses, and Ethan had been holding it in place with his knee so that he could use the plane with both hands. Along with several others, that particular piece of walnut was going into a wardrobe he was lovingly crafting for Anne. He himself had made practically all the furniture he had figured his bride would need, staining and waxing each piece as he'd finished it until it shone. And since he was one of those fortunate—in that one sense, anyhow —people who are born with the knack of working with their hands, and was blessed in addition to that with a patience that was almost Oriental, plus a love for beautiful things, the furniture he had made for Anne was very fine. It transformed the gloomy interior of the sod house, made a home of it. . . . 'Or as much of a home as a house can be that hasn't a woman in it yet,' he thought.

"Yes," he said shortly, then, conscious of the brusqueness of his tone, he immediately softened it. "Yes, Cora," he said; "Why?"

"The next time you go there," Cora said quietly, "I want you to do me a favor. Find—Hank Atkins. Ask him to—come to see me . . ."

Ethan stared at her. A long, slow-crawling time. And his blue eyes were as wintery as a December sky. Then he sighed.

"All right, Cora," he said.

"Don't look at me like that, Ethan!" Cora said angrily. "You're— getting married at Christmastime. So—I can't depend upon *you* for my salvation. And I can't run that place alone. Big as I am, I'm still a woman and—"

"With child," Ethan finished for her. Like that. Flatly.

Her brown eyes, always curiously light in color when contrasted with the mahogany and teak darkness of her hair, flared amber, yellow, in her deeply tanned face. She looked away from him. Upward into the man-dwarfing immensity of the prairie sky. Downward at the grass-covered earth.

"So—it shows," she whispered.

"No," he said, "I guessed. Something about your eyes. A special look —that gravid women get. Forgive me. I didn't mean to hurt your feelings. Besides, you've nothing to worry about, my dear. The child will be born well within nine months after poor Tom's death and—"

She laughed. The bitterness of that sound was physically hurtful. It felt as if someone had slammed two palmsful of broken glass against his ears.

"Except that it's going to be—a 'breed," she said quietly. "And will look like one, sure as hell. I'm—dark. I even look a little like an Indian myself. D'you know what those horny red bastards called me?"

"No—what?" Ethan said.

"*Ptesanwin.* White Buffalo Cow Woman. Delicate, weren't they?"

"How'd *you* know that, Cora?" Ethan asked her. "You don't speak any of the Indian languages."

"The Old Timer," Cora explained. "It seems he knows them all. And I'm absolutely *sure* my baby's going to be a half-breed. Tom hadn't— touched me for weeks before that happened; and he never did again, afterwards, though I tried to get him to—as a precaution—so there'd be a reasonable doubt in his mind. So now there's none, especially not in mine. That's why I asked the Old Timer for two Osage/Kansa names for it: *Owanyake Waste,* 'Handsome Man,' if it's a boy, and *Tawiyela,* 'Doe Child' if it's a girl . . .'"

"They're—beautiful names," Ethan said gently; "Indian names generally are. But aren't you being more than a mite foolish, Cora? Doesn't seem smart to me for you to call your child by a name everybody and his brother—or rather his *sister,* which is a hell of a lot worse!—will know at once is from an Indian language? That's flaunting your—well—misfortune in their faces, my dear."

"So—all right. I'll call him, John, or her, Mary. And what the hell difference will that make, Ethan Lovejoy, since the poor little bastard tyke is sure to have redskin written all over him, or her? Better to flaunt it. I won't crawl, damnit! I was *forced,* I tell you. So—"

"Lay on, MacDuff! And damn'd be him who first cries, 'hold, enough!' " Ethan quoted solemnly.

"Yes! Exactly. That's Shakespeare, isn't it? But you've caught my idea, lover! When you crawl, belly down like a mongrel bitch, people step on you. They won't do that to me—or to my baby. Indian or not—it's *mine.* But you'd have to be a woman to understand *that*—"

"Nevertheless, I do understand it," he said gravely; "what's more, I applaud it, Cora. Your attitude is—noble. Tell you what: If you'll allow me to, I'll stand as godfather to your child . . ."

"Oh, Ethan!" she breathed. Then she bent her head and wept. Straightened up, smiling, the tears golden on her face in the sunlight.

"Given my druthers, I'd druther you stood as stepfather," she said with that deep, leonine chuckle of hers; "but that would be doing poor little Anne a sight too much dirt, wouldn't it? So, go get me Hank, will you?"

"All right," Ethan said; "But what are you going to tell him?"

"The truth. Hank—loves me, Eth. He only skipped because I was married, and he didn't want to make no trouble 'twixt me and Tom. Said that if I were free, he'd grab me in a minute. So—now I *am* free. Only I aim to play it straight. I could lie and tell him the kid's Tom's; but since, once it's born, he'll *see* it ain't, lying is kind of stupid under the circumstances, isn't it?"

"It's stupid, period. Under any circumstances whatsoever. All right, I'll take a train to Salina tomorrow . . ."

"So pore ol' Tom is daid," Henry Atkins, the well digger, said.

"Yes. And Cora wants to see you. She sent me all the way out here to Salina to tell you that," Ethan said drily. "Are you going to visit her, Hank?"

"Don't know. Thet there big woman scares the hell outta me, Prof! Don't know why. But there's sumpin' in th way thet she eyes a fella, thet—"

'Oh, God!' Ethan thought despairingly; 'Don't let this fail me, too. Cora with a husband—especially a lean, sinewy, rawhide and whipcord specimen like this one who'd keep her worn-out and happy abed—would be one distinctly bearable matter. But a lonesome widow, hot-blooded and yearning as my—our—nearest neighbor—Lord Jesus!'

"Tell me this, Hank," he said quietly; "aren't you fond of Cora—even a little?"

Hank considered that question in his slow, judicious way.

"Th truth is, reckon I loves thet there outsize female critter," he said. "But then I done seen how much pure hell she pinned on pore Tom most o' th time . . ."

"Tom had it coming. You wouldn't," Ethan said.

Hank also considered that, and for just as long.

"You thinks I oughta go 'n see her, Prof?" he asked solemnly.

"Yes. She's got troubles, Hank—over and apart from Tom's death. In fact, his passing was probably a relief to her. He wouldn't, or couldn't, work; and a spread like that one needs a hard-working man. Which brings me to another point: digging wells will never make you rich, you know. Or even halfway well off, come to think of it. But a gentleman farmer, owner of one of the prettiest three-hundred-twenty-acre spreads I've ever seen—that's something to think about, isn't it, my friend?"

Ethan saw—with a relief-laden surge of hope—the shrewd, avaricious look creep into Hank Atkins's eyes. That he could depend upon. Hank was nearing fifty, he judged; and at that age, "The heyday in the blood is tame, it's humble, And waits upon the judgment—" but greed, unlike lust, is a constant that lasts until a man dies.

But Hank surprised him then.

"What kinda trouble is she in, Prof?" he said.

Ethan stood there, thinking about how to answer that question.

"I can't tell you that, Hank," he said; "because it's not my place to. I'll admit I know what Cora's trouble is, but only because I was a witness of—not that trouble itself, but of the circumstances surrounding it, so I was able to put two and two together and guess what had happened. But it's your life, and your future, old fellow, so I'll be damned if I want to be guilty, even by accident, of influencing you one way or the other. My advice to you is that you go to see Cora, let *her* explain the problem to you. My hunch is that she's going to tell you the whole and honest truth. I *know* that that truth doesn't shame her. After you've talked with her, if you have any doubts, come to see me. Since Tom, himself, told me what actually happened, I can confirm what she tells you or let you know if she's lying. You have my word, as a friend of yours, that I'll do that, Hank. But only after you've thrashed the whole thing out with Cora. Fair enough?"

Hank Atkins stood there, lathe lean, somber, tall.

"Fair enough, Prof. Tell Cory I'll drap by day after tomorrow—'n then we'll see," he said.

When Ethan got back to Abilene, marveling as always that the round trip between the two towns was now a matter of two hours instead of the two full days it had been before the railroad connected them, he walked from the station toward Luke Prevost's livery stable, where he had left his horse and the surrey that he, Cy Curtiss, Jr., and Will Trainer had built between them, thus saving him at least a hundred and fifty of the some two hundred dollars that a well-made surrey cost in those times. Young Curtiss and the blacksmith were seriously considering going into the carriage, cart, and wagon manufacturing business, now that the far more complicated and risky farm machinery factory that Will and Ethan had planned hadn't worked out. Cy, Sr., pleased at seeing his formerly wild and boisterous son showing such evident signs of settling down, was calculating how much money he could afford to back the new venture with. He'd promised Will and young Cy a definite figure within a week or two. . . .

What the saloonkeeper didn't know but Ethan—because young Cy had confided fully in his former teacher—did, was that the cause of the boy's conversion to sober industrious ways was less Ethan's influence upon him than biology's. The truth was that Cyrus Curtiss, Jr. had, as eighteen-year-olds will, lost his heart. The object of his adoration was seventeen-year-old Nancy Burton, sister of Tyler Burton, his crony and fellow culprit in the school wrecking attempt.

And, Ethan had been assured, Cy, Jr.'s affections were fully recip-rocated. The doting couple planned to be wed next spring, on Nancy's eighteenth birthday, if they could get what neither of them so far had dared to ask—their parents' consent.

"You'll speak to Pa, won't you, Prof," young Cy had pleaded; "he respects you more'n any man in this town. I dasn't ask him. He'll hem 'n haw 'n mebbe turn me down; but if you ask him for me, he—"

"Let's wait until you and Will get your wagon works started, then I'll broach the subject," Ethan had said. "Give me a stronger argument: your being able to support your bride—"

"Tha's so," Cy, Jr. said; "but, O Lord, Prof, it's so hard to wait!"

So now, as he walked toward the Hotel D'Horse, Ethan was thinking about the whole Curtiss family for a change, not merely about Nora, as usual. He pitied Cyrus, Sr., profoundly. The brutal gang rape of his daughter had sunk the saloonkeeper into a melancholy so profound that it seemed to all his friends a prelude to actual madness. Ethan, of course, had done what he could to lift it. Some weeks ago, he had gone into the saloon and called Cy, Sr., aside to the far end of the bar.

"Cy," he had said, "I'm going to ask you something that's absolutely none of my business, but that I've simply *got* to know. Is Nora—in the family way? I'm sorry! Don't bristle at me like that, my friend. I've a good reason for asking. A girl child as young as your daughter is oughtn't be saddled with an unwanted baby— especially not one that will wreck her whole future by robbing her of any hope of an honorable marriage by its very presence. That's one thing. Another is what it'll do to her chances for any kind of happiness or peace of mind by reminding her, every time she looks at it, of what happened to her against her will, and through no fault of her own. So, if she is, I'm going to write to Anne and get her consent for us to—adopt it. That way, the poor little tyke, who's damned well not responsible for how he was got, won't suffer all his life, and Nora won't either. Come on, Cy, tell me: Is she?"

"Damned if you ain't the whitest man alive, Eth Lovejoy!" Cy Curtiss whispered. "And here's my hand on that. But no, reckon my poor daughter was kind of lucky in that regard—if you can even call it luck. Because the sad fact is that the docs in St. Louis said them dirty dogs done tore her up so bad that they doubt she'll ever be able to have a baby of her own. A pity, ain't it? Nora was plumb born to make some man a good wife 'n his kids a lovin' mother.

" 'N you know what? I was kind of hoping things woulda worked out somehows so *you'd* be that man, Prof . . ."

'So was I,' Ethan thought. But he didn't say that. Not aloud, anyhow. It was bad enough to have even admitted it to himself.

And now, as the livery stable came into sight, he remembered the rest of that conversation. Nora, her Aunt Mildred complained in her letters to her brother, had become—difficult. Moody. Often ill-tempered. Given to waspish speech, sardonic turns of thought. "I just don't know how to reach her!" Mrs. James had written.

'Natural enough,' Ethan sighed to himself as he moved toward the stable; 'A wound in the very texture of your soul is hard as hell to heal . . .'

Then he saw—again—one of the things that reminded him of his resolve to give his patronage to another livery stable, not because he had anything against Luke Prevost or his services, but for the very simple reason that Luke's establishment was located much too close to "McCoy's Addition" or "Hell's Half Acre."

A runty, bowlegged cowboy was standing on the sidewalk, revolver in hand, and laughing his obviously drunken head off. The muzzle of his six-shooter was pointed at a soberly dressed man who was wrapped—to his marked distaste, even shuddering disgust—in the arms of one of the cowtown doves.

And then Ethan saw who the victim of this prime example of range-hand humor was: the Reverend Milton Brownley, pastor of the church he, Ethan, was a member of.

Ethan stood there. He wondered whether it might not be wiser to go and look for the town marshal. Then he remembered: there wasn't any town marshal. The cowboys had "hurrahed" him: run him out of town. 'That makes number six; and two of them were carried out, feet first,' he thought dismally.

He started forward then, moving from one rain barrel to another, so he could duck behind one if he had to, as quietly as a stalking Apache or a Cheyenne. On the frontier, making too much noise, or even any noise at all, quite often was the last mistake a man ever made. Ethan kept his boots well oiled and imitated the redskins' toed-in way of walking. But now he saw he needn't have bothered: the cowboy, immersed in his sport, wouldn't have heard even the final trump or the crack of doom. What was more, just before Ethan reached him, the little trail driver got a newer, better idea.

"Turn 'im loose, Molly!" he ordered; " 'Pears like he doan go fur lip-brandin' o' sweet lovin' neither one, so mebbe dancin' is his favorite kind o' sin. Le's see if he cain't cakewalk, nigger strut, cut hisself a buck 'n wing. Turn this Mister Pilgrim Holy Reverend Preacherman loose, 'n stand well back; doan aim to burn yore prutty bunions none a-tall!"

The cowtown dove turned Reverend Brownley loose, scurried a yard or two away. Then the drunken cowboy proceeded to make the pastor dance by shooting as close to that good man's feet as he could put his bullets. It was, Ethan had to admit, a comical sight. And a sad one. Tears of rage, of fear, of bitter shame, were pouring down the minister's face.

But Ethan didn't move. He waited, enwrapped in almost Olympian calm, and counted those shots. When the sixth one went off, he stepped forward, silently, swiftly. His left arm shot out, wrapped itself around the little cowboy's neck; his knee came up, crashed into the small of that fun-loving Texan's back. His right hand gripped the rangehand's right wrist and slammed the man's gun hand against a hitching post so hard the small bones in it went. He could hear them cracking. The cowboy gave a yelp that any coyote would have envied. His stiffening fingers opened, his six-shooter—empty now, of course, but still useful as a club to beat a man's head in with—clanked to the wooden planking of the sidewalk. Ethan whirled him around then, sank a left jab into his middle just above his gun belt, crossed with his right to the cowboy's jaw, and the fight— and the fun and games—were over. All over.

"Aw, Mister Pilgrim," the cowtown dove whined; "Dry Gulch didn't mean no harm a-tall. He wuz just havin' hisself a little fun with th preacher and—"

Ethan looked at her. His eyes were ice. The words died in her throat. Choked her.

"Get going," he said, "before I take a quirt to your filthy, pox-rotted tail."

Then he bent, picked up the revolver. The barrel of it was still hot from all that rapid fire. That gave Ethan an idea. He walked over to the nearest rain barrel, dropped the six-shooter into it. 'I'm—repeating myself,' he thought sardonically. 'So—how about a little variation? An improvement?'

He leaned over the unconscious cowhand, caught him by the gun belt with one hand, by the scruff of his neck with the other. Then, lifting him with effortless strength, Ethan dropped him, head down, into the rain barrel.

Smiling, he turned to the preacher.

"Well, Reverend," he said; "shall we go?"

And until they were completely out of "McCoy's Addition," they could hear the squawks, the splutters, and the splashes, loud on the cool evening air.

For a week after that, Ethan took his Winchester with him as he went about his chores on the farm and kept it on the floorboard of his surrey when he drove into town. But he needn't have worried. "Dry Gulch" Deeter had to carry his gun hand in a sling until long after his particular outfit had left Abilene. Besides which, his Texan's pride just wouldn't allow him to confess to the boys in his band that he'd been taken by a "pilgrim," "hurrahed" by a "dude." He swore his pony had shied at the sight of a sidewinder and tossed him into Turkey Creek. And to that motive for keeping his trap shut, he had to add the dismal certainty that nobody who knew him would bother to draw a six-shooter on his behalf. He wasn't a popular man. As the trail drivers put it: "His cinch is plumb frayed, even 'mongst his own kind . . ."

But Ethan soon left off going armed, even as a precaution, for two good reasons: the very idea of killing still repelled him utterly, and Christmas was at hand. . . .

Looking out of the window of Gerald Purvis's Eating Saloon—as restaurants were still called on the frontier—it came to Ethan that in one sense his decision to marry Anne at Christmastime had been wise. Late in November, the trail always closed up because the "Blue Northers" came howling down out of Canada and swept as far south as the Texas panhandle, freezing the very ground. So there weren't any cowboys in town to play rude jokes and inflict rough horseplay upon Ethan Lovejoy and his Anne.

His Anne. Mrs. Ethan Lovejoy as of one full hour. Since Reverend Brownley, stumbling nervously over the words, had said: "I now pronounce you man and wife!" Ethan realized, and was saddened by, the reason for the pastor's nervousness. It arose out of the fact that he, the presumably happy groom, had been a witness of Reverend Brownley's display of cowardice; and, what was perhaps even worse, had placed the good man of God under a painfully acute moral obligation by the act of saving him from a real and physical danger, demonstrating all the time the very coolness and courage the minister had lacked.

Still Reverend Brownley was a good and gentle man, and Ethan was very sorry that his shame at a very pardonable failure was going to come between them in the future, making their relations, religiously, and socially, difficult.

But now wasn't the time to think about that problem, or consider how to solve it. He owed all his attention to his Anne. Not yet his, of course, except by word and vow; but sure to be his, in every sense, sometime before morning. 'Or even in full daylight,' Ethan thought sardonically, 'if this celebration doesn't break up before then!'

As it was showing absolutely no sign of doing. In a little prairie town, a state to which Abilene reverted in the winter, when the vast herds of Longhorns and dogies no longer came bawling up the trail, there was seldom anything much to do, so any event, such as a wedding, and especially the banquet following it, was enjoyed to the fullest. Looking around the big, barnlike hall, Ethan could see it was absolutely packed. All his friends were there: Phil and Martha Harris, Ned and Nellie Tyler, Matt and Sarah Hendricks, Will and Molly Trainer, Rad and Grace Stevens, Cy Curtiss, alone, as befitted his state as a widower, and the new couple, Hank and Cora Atkins, married one week before in a quiet ceremony at the rectory, with Ethan and the Harrises as witnesses.

"Ethan," Anne whispered; "why are you looking at Cora like that? D'you think the child she's carrying isn't—Tom's?"

Ethan turned and looked at his bride, and his heart sang hosannas to the Most High. Anne's wedding gown made her look rather like a small, snow-covered haystack. The bodice of it was white satin and fitted her upper trunk—laced in so tight by the corsets she absolutely didn't need that Ethan could, and had, spanned her waistline with his two hands—like a second skin, except that it had a flounce of pleated, eggshell-colored chiffon at the level of her breasts that defeated all his efforts to determine if they weren't a trifle fuller, more rounded than he remembered them as being. Her sleeves were the celebrated pagoda type, a mode so new it hadn't yet reached the frontier; they flared out from the shoulders from below that breast-level flounce that went, actually, all the way around her, until they made the shape of a lampshade, say, then they were tucked in sharply at the elbows, from which, beneath still another eggshell chiffon flounce, they flared out again, to end in a skirt-like scallop at least half a yard in circumference above her wrists and the short white kid gloves—now removed or else it would have been impossible for Ethan to slip the wedding band on her finger—that had covered her slim hands. From her incredibly tiny waist, beneath one more eggshell chiffon flounce, her skirt billowed out, yards wide over the steel hoops of her crinoline, cascading down in alternating waves of pleated chiffon and brocaded white satin until it reached, and completely hid, her little, white satin slipper-clad feet.

The women of Dickinson County were almost physically stunned by the magnificence of that wedding dress. Anne had spent the last penny of her savings on it, and now, seeing those envious eyes, she counted it well worth the cost.

"Eeeethaaan!" she hissed; "I asked you a question!"

Ethan grinned at her.

"Which I'll answer later on. Tonight," he drawled. "No, tomorrow. Mean to put what little breath I've got left to a much better use than to waste it talking . . ."

Whereupon Anne raised her right hand and smacked him smartly across the cheek with the glove she had in it.

"Tha's it, honey!" Phil Harris roared; "Give him a good'un! Show him right now who's gonna wear th pants in th Lovejoy fambly!"

"Oh, he knows *that* already," Anne said with wicked demureness.

Ethan's gaze swept over the Eating Saloon. He turned then, and looked at Anne. Saw that she too was sweeping a searching gaze over the whole Saloon, letting her eyes linger deliberately over the young, unmarried girls present. She studied each of the teen-age maidens with some care until she was sure; then she whispered to her brand-new husband:

"Where is *she?* Don't tell me you didn't invite her!"

Ethan's lean face tightened with remembered pain.

"Didn't is the wrong word," he said quietly. "Couldn't is more like it. She's not here any longer. She's gone to live—permanently—with her aunt in Chicago . . ."

Anne studied his face, his eyes. Said, softly, slowly, clearly: "Thank God!"

"Anne!" Ethan said.

"You're all I've got, Ethan," Anne murmured. "Maybe I'll have some news of my father and my half brothers someday, but it isn't very likely, is it? She was—*is*—very beautiful, husband mine, a state of which I see you need reminding! And what's even worse, from my point of view, she was, and very likely still is, in love with you. You're—a good man. But resisting temptation isn't exactly one of the human male's strong points. Especially not that much temptation. So, yes; I'm glad she's gone. I do, indeed, say, 'Thank God.' And I'll pray to Him, every night, to keep her away from here—forever."

He looked at her, his eyes colder than a Blue Norther. Then he sighed.

"I only hope you'll have the Christian charity—or the simple grace —to be a little less happy over it when you find out *why* she left," he said.

"Eeeethaaan!" she gasped; "You—"

"I had nothing to do with it, Anne," he said gravely. "I'll tell you the whole story later. On the train to Wyandotte. Or on the boat to St. Louis . . ."

"Ethan! You didn't tell me we were going on a honeymoon! I thought we'd go straight home from here and—"

"And *what?*" Ethan said solemnly, though his eyes were alight with mischief.

"Oh, Lord! Men! Don't any of you *ever* think about anything else?"

"No'm. What else is there to think about, especially on our wedding night?" Ethan Lovejoy said.

They stayed the few hours that were left between the broad daylight —it was well past dawn when the festivities finally broke up—and the noon eastbound train at the house of Mayor and Mrs. Tyler. To Anne's vast and obvious relief, Ethan made not the slightest attempt to consummate their marriage during those hours, although Ned and Nellie, with sly winks and knowing grins on their faces, conducted them to an upstairs back bedroom and left them there.

Ethan, being both an intelligent, and a sensitive man, could see what a state of nerves his bride was in by then. But he wisely pretended not to notice that anything was amiss at all and said very calmly: "Come on, let me help you out of all those ten million yards of satin and chiffon so that you can slip on your traveling outfit. You'd be a heck of a lot more comfortable; and, besides, you've got to pack that wedding gown anyhow. And in a hurry, too. It's all of ten o'clock now, and our train leaves at noon . . ."

"Oh, no!" Anne gasped. "Go call Nellie to help me. And you wait outside in the hall until I've changed, and—"

"I will *not,*" Ethan said. "That would be downright unkind to our hosts, Annie, me darlin'. Right now, they're probably in the seventh heaven of sheer bliss, contemplating their mental image of what they think is going on up here. That is, if they haven't taken it upon themselves to imitate such delectable and delightful carryings-on. Why disappoint them, dear heart? Or interrupt them, which would be even—worse?"

She came to him then, put her arms, still clad in all those yards and yards of satin and chiffon, around his neck.

"Ethan—forgive me," she whispered. "I'll admit I'm as nervous and jumpy as a sick cat. Only I can't help it. I've never been alone in a bedroom with a man—except that time in Atchison with *you*—in all my life. Have patience with me, please? I'm going to—to try to—get a grip on my nerves—by tonight. I warn you, I may fail. But I'm honestly going to try . . ."

"All right," he said wryly, "if you'll also promise to be patient with me, since I'm at least twice as nervous as you are, and three times as scared!"

"Of—*me?*" she whispered, breath gone with astonishment.

"Of you, no," he murmured; "of—spoiling things. Of not making the beginning of our life together the joy and the glory it ought to be. I'll freely confess I've been no saint; but then I've been no great shakes as a sinner, either. Put it this way: nothing—or no one—in my past has prepared me for what's going to be the most important night in all my existence, and that will remain just that until the hour I die . . ."

She kissed him then; and he felt, on her lips' warm softness, the ebbing of her fear, the slow, uncertain but nonetheless dawning recognition of the fact that she now had the perfect right to dispense with all the "Thou shalt not's!" that up until this very moment had hedged her life round about, as they did—and often warped and ruined—the lives of most women of her time.

She drew back then, looking up into his face. Then she became conscious of the fact that she wanted him. Wanted this man who was her husband, physically. Her face flamed scarlet. Confusion seized her. The transition from what had been wrong, a sin, metamorphosed by words, a book, a ring, a vow, into right, a duty, even—perhaps!—a joy, was too abrupt. She whirled away from him.

"Unbutton me, Ethan—then, *please* turn your back!" she said.

On the train to Wyandotte he told her of Nora's tragedy and of Cora's now possibly redeemed one. She had the good grace to weep for Nora, and to sympathize with Cora's need to marry again in such unseemly haste. . . .

Ethan blessed her for her charity and felt a surge of relief at its obvious sincerity. He realized that had she proved vindictive, rejoicing at the fate of a younger, prettier rival brought low, his still uncertain love for her would have suffered one more disillusion hard for him to sustain. He was going to spend the rest of his life with this small, plain, often irritating woman. He meant to learn to love her fully; but she would have to help him far more than she knew to achieve that blissful state. . . .

The steamboat trip downstream from Wyandotte to St. Louis took, in those days, anywhere from a minimum of sixteen hours to a maximum of twenty-four. That night, in their stateroom, they became finally husband and wife. The best that could be said for that tender occasion was that it wasn't as bad as either of them had feared it might be. Anne was, as she'd claimed, virgin and intact. There was, therefore, a certain, irreducible minimum of pain involved, some slight bleeding. But Anne realized how careful Ethan had been, saw his abject distress at having hurt her the little that he had, and found, even under those trying circumstances, the whole experience rather more pleasant than not.

The next night, in St. Louis, in the hotel's dining room, he treated her to an extravagant bridal supper, complete with oceans of champagne.

Going upstairs, she giggled like a schoolgirl, swayed on uncertain feet against his arm. She was delightfully tipsy, but not drunk, for long before the supper was over, Ethan had flatly refused to fill her glass anymore.

"Too much will put you to sleep," he said solemnly.

"Which heaven forbid!" Anne said.

Her inhibitions vanquished, their lovemaking—and it was truly that, filled with worshipful little tendernesses far removed, and carefully sublimated away, from the mere physical manifestations of sex—was immediately acceptable and, ultimately, very fine.

Too fine—in a way—to suit Ethan Lovejoy's rock-ribbed New England temperament, his caution, his prudence, his benighted idea—shared with nearly all his male contemporaries—of what a *good* woman was, or should be.

For, in the morning, as she surged up against him once again, kissing his eyes, his mouth, his throat, whispering joyously: "Oh, I *am* awful, aren't I? Wicked! Depraved! But you *are* my darling husband, aren't you? So, Mister Ethan Lovejoy—will you be so kind?"

And then she saw his eyes.

"Oh!" she said; then: "Ethan—I'm sorry. I've shocked you, haven't I? I—I told you I was my mother's daughter! I told you! Forgive me. Please forgive me. I'll try to be—more restrained. I'll honestly try. Only—"

"Only what, Anne?" he said.

"I'll fail," she said miserably; "I'll *always* fail. I—Oh, God!—I love you too much! Even—this way. No—*especially* this way . . ."

'I'm being a fool,' he realized then; 'a frozen New England puritan —with ice floes in my blood. *I'm* the one who's spoiling this, not Anne . . .'

He bent then, found her mouth. And made love to her, not gently, tenderly, as he had before, but with big, fine, honest passion. And thereby saved their marriage.

At least for a certain length of time.

13

On the last night of September, 1868, Anne Jeffreys Lovejoy sat by the window of the sod house her husband had built for her, with her little twin-barreled Remington derringer in her hand. She had no hope at all of being able to stand off the howling, whooping rush of Cheyenne warriors with that puny little weapon. No; the little pocket pistol was to make sure they wouldn't take her alive if they came. It was a choice white women on the frontier often had to make these days.

The night was very clear, so she could see Ethan standing by the big gate, fifty yards from the house, talking to Phil Harris, who sat in his buggy, making no move to climb down. Since timber was still hard to come by in Kansas, and would continue to be so until the railroads linked them, finally, with the great forests beyond the Rocky Mountains, Ethan had planted Osage orange, a prickly hedge, to mark off the limits of the acre on which their sod house stood. It made a good fence; but at fifty cents a perch, it was too expensive to set out around the borders of the whole farm. Still, the Ho-ta-min-tanio braves would have to break through it, or jump over it, to get to the house itself, so they couldn't keep up their usual tactic of worming their way like adders through the grass. And, at that distance, a marksman as skilled as Ethan was could easily pick them off. Only he didn't trust his ammunition. His beautiful Winchester was a fine weapon indeed; but he swore that "rimfire cartridges are no damned good!"—whatever on earth *that* meant.

She shuddered and emptied her mind of all thought, even of her lively curiosity as to what Ethan and Phil were discussing so earnestly down there by the gate. Instead, she sat there very still and looked out at the night. It was cold. The stars made frozen fire in the awesome immensity of the prairie sky, except in the quarter where a full moon hung, spilling silver over half the world. There, its white blaze washed them out, effortlessly drowning their distant twinkle, dropping a curtain of pearl, mist soft and shimmering between them and the seeking eyes of men.

Then, looking toward the gate again, she saw that Ethan had shifted the Winchester to the crook of his left arm, and that he and Phil were shaking hands. After that, Phil drove off, while Ethan turned back up the footpath toward the sod house. And the whole time he ambled toward her without any particular haste, Anne Lovejoy held her breath.

The first thing he did when he came in the door was to hang the Winchester over the fireplace. Which meant a great deal, the resurrection of hope maybe, because he hadn't had the rifle more than six inches from his hands in five days, not even while bolting down the sparse and simple meals she'd fixed him. When he turned to her, he was smiling. He pointed to her little lady's pistol.

"Give me that," he said.

Anne breathed in, breathed out. Her breath rasped, pulsated, gurgled throat-deep, stopped. Started up again.

"So—they—won't come?" she said. "Ethan, are you *sure*?"

"I'm sure," he said peacefully. "They just got the news in town. Colonel Forsyth's Volunteers caught up with the dog soldiers on the banks of the Arickaree . . ."

"Where's that?" Anne asked.

"It's a branch of the Republican River and cuts across the extreme northwestern corner of Kansas just before you get to the Colorado line. Anyhow, Forsyth and his fifty heroes, any one of whom was, in his own modest opinion, 'More'n a match fur all th Injuns they ever wuz, by gum!' were camped on the banks of the Arickaree, which is a broad, shallow stream from what Phil says. And the next morning, the seventeenth, eight Cheyenne braves stampeded some of their horses and made off with seven of them. So Forsyth and his men retreated to an island in the middle of the river—no trick at all, since the water didn't come up to a man's knee —dug rifle pits with their knives and made a stand . . ."

"But Ethan," Anne protested; "You said that Colonel Forsyth's Volunteers caught up with the Indians; but from what you're saying, it looks like the Indians caught up with *them!*"

"Exactly," Ethan said with a grim chuckle. "And the only thing that saved them was the fact they were armed with Spencers, and the dog soldiers had never come up against repeaters before. Anyhow, Forsyth and company beat off the Brulé Dakotas, the Arapahos, and both the Northern and the Southern Cheyenne. But they lost twenty-three dead or wounded, including Colonel Forsyth, who took a bullet through his thigh; Lieutenant Beecher, the second in command who was killed outright; and Dr. Moorehead, the surgeon, who was so badly hit that he couldn't attend the other wounded and died three days later. Every horse the troop had was killed in the first hour. But Forsyth's sharpshooters brought down the greatest of the Cheyenne chiefs, Sauts. That means "The Bat" in English. He was a huge man with a nose like an eagle's beak. The troopers have called him "Roman Nose" for so long that the Cheyenne themselves have accepted the nickname and renamed him Woquini—'Hooked Nose.' A little later the Volunteers also picked off Dull Knife, the bravest of the Dakota chiefs. The redskins' morale seems to have broken at that. They rode off the field and left Dull Knife lying there; but the squaws came out with sticks and clubs and beat the warriors back into the fight . . ."

"I don't understand how *any* of the Volunteers survived," Anne whispered; "there were only fifty of them to start with and there must have been hundreds of those Indians—"

"Several hundred," Ethan said. "But they were used to charging troopers armed with single-shot carbines. So they tried their old trick of drawing fire and then dashing in before the cavalry could reload. Didn't work this time; a Spencer repeater holds seven shots in its magazine. Then, seeing that attacking head-on into that kind of fire was suicide, the dog soldiers laid siege to the island, hoping to starve Forsyth's men out. The siege lasted nine days. During that time, Forsyth sent out four scouts. All four got through. The last two guided Colonel Carpenter of Company H, Tenth U.S. Cavalry, back to the island, and saved those still left alive after nine days of suffering from untended, flyblown wounds, drinking muddy water, and dining off putrid horseflesh, with gunpowder sprinkled over the meat to kill the stench. But thanks to those brave damned fools, we're safe —until next summer, anyhow. The redskins have retreated into Colorado and Wyoming—and in winter they'll keep to their lodges. They only raid in the summertime. This is the first time in my life I've ever been inclined to be grateful for the sheer overconfident idiocy that we lordly palefaces seem to have the exclusivity of. Hell, in this one case, I am thankful for it. And for Christopher Spencer's fine repeating carbine. Not to mention the Tenth Cavalry. I'll have to tell Randy that. He'll be as pleased as all get out . . ."

"Randy will be pleased? Why, Ethan?"

"The Tenth Cavalry are black troopers, Annie, me darlin', and among the best fighters the frontier has ever seen. The redskins call 'em 'buffalo soldiers' because their kinky hair resembles the wool on a buffalo's head. So now, my love, at long, long last we can quit being scared spit-less . . ."

"I wasn't afraid," Anne said then, quietly.

Ethan turned and looked at her. She was very great with child by then. If his calculations were right, their son—or their daughter—should be born by mid-October. And she was a pitiful sight: as the great tun of her belly had swollen, the rest of her had shrunk. Her arms and legs were matchsticks; her face, hollowed; her neck, scrawny. He wondered—again and for at least the thousandth time—whether it was even possible for her to survive the ordeal of giving birth.

"You weren't afraid?" he said wonderingly.

"No," she said. "Not for me, anyhow. Nor—for you. We've had our lives. Almost—a year together. A good year. The best, Ethan. And we— owe God a death. Who said that?"

"Shakespeare. 'Now by my troth, do we owe God a death; and he who pays his debt this year, is quit of it the next.' Or words to that effect; I'm quoting from memory. Anyhow, it's a noble sentiment. Very—"

"But I *was* afraid for our baby. We owe him his life, Ethan."

"Her, *her* life," Ethan teased her solemnly. "It's going to be a girl and look just like *you.*"

"Which heaven forbid! You know what I was thinking while I was sitting there with that little pistol in my hands?"

"No, what?" Ethan said.

"That since this was going to be my last night on earth, or at least above it, I was—grateful—I could spend it with you, my love. Ethan—I thank you for this year. The one wholly good, big, fine, wonderful year I've had in all my life. And I thank you for—my baby. If only God—and the Cheyenne—will let him live."

"Anne, I told you the danger is over," Ethan said reproachfully.

"Until next summer. Ethan, how many people—white people—have they killed so far?"

"One hundred seventeen. All of them in the Solomon and Saline river valleys—west of here. Twenty-five raids this summer. Seven white women carried off into captivity—the fate worse than death, I suppose. Of course, Cora Bellamy Atkins might not agree with that point of view . . ."

"Her baby is—beautiful," Anne sighed. "Doe Atkins. Except that Hank had nothing to do with that little papoose. Poor Cora. Poor baby Doe Child. The women hereabouts are downright *mean!*"

"They share the opinions of their husbands. And are equally bigots —racially and religiously. A point of view you ought to understand. You almost cost me my tenants, even knowing how much I need them . . ."

"Ethan! I've told you and told you I said not one word to Cindy Otis! I don't even know why they started to leave—"

"You looked at her children, Cindy's children, as though they were —animals. Repulsive and loathsome animals. One of the kids reached for your hand, trusting you, believing that grown-ups are kind, regardless of the color of their hides. And you—shrank from the touch of that small, innocent black hand—shuddering. Do you wonder that Cindy was insulted, wanted to leave? Took me two hours of pleading to make them stay. Suppose someone were to treat your child like that?"

"But *our* child, Ethan Lovejoy, will be—"

"White. And, therefore, but little lower than the angels, crowned with glory and honor. A citizen of the nation that has signed over three hundred treaties with the red men between 1778 and now, and broken every single one of them. An example of sheer perfidy, even infamy, unequalled by any other civilized nation. The Plains Tribes are only trying to preserve their way of life, Anne, dear. A way of life we've doomed by firearms, liquor, disease—and the slaughter of the buffalo. A primitive way of life—often cruel, to be sure, but strangely noble for all that. I admire the redskins, most of the time, anyhow; but I'm seldom able to admire our own people, love. The cowboys, gamblers, cowtown doves, fanatical fundamentalist preachers, buffalo hunters, claim jumpers, and bunco artists have taught me not to."

"Ethan, that's unfair! There are decent people in Abilene, just as there are in Omaha, the only two Western towns I know. For instance: the Harrises, the Tylers, Mr. Curtiss, the Hendrickses, the—"

"Every damned one of whom is capable of cutting poor Cora off even from the usages of common politeness, not to mention ordinary social intercourse because she gave birth to a half-breed child, conceived through absolutely no fault of her own. Every good wife among the pairs you've named is going to go out of her way to be as nasty to poor little Tawiyela Atkins as possible, while their children, following their mothers' examples, are going to make that innocent baby's life a sheer hell from the moment that she's old enough to go to school. Anyhow, we've talked enough tonight. You must be tired. Besides, you've got to take care of Annie, Two. Let's go to bed . . ."

"No," Anne said; "I—couldn't sleep. And I'm just as comfortable, if not more so, sitting up. Let's pursue this a little further—the aspect of it that interests me, anyhow . . ."

"And that aspect is?" Ethan said quizzically.

"The—well—motives behind your exceedingly strange behavior, husband mine. Oh, I grant you the rightness, even the nobility of all the lofty principles you've been giving vent to for the last half an hour. But I'm a woman, and my female mind tells me that people don't work by generalizations and abstractions, but only by reactions to concrete cases. *You,* for instance. You've only become such a fiery advocate of Indians' rights since you had that terrible fight with that man in Cy Curtiss's saloon —to which you go, dear faithful spouse, since you don't even like whiskey and seldom touch a drop of the stuff, to inquire after your darling little Nora!"

"I'm going to have to keep a list," Ethan said solemnly, "of all the beatings I owe you, so I won't forget to lay 'em on—with a rod no thicker than my thumb, of course, as the law allows—once you've brought my daughter safely into this world . . ."

"Your son and heir. And I wouldn't put it past you. To start beating on me, I mean. Whereupon I'll leave you, taking our offspring with me, so take care, Ethan Lovejoy! But, as I was saying, I know, because you admitted that much, that the fight was over the Indian question. Ugh! When Phil and Ned brought you out here, I almost fainted. If I hadn't remembered my—our—baby in time to get a grip on myself, I'd probably

have fallen flat on my big tummy and had a miscarriage. You were all—
bloody. Covered with bruises. One eye swollen shut—"

Ethan grinned at her.

"You should have seen *him,*" he said.

"Oh, I gathered that you won that fight," Anne sighed; "but I
just can't understand your fighting at all. Usually you're so calm, so—
peaceful . . ."

"And, therefore, exactly the wrong kind of a fellow to pick on,"
Ethan drawled. "I didn't start that fracas, my dear. I simply punched back
when punched . . ."

"But why should he have hit you? A man he didn't even *know?*"

Ethan stared at her, and his eyes were somber.

"Anne, don't ask me that," he said quietly. "That information isn't
an item likely to add to your happiness, or your peace of mind . . ."

"Ethan, now you're going to tell me the truth! Or else I'm going to
sit right here until you do. So, if you care about me, or our baby, you—"

"The female mind in action," Ethan quipped; "Of logic all compact!
All right, but don't complain when what I say shocks you. It seems he
got the idea that I objected to his indumentum. He was right; I did.
Violently. But I didn't say anything. I suppose he must have read the
expression of disgust, of near nausea upon my homely face. You see, he
was from Colorado, from, more exactly, Denver, a place where, as I've
already told you, they offer a ten dollar bounty for each Indian scalp
taken and make no specification that said scalps have to be torn from the
heads of warriors . . ."

"He'd—he'd scalped—*women?* Squaws?" Anne breathed. "But,
Ethan, how on earth could *you* know that?"

"Because he was wearing a cap made of human skin, and hair, and
bragging about what he'd done to those women from whom he had
bloodily ripped those particular trophies before he'd killed them. And
their children, of course. Then he saw how I was looking at him and
punched me in the snoot . . ."

"You mean—you actually mean—that he was wearing a cap made
out of the scalps of Indian squaws?" Anne whispered.

Ethan stared out of the window into the shimmering moonwash.
Turned back to his wife.

"Well—that's one way of putting it," he said.

"Ethan Lovejoy, you drive a body wild! Was his cap made of women's
scalps, or wasn't it?"

"No," Ethan said softly, sadly; "it wasn't. But then—the head isn't the only place that the human body, even the human female body—grows hair . . ."

Anne stared at him. A long time. A very long time. Horror invaded her eyes. Grew until they blazed with an icy, swimming sickness brighter than the moonlight.

"Oh! Oh, my God!" she said.

"Amen. And the bastard was bragging about *that*. For the first time since Jonathan—died—I had the honest and wholehearted desire to kill a man. But I restrained myself and limited my efforts to giving him a good beating, which wasn't hard to do, since I practiced boxing as a sport in college. The only problem I had was a tactical necessity to protect my shot-up middle, because one good punch there would have finished me. But at the end of it, Anne, dearest, I made my one mistake, though I have to admit that that one came close to being fatal: seeing him down, and apparently out, I turned to walk—or rather stagger, because, as you saw, I caught quite a few myself—away from there. But he wasn't out—or maybe he was one of those tough hombres that recover fast. Anyhow, he came up from the floor with a buffalo skinner's knife in his hand. It seemed he worked as a skinner for some buffalo hunters operating out of Fort Dodge . . ."

"Ethan," Anne whispered; "but if he had a knife, and your back was turned, how—?"

"Cy shot him. Dropped him in his tracks, dead before he hit the floor. So now I've one more moral problem to wrestle with: I'm glad he's dead, Anne. That's a terrible thing to say, or even to think, but there you have it. My heart tells me, and even my mind, that living—breathing air—is a privilege that oughtn't be extended to obscenities like him. Not for any length of time. They do too much harm . . ."

"And I'm glad, too. Not only because, in spite of all your faults, you're an old sweetheart of a husband and I love you, but also because I have absolutely no desire to become a widow anytime soon. And especially not a pregnant widow. You see, there aren't any more Hank Atkinses left running around loose. Which would make matters awfully hard for me and Ethan, Jr., wouldn't it?"

She stared up into his suddenly stricken face. Laughed merrily. Said: "Good! I see I've won that round! Come on now, let's go to bed . . ."

It was exactly three weeks from that very night that Anne turned to Ethan in the darkness and whispered:

"Ethan—are you awake?"

"Huh?" Ethan grunted sleepily; then: "Yes, honey, I am—now. Why?"

"You'd better—drive into Abilene—and get me Doctor Baines," Anne said.

Ethan's bare feet hit the planked floor with a double thud.

"You—you're sure, Anne?" he croaked.

"Yes. My—pains—contractions—are coming—every—few minutes, now. Oh, Ethan, dearest—hurry!"

"All right," Ethan said as he shoved one hairy, skinny leg into the wrong leg of his pants; "but first I'm going to rouse Cindy out and get her to sit with you . . ."

"Oh, Ethan—no!" Anne said.

"Good Lord, Anne! She's a woman, and she's given birth to six kids herself. The last one three weeks ago. Saw her nursing it, yesterday. What's her color got to do with this? I can't leave you all alone, and fetching Cora Atkins would take me too long. That's a mile away, round trip, and she'd still have to get up and get dressed, and—"

"No," Anne said; "not Cora! I'd prefer even Cindy to *her*. I don't need anyone right now. And I won't for hours yet. But after all, Abilene is three miles away. Oh, Ethan, get started, please!"

"Anne, you're going to have to put up with Cindy, that's all," Ethan said grimly; "because I'm damned well not going to drive *six* miles—three going and three coming back—and leave you all by yourself, and in the throes of labor!"

"But Ethan, she—she *hates* me. She doesn't talk to me at all—except when she can't avoid it; and even then—she's—as insolent—as she dares be. She might—do something to me. To—my baby . . ."

"Hogwash!" Ethan snorted. "Cindy loves babies. Look how she spoils and pets her own. And I don't believe even all the good reasons you've given her to dislike you will matter to her, right now. She'll see a poor, forlorn female 'critter' who's trying to give birth to her first baby. And Cindy's been through that business six times to date. So I'm going to call her and that's that. Or else I'll go crazy before I even get to Abilene to wake up Doc Baines. You don't want a gibbering idiot for a husband and the father of your child, d'you?"

"No-oh," Anne faltered. "All right. Go call her. I'll just have to stand —her presence—that's all. If she—only—looked a little less—like—an orangutan, I—"

"Maybe if you weren't the spitting image of a nanny goat," Ethan teased her solemnly, "she'd like you a little better, too. That's what she says *you* look like, Anne o' my heart. A white nanny goat. No, she didn't tell *me* that. I overheard her saying it to Randy . . ."

"Well, I never!" Anne gasped.

"There's no accounting for tastes—or opinions," Ethan said, and kissed her. "Hold on to everything, Annie, me darlin'—including that outsize belly, 'cause I'm on my way!"

But as he might have expected, and as was usual in the miserable existences led by general practitioners on the Great Plains, Josiah Baines wasn't at home. He was out on an emergency call, attending a farmer suddenly striken with terrible belly pains that involved all the symptoms of acute appendicitis. To make matters even worse, Mathilda Baines had been three-quarters asleep when the farmboy had come to summon her husband to his father's bedside, so she didn't know, or couldn't remember, the name of the man Dr. Baines had driven out to attend. So Ethan did the wisest thing he could do: he waited, and came to the very borders of a nervous breakdown through anxiety and fear before Dr. Baines, gray and trembling from fatigue, returned, at nine o'clock the following morning, to his house.

"Let me get some breakfast under my belt, son," the doctor sighed; " 'Specially some hot, black coffee to wake me up a mite. Don't worry: It's your missus's first kid, ain't it? Hell, Eth, we could drive out to your place day after tomorrow and still be in time . . ."

Since by then the doctor's swaybacked, wind-broken nag was an obvious candidate for the glue factory, Ethan drove Dr. Baines out to the farm in his own big wagon and had the good sense, in spite of the gnawing anxiety that clawed at his shot-torn gut, to let the good practitioner, who was at least no more ignorant than most medical men of his time, and probably a great deal less so than most, sleep all the way.

Only to be faced with the happy necessity of turning around and driving him right back again, for Anne, a hint of color beginning to steal back into her snow white, corpse white, face, lay smiling peacefully through swollen, blue bruised, hard-bitten lips, with their firstborn—a tiny, perfect boy—cradled in her arms.

"Damn stubbornes' woman I ever did see!" Cindy Otis chuckled. "Tol' her to let go 'n yell—screamin' yo' haid off mebbe doan help none a-tall, but hit sho' Lawd meks you feel better. But her, nosireebobtail!

Her's a white lady, 'n white ladies doan yell. 'Neath they dignity to cry 'n carry on lak us po' niggers does. 'Sides, 'pears lak she done gone 'n give you her Bible word that effen she ever starts in t'moanin' low over 'bout how hard this here way o' livin' is, you's got a perfect right t' up 'n leave 'er. Well, tell you one thing, Prof Lovejoy, suh—you's purely stuck, 'cause she ain't let out the teeniest li'l squawk. Nary a whimper, let alone a honest-to-Gawd birthin' woman's yell. Braves' li'l ol' skinny nanny goat o' a white gal I ever did see!"

"Cindy, you stop it!" Anne whispered; "Insulting me that way. . . . Ethan—she—was wonderful. She—very—likely—saved my life . . ."

"Aw, you wasn't in no danger, honey," Cindy said. "You's got good wide hipbones, even skinny as you be. You birthed that young'un real easy fur a fact. Well, Prof, how does you lak yo' baby boy?"

"That's *my* question, Cindy!" Anne said sharply; "And it's my place to ask it. Well, Ethan, dearest—how do you?"

"Well, he's mine all right," Ethan said solemnly. "Maybe he could be a little uglier if he tried harder; but give him time. Come here, you little monster, and meet your pappy. Lord, what a sight! Doc, don't you think maybe we ought to put him back and let him cook a little while longer? Looks a mite underdone to me . . ."

"Well, I never! Men! That's gratitude for you!" Anne said.

"Hell, son, all new babies look like that," Dr. Baines chuckled. "Don't even start to look human 'til they're about three months old. Lemme have a look at him, Missus Lovejoy. Your cullud woman attend to you? Seems to have done a good job. You had midwife training—wha's your name?"

"Cindy, suh. Nawsuh, I jes' learnt birthin' my own . . ."

"Hmmmn. Cord tied neat. Not too short. A mite too long, but better that way. When this here drops off, he'll have the prettiest li'l belly button anybody ever did see. Now, how's about you, ma'am? Hmmmmmnn—cleaned up nice. No excessive bleeding. Use b'iled white cotton cloth for napkins, no dyed stuff, y'hear? 'N change 'em frequent, 'til it stops. Cindy gal, what did you do with th afterbirth? Throw it to th hawgs?"

"Nawsuh. We'uns most in generally buries it. But I ain't had time. Hit's in that slop bucket over theah . . ."

"Hmmmmnn, lemme see. Normal. Absolutely normal. No pus. No purple streaks. Awright, Cindy, gal, you can get rid of it, now. . . . Missus Lovejoy, your newborn wakes up 'n starts in to yell, give him your breast. You won't have no milk 'til this time tomorrow, but th li'l fella's pulling on it will stimulate lactation. Well, Prof—how's about fetching me along back home? I mean to sleep all day if my patients will let me . . ."

"Ethan," Anne whispered; "if you're—pleased, I must say you're concealing it awf'ly well!"

Ethan bent down and lifted the tiny infant from Anne's side. The baby scarcely filled one of his big, knobby-knuckled, work-hardened paws, not to mention both of them.

"My son and heir," he whispered. And all of a sudden tears stood and glittered in his eyes.

"Ethan!" Anne gasped.

"It just—hit me, Anne o' my heart," he croaked. "The meaning of it. I'm—a father. A real, honest-to-God father! This is—our image. Our continuation in time. Here, take him back, for God's sake! I'm shaking so, I just might let him drop . . ."

"Don't you dare!" Anne cried, and took the baby. She lay there holding it and smiling at it tenderly. To her, as to all new mothers, that tiny, red, wrinkled, hideous little lump of scarcely human flesh was— beautiful. . . .

'As it is. As all new babies are. It takes time and disappointment and bitterness and anger to make them ugly,' Ethan thought. 'The loss of trust. The souring of love. Sin. Hatred of one's fellows. In short, growing up. Maturity. The death of dreams, of hope. So you'll get there, son of mine, God pity you!'

He turned to the worn-out little physician, and his smile was sad.

"Well, Doc," he said softly, "shall we go?"

Which should have practically ended the matter of the Lovejoy succession—barring the usually manageable problems of childhood diseases and accidents—at least until the next baby came along. But it didn't. For Anne hadn't any milk. Her small, rather shapely breasts didn't swell, become globular. They stayed exactly the way they were before their first offspring arrived upon the scene. By the next night, the baby's cries were a thin, ever weakening wail.

"And," Anne wept, "all the cows are dead, thanks to the fever those ugly Texas Longhorns brought! Oh, Ethan, what on earth are we going to do?"

Ethan thought about that. Then, without a word, he got up and went out into the night. Ten minutes later he was back, bringing Cindy Otis with him.

"Give her the little fellow, Anne," he said.

Anne's blue eyes widened. Then they went very cold and still with what was very surely horror. In that moment, Ethan saw what the redskins meant when they declared that the pale eyes of the Nordic segments of the white race didn't look human, that they were the attributes of evil spirits, ghosts. That was what Anne's looked like at the moment: the icily glaring orbs of a small, square-faced she-devil.

"No!" she grated shrilly; "God, no!"

Cindy put one hand down the front of her own shapeless Mother Hubbard dress, came out with one glossy, velvety black breast, squeezed the nipple between her thumb and forefinger. Drops of milk came out of it, trickled down.

"Hit's white as yourn," she said calmly. "Naw—whiter, 'cause you ain't got none."

Ethan stared at his wife. At the moment, his own eyes, as blue and as pale as Anne's, would have earned him easy entry into the ranks of the *himunga,* "those mysteries to be dreaded."

"Give her the child, Anne," he said.

He didn't raise his voice, but the authority in it was like sudden stone. Anne stared at him, and for the briefest instant rebellious anger flared in her eyes. For the duration of that same instant, she hated her husband utterly, hated the patriarchal force in him, rock solid and complete, with no weakness in it anywhere. Then her gaze softened, became unsettled, walled vision out behind a sudden scald of tears.

"Oh, Ethan, I—" she sobbed.

"Give her *my* son," Ethan said. "*Mine,* because I wouldn't deny him —life. Not for any reason. Certainly not for motives as downright shameful as yours. Don't make me take him from you, Anne. I will if I have to. So, don't make me."

Wordlessly Anne passed the baby up to him. Ethan handed the child to Cindy. Stood there while the black woman nursed it, and gazed sorrowfully at his wife's small back, shivering and shaking from the galestorm of weeping that tore her as she lay there face down, muffling her sobs in the pillow, soaking it with her tears.

And it came to Ethan Lovejoy that, while he more or less understood, even accepted the force of a repugnance Anne simply couldn't contain, and though he didn't confuse it with a prejudice, since prejudices have a certain intellectual content however irrational that content might be, it was going to be awfully hard for him to forgive her for putting that visceral revulsion, even momentarily, before their child's life. That, or anything. For it seemed to him a failure of the very maternal instinct, and thereby of womanhood itself. Which, quite simply, to his stern New England mind, wasn't pardonable. Whether she liked Blacks, or loathed and despised them, or—more accurately in her case—found their physical characteristics utterly repulsive and was very simply afraid of them, was a total irrelevancy. She had—instinctively, *meaning* it—put something, *anything,* because what that something was didn't matter, above the continued existence of her own child. And—his.

"Doan worry bout it, Prof Lovejoy," Cindy said. "Her's a Yankee, 'n Yankee wimmen jes' plain ain't used to us th way Southern white folks is. Lawdy me! White plantation ladies had a-been worried 'bout a niggergal shovin' her coal black tit into they babies' li'l pink moufs, wouldn't be no 'ristocratic Southern white folks left. 'Cause them ladies brung they babies to us not 'cause they didn't have no milk, but 'cause they didn't want they shapes ruint by havin' they titties drug down to they belly buttons by a greedy li'l critter like this 'un pullin' on 'em. Lawd Jesus, but he sho' hongry, th po li'l fella . . ."

Anne whirled then, sat up in bed; whispered:

"Cindy—I—I'm sorry. I—apologize—humbly. Ethan—?"

"Forget it," Ethan said; "I've decided on a name for him. I'm going to call him—Jonathan. Any objections?"

It took Anne three tries to get the words out.

"After—after—your—brother? But, Ethan—that's—bad luck! Your brother died—horribly, and—"

"My father's name is also Jonathan. And the old man will live past ninety, sure as hell. Objection overruled. Jonathan, it is. So you've finished with your first dinner, Jon? More of a banquet, I'd say. Here, Cindy, give him to me . . ."

"Not yet, suh. I'se purely got to make him bring up all that air he done gone 'n swallowed along wit my black nanny goat's milk. Else he git gas pain in he li'l belly 'n he cry all night," Cindy said. "Y'all won't git a lick o' sleep fo' mawnin' . . ."

Anne sat there, upright in the bed, watching as Cindy patted the baby's tiny back to make him belch. Then she felt Ethan's steady gaze upon her, and half turning, saw his eyes.

"Ethan—I—I've—lost you. Lost you forever, haven't I?" she whispered brokenly.

Ethan considered that question a long, slow, dead-stopped time. Then he sighed.

"No. But let's say you came a mite too close for comfort that time, dear," he said.

14

"Have you seen her?" Anne said.

Ethan looked at his image in the standing mirror. The sight wasn't pleasing. He saw a gaunt, rangy figure in a rusty black broadcloth suit, frayed at both the sleeves' and the pants' cuffs, that looked as if he had borrowed it from a far fatter and a much shorter man. His face, as he already knew from their comments, reminded people of the late and martyred President Lincoln's, all bones and hollows, though the otherwise striking resemblance was somewhat diminished by his truncated nose tip, and the great blaze of the scar the now departed Bart Lee had burnt across his cheek with a bullet. Otherwise, he hadn't changed much in the nearly five years he had now lived—and bent and gnarled his body working— in Kansas, except for a web of fine lines that drew crow's feet traceries about his pale blue eyes. His medium brown hair was longer. Trips into Abilene to get it cut cost him too much time so he seldom made them until Anne started in to nag, at which, like all loving wives, she was very good indeed. And already, though in that summer of 1871 he was still only thirty-two years old, his temples and his sideburns were thickly silvered. Oddly enough, the heavy mustache he had grown in the spring of 1870, a year ago, apparently had no white in it at all. Or if it did, the white didn't show; for, like his eyebrows but unlike his hair, which was curiously dark for a man as fair complexioned as he was, his mustache was blond. As blond as his twin brother Jonathan's hair had been. As blond as were the fine-spun baby locks of the third Jonathan, his not quite three-year-old son.

"I asked you a question, Ethan," Anne said.

"I heard it," Ethan said drily. "And the answer is No, I haven't. They're staying at the Gulf House. Time enough to offer our condolences after the funeral. The two of us, together. Somehow, at a time like this, I didn't feel I should intrude . . ."

"They?" Anne whispered.

"Nora and her husband. A man named Price Andrews, about whom I know nothing, so don't ask me. Not even what business or profession he's in. The one piece of information I had forced upon me by the Sisterhood of Hen Buzzards and Associated Witches, Abilene chapter, is that he seems much older than you'd have expected a husband of a girl of her age to be. The estimates run from forty to forty-five . . ."

"Exactly what *I* should have expected," Anne said; "and I'll even wager he looks a great deal like you, physically."

Ethan stared at his wife. But what came to his mind, hung bile-bitter on his tongue tip, he didn't say. He had long since learned the lesson that it takes two to quarrel. And today was no time for even verbal bickerings, not with Cy Curtiss—his good and true friend, the man who had once saved his life—lying dead in his blood, gunned down like a dog.

"What have you done with the kids?" he asked Anne calmly, quietly.

"Cindy's keeping them until we get back from Abilene. She's also keeping little Doe Atkins, since Hank and Cora are going to the funeral, too—in *our* surrey, with us. Hope you don't mind!"

"No," Ethan said; "I don't. Cora's become distinctly bearable since Hank's taken both her and the farm in hand. And I've always liked Hank. Do we pick them up, or are they coming over here?"

"They're coming here. That's why we're waiting. Poor Mr. Curtiss! I liked him, too, Ethan. And now look—five whole days above ground in this heat. Ethan—didn't that present a problem?"

"It did. Especially since we've no regular undertaking establishment, qualified to do embalming; but Phil, Ned, I and the new mayor, Joseph G. McCoy, elected by the grateful citizens for his most excellent and appreciated services in turning our little one-horse burg into 'The Queen of the Cowtowns' solved that among us. We sent Ned by train to Junction City to buy half a boxcar of ice. They've got an icehouse in Junction City, you know. They cut it out of the Big Blue River up near the Nebraska line in winter, and store it in a frame structure that's got double walls, and a double roof, with sawdust packed between. You'd be surprised how long ice lasts when kept under those conditions, even in the hottest weather. Of course, it would have cost us a pretty penny except that Joe agreed to pay for it out of the town's currently overflowing treasury, as a token of the high esteem in which poor Cy was held by nearly everybody. . . . Well, here come the Atkinses. I'd better go open the gate . . ."

"Who killed poor Cy, Ethan?" Cora asked. "And for *what?* Believe it or not, we only heard he'd been shot day before yesterday. As the town's Official Fallen Woman, mother of a half-breed Injun brat, I stay out of Abilene all I can, because I see no sense in going to jail for snatching one of the local witches bald-headed, or wiping up all the horse droppings off Main Street with her carcass. And I manage to keep poor Hank, here, real busy, so he don't get there much either . . ."

"This here woman," Hank groaned, "has gone 'n repealed the Emancipation Proclamation all by herself!"

"But I treat you real good, nights, don't I, honey?" Cora said with that deep, dark, feline chuckle of hers. "But, as I was saying, I just don't understand it. Cy didn't have an enemy in this world. Everybody liked him. Of course, keeping a saloon isn't the most respectable business a body could make a living at; but people did respect Cy. And most of 'em admired him. I did. He was a fine figure of a man . . ."

"I purely admired him, too," Hank said sorrowfully.

"Well," Ethan sighed; "it was just another of what has come to be known in local parlance as a 'corpse and cartridge occasion,' one of those senseless killings that happen all too often these days in town. It seems that two Texans, with a sight more liquor in their bellies than their feeble brains could ballast, decided it would be great fun to take their next snorts mounted. So they rode their mustangs into Cy's place and ordered drinks from the saddle. Cy accommodated them at first, for peace's sweet sake. But those miserable Texas Cayuses hadn't been housebroken; and when Cy saw all that fresh and stinking horse dung on his floor, he ordered the trail drovers out of his place in no uncertain terms. The discussion heated up fast. And one of the cowboys shot him. Or maybe both of them did. We'll never know."

"Why not, Ethan?" Anne said.

"Because the new town marshal, James Butler Hickok, better known as 'Wild Bill,' heard the gunfire and came on the double. He killed both of those drunken scoundrels as they galloped out of Cy's place. One of 'em started up the street, and the other, down it, but our sterling marshal dropped them both so fast that a boy who witnessed the whole thing swore he killed them with a single shot . . ."

"Wild Bill," Cora said fervently, "is the handsomest man I ever saw!"

"He is that," Anne agreed; "but he gives me the creeps somehow. He's not quite—human. Those eyes of his—like blue ice. Without—any pity in them. None at all. How many men has he killed so far, Ethan?"

"Some say forty-three. Some, even more. And rumor has it that he plans to raise his score to an even hundred before he retires . . ."

"He's sure Lord calmed Abilene down more'n a mite," Hank Atkins said.

"Except my darling husband whom he fairly dotes on!" Anne said mockingly. "Tell us, Ethan, dearest, why *is* he so fond of you? He's always inviting you to have drinks with him, y'know . . ."

"Which I always accept, and stand him a few in my turn," Ethan said with a wry chuckle. "Wild Bill's a good man to have as a friend. But do you know the reason for his sudden interest in me?"

"Wal, now," Hank drawled; "seeing as how you shore ain't pretty, 'n you doan wear no lace on yore drawers, I purely cain't imagine. Why has he taken sich a shine to you, Prof?"

"He's become envious of the fact that the fame of his old sidekick, Buffalo Bill Cody, has already been recorded in literature, and his hasn't. So now he's considering me—as perhaps the most highly educated man hereabouts—as his official biographer. A position I don't relish, and am quietly and subtly resisting. He got the idea from reading the pure, unmitigated, plain damn lies that an Eastern writer of dime novels called Ned Buntline wrote about poor stupid Bill Cody. I wish he'd just forget it. And that all of you, or rather all of *us,* including me, would shut up. Something unseemly about a bunch of people chattering away like magpies on their way to the funeral of a murdered friend. A little meditation is in order, wouldn't you say? About the vanity of human hopes, for instance. Or on the efficacy—of prayer. So let's be quiet, shall we? Besides that's Abilene up ahead. . . ."

Ethan swept off his black Western slouch hat, and bowed stiffly over Nora Andrews's—Mrs. Price Andrews's—hand. He was fully and dismally aware that he was going to "catch it" when he got back home, for during Reverend Brownley's long and moving sermon, Anne had hissed at him: "If you don't quit staring at her like that, I'm going to slap you, Ethan Lovejoy! Here and now. At her father's funeral. In this church. Before everybody. And I don't care how much of a scandal it causes!" But Ethan hadn't really stopped enveloping and consuming Nora in the pale luminosity of his gaze; he had simply been more discreet about it thereafter. He wasn't the only culprit in that regard: all the men at Cyrus Curtiss's funeral—with the sole and logical exception of the saloon-keeper's heartbroken and weeping son—fixed that small and utterly ravishing figure as the common focal point of a hundred stunned, bemused, lost, and hopelessly yearning stares, while the good wives of Abilene concentrated enough malevolence into their baleful glowerings—had she been aware of them, which, sitting there, head bent and silent, locked within the invisible walls of her private grief, she wasn't—to have shriveled poor Nora to a cinder like a moth caught in their collective flames of envy, and of hate. But now the services and the burial were over. And yet the forms, circumstances, and shibboleths of social intercourse, however hypocritical, had to be maintained. For a while longer, anyhow.

"My dear," Ethan said quietly; "words are pretty useless at a time like this, aren't they? Useless—and meaningless. I'm sorry and grieved that your father—died. Wish I could invent a new and better way of saying that; but I can't. He was my friend, faithful and just to me, which he proved by saving my life at the risk of his own. And when it could have—*should* have—been my turn to do as much for him, I wasn't anywhere around. That's the third thing I'm going to regret all the rest of my life . . ."

"What are the other two, Ethan?" Anne said from where she stood by his side.

Ethan sighed.

"My brother's death, and the manner of it," he said. "But the second one I'll hold in abeyance. Nora surely knows what it is, so it needn't— and probably shouldn't—be discussed right now . . ."

"You mean—not before my husband, Ethan?" Nora said with quiet but noticeable bitterness. "Don't worry; I've kept no secrets from Price. He knows my history—*all* of it. But if the subject interests you, yes, I *did* hold that against you for a good long time. Not your failure to be on the spot in time to save me from—from what happened to me, because you very seldom stayed in town after dark, so there was no logical reason for you to have been there. But when I found out—was told—*why* you had left not just Abilene but the county on that particular night, that you'd put your very life in jeopardy to save another man's wife from the Indians instead of risking it for me, I resented it bitterly. In fact, I was furious. But then I was terribly in love with you in those days . . ."

"And now you're not?" Anne said, frost and flint in her voice.

Nora gazed at her. Studied her, really.

"Should I be?" she asked; "This is my husband, Price Andrews. Use your eyes, Mrs. Lovejoy; make the comparison—or rather the contrast— for yourself."

"Honey," Price Andrews drawled; "any meaning a body could hang on that one, it comes out sounding impolite, and unkind, both. In fact, to tell the truth about it, that there remark of yours is just plain she-cat mean."

He put out his hand to Ethan.

"I'm mighty pleased to meet you, Prof Lovejoy," he said in his rich, musical baritone; "I have to admit you've cost me many a sleepless night. Every time li'l Nora is peeved at me, and that's downright frequent, the memory of all your manly perfections is the stick she uses to beat my so-called brains in with . . ."

"But now that you've met me, surely you stand reassured," Ethan chuckled, and took the proffered hand. "You never met your late father-in-law, did you? Very well, I'll offer you my condolences for that. Cy was well worth knowing. His friendship honored any man he bestowed it upon, not the other way around . . ."

Anne got a grip on herself, remembered her manners then.

"Nora—or rather Mrs. Andrews," she said; "may I offer you my sympathy? And not for form's sake, my dear. I got to know your father well in the last three years. And to admire him wholeheartedly as much as Ethan did. He was entirely admirable."

"Well," Ethan said awkwardly then, "I guess everything meaningful has been said, so—"

"No. Don't go yet," Nora said a little sharply; "Walk us back to the hotel, won't you? You have to go there anyhow, since that's where the meeting is to be held. Price, take Mrs. Lovejoy's arm like a good boy, will you please? And flirt with her nicely in your own inimitable style. I'd like to talk to Ethan a little while longer. I know you don't mind. And as for Anne—Mrs. Lovejoy—she'll just have to put up with it, that's all."

"You've the advantage today, Nora," Anne said with icy calm; "I won't be drawn into a quarrel with you half an hour after your father's burial. I must say, though, that you've had far better teachers than my poor Ethan must have been. Your speech has become—beautiful. Don't know when I've heard grammar more precise, or phrases better chosen . . ."

"My aunt sent me to Mrs. Wheatley's School for Young Ladies in Evanston," Nora said. "But my teachers there weren't really responsible for my grammar, beyond giving me endless opportunities to practice it. *You* were, Anne. It was the—attainment—I most envied you. Next to your possession of Ethan himself, of course . . ."

"But now you have no further need to envy me anything," Anne said.

"No," Nora said quietly; "A pity, isn't it? I'm sorry I ever had to come back and see him—find him—so sadly shrunken, reduced, diminished—Oh, I don't know the word!—tired, stooped—even old. But that's the way with dreams, I suppose. We outgrow them, let them die, without being able to even grant them a decent burial . . ."

" 'Think you there was, or might have been,' " Ethan quoted solemnly, " 'such a man as this I dreamed on?' No, Nora, there never was. You created that nonexistent image in your mind. The mind of a schoolgirl. A schoolgirl who no longer exists, either. Though I must say I much prefer your present avatar. She's quite something, isn't she, Anne?"

"She's absolutely stunning, for all the good that's going to do you now, Farmer Lovejoy!" Anne said with a snort of bitter laughter. "Mr. Andrews, I'd venture that being the husband of so young and so beautiful a wife must be nobody's easy task. I'll wager that you have to keep your eye peeled and your six-shooter ready at hand . . ."

"Well now," that slow, flat, utterly emotionless voice drawled from behind and a little to the left of the four of them; "That there's a point that's been troubling me a mite, Missus Lovejoy. Price, you know we've got an ordinance in this town against gun toting, don't you?"

Price Andrews whirled. Then he grinned; said:

"I'm—clean, Bill. Packing a shooting iron to my pappy-in-law's funeral didn't seem a gentlemanly thing to do . . ."

"All the same, reckon I'd better make sure," Hickok said. "I know you of old. And fellows who make a habit of trusting sidewinders like you, Price, have a funny way of running clean out o' breath. Raise your arms shoulder high. No false moves now. Your—latest—is a sight too pretty to have to spoil her pretty eyes a-crying . . ."

Nora took in the tall, almost unbelievably handsome marshal with one swift, bitter flash of her eyes. James Butler "Wild Bill" Hickok was a sight to see. From under his black slouch hat, his light brown hair swept down to his broad shoulders. As usual, he wore a long-tailed cutaway, a fancy vest, blue trousers tucked into boots polished to a mirrorlike gleam. His white shirt was snowy, his string tie knotted with carefully careless art. There was no doubt that Abilene's marshal was the best-dressed man on the frontier, and the deadliest.

"Mr. Sheriff—" Nora began, her voice high, tight, breathless.

"It's Marshal, miss," Wild Bill said; "Though that don't make no nevermind. Have patience with me; don't mean your—gentleman friend —a mite o' harm. Just want to see if he's got a hideout gun on him. Price can do a mighty heap o' damage with a stingy gun. Across a card table, anyhow."

"Mr. Marshal," Nora said bitterly; "my husband gave up gambling when he married me. That was the condition I put upon accepting him. And he's kept his word ever since. We run a restaurant in St. Louis. And we've just come from burying—my father. So I beg you to leave us in peace!"

Hickok stared at her. For once in his life, his ice blue eyes showed emotion. And that emotion was, Ethan saw, astonishment.

"You're Cy Curtiss's daughter, miss—I mean ma'am?" he said.

"Yes, I am," Nora said.

Again a flicker of feeling passed over that too handsome face. And this time the feeling was—clearly—sorrow.

"Price," the marshal said heavily: "This'un's pa was a friend o' mine. So I won't search you. I'll take your word for it that you ain't got a Derringer or a sawed-off Colt somewhere under your clothes. I'm making you that concession as a favor to this little lady who is purely an angel, and as pretty and sweet as they make 'em, as any fool can plainly see. So, if I find out you've gone and done what I'm damned nigh sure you have —or even if you ain't, which I doubt—and I ever hear about you low-rating her, or treating her bad, I'll look for you all over hell, and send you there, too. Reckon it's your natural destination, anyhow . . ."

"But just what do you think, or rather are almost sure, he's done, Marshal?" Anne demanded. 'With a damned sight more eagerness than is seemly,' Ethan thought.

Hickok stared at her. Then he swept off his broad-brimmed hat. To ladies—*real* ladies—Wild Bill was always impeccably polite.

"Well now, Missus Lovejoy, reckon that's a matter that lies between Mr. Andrews and me," he drawled. "And since I could be wrong, I'd be doing him an injury to air it . . ."

"But you don't think you're wrong, do you, Marshal?" Anne persisted.

"Anne, for God's sake!" Ethan said.

"No'm," Wild Bill said; "I don't. In fact, I'm pretty sure I'm not. And that being so, I'd be doing this sweet, innocent girl, who's let her heart get ahead of her head and got herself mixed up with a lump of polecat's puke like Price Andrews—"

"You mind what you say, Bill Hickok!" Andrews flared.

Hickok stared at him. And Ethan saw then, in that instant, why the marshal always won his gun battles. When he looked at a man the way he was looking at Price Andrews now, that man froze. It was all but impossible to move when you were staring into the eyes of—death. Which gave the marshal, who was anything but a quick draw artist, all the time he needed to leisurely take out one of his single-action Colts, aim it with professional care, and shoot his opponent dead.

"And that being so, Missus Lovejoy," Abilene's marshal went on imperturbably; "since this poor li'l thing has gone and took up with the kind of a critter apt to turn the stomach of a turkey buzzard, reckon my talking about it would hurt her a sight more than she's up to bearing today. Good evening, Missus Lovejoy, Professor—and to you, li'l Miss Curtiss, I mean—Missus Andrews. Price, you take care!"

Then he turned and moved away from them with that peculiar walk of his, which one of his many biographers described as being "as light and as proud as a buck's in the rutting season . . ."

"Price!" Nora stormed, tears in her lovely eyes and already streaking her cheeks; "Why'd you let him make you take low like that?"

"I was telling the truth, honey," Price sighed; "I really don't have a shooting iron on me . . ."

"And—if you had had, Mr. Andrews?" Anne asked, her voice brittle with sudden—and sure—contempt.

"I wouldn't have drawn it. I'd have taken low just the same," Price Andrews said honestly. "That there is Wild Bill Hickok, and I mean to live a long, long time . . ."

The meeting, called to determine what steps might be taken to curb the general lawlessness that had the Eastern newspapers calling Abilene "The Wickedest Town Since Sodom and Gomorrah," and provoked into urgency by the widespread and sincere public outrage over the senseless murder of Cyrus Curtiss, Sr., was, of course, and as was usual in those illiberal times, confined to the male citizens of voting age. But it must not be imagined that the good ladies of Dickinson County didn't resent their exclusion. They did, both loudly and angrily. Kansas women from the very beginnings of white occupancy of the territory didn't accept tamely either male domination or the bad habits of their men, as their saloon wrecking campaigns two years later, in 1873, and again in 1899–1900 under the direction of the famous hatchet-wielding Carry Nation were to amply demonstrate. In 1867 Lucy Stone and Susan B. Anthony had already stumped the state on behalf of women's suffrage; and just two years before, on February 4, 1869, a convention agitating for granting the women of Kansas the right to vote had been held in Topeka.

But so far, male conservatism—and/or chauvinism, though that term had not yet come into general use—prevailed. The ladies were excluded by the rather cowardly stratagem of holding the meeting in the Gulf Hotel's barroom, which no self-respecting lady would dream of entering —one of the reasons, Ethan realized two years hence when the saloon wrecking campaign was being carried out, that the good wives of Kansas entered into it with such genuine enthusiasm.

All Ethan's friends were present, and the vote was unanimous: the male citizens of Abilene, and those of Dickinson County in general, voted to have a circular printed on the *Abilene Chronicle*'s press and passed out to the trail drover's range bosses inviting the Texans not to come back anymore. Even Mayor McCoy, who had been responsible for their coming in the first place, voted in favor of the measure.

Which was hardly surprising because the town dwellers, despite the fact that the silver dollars spent by the cowboys paid off at the end of the trail, and the cowpunchers in the railroad yards brought considerable profits to certain types of enterprises, were disappointed at the evident fact that all that money went to very few businesses indeed.

For, as Phil Harris put it: "If you ain't a saloonkeeper, a hotel manager, a restaurant owner, the boss of a gambling joint, or a whorehouse madam, you don't see one thin dime!"

Beyond such mundane considerations, there was the sheer nuisance factor or, to again quote Phil, "the plain pain in the assedness" of being forced to live in a cowtown. Though such fearless lawmen as Tom Smith of Kit Carson, Colorado, Abilene's first great marshal, and his even greater successor, "Wild Bill" Hickok, had sharply reduced the outrages perpetrated by drunken cowhands, they hadn't been able to end them altogether, nor even the plague of wholesale murder from which all the cowtowns suffered, though "Wild Bill" is said to have killed from twenty to thirty men in Abilene's "Hell's Half Acre" trying to do just that.

Then, the good citizens of Abilene were nearly all married men. And during the town's reign as The Queen of the Cowtowns, their wives developed an edge to their tongues that would have "raised blisters on a boot," as more than one of them mournfully put it. The causes of the widespread domestic infelicity were just three: the saloons, the gambling joints, and the cowtown doves. And while the first two gave the respectable women of Abilene and Dickinson County good and sufficient causes for their ire by diverting from the household exchequer sums almost no family in that region and in those times could afford, it was the third— naturally enough!—that really got them wild.

And so it was that though the meeting, its mission accomplished, was over in less than ten minutes, none of the men present, including, be it sadly said, Ethan Lovejoy, were in any special hurry to rejoin their ever loving wives. The ladies, at that moment, were waiting in the Gulf Hotel's Grand Salon, drinking tea, and avidly discussing the most minute details of Nora Andrews's really smart clothes, agreeing without a dissenting voice that she'd gone downhill, grown hard-looking and sullen at the ripe old age of twenty-one, and speculating on how she had ever managed to catch herself so splendid a specimen of manhood as Mr. Andrews! About Price Andrews, the good wives of Abilene—again without a dissenting voice!—waxed positively lyrical, feeling perfectly free to express such opinions in the absence of their husbands, and because Nora had, of course, retired to her room with the object of all that un-, sub-, and—in some few cases, anyhow—entirely conscious mental adultery. Anne Lovejoy, after having agreed that Andrews was at least as handsome, if not a little more so, than Marshal Hickok, had withdrawn from the conversation. She was examining her own reactions to the—supposedly!—ex-gambler. And being an almost painfully honest little soul, she had to admit to herself that they were shocking. Having admitted that, she began to revise the stern and lofty wifely talking-to—on the subject of Nora Andrews, of course!—she had planned to vent upon Ethan's defenseless head once she had him safely home again, moderating it considerably, softening its tone. For a number of old saws, including the one about which activities a dweller within crystal walls must refrain from, and the other alluding to the futility of a discussion over the comparative hues of kitchen utensils, had popped hurtfully into her mind. She was just getting to the Biblical reference to motes, beams, and eyes, when she saw Cora Atkins storming furiously out of the Salon. Later she found out why: one of the local Broomstick Wranglers had bent over the big woman and asked: "And how's yore cute li'l papoose, Cory, dear?"

Ethan stood at the bar having a few with Phil Harris, ex-Mayor Ned Tyler, actual Mayor Joseph McCoy, Will Trainer, Rad Stevens, and Matt Hendricks. The question being discussed was how the hell—short of a full-fledged shooting war—they were going to keep the Texans out of Abilene, if the trail drivers decided to come back anyhow next year, circular or no circular.

"Leave it to me, boys," Joe McCoy said; "I got you into this mess for which I'm rightly and humbly sorry, so it's up to me to get you out.

That I didn't know what I was letting you in for—being an Illinois boy, myself—isn't any valid excuse. But I've got a mighty good idea of how to get us shut of cowboys, cows, and all that goes with 'em, including cowtown doves . . ."

"Joe," Ethan said; "how do you propose to rid us of the Texans?"

"By sidetracking 'em to another town. The Atchison, Topeka and Santa Fe Railroad has just got to Newton, as of last week. So I'm going to sell the Newton folks, who're kind of envious of our prosperity, a bill o' goods: the advantages of being a cattle shipping capital. You see, Eth, since the KP *and* the AT and SF run through Topeka, the trail drivers can drive their steers into Newton, which being farther south than we are will shorten the trail by three or four days' hard driving. 'Cause they can ship the filthy beasts over the Santa Fe from Newton to Topeka, and by the good old KP to Wyandotte as usual. That'll make sense to the trail bosses . . ."

"But the people of Newton? How're you going to persuade them of the joys and delights of being a cowtown, Joe?" Ethan persisted.

"As a favor to us," McCoy said with a mocking grin. "Don't worry! I don't mean to admit we're planning to get out of the cattle shipping business altogether; I'm going to tell 'em—and it happens to be the strict truth—that our facilities for receiving Southern cattle are plumb overrun, which, with all of eight hundred thousand head expected this year, they purely are. So I'm gonna ask 'em as a neighborly favor to us to take some of those lovely, beautiful, money-making Longhorns, and the nice, sweet, gentlemanly, abstentious, clean-living Johnny Reb rangehands who drive them, off of our hindquarters . . ."

"D'you think it'll work, Mayor?" Rad Stevens said.

"Of course it'll work, Rad!" Joe McCoy said. "Like all new towns they're hard put for cash money. And next year, when the Santa Fe finishes backtracking to Wichita, it'll work even better. So you boys can quit worrying about that problem. Leave it to me . . ."

"Prof," Will Trainer said to Ethan then; "how's your self-binder coming along?"

"It's not, Will," Ethan answered the blacksmith sadly; "I've quit working on it. That's a mighty complex piece of machinery, you know. Oh, I'm sure I could solve all the remaining technical problems within eight months to a year, say; but why bother? If we couldn't manufacture a simple machine like our harvester cheaply enough to sell at a reasonable asking price, we're sure to take an even worse beating with a self-binder.

It will look like the inside of an oversize clock designed by a candidate for the lunatic asylum at Osawatomie with all those wheels and belts and cogs; and it will be so damned heavy we'll need a three- or four-horse team to pull it through a wheat field. Seems a poor investment of our time and work to me . . ."

"But it don't to me," Will said eagerly. "Git back to work on it, Prof, will you? I need some ready cash to expand my wagon works, what's going great, even though I'm losing young Cy . . ."

"You're losing Cy, Jr.? Why, Will? I thought he was working out just fine . . ."

"He was, and I'm mighty sorry to see him go. But he swears he can't stand living in Abilene no more, after what happened to his pa. And you can't blame him, there. He's moving out to Californy—easy enough to do nowadays since the Union Pacific done jined up with the Central Pacific 'n you can take a train clear from the Missouri River to the Pacific Ocean. Hell, you kin take one from coast to coast, you don't mind changing cars right pert frequent. He's taking his pretty li'l wifie Nancy with him—good thing they ain't had no babies yet—and he's planning to open a woodworking and cabinetmaking shop out in Sacramento or Frisco with th money his pore pa left him. He'll make a go of it, tha's sure, thanks to the first-class training in carpentry you give him, Prof . . ."

"Thanks to his own skill and willingness to work, both of which he's got in God's own plenty, Will. I'm sorry to see him go, too; yet, as you just said, under the circumstances, who can blame him? But to get back to what we were talking about, how the devil do you figure to make money out of a machine too blamed complicated for us to manufacture at a resulting asking price our neighbors can afford to pay?"

"That's jes' th point," Will said happily; "we don't even try to manufacture it. We builds just *one* between us, patents it, and sells the manufacturing rights to some big company like Buckeye, Bradley, Sucker State, Peoria, or Marsh on a royalty basis. You know who give me that idea? Remember the fella who came through here, spying out our harvester? Well, th other day, he was back in town ag'in, 'n he drapped by my wagon works on purpose to ask about *you.* Wanted to know if you'd gone 'n invented sumpin' else. I told him you was working on a mighty fine idea, but allowed I wasn't at liberty to tell him what it was. So he gave me his card, told me he was an agent from the Sucker State Company, and asked me to tell you he'd be mighty interested in buying the manufacturing rights of any good machine you turned out, for his company, on a royalty basis. Said you could patent it yourself, or his company would patent it for you, jointly in their name and yours—he leaned hard on that joint patent idea, said it over three times, 'n he give me his personal guarantee that the company would deal square with you, 'n that you wouldn't be cheated. Sounds mighty good to me, Prof!"

"And to me," Ethan said slowly, a little glow of hope beginning to show in his eyes. He was thinking that with a steady and reliable supply of cash money of even moderate size coming in, he would be able to improve his farm, and the quality of his and Anne's life on it, considerably. 'Build her that long-promised frame house,' he mused; 'Plant her that grove of shade trees next to it, she's been longing for. And with the Texas cattle gone, the fever ought to die out, so I'll be able to buy the cows we need without fear of their dying on us . . .'

"Well, Prof?" Will said.

"I'll do it, Will. I'll start working on the damned thing again, tomorrow," Ethan said. "Now, if you'll excuse me . . ."

"Aw, Prof, stay 'n have a couple o' snorts on me to celebrate our binder!" Will said happily.

"Can't. Our marshal just came in, and I've got a turkey buzzard-sized crow to pick with him before Joe and Phil and Ned and the rest grab him to liquor him up and pry tales of his gunfighting exploits out of him. I'll pass by your place next week so you can help me out on some tricky points of the design. Be seeing you, Will . . ."

Ethan headed Wild Bill off before the marshal even got to the bar. He caught Hickok by the elbow with an iron grip and steered him unceremoniously out of the barroom and through a side door that opened on the service alley, since he damned sure didn't want the most wifely of all wives seeing him talking to the marshal. Not after that peculiar conversation all three of them had engaged in with the Andrewses. She'd put two and two together and arrive at six, as women always did, if he committed so gross a tactical error as that in the eternal warfare between the sexes.

Cheerfully, and with a mocking gleam in his eyes, since he obviously wasn't puzzled even slightly by Ethan's motives for almost dragging him out of the Gulf Hotel's bar, the most dangerous man in the West allowed the least dangerous and the mildest to lead him out of the service alley, across the dusty, wheel-rutted, horse dung-festooned street to a saloon directly opposite the hotel. They sat down at a table, and Ethan called for a bottle of the marshal's favorite rye. But when he broached the subject that was preying on his mind, Wild Bill surprised him.

"Figgered that was what has gone 'n put a cocklebur under your cinch ring, Prof," Hickok drawled; "but I purely don't aim to tell you one damn thing about it, my friend. It's too delicate-like. Besides, I saw how you was looking at that pretty child, and not being a spavined, wind-broke, stone-blind fool, I saw just as quick that your good missus was fair b'iling over with female jealousy. Th information wouldn't do you any good anyhow. Ain't a damned thing you can do about it, so why upset yourself and get into one hell of a lot of trouble with your lady?"

"Please, Jim!" Ethan pleaded. He was suddenly glad he was one of the few people whose friendship with the marshal was close enough to allow him to call James Hickok "Jim" instead of that "Wild Bill" nickname that made no sense that he could see, since the marshal certainly wasn't named William and was the exact opposite from wild, being the calmest, coldest, most self-sufficient man Ethan had ever met. "I taught Nora once when I ran the school here and—"

"She was head over heels in love with you. Heard that story, Prof. In this town you hear everything about everybody. I know why she had to leave here, too. A pity. Maybe if she could've stayed, she wouldn't have got mixed-up with a puking polecat like Price Andrews . . ."

"Tell me that much, then," Ethan said. "Why are you so down on Andrews, Jim?"

Hickok took a sip of the rye.

"Mighty good drinking whiskey, this," he said solemnly. Then he grinned. "All right, Prof, I'll tell you about that there, 'cause if I don't you gonna go hog-wild and worry your head 'til you're crazier than a bronc that's been eating locoweed for a month o' Sundays. And, don't fret, I won't even hold you to writing my life story for me. Done changed my mind about that. Give too damn many ambitious young fools, what's got the price of a six-gun, ideas, my name was to appear in print too frequent, like that idjut Bill Cody's . . ."

He took another snort of the rye.

"But one thing, Prof: I want you to give me your word of honor as a gentleman and a scholar you won't tell your missus *nothing* about this here. That you won't even mumble about it in your sleep. I know, I know —she's a loving wife and a good woman. And than that, my friend, in a case like this, there ain't nothing worse . . ."

"You—you think," Ethan breathed; "that they—that Andrews and Nora aren't really married?"

"Don't think," Wild Bill drawled; "I know damn well they ain't.

Unless the wife he's got in St. Joe has dropped down dead or petitioned the Missouri state legislature for a Bill of Divorcement. Neither of which is very likely, Prof. Hell, I know that skunk from way back yonder. He used to work the boats; then, after they kicked him off the packets for pulling every dirty trick in the books: spring-loaded sleeve cuffs that could shoot a pair o' cards to fill an inside straight into his hand so fast you'd never notice it; rings with mirror glass in 'em 'stead of diamonds so he could see who was gettin what when he was dealing; box with tar on the top of it he could stick to the bottom of the table when he sat down, said box holding a whole new deck, marked as pretty as you please to be rung in when he felt th need of it. You name it, Prof; if it was crooked, Price Andrews invented it. Where was I? Oh, yes, after there wasn't a steamboat cap'n on any river in the West what would let Price aboard, he ran shell games and sichlike in the towns. First run into him in Leavenworth. Bill Cody 'n Price Andrews both used to live there back then. That there writing fella says I used to hang out with Bill in them days, but I didn't. Not because I had anything ag'in Bill, who ain't a bad sort, but because I'm nine years older than he is, and he wasn't more than a snotnose when I was in Leavenworth. Hell, I don't even remember him from there. But Price I damn sure do remember, 'cause he stole my best girl from me . . ."

"And that was what soured you on him?" Ethan asked.

"No. Hell, no. Reckon he plumb did me a favor that time. I ain't the marrying kind, and Sadie—that was her name, Sadie Nelson—was a even bigger pain in the ass than most wimmen are. What got me riled with Price was the way he treated her afterward. Even being as big a hurting in the hindquarters as she was, she didn't deserve being treated that way. Like a dog. Except that no halfway decent fella would treat even a dog that damn bad . . ."

Hickok took another slow, thoughtful sip of the rye. Went on quietly: "You see, he married her ag'in his will, because he wasn't no more given to getting hitched in double harness than I was. The trouble was, that although he knew damned well he'd got her in the family way, he just couldn't bear to leave town 'cause he was running the oldest floating crap game in the state of Missouri—some say it got started back when Andy Jackson was President—in some warehouses down by the river, and his luck—or his loaded dice—was holding up mighty fine. So her pa caught up with him. Big cuss, Sadie's pa. Rough. Mean. And a fine hand with a scatter-gun. So Price went through with it. Lived with her all of five years, and give her two more kids before he took leg bail from all that wedded bliss. Left her 'n the kids flat, and without a dime. At that, she was lucky. He hadn't turned Mack, then, recruiting for the parlor houses . . ."

"Jesus!" Ethan whispered; "You mean Andrews is a pimp?"

"Yep. Got into that because wouldn't nobody play cards or shoot craps with him no more. Top hand at it, too. Recruited every decent-looking filly Gashouse Gertie's got, hisownself, personal. Gert 'n him have an agreement. Price is a good-looking maverick, you know. And such a smooth talker that butter wouldn't melt in his mouth. So he gets the poor little innocent critters filly-wild over him and his charming ways, pulls up their skirts, yanks down their frilly unmentionables, and once he's got 'em properly ruint, sells 'em to old harridans like Gert for cash . . ."

"But Nora!" Ethan got out; "Nora, Jim! What about *her*?"

"I ain't sure, but I don't think he dared try his old tricks with a filly *that* fine, Prof. My guess is that he went through a wedding ceremony with her, without bothering to tell her he's got a living wife in St. Joe. You heard how she insisted to me about him being her hubby, didn't you? I think she honestly believes he is . . ."

"I do, too," Ethan said sadly; "Nora is one of the most thoroughly decent girls I ever met . . ."

"Exactly the kind Price preys on," Hickok said. "Now the trouble with all this, Prof, is that his first wife could be dead. Of starvation, likely, 'cause I'll eat my boots with the spurs still on 'em if I believe Price ever got around to sending her a red copper. Or maybe she met some fellow with a big heart and a soft head, petitioned the Missouri legislature, got shut of Price by law, and married again. In either case, his wedding to li'l Miss Curtiss would be legal. You see that, don't you?"

"I see it, but you don't believe it, do you, Jim?" Ethan said.

"Naw. I purely don't. Sadie was a healthy girl, and mighty few fellas want to take on a ready-made family. But I lost touch with Sadie ever since she got hitched to him, so I can't swear either one of those two things haven't happened, Prof. Tell you what: Why don't you think up some excuse to take a trip up to St. Joe? Tain't that far, and you kin go all the way by train these days. KP to Wyandotte, and the Hannibal and St. Joe from there. Figger out some reason for going there your missus would believe. Then, if you find out that Price is doing that there poor sweet pretty child dirt just like he always does, you come back and tell me, and I'll crowd him into drawing on me the next time I run across him. Better that way. Believing that she's a lone widow woman will hurt li'l Nora less than finding out she's been a fancy article, kept on the side. And by a gambler and a pimp at that . . ."

"No, Jim," Ethan said slowly; "I'm still against killing—even a skunk like Andrews . . ."

Wild Bill Hickok studied Ethan. A long time. With wonder and with care.

"Then reckon we'll just have to let the whole thing drop, Prof; 'cause sides from that, there ain't no other out I kin see," he said.

"She is *not* married to him," Anne said with total conviction. "Your dearest, darling Nora is living in sin with that tinhorn gambler. And Marshal Hickok knows it, Ethan. He kept calling her 'Miss Curtiss'; and when he finally got around to saying 'Mrs. Andrews'—and then only because he couldn't avoid it—the words almost choked him!"

Ethan didn't say anything. What was there to be said, really? Besides, any word he voiced now was going to be wrong from his beloved Anne's point of view. That was surer than old hell. So he clamped his jaw shut and drove on.

"And there she was, little Miss Hoity-Toity, low-rating you, putting you down. Loftily inviting me to make the comparison or the contrast between you and him!"

"Anne, dear, all Nora said was that I seemed—reduced, diminished, tired—old. And she's right. I am. All of those things . . ."

"Don't defend her, Ethan! Don't you dare!"

"I'm not. But only because she needs no defense. And you might consider that that business of contrast and comparison works on the distaff side of humanity as well, my dear."

"Eeeeeethaaaan Lovejoy! I—"

"Anne, let's not quarrel. Please. I'm much too sick at heart—"

"Because your perfect little angel proves to have feet of clay—and— elastic morals, Ethan?"

"No, because she has neither. Because, in that regard, she's as good and sweet as she has always been. Which makes it all the more tragic to see her fallen into the hands of that bounder."

"Ethan, you think—you believe—that Andrews has tricked her, don't you? Or rather, you *know!* Because I saw Marshal Hickok going into that barroom long before you came back into the Salon! So you had a heart-to-heart talk with him and he—"

"Told me the details of Andrews's past history. But not, I assure you, Anne, one word about the man's relations with Nora. He couldn't tell me anything about that, my dear, because he hasn't seen Price Andrews for several years before today, and simply doesn't know that part of the story. But what he did tell me makes your supposition of sheer innocence being taken advantage of—and by a man to whom the very concepts of either honor or shame are utterly foreign—seem very probable . . ."

"Hardly sheer innocence, Ethan," Anne said with icy quiet; "there were—after all—those Irishmen . . ."

Ethan looked at her. Looked away. Said slowly, flatly:

"Don't talk anymore, Anne. I ask you that. Please."

"So now I've offended you—by telling you the ugly truth about your dearest love?" Anne grated.

"So now you've offended me by—maybe—being yourself. By convincing me—again—that the want of compassion, understanding, and forgiveness—for all those without or who seem to you to threaten the little fortress that you mean to have and hold—is part of your very nature. That distresses me, Anne. That makes me sad. You just can't imagine how sad it makes me feel."

"Sadder than seeing *her* in the arms of another man?"

Ethan looked at her. Studied her, really. Said:

"Much sadder. The only thing that troubles me about that—and I have to admit it troubles me badly—is the nature of the man. If Nora had married a young fellow in any way worthy of her, I should be as happy for her as for my own daughter in such a case. But she didn't. From what Jim Hickok told me, Andrews is one of the most degraded and unconscionable scoundrels ever to draw the breath of mortal life. But there's nothing I can do about that, and Nora has yet to find it out. As she will, God help her! We always find out much too much, far more than we want or need to know, about the persons whom we marry . . ."

"Which is either a veiled insult—or a hidden threat. Are you—insulting me or threatening me this time around, Ethan?"

"Neither. Insults are puerile, demeaning to the one who proffers them; and threats are bootless when the means for carrying them out don't even exist. As in my case. As in the case of any man married to the mother of his two helpless infant children, however much that woman may occasionally displease him. I'm trying to retain some fondness for you, Anne. A little respect. The lubricants that make a marriage run with reasonable smoothness. I married you of my own free will—though I sometimes wonder why!—and I mean—in fact I've got to—to live with you all the rest of my life. All I'm asking you is not to make our lives together a minor purgatory, a diminutive, mean-souled hell. Let's try to be, if not happy— an obvious impossibility, since it's my conviction as a thinking adult that happiness doesn't and can't exist in this senseless and cruel world—at least content with one another. And being as nasty as possible about a young woman who is absolutely no threat to you, or to our union, however fond I may be of her, is no way to achieve that contentment, my dear . . ."

"So you admit you're fond of her?" Anne said bitterly; "Why don't you go on from there and admit you're in love with her, Ethan Lovejoy!"

Ethan considered that.

"Because I don't think I am," he said quietly. "Just—fond. Maybe that fondness could grow into love, if it had any continuity to it, anywhere to go. But it hasn't. I haven't—before today—seen Nora since the summer of 1867; I shall, in all likelihood, *never* see her again. Her brother is moving to the West Coast, her father is dead, so all her ties to Abilene are broken. And there's no conceivable reason for me to go to St. Louis, except, perhaps, a vacation, pleasure trip, in which case I'd take you with me . . ."

"I thank you for *that,* my Lord!" Anne raged.

Ethan looked at her. Sighed, long and deeply; said, with utter weariness:

"To repeat—let's stop talking, shall we?"

Anne shut up then. Bent her head and cried, noisily, angrily, despairingly.

Ethan let her cry. He was lost in the dismal contemplation of the fact that he no longer loved, even slightly, the woman at his side, his wife, and the mother of his children. And he was torn with bitter shame at the recognition that this somber state of affairs was far more his fault than hers. Anne was often irritating; but what human being was not? His own dour ways, he was well aware, often drove her to the edges of a nervous crisis. And the hardships and the dullness of prairie life were enough to try the patience of any woman who was even slightly less than a perfect saint, which was to say any woman whomsoever. He had to admit that Anne had borne the endless drudgery, the loneliness, the monotony, the inescapable dirtiness of a sod house, the sound of those unceasing winds, the teeming insects, the deplorable hygienic facilities—an outhouse, even with unslaked lime below the seats, he had to admit was a pure abomination!—all the drawbacks of the life he'd inflicted upon her, including the grinding poverty he hadn't yet been able to break free of, and last but not least, the presence of his Black tenants whom, try as she would, she simply couldn't abide, very well indeed, and with an inescapable and entirely permissible amount of complaining. . . .

Why then had he ceased to love her? Not, God knew, because of her jealousy, which was rather flattering, if anything. He thought about that question as he drove toward Matt Hendricks's farmhouse until the answer came. It was very surely because he had never loved her enough in the first place to make the wear and tear of married life endurable. He wondered suddenly whether, if he had taken little Nora to wife instead of Anne, their marriage would have reached this bleak plateau of utter hopelessness.

He doubted it. He doubted it profoundly. Even conceding that Nora had the capacity—as she'd demonstrated this very day—for being quite as irritating as Anne was, or even more so, he was certain that a marriage with her would have worked. The way he would have loved Nora, if the Moirai, the Parcae, had allowed him to love her at all, would have insured that. For the intensity of that love, its passion, its tenderness would have been total. And therefore proof against weariness, anger, the grinding years. Proof against all things except death itself. He was very sure of that.

Then suddenly Anne spoke up.

"Why," she gasped; "this isn't the way home, Ethan!"

"I know it isn't," he said; "I have to stop by the Hendrickses. I need to ask Sarah something. And it didn't occur to me at the funeral . . ."

"Which is?" Anne said darkly.

"Gordon Lee's address in St. Joseph, Missouri. He's her nephew, you know . . ."

"That pretty, effeminate boy who was so much in love with you?" Anne said mockingly.

Ethan looked at her. Said calmly:

"The same. Maybe being married to you, my dear, inclines me to change my luck . . ."

"Ethan," Anne whispered; "why do you want to know Gordon's address?"

"I want him to find out one thing for me: a detail from Price Andrews's past that will either confirm your suspicions—or negate them," Ethan said.

"And—" Anne got out, "if it *confirms* them, what then, Ethan?"

Ethan sat there, hunched over the reins, thinking about that. When he had come to the only conclusion possible under the maddening circumstance hedging his life about—and Nora's!—he said slowly, softly, sadly:

"Nothing. Confirmation or denial, there's nothing I can do, Anne. The matter's beyond my reach or grasp. Moreover, it surpasses my comprehension of Fate's workings—or God's. And you and I have given our hostages to fortune. So, if you'll let us be, we're safe . . ."

Then he drove on, toward the Hendrickses' house.

15

"I'll be damned if I can see," Ethan growled; "why the devil you accepted an invitation to spend all day today with the Atkinses. . . ."

"Because it's Easter," Anne said. "Besides, I feel so sorry for Cora, being the outcast of the town through no fault of her own. Don't be an old sore-headed bear, Ethan!"

"I'd thought we were going to drive into town and attend Easter services at the church. After that, we could have visited Phil and Martha. Their spread is close enough to town for that. Or Ned and Nellie, who're only three blocks from the church itself . . ."

"Ethan, dear, apart from the fact that Reverend Brownley's sermons bore me stiff, and probably you as well, though you won't admit it, I just don't feel up to driving all of six miles today. That's what it amounts to, you know: three going and three coming back. I'm tired, friend husband. And you must admit I have some right to be . . ."

Ethan put down the cup of scalding coffee he had been drinking— it was very early in the morning of April 13, 1873, so the two of them were having breakfast—and turned to her. He reached out his big paws and took her small hands. The feel of them shocked him. They were almost as calloused, as work-hardened as his own. He stood there, looking into her eyes, and his gaze was deep and sorrowing.

"Anne, forgive me, will you?" he said.

"Lord, Ethan—for *what?*" Anne whispered.

"For being a failure," Ethan said.

"You're not a failure," Anne said gently. "We hold our lands free and clear. Of how many other farmers hereabouts can that be said? Rad Stevens, of course. But who else? Tell me, Ethan, who else?"

"Matt Hendricks—I think," Ethan sighed. "But I'm not sure of even him. That's not the point. The real question is: *Who* has been the chief sufferer from the effects of my refusal to take out a mortgage on our place? You, my dear. Even granting me that what I believe is mostly so: That going into debt is always dangerous, and can be ruinous—look how many foreclosures there have already been this year—"

"This is a panic year, Ethan, dearest. Back East, the banks are closing right and left . . ."

"Even so, I should have taken a chance. Here we are, at Eastertime, 1873, married nearly six years, five and a half to be exact, since our sixth anniversary isn't until Christmas Day, and we're still living in this pile of dirt . . ."

Anne sighed, long and deeply. Said: "I won't lie; I hate it. It's damp in winter, dirty in summer, and dark all year long. All the same, I don't want you to go into debt to build me a frame house. I'm resigned to living in this 'soddie' until we're better off financially. When d'you think that'll be, Ethan?"

"God knows," Ethan said gloomily. "Nothing seems to work out for me. My winter wheat freezes. My summer wheat burns up. And I can't get that balky, thrice-be-damned-and-consigned-to-hell-forever self-binder of mine to work for as long as five full minutes at a stretch. Maybe I ought to take out life insurance, and then drown myself in an irrigation ditch. That way, maybe my *widow* would be able to build herself a decent house. And buy herself a young and lusty husband, too; come to think of it . . ."

"Fat chance!" Anne laughed. "But you shouldn't be so despondent, my love, because you really haven't done so badly. You've bought us cows again to replace the ones that died. Looks like these new ones are going to live, too, now that those *awful* Texans, and their Longhorns don't come here anymore . . ."

"Thanks for trying to cheer me up. Speaking of cows, I forgot to tell you: I've bought a two-year-old bull from Dr. Switzer in order to increase our herd, or at least to keep the cows happy," Ethan said with a grin. "Doc Switzer's place is west of Salina, and the Texas fever didn't affect his stock, largely because they never came into direct contact with Longhorns, I suppose. He'll ship it to me, by railroad, next week. And, while you're enumerating my many virtues, don't forget I put in a pump so that you no longer have to haul the water up from the well in buckets . . ."

"A lot of good that did!" Anne snorted. "The pump is almost as bad. In fact, it wears me out!"

"A problem that's going to be solved before the end of this summer. You see, honey, I've ordered us a windmill . . ."

"Oh, Ethan!" Anne said, and kissed him.

"I really ought to keep my big mouth shut," Ethan said honestly, "and take credit for being a thoughtful, considerate husband; but the truth is I need the windmill to pump water into the irrigation ditches I'll have to dig to keep alive the saplings I'm going to set out on our tree acreage . . ."

"Oh!" Anne said. "Then give me my kiss back, since you don't deserve it, Ethan Lovejoy!"

Ethan kissed her, thinking: 'Thank God she's in a good mood for a change!' He said:

"Of course you'll benefit from it, honey. I'm going to put pipes into the kitchen, so you'll have tap water directly into a sink . . ."

"And the dirty water, Ethan? Will I still have to haul it out of the house in buckets?"

"Hadn't thought about that," Ethan said; "but it ought to be easy to rig up some sort of a drainpipe, running through the back wall of the kitchen into the yard . . ."

"Wonderful!" Anne said. "But speaking of water, how many cylinders do you have charged for the stove, Ethan? I ask you that because, before we go over to the Atkinses, I have to bathe the children; and, what's more, I'm going to have a nice all-over bath myself. What about you, love?"

"The work will almost kill me, but I guess I will, too. Damned if I want to go around stinking as bad as Hank and Cora do . . ."

"Like most *men,* Hank simply doesn't wash," Anne said tartly; "but in Cora's case, I suspect she has such a strong odor because she's so blamed big. People her size sweat a lot. She's clean enough, as prairie women go. Ethan, why don't you invent a better hay-burning stove than that miserable thing? If you did that, keeping the house warm, and cooking, and heating water wouldn't be such awful chores . . ."

"Two reasons," Ethan said; "the first being that what with the new shallow mines in the southeastern part of the state, which are coming into production at the rate of a new one almost every day now, by next year coal ought to be downright cheap. And the second is that this weird contraption is about as good as hay-burning stoves can get to be. In fact, it actually works better than I'd thought it would. Hay just burns up too fast, that's all. But I guess that if I fill all the extra magazines they sold me with the stove, you can heat enough water for the whole family to scrape most of the scum off our grimy hides . . ."

"I'll bathe Martha Anne and Jon at the same time. That'll save *some* water," Anne sighed. "That is, if you can even catch Jon. Don't tell him I mean to bathe him, or he'll run off and hide. Playing with those *filthy* Otis children has got him so he *hates* being washed. . . ."

"Cindy's got too many kids for her to be able to even start to keep 'em clean. They do smell Lordawful, don't they? Catching Jon's no problem. How fast can a four-and-a-half-year-old kid run? All right; I'll get busy filling the magazines for the stove . . ."

"No," Anne said; "sit and rest a while longer, Ethan. It's early yet. We're not expected at the Atkinses' until around noon. You look so tired. You never complain—a petty vice I'm all too often guilty of, even though I promised you I wouldn't be. Talk to me. You very seldom do, anymore —for fear I'll snap your head off, likely. Tiredness causes that too, Ethan —bad temper, I mean. And yet you always hold yours almost perfectly in check . . ."

"My mother was always saying to me when I was a kid: 'Keep your temper, son; nobody else wants it.' All right, Anne; what'll we talk about?"

"Oh, I don't know. Anything. Out here, one gets so that one's ears ache for the sound of a human voice. Oh! I just thought of something. Something that *does* interest me. Tell me, good and *faithful* husband, did your little friend, Gordon Lee, ever answer your inquires about Nora's husband?"

But, by then, Ethan had learned Lesson Number One for maintaining marital peace: As any seasoned husband knows, if you want to avoid being driven completely out of your mind by your ever-loving spouse, there are numerous, if not daily, occasions on which you simply have to put into practice the high art and rigorous intellectual discipline of barefaced, shameless, unconscionable lying—and keep a perfectly straight face while doing so.

"No, he never did," Ethan Lovejoy, lapsed man of honor, said.

"That's odd. He always impressed me as being most devoted to you. So—why didn't he?"

"My guess is that he never got my letter," Ethan said with the calm confidence in one's powers that the daily practice of the art of barefaced

lying gives. "About that time—the summer of 'seventy-one, wasn't it?—
he changed jobs and cities. Now he's working for a newspaper in Chicago.
Incidentally, he's married, which takes care of his supposed effeminacy,
doesn't it? Matt told me that some time ago. Didn't I mention it to you?
I guess I didn't. Hardly an event of world-shaking importance, so I suppose it slipped my mind . . ."

"But," Anne persisted, worrying the subject as a terrier does a captured rat; "couldn't you have got his new address in Chicago and written
him again, asking him what you wanted to know?"

"No point," Ethan drawled; "Gordon doesn't have, and has never
had, the information I was trying to get my hands on, honey. It was his
physical presence in St. Joseph that was important at the time. You see,
Price Andrews used to live there. So I asked Gordon to find out *in that
city,* a detail about Nora's darling hubby's past that I was curious about.
But now that Gordon no longer lives there, and what's worse, since I don't
know, in the sense of not being acquainted with, a single other soul who
does, my chances of obtaining that information have become nil. Besides,
having had time to think the matter through calmly, I'm quite sure I don't
even want that information anymore, for the very simple reason that it
would be of no use to me or to anyone else if I had it . . ."

Anne stared at her husband, passed a pink tongue tip over lips gone
suddenly dry and pale.

"What was that information, Ethan?" she whispered.

Now was the moment, Ethan realized, to employ the highest refine-
ment of the liar's art: slipping in a large dose of bitter truth. He had
stumbled upon one of the most difficult-to-accept facts of human morality:
that no act whatsoever is either good or evil except in so far as the
circumstances surrounding it make it one or the other. Man, he was
beginning to realize, does not live by ethical dichotomies, but only by
intelligently thinking through the ramifications of each individual problem
as it presents itself, and making decisions as wise and as sober as his own
intellectual capacity allows him to. This First Law of Moral Relativity was
going to serve him well in the future, especially after he finally was able
to evaluate the question of his twin brother's death in the light of it, and
extend it, as a principle, to all aspects of his life.

"I asked him to find out whether Andrews's first wife, the mother of
his three children, was still alive," Ethan said quietly.

"Good Lord!" Anne gasped. "So just as I thought, they—"

"Are living in sin? It's possible," Ethan said. "Long before he left us
to take the stellar role in that traveling Wild West show, our ex-marshal,

'Wild Bill' Hickok, told me that Price was married some years ago to a girl from Fort Leavenworth. Come to think of it, he gave me that information right after Cy Curtiss's funeral. But Jim Hickok didn't know either one of the possibilities that could conceivably matter, and they only to Nora herself: whether Price Andrews was a widower when he and Nora were wed, or whether either he or his first wife had petitioned the Missouri state legislature for a Bill of Divorcement, and had been subsequently granted it. One thing Marshal Hickok was absolutely certain of—and if you've got an ounce of fairness left in your heart, you'll concede that it absolves poor little Nora of any fault, or even sin. The marshal, who knew him of old, was convinced that Andrews is scoundrel enough and to spare to have lied to Nora about his marital state, and to have gone through a second, bigamous wedding ceremony with her. You met Nora, talked with her. Did she seem to you the type of girl who would deliberately go to live with a man knowing he was married to another woman?"

Anne stared at him, long and thoughtfully.

"Yes," she said with icy calm; "I'm quite sure she would."

"Good God, Anne!" Ethan exploded; "How unfair can you be?"

"I'm not being unfair, Ethan," Anne said sadly; "I'm only telling the ugly truth. She would, which is no special reflection upon her, because *I* would too, and so would any woman who is a *woman* in any real sense of the word, under heaven. If you had been married when I met you, I should have lived in flagrant sin with you out of the simple inability to give you up, Ethan. Ethan—there's no such thing as a good woman in a situation where one of us is brought suddenly—and shockingly, even to ourselves!—face-to-face with our basic needs. For if nature—or God—or the Devil!—hadn't made us so, then good-bye to the human race! Every woman who sits of a Sunday in her church pew with her head held high, sits there by sheer default: that she's been lucky—or unlucky—enough to have never met the one man alive who can glance at her out of the corner of his eye with that sardonic, teasing mockery that both you and Price Andrews possess—though he far more than you, my love!—and make her hang there, breath gone and helpless, her throat tight and dry, self-strangled, her very bones melting inside her, waiting for him to lead her away to some reasonably private place where he can do what he wants to with her, what *she* wants, too, on the spur of that same instant a thousand times —no, ten thousand!—more than he does!"

"He tempted *you?*" Ethan said then, much too quietly; "You found him attractive—*that* way?"

"He tempted me. I found him—enormously—attractive *that* way. It is—entirely possible that if he were around me any length of time, and really wanted to, he could make me be—unfaithful to you. So now you've got two reasons to want to kill him, instead of just one . . ."

Ethan stared at his wife, and his eyes were very bleak. He realized —sadly—that he had again underestimated the human female's capacity for fine—or rather superfine—bitchery. But then, being possessed of both a subtle and an endlessly ironic mind, the perfect answer to Anne's confession—or her taunt, for which it was, he realized he'd never know—came to him.

"No," he said almost gently, "I still have only one. And I'll let you —amuse yourself, for all the rest of your life, maybe, trying to figure out what—or whom—that one reason is . . ."

"Ethan!" Anne got out.

Ethan pushed back his chair, stood up.

"It's getting late. I'd better go pack the stove's cylinders with hay if we're to all have time to bathe," he said. Then he walked out of there without a backward glance at Anne's small, white, stricken face, leaving her much too stunned to cry.

Into the very first cylindrical magazine of the hay-burning stove, well mixed with the dried grass and twigs, Ethan packed, carefully torn up into tiny pieces, Gordon Lee's reply to his letter asking his former pupil to do a little quiet detective work for him. Ethan didn't know himself why he'd kept the young cub reporter's answer. 'Except,' he thought sardonically, 'a strange and goddamned perverse desire to enshrine and enjoy my own suffering . . .'

Before he tore it up and burned it, Ethan read Gordon's detailed report of his investigations over again, for no conceivable reason at all unless it were the forlorn hope of jolting his poor, malfunctioning head into coming up with an idea that might help or save the hellish situation poor Nora now was in. The only thing his rereading convinced him of— again—was just how hopeless that situation actually was.

"I had no trouble at all," young Lee had written on that long past day in September 1871, "in finding the person you asked me to. A Mrs. Price Andrews was listed on the city census rolls, taken, as censuses usually are, every ten years, which means that last year, 1870, was when it was compiled.

"I hastened at once to the address given there, for fear Mrs. Andrews might have moved, since, as we reporters know only too well, to trace a person who has changed his address, it behooves one to make inquiries in his old neighborhood as quickly as possible after he has left it, or the whole thing slips people's minds.

"But Mrs. Andrews hadn't moved. I found her in that dreadfully poor quarter in a one-room shack, which smelled to high heaven of boiled cabbage and other aromas that I can't even enumerate, and any divulgation of whose nature and origins the canons of good taste instruct me not to inflict upon you!

"She is a large, florid woman. She reeked of cheap gin. Two little girls tugged at her none-too-clean skirts. The boy, Price, Junior, was not at home. He was out with his shoebox, shining shoes, and earning money by other means, which, I gathered, include picking pockets, sneak thievery, and other types of skulduggery of a very low order. 'Takes after his dirty dog of a pa!' Mrs. Andrews said.

"She works in a hand laundry and supplements her earnings through occasional prostitution—a fact I discovered when she made a halfhearted attempt to interest me in the purchase—or hire—of her blowsy, unwashed charms. I turned her down as politely as I could and launched into my spiel. I was, I told her, writing a book about colorful Western characters —especially gamblers. 'Your husband,' said I, '*is* Mr. Price Andrews, the Prince of the Riverboat Cardsharps, isn't he?'

" 'That he is,' says she, 'the unprincipled scoundrel!' Or rather that, my good Professor, is an acceptable substitute for what she actually did say, a totally unprintable phrase that called into question the legitimacy of his birth, the cleanliness of his person, the morals of his mother, and even her membership in the human race, attributing to her, of course, the at least nominative inclusion in a far lower order in the animal kingdom . . ."

'Kind of heavy-handed with your irony, aren't you, son?' Ethan thought, again; 'but then, simplicity is the hardest of all qualities to attain, and you'll get there, given time.' He went on reading.

"I then asked her if her husband were at home. 'Why, hell no!' she flared; 'I ain't seen that (unprintable obscenity) in years!'

" 'Then the two of you are separated? Even perhaps divorced?' I asked her then.

" 'The dirty (more clinically descriptive epithets, uncomplimentary to a most picturesque extreme!) left me and his poor kids flat years ago. Ain't sent us a red copper since he lit out for parts unknown. Divorced? Ha! Ha! Don't make me laugh, young fella! Pushing a Bill of Divorcement through the state legislature costs a barrel o' money, and I ain't got one thin dime. Him? Hell, son, he'd never bother. 'Sides, like all gamblers, he's either flush o' flat broke. And when he's flush, he's living it up, drinking champagne out o' th dainty slipper of his latest light o' love and sichlike carryin'-ons, doncha know . . .'

" 'Do you,' I then asked, 'have any idea where I might locate Mr. Andrews? It's important for my work to actually talk to him . . .'

" 'Heard tell the four-flusher's hanging out with a li'l blonde (four-footed female member of that animal species usually led around on a leash) in St. Looie, helpin' her run a restaurant her rich fambly staked her to. That won't last, I kin tell you, young fella. Price gets tired o' his wimmen awful damned quick. Then he either leaves 'em flat, jes' like he done me, or puts 'em out on th streets to hustle their dainty li'l bustles for him, his cut being jes' about all o' the poor dearies' take. Pity I ain't got no money. Had some, I'd take a steamboat down to St. Looie 'n pistol the polecat. Take a buggy whip to his hoor (her pronunciation of that unlovely word!) or splash a bottle o' oil of vitriol into her baby doll's face so she won't be able to hook no other decent woman's hubby ag'in as long as she lives . . .' "

At which point Ethan stopped rereading the letter, tore it up, and stuffed it into the iron cylinder magazine along with the hay. Keeping it was futile. But then it had always been.

"Ethan—" Anne whispered as they started walking across the half mile of prairie that separated their sod house from the Atkinses'; "I'm— sorry for what I said. I—I didn't mean it . . ."

Ethan looked down at his three year old daughter, squirming happily in his arms. Martha (after Phil's wife) Anne (after her mother) had white blond hair and looked like a cherub. She was the greatest joy in Ethan's bleak existence; and little Jonathan, scampering along ahead of them across the prairie like a well scrubbed, chubby little pink pig on that surprisingly warm Spring day, only a trifle less so.

"Forget it, Anne," he said.

"Have *you* forgot it?" she whispered.

"No. But I'm going to. Tormenting each other serves for nothing, my dear. We've got to go on together. These two make any other course unthinkable. I'm not going to let anything, not even the way you confess you feel about Price Andrews, nor the way I've never really allowed myself to feel about his wife, destroy what is, after all, despite its creaks and groans, and the occasional breakdowns the flesh is ever heir to, a going concern . . ."

"His wife," Anne said bitterly; "Is she, Ethan? Is she really?"

"That's very simply none of my business, Anne," he said quietly; "and certainly none of yours. As long as they live together calmly and quietly, as they seem to be doing—"

"Ethan," she said sharply; "how on earth do you know *that?*"

"I checked," Ethan said. "I asked Farley Evans, who runs Abilene's combination Gents Haberdashery and Ladies Wearing Apparel store and therefore, for business reasons—replenishing his stock, keeping abreast of the changes in fashion, and the like—makes frequent trips to St. Louis, to inquire into how the Andrewses are getting along."

"Ethan," Anne's voice retreated almost out of sound, "why did you do that?"

"Because Cy Curtiss was my friend. Because he saved my life. For those two reasons alone, I didn't feel I could stand idly by and allow his only daughter to be abused, mistreated, betrayed. And, yes; because I am fond of Nora. I believe that fondness is innocent, that it does not extend as far, or go as deep, as love. But, in the worst of cases, there's absolutely nothing I *could* do about her, my dear. I am the husband of a reasonably good wife who is only occasionally a pain in the posterior—as what wife is not?—and therefore have—so far!—insufficient reasons for leaving her unless, or until, she succumbs to certain fond and foolish fancies she admits to, and gives me valid ones! I am the father of two helpless infants whom I'm not ashamed to confess I adore. And I'm hardly rich enough to keep a mistress, however charming, on the side. Therefore the only thing I could do for that poor, dear girl would be to suggest to her that she leave Andrews and go back to her aunt's house in Chicago, which I would do only if it turns out that their union is unlawful, without her knowing that it is. Please take careful note of that qualifying phrase, dear Anne! Or if he is treating her badly physically or cheating her financially . . ."

"Oh!" Anne said; "and is he? Either one?"

"Papa!" Jon shrilled; "gimme a stick. I wanna dig up a prairie dog!"

"No, Jon; you'll get all dirty," Anne said. "And you must stay nice and clean to play with Doe Atkins. . . ."

"Damn Injun!" Jon said.

"Now where the hell did he get *that* from?" Ethan said.

"Where'd you expect? The Otis children, of course. And they from

Randy and Cindy who talk about *everything* before them. Ethan, is Andrews taking advantage of Nora? Strange, I liked her—until she came back to her father's funeral and demonstrated to me that she could be as nasty as even I can. Is he, Ethan?"

"It seems not. And it finally came to me why. Cy Curtiss left a considerable amount of money to Nora and to young Cy, Anne. After all, he was in the third most profitable business that one can engage in in the West, y'know . . ."

"The third?" Anne said; "What are the other two? Jon! You get up from there!"

"Aw, Mummie!" Jon said.

"Obey your mother, Jon," Ethan said sternly; "Or else I'm going to paddle your little fundament!"

Jon got up from where he was rolling in the prairie grass, came up to his father, took his big, rough hand.

"I'll be good, Papa," he said.

"See that you do," Ethan said. "Where were we, anyhow, Anne?"

"You were about to explain to me what two businesses are more profitable than running a saloon," Anne said.

"Useless information since you're unlikely to engage in either of them; but, if you must know, they're gambling joints and whore houses, my sweet!"

"I just might apply for work in the latter," Anne said sweetly, "considering how much tender love and gentle affection I get from *you,* husband mine!"

"Bitter truth, spoken in jest," Ethan sighed. "Anne, I'm sorry. I have —neglected you, I suppose. The truth is I'm worn to a frazzle by too goddamned much, hard, backbreaking work. And so are you, my dear. Still, I promise to try to do better in that regard in the future, if only to get your mind off Price Andrews . . ."

"See that you do, for, among other less important ones, the very simple reason that a little less—monkish continence—on your part, would probably stop you from brooding over your lost Nora! Which brings me back to *that* subject again. What has the money her father left her got to do with Nora's—so-called—husband's behaving himself?"

"Everything. A man like Andrews is entirely unlikely to leave an heiress. At least not before he's fleeced her of the last red cent she has. Therefore, if little Nora keeps a tight hold on her purse strings and is smart enough not to let Friend Husband—legal or not!—get his sticky fingers on any sizable part of her inheritance, her marriage, even if it turns out to be only common law, is both safe and rock solid. All she has to do is to dole Price out sufficient cash for his creature comforts and to make a brave show before his cronies, but never so much as to afford him even the possibility of making a killing at draw or stud. Let him get his hands on that much, honey, and temptation, since gambling actually is a kind of psychological disease just as drunkenness is, will overcome him sure as old hell. The only thing that worries me is that nothing I know about Nora inclines me to believe that she's that smart . . ."

"That's where you're wrong, Ethan, dear," Anne said; "She's smart enough and to spare to handle him. She's had a very bad time of it—and of a kind that either crushes a woman, utterly defeats her, or makes her hard as nails. Your angel-baby sugar-pie doesn't exist any longer. You'd better wake up to that fact. For, among other reasons, the recognition of it might help you realize that your chances of prying Little Nell out of the Dastard's clutches are nonexistent, too. She *isn't* deluded about Andrews, lover; she isn't at all. She's simply a victim of a common female perversity that nearly all us women share: the strong tendency not only to adore such utter—and what's even worse—*obvious* blackguards as Price Andrews, but to actually prefer them—and by long odds!—to such good and gentle men as you are, my love . . ."

Ethan turned and looked at her, cradling his baby daughter against his gaunt, sun- and wind-creased neck as he did so.

"Anne," he said; "you're beginning to worry me, now. Seriously."

She smiled at him, in mockery, in triumph, in sadness, and in truth.

"You have nothing to worry about on that score, Ethan. Reason number one being that Price Andrews wouldn't have me as a Christmas gift. He can do far better and knows it. He *has* done better: Nora, for instance. Then all the coexisting conditions that would drive me to commit a piece of folly that idiotic—and that gross!—would be practically impossible even for Fate's malevolent juggling of evil coincidences to unite at the same place and time. Your having hurt me unbearably, leaving me wild with rage, insane with the desire to even the score, for one. Or your having subjected me to so prolonged a stretch of—of sheer physical neglect—Oh, I'm being impossibly frank, shamelessly honest, aren't I?— that the ardent blood I inherited from my whorish mother would rise from my scalding loins and boil my brains away. Or my being at the same place at the same time as a man who possesses that precise kind of dark, perverse, Luciferan charm; said occurrence coinciding with a prolonged absence on your part. None of which is likely to happen in three lifetimes, not to mention one. So don't worry about it—or me, my love!"

"I don't. But that you're even beginning to think like this means that our marriage is on damned shaky ground. My fault? Yes. Most of it. Anne —I'm sorry I haven't known how to be the husband and the man you want —and need . . ."

"Oh, Lord!" she said. "Ethan, I love you! You *know* I love you! It's only that I'm—so tired. So mixed-up. So—scared . . ."

"Don't be, Anne," he said gently. Then he stopped. Said: "Take the baby, Anne. Jon, come here! Right *now*. That's it. That's it, son. Put your arms around Papa's neck—and hold on tight. Anne, can you run in those shoes? If you can't, take 'em off, put 'em in the pockets of your coat . . ."

"Ethan!" she wailed; "What—what's happening? It's high noon. Or it was. But now it's getting dark—dark as night! And—and *cold*. Brrrr! This wind is like ice! Ethan, what on earth—?"

"Hold Martha Anne as close to you as you can. And stay directly behind me, stepping almost on my heels, never getting more than a foot away. It's a freak storm—like the one we had in November 1871. Remember that?"

"Do I! We were snowed in for three days. But Ethan, it's the middle of *April!* It can't snow *this* late; it simply can't!"

"What the devil d'you think that is that's falling out of those clouds *now*, dear heart? Flour? Refined sugar, maybe?"

"No—but it's not snow either, Ethan—it—it's sleet! My God, how it stings! It feels almost *hot* . . ."

"Which is even worse. And before I forget: Bless you for nagging me into wearing my Army greatcoat; I wasn't going to, it seemed so warm this morning. Anne, cover Martha Anne's face with your shawl. This fine sleet gets into her nose and mouth, it'll strangle her sure as hell . . ."

"But—Jon?" Anne whispered.

"My scarf. Come on! Let's get going now. We've got to get back home before it really hits. Oh, Christ, if we hadn't been talking so much—and arrant nonsense at that!—I'd have paid more attention to those clouds. I noticed them piling up above the Smokey Hills, beyond the river, a little while ago. But you were practicing the delicate wifely sport of husband-baiting, y'know: 'What'll I say next to get the poor devil wild?' and succeeding at it so splendidly, that I half forgot 'em. Jesus, an old prairie hand like me! I *know* you can never disregard heavy clouds out here, summer or winter—cause when it's hot they're cyclones, and when it's cold, they're blizzards! For God's sake, Anne, come on!"

"Ethan—I'm sorry!" she wailed. "Oh, Lord, I can't even *see* the house any more. Maybe we'd better head for Cora's—"

"It's even farther off. I estimate we haven't come even a quarter of the distance between our house and theirs. Jon was walking, remember. Or rather zigzagging as usual. We had to slow down for him. I should have picked him up and carried him from the outset. We'd have been practically there if I'd done that. Besides, neither house is visible any longer. No point trying to run, now. We'd better save our breath—for prayer, among other things. And here's my first one: 'O Lord, keep us traveling in a straight line. Amen!' "

"Ethan, we couldn't get lost," Anne got out; "we aren't even a quarter of a mile from the house and—"

"And in that freak storm two years ago, people got lost—and froze to death—between their houses and their barns. They tramped around all night and died because anything more than a rod away had become invisible in that driving snow. Now I'm going to shut up, and I beg of you to stop talking, too. You let sleet this fine get down your throat, it'll sear it shut and ruin your lungs forever. Keep my baby's face covered, will you?"

"Pa-pa!" Jon gasped; "I'm—cold!"

"I know, son. Keep your head down. And your nose and mouth under my scarf. But don't go to sleep, huh, Jonathan? Whatever you do, don't—go—to—sleep!"

"Don't wanna sleep. Wanna pee," Jon said.

"Oh, Jesus! Anne, come here. Spread your skirt as wide as you can with one hand. I'll try to keep as much of this confounded wind off him with my legs as I can on this side . . ."

"But—Ethan! You can't take his poor little thing out in this cold! It'll freeze and drop off him!"

"Thus ending the Lovejoy succession," Ethan said with grim humor. "I'll shelter his little pink wiener sausage all I can with my hand. But if we let him wet his pants, he's done for, Anne. He'd freeze then, in spite of anything we could do. All right, big boy! Squirt away, will you?"

"Wheeee!" little Jonathan laughed; "I'm making icicles!"

"Good God!" Ethan breathed. It was perfectly true: the steaming arc of the child's urine tinkled to the sleet-covered earth in a brief cascade of yellowish ice, frozen before it hit the ground.

They plunged on through the storm. It was warmer now. Ethan knew that because the sleet had turned into snow, not because he felt any better. Worse, if anything. He was grimly sure that if they stopped moving for an instant, they were all going to freeze. And if they didn't find some sort of shelter soon, they were going to freeze anyhow, dropping in their tracks as exhaustion overcame them. He tried to estimate how long they'd been traveling since they'd turned back. He couldn't get at his big American Horologe watch that, like nearly all watches of those times, he had to keep wound with a separate key, attached to the massive chain that looped across his vest, to make out what time it was. Then he realized that even if he did fish it out of his waistcoat pocket, he wouldn't be able to see either the hands or the numbers amid that driving snow. . . .

Surely they should be close to the house by now. But they couldn't be, for he'd seen no sign of the Osage orange hedge, or the big cottonwood gate. The dismal conviction grew within him that they were traveling in circles as the lost and snowbound always do. There were no visible landmarks to orient themselves by; the blizzard, howling down out of Canada, had obliterated them. In that white, subzero hell there were no signs that the puny, scant-furred ape-mutant called man had ever existed in all this frozen world.

Then he saw that white hump rising out of the snow-drifted prairie. It took him some minutes to recognize it for what it was: a haystack. Which meant that the house and the barn were somewhere very close. But dared he try to find them? Old Man Wilkes, a neighbor to the west of his spread, had died in the November storm *twelve feet* from his own front door, because, at four scant yards from his house, it had been completely invisible through the snow.

Ethan stopped. The chance was too great to take. His hedge was fifty rods from his house, but there was no way for him to tell if this particular haystack was within the natural fence he'd planted to protect the house and barn from redskin raids, or without it. Without it surely, unless the snow had drifted so high, and had been packed down so hard by the howling winds, that they'd passed over the hedge without even knowing it. But he doubted that. And he had haystacks all over the place. On a four-hundred-eighty-acre spread, this one could be three quarters of a mile from the house. You could die in three quarters of a mile. Hell, in a storm like this you could die within ten feet!

Anne came up to him. She was shivering violently. Her hair, her brows, her lashes, were caked with ice. Her breath plumed from her slim nostrils upon the Arctic air.

"Take Jon," Ethan said. "Hold him and the baby close to you. Keep them as warm as you can. I'm going to dig into this haystack. It'll be well above freezing inside. Then you scramble in, and I'll hand you the kids . . ."

"And—you?" Anne breathed.

"No. I'll have to tramp around all night, calling out to you to keep you awake. You go to sleep, and you'll never wake up, my dear. I say this to give you a reason to fight off sleep, because in blizzards the temptation to let go and slip away into blissful slumber is awfully, awfully strong—you've got to stay alive so your body's heat will keep the kids from freezing . . ."

"But Ethan! Your coat's so thin! And you haven't any gloves and—"

"I'll manage. Take Jon, Anne!"

His hands were bleeding within minutes from the frozen straw, but he kept at it. When he had the cavity just big enough, he growled:

"Give me the kids first, then in with you, my dear!"

"Ethan," she got out; "kiss me?"

"Lord God, Anne!"

"If—we're going to die. I want to kiss you—good-bye. Tell you—I love you. Say—"

"Not another goddamned word. You kiss me and our lips will freeze together. Tear all the skin off, getting 'em loose. And they'll bleed. We can't afford that, dear heart; blood is warmth. Get into that hole, damnit!"

Anne scrambled into the black hole in the haystack. Ethan handed her the children. They were both sleeping peacefully—which was dangerous. But their little bodies still felt warm to his touch. He decided to let them sleep. Three human bodies crowded together generate a surprising amount of warmth, especially with several yards of hay keeping the wind and snow off them, and they'd be more comfortable asleep. Then he covered up the opening with some of the hay he'd dug out of the hole, explaining to Anne that enough air would get through anyhow to ward off suffocation, and closing them in would keep out most of the cold.

He was perfectly right, as far as he went. But during the night, the careful training Anne had already instilled in them upset by the strange and uncomfortable conditions they found themselves in, both children urinated, wetting their clothing through, not once, but several times. Ethan hadn't thought about that, and there would have been nothing he could have done about it if he had. So he stamped around that haystack all night long, beating his arms against his thin, ill-clad body to keep himself warm and calling out to Anne insistently every few minutes until she answered him to make sure she stayed awake. When you went to sleep in that kind of cold, you died very quickly, and, most people agreed, peacefully; but however you died, you were dead.

When the dawn filtered through that iron gray haze, he saw the roof of the sod house not a hundred rods away. The snow had stopped, but all the world lay drifted deep in purity, in silence, and in a curious kind of peace.

'The kind that comes when you've moved beyond all pain,' Ethan Lovejoy thought.

Feverishly he dug into that haystack, dragged his wife, his children out. The baby, Martha Anne, sneezed as the icy rush of air poured into her tiny face, then started to cry.

But little Jon was still.

"Jon," Ethan croaked tentatively, poking him with one finger, blue and black with cold; "Jon—"

The child didn't move. Ethan put his truncated, frostbitten nose close to the boy's nostrils and his mouth, and sniffed noisily.

"Ethan—?" Anne said.

"He's—dead, Anne," Ethan said woodenly, and took a step away in the direction of the house. But a yard from the frozen haystack, from a woman all but dead of shock, her mouth and eyes opened wide, stricken beyond even the possibility or the relief of tears, he stopped. His knees buckled beneath him.

And Ethan Lovejoy, sober citizen, good Christian, man of iron will, lifted his head toward the leaden heavens and roared out his grief, his rage.

Howled like a rabid dog.

16

Ethan ran across the grassy prairie in the moonlight. He ran faster and faster, but the effort of it didn't tire him, and neither his breathing nor his booted feet striking against the sod made any sound. He could see his twin brother Jonathan up ahead. But although Jonathan was walking very slowly, and he kept increasing his pace until his legs were pumping like the pistons of a locomotive, he couldn't catch up with his brother. He couldn't at all.

Jonathan had both little Jon and Martha Anne in his arms. Ethan figured it was all right for Jonathan to carry the boy off like that, because, after all, both of them, uncle and nephew, were dead. But he had to stop his twin from bearing Martha Anne away too; because if he allowed Jonathan to do that, it would mean—

What?

He didn't know. He only knew that he had to keep on running after the three of them, although he was on (his life had become) a treadmill suspended beyond both space and time so that no matter how fast he ran he wasn't moving forward, but only hopping up and down in one place like one of those wooden monkeys on a stick they sold in the toy stores at the Christmas season.

Then Jonathan turned and smiled at him and Ethan saw that his twin's face was intact that it wasn't mutilated had its lower jaw in place no bullet hole in its left temple and that the crotch of his cavalryman's riding pants wasn't bloody shredded torn. . . .

There was something wonderfully peaceful about Jonathan. The moonlight spilled soft melted pearl all over him and the sleeping children in his arms. Ethan quit running, stopped jogging up and down.

'It's over he's forgiven me and I won't dream about him anymore,' he realized. He said:

"Martha Anne Jonathan turn her loose put her down she's not dead yet you know not yet not yet not yet not yet—"

Then all the prairie exploded into sudden flame, skytall horizon to horizon reaching, and Jonathan and the children were walled out behind that leaping, broiling rush, disappearing into orange red yellow white glare into inky sooty heavenward billowing pluming. . . .

And he hanging there on the rim edges of forever on the frontier line the sunset border between now and eternity saw the Old Timer coming out of the holocaust leading little Martha Anne by the hand. The old man's face was a bloody mess out of which his eyes glared lidless and his toothless mouth grinned in a way that was both horrible and obscene. His chest and belly were festooned with feathers, said feathers being attached to him by slim wooden shafts. He was—changed—in other ways too, but he stank as bad as ever or maybe a little worse and his voice was just the same as he cackled:

"Here, take her. I brung her back. She's a mite damaged but thet doan mek no nevermind—"

And he, Ethan, reaching down to pick up his little daughter, recoiled away from her in sudden horror because the left side of her face was—

Unbearable.

But he didn't know why. And now he would never know, because he was wide awake and his nerves were jangling like telegraph wires in a high wind and the dream with all its senseless mingling of past, present, future, with its menace and its auguries was—gone.

Ethan sat up in the bed. At once he saw that Anne was no longer lying there beside him. He threw the covers back and got out of bed. He took one long stride toward the cradle and almost fell, because he had forgot that he couldn't step forward like that—at least not without his stout walking stick, anyhow—for the night that had cost him his only son, had also left him with the ugly, rolling, lurching gait of a cripple, because three toes on his left foot had been so badly frozen that Doc Baines had had to take them off. Crossing the room, limping carefully, he reached the cradle and bent over it. Martha Anne was in it. She was sucking her chubby little thumb and sleeping peacefully. There was nothing wrong with either of her cheeks. Nothing at all.

Ethan stood there, very still, and waited until the dream, with its absurd commingling of unreality, horror, and shock had turned him loose. Then he went looking for Anne.

It was a warm night in May 1874, a year after little Jonathan's death. But Ethan didn't trust warm spring nights anymore. Of course the month of May was ordinarily too late for snowstorms, but a hard rain could do almost as much damage, especially to a woman as frail, as emaciated as Anne was now.

He found her at once, and without any difficulty, because she hadn't wandered off as he had feared. Clad only in her nightgown, she was sitting on the doorsill, staring out across the prairie, moonwashed and silvery, the grasses sweet sighing in the wind. Above their heads the new windmill creaked and groaned. Occasionally it slammed itself completely around with a tinny crash as the tail vane that kept it pointing into the wind caught up with the veering, quartering motion of that moving mass of air.

Ethan stood there, looking at his wife. Her hair was a wild, tangled mess, because she hadn't combed it in two months. She smelled faintly of sweat, and although he couldn't see them in that luminous semidarkness, he knew that lines of dirt were ground into the creases of her scrawny neck. If he didn't remind her to, she simply didn't wash herself anymore. Anne—who had been neatness, cleanness personified.

He had learned to come home from his spring plowing an hour early, because she often forgot to cook not only his dinner—which didn't matter much, for eating was a chore he did to keep alive, not a thing he especially enjoyed—but her own and little Martha Anne's as well. He'd solved that problem finally by paying Cindy Otis a small salary to cook and clean for Anne. Which meant that Cindy had to neglect her own ever increasing brood while Anne sat there idly staring out into space. Her life—and his —had been reduced to that silent gazing upon the empty horizon, upon that sweep of desolation, of loss.

As now.

"Anne," he said gently, keeping all reproach out of his voice, "Come on—let's go back to bed . . ."

"It's—an eye," Anne said calmly, quietly; "It's a huge eye. Like Cyclops. At night, it's silver. In the daytime it's green—or golden. Depending upon the time of year. But always—it's an eye. And you and I, Ethan, darling, are motes in that golden eye. One day it will close, very, very slowly. And that'll be the finish of you and me, my love. Of everybody. Cyclops the Giant shuts his one huge eye to sleep, and that's the end of the world . . ."

Ethan felt the hot tears sting his eyes. He raised his face toward the mist-pearl and silver of the night sky, and whispered:

"You're supposed to be a God of loving kindness, aren't You? Of mercy? Well, I could use some now. Some kindness. Some mercy. Or both . . .

"Anne—" he said.

"Is—Jonathan sleeping?" she asked brightly. "He's—so fretful, poor baby. That's because he's teething, and—"

"Anne," Ethan said harshly, angrily, trying to see if shocking her would help. "He's dead. Jonathan is dead. He died of cold in that snowstorm last April. A *year* ago, my dear. For God's sake get that through your head!"

"Yes," Anne whispered; "he's gone. I—I killed him. I—rejected him. I hadn't—any milk—and he starved to death . . ."

"Oh, Jesus!" Ethan said.

"No!" she shrilled; "That wasn't the way it was! You gave him to that black she-ape, and her milk—poisoned him! Human beings can't drink monkey's milk, and Cindy is—a monkey. Ugh! Sticking her horrible big black purplish nipple in my baby's poor little mouth and—"

"Anne," he said; "Stop it. Stop it, *now.*"

"All right," Anne said; "it's stopped. Sit down here beside me, and gaze into Cyclops's eye. We're only—figments of his imagination, anyhow. Dreams in the mind of—God. Bad dreams, at times. Nightmares, maybe, but—"

He caught her by both arms, dragged her to her feet.

"Come on, Anne," he said, his voice drowning in despair, in sorrow; "let's get back to bed . . ."

He was plowing his nothernmost fields, just on the border of his tree acreage, next to the rows of cottonwood saplings, green and silvery in the morning sun, that he had set out, when he saw Will Trainer coming toward him, driving a pair of splendid Morgan-Percheron crosses, even bigger than Ethan's own huge plow horses were. Which meant that Will was bringing him the new, case-hardened pinion and bevel gears for the harvester–self-binder, and the much smaller wheels he'd also ordered for it.

It was those smaller wheels that had solved the last of the problems that had plagued his invention for so long. After the mower had cut the grain, and the reel—a whirling arrangement of wooden slats that looked something like a river steamer's paddlewheel—had swept the cut grain onto the platform behind the driver, a treadmill-like endless belt running across the platform and over the right wheel of the combination harvester–self-binder delivered the grain to the automatic twine binder that spun a loop of cord around a roughly measured sheaf of grain, cut that cord, dropped the sheaf to another low platform from which the self-raker kicked it off. But since the endless belt had to carry the loose grain up over the machine's right wheel, normal-size wheels made the slant of the belt's upward travel too steep, hence the constant jamming of the whole works.

And, Ethan realized ruefully, it was the very simplicity of the solution—that is, reducing the size of both the machine's wheels, thereby cutting down the height the grain feed belt had to climb to get over the right one—that had made it so difficult for him to see. Over the years 1871–1874 he'd worked out two dozen pieces of brilliant, complicated machinery to do the job of delivering the cut grain to the already—by mid-1872, anyhow—successful automatic twine binder. And none of them had worked. Then one August day, flopped down on his back on the prairie to rest after another unsuccessful tryout of the machine, his very supine position had forced him to see clearly how steep the uptravel of the endless grain feed belt was. He'd thought, 'If I raise the platform behind the mower, then—' But he knew that wouldn't work, because the reel would then throw the cut grain beneath the raised platform onto the ground. "So lower the belt's upward travel—reduce that goddamned slant—by using smaller wheels! Well, I'll be hog-swoggled and confounded, both! Why didn't I think of that before?" he'd roared aloud and leaped to his feet.

Two days later, fitted with a pair of homemade, smaller wooden wheels without iron tires on their rims and which weren't even really round so hastily had he thrown them together, and with, of course, the feed belt's upward climb reduced to a much more gentle angle, Ethan's self-binder had worked like a charm, and kept on working until he'd sacrificed a whole acre of unripe wheat to testing it.

So now, with the new parts that would have all of Will Trainer's superb workmanship to guarantee their quality, this fall he'd be able to test a fully finished and truly practical self-binder on his entire grain harvest. The drawings were already in the patent office. And after he'd cut and bound enough acres of wheat to be absolutely sure, he'd have Will wire the Sucker State Company's agent to come and watch the machine in action.

Then all his problems would be over. Except the main one. The one that would never be over now. He'd have a lovely frame house, painted snow white. Shade trees around it. A flower garden. And in that house, under those trees, among those flowers—a mentally deranged woman. A wife whose mind was—gone.

'From too much hardship, suffering, loneliness,' he realized now. 'Jon's death was only the last straw, that was all. Oh, Lord, maybe this will pass with time. Maybe something will snap her out of it, maybe—'

But he knew better than that. It wouldn't pass. Nothing would snap her out of it. Nothing. The destruction was too complete.

"Howdy, Will," he said; "You've brought the new parts, haven't you?"

"Shore did, Prof," Will said. " 'N I brung you sumpin' else, too. Couple o' pieces o' news: both of 'em bad, I'm sorry to say. A telegram from yore folks back East. Happened to be in the telegraph office sending a wire to that foundry in Atchison, ordering some sheet iron to make rims outta, 'n a couple o' tons o' pig, when this'un came in for you. So I told th operator I'd take it to yore place seein' as how I had to come out here today, anyhow. 'Pears like yore ol' grandpa is dead. Naw, I didn't read yore telegram. The telegrapher told me that. He had to listen to th message in Morse code, 'n then write it down, y'know—"

Ethan bowed his head. How old would his Grandfather Daniel have been this year? He'd been born, according to the records in the family Bible, in September 1788, just after the Revolutionary War in which his father, Great-Grandfather Josiah Lovejoy had fought. "And deserted from," Grandpa Daniel had always said happily. "That's howcome he stayed alive to sire me! Smart fellow, my old hayfoot, strawfoot, country bumpkin of a pa was!"

So now, Grandpa Daniel was just short of eighty-six years of age. A good, long, full life. 'I loved him,' Ethan thought sadly. 'And he loved me in return, which is more than you can say for my father . . .'

He took the telegram from Will's outstretched hand. It read: "Grand-father Daniel died last night. Can you come to funeral?" it was signed: "Mother."

Ethan thought about that. He realized that he could catch the midnight train out of Abilene tonight and be back in Pittsfield in three days—or less. If they had had the body embalmed—as they probably would—he could easily attend the funeral. He owed his grandfather that much—honor, respect, even gratitude for all the things the old man had taught him: woodsmanship, carpentry, how to run a farm, and more. 'How to be a man is what it adds up to really,' Ethan thought.

'But what about—Anne?' he mused. Then, suddenly, rebellion rose in his mind and heart. He was ashamed of that, but there it was. For nothing is more trying than to have to deal with even the mildly insane, the person who, while not dangerous, simply cannot be reached or communicated with. So much of life is based upon compromise, persuasion, talking things out. But the mad—even the gently mad—are impervious to all three. 'Which is why,' Ethan thought bitterly, 'that madness is contagious. She is driving me very slowly out of my mind, as well. And I can't let her do that. There's Martha Anne—who needs me all the more because she hasn't—*cannot* have—a mother—'

He said: "I'll write out an answer to this, and you'll take it in and send it, won't you, Will?"

"Why, shore, Prof," Will said lugubriously.

Ethan, caught by his tone—for Will was generally a cheerful man, his competence in his work and his confidence in his giant's physical strength combining to make him so—stared at the blacksmith.

"What was that second piece of bad news, Will?" he asked.

"Th Ol' Timer," Will said; "You know th pore ol' buzzard had gone got hisself a job, didn't you?"

"No, I didn't," Ethan said; "And I can't even imagine him even looking for work—on a steady basis, anyhow. Handyman's jobs, such as the ones he did for me, yes; but working six days a week, that I'd have never believed, Will . . ."

"Did, though," Will said. "Reckon it was 'cause he finally found one to his liking: lookout man 'n scout for Pat Hennessey's freighting company. You know Hennessey operated a wagon freighting outfit out of Wichita, picking up the goods off the Atchison, Topeka and Santa Fe, 'n hauling it south into Injun territory where there ain't no railroads yet. Good job for th pore ol' fella. All he had to do was to ride on ahead o' th wagons 'n keep his eye peeled for Injuns. Dicker wit 'em, too, they wuz friendlies, cause that ol' buzzard could talk jist about every Injun language there is . . ."

"I knew that," Ethan said; "Lord God, Will, get to the point! What happened to the Old Timer?"

"He's dead, Prof," Will sighed. "Kiowas ambushed Pat's wagon train on th way to Anadarko. Kilt every man in it. They got th Ol' Timer *first* 'cause he was scoutin' out th route ahead o' th wagons. Didn't kill him outright, th pore ol' fella. Been better if they had. 'Cause they tied him 'n Pat—who was took alive too—to a couple o' wagon wheels laid out flat in that desert country. Shot 'em full o' arrows. Then they sliced the lids off'n their eyes 'n left 'em to gaze up into that sun without bein' able to close 'em. Th lips off their mouths, too. Gelded 'em. Stopped th bleedin' down there with axle grease so they wouldn't die too fast. So, as a real good friend o' yourn, Prof, I'm axin' you mighty kindly not to take up for them Gawdamned savages like you always does. 'Cause as any white man in th West, 'ceptin' maybe *you,* knows damn well, th only good Injun is a dead'un, 'n that's a livin' fact!"

'That nightmare,' Ethan thought. 'Why is it that when I dream horrors they always happen?' He said slowly, quietly: "I'm awfully sorry to hear that, Will. And I won't defend the Kiowas. Savagery has no excuse, no matter who commits it. I've never upheld the redskins' cruelty —it's other aspects of their life that appeal to me. But, my friend and partner in a venture that's going to make both of us a fair amount of money, because now the damned binder works, Will, and you have my word for that, will you let me say, or rather point out, three or four things on the other side of the picture, call it?"

Will stared at him. "All right, speak yore piece, Prof . . ."

"Last spring a wagon train operating out of Wichita—and it could, or could not, have been Pat Hennessey's—that point I don't know—beat off a Kiowa raid and took a young brave alive. They bound him to one of the wheels of a freight wagon, spread-eagled, and drove across the desert with him turning with that wheel, head up, head down, head up again, all day long until he died. Those were white men who did that, Will . . ."

"Wal now, freightin' fellas kin be awful rough but—"

"But do you remember the buffalo skinner Cy Curtiss killed when he was trying to knife me? Do you know what he was called? Do you, Will? And *why* they called him that?"

"Yep. They called him Pussy Cap Carrington. But he wasn't but one crazy mean bastid and—"

"A member of the Second Colorado Volunteer Cavalry, who under Colonel J.M. Chivington stormed Black Kettle's Cheyenne village at Sand Creek in 1864. They killed three hundred Cheyenne. Seventy-five warriors. Two hundred twenty-five women and children. Or, if you prefer, squaws and papooses. And they exhibited more than a hundred scalps in a theater in Denver afterward. Plus the private parts hacked off men and women alike. So Carrington was more than one, Will. In fact his name was legion . . ."

"But, Jesus, Prof—th pore Ol' Timer didn't have one damn thing to do with either o' them things—"

"His skin was *white,* Will. Maybe the Kiowa and the Cheyenne and the other allied tribes have decided that the only good white man is a dead white man, my friend. God knows we've given them reason enough to . . ."

He stopped, looked into Will's troubled face, sighed, said:

"I'm sorry the Old Timer's dead, and sorrier than that, that he died so terribly. I was fond of the old cuss. Very fond. But he killed his share of redskins while he was alive, and debauched more than his share of their women. So I can't say he didn't have it coming. But then, we all do, maybe. . . ."

"Jesus, Prof, you shore have got a funny way o' thinkin!" Will said.

"Haven't I, though?" Ethan said. "Only my way of thinking isn't funny, Will, my friend—it's sad. And I apologize—humbly—for inflicting it on you. Maybe one day I'll learn to keep my big mouth shut—probably the day that somebody stuffs it full of dirt with a shovel in the graveyard, so consider this highly unpleasant subject dropped. Say, would you mind driving me over to the Atkinses'? After we unload this stuff inside my barn, of course. It would save us a heck of a lot of time. . . ."

"Why, nach'ly, Prof," Will said; "but I'd shore appreciate you tellin' me how goin' over to Hank 'n Cory's place is gonna save *us* time."

"The telegram I want you to send for me. I've got to ask Cora to stay with my wife while I'm back East. Anne isn't well, Will. And if Cora can't stay with her, I can't go to Grandpa Daniel's funeral, so asking Cora that favor comes first. . . ."

"Yes, I see that," Will sighed. "Prof, you gonna be gone long?"

"Two weeks. Don't worry, I'll have our new self-binder built and operating long before harvest time. A trip back East to pay my last respects to a grand old man will delay me little, if at all . . ."

When he got off the train in his hometown of Pittsfield, Massachusetts, there was no one at the station to meet him. That fact, of course, was hardly surprising, because his family hadn't known either the hour of his arrival or the railroad line he'd be returning to Pittsfield on. They hadn't because he had failed to notify them, having wired merely: "Will attend funeral. Love, Ethan."

As the hansom cab he took at the station clipclopped and whirred and jangled up West Street into East Street and then southward on Pomeroy Avenue toward his father's house, Ethan was rather dreading, if anything, his reunion with his parents. It had been only two years ago, in 1872, that he had resumed correspondence with his mother; and, even so, he hadn't been able to bring himself to notify her of the death of her only grandson. He was now going to have to tell her that melancholy piece of news. That it was going to upset her considerably, he was sadly sure. He was even surer that his father was going to take the tragic notice almost as a personal affront; for the first Jonathan Lovejoy—now, at his advanced age, by one more example of Fate's unfeeling clumsiness, the only survivor of the three Lovejoys who had borne that august and patrician name—would see at once that his ancient line was in grave danger of ending when his sole living son was gathered to his reward. 'Or hurled howling to my just deserts down below!' Ethan thought sardonically.

As for Anne's illness, as he euphemistically called it, even to himself, Ethan planned not to tell them—*them* including, of course, Horace and Edith, for the Willoughbys, he'd gathered from his mother's long, rambling letters, had become a sort of surrogate younger generation of the family to his mother and father—one single word. It was none of their business, anyhow; and, apart from him, what other way did they have of finding out his private tragedy?

He had no sooner climbed down from the cab, taking his lone valise with him, and handed his fare plus a generous tip up to the cabdriver, when he saw Edith Craddock—no, Willoughby—come scampering like a schoolgirl down the flagstone walk that led from the steps of the mansion's austere and beautiful portico down the gently sloping and impeccably kept lawn to the wrought-iron fence and gate that protected the Lovejoy manse and its inhabitants from the lower orders. 'The lower orders being, of course,' Ethan thought with solemn mockery, 'according to the famous phrase, anybody not named Lowell, Cabot, Lodge, Lovejoy, Craddock— or God. That is, if father's even on speaking terms with God these days.'

He stood there very quietly and waited until Edith had snatched open the iron gate with considerable force and come out onto the sidewalk where he was. There she stopped abruptly and hung there, staring at him.

Ethan stared back. She hadn't changed much in the eight years since he'd seen her last. She was still the single most—superbly and splendidly —beautiful woman he had ever known. Her hair was still like a darkling flame, and her eyes—since true redheads are a mutation of the brunette not the blond—were a brown so dark as to seem almost black. They still smoldered, lit from within by the passions—or the screaming nerves!— that consumed her. A year short of her thirtieth birthday, she was close to the peak of her female—and obviously starved—sexuality. Which was one of the things that had been troubling Ethan all the way back East: how to handle the degree and kind of temptation Edith was sure to flaunt before him. He remembered only too well how they had parted, to what raging and ravenous extent their entwined naked bodies had lit the night with flame. 'Adulterous flame at that,' he thought mockingly.

Then he read what was in her eyes very clearly: disappointment. Deception. Even—dismay.

That hurt. It hurt like hell. He was wounded in the human male animal's weakest spot: his vanity. Even in his pride of self. But there it was.

"Oh, Ethan! How *awful* you look!" Edith Willoughby, née Craddock, said.

"You're both young," Jonathan Lovejoy said; "You'll have more children! Lord God, Eth, boy—you've got to!"

Ethan stared at his father. He was thinking that you couldn't call the old man Jonathan Lovejoy, "Senior," anymore.

"Doesn't depend upon me, Father," he said. Then, ignoring the old man's outraged mumbling, he glanced out the window of the family carriage that was bringing them back to the mansion from the graveyard of Saint Stephen's Episcopal Church, where Daniel Lovejoy now reposed forever among his fathers.

"Why doesn't it depend upon you, son?" Emily Lovejoy, Ethan's good and gentle mother whispered; "You haven't—well—undermined your health, working so hard?"

"No, Mother," Ethan sighed. "It's Anne who's not too well. Losing little Jon in that terrible way grieved her beyond all bearing. It's been a year now, and I still have to almost use force to get her to eat. I actually don't think she'd survive bearing another child . . ."

"Stuff and nonsense!" his father roared. "Just what she needs to take her mind off—the other. And you *owe* me a grandson! Owe it to the family! God, boy, you can't let the Lovejoys die out! We came over on the *Mayflower* and—"

"Father," Ethan said wearily, "we did *not.* Our first ancestor in the New World arrived with Captain Thomas Wollaston and Thomas Morton in 1625. Landed at Quincy, not at Plymouth. And was a tosspot and fancier of redskin wenches—tendencies that have remained in the Lovejoy bloodstream ever since, to judge by Grandpa Daniel and my brother, Jon. And he was nobody's aristocrat, being an indentured servant, a matter you conveniently forget, old party! Spent a good many hours in the stocks for swilling rum, pinching bare and dusky bottoms, dancing around the maypole, and raising general hell. Fine ancestor to have. I'm proud of him. He was a human being, which is more than can be said for most of his descendants—"

"Lord God, boy!" Old Jonathan said in a baffled tone. "Where on earth did you get that peculiar turn of mind?"

"From me, I suspect," Emily Lovejoy said; "Besides, a steady diet of sheer humbug would throw anybody off his feed. Ethan—the child, my little granddaughter, she's—all right, isn't she?"

"She is, Mother. And if you'll pardon the paternal pride, she's the most beautiful little angel imaginable. I keep hoping that one of those itinerant photographers will come through Abilene so I can have some photographs made of her to send you . . ."

"See that you do," his mother said. "And, Ethan, when she's older, I do wish you'd send her back here to live with me—in a civilized part of the country. How can the poor child *ever* acquire the faintest vestige of culture in that wild and savage place?"

"From her father," Ethan said drily, "who isn't exactly an ignoramus, Mother, dear. And from her mother, who, for your information, is from Lynn, Massachusetts. Which makes her an authentic Down Easterner, doesn't it? Not to mention the fact that Anne's one of *the* most cultured and refined girls I've ever met. Main reason I married her, because she's not much for looks. Fact is, she's rather plain . . ."

"A Massachusetts girl, eh?" Old Jonathan rumbled. "Hmmmmn. That's better! What did you say her family's name was?"

"I didn't," Ethan sighed; "But, for your information, it's Jeffreys. Does that mean anything to you?"

"Hell, yes! They were all King's Men. Tories. My father said that the whole scurvy lot of 'em went back to England with Cornwallis after the Revolutionary War to save their hides!"

"Father," Ethan said; "Grandpa Daniel was born in 1788, after that war was all over. So how the devil could he have known what happened to the Jeffreys family?"

"From *his* father, my Grandfather Josiah," Old Jonathan said, "who treated old Benjamin Jeffreys to a suit of tar and feathers—and in Lynn itself, come to think of it!"

"And then proved his patriotism by deserting from the Army two weeks after Lexington," Ethan chuckled; "and never firing a shot thereafter. Smart fellow, Great-Grandpa Josiah! He knew that staying alive was the principal thing. If he'd got himself heroically splattered with grape or canister or bayonetted, there wouldn't have been any Lovejoy family, y'know . . ."

"And there won't be from here on in if *you* don't do something about it!" Jonathan Lovejoy roared.

"Father, isn't that in the hands of the Lord?" Ethan sighed. "Who can guarantee the conception or the birth of a child? Or that that child will be male when born? Have patience with me, old party. I'm doing the best I can . . ."

"That's better. That's distinctly better. I thought you'd given the matter up altogether," his father said.

Ethan looked at Horace Willoughby, his own good friend, Edith's husband, his father's former manager, and now, to all practical intents and purposes, owner of the shoe factory that had been renamed "Lovejoy & Willoughby," since, although Old Jonathan retained a minor token partnership, he had finally surrendered his last hope that Ethan would come back East to live and to manage the family business as it was "his bounden duty to!" from the old man's point of view. They were all sitting around the table in the Lovejoys' dining room. Like the whole house, that room was chastely elegant. On the walls were two portraits: the first of them was a stiffly primitive likeness of Josiah Lovejoy, done by one of those unknown itinerant painters of coach and tavern signs who carried about with them fully painted male and female figures dressed in the mode of those colonial times, but with the faces left blank to be daubed in within an hour if the client agreed with a minimum of haggling to the painter's asking price; while the second was of Grandpa Daniel, also unsigned, but a rarely spirited and accomplished work that the family attributed to Copley. Ethan, with his engrained skepticism, doubted the attribution. By Grandpa Daniel's manhood, Copley was already living and working in England. He'd meant for years to ask his grandfather who the artist had actually been; but he had delayed too long, and now he never could.

All the silverware was from Paul Revere's excellent and talented hand. And it was authentic, which was due to Old Jonathan's ostentatious patriotism, not to his dubious taste. Emily Ware Lovejoy had supplied the taste. But, all in all, the family had been fortunate, because they'd lived through epochs when money could still command really splendid talents: both Bulfinch and McIntire had collaborated in the design and building of the Lovejoy manse—and the skill of Massachusetts's two supreme architects and master builders showed, for the red brick Georgian house was quietly beautiful.

Sitting there with his parents and the Willoughbys, while the imported Irish servants deftly cleared the remnants of a marvelously well-cooked meal, Ethan was sadly aware just how much beauty, comfort, and sheer graciousness of living his choice of immigrating to the wilds of Kansas had cost him. 'I'll build a house like this one out there yet!' he swore. Then he remembered. 'A house like this for whom? For what?' he added sadly in his mind.

"What's the matter, Eth?" Horace squeaked. Like many short, fat men, Horace Willoughby had a high-pitched voice. Yet there was nothing effeminate about the little industrialist. Ethan, who'd always had a big-brotherly fondness for the chubby little bald man—Horace was a year younger than he—knew that very well. Before his marriage to Edith Craddock, Horace had been a reluctant and shamefaced patron of the village whores; but an assiduous one for all that. "Lord, Eth," he'd often groaned; "I know I'm doing wrong—risking my own health, maybe. But none of the girls hereabouts will look at me out of the corner of one eye. And when they do look, they burst out laughing. So what's a fellow to do? Go crazy, maybe?"

"What's the matter how?" Ethan said.

"You look downright sad," Horace said. "And you oughtn't be. After all, Grandpa Dan'l lived a full life, and a happy one. He wouldn't even appreciate your grieving over him this way . . ."

"I'm not," Ethan said. "Grandpa Daniel's gone, and presumably at peace. I'm sorry I didn't get to see him again before he died, but that's about the size of it, Hor. Death is—curiously acceptable when it comes to a man that age . . ."

"Which means you're thinking about your little boy," Edith said gently.

"Yes—and envying the two of you, yours," Ethan said. "By the way, when am I going to get to see him? I swear if I'm not beginning to believe you're hiding little Horace from me on purpose!"

"Little Ethan!" Horace corrected happily. "We named him after you, old boy. *I* insisted on that. Edith wanted to name him after Jonathan; but I was afraid he might take after Jon in his ways as well, seeing as how the Lovejoys and the Craddocks have so many ancestors in common. I don't mean any disrespect to the dead, but you've got to admit that old Jon was awfully wild. That's just the plain and simple truth . . ."

"My name is Jonathan, too; remember that, Horace!" Old Jonathan thundered.

"And begging your pardon, sir; you were nobody's saint in your younger days, I've been told!" Horace said with a gust of near soprano laughter.

"A better reason is that the name seems to be unlucky," Ethan said sadly. "Look what happened to my brother—and my son. And you, Father, haven't been that fortunate either—especially not in *your* offspring."

"If you hadn't been a rebellious ingrate, and settled down here—with the Rawlings girl, as I'd planned it—things would have been different, son of mine!" Old Jonathan growled.

"Maybe—and maybe not. Fate is not a matter of a specific geographical location, Father. It finds you, wherever you are. But to get back to my complaint: When am I going to see my namesake, Edith, Hor?"

"When do you have to go back to Kansas, Ethan?" Edith asked.

"Tomorrow," Ethan said. He had decided that only an hour ago. He wanted nothing from Edith anymore; he had come back to Pittsfield fully prepared to resist her blandishments, her arch, teasing invitation to a renewal of what there'd been between them; but her indifference irked him, her calm, apparent, and bored distaste for he who had been—at least for one tempestuous season!—the object of all her passion, tenderness, even love. 'She cuts me down to two feet high, looking at me the way she does now,' he thought.

"Well," Edith said. "Your namesake has a touch of the flu, Ethan. I'd expected you'd stay here at least a week, so—"

"He's got to," Old Jonathan growled; "To hear Pa's will read and probated, anyhow. Since the old fool's very likely left every red cent he had, and that farm of his, to you, son, don't see how you can possibly rush away . . ."

"In that case, I can't," Ethan said soberly. "The trouble is that Anne's far from well—and though I left her in good hands, I'm worried about her. But since, as all of you can plainly see, I've been no rip-roaring success as a farmer, I actually need whatever money Grandpa Daniel left me. It'll probably put my place on an efficient operating basis, and give me a breathing space, as it were . . ."

"I take it you mean to sell the farm Grandpa Dan'l left you?" Horace said.

"Yes, Hor. I can't farm two spreads nearly two thousand miles apart, you know . . ."

"Then let me handle the sale," Horace said, the iron man of business showing through his rotund, mild-appearing exterior. 'Horace,' Ethan thought, 'looks like mutton suet but is as tough as pig iron.' He said:

"Would you, Hor? God knows it would be a lifesaver for me."

"I'll do better than that. I have a buyer already. A New York man who wants to build a resort hotel out there. Tennis courts, bridle paths, swimming and boating on Grandpa's little lake. How much d'you want for it, Eth?"

"God knows. What's it worth, Hor?"

"I'm going to ask Mr. Swanson—Murray Swanson, banker, millionaire, sportsman, and dabbler in real estate—seventy-five thousand dollars for it. I tell you right now I won't get that much for it. But I will get fifty—"

"Fifty thousand dollars! Lord God, Horace!"

"Yes," Horace said complacently; "That's the way the game is played today, Ethan. If I ask him the twenty-five to thirty that farm is actually worth on today's market, he'd haggle and bargain until I'd have to settle for fifteen. Never pays to play oneself cheap, y'know. Incidentally, Eth, you stay out of this; keep completely out of sight until I clinch the deal. You're much too soft; that old pirate would take you with the greatest of ease. So stay in town at least a week, will you? By then I should have definite news for you . . ."

"Including your commission, Hor?" Ethan said.

Horace looked him straight in the eye.

"You've paid it already. Edith—and the son she's given me—are beyond all price, Ethan. Of course when we married we both believed you were dead; but—"

"You did well, both of you," Ethan said quietly; "Edith and I would never have worked out, Horace, my friend. She needed—and got—a man with a head on his shoulders, never a dreamer, and a fool . . ."

"A dreamer, yes," Edith said then; "but a fool, never, Ethan Lovejoy! I still have faith in you. I believe you'll make good yet. I—I want you to. My memories of you—are all good ones. And neither Fate nor God could be so cruel as to let a man so—so essentially noble as you are— fail . . ."

"Now you're embarrassing me, honey," Ethan quipped; "but thanks for those kind words, anyhow . . ."

The next night Edith drove back out to the Lovejoy mansion in the smartest victoria Ethan had ever seen, driven by a liveried coachman, with an equally liveried footman perched beside him on the high driver's seat. The victoria was paneled in rosewood, mahogany, and teak, upholstered in the finest top-grain calfskin. It had a coat of arms belonging to the Willoughby family of Pelham, England, baronets and viscounts all—to whom Horace's relationship was nebulous in the extreme, if it existed at all, which Ethan doubted. But he kept his mouth shut. He was beginning to realize one had to allow people their small vanities. The victoria was drawn by a splendid night black pair, and—

The whole ensemble fitted Edith, and she it. In a region where ancestor-worship, and not the dour Anglican-Episcopal brand of Protestantism given lip service to, is the true religion, he knew the Craddocks' history. He had to, for almost from the beginning it had mixed and mingled with that of his own family. From the time both families were firmly established in New England—the Lovejoys having scrambled ashore at Quincy in 1625 —"One jump ahead of the Royal hangman!" the Craddocks sniffed, with some exaggeration, but also with some measure of historical truth; and the

Craddocks, in their turn arriving more grandly with John Winthrop at Salem, five years later, the seductions, duels, elopements and marriages between the two clans had been going on without let-up in every generation until by Ethan's boyhood, one would have been hard put to prove that the Craddocks and the Lovejoys were really separate families anymore, so entwined had their ancestral trees become.

'Would have been damned close to incest to marry Edith, anyhow,' Ethan thought as he climbed up to sit opposite her in the backward facing seat of the victoria.

"So I'm to be rewarded?" he drawled. "How's the little fellow, Edith?"

"Better," Edith said. "By the way, before you give Horace credit for too much generosity, our son's name *is* Horace. Horace Ethan. Has a nice ring to it, hasn't it? Horace Jonathan sounds horrid, I don't know why . . ."

Ethan thought about that.

"It's a matter of poetic scansion," he said gravely. "Horace Jonathan combines a trochee and a dactyl, two metric feet that just don't go together easily in English. While Horace Ethan makes two trochees, which combine almost as readily as two iambs do. Though, actually, iambs and anapests make up the natural rhythmns of English—our speech normally falls into the short-long stress pattern, not the other way around. Horace is a classical Latin derivation, and Ethan is Biblical—Hebrew—I suppose. That's why they reverse the usual stress patterns, accents of our language, being rather foreign, themselves . . ."

Edith stared at him, loosed a soft gust of delighted laughter.

"So you haven't changed," she purred; "you remain a gentleman and a scholar in spite of your outward metamorphosis into a sort—of Daniel Boone, say . . ."

"Not into a Boone, who was a frontiersman and scout. Into a farmer, which is far less interesting. A failed farmer, at that. I knew life out there was hard; but I hadn't realized how hard it was going to be . . ."

"But now, with your inheritance from Grandfather Daniel to help you along—" she murmured.

Ethan sighed.

"It won't help," he said; "For don't you see? My defeat is moral, my dear. What good is a *deus ex machina* at this stage of the game? And a belated one at that."

"A *deus ex machina?*" she said; then the puzzled frown crinkling her smooth patrician forehead disappeared. "Oh, yes—I see what you mean:

at the point where your life had reached a dead end, when your problems seemed insurmountable, you receive this gift from heaven—"

"That I didn't want. At a cost that's much too high: Grandpa Daniel's life. That bails me out of my failures; it doesn't demonstrate my worth. That arrives far too late to change things in any important way. But then the gifts of the ribald gods who actually control man's destiny, human fate, always come too late, don't they, Edith?"

"Ethan, now you've lost me!" she said.

"Look, Edith—my farm will work now. I'll have the money to force it to. Which proves what? That in this one instance, and in that one way, I've been a lucky fool, never a man of endurance, stubborn will, real worth. So I'll be well-off again; perhaps with this boost from Dionysus, Hermes, Pan—or from Zeus himself, the worst trickster of the lot!—wealthy. Again—what? I'll be able to place my daughter in our —yours and mine, dear!—accustomed sphere of life, *buy* the right sort of husband for her. But—the Lovejoy family is—finished, Edith. Anne can never have another child . . ."

She smiled at him then, with pure, delighted mockery.

"You should have accepted—my offer, Ethan," she said. "I know, I know. That business about—the name. 'What's in a name? A rose by any other—' "

" 'Would smell as sweet.' Especially when fertilized in the rank compost of—sheer dishonor . . ."

She laughed then, bitterly.

"You're still a fool. Well, here we are. Come on," she said.

But she didn't take him upstairs at once to see the boy. Instead she sat him in the little sitting room, had her butler bring them wine and cakes, sat down herself across the table from him.

"You're right," she said; "those ribald gods gave you back your life after keeping you hanging by a spider's thread between here and eternity for almost a year. Then they allowed *me* to discover you were alive only after I'd given up—and married Horace . . ."

He gazed at her with bleak and bitter eyes.

"A piece of arrant cowardice on your part, Edith!" he said.

"So? Or say rather a realistic acceptance of the way life really works, Ethan. I'm not a romantic, y'know. Would you be surprised if I told you —I've been quite happy with Horace?"

"Surprised, no; I'd simply call you a barefaced liar, Edith, dear," he said with bone-dry mockery.

"Only—you'd be wrong. I have been happy. Horace is—quite endurable as a husband, and a man, both. *You* wouldn't have been. The degree of *Sturm und Drang* existing between us would have wrecked both our lives completely . . ."

"That's German, isn't it?" he said. "What does it mean? I was a Latinist, you know; the Romance tongues come easily enough to me; the Teutonic ones escape me completely . . ."

"Storm and stress," she supplied; "All that—passion—would have burnt us both to ashes far too soon. Will you accept *meden agan* as a far wiser rule on which to base one's life?"

"*Meden agan*—the middle way. Or better still, *aurea mediocritas*—golden mediocrity? How can I, not being wise? One day—one *hour*—of what we had together, Edith, seems to me better far than a life wanting in all fire. Burn me up in an instant; don't—leave me to be nibbled to death by the little mice of time . . ."

"Then—your wife, your darling Anne—had proved—disappointing, *that* way?" Edith asked.

"No," he said easily; "far from it. It's the other way around. I disappoint her. For which, in self-defense, I put the blame on overwork, my dear. Only that problem's over. Or rather it's been replaced by another one—"

"Which is?" Edith whispered.

"Grief. The loss of our son—is killing her, Edith. Very slowly but irreversibly. She'll be gone before three more years are out. Five, at the most . . ."

"Whereupon," Edith pointed out acridly, "you remarry—and save Clan Lovejoy from extinction . . ."

"I've had one solution to my problem that cost—a human life," Ethan said bleakly; "I can do without another, thank you! And Anne is very dear to me. All right! Quit stalling, will you? Take me up to see your son . . ."

"Very well," Edith said slowly, mockingly; "but before we go, let me —supplement our lessons in linguistics—we've been through German, Greek, and Latin so far, haven't we?—with a brief review of mathematical principles. Ethan, darling, exactly when was it that you left here? D'you remember that?"

"Of course. And especially the night which preceded my departure, I'll be ungentlemanly enough to say. I left here on the twenty-eighth of July 1866, Edith. Why do you ask?"

"You'll see that soon enough," she said a little sadly. "But to continue our exercise in elementary arithmetic: Ethan, how long is it from July of one year to June of the next?"

He thought about that; said:

"Since July to July would be one full year; July to June would be eleven months. Edith, in the name of God! Why these riddles?"

"Come with me now, Ethan," Edith said.

He stood there looking down at the sleeping child. At that eight-year-old boy who was—his image. Himself recreated in roseate tender child-flesh. The hair a trifle darker, more reddish. The eyes—he couldn't see the eyes. Little Horace Ethan had them closed in slumber.

"They're—blue," Edith said. "Like Jonathan's. Like yours."

"Edith! Oh, Edith!" he moaned.

She held him with those midnight eyes of hers, and they were cold as death, as cruel.

"My son—and Horace's—was born on June the twenty-seventh, 1867," she said quietly; "Eleven months after—your departure for the West, Ethan . . ."

He didn't answer her. He stood there and crumpled behind his eyes. Died a little—one of the daily, partial deaths we pay God on the installment plan. 'Advances against the final one,' he thought.

Then he turned and limping more heavily, more clumsily than usual, went back down those stairs.

17

All the way back to Kansas, Ethan Lovejoy puzzled his head over the freakish sport of jesting nature or of the ribald gods that had given fat little Horace Willoughby and his tall and stately wife, Edith, a son who was his very image. But when the logical explanation came to him, it was of scant comfort, or none at all: the Lovejoys and the Craddocks had been marrying one another for close to two hundred years now; therefore, in Edith's ancestry there surely was—had had to be!—a female Lovejoy, married to a male Craddock, who had transmitted to her, and through her to her son, the dominant characteristics of the Lovejoy line.

Human gestation took nine months, a fact that Edith, herself shocked by how much her son looked like the Lovejoys—that shock reinforced by the memory of their brief, but passionate, and adulterous, affair—had been careful to point out to Ethan ahead of time.

The only degree of consolation Ethan could draw from the whole disconcerting and cruel business was the bitter reflection that if he and Edith were indeed as closely linked by ties of blood as that glorious manchild seemed to demonstrate they were, then they'd been lucky not to have been able to marry each other, since that degree of consanguinity generally produced monsters, dwarfs, mongolian idiots, and other congenital disasters in the human race. But, all the same, he got back to his farm bent under the feeling that he had lost two sons, not one: Jonathan to the icy blasts of one of the most devastating snowstorms in living memory; and little Horace Ethan to—what? Name of God, to *what?*

'To—my own lingering weakness from my shredded gut,' he told himself; 'To shooting wadded blanks. To nature's taking damned good care to make what must have been near incest fruitless. Who knows? Merciless God, who knows?"

So thinking, he got down from the buckboard he'd hired from Luke Prevost after his arrival in Abilene and stood there a moment watching Luke's eldest son driving it back toward town again. In his billfold he had two certified bank checks; one for the twenty-five thousand dollars in cash his Grandpa Daniel had left him, fruits of the old man's war profiteering in wool and mutton; and the other for thirty-five thousand, acquired through the sale of the farm that had been the other part of his inheritance. And which, Ethan realized, represented a clear defeat for Horace Willoughby, since that comparatively modest sum had been all he'd been able to beat out of a man every bit as hardheaded, flinty-hearted, and tightfisted as he.

Still, sixty thousand dollars wasn't to be sneered at, so once he'd got past his irrational impulse to tear both checks into tiny bits and let them blow backward out of the train window, Ethan had resigned himself to the—to him!—shameful fact that he had become well-to-do again through absolutely no merits of his own. He was going to need that money to make a decent life for his daughter, to see that Anne had adequate care. . . .

And now Cora Atkins came out of the sod house. It was hot. Cora was wearing a short-sleeved dress, and her upper right arm was thickly bandaged. Even so, that bandage was splotched with seeping red.

"Good God, Cora!" Ethan said.

"Her," Cora said with a weary grin; "Swear to God, Eth, never would have believed a woman that small and skinny could be so dadblamed strong. Had to hit her over the head with the seat of your chair—we'd already done made stove wood out of it, fighting—and knock her clean senseless before I could tie her up . . ."

"Fighting? You and Anne? Lord Jesus, Cora—why?"

"Well now, I kind of objected—real mildly, Eth—to her starting to stick a hog butchering knife into Martha Anne's tummy on the grounds that since li'l Jonathan has passed away, then the Good Lord didn't aim for her to have any children, so Martha Anne would be better off dead, too. She put that knife halfway through my arm before I could get it away from her, the pore, loony she-critter . . ."

"But—but Martha Anne?" Ethan got out through lips gone parchment-dry.

"Nary a scratch. I'm fast for such a big buffalo cow of a woman. Scairt out of her wits, though, th pore li'l thing. . . . C'mon in, Eth. Anne's —all right now. She don't even remember—that. Keeps on whimpering: 'Cora, why have you got me tied up like this? I'm not crazy! I'm *not!*' "

"Jesus! Jesus! Jesus!" Ethan moaned. "Cora, what on earth am I to do?"

"Well now, Eth—if you was *smart,* which you *ain't,* you pore, sweet, good-hearted fella, you!—you'd pack her things, take her back East to Osawatomie, and leave her there, safely locked up. Doctor Baines would sign the commitment order sure as hell. 'Cause failing that, you ain't a-going to be able to do a lick of work. You'll have to stay home and watch Anne all the time. Like I told you, right now she's just fine. Clothed and framed in her right mind. But who knows how long she's gonna stay that way? Or what she'll do in her next spell, and you out in your fields, likely, half a mile away?"

Ethan hung there, lost in thought.

"Cora," he said; "Take Martha Anne to your house—to stay—until I decide what to do. Another kid underfoot wouldn't make that much difference to you, would it? I can't push the poor baby off on Cindy Otis, because she's got too many kids of her own, and besides that would really get Anne wild . . ."

"Sure would! She's pure death on niggers, Anne is. Strange in a Yankee woman like her, isn't it? Sure, I'll take Martha Anne. She'll be company for Doe Child, and having her around will be a pleasure, Eth. Now come on in, lemme rustle you up some grub . . ."

"No," Ethan said; "God, no, Cora!"

"You gotta eat, Eth. You're gonna need your strength, y' know . . ."

But what he needed was patience of an almost superhuman kind. And, needing it, he found it. The women of Dickinson County praised him to the stars, called him a saint, seeing the gentleness, the kindness, with which he treated his mentally ill wife. That is, they praised him after they found the time to even talk about the Lovejoy family's tragedy.

For two weeks after Ethan Lovejoy got back to his farm, the grasshoppers came.

He was sitting outside of the sod house with Anne, resting after their noonday meal. Anne was complaining bitterly:

"Cora's a liar, Ethan! You had no business listening to her and taking my baby away from me! I—hurt my own child? Lord, Ethan, she's the crazy one, not I! Martha Anne's all I've got now, and—"

Ethan looked at her sadly. He'd learned one thing very well by then: the insane never know, or at least refuse to believe, that they are.

"Anne," he said quietly; "do you *remember* sticking a butcher knife through Cora's arm?"

"No," Anne said miserably, "I don't. And I didn't! She—she did it herself, so you'd believe her lies!"

"She's not lying, dear heart. The next time she's over here, look at her arm. People scratch themselves accidentally, or even sometimes cut themselves a little in a fit of rage. But a wound like that one, bad as it is, and located where it is, simply couldn't be self-inflicted. You stabbed her, Anne. Believe me. Face that one fact. You've got to start doing that again, standing up to harsh reality, or you'll stay—sick as you are, forever . . ."

"Ethan—you—you don't love me anymore, d'you?"

"I love you. If I didn't, I wouldn't care for you, take care of you, the way I do. You're good and sweet, and a lovely wife. You've even remembered to keep clean these last few days, haven't you?"

"That's—because," Anne whispered; "I—I want—another baby, Ethan. A little boy to take Jon's place. And you won't come near me— if I smell bad . . ."

'Oh, Jesus!' Ethan thought. Then raising his head toward the northwest, he saw that cloud.

It was the thickest, blackest cloud he'd ever seen. It didn't look like dust, or rain, or a cyclone, or a tornado; and it couldn't be a blizzard in July. He sat there watching it sweep ever closer.

Five minutes later it rained down grasshoppers from the sky. They crashed against the roof of the sod house like hail. In minutes the ground was six inches deep in them. In half an hour they destroyed everything that grew on Ethan Lovejoy's four-hundred-eighty-acre spread except his sorghum cane, castor beans, and grass, all of which, oddly enough, they refused to touch. But they ate the bark and the leaves off the cottonwood saplings in his tree acreage, leaving not one alive. They totally destroyed the truck garden Cindy Otis cared for, eating the onions, turnips, potatoes, and carrots clear down into the ground. Cindy came out with her family's bedding to cover up the tomatoes, in an attempt to save at least that much. The grasshoppers ate holes through the bedding and wiped out the tomatoes, bushes and all, then bored into the earth and devoured the roots. In the cornfields, amid the wheat, they sounded like a herd of cattle feeding.

They ate the wooden handles off the farm implements; they gnawed the farm wagons until the wood looked as if it had been planed white and smooth. They polished into apparent newness the house and barn doors, stampeded the horses, the cows, and the bull by crawling into the animals' eyes, their nostrils, their anuses. The chickens and the pigs fought back in a gallant war of gluttony versus greed. Both ate the "Rocky Mountain locusts"—which some people claimed they were, swearing they were too big to be ordinary 'hoppers—until pigs and chickens lay sprawled out, too full of the voracious insects to move.

Randy Otis and Ethan kept the well water relatively unfouled by lowering one of the smaller Otis boys down the well on ropes tied around his skinny waist and looped under his armpits, then slanted in a double cross over his thin chest so there'd be no way he could slip out of them and drown, even small and slight as he was, to dip the grasshoppers out of the water with a sieve.

The fight went on for three full days and nights. Smudge pots, prairie fires deliberately set, beating through the fields with blankets, nothing availed.

Cora came over clad in Hank's pants, with strings tied around the ankles tight enough to keep the hoppers from crawling up her legs, and helped Ethan put Anne to bed, tying her to it by her wrists and ankles. They left her there, screaming in hysterical terror as the grasshoppers invaded her hair, crawled up under her clothes, left their fetid, dark brown slime all over her poor thin body. There was nothing else to do. They were far too busy to be able to watch her every minute to see that she didn't harm herself. Hot as it was, Cindy Otis sewed all the children—Martha Anne, Tawiyela Atkins, and her own—into their long winter underwear and bound up their hair in cloths. Even so, the children had a miserable time of it, for all the bigger Otis kids could do was pick the grasshoppers off the smaller ones, including the two little white girls, since Martha Anne was only four years old at the time, and Tawi, six.

It wasn't until after another rising wind had lifted the grasshoppers, blown them away to devastate farms farther south, that Ethan discovered the magnitude of the disaster. From the middle of the state of Missouri to the Rockies, from the Canadian border almost to Mexico, *every* farmer was completely wiped out. For days on end the trains couldn't run because their wheels, crushing the mountains of insects with which the tracks were covered, became so befouled with the oil from the grasshoppers' bodies that they spun helplessly without gripping the rails at all, and the trains couldn't advance an inch. The railroad crews had to tie on flatcars piled high with sand and spread it on the rails yard by painful yard to get the locomotives into motion again.

The aftermath of what Westerners, Sons of the Middle Border, called afterward simply "The Grasshoppers" was even worse. In one short week every farmer in that immense region was reduced to abject poverty. In Dickinson County, only two men had the wherewithal to withstand the catastrophe: Rad Stevens, who, by his exceptional skill as a farmer, a large dose of sheer luck, and the wise choice of his holdings in the first place, had accumulated a sizable bank account, and Ethan Lovejoy, because his grandfather had died and left him money.

Ethan was bitterly ashamed of the fact that his survival was due to an act of God, not to his own deserts; but he had reason to be glad of his inheritance at last, for the wagons passed his place all day long, loaded with the household goods of ruined farmers fleeing the county, bearing signs that read: "Leaving Sodom, where it rains fire, snow, and grasshoppers!"; "Going Back East to Live On My Wife's Relatives!"; "Give Kansas Back to the Indians! They're all It's Fit For, Anyhow!"; "Nobody but a Jackass would try to farm out here, and my Ears ain't Long & Hairy!"; and the like. Within ten days, the county was almost emptied of its farmers. When Cora told Ethan that she and Hank were going to have to pull out too, he wrote the Atkinses out a check on the Abilene Citizens State Bank for two thousand dollars on the spot. Hitching up his big wagon, he drove, with Anne sitting beside him vacant-eyed, out to Phil Harris's, to Matt Hendricks's, to other close friends of his, handing out checks without signed I.O.U.'s, without any guarantees, mortgages, or interest charges whatsoever. Phil Harris stood there holding that piece of paper that represented salvation in his withered hand, and the tears rolled down his cheeks.

"Gawd bless you, Ol' Hoss!" he croaked. And Martha Harris threw her arms around Ethan's neck and covered his face with kisses. Learning what Ethan was doing, Rad Stevens made unsecured loans to his friends, too. Between them, Ethan and Rad managed to keep eight farmers from leaving the county and the state. But even so, central and western Kansas became, in that summer of 1874, a graveyard of deserted farms.

Back East, during that summer, relief movements were undertaken. They bogged down in thievery, fraud, error—the Easterners, with the best of intentions, didn't know *what* to send—and mismanagement. But they kept Kansas from losing fully half her entire population, a fate the state was seriously threatened with that year.

Ethan set about mending harnesses—a tasty tidbit to the grasshoppers—plowing under his ruined crops, setting out new saplings brought from eastern Missouri to replace the ones on his devastated tree acreage. He finished his self-binder. Only he couldn't test it. There wasn't a single blade of grain left standing in the whole vast Middle West.

Greatly to his relief, Anne came out of their ordeal calm and quiet. Her speech and bearing became so rational that Ethan took the risk of bringing Martha Anne home again. Anne cared for the child with tenderness, with skill, until Ethan would have believed her cured but for the fact that she let days on end go by without uttering one single word to him or the little girl, and spent long hours gazing out over the empty prairie with utterly vacant eyes.

In September Ethan took her out to Salina on the train, then by rented buggy out to Dr. Switzer's farm. He wanted to consult with the good doctor about her case. Dr. Switzer was a far better trained and more cultured man than Dr. Baines. But when he got there, Ethan almost forgot his mission, for several of Dr. Switzer's fields were knee-high in green, growing plants.

"Lord God, Doc!" Ethan said; "How'd you keep the 'hoppers out?"

"Didn't, Eth," Dr. Switzer said; "They stripped me as bare as a baby's behind, just like they did everybody else. But that plant you see out there is alfalfa. Got it in California. And although the grasshoppers ate it down to the ground, it came up again all by itself after they had gone. Which means it's the crop for Kansas, boy! It's a grass; good for animal fodder. Cost me fifty cents a pound for seed. I'll ship you a hundred pounds if you like, and you can pay me when you get the money . . ."

"I'll pay you now," Ethan said; "Came into a windfall, Doc, though a sad one. . . ." Slowly, quietly, he told the good doctor about his grandfather's death. Then, taking a deep breath, he launched into his real errand.

"Well, Eth, I just don't know," Dr. Switzer said when Ethan had finished his brief, clear exposition of Anne's case. "Very few kinds of insanity are inheritable. Syphilitic paresis of the brain is the only one that comes readily to mind. So you can forget about any new child's being born retarded. You've said that your wife was a remarkably intelligent, even a brilliant woman before this tragedy drove her around the bend? That fits, too. You've got to have a mind to lose it. Stupid people never go mad. Would having another baby—especially the boy you say she's longing for —improve her condition? Don't know that, either. It might. Or it might worsen it. Childbirth's one hell of an ordeal, you know. Lord God, how little we really understand about the human mind! One thing, though, if you impregnate her, and the child turns out to be another daughter, she just might reject it. Which could set up a mighty unhealthy mental set in the child itself. In fact, if your missus switched from this quiet phase she seems to be in now to another violent one, you'd better consider sending her away. I know, I know, insane asylums are pretty dreadful. But, barring a miracle, you've lost your wife already. And you have to think about the terrible damage—emotional, moral, mental, even physical—she could do your child . . ."

So, as he drove back toward Salina to take the train back to Abilene, Ethan was acutely aware that he had solved nothing. Like so many of life's serious problems, Anne's illness really hadn't any solution—except her death or, what was even worse, that death in life, that living hell that the insane asylums of that epoch were. He hoped it wouldn't come to that; but just as all men owe God a death, he, as a father, owed his four-year-old daughter her life. A normal life, untwisted by her mother's madness.

He was thinking that when he passed by a farm and saw a group of heavily bearded, oddly-dressed farmers sowing what was evidently wheat. Sowing wheat in September!

'Which means these crazy-looking old coots have—or think they have—a *winter* wheat!' he thought. 'Good Lord, I know who they are: those Russian farmers the railroads are inducing to immigrate out here to take up the alternative sections the government granted to the lines as part of the construction expenses. The Union Pacific and the Kansas Pacific —the same line really, heard they've merged or are going to—have to have people on those lands or what the hell will the trains have to haul? Farmers mean railroad clients—hence these Russkis. Jesus, I hope one of 'em speaks English! Because if they've brought with them a wheat that will grow in winter in a place as cold as Russia, God's granted me another miracle!'

He jumped down from the buggy. Anne paid no attention. *She* wasn't there. Only her body was.

"Howdy!" Ethan said to the nearest sower.

"Grüss Gott!" the man replied.

'Oh, Jesus!' Ethan thought. He said, very slowly: "Do—you—speak —English?"

"Nein," the man said; *"Ich spreche nur deutsch."*

"Dutch?" Ethan said; then it hit him. *Deutsch!* The man was speaking German! 'Fat lot of good that does me,' he thought, 'Russian or German, I know not one word of either.' He pointed said: "Is that— wheat?"

And since English is a Teutonic language, for all that it is loaded down with Norman-French Latin derivatives that nobody who speaks it well or simply and idiomatically *ever* uses, the Mennonite farmer understood him.

"Ja," said he; *"Das ist der Weizen. Sehr gut. Es ist das Türkischrot. Für dem Winterfrucht—verstehen Sie sich?"*

"Not one damned word!" Ethan groaned. But it came to him that he had gained a slight advantage. The man spoke German. There were already a large number of German immigrants in Kansas, some of whom already had been here long enough to have learned comprehensible English. Finding an interpreter for German would be difficult but not impossible. Russian would have been out of the question.

"Thank you very much," he said politely. "I will come back next week—understand?"

"Jawohl," the bearded farmer said. *"Heute in acht Tagen. Grüss Gott, mein Herr!"*

As he climbed back into the buggy, it suddenly struck Ethan what he had better do: turn around and go back out to Doc Switzer's place. He'd never thought about it before, but from his very name, Switzer had to be of Swiss descent and from that part of Switzerland where they spoke German, at that. Of course, there was no trace of an accent in the good doctor's speech, but—

Ethan hauled the rented nag's head around.

"Lord, Eth, of course my father was from Switzerland, but I was born here in the States," Dr. Switzer said. "And the little *Sweizer-Teutsch* I picked up as a child, I've clean forgot. Besides, it's awfully bad German, anyhow. Why do you need someone who speaks German?"

"Those old Russian farmers down the road," Ethan said earnestly. "They were planting *wheat*, Doc! *Now*. In September. But when I tried to ask 'em what kind of wheat it was, they answered me in *German*. I've heard enough German to recognize it as such when somebody says something in it. Russian I couldn't even identify. But that old fellow was speaking German. I'm sure of that . . ."

"Naturally he was," Doctor Switzer said; "Those new settlers are Mennonites, and the Mennonites are a *German* religious group. They migrated to Russia back in the eighteenth century because Catherine the Great promised them religious freedom, exemption from military service —they're pacifists, y'know—and that they wouldn't have to pay taxes for the first thirty years in that country. Only being a mighty clannish folk, they didn't assimilate. I suppose they do speak Russian; they'd have to in official matters, wouldn't they? But among themselves, they've gone right on speaking German. A *winter* wheat, you say? Lord God, Eth; that's just what we need out here!"

"I know it is," Ethan said; "but since back East where I come from, it's considered elegant to speak French or Italian, I don't know one word of German. And right now, knowing a little would make one hell of a difference. For if those old fellows have a wheat that will grow in a Russian winter, it ought to grow at the North Pole, not to mention here. Our winters really aren't that bad except for freak snowstorms like the one that cost me—my boy. And how often do they happen? Only every three to five years. So if those—Mennonites, you called 'em?—really had a hard-stemmed winter wheat, they'll be the salvation of western Kansas as far as farming is concerned . . ."

"Let me think, let me think," Doctor Switzer said; "It seems to me I treated a Mennonite not too long ago, who speaks English . . ." He turned to his desk, picked up an account book, turned the pages. "Yes, here it is: Mr. Bernard Warkentin of Newton. . . . Or rather he has a flour mill at Halstead, twelve miles west of Newton. He's a Mennonite, but unlike most of his coreligionists, he struck me as a highly cultured man. His English, I recall, was fluent and good. Somewhat accented, though. He told me that the AT and SF is dickering with him to go to Russia as their agent to lure more Mennonites to Kansas. You see, the present tsar had revoked the privileges that Catherine the Great granted them, so the Mennonites are in a terrible stew, since to them military service, with its implication of killing people, is an absolute evil . . ."

"They're right. Maybe I'd better learn German and join their church, because I agree with them two hundred percent, Doc," Ethan said. "How the devil do you get to Halstead—besides driving down there in a buggy, I mean?"

"You take the Union Pacific—the old KP, but they've consolidated now, you know—to Topeka, then the Atchison, Topeka and Santa Fe to Newton. From there, you could take the branch of the AT and SF that goes to Dodge City and get off at Halstead. But that may not be necessary; Warkentin sells practically all his flour in Newton, so you're very likely to find him there . . ."

"Thanks, Doc; and if those old longbeards do have a winter wheat, I'll let you know!" Ethan said.

"Why, yes, Mr. Lovejoy," Bernard Warkentin said gravely in his good though noticeably accented English; "My people do have an excellent hard-stemmed winter wheat. It's called Turkish Red—*Türkischrot* in German—because it originally came from Turkey. But you must not expect miracles of it, for it only grows well in *southern* Russia, that is below the Volga River, roughly . . ."

"How cold is southern Russia, Mr. Warkentin?" Ethan asked.

"Colder than here. Much colder, except around the Black Sea, the Caspian, and in the Crimea. Quite a lot of southern Russia is subtropical, you know; but, unfortunately, most of that part is also desert country. I'd say that the regions where Turkish Red has grown well are about as cold as the Dakotas or southern Canada. That's why I advised my people to bring it. Here in Kansas, it should do very well indeed . . ."

"Sir," Ethan said; "Could you give me a letter—in German—asking your people to sell me some of that seed? And they can just about name their price."

"Unfortunately," Warkentin said; "they probably have no surplus to sell, Mr. Lovejoy. My people came here as virtual refugees, so they were able to bring very little of anything. Of course, if you can wait a few years, until they have accumulated a surplus by natural increase, why then—"

"Oh, God!" Ethan said.

"Then—there's one alternative: by your speech, you seem a highly educated man—and an Easterner. From, I'd judge, a relatively well-off position in life. Why don't you make a voyage to Russia—as the agent of the farmers of your district or county, say—and buy your Turkish Red seed directly there? That way, you could purchase all you want and have it shipped back to Kansas. It would surely reach here by ocean steamer and the railroads well within six months. Too late for this year's planting, but in ample time for the next's—"

Ethan thought about that.

"That's an awfully tempting idea, sir," he said; "but since I speak neither Russian nor German, how could I dicker with the farmers?"

"Come along with me," Bernard Warkentin said; "I'm sailing, as an agent for the railroads, from New York to Odessa by way of the Mediterranean and the Dardanelles to the Sea of Marmara, then through the Bosporus to the Black Sea. A long voyage. I should be glad to have company on it . . ."

"When do you leave?" Ethan said. His pulse was racing. The very names were magic. He hadn't been abroad since his college days, when he'd spent a summer wandering around Italy and France, with only a few days in England before crossing the Channel and heading South. . . .

"In November. Don't worry, Odessa is an ice-free port, and Black Sea winters are mild, except for the Bolshoy district on the east coast where it gets plenty cold. What do you say, Mr. Lovejoy? Will you be able to come along?"

Ethan's answer surprised even himself. Because he *knew* he couldn't go abroad, even though he did have the money to. Not with Anne sinking deeper into apathy with every passing day. But he did so want to go! To get away from the West, from terrible, tragic Kansas that had robbed him of his son, broken his wife's spirit and her mind, was bowing him ever closer to defeat, surrender, age—death. To get away from—Anne. That thought shocked him, but there it was.

"When do I have to let you know?" he said.

"Any time before I leave," Warkentin said. "Your coming along won't change my travel arrangements, you know. But, as I said, I should be glad of your company. You seem—a civilized man. And there are so few of that kind out here . . ."

He wanted to, and he had the means. He even had a convincingly valid excuse: if he could sow the majority of his acreage to winter wheat, his farm would not only become immediately profitable, but would probably remain so, the rest of his life. Wheat was the money crop, not corn. Moreover, with the profits from his wheat and the royalties from his self-binding harvester, which now worked perfectly, he could begin to buy up the farms that the plague of grasshoppers had forced the homesteaders to abandon all around his spread. If he could persuade Hank and Cora to sell, thus freeing his southern borders, he could assemble two full sections—one thousand two hundred eighty acres—two beautiful square miles—into a solid block around his three original quarter sections. His spread would then sweep north to the Smokey Hill River, thus ending his water supply problem forever, and—

Insure his only daughter a good life: an education in the East, topped off by a university degree if she wanted one, in one of Massachusetts's excellent female colleges; see that she met the right sort of young fellow and—

As Anne had. A gentleman and a scholar—transformed into clodhopper, country bumpkin, hayseed, oaf. Metamorphosed into—scoundrel prepared to shove her aside, desert her, when it was the very life he'd inflicted upon her, plus, doubtless, his own dour ways that had wrecked her really splendid mind!

But procuring that winter wheat was vital. His grandfather's legacy wouldn't last forever. A way must be found to "absent him from *in*felicity the while," to misquote Hamlet, long enough to do what he had to do.

So Ethan Lovejoy found that way.

"Why, yes, Prof," Dr. Baines drawled; "I do know of a female rest home that takes nervous cases. Run by an ex-classmate o' mine in med school back in Missouri. It's in St. Looie. Ain't cheap, though. Fact is, it'll cost you a pretty penny—"

Ethan explained the matter very carefully to Anne, pointing out that his procuring a solid supply of the new winter wheat would mean a definite end to the grinding poverty that had oppressed them so long.

"I'll build you your frame house, plant your shade trees, a rose garden, hire you a servant girl, give you a little of the comfort you deserve," he said.

But when he had finished his little speech of persuasion, he was unsure whether or not she'd understood, or even listened to it. For—

"All right, Ethan; anything you say," she said.

*   *   *

His long voyage to Odessa on the Black Sea was troubled by two things: his feeling of guilt over what seemed to his mind the extremely callous act of leaving poor Anne in the hands of strangers, albeit professional and apparently competent medical people in St. Louis; and the fact that the Andrewses, Nora and Price, had disappeared from that city, leaving not a trace behind them.

He knew that because instead of immediately taking a train for New York, where he was to join Bernard Warkentin, he laid over in St. Louis one more night even after he had safely installed Anne in the rest home with the deliberate intention of visiting his (achingly beloved!) former pupil and her husband with the flimsy excuse of taking a meal at their restaurant. He had the address of their establishment from Farley Evans, the Abilene haberdasher, who had looked it up for him during one of that shrewd merchant's frequent business trips to the city that was his chief source of supply. But when Ethan got there, he found the restaurant padlocked, and with a huge For Sale sign nailed to the front door.

It was far too late to call upon the real estate dealer listed upon that sign, so Ethan stayed over another night, thus cutting the week's sojourn he'd allowed himself in New York City, largely to buy himself some decent clothes, down to a scant three shopping days and eliminating any possibility of making a quick overnight trip up to Pittsfield to visit his parents altogether. But, the next morning, when he reached the agent's office, to his acute chagrin, the man knew nothing about the Andrewses' whereabouts.

"You see, sir, I don't represent the former owners," he said; "I'm representing myself. I own that place now. Bought it on speculation from the city for back taxes . . ."

"You mean they'd done so badly with their restaurant that they couldn't pay their taxes?" Ethan said.

The real estate dealer hesitated.

"How well do you know Price Andrews, sir?" he said.

"Not well at all. His wife's a former pupil of mine and the daughter of one of my best friends. A man who once saved my life, in fact. It was she I was interested in getting in touch with, not her husband. All right —I do know, or rather have been told, that Andrews has a bad reputation. That he's an ex-gambler—and a crooked one. That's why I wanted to see if Nora were all right . . ."

"Can't help you there, Mister Lovejoy. Haven't idea one where Mrs. Andrews is. I happen to know they've separated. Andrews ran true to form: he pocketed the money she gave him to pay the taxes, which was why they lost the place, although, thanks to her, their eatery was doing exceedingly well. And when she reproached him for that, the very next day he skipped—after withdrawing her last cent out of the St. Louis First National on the basis of a power of attorney over a masterly and artistic forgery of her signature . . ."

"Dear God!" Ethan grated; "Somebody ought to pistol that polecat!"

"Well, sir," the agent said; "if you feel up to doing society that favor, I can tell you where *he* is—roughly. In Kansas. Wichita or Dodge City, whichever one's got the gambling halls and the cathouses going at the wilder clip. That Mrs. Andrews also has left St. Louis, I've been informed, though where she's gone, I haven't the faintest idea . . ."

From the real estate dealer's, Ethan went directly to the telegraph office and sent a wire to Mrs. Wilbur James in Chicago. He had Nora's aunt's address because Nora had given it to him in the summer of 1867, just before her departure from Abilene. He hadn't made any special effort to conserve it; he had it still because he had jotted it down in his address book, and an address book generally lasts a man half a lifetime unless he loses it or the conditions of his existence change so drastically that he has no further need of the information therein contained.

His message read: "Is Nora with you? Anxious to know. Please wire me collect, Grand Hotel, St. Louis, Missouri." He signed it, "Professor Lovejoy." Two hours later the answer was in his hands: "Nora's whereabouts unknown to me. Sorry. Mildred James."

And that was that. He couldn't suspend his voyage to Russia to search for Nora no matter how badly he wanted to, not when he didn't have any idea where to begin that search. Collaring Price Andrews and half strangling the information out of him, however emotionally satisfying that procedure might seem, had the double drawback that Price probably didn't know where Nora was either, and most certainly wouldn't give that information to one Ethan Lovejoy even if he did. . . .

But Ethan's disquietude, added to the fact that Russia is a gloomy country to visit, its cities, with the lone exceptions of St. Petersburg and —stretching the point wildly—Moscow, drearily dull, practically ruined his trip for him as far as any pleasure went. The business side of the voyage, however, was eminently successful. He was able to buy several hundred bushels of Turkish Red wheat seed and even saw his consignment loaded on a steamship at Odessa for shipping directly to New Orleans— from where it would be transshipped straight up the Mississippi and the

Missouri to Atchison, and by rail to Abilene—before he left the grim and forbidding land of the tsars.

He did not return home by the same route by which he had come to Europe. While his ship lay anchored before the fair and smiling city of Nice—Nizza la superba!—he suddenly bade farewell to Bernard Warkentin, went ashore, and took a train to Paris.

His reasons for doing that were very simple: since the death of his little son in April 1873, he had not had sexual relations with his wife. Further, he doubted that he'd ever risk having them again. To inflict another child upon a mad mother, and worse still, a mad mother upon a helpless child, seemed to him unthinkable. He was a human being, and male. Prolonged abstention was no easier for him than it is for any other man not certifiably defunct. And, *les poules de Paris,* he already knew from his university grand tour, were clearly the best that Europe had to offer, which was to say that they were merely dreary, not ranging from dismal to ghoulish as in most towns on the Continent; and a world above the appalling hags that London had on display.

So he went to Paris and let off steam. A very pardonable, minor, venial sin. That done, he took a ferryboat across the Channel to London.

What he did in the English capital sounds like a bad scatological joke, except that it wasn't. He spent a goodly part of his time there making detailed sketches of the mechanisms of the new water closets coming into vogue in that great city. For at that time, 1875, when it came to sewage, drains, and hygienic conveniences, London was the most advanced metropolis on the face of the earth.

Now Ethan Lovejoy, with his prominent—if somewhat truncated—nose and his weak stomach, had always been an acute sufferer in the presence of vile odors; and the outhouse on his farm, no matter how frequently he replenished the quicklime beneath its seats, was a sheer torture to him. Therefore, the new English "loos"—not so new at that, since the first flushable W.C. had been built in 1596 for no less a personage than the Virgin Queen herself by one Sir John Harrington, her own godson —delighted both the puritan and the inventor in him.

He was less delighted with the English bathtubs, after having been parboiled to a rich lobster color in the bathroom of his hotel in a metal tub that had the naked flames of gas jets burning beneath it to heat the water to the proper temperature. The trick was to pop one's self in while the water was lukewarm, then pop out before the flesh dropped off one's bones. Only poor Ethan went to sleep in the fiendish contraption and narrowly escaped a sudden if highly sanitized departure from this world.

He sketched other things besides bathtubs and loos for the house he meant to build for his poor darling Anne, for English country houses were then and still remain among the most beautiful in all this world.

So came he home at last—to near tragedy. He was forced to go to considerable trouble, and no little expense, to get Anne out of the insane asylum at Osawatomie, Kansas, to which the head doctor at the rest home in St. Louis had packed her off, when, after three months of perfect behavior—or, more accurately, total apathy—she had suddenly become violent and reduced the furnishings of her room to shreds, splinters, and what was even worse, ashes, for among the things she smashed in her screaming rage was a lighted kerosene lamp.

At the very sight of Ethan, Anne became a perfect little lamb, which convinced the head keeper of the asylum, which the state of Kansas had built on a little hill above the Marais des Cygnes River just outside of John Brown's hometown in the middle 1860s on grounds donated by the fiery antislavery prophet's own nephew, Charles Adair, that her husband could demonstrably do far more with her than they could. So they released her to his care.

Which was a tragic error. But then, everything in the Lovejoys' existence had become an inevitable tragedy since little Jonathan's death had deprived his mother of her reason.

And the very worst of that tragedy was the fact that it took so long to fulfill its fatal auguries.

18

On the last day of June 1877 Ethan Lovejoy stumped heavily down the steps of his magnificent white frame house, which was an exact replica of one of the big, four-square Colonial houses of Salem and, for that very reason, looked out of place in Kansas. It seemed to him that his awkward limping gait, a bitter souvenir of the night he'd lost his only son, was getting worse as he grew older. Of course thirty-eight wasn't really old; but a man was as old as he felt, and, by that token, he was a surviving contemporary of Methuselah.

At the foot of the stairs he climbed into the buckboard one of his hired hands had brought up to the house. How many hands did he have now? Sixty? Seventy-five? He really didn't know. Taking the reins from the young fellow's hand he drove northward toward what he called his "River Section" because it actually bordered on the Smokey Hill River.

Parts of his spread were only a mile and a half from Abilene now, instead of the three miles that had been as close as his borders had approached the town previously. As he drove, he could see fifteen combines—as the harvester–self-binders of his own invention, now being sold all over the West and pouring gold into his coffers, were beginning to be called—moving through the fields of Turkey Red winter wheat he'd planted in September 1876 and that by June and July of 1877 were in perfect state for harvesting. His five threshing machines, with six teams of horses moving in circles towing the sweeps that powered each thresher, were already beginning to thresh the grain from his southernmost fields. He owned one thousand six hundred acres, ten quarter sections, or five half sections, or two and one half sections—two and a half square miles of magnificent prairie earth.

He had a herd of fifty dairy cows, a hundred hogs, uncounted hundreds of chickens. His truck garden fed his hired hands, his family, and himself, and was the main source of fresh vegetables and fruit for nearly every grocery store in town.

He was a success. A wealthy man. A legend in the county. On his way to becoming a giant in that sweep of prairie earth.

And one of the most miserably unhappy men alive.

He had not—first of all—been able to find the slightest trace of Nora Curtiss. It was as if the earth had opened up and swallowed her. He had spent, and went right on spending, small fortunes in the hiring of private detectives who combed the entire Middle West in search of her to no avail. Later, he would learn that it was he himself who had condemned their efforts to failure. For in his instructions to his agents, he always included the notation: "Miss Curtiss—or Mrs. Andrews as she believes herself to be—left St. Louis in the fall of 1874; and since that time has not been seen by anyone who knows her . . ."

The trouble with that notation was that it was completely wrong. All the time that Ethan was moving heaven and earth to find her, Nora actually was in St. Louis, a day's train ride from Abilene. In fact she had never left that city and worked there still as a waitress in a restaurant run by a family who, though they had been her chief business rivals, had admired her gallantry and courage, and did what they could to help her survive the financial ruin into which Price Andrews had plunged her. But Ethan had taken the real estate dealer's misinformation as sober truth for the simple reason that the man had given it sincerely, believing it factual, and therefore the conviction in his tone had been both honest and real.

Still Ethan had the search continued. He didn't know what the devil he could do with Nora if he found her—beyond offering her what monetary aid she might accept. 'I'll buy her a new restaurant,' he thought; 'Putting the matter as a loan to salve her pride—and investing the money for her in stocks and bonds in her name if she tries to pay me back . . .'

But to do that, he had to find her. And by now—after three full years of fruitless search—the thought went creeping through his mind: 'Is she —could she be—dead?'

He turned shuddering from that thought, banished it by considering his other problems.

He lived with a woman who was a silent ghost for ten months of the year, then for the other two, a screaming, destructive maniac who had to be bound to her bed until her senseless rages passed. He had a seven-year-old daughter, as lovely as a pale, wan angel, but who had never known the spontaneity, the joy, and playfulness of childhood because she was utterly terrified of her mother. He also had a ward, who was the only true ray of sunlight in his life. For nine-year-old Tawiyela "Doe Child" Atkins practically lived on the Lovejoy farm—at his invitation. The reason for this was simple: after she had been beaten black and blue, her long Indian braids hacked off, her face daubed with both axle grease and paint, called papoose, squaw, dirty 'breed, and the like by her schoolmates, who thus lived up to the very best traditions of Anglo-Saxon swinishness, blond bestiality, and/or Northern barbarity, poor Hank and Cora had given up any hope of trying to obtain a formal education for Cora's stunningly beautiful half-breed child, whom—to his eternal credit be it said!—Hank Atkins loved as much if not more so than Cora did. Whereupon Ethan volunteered to tutor her, with the result that at nine years of age, Tawiyela was by long odds the best educated child in the county, far and away superior in learning, intelligence, and poise even to his own daughter.

Moreover, out of his stern New England sense of duty, Ethan also gave lessons twice a week in the three R's to the black Otis children, for, although on March 4, 1876, the state legislature had abolished all color distinctions from Kansas laws, Randy and Cindy were simply afraid to send their brood to school in Abilene itself. "They beat up a prutty half-Injun chile lak li'l Doe that bad, whut they do to a po' li'l ugly nigger?" Cindy moaned. Half a generation out of slavery, the Black children did, by comparison, poorly. But Ethan realized that the comparison was itself unjust: when you lived in a dugout that hadn't a newspaper in it, not to mention a book, when both your parents were illiterate field hands, that you learned to read, write, spell, and cipher at all was something of a minor miracle. And that miracle, at least, the Otis children achieved.

His house had a grand piano in it that both Martha Anne and Doe Atkins were learning—well, call it adequately—to play. There were pictures on the walls, most of them Western scenes by local artists Ethan tried to encourage by his patronage in a region where most people saw no conceivable need for any kind of art. The house boasted a magnificent kitchen with a huge, coal-burning range, running water in the sink, fed by a gravity tank above the house, said tank being kept full by the windmill which pumped water up to it from the well, thus putting those prairie winds to good use at last. In the kitchen there was also, among other things, a treadle-operated washing machine that left the family's clothes only a little less dirty than not washing them at all would have, but was a considerable relief from doing them by hand in the hard, somewhat alkaline prairie water. And it could be argued without much fear of contradiction that the Lovejoy farmhouse was probably the only private house in Kansas at that early date with a bathroom in it, though it must be admitted that the water for both tub and washbasin had to be heated downstairs in the kitchen, then laboriously lugged upstairs in pails. All Ethan's friends considered that bathroom "plain showing off," and nobody felt called upon to imitate the innovation. Washing their grimy hides wasn't a thing Westerners held to be a grave necessity, at least not too frequently, anyhow. But his functioning, flushable water closet—with its hardwood seat and a bowl fashioned out of galvanized sheet iron by Will Trainer's wonderfully skillful hands—was the wonder of the county, or the derision, or scandal, or scorn, depending upon the temperament of the persons who had either heard about it, viewed it, or, even, as a visitor to the Lovejoy place, used it where it sat in lonely grandeur in its own small Greek temple some yards from the house. Ethan knew that in England— since 1848, anyhow—people had built their loos—a word derived from the

French *le lieu,* "the place"—inside their houses, but his big Lincolnesque nose told him that his was far from sufficiently odorless for him to go *that* far.

Presiding over his household with silent grace was sixty-year-old Ruth Quindaro, a three-quarters white to one-quarter redskin woman of the Wyandot tribe. Ruth had formerly been the late Cyrus Curtiss's housekeeper, and Nora's nurse, and Ethan had gone all the way down to Indian Territory to find her.

His own study was filling up with books. He read endlessly in his never ending efforts to find some meaning to the senselessness of human existence. He was moody, sometimes irascible, always sad, and obsessed by the not entirely mistaken, and even somewhat self-fulfilling conviction that he was slowly drifting into actual madness himself.

So stood matters for Ethan Lovejoy as he drove through his fields on that last day of June 1877, the day his descent into hell, and ultimate resurrection into life, began.

He was sitting there, contemplating with the dour satisfaction that was all he permitted himself, the walnut and cottonwood saplings he'd set out in his tree acreage to replace the ones the grasshoppers had destroyed. Of course, the 'hoppers had reappeared in both 1875 and 1876, but in much smaller, easily controllable numbers. This year, however, they hadn't come at all, and his harvest of winter wheat was nothing short of magnificent.

He was silently thanking God for that when he saw Ned Tyler driving toward him up the internal road leading from the house. Which meant Ned had gone to the house first, looking for him, and had been told what direction he had taken.

Ethan sat there, waiting for Ned to come up to him. Next to himself, Ethan considered Ned the most badly troubled and unhappy man in the county. There was one great similarity between their cases: both were eminently successful economically, but their married lives had gone to hell. Since he'd lost out to Joe McCoy in the last election for the mayoralty of Abilene, Ned practiced law and served as an officer of the local bank. This very spring, he'd been elected president of it by the board of trustees, so it looked like banking was going to win out over the law in his case.

But he and Nellie lived together in a silence that, if not total, wasn't broken by ten whole words a day. Which was a pity, a very great pity; but there it was. . . .

Ned came up to where he waited.

"Eth!" Ned gasped, or groaned, or both; "Sweet Baby Jesus, Eth!"

"Hell, Ned, what's eating you?" Ethan growled; "You look like you've just seen a ghost—or something . . ."

"Did," Ned moaned; "Lord God, how on earth am I ever gonna tell *you* this!"

"You might try starting at the beginning," Ethan said dourly.

"Tha's just th trouble: what *is* th damned beginning? All right! Eth, I reckon you know that I stops by ol' Gashouse Gert's in Wichita oncet in a while, don't you?"

"Stale news, Ned," Ethan drawled; "And if I hadn't seen you lift your hindleg to wet a tree on occasion, I'd have sworn it had turned blue, started in to rot, and dropped off of you by now . . ."

"Aw, Eth, Gert runs a *clean* house. Changes her ridin' fillies right pert frequent, keeps a pill pusher on call, and—"

"You should know. Which reminds me: this is absolutely none of my goddamned business, but I wish you'd explain me howcome Nellie hasn't kicked you out of the house long before now?"

"Jesus, Eth—that's a rough question to answer. But—all right—you know how to keep that Yankee clamshell of a jaw o' yourn shut tight. Betwixt you, me, 'n th gatepost, 'twas Nellie who *sent* me to Gert's in the first place . . ."

"*Nellie* sent *you* to Gert's? Ned, for chrissakes!"

"Did, though. Look, Eth—that there's a mighty sad story, but here goes. Even while I was courtin' Nellie, effen I hadn't been a stone-blind jackass, I'd've noticed she was colder'n floe ice. She useta keep my jaw swole up slappin' me windin' ever time I tried to buss 'er one. On our weddin' night, my friend, Nellie decided that what a couple plainly has got to do to git theyselves some kids just wasn't to her likin'. Course she was a dutiful wife for several years, 'n put up wit what she called 'that nasty 'n disgustin' business' or 'you horny male critters' ani-mule natures' 'cause she wanted children so damn bad. But th kids just didn't come, reckon 'cause she's done froze it so solid that it's proof ag'in whatever dose th filthiest cowtown slut alive could give me. So a few years back she comes right out with it. Sez she: 'Ned, I jes' ain't a-gonna put up with this here no more. I've tried 'n tried but the whole business keeps right on turnin' my stummick. So I'm axin' you mighty kindly to let me plumb alone. 'Cause effen you don't, I'll be purely forced to leave you!' "

"That's—really sad," Ethan said; "What did you say to that, Ned?"

"What d'you expect? 'Lord Jesus, Nell—what am I gonna do?' 'Wal now,' she sez, cool as you please, 'you feels like you gonna bust, you visit Gashouse Gertie's. On th quiet, takin' care nobody finds it out. 'N make sure th wench is—clean. Don't want you bringin' me home sumpin' awful . . .' "

"So that's it," Ethan sighed; "A pity—a real pity, my friend. All right, Ned, what did you come tearing out here to tell me?"

"Oh, Gawd!" Ned groaned; "reckon I gotta. But I'd give ten years off o' th tail end of my life not to hafta be th one who tells *you* this . . ."

"Come on, Ned!" Ethan growled.

"All right! Last night, havin' reached th bustin' point, I took a train down to Wichita. 'N when I come into Gert's parlor, Old Pusgut 'n Blubber took me by th arm all sweet-like. 'Ned,' sez she, "got a reeeel treat fur you, my friend. Gal my best recruiter jes' brung in. Guaranteed un-broke—virgin stuff, you ol' heller, you!"

"And you believed *that*?" Ethan said disgustedly.

"Naw. Hell, naw! I ain't no fool, Eth. That business about th House Virgin is always a Gawdamned lie. But most in general they *is* young gals what ain't been pounded to pieces 'n used up yet. Fillies new in th tail-peddlin' trade. I seen some of 'em what looked pure 'n sweet as angels. Fact is, this'un did . . ."

"Get on with it, Ned!" Ethan snarled.

"All right, all right! Well, I'll admit I ain't one to turn down a chance at fresh young tail—fresh as it kin be found in a parlor house—which kin be a damn sight less spraddle-legged, stretched loose 'n worn-out than many a fella's done got stuck with permanent outside o' one. 'Cause effen all th men what's done found out on their weddin' nights that they could drive a farm wagon up it was laid end to end, they'd stretch from here to Californy, and—"

"Ned, for God's sake!" Ethan said; "will you please quit stalling?"

"I am, ain't I?" Ned sighed. "All right, Eth—grab a hold onto yore buggy seat, 'n brace yore feet ag'inst th floorboard. I shore Lawd doan want you fallin' flat on yore face 'n hurtin' yoreself—'cause that there cute li'l House Virgin, so called unbroke whore was—Nora Curtiss, Eth, my friend . . ."

Ethan sat there. His blue eyes glittered in his tanned face like those of a prairie wolf. His jaw clamped shut. In the sudden silence, Ned could hear his teeth grinding together like the stone rollers of a grist mill. A knot of muscle appeared above his jaw. It seemed to have an independent life of its own. Ned couldn't take his eyes off it. He hung there fascinated, watching it as it jerked and jerked and jerked.

"Oh, Lawd!" Ned moaned.

The glare in Ethan Lovejoy's eyes was madness's blue-flamed self.

"Was—she—good?" he said.

"Jesus, Eth, what d'you think I am?" Ned flared.

"A self-confessed whorehopper," Ethan grated; "A fancier of raddled she-meat. You're going to sit there with your bare face hanging out and tell me that you didn't?"

"I didn't," Ned said quietly; "I walked into that bedroom 'n saw th only daughter of one of the best friends I ever had in this world, standin' there bare-assed, mother-nekkid. Afterward I found out Gert had done took away her clothes so she wouldn't try to run off ag'in. She'd done tried it three times in th week it wuz since Price Andrews brung her there . . ."

Ethan raised his eyes toward heaven.

"I'm sorry, God," he whispered; "but I take it back. I've got to now. You can burn me in hell forever if You want to. It's—worth it. I take it back."

"Eth," Ned said worriedly; "You—you shore you're all right?"

"I'm all right. Go on, Ned."

"You don't look like it," Ned said. "Anyhow—I come as nigh to faintin' dead away as I ever have in all my born days. 'N I laid in front of Nashville a whole day with a minié ball in my guts 'n didn't pass out. So swoonin' don't come easy to me, Eth, my friend. I got th shakes 'n th pukes, both. At that I was lucky. She didn't—recognize me. I think she was—drugged, Eth. A strong dose o' laudanum, likely. She just stood there, bent over, stooped over, trying to hide her babygirl's fuzz 'n her tits with her pore li'l hands—'n cringin' like a whipped setter bitch. That was when I got to th point I couldn't stand it no more; not one more second, boy. I turned away from her 'n puked my guts up on th carpet just outside her door . . ."

"And then?" Ethan whispered, his voice grave earth, tomb moss, silence.

"I got outta there. Didn't even try to get th fifty whole bucks back that Gert had done pried outta me as her askin' price for bustin' into a pore li'l virgin. Went straight back to the station, took the next train I could get outta Wichita . . ."

"And Andrews? Did you see him?" Ethan said.

"Naw. That pukin' polecat's puppy has done skipped, as usual. Gert told me that. I axed her. Said he told her he was headed for Chicago."

"All right. Ned, drive back to my house and tell my housekeeper I've been called out of town. Tell her I'll be back in a day or two . . ."

"Lord, Eth—whatcha gonna do?" Ned breathed.

"Get her out of there. Then bring her home with me. Where she belongs. To stay."

"Eth—you can't! What about—Anne?"

"Anne—doesn't exist," Ethan said. "Only—her body does. And I've no use for that. Get going, Ned!"

"All right. But, before I do, I want to be all the way in the clear. That there prayer you said: whut wuz it *fur*?"

Ethan's gaze wrapped his friend's face in a cold luminosity that united the utter contradictions of ice and fire. Sapphire ice. Blue crystaline fire.

"During the War," he said quietly, carefully, "I killed my own twin brother, Ned. Maybe it was mercy; maybe it was murder. I had grounds for both, so I'll never know. Anyhow, I swore before Almighty God I'd never kill another human being again as long as I lived. Not even in self-defense. That I'd die myself first. I just took that vow back. Because I'm going to kill Price Andrews. If I have to hunt him through the bowels of hell, I'll find him. And when I do—he's dead."

Ned Tyler sat there in his buggy, staring at Ethan Lovejoy.

"And effen you miss, effen he takes you, *I* will," he said.

Gashouse Gertie was tremendously impressed with Ethan. His clothes, for instance, immediately took her expert gold digger's eye. While in London, on his return from buying winter wheat seed in Russia, Ethan had himself outfitted very completely in that city that has always been as preeminent in male fashions as Paris is in female ones. Never again would anyone call him a country bumpkin if they judged him by his attire. But Gert—nobody's fool—based her estimation of him on a far more subtle yardstick than his clothing. For, as Anne had once remarked, he had actually come to resemble a dour, forbidding protagonist of a Brontë novel: a Heathcliffe, or a Rochester, say. The somber fire of unrelieved suffering that glowed behind his eyes, the quiet control that informed his every movement—he even limped with a certain rugged grace—were far more exciting to any adult and experienced woman than the spectacular good looks of such extraordinarily handsome men as Price Andrews, and the now dead "Wild Bill" Hickok—murdered at Deadwood, South Dakota a year earlier—ever could be, even to the silly schoolgirls to whom male beauty generally appeals. For in 1877, with his stern, Lincolnesque ugliness, with the implosive impact the monumental stillness of his bearing always made upon female respiration, with his air of unalloyed savagery held in iron check, Ethan Lovejoy was, or had become, one of the most impressive men to be found in all the West.

Gert momentarily forgot her age and bulk and fluttered like a girl in her teens. Ethan cut off her arch protestations in her fat, crêpey throat with one withering slash of his gaze.

"The new girl. Ned Tyler told me about her. I want to see her," he said evenly, slowly, flatly, and handed Gert a hundred dollar bill. Gert found his low, harsh, slightly grating voice thrilling. Besides, from lifelong habit, any large denomination greenback always stimulated her Bartholin glands, set them hotly, wetly aflow. She wiggled her overstuffed form like a cow elephant in estrus.

"Right this way, sir!" she said.

She opened the door, let him in, locked it behind him, cooing:

"Ring for me when you've finished, dearie! And pray do take your time!"

Ethan didn't even hear her. He was staring at Nora, who was bent over, doubled up, cringing before him in that ugly, awkward Aphrodite Kallipýgos posture, trying, vainly, to cover her lovely breasts, and the small, triangular, gold-thatched proof that she was a true blonde with her widely spread, wildly trembling hands.

Ethan didn't say anything. He couldn't. He dragged air into his lungs. It was noxious, rank with brothel stenches. Perfume. Sweat, used whore-flesh. Stale cigar smoke. The stink of rutting male. His throat clamped shut, locked it in. It burnt him, made him strangle.

He took a step toward her—a clumsy, lurching, cripple's stride. Stopped. Saw her eyes flare. Saw—recognition invade them. Her lips, gone snowy, whiter than the bitter, ravished winterscape of her face, formed the shape of the word "You!" But no sound came out of them. No sound at all.

He saw what got into her eyes then, and it paralyzed him at the exact instant when most he needed speed, strength, motion, voice. He hung there frozen, acutely, painfully, idiotically aware of his own sensations, even those of them that were phantasmal: the toes that Dr. Baines had hacked off his half-frozen left foot ached, seared, burned like ice, like fire, although they were not there.

It was the crash of the heavy pitcher from the washstand as she smashed it through the window panes—negating in one blinding second, in one smooth swift incredibly graceful linked chain of whitefleshed naked motion, all Gert's professional precautions, learned in a lifetime of practice of the genteel art of reducing decency to whoredom, modesty to sluttishness, against precisely such a contingency as this—that released him. But he had been still too long: his crippled left foot had become a lump of inert, maddeningly heavy flesh; the calf of the leg it hung from knotted into an agonizingly painful cramp. Which didn't stop him, of course. He lurched forward like a hamstrung, raging bull, roaring "Nora!" as he came. But that one more demonstration of Fate's essential malevolence slowed him the two seconds, three, that were all Nora needed to complete her Classic Roman woman's vindication of what wasn't even the oversimplification of outraged virtue, the semantic irrelevance of honor betrayed, but a sure rejection of even the remotest possibility of living on to face the daily, hourly contemplation of the ruin of her selfhood, her conception of who and what she was, reading—by truly tragic error!—in his eyes the utter wreckage of her womanly dignity, her female pride; for well within those three clock ticks she found—or seized—time enough and to spare to perform an appalling amount of sheer, hideous butchery upon her slim, white form.

Thrusting her arms through the smashed window, she sawed both wrists to the bone; then, as his big bony hands clamped down on her bare shoulders, she bent, twisting her sweat glistened flesh out of his grasp, swooping in one sight-blurring, heart-breath mind stopping motion, and snatched up that accidentally murderous blade of crystal, that dagger of broken glass formed by the mindless—or cooperative?—malice that informs all of human destiny, into the right, the perfect shape for what she meant to do with it, and, pressing its edge a little behind and below her left ear until it bit flesh, raked it diagonally downward and across her slender throat, which opened like a second, obscenely grinning mouth and vomited up a solid sheet of blood.

He hung there, the death sickness in him, seeing her life flooding out of her, dyeing her whole upper trunk red, watching the black-scarlet rivulets race down between and around her breasts, trace spreading horror across her belly, descend her thighs, and still she stood there before him, rock-steady, unwavering, holding him with those morning star eyes of hers that were performing the gut-crippling alchemy of fracturing what little light there was in that close and fetid room, transmuting it into liquid diamonds, beading upon her lashes, mist silver, trembling there in fragile resistance to the whole ponderous downpull of the world for what seemed to him an almost unbearably prolonged halting of the very flow of time before each one of those individual distillations of her utter desolation, her terminal despair, broke free to flash white fire one luminous instant down the dark and fall and fall and fall—

Her voice came over to him, laden with a quiet bitterness that was going to haunt him forever, but speaking slowly, clearly, simply, with no stress or stridency in it, nor any special emphasis, pushing the words out on little blood-drenched and gurgling spurts of breath:

"A—whore. A—riding filly—for—dead game—sports. Dirt—cheap —goods—for sale. Anybody's—woman. Everybody's. But—not—*yours* —Ethan. Not—*this*—way. You—haven't—got—my—price . . ."

Then abruptly she loosened all over, went down. The soft thud her body made striking the carpet was drowned in the trochee of her name exploding in hideous maniac shrillness up his throat. He lurched forward through its echoes, dropped to his knees, disemboweled, blind.

And snatched her up from where she lay—in expiatory self-immolation before the pitiful altars of all the outraged chaste—bleeding her life away upon a brothel's floor.

19

There were neither sheets nor covers on the bed, only a bare mattress splotched and spotted with the dirty white of semen stains. The window had thick wooden shutters outside its now shattered panes, but no curtains. Gert was an old hand. She knew better than to leave anything around a new girl, not fully broken-in yet, that the poor little bitch could use to hang herself with. Suicide was one of the nightmares of a whorehouse madam's existence. Riding fillies who did themselves in were bad for business. Their sudden and usually messy departures from this world of sin threw the clients off their feed. Worse still, they could get your place padlocked, if you didn't have the local marshal solidly bought with cash and/or hooked on some fine little piece of—for him, anyhow—free tail. And if the dead girl had been popular with the rougher element, her voluntary immigration to a higher sphere—or to a lower, warmer clime! —could even get you run out of town, profusely decorated with tar and feathers and riding on a rail.

So the only materials Ethan Lovejoy had for tourniquets were his necktie and his belt, while for bandages, his pocket handkerchief, and, after it occurred to him, the shirt off his back, ripped into strips, had to serve. He had just finished doing an ex-combat veteran's rough but effective job on Nora's self-inflicted wounds, when he heard the key turn in the lock.

There stood Gert, all two hundred sixty pounds of her, giving a quite remarkable imitation of a beached white whale.

"Where's your doctor?" Ethan growled at her.

"No. Oh, no! She dies here in my place, and I'm ruint. You git her outta here, and right now, mister!" Gashouse Gertie said.

"Wal now," Dr. Halston, Wichita's leading physician and surgeon said; "Cain't guarantee you nothing, mister—Lovejoy, you said yore name was, didn't you?"

"Yes," Ethan said; "Ethan Lovejoy. Get on with it, Doc. You were saying?"

"That I cain't guarantee you nothing. With bedrest, soft foods—she's done messed her neck up for fair!—'n a whole lot o' keerful nursin', she oughta pull through. You got anyplace to take her?"

"Good God, man! You said yourself she oughtn't to be moved!"

"Knows damn well I did. But I knows even better'n that, that this here pore li'l delicate critter is one o' Gashouse Gertie's fancy articles. A fresh recruit from the looks of her. Ain't wore-out hardly none a-tall. But I got a wife, Mister Lovejoy. I wuz to try to keep this carved-up li'l piece o' commercial tail in one o' th three beds I got for bad-off cases in the annex behind my office, I'd be a lying-in patient for one of the town's other two sawbones before tonight. 'N so would you, sir, you wuz to argue wit my old woman erbout it . . ."

"The other two doctors?" Ethan said.

"Same deal, Mister Lovejoy. I cain't fault you none fur gittin' mixed-up wit a soiled dove this daggummed fine; but you've gone 'n done it. So it's purely up to you to arrange matters as best you kin. I'm likely to lose half my wimmen patients in this here town fur even botherin' to sew her up. Respectable ladies is purely down on whores; and ninety-nine percent of 'em, including my own ever lovin', will come straight out 'n allow that I oughta have let her die, seein' as how that was what she wanted to do in th furst place. So it's *yore* problem, sir, I'm mighty sorry to say. Tell you what I will do, though: I'll call in Gwendolyn Burton, who does midwifing hereabouts, to set with her whilest you're finding someplace to put her. You'll have to pay ol' Gwen, nacherly, and a mite extra to keep her from feeling too put on 'n insulted, bein' axed to set with a whore . . ."

"All right. Give me an hour, will you?" Ethan Lovejoy said.

But it took him far longer than that. The story—with its gamy whiff of scandal—was all over Wichita by then. And it made the task of finding some place of refuge for a girl hanging on the borderline between life and death extraordinarily difficult.

No respectable hotel would take her in. And the disreputable ones were out of the question: filled with bellowing, quarrelsome cowhands and equipped with hygienic facilities—when they had any such facilities at all —whose stench would have turned the stomach of a goat, to have installed Nora in one of those noisy and noisome fleabags would have ended her chances for survival then and there.

There were no hospitals, nor even a clinic in town. All three of the doctors had, of course, two or three beds in single rooms next to, or behind, their offices, where serious gunshot wound cases—the majority of their practice now that Wichita had become Queen of the Cowtowns— could lie in until they recovered sufficiently to be moved or, as was far oftener the case in those days of rough and ready pioneer medicine, died. But all three good physicians were married men, and Dr. Halston had already explained to Ethan what a dim view their wives would surely take of their accepting her as a patient in their establishments.

Ditto the spouses of the men of God. "Bring a cowtown dove into the rectory? Why, Harry, honey, you'd lose your church 'n never be called to another one—in this state, anyhow—as long as you lived!"

To make matters worse, the city marshal went looking for Ethan to see whether the possibility didn't at least exist of booking him on a nice hangable charge—public hangings being one of any Western town's favorite spectator sports. But Ethan got out of that danger easily enough, for the very simple reason that Alexander Wilkes, Wichita's city marshal, was a professional police officer and therefore a rock-bottom realist. Now all professional policemen know who their towns' untouchables are, the influential citizens whom—however guilty of high crimes or low misdemeanors —you throw into jail only if you're sick and tired of your job. More, Marshal Wilkes was a shrewd enough judge of character to be able to quite easily decide which visitors to Wichita should be granted the courtesy of temporary untouchability, or—for public consumption!—a distinguished visitor's status. One good hard look at Ethan Lovejoy, three minutes of listening to the polished speech—though a slight Western twang was slowly creeping into it by then—of this tall, self-assured, well-dressed, and quiet man, and Marshal Wilkes not only didn't arrest Ethan, but invited him into a local saloon to "have a snort on me, 'n talk th matter over, Mister Lovejoy, suh. . . ."

Ethan accepted at once. The town marshal was the best ally any man in the kind of trouble he couldn't be shot, jailed, or hanged for, could possibly enlist to his cause. Besides, it was high time the other side of the story reached sympathetic ears. Because, even if Nora recovered at all— an outcome to her tragedy far from assured at that bleak, anxiety-freighted moment—he was going to have to stay in Wichita for at least three weeks, and probably even a month, before he dared take the risk of moving her —and that by chartering an entire pullman car—up to Abilene.

So he told Marshal Wilkes as much as he felt was useful of her story, including what was, from the legal point of view, the most significant part of it: Nora had been brought into Gert's parlor house bodily by Price Andrews while under the influence of those strong narcotics known variously as "knockout drops" or a "Mickey Finn," which have always been one of the last-ditch expedients of the white slaver's trade.

Ethan had found this out because Gert, upset by all that blood, or perhaps prudently desiring to avoid the immediate consequences should "the law" show up along with the horse-drawn ambulance Dr. Halston had sent for, beat a hasty retreat from the premises, thus giving not merely one, but no less than three of her doves, themselves former victims of Price's black arts, the perfect opportunity to revenge themselves upon him and Gert by telling Ethan the exact details of Nora's case—and their own! —while he waited for the ambulance.

For Price Andrews's methods never varied: to procure Gert an ever fresh supply of poor, stupid, sweet innocents who didn't even *look* like prostitutes—which was Gert's chief selling point—he promised them anything from honorable matrimony to stellar roles in the theaters and/or music halls of the greater Western cities, and delivered them drunk or drugged or both into Gert's virtual fortress, where they were submitted to marathon rape by the old harridan's richer clients until they broke down morally, gave up physically, and admitted to themselves that they were whores.

How Price had got his hands on Nora again, Ethan didn't know. And the point was unimportant. What was important from the law's standpoint was that she hadn't walked into Gert's bordello of her own free will, that she had been sold—for hard cash at that—into a state it had cost the nation over a million lives to abolish a little over a decade earlier. And the name of that state was slavery.

"I fail to see how the color of her skin changes matters much, Marshal," Ethan drawled as he concluded his recital of the facts. "Selling a human being, Black—or blonde, as in this case—is plainly against the law. Not to mention bigamy, of which Andrews is also guilty. Kidnapping. Endangering the poor girl's life with dangerous drugs. I could think up two dozen more charges on which he could be jailed for life, if you gave me a little time; but the ones I've spelled out are enough, aren't they?"

"They sure Lord are!" the marshal sighed. "But, Mr. Lovejoy, you've done gone and managed to put me in a mighty ticklish spot. I know white slavin' is a criminal offense, 'n I'm duty bound to shut Gert's parlor house up 'n haul her fat carcass off to th hoosegow, you wuz to press charges, but—Good Lord, sir, whut I means is—"

"That you don't want me to press them," Ethan said evenly. "Too many of the town's leading citizens partake of the fleshpots at Gert's. Don't worry, Marshal; it's been a long time since my sixteenth birthday. I know better than to call the kind of poker hand Gert's holding. Punishing that overstuffed sow doesn't even interest me. All I want is a clean, decent place I can put Nora in, and where I can stay to care for her personally until I can bring my housekeeper down here to take over. Got any ideas on that score, sir?"

"Yep. Shore have. You can bring her to *my* place. I've got some fairly comfortable old bachelor's diggin's up over my office. Though I'm a widower, not a bachelor, to tell th truth about it. Anyhow, it solves the main problem: I ain't got no woman to raise hell with me fur takin' in a pore li'l filly what's been ruint ag'inst her will. 'Cause effen you knows anything about wimmen, you gotta allow that ruint is ruint to them 'n whose fault it wuz don't matter a good goddamn. C'mon, le's mosey over to my place so's I kin throw my plunder into my possibles bag 'n cart it over to th Weary Cowboy's Bunkhouse and Chuck Wagon, across th street. Tha's a hotel 'n restaurant, y'know . . ."

"Yes, I do know. I tried there, too. They would only take me *without* Nora. And, Marshal, aside from my heartfelt thanks, I'd like to say I'd consider it a favor if you'll allow me to pay for your lodgings and your meals while I'm—we're—occupying your place . . ."

"No need for that. Bill Farrell won't charge me a thin dime. And I always eats where I'm nearest to, come mealtimes. For free. Being marshal carries some privileges with it, y'know. You kin pay my cleanin' woman, though. She's a 'breed. Half Cherokee, so yore li'l friend won't upset her none a-tall. I'll have the Chuck Wagon send you over yore meals 'n yore li'l lady's. Reckon hern has got to be special, ain't they?"

"Soups, broths, nothing solid. I'll pay 'em for the extra trouble, of course . . ."

"Ain't none. They'll be glad to do it, I ax 'em to. Naw, don't thank me. After th hard time this here bone-mean town done give you, I'm only tryin' to make it up to you a little. 'N I'm gonna try to do you th only *real* favor I kin: set folks straight as to what really happened when they ax me. 'N they're gonna ax me, sure as shootin', they find out I'm loanin' you 'n her my place . . ."

"Marshal, you're one of nature's noblemen. And a prince," Ethan Lovejoy said.

Before carting poor Nora's inert, unconscious form in a horse-drawn ambulance to the marshal's apartment over his office, Ethan wired Ruth Quindaro to put everything in Cindy Otis's hands and come to Wichita at once. He knew damned well he was taking an awful risk by doing that. There were times when the mere sight of Cindy's Black face could throw Anne into one of her maniacal rages. But he had no choice in the matter. Though still occupying it physically, Anne, the wry, fey, interesting, and even exciting woman he had loved, had departed to all useful—even to herself!—intents and purposes from this life. He could never reach her again. She had flown—or had been driven—much too far down an oblique tangent out of time and mind. And Nora—his Nora!—had to be saved. Those were the hard facts. He simply had to accept them. He had no other choice.

But prior to Ruth's arrival that next afternoon, Ethan caught hell. Aided by Marshal Wilkes and surrounded by a crowd of tobacco-chewing, evil-smelling cowboys and barflies of other trades or none at all—said crowd including even two or three members of the Broomstick Wranglers

Association, driven by an all-devouring curiosity to enter a part of town they ordinarily wouldn't have been found dead in and to rub shoulders, and even bustles, so tight-packed was the mob, with men they usually wouldn't have touched, 'Even with the butt ends of their favorite means of transportation,' Ethan thought sardonically—he tenderly carried poor Nora upstairs and put her to bed. But that much accomplished, he found his troubles had just begun.

For one thing, although the flexible rubber urethric catheter for permanent use by bedridden female patients had been invented a full decade before, no frontier doctor, and probably very few anywhere in the medically backward and primitive country that the United States was at that time, had ever heard of it. Ethan solved—somewhat—the problem of the bedwetting that the unconscious girl simply had to do by sending the cleaning woman out to buy a cowboy's oilskin at the dry goods store, and several changes of bedclothes at the General Merchandise Emporium. Fortunately for him, the even more serious problem of defecation didn't even arise, since not one mouthful of solid food had passed that outraged and abused young woman's lips in more than a week. But keeping poor Nora dry and warm proved a monumental task, and feeding her an impossibility.

Dr. Halston, who had been told by Marshal Wilkes Ethan's side of the story, looked in on Nora several times during that first day, obviously moved by shame at his earlier uncharitable behavior. He warned Ethan not to try to feed her until she was fully awake, because in the state of almost total insensibility that she lingered, the clearest broth would be sure to choke her.

Due to the fact that the blood had flowed, not pumped or spurted from her wounds, the doctor was sure she had had the almost miraculous good fortune not to have cut into an artery, though the veins she had severed had been of considerable size. A human being could die of cut veins, of course, he explained to Ethan, but it took considerably longer. A major artery slashed through would have emptied Nora's slight body of blood in one and a half minutes. That piece of luck—or that stroke of ribald Fate, considering all the devastating consequences that were sure to result from Nora's survival—had given him time to save her.

Only she seemed to Ethan to be growing steadily weaker. What she desperately needed, a transfusion to replace the appalling amount of blood she had lost, Dr. Halston quite correctly refused to perform. In 1877 any good surgeon knew *how* to do a transfusion; what no medical man on the face of the earth then knew was a method of selecting the donor and thus preventing the inevitable death of the patient if "the other party's blood don't agree with 'em," as Dr. Halston put it.

Which, of course, didn't help matters a good goddamn.

By midnight, out of pure desperation, Ethan was bending over her still form calling softly, endlessly: "Nora! Nora! Wake up! Oh, dear God, let her wake up! Nora, please!"

But she didn't move. Her breath was slowing, her pulse rate so low that he groped long minutes along her inner arms above her thickly bandaged wrists before he could find a place where the beat of it was perceptible. Her lips were paling out of life.

Seeing that, Ethan Lovejoy, frontiersman, farmer, combat veteran, decorated hero in his country's service, wept. And not with quiet, manly dignity. He opened his mouth and cried aloud like a whipped child, harshly, hoarsely, angrily, terribly. His tears dripped down into her face. They were scalding.

And God—some god—Aphrodite, Pan the satyr, Eros—who knows? Maybe even tender Baby Jesus. Mary, his mother. Isis, Mater Dolorosa of the Resurrected Horus—Ra, the Sundisk, Apollo, Lord of Healing— does it matter?—granted him a miracle.

Her eyes fluttered open—unfocused, mindless, blank. Then they cleared. Sculptured his face upon the dark with chisel strokes of purest light. Saw, perceived, his tears.

"No—" she murmured, making with awful effort an almost silent sound he had to bend so close to her to capture that her lips fluttered like pale moths' wings against his ear; "Not—worth—one tear—of yours. Not fit—not fit—"

That was as far as she got. His mouth against her whispering mouth poured—by sheer osmosis!—anguished joy, wild hope, all the frustrated tenderness he had been forced to deny her for ten long, bleak, hopeless years into her three-quarters-dead body through those lips of hers that were parchment-dry, blood encrusted in their corners, salt to his taste, ice cold, but warming now, going moist, moving under his, opening, parting, receiving, accepting, welcoming—life.

A transfusion of sorts? Psychosomatic medicine? Faith healing? Love's idiotic magic? Witch doctoring?

Words. The scrawls, scribbles, sounds standing forever between us and meaning. Words.

By that next morning, she was gazing at him with adoring eyes and struggling to sit up in bed.

20

"They sent me on this here errand, Eth," Phil Harris said sadly; " 'Cause they knows what good friends you 'n me is . . .''

Ethan looked at his oldest friend in Kansas. Phil quailed a little at that look. For, by then, Ethan's eyes had taken on the aspect they were to keep for the rest of his life: a steady, unblinking glare characteristic of the great birds of prey, who, far more than any earthbound species, are immune to any consideration of fear.

'Jesus!' Phil thought; 'Looks like he's done gone 'n worked hisself up into hating th whole damn world . . ."

But Phil was wrong. Ethan didn't grant his fellow citizens and former friends the grudging esteem or the soured respect, sometimes even admiration, that are core components of hate. To hate a man, you had to admit he was a man; and, to Ethan, the behavior of the people of the county and the town was that of lice. Or of something even less, if there were anything less. What Phil saw in those steady cold blue eyes was something far worse than hate: it was contempt, pure and unalloyed.

"All right, Phil," he said quietly; "You have my resignation, effective as of now, as master of the local grange. And as a member of it, too. D'you want that in writing?"

"Reckon that would be better, Eth," Phil said uneasily.

Ethan turned to his desk, drew out paper, a bottle of ink, a steel-tipped pen. From another drawer in the rolltop desk he took the heavy spectacles most people had never seen him wear, not because of vanity, but because he only needed them for reading or writing and therefore usually forgot to even take them with him when he left the house. He wrote swiftly, signed and dated the note, passed it over to Phil.

"Will that do?" he said.

Phil read the note.

"Yep," he sighed. "Eth, do I hafta tell you that I voted ag'inst axing you for yor resignation?"

"No. I know that. You, Matt Hendricks, and Rad Stevens. You, out of friendship, loyalty, I suspect. Matt and Rad, too; but not unmixed with self-interest on Matt's part. Or at least he's got sense enough not to let moral indignation play tricks with his memory. Anyhow, whatever your motives—and theirs—were, they've kept you off this list I'm sending to Ned, as president of the bank, and by you, Phil. I think maybe you'd better read it, too . . ."

Phil read the list. And the note accompanying it. He looked up at Ethan with badly troubled eyes.

"Jesus!" he whispered; "You're calling every note you've got outstanding—'n every damn one of 'em long overdue, I grant you that—ag'in all th folks who owe you money. 'N since you've always been mighty white, 'n generous to a fault, that means practically everybody in th grange who axed you to—"

"Resign. Yes. They've had themselves more fun than a band of monkeys let loose in a warehouse full of peanuts. They've allowed that flock of hen buzzards they're married to to say that maybe Nora went looking for those construction crew Micks the night you and Ned had to use your six-shooters to get her away from them—too late. Nobody's raised a dissenting voice to the widespread opinion that she walked into Gashouse Gertie's place in Wichita on her own two feet and offered her services in the bustle hustling trade. And they've elected me Head Sultan of the whole damned state of Kansas for keeping a harem consisting of one poor, totally deranged wife I never touch because to get a woman in her state with child would be an offense in the nostrils of God, and one poor physical wreck of a girl—no, Nora's every inch a woman now—who the ardent attentions of the rampaging old billy goat I'm supposed to be —any time in the past few weeks, anyhow—would have killed outright. So all I'm saying, Phil, my friend, is that in this world of sin, fun seldom comes free of charge. They've had theirs; now let 'em pay for it."

"Eth—" Phil said; "You realize—that havin' these here notes called is a-gonna ruin outright th majority of th folks you hold 'em on. That they're gonna lose their spreads 'n have to leave here? People with scads o' kids? Lord, Ol' Hoss, you gonna be th cause of a bigger exodus than the grasshoppers was!"

"I'm not going to be the cause of anything," Ethan said drily; "their own filthy minds, loose tongues, and mighty short memories are. But between you, me, and the gatepost, Phil, I don't mean to put one single family off the land. Mind you, I damned well am going to foreclose; but I'll let 'em stay on—as tenants, or hired managers, whichever suits the individual cases best. Then, every Saturday night, when they draw their pay, they can get drunk and cuss the boss. Behind his back—and quietly. But at least they'll know who the boss is . . ."

"Lord, God, Eth; I didn't know you had that much pizen meanness in you!"

"I didn't. The Abilene Association of Hen Buzzards and Broomstick Wranglers lent me my fair share. Assisted by their henpecked husbands, of course. Now come on . . ."

"Come on where?" Phil said.

"To see Nora, of course. I want you to give Martha, and, if she'll listen, Nellie Tyler, a detailed report as to what shape I've left her in, pounding her to pieces every night. You heard me, Phil; come on!"

As they got to the top of the stairs, they could hear Anne's voice. The odd part of it was that, considering what she was saying, it wasn't loud, and didn't even sound particularly angry. She was chanting in a monotone as though she didn't know or understand the meaning of the words she was pronouncing so slowly and carefully:

"Bitch. Slut. Whore. Husband stealer. Adulteress. You are, y'know. That's why—I'm going to kill you, Nora. I've got to. You understand that, don't you, dear?"

Nora's voice came through the door, flat, calm, utterly toneless, dead:

"Yes, Anne. You're—perfectly—right. So what are you waiting for? Go—ahead. But—come—closer. You might—miss me—from—way over —there . . ."

"Jeee-sus!" Phil gasped.

Ethan's big hand clamped down on Phil's arm, halted his rush toward that door. Phil turned and looked at him wonderingly. Ethan bent close to his friend's ear. His breath poured a harsh, grating whisper into it, growling:

"She won't. She can't. She hasn't got it in her. Nor anything to do it with, anyhow . . ."

He hooked his long fingers around the doorknob, turned it slowly, quietly, pushed the door open. Not even the hinges squeaked.

"Lord God!" Phil Harris murmured.

"Is that all you've got to say for yourself, Nora?" Anne said in an odd, bright, birdlike voice; "Can't you think of—any excuse—for your behavior? I really don't want to shoot you, y'know . . ."

Phil was staring at Nora. What he saw was a living skeleton: white flesh stretched tight over all too visible bones that were threatening to burst through it at every place that could be seen above her nightgown.

Dr. Baines had long since taken the bandages off, so the long, diagonal, downward-slanting scar showed livid, bluish-red against the corpselike pallor of her throat. The only words that Phil could think of that fitted it were: 'Plumb horrible!'

"Look at her wrists, Phil," Ethan murmured. He was paying, Phil saw, not the slightest attention to Anne, nor to the little double-barreled derringer in her hand. 'Likely he's got th damned thing spiked, or th trigger jammed,' Phil thought. He glanced at Nora's wrists. They were scarred, too. The scars were—ugly.

'Plumb horrible!' Phil thought again; 'Th pore li'l thing shore Lord wuzn't playin' games!'

He looked at Anne now. He hadn't seen her in several years. Since her madness was serene most of the time, allowing her to live in bemused acceptance of everything that was done to, for, and around her, she had put on flesh, gained weight. Not too much, but enough to make her pleasingly plump. In fact, in comparison to poor Nora, she was a ravishing beauty until you looked into the utter vacancy of her eyes.

"All right," she sighed; "Say your prayers, little Miss Nora Curtiss, 'cause now you're going to die . . ."

"That's enough bad melodrama for today, Anne," Ethan said wearily from the doorway. "Give me that pistol, will you? And go to your room. Don't worry about it, Nora; it isn't loaded . . ."

"That's what you think, Mister Vile Lecher Ethan Lovejoy!" Anne said in the stilted, artificial declamatory tone of voice so beloved of second-rate actors and actresses in the third-rate melodramas of the time, sounding as though she were on some tent show's or cheap theater's stage; "See for yourself!"

And in one half heartbeat, almost converted melodrama into tragedy. The derringer bucked and thundered in her hand, spat flame, smoke. Splinters flew up from the headboard of the bed, scant inches to the right of Nora's pale, drawn, curiously impassive face. Ethan lurched forward like a clumsy, half-starved bear, caught Anne's wrist, twisted it cruelly, powerfully. But the second shot in the until that moment unfired lower barrel of the derringer ploughed into the ceiling before he got that little pocket pistol away from Anne.

Madness flared in his own eyes then. He dropped the derringer into the side pocket of his jacket, drew back his hand, and slapped his poor, deranged wife so hard that her head turned sidewise under the impact of his big, bony hand. The blow exploded against her face with a sound much louder than the derringer's quite respectable .41-caliber cartridge had been able to manage. Anne crumpled to the floor, lay there, whimpering.

"Ethan!" Nora said reproachfully; "She—she's not responsible, poor thing. Besides, she's—right. I'd be—better off—dead. I'm only sorry—that she missed . . ."

"Shut up, Nora!" Ethan snarled. "Anne, where the devil did you get those bullets from?"

Anne stopped whimpering and grinned at him. Her small, square face took on the expression of a naughty child's. "Out of your desk," she said triumphantly, pleased as punch with herself and showing it; "I picked the lock with my little letter opener. Wasn't hard to do at all. Then I stole two bullets for my lady's pistol out of the box you'd so thoughtfully written forty-one caliber on, and put the box right back in the pigeonhole you had it in. I knew you'd never think of looking in the box to see if the bullets were all there, because, to tell the truth, you're not very clever, husband mine!"

"She's right, Ol' Hoss," Phil said; "You should've messed up that derringer so it wouldn't shoot no more. Or throwed it 'n the bullets clean away. Howdy, Nora—there, there sweet baby, don't you go 'n cry thataway! Lord, sugar—you'll have me bustin' out 'n bawlin' myownself in a minute!"

"Welcome to my happy home, Phil," Ethan said drily; "Or rather to my den of iniquity. And while you're here, you might take a good look at these two mighty fine odalisques I've got. One of 'em half dead, and the other mad as a hatter. Some sultan, aren't I? Hell, I probably couldn't even get a job as Second Assistant Eunuch, guarding the seraglio's back door . . ."

By then, Phil was sitting on the side of the bed, cradling Nora's bright golden head on his shoulder, patting it clumsily, letting her cry.

"Ol' Hoss," he groaned; "I begs yore pardon, mighty humble-like. 'Cause I gotta admit I did think there was a little somethin' to them stories. Not much, but a wee bit, anyhow, seein' as how this pore abused baby always has been long gone over you . . ."

"I *still* am, Phil," Nora whispered. "It took being married to—an utter swine—to teach me—just what Ethan is. The finest man alive, as far as I'm concerned. The noblest—and the best. A giant in the earth—morally, anyhow—who stands so tall above other men, he makes 'em look like pygmies. Gulliver among the Lilliputians! Who's all I've ever wanted —all I'll ever want. And I—can never have him. There *she* is, ruining his life, just like she's always ruined it. And if she weren't there, didn't even exist, he'd still have a right to—a decent woman. Not a—a *thing*—like me. A broken, used, dirtied thing. Goods on sale. Dirt cheap. For me, dear Phil, Gert charged ten whole dollars! Not—even—human anymore. A— dog. A *she*-dog. A mongrel—a bitch—crawling toward him—on her belly —so she can lick his boots. And hoping he won't kick her. That maybe he'll fondle her ears, pat her head. And living only for that. One careless touch—of his. One word of—kindness . . ."

"Oh, Jesus!" Phil all but wept.

"Amen," Ethan whispered; "You see what I'm up against, my friend?"

Two months from that day, Ethan took Nora into Abilene in his surrey, with the intention of traveling with her by train to Topeka, the capital of the state, where he meant to either rent, lease, or buy her a house to serve as her permanent residence and set her up in a business that would enable her to be not only self-supporting, but independent—financially, anyhow—of the whole greedy, conniving, and, above all, horny male sex. But once they'd got into town and were driving toward the railroad station, he found himself confronted with a problem: should he leave Nora in the waiting room with their baggage, while he drove the surrey over to Luke Prevost's livery stable, where, for a daily fee, of course, both horse and vehicle would be cared for until his return; or should he leave only the bags and drive, accompanied by Nora, over to the Hotel D'Horse, accomplish that necessary business, and then walk back with her to the station?

Since Nora was now fully recovered from the effects of her suicide attempt, there was no physical impediment to his doing either; while as far as time was concerned, they had a full hour before the train would pull out for Topeka. The real question was simpler and uglier: Which of the two procedures involved the lesser risk of having Nora insulted by the self-appointed guardians of public morals, and to her very face?

In the end he decided to drive over to Luke's first, then stroll back to the station with Nora on his arm. His reasoning was impeccable, though put a trifle metaphorically: "To craven dogs, never show your back!"

As they passed through the streets, all conversation died. Women came out of their houses and stood on the dusty sidewalks to openly stare. A chorus of "Wal, didya ever!" and "No, honey, not never!" with the "See a thing like this!" unstated but understood, floated behind them on the summer air.

"Thet thar Eth Lovejoy's got more nerve than a brass monkey! Jes' 'cause he's done got to be filthy rich 'n has bought up th whole goldurned county, he's sartin shore he kin git away wit eny damn thing!" the good burghers growled sotto voce. " 'N her, th barefaced li'l hussy!" their wives edged, and shrilled, and screeched even their whispers; "She jes' plain ain't got no shame!"

Still, they were spared a direct confrontation—though poor Nora was ghost white and trembling, visibly fighting back her tears by then—until they had almost reached the station. Then Molly Burns—the one woman in town openly given to drink instead of following the discreet example of her more respectable sisters of taking multiple daily doses of patent medicines whose heavy alcoholic content had reduced a surprisingly large minority of North American housewives to secret dipsomania by then, when, as was even more frequently the case, the amount of laudanum mixed into the often deadly quack nostrums of that day hadn't made hopeless opium addicts of them—took it upon herself to personally express the whole town's outrage at this visible, public, and defiant flouting of its moral code. She reeled out of an alley and stood before them, hands on hips, glaring.

"Nora," she said; "I swear t' Gawd effen you ain't the brazenest li'l hussy enybody iver did see!"

Nora quailed before that massive, Junoesque figure, almost overcome by the reek of snuff, raw onions, and cheap whiskey on Molly's breath, not to mention the other deadly vapors emanating from the outsize body of a woman on permanent vacation from soap and water. But Ethan's voice, raised just enough to carry with maximum effect to the ears of all the quickly—and thickly!—gathering curious, cut through that warm noonday air like a blade of ice:

"Molly," he drawled; "I gave your husband a breather before foreclosing on that miserable place the two of you have let go to rack and ruin. Well, I've just changed my mind; or rather you've just changed it for me by not knowing how, when, or where to keep your filthy trap shut. You tell Tim I want you, and all your possessions—if you haven't pawned the lot of 'em for drink by now—off the place by nightfall. I hope you won't make me send the county sheriff to dispossess you, for, as unpleasant as that procedure is, I will. Come along, Nora, dear . . ."

"Oh, Lawd!" Molly moaned; "Eth—Mistuh Lovejoy, you—you *wouldn't!*"

"You should wash your ears once in a while, Molly," Ethan said dourly. "That way you'd hear what's said to you. To repeat, I'm foreclosing. I want you off the place by tonight. *This* night to make myself entirely clear."

Nora whirled to face him, caught him by both his arms, peered up into his face with tear-blazed eyes.

"Ethan, please!" she said.

"Please *what*, my dear?" Ethan said; "I'm afraid I don't understand—"

"Don't put them off the place. Not—poor people like them," Nora begged. "People—with children, surely—" She turned to Molly, said breathlessly: "You do have children, don't you, Mistress Burns?"

"Five pore wee'uns," Molly said lugubriously; "Nora—Miz Andrews, I begs yore pardon real humble-like! Ax him not to! Tell him—"

"Hell and Death!" Ethan growled; "People who can't feed their brats shouldn't get them. And a debt's a debt. Especially one so long overdue. Don't intercede for her, Nora. She's got to learn, and spread the news, that discourtesy to *you*, my dear, can get to be pretty costly. Come on now, or we'll miss our train . . ."

"Ethan, please!" Nora said tearfully; "Not for *my* sake. I don't care what she says about me. You and I know the truth, so what does it matter? To—to punish a whole family like this just because she—insulted me, or tried to—your doing that hurts *me*, my darling! Makes me ashamed. So don't. I ask you, I beg you, please!"

"She's lucky I haven't taken my cane to her," Ethan said drily; "but since you wish it, very well. . . . All right, Molly, you've got a reprieve. But the next time you forget the respect due your betters, I'll not only put you off the place, I'll run you out of the county. Now, for heaven's sake, Nora, come on!"

Half an hour later the two of them were on an eastbound train.

"But the main reason I chose Topeka," Ethan told her as the train bore them away from Abilene, "is that nobody knows you in the capital, my dear. There you'll be able to easily remake your life. The kind of establishment I mean to find for you, in the sort of location I'm going to insist upon, will insure your clients' being distinguished people—with at least a few fine, upright young unmarried men among them. I only hope you'll make a wiser choice this time. . . ."

Hot rebellion flamed in Nora's heart.

"Are you—trying to—give me away, Ethan?" she said in the husky contralto whisper that was all that blade of broken glass had left her of her formerly almost silvery, lyric soprano; "Are you, Ethan?"

"God no! But—"

"But nothing," she husked; "I made my choice—my lifelong choice! —when I was a schoolgirl of sixteen. Only I didn't have sense enough to stick by it. But now I do. I've been taught the hard way. I'm yours, Ethan. 'Til death us do part. I can't be—your wife, so I'm going to be your mistress. Wait! Don't say anything. I've suffered enough. And so have you —married to a madwoman. Oh, I don't blame poor Anne! Losing a son of *yours* would drive me insane, too. And that's another thing: How many times have I heard you say that the Lovejoy family is going to die out with you? Say it with a sadness it almost broke my heart to listen to! Well, it won't. I won't let it. I'm going to give you the son you're longing for, and three or four more to make the matter certain!"

"Nora! Oh, Nora!" he murmured prayerfully.

"So tonight, when we get to Topeka, you're *not* going to take a separate room for me, or register me as your niece. You're going to sign us in as man and wife—and once we're alone, and naked, and in bed—I'm going to teach you every filthy whorish trick I learned at Gashouse Gertie's!"

She was crying by then, and smiling at him at the same time, so that her face was like an April sky filled up with sun and clouds and rainbows, and he loved her so much he hurt. But, being the rock-ribbed puritan he was, he had to protest, to say:

"Nora—I can't. We can't. To wreck your life like that—*again* is— would be—unpardonable. Who's going to believe that a man who lives somewhere else, and who comes to visit you once in a while is really your husband? Absolutely nobody. And—"

"Who gives a tinker's damn what anybody believes!" she raged. "Ethan, you gave me back my life, so don't take it away from me all over again. I've very simply got to the place where I can't possibly live without you, and I don't propose to even try. So hear this, you dear, sweet, impossibly noble fool: either you make me yours, now, henceforth, and forever more, or I will not stay alive one hour after you've left Topeka. I swear that by God, and by my love for you. And on the honor I haven't even got!"

"Nora, you wouldn't!" he croaked.

"I would and I will, and you know all too well I'm capable of it. Only I'll make sure this time. With a gun. No. First I'll commit hara-kiri like a lovelorn Japanese maiden. Then, after that, I'll drink a *pint* of vitriol.

Then I'll soak my bed in kerosene, lie down on it, and set it afire. And, last of all, I'll shoot myself. You've already discovered it takes an awful lot to kill me, haven't you? Little Nora, the Iron Maiden—maiden—ha! The bulletproof, armor-plated—hussy!"

"Nora—Oh, Lord! I just don't know what to say—"

"Then don't say anything. Shut up and kiss me," Nora said. And that was—almost—that.

First in the morning, the sunlight came through the window of that hotel room, and washed Nora's sleeping form in a soft pale radiance. The covers had fallen to the floor so she made a Botticelli Venus on the half shell, as close as that to sheer perfection. He lay there propped up on one elbow looking at her, enjoying the sight. She was still much too thin, but apart from that, her body was just about as beautiful as the female human form ever gets to be. The only thing that marred it was that hideous scar, which was going to force her to wear high-necked clothes and even bathing dresses that buttoned up to her chin for the rest of her life.

Then it came to him that, ugly as it was, it was also a badge of honor, and the highest tribute anyone had ever paid him in all his life. So high, in fact, that he found it both crippling and humbling; for it was totally indisputable that she had preferred death itself to being shamed before his eyes. Thinking that, those eyes blurred, misted, stung. He bent over her and kissed her throat, letting his lips slide with anguished tenderness slowly down that scar.

She came awake and almost strangled him, sobbing aloud, kissing him every place she could reach. . . .

"Nora!" he got out worriedly; "What's wrong?"

"Nothing!" she wept; "Nothing at all! Life is so beautiful that I can't stand it and if you don't make love to me right now this minute I'm going to die!"

"If that's what it takes to keep you alive, you're going to see ninety sure as hell," Ethan said solemnly.

Thereafter, of course, he obliged.

Living in sin—especially when one of the two remarkably happy and entirely unrepentant sinners dwells, or resides (for, of course, they *lived* only when they were together), in a certain town and the other in another, said towns being one hundred seventeen miles, or five hours by train, apart —has much to recommend it. In the first place, their prolonged separations transformed their brief days, or sometimes, rarely, weeks together into renewed honeymoons. In the second, their "arrangement," as they called it, was quiet, discreet, and almost completely decent, far more so than many legal marriages are. They were absolutely faithful to each other and hurt no one at all except poor Anne, and her only occasionally in those rare intervals when she was lucid enough to be aware of Ethan's absences and to guess, with that sure and destructive female instinct that has no need for reason, having evolved—in the distaff half of humanity, anyhow! —long before cerebration finally did, where he'd gone. In the third, the very intermittency of their tender, and largely involuntary, violation of the laws of Church and State, gave it all the advantages of matrimony and none of wedlock's drawbacks.

"Ethan—" Nora whispered once, "are—you—cheating? Even—with —Anne? That's your right, of course; but if you are—"

"If I am, or rather, if I were—what?" Ethan drawled, down-curving his lips beneath his heavy mustache to keep the smile he was fighting against from overcoming him and tugging their corners upward.

"I'd die!" Nora wailed; and there were the tears, hot and bright and sudden in her lovely eyes.

He drew her to him, kissed the top of her head.

"No, I'm not," he said with the almost funeral solemnity of tone he employed when he was teasing her; "Are you?"

"Why, Ethan Lovejoy!" Nora flared; "Just *what* d'you think I am? Oh. Ohhhh, Jesus! You don't have to think, d'you? You *know*. A—whore. A creature you found in a whorehouse and—"

"Who carved the price she set—upon—her honor—into her own sweet, tender flesh," Ethan said in the same tone of amused, tender, and wildly exaggerated gravity; "Who was dragged through the mire and emerged—spotless. Who was thrown into hell and came out of it with her white wings and her halo firmly attached. In just the right places, at that. In short, an angel. *My* angel, whom I'm going to worship on my knees and thank God for the privilege of being able to until the very day I die . . ."

"Ohhhh, Ethan!" she sobbed, and she threw her arms around his neck and started kissing him from his Adam's apple to his chin, which, due to the great disparity in their respective statures, was as high as she could reach until he bent a little and made matters easier for her. Which, of course, ended all conversation.

For the rest of *that* night, anyhow.

*　　*　　*

But when he awoke with the eastern sun's rays in his eyes, and stretched out his long limbs blissfully, lost in that peace beyond understanding that pervades a man's very soul the morning after a sublimely busy night, he found her propped up on one elbow, staring at him, and the tears were rolling down her cheeks, in an unending, linked crystal chain.

"Now, what the hell?" he groaned.

"Nnnnnothing . . ." she sniffed, trying to hold back, or dam up, those tears.

"Come on, Nora! Out with it," he said.

"Oh—all right! You—you're going to get mad at me; but I—I've got to say it! You—you're going home today. And the way I feel about *that* is getting worse. I could always wait until you were safely out of the door and even sometimes wave to you as you drove away in a hack toward the station, before falling back into bed and crying 'til my eyes have swollen so shut I can't even get them open and have to stumble around three-quarters blind for half the morning—"

"Nora!" he said.

"But this morning I couldn't even wait. I have to cry—right now. I can't help it. I—I—thought I'd get used to it—to your leaving me, I mean. But I—haven't. And I won't. It's like being condemned to death every time you go. Even the—resurrections—the hearing the horse's hooves dancing to a stop, the harness jangle, the cabby's 'Whoaaa!' and then your footsteps—they don't sound like *anyone* else's, y'know—coming up the stairs . . . and standing there going so weak from sheer joy that I have to catch hold of something or lean against the wall to keep from falling down —aren't enough anymore, Ethan. I want you here with me *all* the time. Every second of the day and night. I'm too lonesome without you. I *hurt* from lonesomeness. I ache with it. At night, the silence—crushes me. The —emptiness. Your pillow—undented. Your long, ugly scarecrow of a body—"

"Lord!" he said.

"That's so beautiful—to me—not here in this bed beside me—"

"Not exactly beside you most of the time," he teased her solemnly.

"Yes," she whispered; "that, too—maybe especially that. Or rather, too *little* of that, which is one of the things that's driving me crazy . . ."

"Why, Nora, sugar," he groaned in mock despair; "I'm a mighty old party, and I do the best I can!"

"Oh, Lord! That's not what I meant, and you know it! Ethan—I don't act like—like a lascivious female, do I? Because I don't think I am. It's —just that—I—I love you. You—the *way* you are. The way you think, react, talk laugh, smile. *You.* Your—kindness. Your—everlasting patience with me. Even the fact that you think I'm a funny little thing and are secretly laughing at me most of the time—"

"And am wholly, blessedly in love with you *all* the time," he said quietly.

"Ohhhh, Ethan!" she wailed; and kissed him.

"Stop that!" he quipped; "It's morning, and I'm tired, and we were having a conversation. Let's talk for a change, shall we?"

"All right. But—don't tempt me. Saying sweet things like that to me does that, you know. I suppose what I was trying to say is that because I love you—it makes—the other—all right—"

"Just all right?" he sighed lugubriously; "Then I'm a failure!"

"No! Ethan—you know how hard it is for me to talk about *that.* I —I haven't the words to say it with. And all the ones I do know—taught me by my darling husband, Price—"

"He's not, you know," Ethan said; "he never was. So if he ever traces you, and shows up here when I'm not around, call a policeman. He has absolutely no legal hold on you, Nora . . ."

"I know he hasn't. That I was his kept woman, not his wife. Though it was the other way around: I kept him. He never hit a lick at a snake, y'know. He told me the truth about our—so-called—marriage, when I asked him—at—at Gert's place—how a man could do to his *wife,* what he'd done to me—"

"Nora, stop it. Get off that subject. It makes both of us unhappy, so forget, will you?"

"All right. I only brought him up to explain to you that *his* vocabulary isn't the one that any self-respecting woman—or man either, for that matter!—could use to talk about—love. And it's the only one I know— all those horrible, dirty words! Oh, all right! That subject's closed. Ethan —along with the hurtfulness of being without you, I'll admit I *am* worried about *that.* What we do together—making love—"

"Good Lord, Nora! I thought you—kind of enjoyed it—"

"I *do.* So much. So very much! With you—it's lovely, perfect, wonderful—"

"Then?" he said.

"Then why doesn't it *work?* That's why I said 'too little.' Not because we don't make love enough while you're here. I—I wear you out, you poor old darling! I'm—*always* after you—as slyly as I can, because I don't want you to think I'm a—a brazen hussy—"

"Braze away, hussy!" he chuckled.

"You're going to be sorry you said *that,*" she giggled. "But Ethan— it's been more than a year now, and—*nothing* has happened. Every month, right on schedule, like clockwork, I start feeling sad or *mean* or both—and sure as shooting—there it is—my menses. Ugh! Why do we women have to function in such—a messy way?"

"I suspect the Almighty has His failings after all. When it comes to female interior plumbing, He's a Lordawful sanitary engineer, isn't He?"

"Oh, stop *joking,* will you? This is—serious, love. Ethan—suppose I —I *can't?* Suppose my poor insides are—ruined? They could be, that's for sure! Those—Irishmen—those railroad construction workers Phil and Ned had to *shoot*—one of them, anyhow—to get me out of their clutches. They were—awfully—brutal, y'know. And then—Price. God knows what he—or some of his friends—might have given me. Ohhh, Ethan!"

Ethan lay there. He was remembering with dismal exactitude the conversation he'd had with her now dead father on this same subject. On that occasion, Cy had told him that it was the opinion of the doctors who had treated her in St. Louis that the damages she had already suff-ered—'A child of sixteen violated by apes!' he thought bitterly—were very probably so great as to preclude any possibility of her ever having a baby. But he couldn't tell her that, not like she was now, sitting there misty-eyed, lost in her dream of sweet maternity. It would very surely break her heart.

"Nora," he said gravely; "You're under absolutely no obligation to present me with a son and heir. In the first place, under our present circumstances, he'd be illegitimate. A bastard, to say it straight out and ugly . . ."

"Whereupon," she said stubbornly; "you'd adopt him. Go to the courts and make him yours legally, which sounds downright silly, seeing as how he'd already be. And who's talking about obligations? I *want* to have your son, Ethan Lovejoy! I want to feel him growing inside me, swelling me up as big as a house. . . . I want you to have the joy—the privilege—of pressing your ear against the great tun of my belly listening for his heartbeat, feeling him kick! Oh, Ethan—don't you know, can't you realize, how *happy* we'd be then?"

"Yes," he murmured, and half turned away from her so she wouldn't see the tears that were blindscalding his eyes.

"Then—after he's born—holding him, singing to him, feeding him—with the milk from my own breasts—Oh, Lord, Ethan—give me a son! I want him so bad! I *need* him so!"

"So do I—" Ethan whispered brokenly.

"You—all over again. A little you—to have, to hold, to keep. Watching him grow more like you with every passing day. Oh, my darling, there's nothing that equals *that.* And without it, there's nothing that really matters . . ."

"I agree," he sighed; "but don't you see, Nora, dearest, that it isn't in our hands, but in those of the Lord? Many couples never have children, no matter how they try, and—"

"But most couples do. Especially those who are together all the time! Ethan, don't go back there. Please don't. Stay here with me. Always. I'm —begging you not to go. You want me to get down on my knees? All right, I will. See?"

"Nora, for God's love!" he howled; "You want to drive me out of my mind? I've got it rough enough as it is, and—"

"There's Anne. That crazy fool. That—murderous lunatic. Who'll—kill *you* one night while you're asleep. Or—your little Martha. . ."

He noticed again that she didn't say Martha *Anne.* That she was refusing to.

"Nora," he said quietly; "You're making me dislike *you* a little now. A thing I thought could never happen. But you're getting there. Look, whatever Anne might do is a risk I have to take. She's my responsibility, by my most solemn oath, sworn before Almighty God. Haven't you had enough of men who behave like swine? That's precisely what you're asking me to do now. Anne is—helpless. No, worse, she's a danger to herself—"

"And *I'll* be a danger to *myself* if you go back to her!" Nora stormed.

He stared at her and his eyes were very bleak.

"That choice is yours—and up to you," he said quietly. "For I haven't any choice, my dear, none at all. I can't permit myself even the luxury of ending a pretty close to intolerable life. There's Martha Anne, eight years old, who needs her father. Who in another eight will need him even more—perhaps as badly as you needed yours at sixteen. I have—a wife who's mad. In you I had—or thought I did—the only real joy in my whole dismal existence. You'd—take even that from me? So be it. It would break my heart. But then you're already breaking it right now . . ."

She came up from her knees in one wild rush, hurled herself into his arms, kissing his eyes, his face, his throat, his mouth, sobbing, babbling, crying: "I'm sorry! Oh, I'm so sorry! I—I didn't mean it! Oh, yes, I did! Every mean, wicked, selfish word of it. I won't lie to you. Not to *you,* Ethan. I—I'm awful. Only you're stuck with me, awful as I am. You—should have let me bleed to death that night! You should never have saved me! You should have let me die!"

"Couldn't," he said gravely; "Too many people depend upon my staying alive—and clothed and framed in my right mind. To a reasonable degree, anyhow. And that would have been the price of letting you get away with that piece of madness, Nora. Scrambled brains or a heart attack. Maybe both . . ."

"Ethan—" she whispered, draping herself around him bonelessly, fitting her slim, incredibly supple form into all his hollows; "make—love to me—now. Please?"

"No," he said. Like that. Flatly.

"Ohhh, Ethan!" she wailed.

"Nora, I don't feel like it. I'm tired. In a bad mood. And that has to be mutual—or it's no good. Besides, I want you to think about a couple of things. Really think. You're no longer a schoolgirl. You're soon going to be all of twenty-eight years old—"

"An old hag!" she moaned.

"A woman, I hope," he said; "You blithely propose I come here to live with you permanently. All right: what becomes of my farm?"

"Sell it!" she said triumphantly; "Invest the money in a chain of restaurants! We'd make a fortune, love! You've seen how I run mine. It's a great success, Ethan! Friday nights and Saturdays I have to turn people away. Even so, some of my regular customers wait two hours—and gladly —for a table. And when I apologize for having had to make them wait, they swear they don't mind, because my food's so good and the atmosphere in my place is so homelike—so cheerful . . ."

"Most of 'em being," he growled in a tone of mock jealousy that wasn't nearly as faked as he thought it was, "good-looking young fellows who're in love with you . . ."

She turned him loose. Sat up. Grinned at him like an imp. Clapped her hands like a child.

"Oh, good!" she laughed; "I'll have to work on *that.* Making you jealous, I mean. For if that's what it takes to keep you with me, I'll start going buggy riding in the moonlight with a different one every weekend!"

"That's what it'll take to get you a well-striped bottom, Nora, girl," he growled; "So if you want to have to eat all your meals off the mantelpiece 'cause you can't sit down, go right ahead!"

She stared at him, her eyes alight with mischief, with a tiny bit of fear, and, curiously enough, with joy.

"Ethan—would you beat me?" she whispered; "If I cheated—only a little, I mean? Like going buggy riding, say?"

"Bloody," he said flatly.

She locked both arms around his neck, hugged him fiercely.

"Ohh, I'm so glad!" she whispered; "You're jealous! You *really* are! Which means you love me! You—do, don't you, Ethan?"

"Women!" Ethan groaned. "All right. Back to my catechism. What would I do—with Martha Anne, Nora?"

"Bring her with you. I'd—love her as though she were my own. I wouldn't hold her being—Anne's—against her. I'm not *that* unfair, Ethan. Besides, she *ought* to be taken away from Anne, anyhow. Haven't you ever thought—don't you even realize—what being brought up in a home with a mother who's not right in the head might do to that poor child's own mind, dearest? Your overdeveloped sense of duty isn't very fair to your daughter, it seems to me. Besides, you've told me that Anne —becomes violent—once in a great while. She stabbed Cora Atkins—for which I thank her, because that big dray horse is in love with you! She tried to shoot me—and I don't blame her, because she was only protecting her home from a certain little loose-limbed female freebooter, namely *me,* who was trying to steal her husband. But suppose one day when you're not around she—"

Ethan shuddered. He was remembering *why* Anne had stabbed Cora. He had never told Nora that. And he had no intention of ever telling her.

"Ruth Quindaro is always there," he pointed out.

"My old nurse," Nora sighed; "I'd love to have her back with me. She'd be—wonderful for *our* children, Ethan."

"If we ever have any," Ethan said.

"Oh, Lord! Why'd you have to go and remind me? Ethan—suppose I can't? Suppose I *really* can't? To end a family like yours. An old, old family. They came over on the *Mayflower,* didn't they?"

"Who told you *that*? Anne, likely!"

"Yes. Well, didn't they?"

"Nope," Ethan drawled; "my great-great-great-great-grandpappy, give or take a few greats, swam across a few years before even that. And was there at Plymouth Rock to greet the Pilgrim Fathers when they landed. With a turkey in one hand, and Pocahontas in the other. Accompanied by forty dozen half-breed bastard brats, of course. That's what makes *me* so wild, all that redskin blood I've got in my veins . . ."

"You are *never* wild, my darling. You are very sweet and slow and gentle. Maybe that's what's wrong. Maybe—you ought to be—wilder. Bulls—never miss, do they? Nor do—stallions . . ."

"Oh, Lord!" Ethan groaned.

"I—I'm only teasing. Ethan, let's say—I can't—as is very likely after all the things that have been done to me. What then? I'd never forgive myself—if you let the Lovejoy family die out because of me. You *need* a son worse than I do. And you want one just as bad . . ."

"Granted," Ethan said solemnly; "That being so, here's a suggestion: instead of my going home today, I stay until Monday, say. But you, my sweet, don't. You take a trip down to St. Looie to buy yourself some fancy duds. But while you're gone, send that cute little red-headed waitress of yours over here to—to tidy up the place, for instance—"

"I saw you looking at her! I saw you! And she was looking right back at you—and smiling at you—the saucy minx! I'm going to fire her! This very Saturday! And—Oh! Ohhhhh, Ethan!"

She bent her head and cried then, really cried.

He held her to him, gently, tenderly.

"Aaaallll rrrright!" she sniffed; "You—want me ttto fffix it ffor yyou, Ethan? Wouldn't be hard. IIII-I'm ssssure ssshe'd be dddelighted ttto oblige!"

He pushed her away from him, peered into her eyes.

"Nora," he said; "any child who isn't *yours,* I don't want. And if God doesn't grant us that, I'll cheerfully forget the whole stupid business. So stop crying, will you?"

"Ethan—kkkiss mmme?" she whimpered.

He kissed her. Straightened up, smiling.

"Now what?" he said.

"You *know* what!" she whispered fiercely. "Oh, Ethan—please!"

But it didn't work that time, either. And, as he rode away in a hansom cab toward the station, he knew in his heart of hearts it never would.

Not ever. A pity. A very great pity. Maybe even a tragedy. But there it was.

21

That next morning, as usual, when he got back from Topeka, Ethan retrieved his buckboard and his team from Luke Prevost's livery stable. And, also as usual, it was one of Luke's hired hands who brought the vehicle to him. But as he climbed up into the driver's seat behind his splendid, night-black pair of trotters, Luke himself came out of the office of his establishment and stared up at Ethan with a worried look in his eyes. At once Ethan drew the horses up and sat there, waiting for Luke to say whatever it was he had on his mind.

"Mighty heap o' horseflesh for such a lightweight rig," Luke said.

"Quit stalling, Luke," Ethan said. "Something's gnawing at your big gut. Out with it, man!"

"Well—put it this way, Eth," Luke drawled; "Don't reckon I'm telling you any news when I say you ain't exactly the most popular man in this here county . . ."

"Nor I, you, when I say I don't give a damn," Ethan shot back at him. "Skip the preamble, Luke; get to Article One of the Constitution, will you?"

"All right. But this much is out in front, my friend: you always treated *me* mighty white, so I figger it's my bounden duty to put a flea in yore ear. Whilest you wuz away—in Topeka, I heard tell—"

"Which is none of your goddamned business; but, yes, I was in Topeka. Visiting Nora Curtiss. So now you can confirm all the speculations, for all the good that'll do anybody. Sorry. Didn't mean to snap your head off. Go on, Luke . . ."

"Tha's just it. He come here. *Her* husband. Knowed him the minute I laid eyes on him, 'cause he's sich a good-lookin' fella. My old woman almost earned herself a beatin' after pore ol' Cy's funeral by carryin' on so long about how handsome Price Andrews wuz . . ."

"So?" Ethan said.

"Ain't that good-lookin' no more. Done got worn-down 'n puffy-jowled. Y'know, too much likker, too many nights sittin' over th cards 'n poker chips in a room filled up wit seegar smoke, too many spraddle-legged li'l fillies, clappin' up his waterworks—"

"Get to the point, Luke," Ethan said.

"He rented a rig. Then he axed me how to git out to yore place. I told him you wasn't home. Then he axed me where you'd gone . . ."

"And you *told* him?" Ethan said.

"Naw. Hell, naw, Eth. You doan even tote a six-gun. 'N fellas like that'un *shoot* when they catch another party wit their wives . . ."

Ethan held the stable owner with his icy, gyrfalcon's stare. Said flatly, calmly:

"Price Andrews's wife lives in St. Joe, Luke. With his three kids. I don't know her. I've never visited St. Joseph, Missouri, in my life. So he has no reason to shoot me. Not that he needs one, of course. All of which is immaterial and irrelevant, as the lawyers say. What was his reaction to the news that I wasn't at home?"

"That 'twuz jes' as well. That he'd mosey on out there 'n see effen he couldn't pay you back in kind. Then he druv off. This mornin', jes' a little while ago, he come back. Paid me fur my rig. Walked away in th direction o' th station. Didn't say nothin', cept'n': 'How much do I owe you, friend?' I tol him that, 'n he paid up without a murmur. Then he strolled away, lookin' as happy as a boar hawg at a full slop trough—after he's done et his fill, thet is . . ."

Ethan thought about that. His eyes became very cold and still. Near certainty invaded them.

"Thank you, Luke," he said.

On the way home to his farm, Ethan thought about the fact that now very likely he was going to have to hunt Price Andrews down and kill him, or get himself killed, trying to. But since that seemed to him a self-evident, inescapable fact, he quit thinking about it altogether.

When he came into the house, the first thing he did was to walk up the stairs to his bedroom. Anne was still in bed, although it was almost noon by then. She was naked.

So he knew he didn't even need to ask any questions, because Anne never slept naked. Like many women of an epoch that even put embroidered covers around piano and table legs, and draped nude statues, she had a perfect horror of nakedness, especially her own. Never again, after their wedding night, when, her inhibitions overcome by a virtual flood of champagne, she'd allowed him to take her nightgown off her, had Ethan Lovejoy seen his wife unclothed. In the old days, whenever she took a bath, she had sternly banished him from the kitchen of the sod house. In their new and splendid frame house, by automatic reflex, once inside the bathroom, she always locked the door.

He stared at her and a slow green tide of nausea crawled up the back of his throat. Her body was pleasant enough to look at. Bearing two children hadn't spoiled it noticeably; and here of late, she had put on flesh, so that it was, if anything, more curving, rounded, harmonious of line than he remembered it as having been on their wedding night.

But what sickened him, made his shot-shredded gut pump bile and acid up his esophagus until he could taste them in his mouth, was her posture. She lay on her back with her two hands beneath her head, sprawled out—a damp rag doll in a wet tangle of sheets, with her brown hair like a sparrow's nest and her legs spread as far apart as she could get them. Her whole body gleamed silvery with sweat; it beaded on the sparse tufts of mousy brown hair in her armpits, ran in discernible rivulets between her breasts and down the curve of her belly. The mat of darker brown pubic hair was sweat glistened, too; and on her inner thighs, the dirty white smear of semen stains.

"Cover yourself up," Ethan said.

"Why?" she said, making a ghoulish grimace meant surely to be a mocking smile; "I thought you liked me—naked, Ethan . . ."

"Right now, I don't like you, period," Ethan said; "Cover yourself up, Anne!"

"No," she said, and lay there sprawled out like that—offensively, obscenely. Then she saw his eyes.

"Are you going to—kill me, Ethan?" she said.

Ethan didn't answer her. He was staring at her breasts. Their nipples were no longer pink, but blue. Mottled blue. Purplish.

'Where that bastard bit them, sure as hell!' Ethan raged, inside his mind.

"Are you, Ethan?" she whispered.

"Am I what?" he said.

"Going to—kill me?" she said slowly, softly.

"No," he said.

"Then—you're going to—beat me?" she said almost hopefully.

'No, *surely* hopefully,' he realized; 'She's violated her own moral code, so punishment would be a relief to her. What are a few welts or even bloody stripes in comparison to shame's acid corroding your guts forever? Only—I'm not God. And these big knobby-knuckled paws are singularly unfit for throwing rocks, especially if I accept the condition the Good Lord put on that at times damned tempting activity, anyhow—'

He lifted his big beak and sniffed the air. It was redolent with sweat stench, much of it male, and carnal, specifically sexual odors, most of them female.

'Like Gashouse Gertie's the morning after a busy night,' he thought sardonically, and took a backward step, stood in the doorway, loose-limbed, leaning his gaunt form against the doorframe.

"Ethan—why don't you answer me?" she said; "I asked you if you were—"

"Going to beat you? No; I'm not. I don't mean to do anything to you, Anne."

Where he was, the air was clearer, so it was the smell of his own body that rose out of his loosened collar and made his big nostrils twitch. 'Wish my olfactory sense wasn't so damned keen,' he thought sadly. 'Hell, I need a bath. And for the same reason she does. A mixture of aromas, not all of them mine. Mansweat, perfume—that chaste scent Nora uses—and—her. Nora, herself. As clean as she always is. But—it's one of nature's weapons, isn't it? That high-spiced musk of estrus. Deliberately designed to be exciting. Which is why it is so potent, striking effortlessly through the bath salts, good soap, perfume . . .'

He lounged there, staring bleakly at his naked, adulterous, unfaithful wife.

"Not—even leave me? Petition the state legislature for a Bill of Divorcement?" Anne said.

"Who'd take care of you?" he said quietly. "Besides, the legislature wouldn't grant such a bill, if I understand anything about the law . . ."

"Why—not?" Anne whispered.

"Because to charge you with adultery, I'd have to contend you're responsible for your actions. And you aren't. You haven't been for a long time . . ."

Her eyes flared into almost maniacal rage; her small, square face became venomous.

"And not because the laws also says that when *both* partners in a marriage are guilty of adultery no divorce can be granted them?" she spat.

Ethan went on looking at her. His face didn't change.

"There's—that, too, I suppose," he said.

"You suppose!" she screamed; "When you're always down there in Wichita, wallowing with your filthy little whore!"

'So she doesn't know where Nora is,' he realized. 'That's a relief, if a small one.' He said with a dry chuckle:

"She smells a heck of a lot better than you do, right now. Anne, stop it. This is futile. We're both stuck with each other, which is maybe poetic justice. Now I'm going downstairs and ask Ruth to heat some water so you can have a bath. You need one damned bad, y'know . . ."

"No," she said with that ghoulish grin; "I—I like his smell. I want to keep it on me. It's—exciting—to me, anyhow. And—he's good at—at *that*. Better than you are, Ethan Lovejoy! He made me—made me—moan. And—and pant. Like—a she-dog . . ."

"The word's 'bitch,' Anne," he said.

"I know," she said with a primness that was madness's very self; "Only I—can't say—words like that. He tried to get me to, but I—wouldn't. Or rather, I couldn't. My throat chokes up on me and won't let 'em out . . ."

" 'For this relief, much thanks!' " Ethan quoted solemnly.

"He told me to tell you what he'd done to me. But I can't say that word either. It's—too horrid. Filthy—"

"But doing it, of course, is not?" Ethan said drily.

"No! No, of course not!" she laughed shrilly; "Doing it is—great fun! And that's just what we did, Ethan Lovejoy, that horrid word, not making love. Making love—is nice. Slow and sweet and tender. But were we ever wild! Like—a stallion and a mare! Funny, you never told me—or showed me—that people—could do it *that* way, too—on my hands and knees, and him mounting me from—"

"Stop it, Anne," Ethan said.

"Oh, so you don't want to hear about it, d'you? Well, you've got to. I'm going to tell you. I want you to know!"

"Anne," he said bleakly, "I know everything men do to women they despise. To raddled she-meat. To bodies emptied of all that counts: being, personality, selfhood, identity, mind. Upon such barely living corpses, they commit their near necrophilia, twisting their practically inert dolls into dozens of distorted, ugly, painful positions, making use of bodily orifices not intended by nature for such employ. I know all that, although I wish I didn't. There's a lot to be said for—innocence, after all. So spare me a recapitulation, will you? I don't need it. I only lie with, bed with, women whom I love. And I'm incapable of loving—even physically—women I don't respect . . ."

She stared at him oddly, almost thoughtfully.

"You're right," she whispered almost to herself, her gaze turned inward, lid-hooded. "With—in—one's mouth—ugh! That's really—nasty, isn't it?"

"Jesus, God!" Ethan whispered prayerfully.

She flopped over onto her belly, suddenly. The motion was oddly graceful. 'Like a slim, white seal's,' he thought.

"He told me to—show you *this,*" she said, twisting her head around on her neck so that she could look backward over her shoulder at the soft rising curve of her hips.

Ethan hung there. The rage that tore him was a totally crippling thing. Into Anne's left buttock, Price had carved his own initials. With the point of a pocket knife, surely, digging in, raking downward, slashing across: P.A. The letters were thickly encrusted with dried blood.

'I'm going to kill him,' Ethan thought; 'I've got to now. It's no longer a question of comparative guilts. My wife—bedded with, opened her thighs to, took inside her body—willingly, eagerly, delightedly—the rampant and rigid male organ—of another man. Accepted the hot jetting of his seed. I've been doing the same—for almost a year now—lying with, tumbling, engaging in sexual intercourse with—another woman. One hand washes the other. So be it. The score is even.

'But this—this is another matter. This is—deliberate insult. He's forcing me to put my manhood on the line. And he's reduced my choices to a sole alternative: to face him, armed. To one brief flurry of gunfire in a sunwashed street, one of us—him or me—dead like a dog in his blood. Or not to meet him at all. To (Oh, go on with the canine simile!) slink about my befouled and violated kennel, snapping and snarling at the mad bitch he took, obliged me to share. Again—like a dog. Like a craven dog, choking on his own dog vomit unable to meet his own hangdog, coward's eyes. So be it. I—'

"He told me to tell you—it was his brand," Anne whispered; "Cut into his—property—to—stake his claim. Or—if you'd prefer, his guarantee—of quality. 'P' for Prime. 'A' for—well, that's another dirty word I can't bring myself to say. But you know what he meant, don't you, Ethan?"

"Yes," Ethan said; "I know what he meant."

She was crying now, bitterly. He let his body relax. He was beginning to feel a little sorry for her.

"Ethan," she said sadly; "I wasn't crazy when I did—while I was doing—that. I did it deliberately. As I told you before: you'd united all those impossibly improbable coincidences. You'd—neglected me too long, and left me alone—for him to come to me. I was quite sane—except for the rage at knowing you were lying in her arms—between her legs!—at that very moment, likely. And—how ugly the truth is!—I wanted him. I'll always—want him. Like that. I don't—love him. I don't even like him. I just want him. To do *that* to me—in the rough, ugly, brutal way he does it. To make me sweat, stink, pant, moan, beg, scream. *That.*"

"All right, Anne," he said, his voice dead, gray, almost soundless; "Let's not talk anymore. There's nothing more to be said—" He thought: 'Not ever again, between us in this life . . .'

"Papa!" that childish voice piped from behind him; "Is that man—gone? Is he, Papa?"

Ethan whirled. Little Martha Anne was standing there, her eyes like huge blue saucers. Tawiyela was beside her, but hers were midnight velvet, slanted, deep as night, unreadable.

"What man, baby?" Ethan croaked. He didn't even glance back over his shoulder at his wife.

"That *man,*" Martha Anne said. "He knocked on the front door, Papa. Ruthie opened it. He asked for you—"

"And?" Ethan got out over the bile and brine and wormwood in his throat.

"Ruthie told him, you weren't home. So he asked for Mama—"

"Martha," Tawiyela said; "I told you not to tell Uncle Ethan! I told you!"

"He's *my* papa, not yours! So I am so gonna tell him!" Martha Anne said.

"All right, pet—tell me," Ethan said.

"Ruthie told 'im Mama was sick. 'N to go 'way 'n leave us alone. So he took a little bitty pistol outta his pocket 'n poked Ruthie in the stummick with it. Made her go downstairs. To the coal bin. He locked her up in it 'n put the key in his pocket. 'N—Oh, Pa-pa!" Martha Anne giggled happily. "This morning Ruthie made pipi all over the coal! Said she couldn't wait any longer since me 'n Tawi couldn't let her out. Isn't that *awful*—an old woman like Ruthie!"

"I suspect she really couldn't wait," Ethan said gravely; "after being locked up all night. And wetting it down a mite won't hurt the coal. Make it burn better, likely. . . ." He looked over his shoulder at Anne. She was lying there on her stomach, and staring straight ahead of her, indifferently. "Then what happened, Martha?"

"Mama came downstairs. And she and that man talked to each other. They didn't talk much. Mostly they just grinned at each other. They looked so silly, grinning like that . . ."

"And?" Ethan whispered, his voice retreating out of sound.

"They sat down on th sofa. Then they started huggin' 'n kissin'. 'N that man put his hand up under Mama's skirt—"

"Jesus!" Ethan whispered.

" 'N Mama said: 'Oh!' Then she said: 'Ah!' Then 'Ahhhhh!' "

The imitation was perfect.

"Christ!" Ethan said.

"Then Mama said real funny: 'Not down here. Take me upstairs.' 'N that man picked Mama up in his arms. Then he saw me 'n Tawi looking at 'em so he put out his hand to me 'n said: 'Come along, li'l missy, time you learnt sumpin', too!' "

"And you—went with him?" Ethan breathed.

"Yes, Papa. 'N Tawi did, too."

"Oh, God!" Ethan said.

" 'N when we got upstairs that man laid Mama down on th bed. 'N he said: 'Strip, bitch!' "

Ethan didn't say anything. He couldn't.

" 'N Mama took all her clo's off. 'N that man took all his off, too. Papa, he was made real funny. He—he poked out in front. 'N he was— all hairy. Papa, are you made like that, too?"

" 'Course he is, ninny!" Tawiyela said. "All menfolks are . . ."

"Jesus, Jesus, Jesus!" Ethan whispered.

"Then him 'n Mama—did things, Papa. Funny things. They wrapped their arms 'n their legs all around each other 'n bumped 'n bumped 'n bumped 'n Mama said: 'Oooooh—that's good. That's—so good, darling, I like it.' "

"Martha," Ethan said; "Go back downstairs. You, too, Tawi. I'll be down in a little while. You heard me, girls—hop!"

The two children scurried away, raced down the stairs.

Ethan went back into the bedroom, stared at Anne.

"You let—my daughter—let little Tawiyela—*see* that?" he whispered. "Precisely *that,* Anne?"

"Yes," Anne said indifferently; "they have to learn, sometime, don't they? They'll be doing it themselves, soon enough . . ."

Ethan loosened his belt buckle. Took off his belt. He was, after all, a man of his times. Perhaps even a little beyond them. Few, if any, of his contemporaries could have rejected the double moral standard for male and female sexual behavior as easily, as completely, as he had. Being, above all, just, he had seen no defensible basis upon which he could arrogate unto himself the right to punish Anne for a sin of which he was not only far more guilty than she was, but that he knew perfectly well he was going to go right on committing at every available opportunity with the woman he loved. He granted Anne, wronged by him, what very probably no other man of his times would have: the perfect right to take her vengeance in kind, and conceded her—if not forgiveness—at least the ethical justice of impunity.

But this was another matter. He could not pardon her for what seemed to him unpardonable: the deliberate corruption of the morals of minor children. For he thought of what she had done as that—as a sort of deliberate, rather perverted exhibitionism, designed to strike at him through two small, innocent beings he loved, regardless of the emotional, moral, or psychological damage done thereby to the two little girls themselves.

That it might equally have been the sheer mindlessness of a woman caught up in estrual rage, uterine furor, the total unawareness of her surroundings, or of the presence of anyone whomsoever of a human female, dehumanized, turned into animal, into maenad, by desire, he didn't so much as realize. Nor did he reflect upon the fact that if this possibility didn't at least occasionally exist, the human race would have long since vanished from the earth.

He swung his arm back, back, back, with that heavy belt dangling from his hand. Brought it whistling down. It wrapped itself around her slender back just below her shoulders, so far around, in fact, that the free end of it bit into the upper part of her right breast. The noise it made, striking against her tender flesh, was loud in that little room. She shivered under the impact of it, cringed a little in anticipation of the next flesh-purpling blow, but she made no sound. Ethan drew that belt back again, the deepest masculine lust, that for cruelty—the male animal's atavistic delight in inflicting pain—rising in him, held it there, savoring that moment—which was a truer perversion than any she had committed, although he didn't know it was—and then he saw her eyes.

They were glittering at him, out of her small, square face, turned upward and backward, wild with macabre triumph, as though something in the twisted recesses of her disordered brain told her that by the very fact of having provoked him into beating her, she had won the duel of wills between them.

'As,' he reflected soberly, sadly, the rage abruptly gone from him, leaving him cold and sick to his shredded gut, 'she has. Made me descend to the level of low comedy, bad melodrama. The cuckolded husband whipping his faithless wife. Declaring: Honey, your narrow little passage into Gan Eden—or to madness!—is *mine*. I'll kill you if you permit the hot, sweet use of it to any other—horny, brutish—male, but me! Thereby accomplishing what? Vindicating my husbandly honor? Or retreating into the hairy apehood from whence we all sprang? If we ever really escaped from it, which I doubt—'

She saw that look of self-recognition invade his eyes, the smile of sardonic acceptance of all human limitations, including his own, steal across his face, perceived the exact moment that his raised right arm, the hand holding that belt began to relax. Rage tore her. She glared at him with terrible eyes, screamed:

"Don't stop! Keep it up! Beat me some more! Beat me—to death!"

He slipped the belt back through the loops of his pants, tightened, buckled it. He thought: 'The pity is that I can't grant myself that relief. Or you, that kindness.' He said: "No. One whack is all the matter's worth." And turning very quietly, went back down the stairs.

He took his Winchester down from where it hung above the fireplace and started to clean it. He didn't have much faith in his rifle, for the 1866 model Winchester had several defects, none of them very serious, except one. But that one could be fatal in a gunfight, because when it happened, the dadblamed gun just wouldn't shoot. And you couldn't rework the rifle to help matters, because it wasn't the Winchester's fault, but rather that of the rimfire, brass-cased ammunition it used.

He shrugged his shoulders. There it was. Life had its inevitabilities built in. He was going to kill Price Andrews—or die trying. And considering the dead end his own existence had got to be then, he conceded it didn't make much difference either way. So he loaded the Winchester. Dumped a handful of cartridges into his coat pocket, turned—

And faced two pairs of staring eyes: one pair sky blue, the other midnight velvet.

"Oh, Lord!" he groaned.

"Papa," Martha Anne piped; "You gonna shoot that man?"

Ethan stalled for time.

"Now just *who* gave you that idea, pet?" he said.

"Tawi," Martha Anne said. "She says you got to. Because—Mama

—cheated on you with him, doing that funny thing they did. 'N lettin' him see her nekkid."

Ethan stared at the sapling straight half-breed child, with her two long, night black braids, and a beaded wampum band around her forehead. She was dressed in a porcupine quill embroidered buckskin dress that Ethan, himself, had bought her for the simple reason that redskin clothing looked so right on her, brought out her racial heritage. Or part of it, anyhow. As a matter of fact, Tawiyela had Caucasian features, and her skin was fair, fairer, in fact, than her mother's; but her hair and eyes were those of the red race. The combination made her singularly, oddly beautiful.

"Tawi," he said gently; "Did you actually *know* what you were saying when you told Martha Anne that?"

"Yes, Uncle Ethan," Tawiyela whispered.

Ethan stared at the grave, completely poised ten-year-old child.

"Then maybe you'd better explain it to me," he said; "because I'm not all that sure *I* understand it, either, sweetheart . . ."

"They were fucking," Tawiyela said serenely; "And when people fuck, they—"

"Tawi!" Ethan thundered.

Tawiyela's slanted Kansa eyes, rain-crow velvet, became jet. Glittered with sudden tears. Her adored Uncle Ethan, the exact center and sun of all her existence, had spoken harshly to her for the first time in her life. Had roared at her like a maddened bull, in fact. Her heart was broken. It really was. Amber tears beaded on her sooty lashes. Ran in topaz droplets down her cheeks. That sight melted Ethan like a stick of butter left out in the sun in mid-July. He put down his Winchester, held out his arms to Tawiyela. She came to him.

"I'm—sorry, Uncle Ethan," she whispered.

"No, I'm the one who's sorry, sweetheart. Didn't mean to yell at you that way. It's your mama I'm going to yell at. She's let you hear—and maybe even see—a damned sight too many things that aren't appropriate for a little girl your age even to know. *That* word for instance. It's ugly. Bad. I don't want to hear you say it again, *ever.* Not as long as you live. Promise me, sweetheart?"

"Yes, Uncle Ethan, I promise," Tawiyela said.

"I want you," Ethan went on gravely, "*both* of you, to stay as sweet as you are for as long as you can. And knowing too much about grown-ups' doings won't help that. Grown-ups can be awfully wicked, I'm afraid . . ."

"Is *Mama* wicked, Papa?" Martha Anne said.

"No, pet. Just confused. She doesn't know what she's doing half the time. No, three quarters . . ."

Tawiyela laughed then, suddenly. Her laughter was pure music, the silvery tinkling of a mountain stream.

"You mean she's crazier than a bedbug, don't you, Uncle Ethan?" she said.

"Yes, Tawi," Ethan sighed; "I suppose that's exactly what I do mean. And it's why we mustn't hold the—strange things—she sometimes does against her."

"Papa," Martha Anne said then, disappointment brimming through her voice; "then you're *not* gonna kill Mama?"

Ethan asked the right question then; the one that mattered.

"Why, honey?" he said with nerve-draining calm; "Do you want me to?"

"Yes, Papa," Martha Anne said clearly, firmly; "I wish you'd shoot her all full of holes so she'd drop down dead."

Ethan stared at his little daughter. This was an aspect of his tragedy that had never occurred to him.

"That's—odd," he said quietly; "Why do you, Martha Anne?"

"She's awful mean, Papa. She yells at me. 'N she hits me when Ruthie's not around. She hits me—for nothing, Papa."

"Even when you haven't been a bad little girl, pet?" Ethan said; "You quite often are, y'know . . ."

"She—she hits me when I'm *good,* Papa—'N—"

"Out with it, Martha Anne!"

"One time when I was really bein' bad, yellin' 'n breakin' things 'n throwin' my dollbabies around—she—she kissed me. Gave me candy . . ."

'I've got to get this child away from her,' Ethan thought bleakly; 'Both these children. Before she damages them beyond repair. But how? Name of God, how?'

He said: "All right, my sweethearts—run along and play now. I—have to go away for a while. I've some business to attend to up in town . . . ."

"Uncle Ethan," Tawiyela said soberly; "We—we're awfully hungry, sir. We haven't had any breakfast. Ruthie couldn't fix us any. She's still locked up in the coal bin, y'know . . ."

"Oh, Lord! I'd clean forgot her! Come on!" Ethan said.

He had to pry the lock off the door to get Ruth Quindaro out of the
coal bin, because Price Andrews had either taken the key with him or had
thrown it away. Ruth was, physically, anyhow, a white woman; but she'd
been brought up as the redskin she was less than a quarter of by blood.
Her dignity was monumental.

"Reckon them kids have done told you what happened, sir?" she said.

"Yes, Ruth," Ethan said.

"Then I'll keep my trap shut about it. Didn't see nothing, nohow. I
was locked in this here coal bin all night."

"I know," Ethan said.

She looked at him. She was getting close to seventy years of age by
then, and her hair was gray, her face, wrinkled. But she'd been a beautiful
woman once. In fact, she still was.

"Palefaces' doings!" she snorted, using, as a bitter joke, the term no
redskin in history ever called white people.

"You're a paleface, Ruth," Ethan said.

"Yes. Reckon I mostly am. 'Cause my people didn't have sense
enough to keep apart from yourn. Plumb ruint 'em—white man's ways.
Us Wyandots are too civilized—your way. We ought to have stayed
redskins 'n not mixed our blood with yourn. 'Cause there ain't nothing
good about white people, sir. Not nothing."

"You're right, Ruth," Ethan said quietly; "Perfectly right. There
isn't, I'm afraid."

" 'Cept 'n you," Ruth said with a wintery smile; "You'd've made a
mighty good redskin, you'd've had the chance. 'Cause you live in the
nach'l world, not ag'in it. Only you ain't learned how to be cruel like a
warrior's got to be. Down in th Territory, us lived next to some Tindes
—the people y'all call Apaches. 'N one of their women opened her legs
to a white trader. So the Tindes led her out into the square between the
wickiups. Then they cut her nose off. All her nose—right up to where the
bony part starts. Took their own sweet time a-doin' it. But she was a Tinde
woman. She didn't make a sound. Hanged herself the next day, though.
Couldn't stand the disgrace. They throwed her body to the dogs. Tindes
don't take kindly to female wickedness . . ."

"You're—getting at something, Ruth," he said.

"Reckon I am," Ruth said quietly. "Beat her, sir. Beat her bloody.
'Cause she didn't fight. Even down in the coal bin, I'd've heard—a struggle. There warn't none. She give in too easy. Or mebbe she offered herself
to him. Wouldn't put it past her."

"Ruth—she's mad," Ethan said.

"Knows that, too. But not all the time. 'N yestiddy, she wasn't crazy worth a damn. 'Sides that, there's a matter a woman's got to put her mind to. The body, by itself, don't work no good at all, sir, not for us wimmen, anyhow. We's purely got to put th thinkin', 'n th dreamin', 'n th yearnin' in. So ask her if she had a good time. 'N if she says 'Yes,' beat her. Beat her good, sir!"

"Ruth," Ethan said quietly; "It so happens that I don't *care* whether she enjoyed herself or not. Or what she did. Or what she'll ever do. She could lie down and spread her legs for the whole Ninth Cavalry, and I wouldn't give a damn. And the Tenth."

Ruth stared at him.

"Them's buffalo soldiers, sir," she said; "Niggers."

"I know. That's why I picked those two troops. To make the matter clearer. It's—Nora I care about, Ruth. *Our* Nora. Yours and mine. You brought her up. I love her."

"Yes. There's that there, ain't there? I done talked to the Great Mystery about that. 'Hey-a-dey, Grandfather! This here is wrong,' sez I; 'awful wrong! But blow th South Wind, blow th North Wind 'n fix it, Grandfather! You kin if you wants to . . .' "

"And did he answer you? The Great Mystery, I mean? The Great-Grandfather of all the Real Men, the True Men?"

Hearing Ethan use those two expressions that the red men call themselves no matter what language they speak, Ruth Quindaro smiled.

"He's a-gonna, now," she said. " 'Cause you jes' made Big Medicine, Ethan Lovejoy. The best!"

When he was far enough from the house for the sounds of the shots not to carry back to it, Ethan tried out the Winchester. He put two full magazine loads, thirty shots, through it. In the first trial, seven of those miserable rimfire cartridges failed to go off; in the second, eight. Out of the fifteen shots the Winchester held in its magazine, it was a dead certainty that more than half were going to fail. And he didn't, and couldn't, know in what order they were going to fail. Ethan thought about that, about what it meant.

But it wasn't a matter that thinking about was likely to help, so he drove on into Abilene, left his buckboard and his team at the livery stable, and started walking back toward the station.

On the way, he met Phil Harris. Phil had his youngest child with him. The boy had been born in the spring of 1867. In fact Martha Harris had been pregnant with this child when Ethan and Anne had first met her. There was a standing, only half-jesting agreement between Phil and Ethan that little Martin Harris was to marry Martha Anne Lovejoy when the two of them were big enough to wed. And already at eight years old, Martha Anne was sniffing, woman-like: "That li'l ol' Martin Harris is a pest!"

"Howdy, Ol' Hoss!" Phil sang out; then said to his son, who, at eleven years of age, was beginning to like the idea: "C'mon, Martin! Say howdy to yore pappy-in-law!"

But at that moment Phil saw the rifle in the crook of Ethan's arm and, after that, his eyes.

"So—" he croaked, "th bastid's gone 'n done sumpin' else!"

"Yes," Ethan said; "he's done something else."

"Mind tellin' me, what, Ol' Hoss?" Phil said.

"Before the kid, yes," Ethan said.

"Mart, you run along to th dry goods store. Tell Missus Pennyfeather I'll be along in a couple o' shakes. You heard me, boy! Git goin' now!"

"Yes, Papa. Be seein' you, Uncle Ethan!" Martin said, and scampered away.

"What's that pukin' polecat puppy done *now?*" Phil said.

"Went out to my place. While I wasn't there. Anne was alone. And she really doesn't know the difference between right and wrong anymore, y'know. Nor the distinction between 'No' and 'Yes.' Called himself getting even for—Nora, I suspect."

"I'm goin' with you!" Phil grated; "You ain't practiced with a gun in years, and—"

"No, Phil. This is *my* business, y'know. And his. Nobody else's."

"I see. 'N reckon you're right, Eth. Where? Wichita?"

"Or Dodge City. One of the two. Only two places he hangs out in now, when he's in Kansas. Why?"

"He's—a good hand with a shootin' iron, Ol' Hoss. So—which God forbid!—he takes you, I jes' wanted to know where I gotta head for. To blow his balls out from 'twixt his mangy legs 'n stuff 'em in his mouth. 'N effen I cain't, Ned will. We owe that much to you. 'N to li'l Nora."

"Thanks, Phil," Ethan said. "See you when I get back."

"Hope so," Phil Harris said. Then he added under his breath as Ethan walked away: "Lord God, how I hope so!"

"Yessir," the ticket agent said; "The stranger you done described to me, Mister Lovejoy, bought a one-way ticket to Wichita—'bout nine o'clock this morning . . ."

"Thanks," Ethan said. "Now will you lend me your inkwell, your pen, and a piece of paper? I've got to write a note. Believe me, it's important, or I wouldn't bother you."

"Why, 'tain't no bother a-tall, Mister Lovejoy! Happy to be of service," the ticket agent said.

Ethan took the writing materials, went over to a bench in the empty waiting room. Sat down upon it, spread the paper out before him. He had, he hoped, stilled public curiosity over the unusual fact of his carrying a rifle through the streets of the town by saying to one of Will Trainer's employees who'd made bold to ask him why he was 'toting a gun,' "It's broke, son; I'm going to send it off to Karl Heinz's gun shop in Atchison to have it fixed." But now he had this one last matter to attend to. Dipping the pen in the ink, he wrote slowly, carefully:

"My name is Ethan Lovejoy. If I am killed, please notify Mr. Philip Harris at his farm three miles east of Abilene on the Smokey Hill River, and Mr. Ned Tyler, President of the Abilene Citizens State Bank, who is my attorney. Last of all, after having informed these two, please advise of my passing, Miss Nora Curtiss, at her restaurant, corner of Quincy and Holliday streets in Topeka. I thank you." He signed it, "Ethan Lovejoy."

He sat there very calmly and waited for the ink to dry. When it had, he folded the paper and put it in his billfold, and put the billfold, in its turn, back in the breast pocket of his coat. He realized that it was exactly the sort of note the Boys in Blue had pinned to their uniforms at places like Shiloh Church, and when sent out to reduce Spottsylvania's Bloody Angle. His chances were considerably better than theirs had been, because when Butcher Grant ordered a frontal attack against a Reb stronghold, the result of said orders usually turned out to be mass suicide. His depended upon his first shot's not missing fire. Maybe it would. Maybe it wouldn't. The odds were fifty-fifty, and therefore good enough.

He walked over to the ticket window and handed the agent back his inkwell and his pen.

"Thank you, sir. Now give me a ticket to Wichita," he said.

"One-way—or round-trip, Mister Lovejoy?" the ticket agent asked.

Ethan thought about that.

"Make it—one-way," he said.

22

When Ethan Lovejoy came into The First & Last Chance Saloon—so called because it was the first place the trail drovers could get their drinks of rotgut when they pushed their Longhorns into Kansas, and the last barroom they could toss down a few within the borders of the state when heading home again—he saw Price Andrews sitting at a poker table, dealing the cards out to three cowboys. By then it was midmorning of the day after Price had left Abilene. The reason it had taken Ethan so long to catch up with him was simple: by the time the ex-Yankee turned Kansas bonanza farmer had finally got to Wichita, it had been already after 10:00 P.M. And since Ethan, as a combat veteran of the Civil War, knew better than to try to stage a gun battle in Wichita's ill-lighted streets in near pitch darkness, he had walked over to the Old Munger House on Back Bay Boulevard, taken a room for the night, and gone to bed.

What was more, he had slept soundly until well past sunrise before getting up, eating a frugal breakfast, and setting out—in a horse-drawn hack, since he didn't mean to wear himself out—to look for Price Andrews. He was able to sleep not because he lacked imagination, but because he possessed the useful capacity of being able to turn his imagination off when it wasn't going to help matters or serve for anything useful. And since the only thing that thinking too hard beforehand about an event you had no way of controlling the outcome of could do would be to make you nervous, and thereby insure that you became the corpse in this one more cowtown "corpse and cartridge occasion," he put the whole thing out of his mind.

Which gave him a certain advantage over Price Andrews. For the gambler had been sitting at that card table ever since he had got back to Wichita late in the afternoon of the day before. Price had the professional cardsharp's hard won attributes—a cast-iron bladder and sluggish bowels —so that when he hit a winning streak, he could sit on hour after hour, riding herd on his luck, without having to leave the card table for an instant, not even to answer a call of nature, as the quaint Victorian euphemism put it.

So now he sat there, unshaven, puffy-lidded, bleary-eyed, and dealt those cards. When Ethan came into The First & Last Chance, Price didn't even recognize him. After all, he had only seen "Prof" Lovejoy, as he always thought of him, just once, and then only for a brief few minutes. His memories of the man who had now become his chief adversary were vague, anyhow. He remembered, of course, that Nora had been inexplicably fond of her ex-schoolmaster. But that hadn't bothered him, because it was one of the gambler's deepest convictions that women generally wore their brains—if any—between their thighs. That she had also both admired and profoundly respected her old teacher more than any other hard-sided, pants-wearing critter who had passed through her life, however, puzzled him considerably, because, starting from the basis of his own rather peculiar system of values, Price could see no reason for it. That she might want to "drop her frillies, lay down 'n spread wide" for Ethan was comprehensible to the gambler. But that she could admire his mind, his spirit, his general uprightness, seemed to Price sheer nonsense. Therefore he recalled very little about how Ethan looked, physically. His mental image of the schoolmaster-farmer was expressed roughly in such phrases as: "A long, tall, dangling hunk of dried beef. Ugliest he-critter I ever saw. And *the* worst dressed, bar none. Fair amount o' schoolin', though. Real fair-spoken for a fact. Didn't talk like a clodhopper, none a-tall . . ."

But, beyond that, nothing. He hadn't even seriously expected any trouble out of that hayseed. All he'd meant to do was to show the "damn-fool sodbuster" that *nobody* fooled around with Price Andrews's wimmen. Not *nobody.* And now that he'd paid the bumpkin back in kind, dog-humped the gangling oaf's used-up country bitch in their own bedroom, made her polish his knob for him, take his heifer prod up her Atchison, Topeka & Santa Fe by the southernmost route, carved his own initials, or the mocking evaluation of "Prime Ass" into her skinny tail, Price was perfectly willing to forget the whole thing and let bygones be bygones.

Even the fact that the apish-looking critter had cost him the services and the earnings of the "little piece" who was *really* prime instead of just hard up and eager the way Lovejoy's old woman had been. Because, being as much of a professional in the pimping/white slaving trade as he was at fleecing suckers at cards, Price had permanently struck Nora off his list of first-class articles. He had done so with a certain degree of reluctance, of course, and only after listening to Gert's gut-churning description of how badly that "stupid li'l cunt" had "messed herself up." Hideously scarred for life, Nora just wasn't valuable anymore. Nothing put the Johns "off their feed" worse than a filly who looked as if she'd thrown herself through a plate glass store window.

For that reason, he had made no attempt to trace her. And he had no intention to, ever. To Price a "riding filly" mattered only to the degree that she could bring in hard cash. He was incapable of feeling the slightest fondness for a woman. Without exception—right down to and including his ancient, wheezing, and only semiretired whore of a mother, who had formed his dismal attitudes toward her sex forever by putting him out into the cold, wet, stinking mean streets of his hometown, Chicago, whenever she was entertaining a client—Price utterly despised the whole female half of humanity. Which was to say he suffered from the occupational disease of his second profession: no man who genuinely likes women, more often than not admires them, habitually thinks of them as persons, even loves them almost as much fully clothed and standing up as he does when they're delightfully naked and supine, could ever be a pimp.

It was probably just as well that Ethan didn't know how Price felt about Nora. For if he had known that the gambler-pimp dared to thus blaspheme before the very altar and fount of all his idolatry, his rage at this one more affront might have unseated his reason, and with it, the cool control he had over his nerves. So being the Victorian gentleman—or utter quixotic fool—that he was, once inside the saloon, he gave Price Andrews a fighting chance.

"Andrews!" he called out.

Hearing that stern voice, Price Andrews blinked his sleepy, bloodshot eyes twice. By the third blink, he acted. Kicking the card table over, sending the cards fluttering and spinning through the air, the silver dollars they'd been using for chips rolling across the floor, he stuck his hand under his Prince Albert frock coat, where he wore his little Wells Fargo Colt in a shoulder holster beneath his left armpit—a belt gun being of no use to a man who made his living sitting down, and with his legs under a card table at that—started to drag it out, sadly, sickly conscious at the time that he was way out of practice, muscles cramped from sitting in one spot all night long, fatally, suicidally slow, when Ethan's voice halted him in mid-motion.

"Wait!" Ethan thundered, his deep tones awful in their authority; "I'm not armed, Price! Hold your fire!"

Price Andrews completed the act of drawing that little five-shot revolver, pointed it at Ethan, but then he hesitated. In those days, in the Old, distinctly Wild, West, a killing that resulted from a gunfight in which both duelists were armed, was generally considered none of the law's business, beyond acquitting the survivor after a perfunctory hearing on the spot. But if you gunned down an unarmed man, that was indisputably murder, the sentence for which, handed down with equal celerity, was hanging, period. And said hanging, to the delight of all and sundry, was usually carried out well within the first half hour after the culprit had been captured or had surrendered. Now Price was in no hurry to descend to his just deserts down below, so he held Ethan covered with the little Wells Fargo Colt, but he didn't fire it.

"Prove it, Lovejoy!" he said.

Ethan opened his frock coat, spread it wide. That he wore neither a gun belt nor a holstered six-shooter was evident at once.

"Hell," Price snorted; "How do I know you ain't got a stingy gun on you somewheres?"

"Send one of your friends over to search me," Ethan said. "You can keep me covered while he does it. That's fair enough, isn't it?"

Price nodded to one of his erstwhile poker partners. The cowboy got up off the floor where he'd prudently flung himself and sauntered nervously over to where Ethan stood. Unlike the gambler, none of the cowboys was armed. The peace officers of Wichita strictly enforced the local ordinance against carrying a sidearm. Price was able to violate the law because he neither was, looked, nor dressed like a cowboy, and the place he wore his small Wells Fargo Colt—with its five-inch barrel sawed off to a mere two inches to make concealing it even easier—that is, in a shoulder holster well hidden under his armpit by his loose frock coat—wasn't likely to attract a city marshal's or deputy sheriff's attention. But cowboys had to ride into town past signs that read: "Anything goes in Wichita. Leave your revolvers at police headquarters and get a check. Carrying concealed weapons is strictly forbidden." Which was one of the reasons Wichita never equalled the records of Abilene, Newton, and Dodge City as the successive murder capitals of these United States.

The trail driver ran his hands all over Ethan. Stood back. Drawled: "Naw, he ain't packing a hawgleg, Price. Not even a Arkansas toothpick, fur as I kin see . . ."

"All right," Price said; "Speak your piece, Professor!"

"I'm going out that door," Ethan said quietly; "And I'm going to wait for you down on the corner of Second Street, two blocks from here. Then I will be armed. And if you don't come out within ten minutes, I'll come in here after you. Anyhow, the quarrel between us is a private matter. I'd like to keep it that way. Agreed?"

"Agreed," Price said; "You got somebody to tend to your burying, Prof?"

"Yes," Ethan said evenly; "I rather imagine that Nora will. Don't keep me waiting, Price."

"Don't worry, I won't," Price Andrews said.

Whereupon, being anything but a fool, Price Andrews did what any revolver artist in his right mind would have: he sneaked out of the back door of The First & Last Chance Saloon, went down an alley to Third Street, out Third Street to Market, and up Market to Second.

His intentions were very simple, and very reasonable. He meant to kill Ethan Lovejoy. That was the simple part. The reasonable one was that he meant to do it without getting killed, or even so much as shot at, himself. Ergo, he intended to murder Ethan by sneaking up behind him, and shooting him in the back.

When he got to Second Street, Price flattened himself against one side of a store and, cautiously leaning forward inch by careful inch, peered with one eye around the corner. At no time did he expose even six inches of his precious hide. Before he ducked back to total safety, he saw his calculations had been correct: Ethan stood there on the corner with his back turned toward the direction the gambler was coming from.

By then, of course, Ethan had retrieved his Winchester from the hackdriver who had driven him all over Wichita that morning in search of Price Andrews, paid the man off, and dismissed him. Whereupon the hackdriver had got an amazing amount of speed out of his half-dead nag as he departed the scene of an action sure to be a sight too lively to suit his generally peaceable turn of mind. So now Ethan stood there, rifle in hand, with his broad back offering a target that would have been child's play for the worst shot on earth, not to mention a man as good with a handgun as Price Andrews actually was.

Neither Ethan nor Price paid any attention to the little knot of spectators who were beginning to edge away from there in every direction as it became apparent to them what the gambler meant to do. Ethan didn't, because they didn't act like the people in Abilene—in the old days when she was Queen of the Cowtowns—would have. In Abilene, in her heyday, they would have stampeded, flying away from the scene of the action at a dead run. But Wichita people, thanks to that city's efficient police, had seen very few gun battles, so they didn't know what danger they were actually in. And curiosity overcame them. They moved slowly, and not too far.

Price, on the other hand, disregarded them completely, because he knew they wouldn't interfere. In Wichita, Kansas, still Queen of the Cowtowns in 1878, because it wasn't until after 1880 that she surrendered that proud title to Dodge City, the rule was, just as it had been in the other towns that had been cattle shipping capitals before her, that you didn't interfere with cold-blooded murder, or even warn the man about to be sent to the Hereafter with his boots still on. For if you did, the murderer, or his friends, might put you on their list as prime raw material for their corpse-making business, and make sure that you kept your mouth shut thereafter, not only in the immediate future, but throughout all eternity.

Price hung there, half hidden, with only his gun arm extended around the store's corner, gazing with one cautious eye at the rear view of Ethan's lean and sinewy form with real appreciation. He was actually enjoying the situation. The target Ethan's broad-shouldered back offered him was so good, he actually took time to savor it in his mind.

That was Price Andrews's only mistake up until that moment. Even so, he might have got away with it, except for the fact that, at that instant, an unanticipated factor entered into that delicate equation between life and death, as in human existence, the unexpected, unforeseen, unplanned for, always does. For among that little crowd of spectators who had stopped edging away and were now waiting at what they thought was a safe distance to enjoy the gut-tingling spectacle of seeing a man gunned down, there was a young woman totally unacquainted with cowtown mores and customs. Nobody had been able to explain them to Hilda Müller—Mrs. Hans Müller—because she didn't speak English, being a member of one of the several colonies of German immigrants that the Atchison, Topeka & Santa Fe had induced to come to Kansas and settle on the lands the railroad held as a free grant from the U.S. Government.

So Hilda, standing there with her three-year-old daughter, Gretchen, in her arms, actually didn't understand what was going on. And nobody could tell her, because her soft, timid, *"Was ist los?"* was as incomprehensible to them as what was happening before her eyes was to her.

But when Price took his little sawed-off .31-caliber Wells Fargo Colt out from under his coat and sighted it on the middle of Ethan's broad back, she understood that readily enough. It was instantly clear to her that one *Nordamerikaner* was going to murder another one by shooting him from behind, which to her pure, Bavarian Catholic way of thinking seemed absolutely *abscheulich,* by which she meant abominable. And being a kindly little soul from—at that time anyhow—a relatively civilized country, poor Hilda didn't realize that she was supposed to stand there and do nothing about it, so she sang out in her clear, fluting mezzosoprano:

"*Achtung! Hüten Sie sich, mein Herr!*"

Now Ethan still didn't know one word of German, but he didn't need to. The urgency in Frau Müller's voice was enough. He whirled just as Price Andrews's finger caressed that honed-down hair trigger. Due to the clumsiness of his all but toneless left foot, Ethan's motion was far too slow. But it *was* fast enough to save his life—for the moment, anyhow. Instead of plowing into his heart or lungs, or smashing his spinal column, that little .31-caliber ball from Price's lightweight, sawed-off, five-shot Wells Fargo Colt slammed into Ethan's left shoulder.

Now .31 caliber was the second smallest and lightest revolver ammunition made, being, actually, only a trifle heavier than a .22, so its impact, while enough to spin Ethan half around and make him drop the Winchester, was insufficient to down a man as tall and strong as Ethan Lovejoy was. What it did do, however, was render the problem that he'd been worrying over for the past two days—that is, whether the Winchester's miserable rimfire ammunition was going to fire or not—academic. Feeling the numbing shock, the white fire tearing through his shoulder, Ethan knew he wasn't going to be able to fire his rifle at all now, and for some considerable time into the future. If he had any future, which was extremely doubtful at that dismal moment.

So he hung there, bleakly facing—out of his stubborn Yankee pride —the man who was going to kill him, because, weaponless, wounded, and helpless, he had no way of stopping Price Andrews from doing exactly that.

There was one thing he wasn't going to do, and that one thing was to beg Price Andrews to spare his life. So he stood there with his mouth clamped shut into a granite line, glaring at Price out of his pale, bleak, fierce eyes.

That glare unnerved the gambler, rattled him even more than he already was at the realization that his first shot had not killed his adversary. So he did the worst possible thing he could have done: he dropped into a gunslinger's crouch and started to fan the hammer of his revolver with the palm of his left hand, which was an excellent way of getting off a series of shots in the least possible elapsed time, and was even effective enough if you were shooting it out across a card table against a man who had caught you ringing in a marked deck out of a spring-loaded sleeve cuff, but that guaranteed that you wouldn't hit the broadside of a bright red-painted barn if you were the twenty-five feet away from said bright red-painted barn that Price was from Ethan Lovejoy.

At that, Price was lucky: one of the four remaining shots he had in his elegant little gambler's hideout gun did hit Ethan, low in the fleshy part of his left side at waist level, but so far out that the bullet missed all his vital organs. What it did do, however, was to bleed like hell. And to down Ethan Lovejoy finally, as big and strong as he was.

But Price wasn't even looking at his fallen foe by then. He was standing there, eyes and mouth stretched wide, staring at, recognizing his own doom, the finish of his miserable life.

Ethan came up then, forced himself up on one knee, and stared in the same direction that Price was looking. Saw what Price was looking at. What—or rather whom—everybody was by then: Hilda Müller. She was standing there exactly as Queen Agave in Euripides' *The Bacchae* must have stood in ecstasy, holding the severed head of her son Pentheus. Only what Hilda held wasn't little Gretchen's head, but her largely headless body. Gretchen was—had been!—a beautiful child: spring snow and pale gold and dogwood pink like a *Mädchen-kind* out of a poem by Heinrich Heine: *"Du bist wie eine Blume/ So hold und schön und rein. . . ."* That is she was—had been!—like a blossom until the exact moment that one of Price Andrews's bullets, flying wild, entered her half-open rosebud of a mouth, crashed upward through the roof of it, mushrooming as it went, lifting the top of her skull—blond curls and all—completely off her small head, and splashed her brains like gray pink mush into her mother's face.

Ethan hung there, staring at that. And understanding at last what was wrong with the Elizabethan, even Shakespearian, concept of tragedy that had nourished his own philosophical perceptions his whole life long: that it only approached the outer limits of the human apprehension of horror, never crossed them, dwelt forever beyond them, as the ancient Greeks did. And that Aeschylus, Sophocles, and Euripides got it right: Man is the plaything of heartless Gods, and his merits or his lack of them, the good in him or the evil, his nobility or his vileness have nothing to do with his ultimate fate whatsoever.

He took a tottering step toward Hilda Müller. Another. Fell like a towering oak axed through, face down upon the earth. Lay there like a fallen titan. Tried to lift his head. He could not. Black-winged night, wind-driven from the Aeolian caves, crashed down upon him through the howling, roaring dark.

Through it, high, shrill, terrible, he heard Hilda Müller scream.

23

When Ethan Lovejoy came back into consciousness and time, he saw that he was back in his hotel room at the Old Munger House, and that Dr. Thomas Halston, the physician who had sewed Nora up like an empty sack after she had slashed both wrists and her throat in Gashouse Gertie's parlor house, was bending over him. At the doctor's side was Alexander Wilkes, Wichita's city marshal. The only trouble was that while Ethan could see them, at least in blurry outline, and hear them very clearly, he couldn't talk to them. He was far too weak.

"Think he'll pull through, Doc?" the marshal said.

"Why, shore, Marshal. These here rawboned fellas whose meat is all whipcord 'n sinew are mighty tough, I kind tell you that. By rights, he oughta be dead by now, considering how much blood he's done lost. The fact that he ain't, proves he's a-gonna live. Be a mite puny fur th next five o' six months, but after that he'll be as good as new . . ."

"Glad to hear it," the marshal said; "Strikes me as a mighty decent fella, this here Lovejoy. He took care of thet pore li'l critter what carved herself up in Gert's place as tender as a woman would've. Reckon this here fracas musta been over her, 'cause I done found out that there gambling polecat who's decorating thet lamp post in front o' The First and Last Chance was th fella what brung her here in the first place. Married th pore li'l trustin' gal without botherin' t' mention thet he's already got a wife 'n three kids in St. Joe."

"How th hell d'*you* know that, Alex?" the doctor said.

"This'un told me. Lovejoy, I mean. But afterward I checked. Axed Gert. 'Why, hell, yes, Marshal,' she allows, 'Price is got a woman in St. Joe—'n reckon thet there weddin' wuz legal, 'cause her pappy laid down a scatter-gun on thet lyin', cheatin' dawg.' So Lovejoy was tellin' th truth. 'Course I ain't got no way o' checkin' on his claim thet Price fed li'l Nory —thet's the pore abused li'l filly's name—some knockout drops in her cawfee 'n sold her t' Gert like a tender side o' heifer while she wuz daid to th world . . ."

"I believe it," Dr. Halston said; "knowin' Gert—and Price Andrews

—I know there ain't *nothing* the two of 'em wouldn't do, not if it's puking rotten, that is . . ."

"Me, too. You done sent for Gwen to sit wit him, Doc?"

"Yep. She'll be here pretty soon. She's tendin' a woman who's birthin' a brat over in that pore section 'twixt the railroad 'n th drainage canal. Sent me word she'd come over soon as she got through. Anyhow, I'll stay with him 'til she gits here. I ain't got no patient real bad off at the moment. So, if you wants to git along, do it, Alex. . . . Reckon you got to tend to cuttin' Price's mangy carcass down off that there lamp post, ain't you?"

"Naw. Let him hang there. 'Til furst dark, enyhow. A furst-class, justifiable lynchin' is good for this here town's soul. Reckon them fellas done pumped 'bout forty pounds o' lead into him by now. Pointed out to 'em they wuz only wastin' ammunition since he's shore Lawd daid 'n gone. So they done quit riddlin' him wit bullets. When I left th scene they wuz throwin' horse 'n mule shit at him. Kinda fittin', ain't it? Wal, reckon I'll mosey along. Gotta send a couple o' telegrams . . ."

"Lord God, Alex—to who?" Dr. Halston said.

"Friends o' hisn. Lovejoy's, I mean. Banker fella in Abilene. Farmer outside o' town. 'N her. Li'l Nory. Seems like our friend here didn't trust his luck. Had a note all writ 'n tucked into his billfold statin' who wuz to be notified if Price won thet there friendly li'l disagreement. He wuz right. His luck wuz mighty bad, wuzn't?"

"Naw. Hell, naw. It wuz plumb, downright *good.* He ain't daid, 'n he's gonna live. 'Sides, he wuz lucky in another way. Him bein' gutshot 'n down kept them fellas from lynchin' him 'long wit Price. After all, they could've figgered that since he staged a gunfight with that pukin' polecat, he wuz damn nigh as guilty o' that pore baby's death as Price wuz . . ."

"Only he *didn't,* Doc," Marshal Wilkes drawled; "Price shot him in th back. He never even got to fire a shot. 'N th only reason he wasn't kilt outright wuz thet pore li'l German lady warned him. In Dutch. But he musta understood her 'cause he whirled around in time to make Price miss his heart o' his lights. Thet wuz whut got the good citizens o' Wichita so wild. They thinks Price shot at th pore woman cause she warned Lovejoy, missed, 'n hit th baby . . ."

"Do you?" Doctor Halston asked the marshal.

"Naw. Eyewitnesses swear he was hammer-fannin' his shootin' iron. 'N you cain't hit *nothin',* hammer fannin'. You's lucky to hit anything wit a six-gun even when you aims th damn things. Wal now, I better be gettin' along. Sit tight, Doc; be seein' yuh . . ."

Ethan lay there, thinking about that. He was weaker than a baby, so the only thing that was clear to him was the evident fact that Price Andrews was dead, and that he had died very badly. And it came to Ethan Lovejoy that, strangely enough, he wasn't glad. Because, as it nearly always was, the price of accomplished justice was too high: an innocent little girl's life. He thought: 'I'll have to find that woman, do something for her.' Then he said a little silent prayer: 'Dear God, if you can find it in your heart to forgive Price Andrews, I do, too. He could no more help being what he was than any of the rest of us can help being what we are. And I ask your pardon for my part in it. Gather that little child unto your bosom, for I killed her almost as much as Price did. But since neither one of us meant to, grant both of us—absolution—and mercy, Good Kind Lord . . .'

Which proved, if anything, that sinner though he was, Ethan Lovejoy was also a Christian. And about as close to being a real one as people ever get.

After that, he sank back down into the Cave of the Winds, into whistling, howling night.

When he came back again—this time to stay, he realized—his side and his shoulder ached him terribly, but the pain was well within the degree of physical anguish that he was capable of bearing. Then, as he turned his head toward the window, he saw that it wasn't Gwen Burton —the midwife and occasional nurse who had been there at the brief flickering intervals when he'd managed to push his eyelids upward against ten tons of solid darkness, the crushing weight of utter night—who sat there beside him, but Nora.

Only she looked so funny. And in both senses: funny, strange; and funny, comical. For one thing, she hadn't any hair, and her shapely little cranium was rosy pink, in the morning light. For another, she stank like hell. Then he realized that her smell wasn't of unwashed female flesh, but rather a sickening chemical odor. And lifting his big, truncated beak and sniffing the air, he identified that stench: it was a combination of coal oil, that is, kerosene, and tar.

"Nora—" he croaked; "Nora, baby—"

She whirled, sprang up from her chair, and dropped to her knees beside the bed. He could see lines of glistening black in the creases of her neck and along the edges of the ridged scar tissue that marked the place where she'd cut her throat with that piece of window glass.

He put out a trembling, all gone hand, and touched those black lines. They felt sticky.

She caught his big paw, turned it palm up, and ground her pale lips against it in an agony of tenderness, tracing little warm wet circles against it with her tongue tip.

'If there's a method to revive the dead she's found it,' Ethan thought. He said, forcing the words out over the green tides in his throat:

"Nora—sweetheart—your—your hair! And—and—"

"They caught me—at the station," she whispered; "The—the women, Ethan. I think the—telegrapher must have told somebody you'd wired—for me, because they were there waiting for me when I got off the train. One of them called out, 'There's the filthy little whore what was the cause of it all!' Then—they jumped me. They used—buggy whips on me. Umbrellas. Their feet. I'm black and blue all over. I can hardly move. One of 'em went into the barber shop down by the station, came out with the barber. I think she must have been—his wife, because he didn't dare not do what they ordered him to. 'Cut all her hair off!' they yelled; 'Shave her head! Le's see how pretty you horny varmints will think she is when she's bald as an egg!' That one way, I was—lucky . . ."

"Lucky?" Ethan croaked.

"Yes. If they had tried to do it themselves, they'd have cut me pretty badly, Ethan. And he—was sorry. Whispered in my ear: 'Pardon me, honey. But these here witches will wreck my shop effen I don't . . .'"

"Poor baby. Then what happened, my dear?"

"They—tore my clothes off me. They did leave me—my drawers and stockings on, but that was all. Then they—painted me with tar. Hot tar, Ethan. Fortunately it wasn't hot enough to take all the skin off me. They broke into the railroad's warehouse to get the tar. But they brought the feathers themselves. I'll bet there isn't a pillow case left intact in town . . ."

"Baby, I'm sorry," he groaned.

She stared at him, and the tears rolled down her face.

"The tar didn't hurt much. The kerosene Mrs. Burton used to get it off hurt worse. My skin is all red from it. Marshal Wilkes told her to do that. Use kerosene, I mean. After he'd finally got me away from those women. They threw—horse droppings—at him—at me, while he was leading me away. This is one of Mrs. Burton's dresses I've got on. It's three sizes too big for me. They ripped my suitcase to pieces, poured coal oil and tar over my clothes, burned them. But that's enough about me. Ethan, you—you're all right, aren't you? Doctor Halston said you were. He told me that neither of your wounds is too bad, but that you'd lost too much blood by the time he got to you. So now I—I've got to take care of you,

until you get better. That is—if you want me to. If you wouldn't rather
—somebody else did it—"

"Somebody else?" Ethan husked.

The tears on her face became a flood. Her lips became a pale pinkish
blur they trembled so violently.

"Yes!" she stormed; "Whoever it was you were trying to kill Price
over! Because it wasn't me, Ethan! It wasn't me!"

"Nora, baby—" he whispered.

"Price hasn't been near me since he left me in Gertie's place!" she
wept. "Guess Gert told him—how—how—scarred-up—and ugly I am! So
—he knew—I—wasn't any good—for *that,* anymore. To make money for
him—on my back, Ethan Lovejoy! And that was the *only* thing about me
that interested him . . ."

Ethan stared at her. He didn't know what to say. There was, very
likely, nothing that could be said. Nothing that made any sense, anyhow.

"So," Nora whispered; "it—has to be—someone else. Another
woman. You neither drink—nor gamble. And if you'd wanted to—to get
even with him for what he—did to me, you'd have done it over a year ago.
Because *you* started that gunfight, Ethan. Marshal Wilkes knew how to
get in touch with me because of that note in your pocket and—"

"That note," Ethan said slowly, weakly; "that had *your* name in it,
Nora. Your address. Not—any other woman's, baby girl . . ."

"Oh!" Nora said. "Ethan—it makes no sense! None of it does!"

"Does anything in this world, baby?" Ethan said. "Listen—I—
haven't—much breath—for talking. Too—damned weak. But he—went
to—my house while I wasn't there—while I was with *you,* Nora—and
took—advantage of—Anne—"

"Anne!" Nora breathed, whispered, almost said; "And for *her,* you'd
kill him, Ethan—wouldn't you? For—your wife—in God's sight, and in
Man's. Not for—your kept mistress—your fancy woman—your—whore.
Oh, Ethan, aren't you going to leave me *any* reason to—to go on living?"

"Isn't that—I love you—enough?" he said.

"No! Because you don't! Because if you did, you'd have killed Price
last year, not this one!"

"I didn't kill him any year," Ethan sighed.

"I know. They were—just taking him down when I got here. Poor
Price! He didn't even look human any more. They'd beat him to death
even *before* they hanged him, the marshal says—"

"And—you're—sorry for him?" Ethan whispered.

"Of course. I loved him once, Ethan. Or else I shouldn't have married him. I know, I know; he lied to me. But *I* thought it was a marriage. I —am—*not* a loose woman, Ethan. Except—for *you.*"

"For me—you're—an angel, Nora," Ethan said.

"But you—killed a man—got him killed—over *Anne,*" she whispered.

"Yes. Only that's too simple, baby. Because—he took advantage of a—a madwoman, Nora. Because he defied *me*—violated my home. And because he—made my baby daughter stand there—and *watch* them while they were doing that . . ."

"Oh, no! No!" Nora said.

"Yes. The final straw that broke the camel's back. First—you. I—I didn't go after him then, because I was fool enough—vain enough—to believe that you couldn't—*wouldn't* have been able to—stand—bear—the news of my death. He was a lot better shot than I am, y' know. He'd killed six or seven men, I'm told. And the truth—the bitter truth is—I was afraid. I didn't want to die. Not with you—back in my life—making it so sweet, so sweet—"

"Oh, Ethan!" she wept.

"But what he did to Anne—was unpardonable. Not because it was *she;* but because—yes! because she was *my wife,* a fact he used to make the insult, the affront to my manhood so terrible. He committed sodomy upon her, Nora—forced or induced her to service him as—a probably willing—which makes it worse—fellatrice—"

"I—I don't know what that means, Ethan," Nora whispered.

"Just—as well. But you *do* know. It's a perversion—at least a semi-perversion—because I've never met—a fellow yet—who's tried it—had it done—for him—who didn't like it . . ."

"Oh. Oh—*that.* Ugggghhh! What I told him I'd kill myself before I'd do. Either—for him—or for any of—the men—he and Gert—were—selling me to . . ."

Ethan grinned at her. His grin was weak; but it was authentic. He could feel—life in him again, slow creeping, soft and warm along all his veins, his nerves.

"Renting—" he teased solemnly. "Because—they—couldn't sell you, baby girl. Nobody's—got—that much money. There isn't that much—in this—world . . ."

"You have," she said bitterly. "For you—I'm dirt cheap. Practically —gratis. I cost you—only an occasional visit. The price of a railroad ticket. A—smile. A—honeyed word. That you don't even mean. Because when you had to put—your life on the dotted line, sign it away, it wasn't for me, Ethan. It wasn't for—me . . ."

He stared at her. He'd thought she had got past the worse of that, but now he saw she hadn't. He said:

"D'you—mean to—leave me, Nora?"

"Yes," she said. "I mean to leave you—forever. I—only ask one thing of you, Ethan . . ."

"Which is?" he croaked.

"That—you'll come to the cemetery—once in a while—and put some flowers on—my grave . . ."

"Oh, Jesus!" he moaned. He was too weak to stand that, to bear the awful fear that she very probably meant it. His eyes went scalded, blind, poured pure anguish down his craggy, bony face.

At once she came up off her knees and threw herself upon his supine body; her arms wrapped themselves around his neck and almost strangled him; she was kissing his eyes, his mouth, his throat, which stung terribly because her lips were still rank with the kerosene Gwen Burton had used to get the tar off her, and the smell of both substances—which would take weeks of daily baths to remove from the pores of her skin finally—rising from her warm young body was enough to asphyxiate a goat, while her weight, slight as it was, was plenty sufficient to make the pain from his wounds go past the bearable into the unbearable. Despite himself, he groaned.

"Oh!" she gasped; "I—I've hurt you! Oh, Ethan darling, I am so sorry!"

"I'm a mighty beat-up old party," he sighed; "So beat-up that I don't think—I could—survive—being without you, Nora. So—I'm appealing to —your generosity—your better nature. Being—a half orphan—with a— crazy mother—is a hell of a thing to wish off on—a baby girl . . ."

"That's not—the way to go about it, Ethan," she said quietly. "Keeping me with you, I mean. Keeping me alive, and in this cruel world with you, really. For being without you is—would be—a death sentence, my dearest. I—I wouldn't *have* to do anything to myself. Without you, I'd just die. As a flower does when it's deprived of sunlight—"

"Then how do I go about it?" he whispered.

"Say—'I love you, Nora.' And—mean it. That's all it takes. That's all it's ever taken. Or ever will, until the day I die."

He whispered:

"I love you, Nora. And if you—don't *know* I mean it, you're the biggest female fool—who ever drew breath . . ."

"I can be pretty silly, sometimes," she sighed; "but generally it's over you. Ethan—couldn't you—send her away? She—she's a menace. She's—destroying—your child. She almost got you killed—She—"

"Had nothing to do with it. My own—irrationality did. Wounded male pride. He—he'd carved his initials into her living flesh—branded her like a heifer. And I—wasn't big enough—man enough—to take that. Or all the other ways—he'd displayed his contempt for me. So I sank to his level—of brutishness, of rage. And that's what nearly got me killed, Nora —not Anne . . ."

"But you *will* send her away, won't you? For *me?* For *us?* So we can be together *all* the time. So we can make love *every* night, all night long until you give me the child I'm dying for! Oh, Ethan, please!"

He stared at her, and his eyes were grave and sorrowing.

"Nora, I can't," he said. "You don't know what an insane asylum's like. I do. I've had to get her out of the one at Osawatomie once before. It's just too cruel. It would—ultimately—destroy—our happiness—to buy it at such a price—"

"Even if—the alternative is—losing—me?" she whispered.

"Even if the alternative is death—which is the exact equivalent of losing you. A slow death, perhaps; a sinking into madness and despair. But a sure one, baby girl. That I couldn't live without you is as certain as that the sun's going to rise tomorrow . . ."

She stared at him, and her eyes matched his own in bleakness, pain. Overmatched them in bitterness, by far.

"All right," she said; "You win, Ethan. I'll go on being—your—fancy woman. The dollbaby, toy, you keep in the back streets of your life. My —shame—will probably kill me one day. But giving you up would kill me here and now. So I'll—take what I can, for as long as I can. . . . What choice have I? What other alternative have you left me?"

"Oh, Nora! Nora!" he wept.

She put her arms around his neck, and cried, too. The two of them lay together like that, mingling their tears. Love is far from a happy thing, which is why wise men and women avoid it like the plague.

But Ethan and his Nora were anything but wise.

24

"But, of course, Ethan! I'll be only too pleased to act as your agent in any matter within my powers while you're laid up," Bernard Warkentin said. "And yes, there is some excellent wheat-growing land out near my place at Halstead. Do you want me to purchase some acreage in that region for you?"

"Not just some acreage, a whole farm," Ethan said gruffly. "A full section, six hundred forty acres. Equip it: seed, plows, a harvester–self-binder, a thresher, draft animals, cows, pigs, chickens. Build the necessary barns on it, silos. And a house. A *frame* house, Bernard. Dig a well. Hell, *drill* a well if you have to. The water table can be several hundred feet down, this far south. Put a windmill-driven pump in that well. Hire some hands—preferably some of your own Mennonite immigrants to get a crop of winter wheat in the ground right now—it'll be September in another week. A tall order. Think you can manage all that, my friend?"

"Of course," Warkentin said. "It only requires time and money, Ethan. You've got the money, and I have the time. . . ." He glanced at the small, slight, too silent woman who sat across the hotel room from them, near the window. She wore a sort of turban of bright printed cloth around her small and shapely head. Bernard Warkentin knew perfectly well why she wore that peculiar headcovering even inside that room. The *Wichita Eagle,* like all Western, pioneer newspapers, wasn't given to calling a spade "an instrument of husbandry." Of course, given the reticences of that epoch, the newspaper had referred to her as "a former Cyprian" instead of as a whore. Which was six of one, half a dozen of the other, Warkentin thought.

Her presence made the cultured German-American uneasy. He was, after all, a Mennonite, and that sect, as all Kansas knew by then, had the strictest code of sexual morality of any Christian community whatsoever. He had never been in the same building, not to mention in the same room with a woman of easy virtue before in all his life—not knowingly, anyhow.

But she was—very clearly—Ethan Lovejoy's woman, so he had to accommodate himself to her presence. He found that fact, that a man like

Lovejoy—whom he'd got to know very well on their voyage together to Russia, when he had succeeded in persuading several hundreds of his coreligionists to immigrate to Kansas, and Lovejoy had succeeded in buying all the Turkey Red wheat seed he'd wanted—had a kept mistress, exceedingly strange. One of the reasons they had got along so well, had become, in fact, fast friends, had been that Ethan Lovejoy's uprightness, his code of morality, matched Bernard Warkentin's own. But there it was. If Lovejoy wanted to explain the circumstances surrounding this—in him —aberrant behavior, he would listen respectfully and politely. But he wouldn't ask. The matter simply wasn't any of his business. He said:

"All right. I'll look around and let you know in two or three days. Do you want to give me any idea as to how much you're prepared to pay? A good place—especially the one I've got in mind—might come fairly high, Ethan . . ."

Instead of answering, Ethan turned to the young woman.

"Nora, honey," he said; "bring me that inkwell and pen off the secretary over there. And in the pocket of my coat, you'll find my checkbook. Bring it, too."

"All right, Ethan," Nora said.

Her voice, Warkentin noted, was low and sweet. Slightly husky, though. And though he really couldn't tell from the few words that she had uttered, it seemed a very cultivated voice. In fact, nothing about her fitted the railroads' immigrant agent's idea of a prostitute.

'Her face—why, it's positively angelic . . .' he thought.

"Push that table over here close to the bed, baby," Ethan said; "I'd thought I'd have got a little of my strength back by now, but—"

"No," Bernard Warkentin said; "Allow me to, miss—"

"Thank you," Nora said icily; "but I can manage very well, Mister Warkentin. Besides, if you touch anything that—an outcast, an untouchable like me has touched, you'd have to go and wash your hands, wouldn't you?"

"Nora!" Ethan thundered.

"I'm sorry, Ethan," she said firmly; "but one of the things you've always insisted upon is that I must respect myself, even within the unfortunate circumstances that I find myself in—or have been reduced to— against my will, and through no fault of my own. So I'm not prepared to be looked at as though I were—dirt. No, offal."

"Nora," Ethan sighed; "Bernard doesn't *know* the special circumstances that are involved in our relationship. All he knows—or thinks he does—is what the *Wichita Eagle* wrote about Price Andrews's death and —our connection with it. I haven't had time to explain it to him. And I didn't want to, before you. There's something, well, intrinsically offensive —and to the woman being so defended—in a man's having to vindicate a woman's presence, her person, and her honor before her very face. Especially when that woman needs neither defense nor vindication, as you don't, my dear . . ."

"Miss—Curtiss, I believe? Or is it Mrs. Andrews?" Bernard Warkentin said; "No matter! In either case I assure you it was not my intention to offend you in any way. And if I have—even unwittingly—I apologize, most humbly . . ."

"All right," Nora said; "I accept your apology, Mr. Warkentin, and offer you mine in my turn. I—I'm not usually so—snappish. But these last few days have been a terrible strain. I'd gladly leave you and Ethan alone to talk, if I could. But since in this enlightened and civilized state of ours, people feel perfectly free to—physically assault a person—whose behavior they don't approve of, I can't even go down to the lobby without running the risk—or rather the near certainty—of being insulted, at the very least. And if I were to go for a walk, I'd need Marshal Wilkes and four or five of his deputies to protect my very life. So—try to put up with—my presence. I never try to influence Ethan in any decision he may take. And I couldn't if I wanted to. He knows I love him more than I do my life, or my—formerly, anyhow!—sacred honor. And that makes me absolutely helpless . . ."

"Now, baby!" Ethan groaned.

"Here's your table, Ethan!" Nora said. Then she flounced over to her chair, turned it away from them so that it faced the window. Then she sat down, with her back toward the two of them.

"Women!" Ethan said.

"If they weren't occasionally—difficult—I suspect we wouldn't find them so—enchanting," Bernard Warkentin said; "It's part of their special charm . . ."

Ethan leaned over the table and wrote in the checkbook. Then he tore out the check and handed it to Warkentin.

"But—but—" Warkentin said; "You've signed and dated this, but you haven't put in the amount, Ethan—"

"I know. You fill in what the spread you choose is going to cost, Bernard," Ethan said. "Save us both time and trouble, that way. Now I'm going to write you another blank check for everything that farm is going to need to put it into operation. Including, of course, your own expenses, and your fee for acting as my agent. And your first step will be to register the farm at the Land Office here, free and clear, as the property of Mr. and Mrs. Hans Müller. You know who *they* are, don't you?"

"Lord, yes!" Bernard Warkentin said. "And, Ethan, permit me to say that this gesture—"

"Only I don't permit you to say it, Bernard," Ethan growled; "Not one goddamned word. Mrs. Müller saved my life—and it cost her her child to do it. So anything I could do for them is too little, anything at all, Bernard. Look—one more stipulation: Try to find them a place as close to yours as you can. They don't speak English, so they'll need your help for a good long time to come. I pay you the high compliment and the profound respect of not even having to ask you if you're willing to give it, because I know you are—"

"Perfectly!" Warkentin said.

"That's why I didn't just give them one of my sections outright," Ethan said. "*Deutsch* escapes me completely. So I'd be of no help to them, especially at the beginning, when they're going to need it . . ."

Bernard Warkentin smiled.

"*Du bist ein Mann, mein Freund,*" he said. "*Ein sehr guter, herrlicher Mann!*"

"Now you're taking unfair advantage, Bernard," Ethan sighed; "but let it go. Another thing: I'd just as soon that the Müllers don't know where their new farm came from. Let 'em think it was given by public subscription, or—"

Nora whirled in her chair.

"Oh, no!" she said; "I simply won't put up with that, Ethan Lovejoy! Mr. Warkentin—tell them. Please tell them. I want *somebody* else to know that he's the—gentleman—no! the angel and the saint *I* know he is. You see, my knowing it isn't enough any longer. I want *everybody* to. Because the next time one of your local witches calls him a whorehopper and an adulterer in my presence, I'm going to kill her, if I hang for it!"

"Now, now, baby wildcat, gentle down," Ethan chuckled. "And let me give you an idea, will you? People defend themselves—or their partners —out of weakness and doubt, never out of strength and security. So when you unsheath your claws, arch your back, and start spitting like a she-cat, you're more than half agreeing with the accusations—"

"I am not!" Nora said; "I just don't want anybody hurting you, attacking you, saying—"

"Baby, my hide is solid granite. New England granite at that, which is the best. And, therefore, as in that children's verse: 'Sticks and stones may break my bones, but *words* can never harm me.' So quit getting so mad, will you? Unless *you* think I'm a whoremonger and an adulterer. Which reduces the whole matter to the same conclusion: if you think so, too, there's no argument; and if you don't, the discussion is still bootless, because trying to convince people that their wrongheaded opinions are senseless is the world's most futile business. If it could be done, there wouldn't be a church or a temple left standing anywhere on earth . . ."

"I've always thought that you were—a believer, Ethan," Bernard said in a troubled voice.

"I am," Ethan sighed. "But then I've never claimed not to be wrong-headed, Bernard. Proof of which is this combination pepper pot and one-woman bombshell, loaded with canister and grapeshot, sitting over there with her fuse cut short and spluttering. Fellows who get mixed-up with *any* kind of woman need their heads examined, but one who takes on a bad-tempered li'l critter like this one, well—"

"Why, Ethan Lovejoy!" Nora cried. Then she saw how he was grinning at her, how peaceful his face was, how filled with blissful contentment. She crossed swiftly toward where he lay, bent and kissed his mouth. When she straightened up, there were tears in her eyes, but she was smiling.

"Forgive me, Mr. Warkentin, but I had to do that. He just paid me the finest compliment I've ever had in all my life," she said.

"Nora," Ethan said gravely; "D'you mind if I explain our situation a little to Bernard? He's my friend, and therefore, by extension, yours. I think he's entitled—if he's going to act for me in this, and other matters with a peaceful mind—to know a little straighter version than the press with its love for sensationalism will ever give him . . ."

"No," Nora said; "I don't mind, Ethan. In fact, you've got to. It's —unkind to keep him feeling so—besmirched, polluted, contaminated by the presence of a—demimondaine—like me. Go ahead. But I'm going to sit in that chair, with my back turned, and my fingers stuffed into both my ears so I won't even be tempted to interrupt, correct, or contradict what you're saying!"

"You really are a pepper pot, aren't you, my dear?" Warkentin said with a wry chuckle. "Ethan, you have absolutely no reason, nor any need to explain anything to me . . ."

"Oh, yes, I do," Ethan said. And did.

"I see," Bernard Warkentin said sadly. "But may I complain that you've left me a badly troubled man, my friend? One of the strengths of our Mennonite faith is its extreme simplicity, which leaves one with the feeling—that you've demonstrated to me just now to be an illusion—that we have the right answers to every contingency. A comfortable position to take, and hold. But you've certainly—if not shattered it—dented it badly. I'm just not prepared to handle a situation like this, nor even to absorb it into my philosophy, really. A mad wife from whom separation or divorce is not possible. A woman—a good woman—whom quite naturally you love—violated not only in her person, but in the very chastity and decency of her wifehood. What a monstrosity! A man like Andrews is—was—unbelievable!"

"No—just pitiful," Ethan said. "A man who didn't know—and apparently didn't care—what he had in Nora, deserved compassion, not scorn. So, if you'll grant us an understandable degree of human frailty, a lack of the capacity for—sainthood—and especially for a kind of martyrdom that's likely to be prolonged lifelong, we'd be very honored, my friend. Because—the lions, the cross, the fiery stake, all the tortures that heathen and pagan could invent, were relatively quick. Nobody was asked to endure them for thirty or forty years . . ."

" 'Let him who is without sin among you,' " Bernard Warkentin quoted, and put out his hand to Ethan. They shook hands, gripping hard. Then the Mennonite leader turned to where Nora sat and extended his hand to her as well.

She stared at it stonily, made no move to take it.

"Please," Warkentine said; "Your friendship would honor me, my dear . . ."

Slowly, shyly, Nora offered her hand to Ethan's friend. But instead of shaking it, Bernard Warkentin raised it, almost reverently, to his lips.

It was exactly ten minutes after that, that they again heard someone knocking on the door.

Ethan nodded to Nora, seeing her troubled face, her eyes.

"Open it," he said; "It'll only be Doc Halston or the marshal. The Broomstick Wranglers or the Necktie Party Boys wouldn't knock. They'd kick the door down and bust on in . . ."

But it was neither the doctor nor the town marshal. When Nora opened that door—with wildly trembling hands—Ned Tyler stood there, more than a little sheepishly. Behind him was Phil Harris.

"The Rapid Dans!" Ethan roared; "The Greased Chain Lightning Boys! The speed you two rode to my rescue has left me breathless. What did you come by, Donkey Express?"

"Now jes' you hold on there, Eth!" Phil said; "There's a damn good reason we'un took so long—or a damn bad one, depending on yore point o' view. Howdy, Nora, honey! Don't yore Uncle Phil rate a measly li'l ol' kiss?"

"All right," Nora said mischievously; "Only that there will cost you foldin' money, pard! Don't you read the *Eagle?* I'm—politely!—'a former Cyprian'—so *my* kisses are for sale! What am I offered, gentlemen?"

"Honey, we ain't got that much money," Ned said; " 'Cause a kiss of yourn is a ruby beyond all price. Lord God, but you get prettier every year that goes by!"

"Even—with my clothes on, Ned?" Nora said bitterly.

"Now, Nora—you know damn well I didn't know that Gert's extra special treat wuz going to be *you,* baby girl. 'N that there sight plumb broke my heart, 'n busted my wind to boot—"

"Not to mention turning your stomach," Nora said.

"Nora, for God's sake!" Ethan said.

" 'Twuz my own shame what done that, honey," Ned sighed. "At my age I oughta've quit bein' a horny ol' varmint years ago. But I ain't. 'Tis th nature o' th beast, I reckon. Eth, I must say you're lookin' great, by which I mean you've got a ree-mark-able resemblance to sumpin' th cat done throwed up on th parlor rug. But that'll pass, I reckon . . ."

"We brung up a bottle o' drinkin' whiskey," Phil said. "You allowed to have any, Ol' Hoss?"

"He is *not!*" Nora said in her most wifely tone.

"Wal now, honey," Phil said; "Hope you doan mind effen Ned 'n me toss down a couple, d'you? 'Cause we'uns *need* it, considerin' what we's got to explain to this here longtall well-ventilated piece o' Swiss cheese. Lawd Gawd, Eth, didn't th Rebs punch enough holes in yore carcass to suit you? Howcome you had t'go out 'n collect yoreself some more?"

"Didn't," Ethan said; "What I set out to do was to perforate Price Andrews. Only he got the jump on me. I was fool enough to think he'd fight fair. Should have known better. Sit down, will you, fellows? Nora, there're a couple of glasses over there on the chest of drawers, aren't there?"

"Yes," Nora said; "only they're—awfully dirty, darling."

"Don't make no nevermind," Phil said; "this here stuff will dissolve a gun barrel let alone a germ o' two . . ."

Nora brought the glasses. Phil poured enough in them to have floored a medium-sized ox. Raised his high.

"Here's lookin' at you, Ol' Hoss!" he said.

"Phil—Ned—what's wrong?" Ethan whispered; "Because something is. I see that now—"

"There shore Lawd is," Ned groaned; "But before we goes into that, I'd kind o' appreciate it effen you'd tell me why th hell you went gunnin' for Price. Phil allows *he* knows, but he's done clammed up on me. Says he don't want to be guilty o' spreadin' thet kind o' dirt around. Doan tell me that gamblin' skunk went to Topeka 'n busted in on li'l Nora, here?"

"No," Nora said with aching bitterness; "I—I'm not that important, Ned. Ethan would never have tried to kill him over anything so—inconsequential as—that. Rather—Price went out to the Lovejoy manse and busted in on dear, sweet Anne!"

"Nora," Ethan said sadly; "You're making me—unhappy now. As always when you tarnish the image I have of you, my dear."

"That image is false!" she said angrily; "I'm not the sweet, silly schoolgirl who loved you, Ethan. I'm a mean, bitchy she-cat of a woman who—adores you. Who is jealous of everything and anyone who comes between me and my total possession of you. Who's prepared to pull hair, claw out eyes, even—kill—any woman who tries to take you away from me. Including—Anne. Maybe especially Anne, who holds you through pity, not love. Because God knows she doesn't deserve you, the randy, rabid bitch!"

"Jesus!" Ned whispered; "That plumb explains it—some of it, anyhow. Look, Eth—is it too much to ask you what Andrews done that made you feel you had to kill him?"

"Tell them!" Nora spat. "Or else I will, Ethan Lovejoy! And you might not like my version of the story. Or the cathouse inmate's vocabulary I'd express it in."

"Nora," Ethan drawled; "remind me to paddle your little bottom when I get my strength back, will you? All right, fellows, here goes . . ."

"Jesus, Jesus, Jesus!" Phil said, when he'd finished it. "D'you reckon you'll ever be able to git *seein'* that outta that pore baby child's mind, Eth?"

"Those baby *children's* minds," Ethan corrected him. "Tawiyela

Atkins saw it, too, witnessed that—exhibition. I doubt it. That damage is likely to be—permanent. Just as—the hurt done to *this* poor child's mind and spirit at sweet sixteen seems to have been. All right, it's your turn now. Tell me what's happened. Why do the two of you look like death lightly warmed over, as Cora Atkins used to say?"

"Hit's Anne," Phil sighed; "She's done turned violent, Eth. Real violent. 'N it don't look like she's a-gonna snap out of it this time. She's been ravin' ever since you left. She tried to—knife li'l Martha Anne and li'l Doe Child Atkins, both—"

"Lord God!" Ethan said.

" 'N when Ruth Quindaro and Cindy Otis got that knife away from her between 'em—and they got cut up pretty bad, th both of 'em, doin' it, too—'n axed her why, she said: 'Tell Jason that when he went to Glauke, he shouldn't have left his children with Medea.' Now what sense do *that* make, Ethan?"

"Very perfect sense," Ethan said, his voice drowning, out of sound; "but don't ask me to explain it, now—"

"Why not?" Nora said sharply.

"Because I can't. Not really," Ethan said. "Remember how I was always quoting Shakespeare to you kids in school, my dear? Well—after Anne lost her mind—I moved out beyond Shakespeare, who, after all, was a reasonable man. Because I'd been forced to see that life isn't—reasonable. Nor human destiny, man's fate. And since, beyond Shakespeare, there're only the old Greeks, I went to them. Filled my bookcase with their plays—in translation. I have some Greek, but not enough to read them in the original. So—she was able to read them, too. Maybe she got even more out of them than I did. On the level of utter horror on which they forever dwell, she, in her madness, could apprehend them far better than I. So she did—and learned from them, too. That's what that reference to Euripides' *Medea* is all about . . ."

"Then them old boys was potty, too?" Ned said.

"Yes. No. Who knows? Maybe they recognized that all the world is mad, and that sanity's the exception. But, Lord God, get on with it! What happened after that?"

"Ruth locked her in the coal bin," Ned said; " 'N now from what you've done told us, I see where she got *that* idea. But crazy people get to be ten times stronger than they are when they're in their right minds. So Anne busted outta there, took a bullwhip, 'n druv th Otises off yore place. They come back after dark 'n got their things. Took a wagon and a team 'n druv away. Randy said he'd bring your wagon and your horses back soon as he could, and to tell you that they were going to a town called Nicodemus. Never heard of it, did you?"

"Yes," Ethan said; "It's an all-colored town founded by the 'Exodusers'—the ex-slaves who have been flocking into Kansas for the last year to get away from lynchers, Ku Kluxers, and Southerners in general. I suspect they'll be happier there. Because, Anne made them see hell, in spite of all I could do—"

"Funny. She wuz a Yankee jes' like you, wasn't she?" Phil said.

"But she couldn't stand Blacks. That feeling was visceral in her—and a part of her irrationality, I suppose. But then racism seems a built-in insanity of the white race. Go on, will you?"

"So Ruth locked her up ag'in," Phil went on; "but in her room this time. 'N took li'l Martha Anne to her own to sleep with her so that pore Anne couldn't get at yore pore child even effen she did bust loose ag'in. 'N thet's just whut she done. Busted loose. 'N she sot yore house on fire, Ol Hoss. 'N being made outta *wood,* y'know—"

"And Martha Anne—Ruth—Anne, herself?" Ethan breathed.

"They all got out in time. 'Pears like killin' herself wasn't what pore Anne had on her mind, Eth—"

"Stop calling that murderous maniac 'poor Anne'!" Nora flared.

"Nora, please!" Ethan said.

"But all of a sudden, she changed her mind. Grabbed yore pore baby chile from Ruth 'n run straight back into thet burning house wit her—"

"God," Ethan moaned, "Oh God God God!"

"But thet there Ruth is part Injun 'n as brave as a Cheyenne warrior wit his sacred medicine bundle round his neck. You know them crazy buggers believes nothing kin harm 'em when they's got thet tied onto 'em 'n—"

"Yes, I do know that! Get on with it, Phil!"

"Ruth dashed straight into them flames. Hit Anne over th head with a dining room chair. Drug her 'n th pore baby out. Ruth got her arms 'n legs parboiled doin' thet; but d'you know Anne wuzn't hardly hurt or burnt none a-tall? Some hair off her head. A blister or two—"

"Oh, damn Ruth anyhow!" Nora said; "She should have left her there to roast!"

"Nora!" Ethan said.

"I'm sorry, Ethan. But she should have. Anne made that hell. Made her own funeral pyre. It would have been—poetic justice—for her to die in it. And it would have solved everything—you'd have been free. You and I—could have given—little Martha a normal, decent life—and our son— if we ever have one—would have been legitimate. But now—"

"The mixture as before. The gods' machine broke down. Left the useless old bastard hanging up there above the stage, unable to pass a kindly—or cruel miracle. As it always does. There're—no answers to anything in this life, baby girl. Nor any solutions . . ."

"Eth, Ol' Hoss—there's sumpin' else yet," Phil sighed. "Your kid, li'l Martha Anne, she got burnt real bad. Oh, no, she ain't in no danger o' dyin'. But th left side o' her pore li'l face is plumb ruint. 'N she wuz sich a pretty baby; but now—"

"But now," Nora said quietly; "She—a girl—a woman—to whom beauty is all important—has to grow up with one side of her face a puckered, red, scaley, twisted horror. Ethan, I told you to put that evil witch away! I told you!"

"Reckon you've plumb got to now," Ned Tyler sighed. " 'Cause this time thet pore woman ain't snapped out of her crazy spell. 'N don't look like she's going to, my friend. Doc Baines says she ain't. We've got her in the county jail, what never was designed for female occupancy. I brung the commitment papers with me—and you'll jes' have to pardon me, Eth, old buddy, but it looks like you ain't got no other out this time but to sign 'em . . ."

"Ned, for God's love! D'you know what Osawatomie is like?" Ethan grated.

"Yep, I know. It's pure hell. But, Eth—she ain't even conscious of her surroundings. She won't suffer none a-tall. And loose, she's a danger to her ownself, to yore pore baby, to you—"

"And to—me," Nora said flatly. "Because I'm not going back to Topeka, Ethan. I'm staying with you, from here on in. You can't make me go. I refuse to leave you. I'm going to live with you until one of us dies. And if you go first, I'm going to enshrine your memory in my heart, and worship it, and you—forever . . ."

"Nora, for God's love!"

"No, Ethan, for yours. I swear that by God, and in the presence of these witnesses. Now, sign that paper, will you?"

"Nora—I won't be able to divorce her, y'know. Ned, what does the law say about that?"

"I ain't sure. Never had a Bill of Divorcement case with alleged insanity as th grounds. 'Pears to me that th law establishes a waiting period to make sure the crazy partner ain't going to come to his or her senses. 'N that there waiting period is the same as in missing person cases, when death can be presumed after seven years. But, as I said, I ain't sure. I'll have to look it up in my law books 'n let you know. But one thing I am sure of, Eth, it ain't *less* than seven years . . ."

"You see, Nora?" Ethan said.

"I don't see. I don't particularly want to *marry* you, Ethan. I just want to live with you, sleep with you—or rather stay busily awake with you—and give you children. A son, anyhow. I love you. And that love is going to go on as long as I do. So what do the forms and the ceremonies matter? A pretty piece of paper with seals and ribbons on it won't make me any more yours than I am now. Nor a ring. Nor Reverend Brownley mumbling foolishly over the Bible. Stop evading the issue as usual, Ethan. Sign those papers."

"Nora—you'll be—a total outcast. We both will. People will swear I committed her to get her out of the way. You'll be a virtual prisoner in my house, unable to go anywhere; without friends; without—"

"I'll have you," Nora said; "Sign those papers, Ethan!"

Ethan stared at her. A long, slow, heart, breath, mind stopping time. Then:

"Give me—the inkwell and the pen, Nora. And you, the commitment papers, Ned," he said.

25

"Eth," Luke Prevost said; "Ned Tyler left word thet effen you got back to town today I wuz to ax you to stop by th bank . . ."

"All right, Luke," Ethan said. He put his valise in the back of his buckboard. Then reaching into his breast pocket, he came out with his billfold and paid Luke the three dollars he owed him for putting up the buckboard in the livery stable, and watering and feeding his team during the three days he had been gone. A dollar a day was all Luke charged for this service, and both of them considered the price eminently fair.

After that Ethan climbed up into the driver's seat and flapped the reins across the backs of his showy pair of black trotters. As he drove through the streets of Abilene toward the bank, he looked neither to the right nor to the left. That way he avoided embarrassing his ex-friends whose wives had forbidden them to even exchange a civil "Howdy" with him, and saved said wives themselves the trouble—or the pleasure—of ostentatiously turning their backs as he passed.

'This sure is a one-horse town,' he thought with grim humor; 'when nobody's been able to come up with a scandal that tops the one Nora and I have been providing the Hen Buzzards and Broomstick Wranglers with, in ten long years . . .'

Reaching the Abilene Citizens State Bank, he began to tie his somewhat frisky and nervous team to the hitching rail in front of it. As usual, he didn't even get to finish that simple task. An office boy came flying down the bank's marble steps, crying out breathlessly:

"Lemme do that for you, Mister Lovejoy!"

"All right, Joe," Ethan said; "And keep an eye on my valise while I'm in there, will you? That is if you haven't any weighty matters of high finance to occupy your attention this morning . . ."

"Well, sir, takin care o' th bank's important clients is part of my job," he said proudly; " 'N seein' as how you're *the* most important client we've got, reckon Mr. Tyler won't mind if I stay out here 'n watch your bag 'n your team, sir!"

"See that you do, instead of all the dainty ankles passing by," Ethan teased him solemnly, and went into the bank.

From their windows and cubbyholes, the clerks and tellers greeted him respectfully as he passed. Their wives might make the same feline noises about "That horny old varmint Eth Lovejoy—who's a-keepin' his pore sweet wife locked up in Osawatomie—course she *is* a wee bit loony, but not nowheres nigh as bad off as *he* claims—so he kin live in open sin with his fancy woman, and in his own house, too!" but said clerks and tellers knew just about the exact balance of his bank account, so the standing joke among them was: "Hell, he kin keep my old maid sister along with Nora Curtiss, he's got a mind to—long as he pushes a little of all that folding stuff he's got piled up my way!"

Ethan went into Ned's office. Ned jumped up, his florid face almost bisected with a grin, and put out his hand to Ethan.

Ethan took it, and the two of them shook hands. Ned made his usual joke about "seein whether a li'l o' yore luck won't rub off on me, Eth!"

"I'm—far from lucky, Ned," Ethan said sadly.

"That you ain't," Ned sighed; "Apart from money matters, that is. But that there ought to make up for most of yore problems, Eth. D'you know that you're the first honest-to-God millionaire this here bank ever had? Yore friend back East, Mister Willoughby—Mister Horace Willoughby—sent you another transfer whilst you was out o' town. Brings yore balance up to two million, five hundred thousand, eight hundred forty dollars and twenty-three cents . . ."

"You're cheating me," Ethan said solemnly; "that last figure ought to be a whole quarter."

"Jes wait 'til you see yore interest statement, Eth," Ned chuckled.

"Well, Ned, what did you want to see me about?" Ethan asked.

"Done told you: th new transfer. And to ax you about pore Anne, of course. How is she, Eth?"

"The same," Ethan sighed. "Actually my visits to Osawatomie are a waste of time. She no longer even recognizes me. Another case of a guilty conscience, Ned—I visit her because I feel obliged to . . ."

"How's—Nora, Eth?" Ned said then.

"Sad," Ethan said flatly. "She's had her heart set on replacing the son I lost—and by now she's practically given up hope. Next week we'll have been together—correction! we've been living in sin, to quote the Abilene Broomstick Wranglers Association—for ten long years. July 1878 to July 1888—and nothing. Could be my fault—I'm forty-nine years old, Ned, and a beat-up forty-nine at that. But since I *have* fathered children, she thinks it's hers. And that makes her unhappy. Very."

"Eth," Ned said, "it ain't none of my goddamned business, but why ain't you gone ahead 'n pushed a divorcement through the legislature, got shut o' pore Anne, 'n married li'l Nory? You kin now. Legally Anne's considered incurable . . ."

"Because Nora won't agree to my doing it," Ethan said; "If she ever finds herself with child, she'll allow me to legalize our relations in order to legitimize our offspring. But she's dead set against my knuckling under to public opinion that way. She swears she won't give the local gossips that much satisfaction. And, in a way, she's right. What difference would it make? Instead of whispering: 'There goes Eth Lovejoy with his whore; they're livin' in sin in his own house!' They'll mutter: 'There goes Eth Lovejoy 'n his whore. Heard tell they's married now. Fat lot o' good that does, after livin' in sin with her for ten long years!' "

"Tha's th truth, if I ever heard it," Ned sighed. "You know one thing, Eth? When I was a young'un, I set out to make a passel o' money. Done made it, too. Course I ain't on your level; but I'm doin' all right. And here we be, th two of us, in th same fix; we both got more money than we need —or know what to do with—and we both done found out it won't buy one thing that counts, not one goddamned thing! Tell me, effen somebody was to offer you anything you wanted at—say—a million bucks a throw —what would you ax for, Eth, boy?"

Ethan thought about that.

"Haven't enough money, Ned," he said quietly; "because I'd need *three* million, my friend . . ."

"Fur three things. Like what?"

"A son—for Nora. And yes, for me. A new face for my daughter, Martha Anne. And—a husband for Tawiyela Atkins—"

Ned stared at him.

"Them's good choices, Eth," he said; "Th best. A boy child to carry on yore name and line. A slight chance—a li'l old miserable teensie-weensie chance fur yore pore baby—I seen her face, Ethan. She showed it to me. She caught me a-starin' at her real curious-like, so she put her fingers in all that prutty brown hair she wears hangin' loose to hide the burnt up side o' her face and lifted it high so I could see—*that*. I ain't gonna lie. It's plumb horrible. I didn't know what to say to her, so I come out with, 'Heck, baby, it ain't *that* bad—' but she quirted her pony 'n rode away from there . . ."

"I know," Ethan said. "She's eighteen years old. A pretty—no—a *beautiful* girl, and that's not just paternal pride talking, Ned. Yet, because of her mother's—madness, she hasn't got a hope nor a prayer for happiness in this world. Nor has Tawiyela. *The* most stunning girl in the whole blame state. And she's going to be an old maid, because these damned ignorant clods think they'd be lowering themselves to marry— a 'breed. She hasn't a suitor. Of course she could have all the company she wanted, Ned, and from young and old, if she were willing to pay the price. But she isn't willing, bless her! She's a Kansa warrior's daughter, very nearly a princess in her own right, so she's not starting to allow herself to be pawed over, slobbered over by an oaf in every conceivable way her inferior, who'll calmly add to the physical injury involved the damned nigh deadly insult of assuming he's doing her a favor by lying with her because his unwashed, sweaty, filthy, pimply skin is white . . ."

"If I had a son, 'n he wanted to marry Tawi, I'd let him," Ned said.

"So would I, if I had one; but since neither of us does have one, her case is also hopeless," Ethan said.

When he got back to his farm, Ethan didn't drive immediately back to the huge—and hideously ugly, although he didn't know it was—Victorian Gothic mansion he had had built on the very spot where the chaste McIntire-style Salem house Anne had burned down had stood. Instead, on that mid-July day in 1888, he did what he often did: he sat in his buckboard and gazed out over his empire. From where he sat, he could see more than fifty harvester-binders crawling like huge, odd-shaped insects behind their four-horse teams, from horizon to horizon across the endless immensity of his fields. To his left, near his barns and silos, self-propelled, straw-burning steam engines thumped and thundered as they drove his threshing machines, having three years ago replaced the teams of twelve horses walking in circles attached to the long sweeps which had powered the threshers before the locomotivelike steam engines had become available. From the threshers themselves the winnowed grain poured in endless streams of gold into the sacks, that, on the morrow, would be wagon-borne to his own grist mill on the Smokey Hill River, and from there, rendered into the finest white flour, to the market to be sold.

He was forty-nine years old. He owned twelve thousand seven hundred acres of the best wheat-growing lands in this state of Kansas. He was one of the richest men in the Middle West, because, besides the bank account Ned Tyler knew about, he had others in the new metropolis of Kansas City, in St. Louis, and in Chicago—this last opened to receive his earnings from the Illinois Farm Machinery Manufactory he held a partnership in. He was getting richer every year.

But his life had stopped dead. And seemingly forever.

Looking up, he saw his eighteen-year-old daughter, Martha Anne, riding her pure-bred white Arabian gelding across the far edge of his enormous domain, as far away from him, or from anyone living, as she could get. He had no trouble recognizing Martha, even at that distance, not only because her mount was so visible, and so spectacular, but also because, as always, she wore her hair loose. After much experimentation, she and Nora, whom she accepted as her stepmother, had discovered that, if parted at an unusual angle, great masses of it could be made to fall in such a way as to completely hide the ravaged left side of her face. And since Martha Anne had inherited the serene loveliness of the Lovejoy women, instead of the Jeffreys plainness, she was a pleasure to look upon, except that, just as Ned Tyler had said that morning, whenever she caught any male gazing at her too insistently—even her own father—she'd push her long, slim fingers into that curtain of hair and deliberately expose the puckered, red, purplish whorls, ridges, and drawn parchment deadness that covered the whole left side of her face.

She was the second loneliest young woman in the entire county. The loneliest was, of course, Tawiyela Atkins—and for the reasons Ethan had pointed out to Ned that very morning. Tawiyela had discovered the cruel fact that every young woman of mixed racial ancestry—when, of course, one of her parents is a member of one of the darker races—in a country whose brutal, crassly insensitive racism and absolutely idiotic prejudices are unmatched anywhere else on earth, soon learns: she is not, and can never be, the object of honorable intentions; to the males of the race to which she only half belongs, she is very simply fair sexual game.

So at twenty years of age, the only masculine company Tawiyela had was still her gaunt, craggy, ugly, old "Uncle" Ethan Lovejoy. But now, as was almost inescapable under the circumstances, a new element had crept into their relations which made them—formerly a sunny, uncomplicated source of happiness to them both—tense, uncomfortable and a strain. Neither Ethan nor Tawiyela knew what to call, or recognized the nature of, this new element; but, of course, Ethan's darling Nora did.

"It's very simple, really," she drawled; "Dear Tawi secretly wants to kick this tired, wrinkled, graying, and—what's worse—*barren* thirty-eight-year-old hag out of your bed and crawl into it herself. If I were sure that the two of you would come up with a boy baby, and that afterward you'd keep *me,* and the two of you would let me keep *him,* I'd grant her the privilege. For as long as it takes for her to go green at the gills, and start up-chucking every morning, anyhow . . ."

"Still consider it—a privilege, my sweet?" Ethan teased her solemnly.

"It is. And the only activity that failing at—no, that's not right. For we don't fail at it, do we? Only to achieve its ultimate results. . . . So, correction: The only activity that failing to achieve its ultimate results, detracts not at all from the pleasure involved in the process. Ethan—I am sorry. Do forgive me, will you?"

"Lord God, Nora! For what?"

"For finishing off your family. For ending Clan Lovejoy's last possible chance of going on into the future . . ."

"Nora, you're only thirty-eight. And that—monthly business stops around forty-five, doesn't it? Forty-eight in some women. Old Doc Baines says he'd had one case where a woman gave birth—to her eighteenth child —at fifty-three. So don't give up hope yet, will you? It could still happen, and—"

"It could *not,* and you know it. Those Irishmen—damaged me too much. Or Price—or some of his gentle friends—probably gave me a dose of something awful. I'd take a trip to St. Louis and have a specialist examine me, except that I'm afraid to find out what I'm practically certain of, is so. Besides, I don't dare leave you alone around Pocahontas too long. You're very honorable and upright and so forth; but if a twenty-year-old Indian maid *that* blamed lovely were to jump all over you the way she's going to forget herself and *do* one of these fine days, you're just too damned male to put up much of a fight!"

"I would, though," Ethan said seriously; "To me that would be incest, pure and simple . . ."

"Not—simple. Not even—incest," Nora said drily; "And *anything* but pure! So, Ethan, old darling, you take care!"

So stood matters, and to such an impasse had his life come on that July day in 1888 as he sat in his buckboard as usual, gazing as usual out over the almost limitless sweep of his domain, and watching, quintessentially as usual, his daughter disappear over the rim of the horizon of his lonely empire of growing things.

Then he saw that light one-horse rig coming toward him. But it was still too far away for him to determine who the driver was. So since the buggy obviously was heading his way, and he'd soon see who the visitor was, he went back to worrying his head over a highly unusual circumstance: last night, for the first time in some fourteen years, he had dreamed about his brother Jonathan.

That troubled him, because he was convinced that somehow his dreams, especially those involving his dead twin, had the curious power of piercing the veil of the future, of foretelling coming events. There was no doubt at all that he had seen the Old Timer's death, and the quite horrible manner of it, some days before it actually happened. And, in that same dream, he had also seen Martha Anne's fire-ravaged face and neck long years in advance of that night of pure horror when Anne, in her madness, had tried to bear her daughter with her into her own improvised funeral pyre.

But then his dreams often failed him. Within the last five years, both his parents had died, leaving him a small fortune, ironically enough, after he had made a much greater fortune on his own. And their deaths had come within twenty-four hours of each other and without any warning at all. He had journeyed East to their funerals, taking Nora with him, and introducing her to his fellow mourners—who were only Horace and Edith Willoughby—as his wife. Young Horace Ethan Willoughby hadn't attended the funerals; he had been away at school, and either he hadn't wanted to come home, or Edith, for motives of her own, hadn't sent for him. There was, Ethan realized, no reason that she should have, for the elder Lovejoys were not the boy's grandparents, though he had been taught to address them as such as an affectionate courtesy.

Between Edith and Nora, it had been undeclared war at first sight. Ethan was far too grieved to realize just how flattering that was. But both of them restrained the hostilities to the level of frigid politeness. The only contretemps arose when Edith said sharply: *"Nora? But I thought you told me your wife's name was Anne?"*

Ethan was forced to fall back upon the ancient art of barefaced lying. He said without a qualm:

"Nora's my second wife, Edith. Anne died—some years ago . . ."

And on the train speeding them westward, home to Kansas, the battle between the sexes was brief and fierce, and poor Ethan lost.

"You," Nora declared flatly; "have been—to bed with that woman, Ethan!"

Ethan was too weary, too sick at heart to lie.

"Yes," he said; "twenty-two years ago. Just before I came out here. When I had yet to learn you were alive, my dear. A very long time, now. So forget it, will you?"

Nora stared at him. Then she sighed:

"All right. But I'm glad you took me with you, this trip. That was —very wise."

Nor had either he or Nora any warning of Ruth Quindaro's peaceful death the year before in her sleep. They'd both wept over her, because the old one-quarter-Wyandot woman had been a true part of their lives.

So now, sitting there in his buckboard, Ethan went over the disturbing features of this latest dream of his. The first of these was the fact that he had dreamed about his long-dead twin at all. For it seemed to him, that, in his last phantasmal reapparition, Jonathan had more or less promised not to trouble his sleep again. But now, thinking about his penultimate escape out of time and reality, all of fourteen years ago, just prior to the Old Timer's death at the hands of a Kiowa war party, Ethan realized that Jonathan had promised him nothing, that rather it had been he who had assumed—from his brother's peaceful aspect, from the fact that the physical horrors involved in his twin's death had no longer been visible upon the ghostly image—that Jon had forgiven him at last for his unwilling participation in it and would no longer cross eternity's dim frontiers to march eerily across his mind.

Yet last night's visitation had been stranger than any other. For the very first time Jonathan's image hadn't appeared in full cavalry uniform. Instead it had been robed in a toga of purest light, through which his brother's form, as handsome as a Phydian male nude statue, shone with a pagan god's serene majesty. And it had been unmutilated—complete— no shot-away jaw, bullet-blasted temple, shredded genitalia. In other words, though Ethan hadn't perceived anything resembling either the wings and halo of the Hebrew-Christian canon, Jonathan had seemed to be an angel.

'Which is stretching God's willingness to forgive outrageous sin to the breaking point,' Ethan thought. 'But, from the evidence, what do we know of the ways of the Almighty? Nothing—or even less. Not even that He really accepts our idea of Him, or our concepts of morality.' Then he heard the soft clipclop of that horse's hooves, the whir of wheels coming on, close now, almost at hand.

"Who're you," he said to the well-dressed, freckle-faced, appealingly ugly red-haired young man who drove that rented buggy.

"Why, Uncle Eth!" the young man laughed; "Don't you recognize me? I'm Martin, sir—Martin Harris. I've been home since I graduated in June; but I just couldn't think of an excuse to come out here before today. . . ."

"Who the hell told you that you needed an excuse, boy," Ethan said, and put out his hand to Phil Harris's youngest son.

"Well—" Martin said; "I know you've had a hard row to hoe, sir; and I didn't want to—intrude. Oh, heck, sir—you happen to be the man I most admire hereabouts, and—"

"A sentiment I thank you for, Mart," Ethan sighed; "but that it wouldn't be wise to express publicly. Reckon you know that, don't you, boy?"

"The heck with being wise, Uncle Eth," Martin said quietly, "I prefer being fair. You live with a good, sweet, decent woman you *can't* marry, because the circumstances just won't let you. There're sins and sins, and that there's a mighty small one, from where I sit. Pa and I are in perfect agreement over that—"

"Is your mother?" Ethan growled.

"Mama's a woman, sir, so she's got her reservations. But she's not all the way against you. It's just that she admired—your wife—an awful lot, and—"

"So did I," Ethan said; "But the Good Lord saw fit to take her away from me. For what's a living *body,* son, when it hasn't a mind in it?"

"You're right. Missus Lovejoy is just the same as dead, isn't she? By the way, here's a telegram for you, sir. I was at the telegraph office, sending off my umpteenth wire, trying to trace my steamer trunk that the train's baggage crew managed to *lose* for me—and between here and Manhattan at that, can you beat that for efficiency!—when this one came for you. Oh, yes, the telegrapher's messenger boy *was* there! Only I wasn't going to let that spoil the first good excuse I've had to visit you all since I got back home, so I volunteered to bring the message out to you by stretching the truth a mite and allowing that I *had* to come out here, instead of only wanting to. Anyhow, here's your telegram, Uncle Eth . . ."

Ethan took the telegram, opened it. The message read:

"Your wife, Anne Lovejoy, died last night. Accidental drowning. Wire instructions, funeral arrangements, disposal of body." It was signed: "H. Morris, Head Psychologist."

'Got to sit up all night, every night, from here on in,' Ethan thought bleakly. 'Because dreaming's a thing I've damned well got to quit doing . . .'

"Sir," Martin said, "is—something wrong?"

"No," Ethan said; "It's from the asylum at Osawatomie. My wife is —dead. I'll have to go there to see after the arrangements. I'm sorry she's gone; but since there was no hope of her ever recovering, in a way it's a relief. C'mon, ride back to the house with me, Mart . . ."

"Sir," Martin said; "is Martha Anne at home? Seems to me I saw that snow white horse of hers heading for the river. I couldn't make out if it was her, riding it, but nobody else does, so far as I know, and—"

"Especially not a female somebody else with long brown hair, and riding sidesaddle," Ethan said with a dry chuckle. "So that's the way the wind blows, eh, son? Look, Mart, I'm not going to play the stern father and ask you what your intentions are at this stage of the game; but maybe you and I had better have a little talk about the problems involved before you go looking for Martha Anne . . ."

"As far as I'm concerned, there aren't any, Uncle Eth. I've been in love with your daughter since I was ten or eleven years old. I mean to marry her—if you approve, sir—and if she'll have me—"

"That there's the catch," Ethan sighed. "Personally, I'd be glad, because I'd be gaining a son instead of losing a daughter. Your pa's place won't support any more grandchildren with your three brothers, their wives, and all their brood already on it. But mine will. And I could offer you the job of assistant manager from the outset—"

"Which I could fill," Martin said proudly. "You're looking at a Bachelor of Agricultural Science from Kansas State Agricultural College at Manhattan, sir! As of June tenth, this year. And I finished in the top tenth of my class, if you don't mind my bragging a little . . ."

"Good for you, son!" Ethan said. "But tell me: Have you seen Martha Anne's face since she got burned in the fire my poor dead wife set?"

"No, sir. She's never allowed me ten whole minutes of her company after that happened. Not even five. It's always: 'Go away Mart! Leave me in peace, will you?' But what difference does her getting burnt make really, sir? Martha's a mighty pretty girl, as the side of her face she doesn't keep hid proves. Cora Atkins told Mama that the left side of Martha Anne's face is pretty awful—all disfigured. But, Uncle Eth, scars aren't inheritable. Anybody who says so is being unscientific. So *our* daughter will be beautiful, and that's what counts, isn't it? Besides, in some courses I took in veterinary medicine, I've seen some awful sights. So a scarred-up face isn't likely to put me off my feed. It's the whole girl I love, not just her face, y'know . . ."

"Only that whole girl includes a spirit, a personality, even a pride of self that have been pretty badly damaged, Mart," Ethan said gravely. "So you can bet on this: she's going to reject you, son—at first, anyhow. Not because you have any rivals, or because she considers you unworthy, but because she doubts herself. Are you prepared to be persistent? Accept rebuffs, hard words, even childish temper tantrums? 'Cause they're what you're letting yourself in for—in the early stages, anyhow. You'll need the patience of a saint, my boy. Have you got it?"

"If I haven't, I'm going to develop it mighty fast, sir!" Martin said with his winning sidelong grin. "Have I your permission to—to ride after her, sir?"

"Of course. But one thing, Mart: If she *shows* you the burnt side of her face, that's a good sign, because it means you're getting next to her. It's her last-ditch defense. Hell, she even uses it on *me* when she can't think of an answer to my arguments that she ought to try to lead a normal life. But, if she does, be prepared to get a grip on yourself. It really is bad, y'know. And if you show the slightest sign of—revulsion, you're lost. But then, if you do find it revolting, you're lost anyhow, as far as any chances of a marriage between you two working out are concerned. You see that, don't you?"

"Yes, sir; I do; and it won't. All I've got to do is remember how the other side of her face looks, and everything will be just fine. Well, sir, I'll see you a little later at your house. With Martha Anne—if I can persuade her to come back with me . . ."

"All right, boy—get along with you. And—good luck!" Ethan Lovejoy said.

Nora was packing his suitcase, and arguing with him as usual, when, looking out of their bedroom window, she saw Martin Harris and Martha Anne riding up the drive toward the house. They were both in the buggy and were leading Martha Anne's white Arabian behind it by his bridle.

"Here they come!" Nora exulted. "And that boy's a heck of a lot better lover, or at least a faster worker, than you ever were, you miserable old stick! Ethan, you've got yourself a son-in-law, or I miss my guess! I wonder how on earth he worked it? For Lord knows Martha can be a perfect pain in that part whereon one sits, not that I blame her, poor child. God knows she has no reason to have an easy temper—"

"I hope you're right, but I doubt it," Ethan growled. "But to get back to what we were talking about—or rather fighting over, which has got to be our habitual mode of procedure, seems to me—Nora, for God's sake! We wouldn't even have to go to the rectory. Reverend Brownley would gladly come out *here* to marry us, bringing Ned and Phil with him as witnesses. And Cora and Hank would gladly serve, too. They're only half a mile away. Bet you Martha Harris and Nellie Tyler would come along, too, and—"

"Oh, God!" Nora groaned; "that would be all I need! But, Ethan, I don't *want* to marry you. I *like* living in sin. It's more fun. You—make love to me as men do to their mistresses—with attention and care. Also —passionately—quite often. Wives are *boring*. I'd rather stay your Fancy Article, your Playtime Girl—your Graduate from Gert's Parlor House . . ."

"Nora, I'm going to paddle your little fundament in a minute!" Ethan howled.

"You won't," Nora laughed; "not now. That would give love and affection a bad name, and those kids need encouragement. There—you're all packed, my ancient lover! That's another reason I won't marry you. If something better—like say younger and more vigorous!—comes along, I can just skip. Now, come on! I want to see how Martin made out. Of course, I scarcely know him, since he's been away at school for years, and dear Martha wasn't starting to let her darling baby boy visit this den of iniquity when he was home on vacations. Though I gather he *has* visited it—the outlying parts of it—on the sly, chasing after Martha Anne; but from what you've told me about him, he seems a very nice boy. . . ."

"He's a fine, upstanding young fellow," Ethan said; "And I'd be more than happy to have him for a son-in-law. But curb your enthusiasm, will you? It's bad form. And very likely if Martha Anne sees that you approve, she won't."

"There you're wrong, Ethan. Your daughter and I are friends. We really are. I honestly believe she likes me. Now, come on!"

Martha Anne and Martin were sitting in the little parlor when Ethan and Nora came downstairs. As they entered it, Martha Anne jumped up from the sofa, and all the visible side of her face was suddenly awash with tears.

"Papa—" she whispered; "Martin—he—he wants to ask you—something . . ."

"Whether I want to get rid of a certain bad-tempered, moody, tearful little wench?" Ethan said solemnly; "The answer's yes, my boy! Yes, of course—and hip, hip, hurrah!"

"Ohhhhh, Pa-pa!" Martha Anne wailed; "You'll make him think I'm —*awful*—and—"

"You are awful, baby. All women are. But we always manage to get stuck with you somehow." He bent and kissed her fondly. Put out his hand to Martin.

"All right, son—speak your piece," he said.

"Sir, I'm asking for Martha Anne's hand," Martin got out breathlessly; "and a quick wedding—before she changes her mind! Next Sunday, if possible. Can that be arranged, sir?"

"No," Ethan said; "it will have to be in about three months, son. After all, there has been a death in the family, y'know. And defying public opinion can be downright painful. You can take that as a fact, from me . . ."

"A—a death?" Martha Anne faltered.

"Your mother, child," Nora said; "Which should be as much of a relief to you as it is to me. It probably was one even to her . . ."

"Poor Mama!" Martha Anne said; "I'm sorry, Papa. I truly am. I got over—hating her a long time ago. She wasn't responsible for any of the terrible things she did. And besides, I've been too busy—hating myself . . ."

"Now, pet!" Ethan said.

"Howdy, Martin," Nora said; "Since I'm to be your stepmother-in-law, it's time we got to know each other and, if possible, make friends. Come here and kiss me, will you?"

Martin made an awkward froglike leap and obliged, with considerable enthusiasm, Ethan thought.

"Martin!" Martha Anne said severely; "Are you going to make me jealous of my own stepmother?"

"She sure is young and beautiful, honey!" Martin chuckled; "But I'm no match for your pa, and that's a fact. Well, I reckon I'd better be heading home. Got to break the news to *my* folks, y'know . . ."

"Will—they approve, Martin?" Martha Anne asked a little plaintively; "I'm nobody's prize, y'know, and—"

"They already do," Martin said happily. "Pa always has, and Mama will have no further objections now that—Oh, Lord! Me and my big mouth!"

"Now that Nora and I can be legally wed, you mean, son?" Ethan said.

"Yessir. That was a kind of sore spot with Mama. She understood your—situation, but she'll feel a lot better about me marrying into your family, now . . ."

Ethan turned to Nora with a grin.

"You see? You haven't a hope or a prayer of escape now, little Miss Flighty and Frivolous! At long, long last the Dastard has simply got to do right by Little Nell!"

"Or vice versa," Nora said merrily; "Mostly vice versa. All right, all right, you win! I won't be a stumbling block in these children's way. But tell me something, Martin: How did you manage? And so fast? You're the original Greased Chain Lightning Boy of Central Kansas and that's a fact!"

"Well," Martin grinned; "I was sort of prepared for emergencies, and—"

"He kissed me," Martha Anne said solemnly; "But it—wasn't just a —kiss, Nora. It was a pledge—of faith. Because when he asked me—if— if I'd have him—I raked my hair up out of the way and showed him the burnt side of my face. All red and raw and scaley like a turkey buzzard's head. And he—didn't even blink. He—leaned toward me—and kissed me —there. On that scarred-up mess. Then he—said—he said—Ohhhhh, Nora!"

Nora put her arms around her stepdaughter.

"There, there, baby, gentle down," she said.

"He said," Martha Anne sobbed; " 'There—that'll make it all well, honey!' Oh, Nora—wasn't that a lovely thing to say?"

"It was," Nora said, her voice gone a little humid, too. "And Martin, thank you. For thinking of that. For—saying it. It's going to be—mighty fine to have you for a son, my boy . . ."

"Ethan," Nora said demurely; "How d'you like my wedding dress, my love?"

Ethan stared at her.

"Why, Goddamn!" he howled; "Where the hell did you get *that* from?"

"Made it myself. I can sew, you know. And cook. And clean. In fact, I'll make you a perfectly darling little wife, if you're still willing to take me on. Are you?"

"In *that* outfit, no. Hell no, in fact. Nora, I told you that both Martha and Nellie are coming to our wedding, and here you are in—what the devil kind of a dress is that, anyhow?"

"Which *proves* you've been a good boy, darling!" Nora laughed. "It's a dance hall girl's costume. All red—appropriate for the local scarlet woman, isn't it? Knee-high skirt. No—a little higher than my knees—give old Ned Tyler a tiny flash of thigh and he'll faint outright, the lecherous old goat! Low neck. Very low. I can't lean forward too far, or I'd spill half the upper part of me out the front of it, wouldn't I? Bet that would cause a riot! Black net stockings—and lace garters with a rosette in 'em. Cigarettes—only I have to practice with them some more; so far they choke me half to death . . ."

"Nora, you go take that outrage off this minute!" Ethan thundered.

"But Ethan, I can't get married in my underwear," Nora teased; "Oh, I know! I'll put on my wedding veil, take my wedding bouquet in my arms, and come downstairs—naked. Give Reverend Brownley a heart attack and—"

"Oh, God!" Ethan groaned.

"But I'm very nice—naked. *You* always say so, anyhow . . ."

"You are. But in private. In our bedroom. And for my eyes alone. I'm a jealous old cuss, honey—"

"No, you're not. Not over me, anyhow. You only went after Price when he took your *Anne,* not because of *me.* So—"

"Aren't you ever going to forget that, Nora?" Ethan said.

"I doubt it. When you came back from Osawatomie—from burying her—with your eyes so swollen from crying, you couldn't open them. When have you—ever wept over *me,* Ethan Lovejoy?"

"The night you cut your throat. And if you'll think back, a couple of other occasions will come to mind. But I don't mean to anymore—ever. I mean to laugh with you, sing with you, dance with you, make love to you, and be crazily happy with you for the rest of my life. Go take that thing off, Nora! Change into something appropriate . . ."

"But *this* is appropriate. I'm one of Gert's Graduates, remember. Ethan—why did you cry over her—so?"

He sighed.

"Guilt, I suppose," he said. "And the way—she died. It was pretty awful. I couldn't have climbed that iron fence; but *she* did. But she must have fallen from the top of it—outside the asylum grounds—for her left leg was broken in two places. Yet she dragged herself down that hill, crawling through the mud to the banks of the Marais des Cygnes River. And drowned herself there—in less than three feet of water. D'you realize what *that* took?"

"Yes," Nora whispered; "Nerve. Courage. Will. And a total determination to die. Ethan—she was very probably *sane* when she did that. She must have remembered—episodes from her attacks of insanity. Realized that they'd surely come back again. That they were—all she had to look forward to. Poor Anne. Poor, poor Anne!"

He looked at her, and his fierce eyes misted over.

"Thank you, Nora," he said.

"Thank me? For *what,* Ethan?"

"For saying 'poor Anne,' finally. For meaning it. So to repeat: I thank you, Nora. I thank you with all my heart."

She came to him then, put her slim arms around his neck. She was thirty-eight years old; her face was tired, a little wrinkled. There were streaks of white all through her blond hair. She looked her age and perhaps even a little more. But she was very beautiful, then; softly, radiantly so.

"Ethan," she said; "I've been—awful about her, haven't I? I—I just couldn't help it, love. When I was only sixteen years old and I'd see you with her—I'd fairly die. And it was death by torture, believe me. I remember once, I was telling Price about you and her—and I burst out crying. I suppose he must have realized then that I didn't love him, that I never could. I—I only thought I did. Remember that time I kissed you like a brazen little hussy in that alley? Just before I was supposed to go to Chicago? I—I'll wear the taste and the feel of that kiss—upon my mouth—until I die. Even through all the others you've given me since—"

"And through Price's?" he growled.

"His don't count. They never did; I know that, now. I—I hated Anne. Because you loved her. Now, didn't you?"

"Yes, I loved her. She was a good woman, Nora. Worthy of my love. Of any man's. That's why her madness and her death were so cruel . . ."

"Oh, God!" Nora wept.

"On the other hand—I adored, I worshipped you," he said quietly. "If there had been any halfway decent, remotely honorable way I could have left her for you, even *before* I married her, I would have done it. And —I think she knew it, sensed it. And it was that, more than anything else, that broke her mind, her heart. Thinking back, I can remember quirks, oddnesses, phrases that were absolute *non sequiturs* of hers that date back to *years* before we lost little Jonathan. She needed only an excuse—to let go, to retreat into madness. It was probably easier than living with the fear of you, with your living ghost, forever . . ."

"As I've had to live with hers," Nora murmured; "and will have to bear the cross—of your memories of her—the rest of my life. I will, won't I, Ethan?"

"Yes," he said flatly; "You will, Nora. So bear it, accept it. There are worse things, y'know . . ."

"Yes. Being without you is worse. Only I don't have to worry about *that,* anymore. In a little while you're going to be *mine,* all *mine,* and 'til death us do part—"

"Not if you keep that dance hall hussy's outfit on, I won't!" he said.

"Oh, Lord! All right, all right—I'll go take it off. I was only teasing, anyhow," she said.

26

Clad in a lovely dress of pearl gray silk, complete with bustle and train, Nora was standing beside Ethan on the front porch under the fret-sawed decorations characteristic of the Victorian Gothic architectural style when they saw that line of vehicles coming toward them up the three-mile-long driveway that led from the borders of their farm to the house.

"Ethan!" Nora breathed; "You said—Ned and Phil—and their wives. Reverend and Mrs. Brownley, of course. But who are all those other people?"

"Lemme give you a list, honey," Cora Atkins said with her deep, dark chuckle as she came out of the house where she had been helping Greta Svensdatter, their newly acquired Swedish housekeeper and cook, with the preparations for the wedding feast; "Them there's Rad and Grace Stevens, Matt and Sarah Hendricks, Will and Molly Trainer, Ned and Nellie and Phil and Martha, natch. I reckon the rest of them folks must be Phil's sons and daughters, and their wives and husbands. 'Cept, of course, young Mart, who ain't got a wife—*yet*. By th way, Martha Anne's done got over her fit o' nerves. She's coming down. 'N you know what, Eth? She asked me to pin up her hair so that a little—just a little of her burnt side shows. Swears she ain't agonna hide it no more. 'If my Mart can stand it, the rest of the world will just have to put up with it, Cora,' sez she. I call that a good sign . . ."

"So do I," Ethan said; "I must say I'm surprised, though. I really didn't expect us to be given absolution and restored to grace so soon, Cora."

" 'N you ain't been, not really," Cora sighed. "Those folks are your friends; and none of them ever blamed you much for th way y'all *had* to live. They just didn't have the nerve to fly in the face of public opinion, that was all. But now that you 'n li'l Nory have plainly gone 'n redeemed yourselves . . ."

"Not *yet*, Cora!" Nora said; "And I still might change my mind!"

"You do that, honey," Cora laughed; "so I kin shoot Hank and grab

Old Eth myownself. Always did have a mighty yen for this here old scarecrow-lookin' rack o' bones, anyhow . . ."

"The understatement of the last twenty-two years," Nora said drily. "And who knows to what extent it wasn't reciprocated? After all, he rode out to save *you* from the Kansa, and left me to the tender mercies of those railroad workers. But, even so, you'd have to rush to beat your darling daughter to him. By the way, where is Tawi, Cora?"

"Don't know," Cora said sadly; "She rode out this morning early, and she ain't come back . . ."

Ethan turned and stared at her.

"You mean she's not coming to our wedding?" he said.

"Oh, Lord, Eth!" Cora said; "Don't tell me you ain't never noticed that my pore li'l Indian child is head over heels in love with you? It's plumb natural. You're the only thing in pants what ever treated her decent, 'cept Hank. 'N she thinks of Hank as her pa . . ."

"And of me, as her uncle," Ethan said.

"No, she don't. She quit thinkin' of you as kissin' kin years ago. Long about when she was fifteen years old. 'Mama,' she told me then, 'I ain't a-gonna kiss Uncle Eth no more. Nor let him kiss me, not neither one. It —it makes me *feel*—so funny!' "

"Why, Ethan Lovejoy!" Nora said.

"Oh, come on, Nora!" Cora laughed; "Eth's so honorable he squeaks. 'Cause any man who ain't never so much as *noticed* how long gone my pore baby is over him is either honorable, or a fool . . ."

"Or both," Nora said tartly. "Cora, you keep your little Pocahontas away from my husband, you hear? Took me a long time to get him, and now that I have, I could do without *that* much competition. Tawi's the loveliest girl in the whole county. And she's twenty years old to my thirty-eight, so—"

"Just like you were sixteen to poor Anne's twenty-one," Cora sighed; "though I hafta admit you didn't try to make her no trouble. You behaved real nice, Nora, back in them days, anyhow . . ."

"No, I didn't!" Nora said bitterly; "Most of the time he had to use a stick to beat me off. Only—thank God!—he wasn't the kind of a man who boasts about his conquests, so—"

"Now, do tell!" Cora whooped; "You doan mean to tell me Old Eth got into your frilly li'l onmentionables even *before* he married poor Anne? Whatcha do, Eth—keep her in after school?"

"Cora, you know better than that," Ethan said. "Now shut up, both of you! We've got to greet our guests . . ."

* * *

"Oh, Lord! I thought they'd *never* go!" Nora said.

"I'm sorry they have, to tell the truth about it," Ethan said. "It—felt good to have friends in, after so many years, honey. Made me realize how much we've missed . . ."

She came up to him with a gliding, graceful stride, meant, he was well aware, to appear feline, tigerish.

"*I'm* going to show you how much you've missed, tonight," she purred throatily. "And, since it seems I have to remind you, this is our wedding night, Ethan Lovejoy! The beginning of our—honeymoon. So, I'm demanding a new bride's rights: that you take me upstairs in your arms, since you can't over the doorsill anymore, and—"

"And what?" he asked her solemnly.

"And pretend you just paid Gert all of ten dollars for me," she said with a wicked gust of laughter; "and that you're out to get your money's worth! Who knows? *That* might do it. If you were to be—really *wild,* just once—knock the bed down with me, fall through the floor, and the dining room's ceiling, continue the—festivities—atop the table amid the dirty dishes and—"

"Lord God, Nora, what d'you think I am?" he groaned.

"An old stick. But I mean to rejuvenate you tonight. Oh, Lord! *Now* what, Greta?"

"Is en jung man. Och en jung leddy. They's askint to see you, sir," Greta said.

The jung leddy was Tawiyela Atkins. And the jung man—

"My God! He's your very image, Ethan!" Nora gasped.

"Isn't he, though? Howdy, Horace. I must say this is a surprise! Didn't you write or wire me beforehand? If so, I didn't get your message," Ethan said.

"Horace?" Ethan's image said; "Oh, that's right: I am named after —father, too, aren't I? Only everybody always called me Ethan, after you, sir, so being called Horace took me aback for a second. But I'll have to get used to it, I suppose. Having two Ethan's around would be more than a little confusing, wouldn't it?"

"Well," Nora said tartly; "We could call you *Junior.* Which is what you probably *are!*"

"Good heavens, ma'am," Horace Ethan said; "That really puts me into a bit of a quandary. . . . By the way, what am I to call *you?* Mistress Lovejoy sounds so—stiff and formal, somehow—"

"You may call me—Mother," Nora whispered; "or Mama if you prefer. Ethan's—son has to be mine, too—"

"Good Lord!" Horace Ethan said; "You—you're crying! Oh, I am sorry! Whatever I said, or did to make you cry, ma'am, I—"

"You didn't say or do anything," Nora sniffed; "You just *are,* and that's enough—to remind me what an abject failure—as a woman, I am. You—you're Edith's son, aren't you, Ethan?"

"Yes, ma'am—"

"Call me Mother! Or Mama, whichever you prefer!" Nora snapped.

"Well—Mother, then. I always called poor Mama, Mama—"

"Called?" Ethan got out. "Past tense, boy?"

"Yes," Horace Ethan said bitterly; "She's—dead, sir. Cancer—of the right breast. Fortunately, it only took her—three months to die. But even so—before the end, it was pretty horrible . . ."

"I'm sorry," Ethan croaked; "I'm very sorry, son. Tell me: How is your father bearing up? He must be bowed down with grief . . ."

Horace Ethan's eyes flashed with deep and bitter anger.

"You've touched me on a sore spot now, sir," he said. "The truth is, Father—I suppose I can go on calling him that; he *was* a father to me, and a good one, I'll admit—had found—other consolations—long before Mama—died. I'm sorry, Mrs. Lovejoy, I mean Mother, if that shocks you. And to you, Miss Atkins, I humbly apologize for mentioning a thing like that before you . . ."

"That—isn't necessary, *Ethan,"* Tawiyela whispered; "We're awfully *wild* out here, y'know . . ."

"All right. I—understand—Father means to—legalize his relations with his little friend. That was one of the reasons I left. I'd have been too —uncomfortable—seeing *her* in Mama's place. Oh, I say! It occurs to me I've been—awfully presumptive about one thing: sir—and Mother—may I *stay?* I freely confess I know not one thing about farming, but I'm a certified public accountant, and it seems to me that that skill ought to be of some use on a place this size . . ."

"It'll be a godsend," Ethan growled; "And if you knew nothing at all, I'd have found something for you to do—like feeding the hogs, for instance! You're mighty welcome, boy!"

"And you—Mother?" Horace Ethan murmured.

"You'd get out of that door only over my dead body!" Nora said tearfully; "I've wanted a son so long, Ethan, Jr. Of course, having a ready-made one handed me on a silver platter as it were is a bit of a shock; but I'll get over *that,* fast enough!"

"Good," Ethan said; "That's settled. C'mon, let's go into the sitting room. Oh, no, you don't, Tawi! Don't you dare try to sneak away! You and I have a buzzard-sized crow to pick, young lady!"

"But, Uncle Ethan—" Tawiyela protested; "This is—a family gathering! Private, sort of, and—"

"You're family," Ethan said; "And you're going to be even more so, if I have anything to say about it!"

Nora stared from young Horace Ethan's face to Tawiyela's, and back again. When she turned to Ethan she was smiling, but her eyes were misty.

"Oh, Ethan! That *would* be perfectly lovely, wouldn't it?" she said.

"Have you had anything to eat, son?" Ethan said.

"No, sir. But that can wait. I've so much to tell you. And to ask you. This—young lady, for instance. She says she's an *Indian.* A wild, wild Indian. And—"

"She *is,*" Nora snapped. "But I can be a whole cavalry regiment riding to the rescue, if necessary! Tawi, where the devil were you all day? Why didn't you come to my—our wedding?"

"Your—*wedding,* ma'am? I mean, Mother?" Horace Ethan said in a tone of utter astonishment.

"*Now* you've gone and done it, Nora!" Ethan groaned.

"No, I haven't. Ethan, Jr., you seem to have jumped out of the frying pan into the fire as far as middle-aged sinfulness is concerned. The ugly truth of the matter is that your father and I have lived together without being married for ten long years. It so happened that it was the only thing we could do under the circumstances existing up until two weeks ago. But since explaining those circumstances would take a month of Sundays, I don't propose to attempt to do so now. I am legally your stepmother as of today. Your father will clear things up for you later on. Will you accept for now that there were good reasons for our unconventional behavior, and at least reserve judgment until you hear them?"

"Of course, Mother!" Horace Ethan said cheerfully; "The chief of those reasons being that my dad is neither blind nor crazy. You're just about the most beautiful woman I've ever seen, ma'am . . ."

"I thought you said *I* was, Ethan—Ethan Number Two, I mean," Tawiyela said in an utterly desolate tone of voice.

"You *are,* Tawi!" Horace Ethan said. "But don't you see the two of you are day and night? Beauties of two different orders between which comparison just isn't possible? Is an apple more beautiful than a pear, or—"

"An Indian squaw than a *white* woman?" Tawiyela said bitterly.

"Tawi, you stop that!" Ethan thundered; "You're one of the loveliest girls who ever drew breath! And I won't have you low-rating yourself. I've always considered you *my* daughter and treated you as such. What's more, I've always been proud of you. The only thing I regret is that you really aren't—"

"I don't—not *now,*" Tawiyela said with a smile that for all its demureness, was a-twinkle with delighted mischief.

"Lord! My head is spinning," Ethan said; "To help which, or to make it spin counterclockwise for a change, I propose to have a snort. How about you, son?"

"Don't mind if I do," Horace Ethan said. "Sir—maybe you and I had better step into another room, apart from the ladies, I mean. What I have to explain to you is—awfully delicate, and—"

"No, you don't!" Nora snapped; "I'm your mother, now, and I won't be shut out. And, for your information, since you seem to be as artless and clumsy about handling women as your father is, I'll tell you that Tawi won't like being excluded, either. Am I right, Tawi, dear?"

"Yes—Nora," Tawiyela whispered; "but what I like, or don't, simply doesn't matter as far as I can see. I—I'm an outsider, and—"

"A state that, if it exists, which I doubt, Ethan and I will fix between us," Nora said firmly; "All right, I'll make it easier for you, Ethan, Number Two. Knowing women, my guess is that Edith—your mother—inflicted a deathbed confession upon you, which was in poor taste, and worse style. She should have told you years ago that this old stick really is your father. That's about the size of the matter, isn't it?"

"Nora, that's impossible," Ethan said grimly. "This young fellow was born exactly eleven months after I left Pittsfield in July 1866—on the twenty-seventh of June 1867. That's right, isn't it, my boy?"

"No, sir," Horace Ethan said.

"No?" Ethan croaked.

"No, sir; it isn't," Ethan II whispered; "I was born on *April* twenty-seventh, 1867. And you—left Pittsfield on July twenty-ninth of the year before, didn't you?"

"Lord God!" Ethan breathed.

"I—I figured it out myself," Ethan II said sadly. "Because, you see, there wasn't any deathbed confession, sir. Mama—couldn't bring herself to do that. I guess she thought I'd lose all respect for her if she did. She was wrong. I—loved her too much for anything to come between us. And she—was a human being. I was fond of Father—I mean Horace Willoughby—but, Dear Lord, sir!—being married to *him,* who could blame her? Especially since she only consented to that wedding believing you were dead. She—tore this page out of the back of the family Bible—and gave it to me. Said—she could hardly talk by then: 'After I'm gone—take this to—Ethan Lovejoy—in Kansas—' That's all she said. Well, sir—here it is."

Ethan took that page. And while he could still see, before his eyes went scalded, blind, he read: "Horace Ethan Willoughby, born This Day of Our Lord, April the Twenty-Seventh, 1867." Only she had traced a line completely through the name Willoughby, and above it, written in the thin, spidery, uncertain script of a woman sick unto death, the single word "Lovejoy."

Ethan stood there, staring owlishly at his son, born to his mind, spirit, consciousness, recognition at twenty-one years of age. He tucked that page into his waistcoat pocket, put out his arms to Ethan II. The young man came to him. Ethan almost most broke his ribs in the wild, sweet, fierce torment of that embrace.

"Now me!" Nora whispered, when finally he turned him loose.

"All right, all right!" Ethan roared happily—he was more than a little drunk by then and showed it—"It's agreed that you're my son, Eth, Jr.! What I want to know right now is d'you plan to be a dutiful one? D'you, boy?"

Ethan II put down his knife and fork, acknowledging that his efforts to reduce the mountains of food that Nora and Tawiyela between them kept piling up in his plate were futile. Across from him, the half sister he hadn't even known existed stared at him with one adoring eye, the other being curtained by the long hair she used to hide one half of her face. She had been brought back home an hour earlier by a red-haired, freckle-faced, ugly young man, who had identified himself as "Martha's promised," and then had driven solemnly away.

"Yes, Dad, I do," he said pleasantly.

"Then I'm going to give you my first order as your father," Ethan said thickly; "Order, hell! This is purely a command, boy! To be disobeyed only on pain of death! I hereby command you to marry Tawiyela. On November the first, the day that Martha Anne and Mart Harris are getting hitched. You don't object to a double wedding, d'you, pet?"

"Why Pa-pa!" Martha Anne gasped; "That's positively outrageous! Just as if he 'n Tawi haven't anything to say about it, and—"

"They haven't. In my castle, my word is law," Ethan growled. "Well, boy; what d'you say?"

Ethan, Junior, threw back his head and laughed aloud.

"Long live feudalism! I hear and obey, my Lord!" he said.

"Good," Ethan grunted. "Well, Tawi, do I have to take my belt to you? I never have so far, but better late than never. What d'you say, sweetheart? Think carefully, child, 'cause a guarantee of two dozen grandchildren is going to be written into the fine print of the wedding contract, with a subheading stating that all the girls have got to look just like you, sugar!"

"But—Uncle Ethan!" Tawiyela wailed; "He—he hasn't even asked me, and—"

"Doesn't have to. I just did, for him. And as I said before, my word is law!" Ethan said.

Nora let her own low, husky laughter beat against the ceiling like the wings of captive doves.

"And so is mine!" she said; "So I'm going to give an even more unbreakable command: Ethan, my boy, go down to the stables, and tell Jake Furnis to hitch your father's team up to his buckboard. Don't worry; you'll find the stables easily enough. You need only to follow your nose! Then take little Pocahontas for a long, long ride in the moonlight. I'm a woman first, and your stepmother only second. So I know what works. And if she doesn't say 'Yes' by midnight, you have my leave to scalp her!"

On the morning of November 2, 1888, Nora Lovejoy lay beside the sleeping form of her husband. She was going over all the details of that double wedding in her mind, savoring them as women will. She was almost completely happy, at long, long last. And she would have been entirely so, if it hadn't been for the gnawing feeling that was churning her insides, whose source—although the feeling, itself, was explicitly physical—was her bitter, jealous pain at the thought that it had been "that *awful* Edith!" who had given Ethan the absolutely splendid son she had acquired by proxy. Which was a miserable way to acquire a son, but there it was.

Then it came to her that the churning in her middle was getting worse, and that she felt positively awful. She leaped from the bed, barely made it through the bathroom door; but, even so, she managed to close it carefully and quietly behind her before that foaming, hot thick tide exploded upward through her throat, poured out of her opened mouth, in an almost death sick agony of retching.

She was as quiet as she could manage, but all the same she made what seemed to her a terrible amount of noise. When it was finally finished, when the racking spasms of nausea turned her loose, she opened the door a tiny crack and peered at her husband's recumbent form. Ethan hadn't moved.

'Men!' Nora thought happily. She turned back to face her image in the bathroom mirror. She looked, to borrow that phrase of Cora Atkins's that Ethan was always repeating, "Like death lightly warmed over." Or was it "slightly"? She didn't remember, and she had no time to search her memory for the correct adverb, because she was too busy praying.

"I'm thirty-eight years old, Dear Lord—so I know it can't be. It can't, can it? But if You would be—so kind, so merciful, I—"

Then she started in to count. She used up all the fingers on both her hands, then the toes on both feet, but she had to go back counting with her fingers again.

"Two months!" she whispered; "For sure, anyhow. Three, likely. Since—the one after we got married? Since August? Yes. Yes! Since August. Only—there's been so much going on, I forgot. I plain forgot! Martha Anne's getting engaged. Anne's—death. Our—wedding. Ethan, Jr.'s arrival. People—being nice, again. Starting to call. . . . And Ethan driving everybody crazy building two new houses on two separate sections for the young couples. Hiring so many carpenters they only get in each other's way. Worse than Simon Legree whipping on his slaves to make sure they'd be ready for the youngsters to come home to after the weddings. For Martha Anne and Martin to, anyhow, since Ethan II decided that Tawi simply *had* to see the East—Pittsfield, Boston, New York. He's right. The poor child's never been anywhere . . ."

She sat there on the edge of the bathtub, hugging herself, and shivering a little. The weather was already getting cold.

'I—relaxed,' she thought; 'Quit trying so hard. Turned my jangled nerves loose. Thought about something else for a change, besides whether it was or wasn't going to—work. And—having young Ethan as a guarantee that Clan Lovejoy wouldn't end with my old stick—the desperation wasn't there any longer. So—'

She got up and, swaying a little, crept back toward the bed. 'Shall I tell him?' she thought. 'No. Better wait until I'm absolutely sure—' She pushed the covers back, slipped carefully into bed beside Ethan. 'But I'm sure now!' she exulted; 'Oh, I'm sure, I'm sure!'

Still—she wouldn't tell him yet. There were some things a woman had a perfect right to keep to herself as long as she could. To enjoy, alone. To—contemplate. To savor.

'And to think I can't even call him—Ethan!' she wailed inside her mind, and bent and kissed her husband's sleeping face.

Ethan Lovejoy only grunted. And went on sleeping like a log.